Epworth Heights – August 1935

A novel in terms of fluid time –

Kathryn Turney Garsten

BOOKS BY JAMES BOYD

ROLL RIVER

LONG HUNT

MARCHING ON

DRUMS

CHARLES SCRIBNER'S SONS

D1457219

ROLL RIVER

ROLL RIVER

By

James Boyd

ॐ

NEW YORK

CHARLES SCRIBNER'S SONS

1935

Copyright, 1934, 1935, by
CHARLES SCRIBNER'S SONS

Printed in the United States of America

*All rights reserved. No part of this book
may be reproduced in any form without
the permission of Charles Scribner's Sons*

TO

MY BROTHER

50564

TO
MY BROTHER

CONTENTS

Book One

BOOK ONE

THE DARK SHORE

CHAPTER I

It was night when the thought first came to him. The nurse had left the room and gone down the corridor. She was having coffee probably, and perhaps ice-cream, with the other nurses. Lying in the darkness he could hear their voices through the crack in his door, held an inch ajar by a small crescent-shaped pillow which hung around the knob. He could not see the pillow but he knew it was there just as he knew each infinitesimal detail of his room, the spidery reach of the bed-table and its arched prehensile feet, the swollen figure of the upholstered arm-chair, a concession by authority to possible visitors from a less ascetic world, the funneled shape of the lamp shade, hard, shining green on top and, underneath, white as the belly of a toad. He knew the shape of the french-gray window frame and of the door veneered in oak, wide enough for the tall bed to wheel through. He knew the floor of some new patent composition that was noiseless, odorless, dustless, scratchless—a triumph of negation, guaranteed to remain devoid of interest through the ages. The walls were of some other composition which seemed to be equally immune. He had searched it, inch by inch, and found no slightest variation in its endless shining.

Through the crack of his door, light a little less dim stole into his room. From time to time this streak was darkened by a shadow, he heard the light clean rustle of a passing nurse. Once there was a cluster of footfalls on the rubber flooring and, in the heart of the cluster, a slow smooth rolling sound. Across the crack of light the shadow lasted longer and when it passed, it left behind it in the air a faint sharp prickle of ether.

All these were mere faint indications of passers-by who were, themselves, mere indications of another world. From these scientifically muffled footfalls, he could make a reasonable guess, as anthropologists from the scratchings in a cave, in reconstructing the persons who had caused them. In theory it should not be difficult. Like the floor on which they trod, the nurses and in-

3

ternes in this best of hospitals seemed carefully and exclusively
designed for their specific function; they, too, seemed to be made
of a synthetic composition, which eliminated the undesirable features of all possible natural materials and retained all their merits
except the merit of appeal. Undoubtedly there were physical
differences between them more subtle than that of male and
female, though what could be more subtle? Undoubtedly there
were tall nurses and short nurses, there were, if not fat nurses, at
least nurses whose weight was greater than that of others. Possibly even there were nurses with red hair. And among the
internes, too, there must be differences. Some were perhaps out-
standingly astigmatic. But that phase of the problem had never
engaged his full attention. In any case, the differences were superficial, the essence was uniform. Any variety they might assume
was accidental, as that of the composition flooring which had
different outlines in rooms of different shapes.

But though this world of medicine about him possessed, beneath the superficial differences of the persons who composed it,
an underlying uniformity, beneath that uniformity lay other differences still, differences far more profound, subtle and complex.
So much so that not only was it impossible from such data as
was given him to reconstruct them, but it would also be almost
equally impossible, had he been given the freedom of the hospital
from birth, to more than guess at some of their more obvious
manifestations. What hopes, delusions, sins and follies lay hidden
in these highly trained automata of science none would ever
know except through the most meagre, fragmentary and accidental glimpses. And even if, by a supernatural dispensation, one
were also made free of this hidden stratum of high variability
where lay the secret thoughts, memories and plans of the apparently composed and routinized inhabitants, one still would not
have mastered, by any means, the knowledge of this little world.
Secret these thoughts were and known only to the jealous and
watchful possessors. But there were other thoughts more secret
still, depths still more cloudy and profound, unknown to those
who harbored them. Known then to whom? Only to a supreme
intelligence, assuming that hypothesis. How then known to himself who had never succeeded in communicating with that intelligence, assuming again that it existed? Well, not known to him
nor to any one, but beginning to be guessed. For from those

depths of dreams and dreads and primal instincts, some accident
or convulsion of nature cast up from time to time an incredible
monster of the deep. These prehistoric and, for the most part,
sinister-appearing specimens were beginning to form the materials for learned speculation and also for much ineffectual exor-
cism, baleful witch-doctoring and demonological imposition on
the credulous. Nevertheless the regions which cast up the monsters must exist, and such was, no doubt, their silent power that
no one could claim knowledge of mankind until he knew
them.

It would be impossible, then, for any man, however distinguished, omniscient even, to acquire anything approaching adequate knowledge of even so small a cosmos as this hospital;
indeed, of even so small a cosmos as that last nurse who just
now rustled by this door. She might be the most commonplace,
colorless, and perfected of nurses, a mere therapeutic function,
yet even so, there was within the cosmos of that nurse a region
unknown to the combined and accumulated wisdom of mankind.
And even were that region some day to be explored, who could
say but that beneath it lay other regions more profound, more
obscure, reaching down in an infinite series ever destined to
elude?

And if this simplified and narrowly focussed hospital world
were basically inscrutable, what of the wide and more spontaneous world that lay below this window? The window was open
to the summer night and to the glow of lights diffused as far as
eye could see, a glow that seemed thrown off by the surf-like
rustle of the town. The horns of taxicabs near by which pierced
this rustle served as a measure of its vastness, reminding one that
the smooth basic hum-note was in fact composed of individual and
sharp percussions which were, however, so infinite in number
and space that they formed an entity of smoothness, as the
smoothness of the dunes is formed by individual sharp grains of
sand. This glow and this continuous almost musical whisper,
results alike of vastness, were mere accidents, unconsidered by-
products, of the life that threw them off. How vast then must
be that life itself? Who could fathom or even count its infinite
and momentarily changing convolutions? And even if one could,
what of that distant bridge whose shadowy bulk and long festoons of glowing pinpoints led to the vaster world they called

America? What, too, of the hoarse voice of that liner casting off her mooring lines for worlds beyond the sea?

And this dark room, this almost silent hospital, this murmuring town, this nation and this earth were merely the first of a series of ever-widening circles in the centre of which he lay. And not he alone; each living being, each animal, perhaps each object called inanimate was also ringed about by its concentric series. With every contact, every thought, these circles changed and moved, approached one another, touched, overlapped, engaged and separated in a bewildering and mystifying flow, like the metal rings of a magician. And as if this ceaseless sleight of hand were not sufficient, above it, the stars which struggled through the city's glowing haze gave trite and yet mysterious evidence of other circles still.

Against the illimitable background of these circles a man appeared infinitesimal. The contrast was mercifully too extreme for comprehension, but if some notion of it seized on one to terrify his sense of dignity, or even what sense of bare validity he had, a man could fortify himself by the reflection that among these inconceivably countless systems one existed of which the centre was himself. Not that he personally required such assurance or was even interested in trying to estimate the value of man in a scale whose values were themselves unknown. What then was the cause of all this reasoning? The exquisitely faint trace of ether, now just about to vanish, just about, as it were, to withdraw a light but warning finger from his bed, reminded him.

It was a subject avoided by authority, avoided with a rigid circumspection which defeated its own purpose and gave it a prominence at once mysterious and all-pervading. He had not been in this hospital long before he began to reflect that some of these passers-by on softly rolling rubber wheels who left behind them sometimes a trace of ether, sometimes no trace of anything whatever, were passers-by in the largest sense of the word, that they were quitting the known world, if for a destination, at most for an unknown one; or that they had already quitted it, leaving behind only a hulk to be disposed of with pious incantations and at unheard of and probably fraudulent charges by the wreckers.

But to-day his reflections, up till now casual or amusing, had like gay flowers on some night of early autumn, suddenly stiffened and then wilted under an almost imperceptible light swift chill. It was at the moment when the doctor, whose visits now were mere routine, had reached out to take his pulse. It was at that elusive yet startling instant that the intimation came. Not from the doctor, whose face, broad and slightly distorted, close yet wholly separated, its glance of interest and inquiry tinged with faint amusement, had seemed to him, quite as usual, to resemble the face of a rather conscientious visitor as it must appear to a fish in an aquarium. Nor was it from his own consciousness. It came rather from his body, that dumb, blind worm whose prosaic crawlings on far lower levels, he had been accustomed to ignore. It seemed, however, that this humble worm might be possessed of knowledge hidden from himself. For at the moment when the doctor's fingers closed upon his wrist, he had felt within him a weak stirring, a straining flutter. The worm, for an instant in contact with a proper understanding, had seized the chance to tell the doctor something. And what the something was, he could read for the briefest instant in the doctor's otherwise professionally assured and jovial eye. A mere interpreter, the doctor had unwittingly conveyed to him a message from the worm—a message of an impending change that would be, certainly for the poor worm, and, for all he knew for himself, more radical than any other that could come.

But except for the first spasm—a spasm in whose grip the worm, knowing then, and knowing that he knew too, had shrunk and trembled, his qualms had been far lighter than expected.

He had had moments of bewilderment, of apprehension and even unjustifiably enough, of self-pity, but his chief thought had been an active one. He thought that he must prepare himself for the event. The notion was perhaps belated. It might be held that there was small excuse for being surprised by the one contingency which, of all contingencies, may most certainly be foreseen. That was hardly fair. Actually he had tried from time to time in a busy life to take in advance some position against this inevitable and final attack upon him. He had read. He had talked, with those supposed to be authorities on the inscrutable. He had even gone so far as to attempt some thinking of his own. But the sum total of these efforts had been merely the disintegration of the orthodoxy with which his childhood had been in theory equipped to deal with all conceivable terrestrial and celestial emergencies. He had ended by concluding, or at least by hoping, that, as often happened in minor circumstances, the emergency when it came would bring with it and confer on him, or else evoke and stimulate within him powers, hitherto unsuspected, by which it might be met. And that seemed to be the case. Ever since this morning, he had felt, lying there, a sense of, to use a phrase recalled from his childhood teaching, girding up his loins. He had felt, not yet it is true any power to meet, that is to understand, his fate; but at least a power to go about that understanding. As if on a Western mountain top, his mind in an atmosphere more clear, more rare, more bracing, seemed to look down from high aloft not only on this city, shrouded by the night, but on all the known world; and not only on the world at this particular, yet ever-changing moment, but also, leading away like valleys from its immediate surface, on vistas of the past. And as an explorer on his peak can, partly from the contours of the country, partly from instinct, tell where his trail should lead, so he, confronted for the first and perhaps the last time by the illimitable scene, guessed that somewhere in those distant valleys lay his path.

CHAPTER II

THE hospital was utterly quiet now, and in the quiet, his mind, like some true and swift and silent mechanism, was running with precision. It was able now, he felt, to take up the thread of life at the beginning, and without haste or error, without discursiveness, to follow it through all its windings that were worthy to be noticed, down to the present, that is, almost to its end. Certainly, near enough to its end for all practical purposes; from now on there would be no further windings, merely a line, straight, and probably short, but long enough, he did not doubt, to give this swift mind of his, time to make some comment on the significance of the long path over which it had passed.

Even while he congratulated himself on the new perfection of his equipment, his mind was bending to the task. He saw already, the first recollected scene of his life. Before him stretched an expanse of green. On it a small brown object stirred. Then across this green expanse of grass moved a white-frocked figure, even then recognized as being a lady, slender, young and tall. Approaching the brown object, the lady with a startling movement, clapped a straw hat over it. Next, the lady, bright lights on her dull gold hair, her silver bracelets, her slender shoulders, stood before him holding out the hat. He peered into its mysterious depths, to meet the beady-eyed, intense and disconcerting gaze of a young sparrow.

Then, and probably not long after, he and the tall young lady were below tall trees that stood on the river bank not far from where he lived. The river was immense and broad and formidable, but where he stood on the sand and gravel it was shallow and lapped gently at his feet. The lady's strong slim hand held his and with it, as his encouragement, he stepped boldly forward. The wetness at first was most disturbing but as it increased it grew acceptable, delightful. In the end, his clothes around the knees were dragging and with his free hand he was beating the water manfully. Surprising drops flew sharp across

9

his face; he blinked and paused and then beat harder. Behind
him, he sensed that people had gathered on the bank. He was
abashed at first but then had realized that he was the centre of
great praise and admiration and of alarming but well-intended
thunders of laughter. That had not been the end of this adventure, for next he knew that he was home, though what home
looked like he could not yet picture. But there was, it seemed,
an altercation between the young lady and a voice, which though
for him still disembodied, he knew to be his mother's. It dawned
on him with some dismay but greater pride, that in walking into
the wetness and splashing it so bravely he and the lady had
shared disreputable adventure.

On these first occasions he had been conscious of no words,
and even on this last, he had merely guessed, as a dog would,
the import of the sounds and intonations. But next in the history of his recollected consciousness, he heard words and exchanged them. He was seated in a buggy, his short legs swinging in space below the green-cloth seat, his left hand grasping
the narrow iron rod that ran beside him, his knee half covered
by a fold of the young lady's white dress. Ahead, the horse's
quarters bobbed and shone. Above, dusty leaves met over the
dusty road. The lady, his lady he felt she was by now, was
speaking to him. "You don't have to whip a horse," the voice was
musical and young.

He must have managed a reply, for the lady was speaking
again. "You just rattle the whip in the socket."

This the lady proceeded to do, but he never could remember,
though the point had often worried him, with what effect on the
slowly bobbing rump ahead of him.

And now, so rapid must have been his progress in the art of
speech, that the young lady next appears hardly as a figure at all,
but rather as a voice and a magician. This voice told him, as he
sat on a rug before a papier-mâché castle whose drawbridge had
been hauled up in preparation for the event, that the moment
now was come. This was the hour of night, when the little page
boy, carried far from his home by the raiding baron, must make
his bid for freedom. The doubled guard, bemused by Rhenish
wine, dozed in the court yard. They did not hear him softly
sawing at the bar; they did not see him climbing on the window
ledge and dropping to a point of rock, just wide enough to

catch him, nor follow him down the steep face of the cliff, a desperate path to safety, now here, now there, by crag and precipice. A finger, the lady's finger, traced its course. Her voice, quiet but quick, insistent, spun the tale. It ceased. The playroom echoed the snores of drunken guards, and the distant gallop of a stolen horse.

But as if she knew that the introduction to birds, rivers, horses and tales of high adventure was not enough, the lady had gone on to make him free of the world of fantasy and of magic. Not free of it by means of the tales which her quick, young and musical voice told him, but free of it in person. What went before he did not know. He had only the picture of a great broad cavern, filled with rows of people and with their heavy smell, and a sense that, in front of them all, were lights and colors and movements and the sounds of music. Then the people went away, shuffling heavily, and he and the lady, alone in the cavern, were whispering together about the bear—the trained bear. Then, for quite a while, he was alone in the now hushed and mysterious vastness until at last he heard the light footfalls which he knew, and saw the young lady beckoning to him from the platform, now dark, where the lights and colors had been seen. Between innumerable rows of seats, he walked clumsily down a sloping aisle which pitched him forward. The lady reached down a hand and helped him up the steep and narrow steps. They stood together, seeming very tiny on the broad, dark platform. The lady still held his hand and smiled.

Greater depths beyond reverberated with the echoes of a foreign voice. There was a sense of movement in the blackness, then a soft padding and light rhythmic clicks. There was the jingle of a chain and the foreign voice again. A floor board creaked. In an instant, dimly foreseen, yet utterly incredible, the bear came toward him. It lay down before him. If, as no doubt they were, they were telling him what to do, there was no need, not even if he could have heard them. He knew. In a dark, soft trance, he went up to the bear and started climbing. Hands pushed and steadied him, superfluously, and voices, their voices, sounded far, far away, offering superfluous advice. He dug his fingers in the bear, he heaved and puffed, his leg slid over a high ridge. He bestrode the bear.

While the voices murmured on, the ridge rose up in front. He clutched two tufts and clung. The ridge rose up behind. They started in a lurching slide. "I on the bear," was the thought that filled his mind. It was a story and a dream.

And then, as it slowly dawned on him, it was being something of a bad dream too. With the lurching, he began to slide from side to side. He clenched his fingers tighter in the hair. But he could not sit steady. The hair he clutched, the hide he sat on was sliding too. It slipped around almost capriciously and with no reference to the fundamental bear inside it. It was a problem, tantalizing, unfair and insoluble, like the problem of a dream.

Then he was lifted to the ground and there were words of approbation and more words between the lady and the foreign man. But he stood alone on the dark stage, withdrawn into himself. The voices were not heard. The world was no longer known. Even the problem of his dream was now forgotten. He stared and stared at the fur mountain and thought, "I on the bear."

After that, there was a long gap in his memory, filled only with the notion that between him and the lady lay a guilty secret, charged with danger and with glory. Floating vaguely in this void of apprehension and delight was simply the picture, sharp enough, but without background of the lady herself. She was really not a lady, at least to call her that could never even faintly evoke her presence. Under the aspect of a young lady of quick grace, darkly golden hair and deep responsive eyes, she was really a young boy, an older, wiser, gayer boy; the source of inexhaustible delight, and possessing a secret of the universe. The secret, he would have called it then if he had been able to call it anything; and even now, here in this darkened hospital, when the secrets of the universe seemed numberless, obscure and perhaps conflicting, he could call it a secret of the universe and perhaps the most precious one; a secret which he could not label or dissect even now after all these years of knowing her, but which had been able, whenever he was with her, to cause a child's world, filled with dreads, obscurities and frustrate longings, to blossom into splendor. A secret which enabled her to live in warm and bright contentment—in itself a sufficient recommendation for any secret—and furthermore to draw those close to her, young or old, who still had any faintest power of response, into an understanding of how life ought to be. That secret seemed nothing more than simple acceptance of all things, an attitude for a child merely natural and obvious, together with a convincing and affectionate belief in the possibilities of all persons and all occasions, a belief short lived enough among children and almost unknown among elders who, far from belief or even acceptance, appeared to struggle, enmeshed in the invisible threads of a gigantic all-pervading and meaningless web. As an older person, sometimes weary of his struggles, he had, when thinking of her, felt a suspicion that this web which he and the world conceived as spread for them by fate, or by a metaphysical demon, might, since obviously it had no existence for her, not exist for themselves. Or if it did that it might be no cosmic web, but their own private labyrinth, created and thrown off by the struggles which it caused. This or rather the essence of it he had felt about her, as strongly as he felt it now, before he had the power of speech and long before he knew that she was his aunt or that her name was Clara.

CHAPTER III

THE second world that he met was the world of his Grand-father Rand. It was the world that one entered up tall brown-stone steps, flanked by fat bay windows in the red pressed brick, which looked out across a dusty street and a narrow park of locust trees to the broad, shallow river and green hills beyond. Downstream the undulations of the covered bridge rumbled to the heavy farm teams, and the trestle bridge rattled to the railroad cars. Up stream lay the tin cans and Irish squalor of Billy-goat Town. But here was peace, reserve and elegant dignity: a park of locust trees above the river's bank, the limestone dust of the street, and, above the brick sidewalk, the house-fronts of the leading citizens, their brickwork sometimes painted gray, their white doors bearing silver knockers and silver nameplates. Among them, Grandfather Rand's stood out. The brownstone trimming made it formidable. It was set back from the street and the office wing was even farther removed behind an iron grille, and a narrow front yard containing two small indeterminate bushes and a white cast-iron stag.

When, as they did in his earliest memories, his small legs had overcome the brownstone steps, he usually turned around to look down on the sidewalk he had just left dangerously far below him; then he looked out across the street and the park and the shining river to the hills on the other shore. There was one more step and he was in a massive vestibule, floored with tile of scrolled pink and black design and blocked by a massive golden-oak door, whose many projecting mould-ings and deep-sunk panels gave it the effect of the natural armour of some prehistoric saurian. In the middle panels were two small and intricate brass grilles, designed, no doubt, to per-mit the inmates to peep out before committing themselves to the hazards of intercourse. But as this arrangement would also per-mit assaulting parties to peep in, and as Samuel, the butler, could be trusted to improvise defenses after opening the door, the grilles had long since been curtained with now faded pink silk.

At the side of the door, a bronze handle shaped like the handle of a mug, when pressed down set up faint reverberations far within. Immediately there was a soft step in the hall, one floor board which creaked, a swift, smooth, noiseless turning of the brass knob, and Samuel stood in the first position, the door held firmly half ajar. Then, of course, it was swung very wide and Samuel creased his black broadcloth waistcoat in a bow. He shot immaculate cuffs out of his black alpaca sleeves and reached forward a soft white, boiled-looking hand in a shake of cordial recognition. "Tommy, how is the young man?" The hand, soft, strong and deft was instantly withdrawn, to curl its fingers neatly under the edges of the black alpaca coat.

Under foot was the deep carpet of a long dark hall, lit faintly by the light from double doors, half opened on either side. The light from the right-hand door was dim. That was the drawing-room. On the left, the library was bright with a fire and well-stuffed chairs and many colored bindings in two alcoves, beneath red-velvet panels bearing two life-sized silver bas-reliefs of George and Martha Washington.

Farther along the hall, a ten-foot mirror, framed in walnut and flanked by marble shelves and hat pegs, reflected the almost life-size cows of a twenty-foot oil painting on the opposite wall. Beyond, a nickel-plated knight in armour on a newel post, held aloft a gas lamp, globed in imitation marble. Obedient to his imperious gesture, the broad spiral stairs mounted slowly under a stained-glass window, pink and green, then on and up into the shadows. Across the hall, the image of the twinkling knight was blurred and caricatured in the golden-oak doors that shut off the dining room and the rest of Samuel's immaculate domain and beyond the stairs a single door always stood open on a dark-red corridor which passed behind the drawing-room to the slightly more cheerful promise of Grandfather Rand's private office. Here, on the left, a very large terrestrial globe, in nickel-plated gimbals, turned Asia and Africa to the glow of a coal grate. On the right, a low bookcase was heavy with the dark cloth bindings of "Moody's Reports" and the "Proceedings of the Anthracite Coal Association." And in between a triple window threw a wide expanse of light on the broad flat-topped desk, the massive figure of Grandfather Rand. He weighed two hundred and thirty pounds but no one could call him, even seated, stooping in his chair, a fat man. There was a firmness and a fineness to the shoulders beneath the well-cut black broadcloth coat, and to the big neck which rose smoothly in a mist of short gray hair above the starched collar whose wide opening at the throat was closed by a dark-blue silk necktie held by one large glowing pearl. There was even a fineness to the paunch against whose stately curves lay the heavy watch chain, like the anchor cables of a noble ship. And there was a fineness to the great calves outlined beneath the gray, striped trousers, and to the great ankles stretching the elastic sides of polished congress boots.

This pile, so still and vast, yet so delicate, was surmounted by a head, perhaps a little small, but showing beneath the thick, short, iron hair the compact strength of a Roman emperor's. His face, on the other hand, seemed large, perhaps because of the nearly white beard, though it and the mustache were short and neatly trimmed. There was about the brow, strongly modelled over bushy gray eyebrows, and the firm nose with its heavy bridge, and the strong, quiet cheeks, a simplification, an abstraction, such as the Greeks gave to the representations of their gods. But this effect was modified by his mouth, soft and shy and humorous, and again by the assurance and acumen of his blue-gray eye.

He sat in a swivel chair resembling those used to hoist painters up factory chimneys and save shipwrecked men at sea; and in fact as he gazed out over the street and over the river while his strong hand, brown with liver spots, tapped a silver penholder in time to the tune which he breathed heavily and softly in a sort of musical whisper, he seemed to be riding safely aloft, above all turmoil and all danger.

It was so, it seemed, that he always had seen his grandfather in his early childhood. At least, it was so that he always thought of him.

Now, as lying in the dark and silent hospital, he saw his grandfather again, saw all the details of that grave and massive figure in its grave and massive lair, time seemed to turn upon itself and lose significance; that moment of his early childhood, when first he truly saw his grandfather, seemed quite as vivid and immediate, the terrestrial globe, the desk, the vast immaculate figure seemed quite as near and palpable as did this hospital, this room, this rather hard and faintly rustling bed on which he lay.

And, more mysteriously, equally real seemed other scenes which happened in that room and in that house before the day that he could grasp them, but which having later projected themselves with telling impact into his life seemed now retroactively to create themselves and form a new part of his consciousness. For having, in his mind, entered the house as a child and made the dark and perilous voyage to the office, he found upon arrival that he, himself, did not as yet exist there; but that instead, announced by Samuel, or by a far more mysterious agency, there was a light step on the parquet flooring of the hall, and a plump little man with a fixed professional smile came through the door. His lips curled softly above his neat chin whiskers, but his light eyes were cautious and detached. His dapper body curved softly, but his steel-gray suit was hard and rigid. Carrying a small black bag in his hand he looked as if he might be a leading surgeon, famous for his professional dexterity alone.

With a slight roll, John Rand turned in his boatswain's chair. "Well, Riser, it's a nice day. Samuel, when you go out, close the door. Sit down, Riser, sit down."

Mr. Riser placed the bag on the carpet beside his chair. He rested his plump elbows on the arms and placed his finger tips together, continuing to smile. His eyes were not quite easy, and when he murmured, "Yes, Mr. Rand, a very nice day," it was with a shade of reluctance that hinted that "Mr. Riser" was the form of address to which he was entitled. But there was also in his voice the faintest contradiction which suggested that he was unable to withhold devotion to one who thus magnificently saw fit to deprive him of his due.

"Well, Riser," said John Rand, heartily oblivious of all minor complexities, "I suppose you know why I sent for you."

"Well, hardly." Mr. Riser repudiated assumptions. "Scarcely," he amended, after a moment's thought.

John Rand looked out the window impatiently. "Riser," he said, "the children grow up. We don't realize it. It seems only yesterday that my son George was in his first pantaloons. Now he has a son of his own."

"Certainly it does not seem long," Mr. Riser said.

"And now my daughter Clara is growing up."

"Ah, yes. Of course." Mr. Riser was cordial but fundamentally noncommittal. "Miss Clara is getting to be quite a young woman now," he said. "I passed her yesterday at Hickory and Tenth Streets; Eleventh, I should say."

John Rand continued to look out the window. "I want to set up a trust for her, one hundred thousand dollars, to become hers outright at thirty, if she is still unmarried; otherwise to remain in trust during her life, and then, if she has children, to be equally divided among them, remaining in trust for any boys until they are thirty, and for any girls under the same conditions as the fund was held for the mother."

"Quite so," said Mr. Riser, "except that in the case of female children the trust cannot again be held for them under the same terms. The law of entail——"

"Yes, I know. It will have to go to them absolutely, I suppose."

"Perhaps," suggested Mr. Riser, "you might leave the sum to Miss Clara outright at thirty with a private agreement, that she herself would set up a trust for herself and children along the lines you desire. That would enable the trust to be extended for one more generation."

"Of course, I know."

"And in a case where perfect mutual confidence exists, such as I am sure——"

"I do not wish her to know that this trust exists."

"Ah, yes. Quite so. In any case it would hardly be quite satisfactory from a legal standpoint, and that, of course, must be our first consideration." Mr. Riser half rose. "May I draw up my chair and make a few rough notes?" He set the bag on the table and drew out a sheet of legal foolscap and a very large ebony pen.

While Mr. Riser wrote, John Rand raised the lid of a mahogany cigar box on the desk. He touched the sponge under the lid to make sure that it was damp. He took the band off a fat, dark cigar and dropped it in the waste basket. With immaculate, square fingers he felt the dark body's plumpness and consistency. He took a match from a ball-shaped glass holder, and struck it on the corrugated side. Leaning back in his chair he smoked slowly, with light, stertorous breathing, surveying the room.

Over the bookcase, facing the fire, hung a geological map of

Indiana and a railway map of the United States. Over the fire-place, a Rogers group on the marble mantel showed a mud-colored widow receiving alms from a mud-colored philanthropist in a high hat; and on the wall above, in a colored reproduction of Meissonier, wheeling squadrons trampled the grain before the bantam in a cocked hat.

From his window he could look across the grass plot in whose centre the cast-iron stag raised a forefoot in perpetual challenge. Beyond the dusty clumps of locust trees he saw the broad, green river, slow and shallow, and the tufted islands far out in mid-stream, narrowed and sharpened by centuries of flow. His family had been following the river for many years. They had stood siege in their own fort on the headwaters of the East Branch in the year of the Indian massacres. And from that dim and legendary time they had slowly followed its course, always pre-sumably bettering themselves at each new stopping place. At all events, by the early part of the century they were in the Three Forks country and his great-grandfather, General John Rand, had emerged from the War of 1812 sufficiently less discredited than most, to cause a grateful citizenry to name Randville after him, and a pack of foxhounds to be sent out from York-shire by the British general who opposed him, and may perhaps have been grateful to him for a semblance of opposition suffi-cient to contribute, however slightly, to his own professional career. Then the times had changed from the days of broad acres and militia commissions, and his grandfather had built the turnpikes and toll bridges, and finally the canal. This last had been a mistake beyond doubt, but the old gentleman had pros-pered and had died, so his father once had told him, before he discovered it. His father, in turn, had started the iron foundry. That, too, had been a mistake, for the railroad was coming in then; in Pittsburgh, the big mills sprang up; and the little coun-try foundries swiftly withered away. So swiftly indeed, that he, himself, was brought home in the middle of the spring term from the boarding academy; ever since, he had been ashamed of meeting any one whom he had known there.

It seemed a long time since then, and he had come a long way. Farther, he reckoned, just to himself, than any of the Rands before him. Certainly he handled more coal than any other one man in the state, and his offices, strung across the

country, from New York to Chicago, were almost more than he
could keep up with now. He could only try to pick good men
and let them do the best they could. But they were hard to find.
Men who had grown up in the home office, here under him,
seemed lost when he sent them out to run an office of their own.
They were always telegraphing for instructions, or else, in a
panicky way, they decided to be bold, and made some blunder.
Again, the young man who was irreproachably honest in every
last detail of business dealing, as, above all, every one of his
young men must be, was often not apt to grasp the ways and
means of getting sidings and coal-pocket sites out of city councils.
And, on the other hand, a young man who was good at that, and
at obtaining special rebates and demurrage concessions from the
railroad, was more than likely, one fine day, to be a little too
smart with a customer. Times were changing, and, no doubt,
for the better. For the better, indeed, in every way, except that
nowadays it seemed as if there were very few young men of
ability who understood the basis of business honesty. He was
glad that George, his son, had married early, and settled down
in the business with him. There was a streak in George; and
he didn't think the coal business meant as much, or would ever
mean as much to George as it had to him. After all, George
would never know what it meant to put all he had in the world
in a single river barge, and float it, loaded with coal and thirty-
day notes, down from the mines, down to where the railroad
crossed the river. That was long ago. He left the barges to the
little fellows now, and hauled by rail. But he could see that
barge as clear as if it were yesterday, floating in at dawn, her
stern lanterns still alight, to the wooden dock where he had
been waiting all night long. He could see the long, humped
pile of coal, its base almost awash, and the ragged shoulders of
the bargeman, hunched over the sweep. George was a first-rate
judge of men, though, pretty smart.

Mr. Riser cleared his throat and looked up from his rough
notes which covered a sheet of foolscap, as fine and close and
regular as a steel engraving of the Constitution. "I presume," he
said, "that this covers it." He read aloud in a modulated but
rhetorical voice, imparting significance to each Whereas. John
Rand held the cigar motionless between his fingers.

Mr. Riser finished reading. He waited. "I presume," he said,
"that this covers it."

"Yes," said John Rand, "it seems to. Better have four copies."

"I had thought of five," said Mr. Riser, "to be on the safe side."

"I want no one to know about this. Not my daughter or Mrs. Rand. No one."

"My dear Mr. Rand, I really think——"

Mr. Rand continued to look out the window. "Yes, yes." He waved his cigar very gently, so that the ash would not fall off. "Let me know when you have the copies ready."

Mr. Riser snapped the clasps of his black bag. "Of course. Good day, sir."

Mr. Rand again slightly agitated the long ash of his cigar. He did not look around. "Good day, Riser, good day. You might leave the door open."

Beyond the road and the narrow park of trees, the river flowed, the green tufted islands seemed to float and tremble in the river breeze; far across the flat swift water, the dark green hills, the summer sky stood steady. Close by, a flatboat, coming up the stream, threw little puffs of smoke and steam and thrashed the flimsy paddle at its stern. She would anchor somewhere and dredge for sand and gravel and washings from the coal mines, a little water parasite that lived off leavings of the mighty. It had been a long time ago when by this river, farther to the east, where he lived then, he had waited for that barge through the night. Back there the river ran, narrow, fierce and swift, through mountains. The mountains that night were cold and towered over him, the river was cold and dark. Then, after the first sickly gray, a thin dawn came and he saw the barge and the pale lanterns and the long mound of coal.

Some one was moving in the hall. The rustle of a dress on the carpet came nearer. His wife's firm, even footstep sounded on the parquet flooring in front of his office door. A fine figure of a woman, he thought uneasily, I wonder what's up now. He knocked the carefully nurtured ash from his cigar and half turned in his swivel chair.

She was a fine figure of a woman. Her close-fitting, braided broadcloth gown showed that. She declared that she could wear that gown without a corset and escape detection, and that, in fact, she once had done so, merely as a test, of course, and secure in the propriety of her sixty years. Her face though finely if conventionally modelled was somewhat coarsely ruddy, and her

nose, though actually large, was lost between her broad mouth
and imperious, pale eyes.

She took her stand in front of the open grate. Mr. Rand made
an attempt to rise, hardly noticeable except for an added straining of his trousers and a light squeak from the boatswain's chair.
As if this squeak met the requirements he relaxed, contenting
himself with a brief, ushering gesture of his cigar, toward a
stuffed-leather chair, beside the fireplace.

"Well, well, Emma. Sit down."

"John," her voice was deep and husky, but musical. "Do you
have to smoke all the time?"

"Why, no, no. If I did, I wouldn't smoke at all."

"I should think you'd remember what happened to General
Grant."

His waistcoat vibrated in a soundless chuckle. "A lot of things
happened to Grant when Jay Gould and that crowd got hold of
him."

Her nose described a short arc. "You'll be sick in this room.
It smells like a saloon."

"Well, you know, I never smelt a saloon. I suppose," he added,
"that a man doesn't need to if he can have a room that smells
like one."

Mrs. Rand placed a heavily ringed hand on her hip. "I want
to talk to you about Clara."

"Is it anything special?"

"Yes, it is."

He heaved up to his feet, pushing hard with his thick arms.
He gave each trouser leg a little shake and moved toward the
door. His step was slow and short, but firm. His heavy shoulders
were stooped and his neck craned forward, but he carried his
head erect and his beard somewhat thrust out. Closing the door,
he steamed slowly back and lowered himself into his chair.
Thrusting with one ponderous boot, he swung round to face
her, then he spread his hands on his knees.

"Well," he said, "what's wrong with Clara?"

"Nothing. Clara's a good girl. You know that."

"Yes. A good girl. There couldn't be anything wrong with
Clara."

"But I mean we shouldn't let her drift into anything."

"Well, I suppose not; not unless she wants to."

You never will do anything about Clara. You leave it all to me."

"Well, what's to be done about Clara?"

"You don't seem to realize that Clara is growing up. You think she's just a sweet little girl."

"Yes. She certainly is a sweet little girl."

Mrs. Rand put the other hand on her hip. "Heaven's alive, John, can't you love the child without being silly about her? I expect I am as fond of her as anybody, she's my own daughter, but I try to do something for her, too."

"Well, what's to be done about her?"

"Haven't you ever thought that some day she might grow up and that somebody might want to marry her?"

"Why, yes, I have, in a way. I thought that everybody might want to marry her. Like to marry her myself."

"John—! John, that's a dreadful thing to say. It's—" her face turned very red. "It's sodomy, or something."

John Rand's beard bristled in a grin. "It's Gomorral," he offered.

"I suppose you know this young Rankin?"

"Well, yes, I've seen him around here lately."

"And I suppose you know who he is?"

"Why, yes, he's from Philadelphia."

"That's what I mean, here he is coming round and all you know is that he is from Philadelphia."

"What's wrong about that? He left there, didn't he? A man can't do more."

Mrs. Rand sat down on the leather-stuffed chair. Her fine figure leaned forward, her elbows were on her knees, her ringed hands clasped together before her. "John," she said. Her tone was that of constrained and exasperated pleading, "let's talk sense. We can't have a nobody coming to the house. Everybody on River Street is talking about it now. Mind you, I don't think there is anything in it, but you can never tell. We mustn't even give Clara the chance of making such a terrible mistake."

John Rand carefully removed the stump of his cigar from the holder and threw it in the waste-basket. He tapped sharply with the amber stem on the arm of his chair. "As far as River Street goes, I don't give a continental." His voice, from within his bristling beard, sounded cold and small. He subsided, but continued to tap more gently on the chair. "I hate to think of Clara marrying—marrying anybody. I hate it more than you do, I expect."

"Well, I'm sure that no one can say that I'm in a hurry to marry her off, especially while she's still so young and foolish."

"Clara's not foolish, she's——"

"But marriage is the natural thing for a girl. You know that. You don't want to see her grow into an old maid, do you, John?"

"I don't think she would ever do that. But what about this young Rankin?"

"Why, just what I told you."

"Well, that's not so bad, you know. He's been to the house a couple of times——"

"Three."

"Three times, but so have lots of other men."

"But we don't know who he is."

"We know he's in charge of the branch of The Keystone Wholesale Hardware Company here. And from what I hear, he's a real business man."

"Good heavens, John, it's not the money that worries me. We have plenty of that to take care of Clara, no matter who she marries."

"Maybe so. But I don't want to see Clara marry a man that can't support her."

"But there's no reason she shouldn't do more than that. She should make a distinguished marriage. There's no excuse for her throwing herself away."

"Well, how did Clara meet this young man?"

"That's what worries me. She met him through Monroe Worrall. You know Monroe has no more judgment. She went up to 27 River Street. Well, this young Rankin was there, and Mun had no more sense than to introduce them. He's trying to be like his father, I suppose."

"Well, Mun is no great shakes, that's a fact, but you know I always thought Judge Worrall was a pretty smart man."

"Oh, he was smart enough, but what good did it do him? I don't believe he left ten thousand dollars, and, what's more, do you know what I think? I think the money to put that plate-glass window in the Worrall's parlor is coming straight from us.

Ellen Worrall is a nice girl, but she's pretty deep. I've got more than a notion that she saves enough from what George gives her to do all sorts of things for her mother. I told George as much the other day."

"What did George say?"

"He didn't say anything, but I think I gave him something to think about."

"George ought not to be bothered. He's doing well at the office and he and Ellen seem to be satisfied with each other."

"Oh, he's satisfied. She can pull the wool over his eyes any time she's a mind, but she ought not to take his money and give it to her family."

"She keeps a nice house for George. Didn't we have a good dinner there, Thursday?"

"That's it. None of you men will say a word against Ellen Worrall, but mark my words, we'll live to regret the day that one of our children married into that crazy family."

"Well, what do you want me to do?"

"I think you ought to talk to young Rankin."

"I did."

"You did? I think you might have told me. What did he say?"

"He said business was fair and they were bidding on the hardware for the insane asylum, and two courthouses up State."

"I don't think that's funny. What did he really say?"

"He said would I mind if he smoked a pipe instead of a cigar, and so we smoked."

"Is that all?"

"That's about all. I thought he was a pretty fair sort of young man."

A short grunt of anguish and disgust was torn from Mrs. Rand's tight-pressed lips. She rose, turned away, turned back again, "John," she said, "will you talk to Clara?"

"Well, I suppose if there's anything in it, she'll want to talk to me, otherwise——"

"Will you talk to her?"

John Rand swung his chair around to the desk and looked out the window. "Yes," he said, "I suppose so."

CHAPTER IV

THROUGH the wall of the office John Rand heard fragments of sound from the piano, thumping vibrations of the bass and, now and then, the sharp tinkle of a high note. He looked up from his copy of *The Iron Age*. Clara must be rehearsing for the musicale. From the bass and treble fragments, he tried to make out the air. It was the Barcarolle, no doubt. She always played it for the musicale and always incorrectly. She cared nothing for the piano, to tell the truth, or for painting china either, but what else was there for a young girl to do? She was a good girl. She worked at these accomplishments methodically, but her attitude toward them was casual and detached. She seemed, and really it was a tribute to her good sense, to feel that they were not important. She also seemed, less comprehensively, always to be waiting, with good nature but with reserve, for something that was going to happen that was important, but of whose nature she had no idea; it was merely going to happen and would be important and delightful, so much so that it cast its radiance before it on the present moment and made it, and all other moments, delightful, too. But without, of course, adding importance to them. He supposed she ought to marry. What else could a girl do? But who was there for such a girl? He knew of no one who would do. And indeed, the girl didn't seem to be thinking about it herself. It was the men she met who did the thinking, and why not? Perhaps some day the right man would come along. Meanwhile, he'd have to talk with this young Rankin: to get a line on him. He didn't want her to marry any one, but there was no use to be severe on Rankin. God knows, no boy was to be blamed for falling in love with Clara, and Rankin seemed better than the most of them. He placed the agate paper weight on a letter. The arms of his chair creaked, as he rose with a strong push.

In the dark hall a flicker of light and shadow through the crack in the double doors showed that Samuel was setting the table for lunch. He passed on between the monstrous herd of cattle and their monstrous reflections in the mirror, on whose marble base a silver platter was heaped with calling cards, which seemed, so juxtaposed, left there ritually by the devotees of some bovine cult.

At the door of the library he paused and glanced in. Warm, cheering light flooded the bay window of plate glass and all the room. The red-velvet chairs slumbered in a sort of bright, gigantic cosiness, on the farther wall the red jacket of the hussar fording a stream stood out brilliantly. On the white ceiling, almost imperceptibly moved and trembled a faint, green tint, the tenuous overflow from the bounty of the trees outside. At her desk, beneath the silver medallion of Martha Washington, he saw his wife's assured and handsome back. If she heard him she made no sign. The other desk, beneath George Washington, had been designed for him, but he never used it. Indeed, he had conferred its privileges on his daughter, Clara. But she did not use it either.

At his back the treble notes scurried like mice underneath the drawing-room door. The bass notes hummed and purred through the walls and floor. If he had not been standing on the carpet they might have tickled his feet. Between these extremes he could make out enough of a blurred jumble to indicate that it was indeed the Barcarolle. Standing there, he commenced to hum the air to himself, correctly.

At the final chord, he rolled back the door. A low shaft of light from under the half-raised shades just reached the back part of the room, the grand piano's rosewood legs, the deep blue folds of Clara's gown. Her head, held slightly to one side, glowed dully, in the shadow. As he advanced, waist deep in sunlight, the gilded chairs along the walls, the gilded picture frames, the chandeliers, glowed also, in shadows deeper still. She turned her head. Her eyes were really enormous. "Hello," she said. Her voice was clear and sexless, like a boy's. "Music hath charms." Her small mouth gave him a delicate, crooked grin.

He clicked his tongue, "You always play it wrong."

"But with feeling." With a long, firm finger against her cheek, she assumed a heavily pensive pose. "I always make people who are not musical, cry."

"Also people who are. Your success is complete," he grunted.

She jumped up from the piano bench and menaced him with a narrow fist. Again there was something boylike in her charming adolescent awkwardness, as she stood there smiling at him, in her close, blue gown. She slid her hand around his neck and ruffled his hair up the wrong way.

"Don't do that," he said. "It really does exasperate me."

He let himself down on the piano bench; she sat beside him, unabashed and smiling to herself.

"Do you think I'm a good accompanist?" she said. "Would you like to sing?"

"Your mother has been talking to me," he said. She curled her long hands in her lap.

Looking away, he stared at the distant bronze head of the Numidian girl, a black silhouette against the sunlight of the bay window. "About young Rankin. She wanted me to speak to him, perhaps." Outside, he heard a double team on the street, and the light puff of a flatboat coming up the river.

"What are you going to say?"

He still looked at the Numidian girl.

"Well, that is what I wanted to ask you about. He doesn't smoke cigars, so it's no use to ask him if he will have one, and I don't know anything else to ask him."

Her hand slid over his and shook it, gently. "You could ask him how is business, wouldn't that be a good thing to ask; it is, always, isn't it? I think you are so nice, nicer than any one. Do you like me pretty well, too?"

He turned and bristled his beard at her. "Yes," he said, "pretty well."

With a small, pushing wriggle, she inserted her hand under his arm and hugged him to her. Her methods, he thought, are obvious and shameless, but they do not impose on me, or rather, they do.

"You are the nicest person of all," she said, "really you are."

"Is that a fact? Well, that doesn't look very favorable for young Rankin, does it?"

"Why are you and mother so worried about him?"

"I'm not."

"Mother, then."

"I suppose your mother thinks you might want to get married some day."

"And she thinks he wouldn't do."

"She just wants to know about him, that's all. She wants to know about all the young men who come around. It's natural, my dear, you are her child and she wants you to be happy."

"You wrote that and memorized it." She gave his arm a shake. "I don't believe you are telling the truth. You never are when you make long speeches." He grunted. "You should be ashamed." He looked away with a grin.

"Ashamed," she said again, "and anyhow, I think it's a nasty way to live."

"Good Lord, what is?"

"To feel that every man you meet is being looked over in—in that way, and that you are being watched, too, to see how—to see how you take him. How would you like it if every woman you met were watched like that and you were, too?"

He swung slowly round to look at her. "You know," he said, "I think I am."

She gave a quick, boisterous laugh, a single "Ho!" that burst out, swift and uncontrollable, and rang through the room. "Well then, you see how it is."

"The case is hardly the same, though, is it? With me, there is no question of marriage."

"Or with me, either. I don't want to get married, truly I don't. I think marriage is horrid."

"Well, well. Good Lord, what do you want?"

"I would like a horse and buggy," she said promptly.

"What for?"

"To drive around; out into the country, everywhere."

"But we have the sorrel and the bay team, and Levi to drive you anywhere you want."

"But I would like a horse that knew he belonged to me, then I could drive by myself."

"But a young lady can't drive around by herself."

"Why not?"

"Well, there are all sorts of things, tramps."

"But I would invite you to drive with me whenever you wanted."

"Thank you very much, but you know how hard it is for me to get away; the horse would be eating his head off." He rocked from side to side in reflection. The piano bench creaked.

"We could get you a spider and Levi could ride behind on the dickey."

"And throw things at the tramps. But would they like that, to have a colored man throwing things at them?"

"Well, what about young Rankin, then? He could ride on the dickey and take care of the tramps."

"No, I don't think that's nice. You are making fun of him."

"Oh, no," he said quickly, "I was just talking nonsense, too."

"Then you don't look down on him, do you?"

"Lord, no. He seems like a pretty smart boy to me. A first-rate man."

"Oh, I'm so glad."

"Why?"

She gave her short laugh again and squeezed his arm, and then subsided and slightly knitted her thin, dark eyebrows. "He is interesting to talk to—I'm glad it is all right to see him."

"Ah, oh, yes, of course. Now about that spider, of course a brewster—" he stared at the piano keys and tapped on them lightly with his immaculate, broad fingers. He felt that those enormous eyes of hers were on him, with a question in them, and were trying to make him look at her. Good Lord, Good Lord, was there no relationship in life where candor was allowed?

A tremendous guttural reverberation, Samuel's conception of a premonitory cough, sounded outside the door. He quickly withdrew his arm. She would have been content to sit there brazenly. He would have got up from the piano bench but there was no time. Samuel's warnings, while ample in volume, were always belated. Heels clicked on the parquet. They stopped, Samuel rocked forward on the balls of his feet, in a controlled ecstasy of satisfaction. "Luncheon is served." He almost beamed on them roguishly.

"All right, Samuel." John Rand got up from the bench. "I must go and wash my hands."

CHAPTER V

Norah was the horse's name, a small bright bay, with black points and, under her feathery forelock, a startled but benevolent eye. As she stood in the carriage, before the door, gently nudging Levi at her head, she was a constellation of winking, moving lights, lights on her ruddy quarters and small broad back, lights on the brass territs and blinker monograms. Lights even on the smooth waves of her black, fresh-wetted mane. Behind her, the fringe of the spider's canopy trembled at her light movements, and even the low-hung sleigh-like spider, deep blue, shining, new, sometimes moved and twinkled too.

To Clara, as she came down the brownstone front steps, all was shining and twinkling, the mare, the spider, the bright trees across the road, the broad river, the islands and the early summer sky. All indeed, but the figure of Levi Mistletoe at the mare's head. A stout, stately Negro in a coachman's livery of steel-gray whipcord and a flat-crowned hat of black straw, he was, of course, not intended to twinkle. But Levi could twinkle even so costumed, and now he did not. His bulk stood planted by the mare's head, square and unresponsive, allowing itself to be nudged but with forbidding patience. As she crossed the sidewalk, pulling on her chamois driving gauntlets, it was clear to her that Levi had not yet reconciled himself to this new vehicle. To a man raised to landaus, barouches and station wagons, it was trivial. Even the brown roll of fat above his white stand-up collar was rigid and grim.

"Hello, Levi."

"Good afternoon, Miss Clara," dutifully Levi touched his hat, but his eyes, brown and bloodshot, like the eyes of an old hound, continued to search for some distant, and presumably better land, across the river.

She took up the reins and whip, "You don't seem very cheerful to-day, Levi. I thought we were going to have such a nice drive."

"Yes, ma'am."

She stepped into the spider and sat down. It swayed gently and lightly beneath her. Norah stamped lightly with a hind foot. "Doesn't the river look pretty to-day?"

"Yes, ma'am."

With her right hand she smoothed her tan broadcloth skirt. "Such a nice day for a drive."

"Yes, ma'am."

"Levi, you are terrible. This is not going to be any fun at all. Why are you so awful?"

Levi swung his tragic eyes to her, "Miss Clara, I ain't."

"Yes, you are; you are awful. You know you are. Norah and the spider look so nice and look at me, all dressed up; and you are awful." She declaimed, "Why, there's not another carriage like this in town."

"That's it, Miss Clara, that's it."

"What's it?"

"Folks around here don't know what to make of this carriage."

"But it's the very latest thing; just this week in *Leslie's* I saw a picture of Mrs. Vanderbilt driving one, in Central Park, in New York City."

"Folks don't know a thing about that, they all making a joke of me."

"They don't do that. Why Levi, you're the most respected coachman in this town."

"Folks turn to laughing mighty quick. Last night a fellow come up to me in the barber shop and says, 'Levi, what's this I hear, you got a new carriage with the coachman's seat on the wrong end?' Everybody bust out laughing."

"Oh, but that was a joke."

"And when I'm in this rig, they holler things."

"What do they holler?"

"When I'm driving behind you they holler 'monkey seat!' Ain't you heard 'em, Miss Clara?"

"Well, I did hear it once, just one bad little boy."

"All the time they holler it—all the boys taken it up now. And when I'm in front, driving to the stable, they holler."

"That's silly, you're not on the dickey then."

"No, ma'am; then they holler—they holler, 'Nigger in the baby carriage!'"

Levi's broad face turned green, his eyes blazed with Basuto fury, his underlip trembled.

"Oh, Levi, that's a shame! They mustn't do that." She moved her tan skirt to one side. "You get in front, here."

He shook his head mournfully, "No, ma'am, Miss Clara; wouldn't look right and it wouldn't stop them. They started and they won't stop. They holler at me now, even on the brougham."

"Well," she said, "we'll just drive up River Street then. There are no bad boys there." River Street was, indeed, consecrated to good little boys and to their mamas and papas.

"Yes, ma'am." The spider shuddered and sank, as Levi heaved his bulk up to the dickey. Norah cast a glance of wonder behind her, shook her mane and started of her own accord. The metal tires rattled lightly on stones, crunched through gravel, ran softly through dust. The River Street houses passed slowly by. Close-built and neatly painted in gray and white and red and yellow, with marble doorsteps and shining bell handles, they presented an unbroken front against the world. But in the mind of Levi Mistletoe, as he watched these fronts against eruptions of small boys from alleyways, floated thoughts of what went on behind this long impeccable façade. Old Mr. Lippitt, whose mind had stayed like a baby's all his life. He had to have a nurse to dress him. Those two mirror boxes, hung outside the upstairs windows of the spinster's house, where Miss Jane sat all day, peering at what went on down in the street. She had lived in that mirror twenty years. Ever since the Colonel had run that Englishman out of town. The new brownstone house of Gus Ringler, the brewer. They said it couldn't be done but Mr. Ringler had busted right into River Street, big fat wife, trotting horses, beer and all. The brownstone mansion of Senator Beaver, with the coat-of-arms carved above the door. Senator Beaver, drunk night and day, and his wife that was so proud, afraid to go around any more. Big doings there last year, when they were trying to pass the railroad bill. Champagne, women from Philadelphia, everything. The Senator's butler told him he was about wore out, bringing some of the gentlemen around in time to vote next morning. There he was now, polishing the door handle. Levi raised a glove, in stately salutation. The Senator's butler spread one black hand on his blue-checked apron, and raised the other in stately reply.

The houses now were less uniform, and though on the left, the river, making no distinction, continued to flow by, still as broad, as shining, as almost theatrically beautiful, on the right were now the modest wooden house-fronts of the merely respectable, broken here and there by the ornately lugubrious brownstone elevations of late-arriving aspirants to social distinction. A great amount of money had been wasted by those anxious dupes, who could never learn that elaboration of façade did not compensate for, but rather emphasized, their lack of proper geographical location.

Against the ineffective majesty of one of these uptown brownstone fronts, she saw the purple plumes and paisley shawl of Mrs. Munkittrick. What was Mrs. Munkittrick doing here so out of place on a concrete walk among oak doors and spiked wrought-iron lanterns? She was going to visit that nephew of hers who had married a girl from the silk mill and never came to parties any more.

"How do you do, Mrs. Munkittrick?"

"Clara." Mrs. Munkittrick bridled, reined back grimly, and walked on. She had taken in Norah and the spider. "And to think," she would say that evening, "that when John Rand came to this town, a sole leather trunk held all he owned." She was proud to know the Rands, but could not help feeling bitter about her nephew and the silk-mill girl.

Ahead, the street lost the last pretensions to elegance, even to respectability; it was flanked on both sides by shacks and shanties, those on the left perched on the narrow strip of river bank, apparently sustained from falling only by mounds of tin cans. The distant figures of two boys, hunched on a flight of crazy wooden steps, rose up. She heard their piercing voices, "Baby carriage! Baby carriage!" She wanted to turn back. The boys of Billy-goat Town were noted. It looked like a bad time for Levi. From alleys and doorways, other figures came running, with whoops and barbarous gestures.

The road was wider here, a vague expanse marked by wandering tracks and packed by the bare feet of the boys of Billy-goat Town. She swung the spider in a circle and touched Norah on her flank. The little mare was trotting back down the river. The cries of "Baby carriage" died away. She pulled the mare, now stirred by thoughts of oats and stable, down to a walk. It

was a narrow world for her and Norah. Down the river, below
the covered bridge, were the railroad tracks and the docks of
river barges; back from the river were dull streets of business and
duller streets of little houses all alike. And up here, the boys of
Billy-goat Town kept a blockade between her and the open
country. Not that she minded them; it would be fun to whoop
and holler. But Levi's dignity must be protected. It was the
basis of his life—to be a Negro no white folks laughed at.

"Miss Clara," Levi rocked forward on the dickey, "your pa
ought to buy them Billy-goat houses. Tear 'em down."

"Why, that would cost a lot."

"Yes, ma'am." Levi's glove fell firmly on the back of the seat.
"No place for them boys—River Street. Them boys hollers and
always will. Lady can't drive."

"But it would cost a lot. It would be better to give up the
sider."

"No use to give it up, Miss Clara. We got it." He thumped
the seat. "What a man got, he got. And everybody knows it.
Tear down them houses. Then we can drive."

"They'll get over it, Levi. It's just a notion. You wait and see."

Levi removed his hand.

"Where we going now, Miss Clara? Can't go home. We ain't
been nowhere."

"We can drive down to the covered bridge. That will take a
little time."

"This little horse don't like that bridge; don't like that rumbling."

Norah walked fast and shook her head. The sun was on the
fresh green leaves and on the lightly dusted roadway. The river
flowed smooth and blue, and on it, reflections of small clouds
were floating down like ice cakes in the winter. On the other
shore, seen between islands, the country was bright and shining,
but to reach it, there was only the covered bridge, a humping
tunnel of a mile down whose dark cavern the farm teams
rumbled dangerously while dust poured up from groaning planks
and swirled in narrow blinding streaks of sunlight. The covered
bridge would never do for Norah.

She heard Levi Mistletoe's subdued salutation. That was the
Senator's butler again. The street from here on would be the
real River Street till she reached her home. Little old houses,

narrow and small compared to the broad-beamed, new brown-
stones, but superior in their air of uncompromising, neat and
delicate decay.

Among the faces of variously painted brick, the red brick of
Judge Worrall's was broken by the big plate-glass window that
Mun Worrall had put in since the Judge's death. There had
been talk about it. The money had come, they said, from Mun's
sister Ellen, and she had gotten it from her husband, George
Rand, who was doing well in John Rand and Company, Anthracite Coal. The window itself might have been acceptable; this
new plate glass was remarkable. In fact, one of Judge Worrall's old political friends, calling on Mun last week, had tried
to spit through it. But Mun used the window as an observatory.
Not that others did not, or even hang out "busy-bodies" upstairs,
those mirror boxes, like the one in Miss Jane's house, which
reflected all that happened on the street below. But people were
supposed to sit withdrawn, or look through curtains. While Mun
—look at him now. And yet she liked him, poor dear.

He stood in the plate-glass window, his thin aristocratic chin-
less head cocked on one side, one hand stroking his light, drooping mustache, the other in the armhole of his checked waistcoat.
His suit of shepherd's plaid was cut on exaggerated lines and a
little too large. His pale blue eyes lit up, he rapped on the pane,
blew kisses, pressed his hands to his heart.

He was on the sidewalk as she drew up. His thin, feeble
frame, overdressed, his dashing pose, hands in his pockets, feet
wide apart, gave an effect common, futile, yet sensitive and
alert.

"The Queen of Love and Beauty," he said, "with chariot and
Numidian. Hello, Levi." His eyes fixed Clara with fatuous
gallantry. "You should be drawn by turtledoves."

"We have no harness for turtledoves."

With his eyes still on her, he shouted, "Fitz!"

For the fourth time, she saw him, and now she could look at
him closely. As he came down the marble steps, one hand was in
the pocket of his narrow dark coat, the other held a cheroot at
which he gazed in melancholy satisfaction. His hair was blond
except for the brown of sideburns on his delicately ruddy cheeks.
His features and brown eyes were fine but a little small for his
tall frame.

Now he raised his eyes and bowed shyly but with faint amusement.

"The Queen of Love," Mun Worrall said, "lacks harness for her turtledoves. What can we do for her?"

She remained silent, merely smiling with attempted easy tolerance. Unless ignored, Mun's gallantries were apt to be elaborated and always for the worse.

Fitz-Greene turned to Mun. "What a question," he said, "to ask a hardware dealer."

"But seriously, Fitz, isn't she beautiful? I ask you frankly."

Clara laughed. "What a question," she said, "to ask a hardware dealer, or anybody else."

Fitz-Greene continued to look at Mun. "It would be hard to convince Miss Rand that the answer was spontaneous."

"Not if you said no," Clara said.

Fitz-Greene grinned at her genially. "I hadn't thought of that."

Mun pinned Clara with a heavily knowing eye. "In talking to a woman, a man must think of everything."

"You oughtn't to tell him that, Mun," Clara said, "you ought to keep it as your secret."

"He's safe," Fitz-Greene said, "even if I know how he does it, I won't be able to do it, too. Like taking rabbits out of a hat."

"Oh, well," Clara said, "never mind, Mr. Rankin. Taking rabbits out of a hat never seems to lead to anything."

"Perhaps that's its advantage."

"Isn't she beautiful?" Mun said.

She felt Levi's bulk rock uneasily behind her. He was looking at the upstairs windows to see if the Worrall's Irish maid, loose-tongued and blatant, was by any chance observing these high doings. The rocking of the spider started Norah. When Clara checked her, she stamped and reached for her bit. Oats and stable two blocks away. The men were saying something; better let Norah go. Mun was in hopelessly good form.

"I must go," she said.

"What! and leave us?" Mun said. "Did you hear that, Fitz?"

"Yes," Fitz-Greene said, "I feel so very sorry for her."

"You don't look it, or act it," Clara said, "so I'm going, really." Norah started.

"Why—" she said. He was seated in the spider beside her. Behind her Mun called, "Hey, Fitz!"

"Well," he said, "here we go."

"But really," he said, "I thought all that talk was pretty silly. You get started and you don't know how to stop."

"Like riding a safety bicycle."

"No," he said, "not at all."

"Oh," she said.

"But never mind," he said. "The great thing to remember is that I'm not as silly as I seem."

"I'll try to remember. I'll make a memorandum."

"I'm the one who should remember, perhaps. Look at those flatboats. They must be racing."

"Yes, they sometimes race home in the evening. The current is swift there between the islands. They go like anything."

"You can see the smoke above the trees."

"They come out under the wooden bridge."

"It must scare the horses."

"I suppose it does. I never go there with Norah. It's so long and dark."

"A long dark place is no place for you and Norah."

"Here is my house."

"I know. It was pointed out in whispers by the citizens." She pulled up to the curb.

"Besides," he said, "I have been there several times."

Shrouded in disapprobation, Levi went to Norah's head. Fitz-Greene Rankin was on the sidewalk holding out his hand. "Three times," she said.

As her foot touched the ground, he made a half salute and walked quickly up the street. She scanned the windows for her mother's foreboding face. They were empty.

"That will be all, Levi," she said. Levi's "Yes, Miss Clara," was a mutter. As she mounted the steps, she heard the spider drive away. At the top, she turned. Downstream, the flatboats had come out under the highest hump of the covered bridge. Steam plumed up, then their puny whistles sounded; like chestnut roasters. That was to scare the horses. Those river boatmen.

Across the river, the sun was low enough to throw a solid copper light on the wide water. The farther shore, between this light and the bright western sky, looked dark and firm and sturdy. High overhead the sky was fathomless.

CHAPTER VI

She knew at once, when she woke, that it must be a perfect morning. Outside, the birds were making what could only be called a din. Robins, song sparrows and chickadees had abandoned themselves; even the English sparrows were doing all that they could with their methodical and uninspired chirping. She thrust her feet, slender enough, but long, through the black rabbit's-fur tops of her red-felt slippers. The window curtains, hanging motionless, glowed with the morning light and with the green reflections from the trees. She pulled them aside, and, kneeling on the window cushion, peered cautiously out. A flight of sparrows fled from the maple tree, below her window. Across the street, in the locust trees along the river's bank, the birds were roaring. There was no other word for it. And, if she could have heard them, no doubt there were other riots in the islands and in the woods along the farther shore.

Resting her elbows on the window sill, she leaned out. On the dark red-brick sidewalk, below the maple leaves, people were already astir. She tried to make out whether they were mere casual passers-by or grocers' boys or neighbors taking an early constitutional. But the height of the mansard window foreshortened all alike to undistinguishable grotesqueness. The world of mortals, in fact, so viewed, became a somewhat ridiculous and pitiful affair. Little did those small individuals, pattering to and fro, engrossed in their trivial enterprises, guess how microscopic and absurd they appeared to her all-seeing eye. Little, indeed, did they guess, that at that very moment, their futility was being noted by Miss Clara Rand, in nothing but a muslin nightgown, with silk chain-stitching around the neck and the short sleeves. In a word, the world was a fatuous place, and she, serene, ironical, sagacious and elated, was far above it. Yet, not so far but that she could wonder whether, if young Rankin were just now to pass below her window, he too would look absurd.

Down below, Johnnie Feistner, the newspaper boy, came along the street. His sack of papers slapped against his thigh. He rolled each paper into a cone, and, without checking his stride, shot it into a vestibule. He was a mean, ingratiating little Dutchman, precocious, she suspected, in all kinds of wickedness. But just now she felt very fond of him. She wanted to holler "Hello, Johnnie!" and wave a bare arm. Just then, Johnnie looked up. She darted back and sat, squatting on the window-seat. She always knew he was a sinful little devil, yet, even so, she could not help, just now, feeling quite fond of him. The morning sunshine felt so warm and fresh and new. The shining river was so delicately, yet brightly, shaded, with the green of rushes and of reflected islands, with steely stretches and broad fields of blue, and with one point of lavender, where the brown of a sand-bar blended with the color of the sky. And here, by her window, the maple leaves, still young, translucent, seemed imperceptibly to float and tremble, in a brief unprecedented moment of perfection, that would never come again.

Back in the room, all white and silver, still shaded, cool and misty, she looked about her, as if expecting other marvels. In the shadows, broken by the first gay lights of morning, it was less austerely virginal. It had the elements of refuge, of mystery, and of a certain grave delight. The ceiling and the gray carpet were mottled with moving flecks of gold and green. The white wooden bed was less noticed than its rosy counterpane. Above it, the eyes of the Infant Samuel, also in his nightgown, raised with saccharine piety to Heaven, were, as yet, obscure. Colors showed above the white-tiled fireplace, the crimson ribbons of cotillion favors and, on the wall, the yellow background of the portrait of a nondescript peasant, smoking a nondescript pipe. It was not a good copy of an original that must have been far from meritorious. But with it she had won a prize for art at the Misses Wherry's boarding school; the art teacher had painted most of it herself.

As she crossed the room, she saw herself in the dressing-table's oval mirror, framed in white and silver curlicues. The light from the window behind, transluminating the muslin nightgown, showed her figure in silhouette. It was a disappointment. On such a morning she had hoped for something a little more opulent and radiant. But it remained high-shouldered and far too meagre. And yet she could see how a little change could accomplish wonders. The waist was slim, yet muscular, and flowed out in delicate, yet adequate, curves into the graceful base of the hips. The legs, while not all they might be perhaps, were long and perfectly straight. On the whole, the possibilities were there. She posed; an attitude of resignation, hands clasped, palms down before her. No, it did not suit her figure. Too near a suggestion of the mendicant. Niobe then, mourning for her children. But that, too, was a failure, the figure so lacking maternal proportions as to suggest that the cause of grief was simple hunger. Mercury, then. She raised a foot, a hand, and balanced on one toe. The pose was impossible to hold. She collapsed. But for an instant in the mirror there had been a flash of something almost perfect, of something lithe and tense and flying. Immensely gratified, she grew more daring. Why not the Venus Capitolinus? That was the slim one, was it not? She thought of slipping her nightgown to the floor. But on the bureau, tight-waisted and tight-haired, their hourglass figures buttoned to the neck in black, a row of the nicest girls in her year at Miss Wherry's, smiled at her with well-bred innocence. And beside them her brother George's broad and kind, but self-assured features above an Ascot tie and boutonnière, bespoke the best type of young Yale graduate.

And reinforcing these intimations of propriety, behind the bookcase's glass panes set in an intricate geometrical design of fluted woodwork, stood the body of her knowledge: the Bible, "Daily Strength for Daily Needs," Paley's "Evidences of Christianity," and, in the secular field, "Hans Brinker or the Silver Skates," "Plutarch's Lives," "Phil the Fiddler," "The World by the Fireside," the Elsie books, and the works of Mrs. Deland.

But yet this morning she felt newly risen from the sea and longed to be young Venus, desirable, provocative, disturbing. At least she could assume the pose. She raised her hands before her and trailed one foot behind. The drooping posture, compound of modesty and invitation, did become her, became her so well, indeed, that she was suddenly overwhelmed. Her hands dropped to her sides. She felt that she hid the germs of evil, that she was in her secret life an outcast from the world she knew. She looked closely in the mirror for the first faint signs of depravity. But her face with its high cheek bones and large nose was at the moment that of an uneasy, slightly scowling boy, the

clear complexion thrown into high relief by the heightened color
of her cheeks and the sombre depths of her big eyes.

"Oh, sugar!" she thought. "What do I care? What's wrong
with wanting to be Venus?"

She turned the photograph of George to face the wall. Again
she was daring and mysterious. The serpent of old Nile. Turning sidewise, she took a pose, angular and tense. It was perfect.
As Cleopatra, she was a complete success. And yet the morning,
so perfect in its sights and sounds and in her waking feelings,
had been flawed. Even here, and on such a day, something, her
conscience, perhaps even God, was watching and correcting her.
She could not be free. Great goodness, oh, great goodness, the
breakfast gong! From the lower depths its reverberations lum-
bered up the stairs. She snatched for hairpins and dashed to the
closet door.

She had to run back after starting down, to turn the photograph to face the room again. She wondered, as she went on
down the walnut stairs to more and more stately depths and
shadows, whether, if she had left the photograph, Miranda, the
German maid, would have guessed the reason. Miranda had a
very good figure; she might have guessed it.

Opposite the knight on the newel post, the dining-room doors
were open.

Her mother, in black satin, glanced past the copper coffee-urn
at her. "Clara, you're late."

"Well, well, well," said her father, giving *The Morning Citizen*
a shake. "Overslept, eh?" There was a trace of impatience in
his kindly tolerance. Samuel was pulling out the heavy leather-
seated chair for her. Silent, she sat down before the orange on
the square, gilded plate, feeling the weight of the heavy linen
tablecloth across her knees. What if she were to say—why should
she not say, "No, I did not oversleep. At dawn, I floated a demi-
goddess, in my nightgown, high above the street, and then the
Venus Capitolinus, in front of my looking-glass. It is I who
have been the busy one. Little you suspect, admirable Samuel,
and admirable mother and dear, obtuse father, what sort of
person you have with you in this elegant, well-established home."
Chilled by the thought, as by the impulse to leap when on a
dizzy height, she felt her face grow most demure and rigid.
Hastily she raised a wedge of orange on the pointed spoon.

It was a room of grapes. Grape clusters, in stained glass, glowed above the golden-oak sideboard, and, in the upper halves of the two flanking windows, grapes were carved on the lower halves of the two oak china cupboards beside the double door into the parlor and grapes were painted on the tiles of the fireplace behind Samuel's unbacchanalian figure. Even the cast-iron fireback of the grate, kept polished and never lighted, showed leaves of the vine in low relief.

She ate fast, Samuel sympathetically assisting her in her efforts to catch up and regain her position in the family. At the last mouthful of orange, the hominy, cream and sugar were instantly presented. The hominy, of course, offered no great obstacle to speed. Another series of Samuel's deft flourishes and she was able to embark on the poached eggs, fried mush and maple syrup, the scrapple, sausages, corn muffins and apple jam, while her parents were still at table. Actually, they had long since finished, but, in compliance with an unwritten rule, which forbade lingering at meals, they both maintained a technical semblance of continuing. Her father, running his second finger down the list of stock quotations, still held, between his first finger and thumb, a last remaining fragment of Parker-House roll. Her mother from time to time performed microscopic operations on a piece of fried mush as she read the morning's letters wherein handsome, slanting feminine hands begged to invite, to regret, to accept, to do something about functions usually involving a philanthropic object and the consumption of rich food.

But beneath her parents' silent absorption, even beneath Samuel's sympathetic ministrations, she had a feeling that all was not well. She hurried on, not stopping to read the letter beside her plate. Not that there was any need; it was in Anna's handwriting, and was, she knew, to ask her if, on next Saturday, she would join an excursion to the cove, which Anna's father was arranging in the Canal Company's steam launch. Anna had already asked her and she had said she would go, but with Anna, it was necessary that a letter should be written and, worse still, that an answer should be received.

The front doorbell rang and Samuel slipped from the room with a caution so elaborate as to be more disturbing than any moderate amount of noise.

"George, I suppose," said Mrs. Rand.

"Yes," said John Rand, "I'll be in my office." Clara hastily folded her fringed napkin and stood up. Tapping his paper lightly against his thigh, her father steamed out into the hall, his mind on his cigar. Her mother, straight and strong and satiny, went through the double doors, into the parlor.

She picked up her letter. Beneath it lay another. She did not know the hand. It was a man's. As she looked at it, and at the postmark, she knew. Rankin. All flaws, all chill, all shackles, vanished from the world. The day was again as it had started, as it was meant to be, perfect. But he should not have written, it was a crazy thing to do. If it had not been for Samuel, blessed Samuel, absurd, adroit and helpful, the letter would have been seen, her mother would have asked. Trouble then, and everything spoiled. But what was there to spoil? It was all in fun and he was really ridiculous, and not at all the sort of man; and yet it was fun to know some one so different, some one foreign, apart, who wasn't always being known about and talked about by every one else one knew.

She heard George's voice in the parlor, a pleasant bass, fresh and young. "Oh, yes indeed, that will be all right, Mother," and with a change almost beyond detection, but one which made her thrust the letter in her pocket, "Where's Clara?"

"She's in the dining room, just finishing breakfast." Her mother's voice was cold. Did she, too, note the change? Hardly, her voice was always so.

She was still standing there, by the table, as he came through the door. First, with the light behind him, he was only a heavy-set, but agile silhouette. As he stopped behind his father's chair, the dining-room sunlight fell on him, on his smooth-shaven face, broad, kindly and assured, above an Ascot tie and boutonnière. His close-cut hair, rather sparse and silky, was like a baby's. His face, with its slight, fixed smile, was like a baby's, too. But the round head and round jaw were strongly modelled. It was the face of a baby Roman emperor. Resting one square-fingered hand on the leather chair back, hooking a thumb in waistcoat pocket, he looked at her, somewhat benign, somewhat stern and perfectly sure of himself. There never was a man, she thought, so like his photograph.

"Hello," he said, "where's Samuel?" As if in answer, a tinny fall of water sounded from the pantry sink.

"Well," he said, "it's all over town."

"What?"

He shook his head in infinitely patient, brotherly reproof.

"Your taking that Rankin for a drive."

"I didn't—we didn't—well, what of it? Anyhow, I don't care."

"I don't suppose you do, or you wouldn't do it."

"Do you have to be so solemn? What difference does it make? I gave him a ride down from Mun Worrall's. Is that important? The town must be hard up for a scandal, to try to make one out of that. It shows how hard up they must be. But I suppose they have to have their scandal; they wouldn't know what to say to one another when they met on the street. They'd just have to bow and pass by."

"There's no scandal. People are just beginning to wonder whether you're going to marry him."

She moved over to the window. The sunlight fell against her blurred eyes, on her hot cheeks and stiff lips. She would like to turn and run out the door, across the startled street, the park of locust trees, and, running still, leap in the river, and swim away, away from the chatter and bustle and scandal, on the bank, away from the little rodents, paunchy and beady-eyed, who lived by gnawing and nibbling at all delight.

"There's no use getting mother and father upset over this," he said. "They don't know about it, now; at least mother doesn't, and that means that father doesn't, so if you just don't do anything more, it will all blow over."

He came up behind her and put one hand on her thin shoulder. A hand a little proprietary, perhaps, but delicate and strong, and really, she thought, terribly affectionate, in a somewhat patronizing and exasperated way.

"What is there," she asked, in a low voice, "so terrible about young Rankin?"

"Why, nothing, nothing at all; he's a first-rate young fellow, I guess. Only nobody knows him but Mun. And you know Mun's friends."

"You sound superior."

"I'm not superior. Fellows like that are just different. As a matter of fact, he probably looks down on us."

"Yes, I think he does."

"He does, does he? Why, Clara, where's your pride? You

can't let a stranger be insolent to you. It would break mother's
heart, if she knew, and I won't stand it, myself." He withdrew
his hand and thrust it in his pocket. "That's the trouble with
fellows of that kind; they're all right in their own place, but if
you give them the least encouragement they make themselves
objectionable."

"You act as if I were going to marry him. I haven't even
thought of such a thing, and he hasn't either. Can't people ever
have a little fun together?"

"He hasn't, eh? I'd like to bet a thousand dollars to ten, that
he has."

She felt a glow of pardonable pride, and of something more.
George did say nice things, sometimes, by accident or mistake;
that made them nicer.

"Think what it would mean," he went on, "to a boy like that,
to marry a girl from this part of town."

"A boy like what? Why, he's from Philadelphia."

"Don't let that stampede you. All kinds of people come from
Philadelphia."

"Oh," she turned away from the window. "I don't know
where all this talk of marrying started," her voice was small and
tired, "and I wish it would stop. I wish—" He was looking at
her, so kind, so interfering, so egregious; a flash of rage shot up,
burst about her. Who was he, or any one, to spoil her freedom?
She was stumbling from the room. She was blinded with spitting
lights and the red glow of fury. "The smug——"

She was running up the stair, wiping at her furious eyes. And
George, she supposed, was still standing there by the dining-room
window. George! she whacked the balustrade. In his Ascot tie
and boutonnière!

Upstairs, the bedroom, not yet made up, looked banal and
tousled, in the full light of day. What had seemed, before she
left it, merely a sweet disorder in its dress, was now frumpiness.
It was always so when you returned to bedrooms not made up.
She felt expatriated, the last refuge gone. If one's bedroom were
uninhabitable, if one could not stay there except harassed between
untidiness and the imminence of the arriving chambermaid,
where else find sanctuary? The letter was in her hand; she sat
down on the window-seat. This was the letter. The chambermaid must not come, not while she held the letter. And the

handwriting was slanting and refined. Would the sheets be ruled? No, they were plain white.

Dear Miss Rand: The carriage ride was a mistake; a nice mistake, but a mistake. I see it now. It won't occur again, and I ask you to forgive me as freely as I forgive myself. And I hope I will soon be allowed to see you in a way which is not likely to make things uncomfortable for you. In fact, I think a letter as considerate as this, deserves that much consideration, don't you?

Yours sincerely,
FITZ-GREENE RANKIN.

What a letter! She was ready to laugh, somewhat nervously. She was pleased, amused, slightly scandalized, uncertain. She had never heard of a letter like this before. Was he silly? Was he impudent? Was he self-conscious and inferior, and trying to hide it? Was he gay, sincere and at ease, or was he,—her cheeks flamed up, burning, was he trying to slide out? She looked out across the river. Mechanically she folded the letter and put it in the envelope. The fire faded from her cheeks. Or, was he nothing in especial, merely that? Just now she had been asking George why people couldn't see each other and talk if they found it amusing. Her thin, dark eyebrows came together. Was this a case in point? Had this young Rankin asked this same question of himself? It might well be so; it probably was. There was no reason why it should not be so. No reason why young Rankin should not have a thousand other interests, more important. No reason why he should not, for all she knew, be engaged to some other girl. Her cheeks flamed up again.

"Well, what is it?" she was saying, angrily.

"Excuse it me, please, Miss Clara. I come back later, make up de bed."

"All right, Miranda. Oh, no; never mind. Come in now, it's all right."

"Nice morning to-day. Oh, so pretty you look, this morning, with those pink cheeks."

CHAPTER VII

On Saturday morning she was in the library, waiting for George and his wife to call for her, on the way to the picnic. It was hot. Summer had definitely come. Though only ten o'clock, the blinds of the bay window were half drawn. Faintly striped linen dust covers shrouded the red-plush, stuffed chairs. As she fanned herself, glancing out the window now and then at an occasional, torpid passer-by, she felt that she would have welcomed dust covers on the red-plush panels of George and Martha Washington and on the scarlet jacket of the hussar. At the desk, beneath the bas-relief of Martha Washington, her mother's pen scratched and her mother's handsomely formed black satin back, erect and motionless, defied the heat and the new fashion of wearing lighter clothes in summer, with special emphasis on the thin, white muslin dress that Clara wore. The dress, reinforced as it was by a heavy, lace-fringed petticoat and bodice, gave only the appearance of coolness, as Clara knew. But even this appearance was, in her mother's opinion, a marked recession from standards. Indeed, the very fact that it was in appearance only, exposed it to additional contempt, as being a sacrifice of convention for no practical advantage. Unless, Clara thought, complacently, one could count it a practical advantage to look charming. She was not quite satisfied that the sash should not have been light blue instead of pink. But the filmy skirt, looped up behind in a faintly amusing suggestion of a bustle, the small, white tie, flying out from beneath the narrow, turned-down collar, the lace parasol, much smaller than the leghorn hat, all these were, she knew, summery, absurd and simply delightful.

The clock on the mantelpiece, surmounted by a bronze female allegorical figure, Ceres, perhaps, or the Spirit of the Philadelphia Centennial Exhibition, struck the quarter. Quarter-past ten. George and Ellen were late; or rather, George was. For, though exacting promptness of mankind, he, himself, was never on time.

With Ellen, his wife, it was the reverse. She was good-natured toward lateness in others—that could be said of her. And she, herself, was never late. Perhaps that was why they married. But now, above the level of the window sill, a very stiff, broad-brimmed straw swam into view. She stood up. Ellen, in a dark-brown broadcloth and brown satin hat that made no concessions to the weather. She was small and trim and her brown eyes were bright and knowing, but her pale face with its small sharp nose and uncompromising chestnut bang was too severe. George, while retaining elegance by virtue of his stiff shirt and stand-up collar, wore a short crash coat and tremendously starched duck trousers. They were blinding and rigid. Each bending of the knees produced a structural collapse, which she imagined she could hear; she turned to the bell-pull, beside the fireplace— When he mounted the steps it would be deafening.

As she spoke to Samuel, she heard George's key click in the lock. He came quickly into the library. "Good morning, Mother. Hello, Clara, are you ready? Where's Levi? Where's the picnic basket? We haven't much time to lose." He stood in the door-way, shaking the wrinkles out of his white duck trousers. Ellen's sharp brown eyes and pointed nose appeared behind his shoulder. "Good morning, Mother Rand," her voice, firm, fresh and rather large, was fluted with a sweet deference, which was not only obviously assumed, but assumed out of implied respect for Mrs. Rand's advanced and almost helpless age.

Mrs. Rand had turned and was sitting sidewise, but still very erect in her chair, her large hands resting, with latent strength, in her black satin lap. "Good morning, my dear. I hope you haven't been keeping George, to make him late."

Ellen's voice was contrite and candid, "I'm afraid I did, Mrs. Rand, I had to see about the baby's feeding."

That is not likely, thought Clara. George was never on time. She's sticking up for him. How well she does it!

"Young wives don't seem to plan ahead any more," Mrs. Rand was saying. "Now you'll have to hurry, through all this heat."

"Where's Levi?" George said. "Where's the picnic basket? Hello, Levi; Levi, where've you been? What? Well, we'll have to hurry."

Burdened by the covered picnic basket, Levi scuttled to open the front door. He had given thought to the problem of how a coachman should dress for the function of carrying a picnic basket to a canal steamer. He wore, above his dark whipcord trousers and buttoned gaiters, a blue serge coat, too tight, and customarily reserved for lodge meetings, a bag-wing collar, markedly too large, a purple tie and an imitation diamond pin. As he closed the front door behind them he placed on his hot, fat head his new coachman's summer hat of white straw, its rolled brim and flat top in the form of a beaver.

"We'll go by Poplar Street," George said, "and pick up Fitz-Greene Rankin."

"Fitz-Greene Rankin?"

"Why, yes," George said.

"Fitz-Greene Rankin?"

"Yes, yes," George said, "why not?"

"I thought you were lecturing me about letting him ride in the spider."

"Yes, of course. Great mistake. You practically admitted it yourself. But Rankin's all right. Met a fellow in my class at New Haven that went to school with him. He went to Princeton, belonged to Aurelian."

"Oh."

"Of course, those clubs there don't stand for things the way we do. But Aurelian is the best."

"But couldn't he get there by himself?" Clara said. "I hope he won't be late, too."

"We won't be very late," George said, "if you girls will just step out a little."

"I don't believe Levi can go any faster, with that basket." Levi's fat scuffling had fallen a little behind.

"And anyway," Ellen said, "it will ruin all Clara's pretty new things."

"The cinders on the boat will do that, anyway," George said. "You girls go on ahead, I'll help Levi with the basket."

"Help Levi? In that crash coat?" Clara gave her small-boy's smile. "But, George, I want to make a good impression."

"On who?" said George, as he turned back. "Fitz-Greene?"

"On you."

"Clara," Ellen said, "you really ought not to tease George when he's upset; it really does annoy him."

"Well, I've tried not teasing him, and that annoys him, too."

"I've never seen you try."

"Well, I'll show you some time. When I'm sweet to him, he belches."

"Honestly, Clara, I think that's a very queer way for a girl to talk. And especially about her brother; honestly, I mean it."

"But why should every one let George walk over them? I think I do George a lot of good; he does so much good to others, he deserves to have some one do good to him."

"Don't you think I'm good for him, then?"

"You make him happy, but you spoil him, too. You're as bad as Mother."

The effect of this was not fortunate. Ellen's small pointed nose swung round accusingly. "Clara!" She closed her small, expressive mouth, her brown eyes looked up at Clara with the contempt of a terrier for a greyhound.

"Well," Clara said, uneasily, "you do. Look at how you took the blame for being late this morning."

"I wish I'd never come on this picnic." Ellen exaggerated bitterness. "I do all I can to get ready in time, and then all I do is get told that—that I spoil George and don't know how to plan and tell lies."

"Who said you don't know how to plan?"

"Your mother," Ellen's voice was tragic, "I never expected you and your mother to combine against me."

"Combine against you, with Mother? Oh, Ellen, my Lord." She turned sardonic. "It looks as if no one wanted Mother on their side."

They were turning down Poplar Street, on which there were no poplars. Old maple trees almost met over the dusty road, and flecked it and the brick-house fronts with shadows and spots of luminous green. Below, their trunks shouldered through openings in the brick sidewalk, their roots heaved up the bricks into ridges and waves. Opposite the second tree, an iron fence guarded hydrangea bushes, a shallow yard, a front porch, and the reclining pongee figure of Fitz-Greene Rankin. Sitting on one of the porch seats that flanked the handsome, sickly brown front door, his trousers were thrust out easily in front of him, one hand was in the pocket of his pongee coat, the other held a cheroot, which he was studying.

He brushed a cigar ash off his coat. He stood up and shook

his trousers down with an air. "Hello, hello," he said. His voice was musical and amused. He waved his hat; the purple and gold band of the Princeton Aurelian Club flashed in the sun.

"Well, well," he said, as he came out the gate. He smiled at them as though he had surprised them in some faintly ludicrous situation. But if he was amused, he was also pleased. There was no mistake that while he laughed at them, he welcomed them with almost affectionate appreciation. It was exciting to be at once on such a footing with this stranger from Philadelphia— although his warmth embraced Ellen's admirable but unappealing presence without, apparently, the least discrimination.

"Hello," he looked back at George. "Need any help?" He walked between them, looking down at them in turn. "It was nice of you to come by. It will give me a standing in the community."

"It was George's idea," Clara said.

"I was afraid so."

"Mun could have brought you anyway," Ellen said.

"Mun has done all he could for me," he looked at Clara. "And this morning, he's busy."

"Mun busy!" Ellen said. "Isn't he coming on the picnic?"

"Yes, but he said he had to go downtown to buy a hat."

"How do you like Mrs. Otten's?" Ellen said. "Are you comfortable?"

"Perfectly. It's Mrs. Otten that complains."

"I should think you'd be the ideal boarder," Clara said. "A handsome hardware man."

"Any one would think so. I give an air to the establishment. Just now on the porch. The effect was that of the highest-toned boarding house."

"Of the highest-toned boarding house, perhaps."

"Well, what more do you ask? A man must be appropriate. Now put me in a private house, and I'll make it seem equally high-toned."

"Higher, maybe."

Ellen turned to him. "Mother says all you do is smoke all over the house and treat her as though she were a young and beautiful princess."

He knocked the ash off his cigar. "You see," he said to Clara, "what you're missing?"

Ahead of them a horse-car bell clanged. The horse-car stopped at the corner and stood, gently swaying. From the car, descended the great black alpaca figure of Good Doggie Trimble, with a luncheon basket in each hand. He raised a big fist to help down his homely sister, but only bounced a luncheon basket off her rugged hip. While he was trying to arrange the baskets in one hand so as to help Miss Meta Betts, whom no one ever took anywhere but Good Doggie, himself, she stepped down unaided, looking very demure and pretty in her blue-checked calico with a tie of green ribbon.

"Hello!" Fitz-Greene Rankin murmured, "a pretty girl."

Behind them George was hurrying up. "Hello, girls," he said, "hello, Doggie."

"Oh, hello," they said, "hello, hello." Good Doggie, bony-jointed, and large, too large for the suit he wore, wriggled his sandy eyebrows and gave a grin. His tall sister grinned beneath her beetling brows. She, too, was large, but formless and some-what hairy around the chops. Meta Betts smoothed down a well-turned torso with a well-turned hand. "So we're all going a-picnicking," she said. "It sounds quite Bacchanalian." She looked around with a sort of obtuse gaiety.

Poor child, thought Clara, that finishes her for the day.

"Well," said George, "we must keep right on going; we're late now. Here, Doggie, I'll take one of those baskets."

"Let go," Doggie said. "Help Levi."

Meta Betts, beside the trudging sister, looked back, still brightly. "We'll wait," she said, "I'm sure you're having a most interesting conversation. I understand," she said, as they came up, "that Mr. Rankin is very clever."

"And witty, too," Fitz-Greene Rankin said. "You should have made fuller inquiries."

"There, you see," said Meta, "a joke right away."

"And a very good one," murmured Fitz-Greene Rankin, in a tone of great dejection. Big Sister beetled at Clara.

"What have you got?"

"What?"

"We've got pimento sandwiches and cold fried chicken."

"I hope what they've got," Fitz-Greene whispered, "is not contagious."

"Why," Clara whispered, "don't you like chicken?"

"Not cold chicken. It's really the skin. It is hard to love the skin of a cold chicken."

"Or of a cold anybody," said Clara.

"A law of nature."

There was now a tailor's shop and an ice-cream parlor and the Evangelical Book Store. Then they came to the corner grocery, whose tree had a wire netting around the trunk to keep the grocer's horse from eating the bark.

That was the last tree. The next block held only blackish wooden boarding houses for railroad men; and on its corner, a resplendent bock beer sign above two dirty swinging doors.

Then they were on cinders and crossing the railroad tracks under the eye of a very old, whiskered man, who carried a soiled white flag. Fitz-Greene Rankin saluted. "A salute to the Flag," he murmured.

"But it wasn't an American flag," observed Meta Betts; "it was just a watchman's flag."

"It is best to salute all flags; nothing happens to the man who salutes all flags."

"Don't you want anything to happen to you?" Clara asked.

"Not at a railroad crossing."

"Superstitious, hey?" Big Sister said. "Well, lots of people are."

Ahead of them, above the canal wharf, the brown stack of the launch fumed impatiently. Figures clustered around it all turned and regarded them. They hurried on. A box car, stranded, grounded on cinders, showed signs of being a bunk house. A high halloo reached them. "Ahoy! ahoy!" A figure came toward them, executing a hornpipe, with much hitching-up of breeches.

"It's Mun Worrall, I declare," said Big Sister. She turned to Ellen, "Where did your brother get that hat?"

"He bought it, I'm afraid," Ellen said, coldly.

"Oh, but he couldn't have," said Meta Betts, "it's just a joke."

"He would buy a hat for a joke."

George had come up behind. "Never buys them for anything else. Hey, Mun, where did you get that hat?"

Mun, immersed in his rôle, ignored him. He cocked the child's white sailor hat, which was perched high on his finely sculptured head, over one pale-blue eye. With a pull or two at his soft, brown mustache and receding chin, he locked his arms in a quarterdeck pose. Making a funnel of his hands, he conned them with the glass. "The harpies of the shore," he announced, "shall pluck the eagle of the sea." He affected to thrust the glass beneath his arm, then walked off in a nautical manner. The others burst into exasperated giggles. Clara laughed softly and more freely. Mun was the buffoon of the world, but it really was wonderful the way he could make his meagre frame and flapping crash suit give the effect of a pea-jacketed tyrant of the quarterdeck.

With helping and murmurs, the girls were climbing down into the launch. Immaculately dressed, Anna Lisle remained on the landing, conceiving that, as hostess, she should receive on the coal-dock rather than in the launch. She wore a hussar jacket with many tabs of green braid festooned about the front and a leghorn hat with black-eyed Susans, Sweet Williams, mignonettes, and forget-me-nots swarming around the crown.

"Oh, dear, Anna, are we late? Are we late?" they asked.

Anna glanced at a watch which hung from a brooch among the hussar braid. "Oh, no," she murmured, "not very!" She gave George a swift, uncertain smile.

"Pardon me." Mun raised his sailor hat. He stepped up to Anna and turned her watch face out. He fell back and raised his imaginary telescope. He made adjustments, blew on the glass, wiped it on the meagre seat of his trousers and brought it to bear on Anna's embarrassed chest.

"Very late," he said. "Eight bells by the chronometer." He thrust the glass beneath his arm. "Tick-tock," he said. "What does baby hear?" He bent down as though to place his ear against the watch. Anna recoiled, pink and rigid.

"Damn it, Mun, have a little sense." The whisper was George's.

The smiles of the young ladies in the launch were forced and politely detached, except for a black-eyed, sturdy girl, who threw back her head and showed broad, perfect teeth. Her laughter was rich, easy and provocative.

"Mun, be quiet!" Ellen's voice was tense. She stepped down deftly, into the launch. Still murmuring greetings, the men took up positions on the forward deck. An expectant hush fell. The boat was about to start. They looked at the smokestack and listened to the clang of the fire-door in the minute engine room. Expectancy then swung to Levi, toiling up with the picnic baskets, his hat now removed from his smoking head. All watched in a foreboding trance.

"Come on, Mun, get aboard," they urged. Any unpredictable disaster might flow from the impending conjunction of Levi and Mun.

"Doctor!" Mun cried, in a loud voice. A broad German grin, well smudged with coal dust, emerged from the engine room. "Shall I cast off?"

"Sure." The head vanished.

While Mun busied himself with the bow and stern lines, Levi arrived on the dock. He had put his hat on for the purpose of touching it in response to their cheerful condescension. "Hello, Levi!" "Levi, how do you do?" "Levi." "Levi."

"Yes, ma'm. Yes, sir. Thank you." His collar was wilted and the purple dye of his necktie had not held up under pressure. He handed the heavy basket to the gentlemen on the forward deck.

"Thank you, Levi— Come on, Mun."

The boat drifted imperceptibly, from the dock.

"Come on, Mun— Thank you, Levi."

"You're welcome, sir. I hope you all——"

The coachman's hat vanished from Levi's head, on which there perched the little sailor hat. The gale of laughter was scandalized, angry, uncontrollable. With hesitation, Levi took the little sailor hat off and held it carefully in both hands. His smile was shy and tolerant.

"Come on, Mun!" their voices cracked with rage and idiot hysteria. "Mun, come on!" But Mun, in Levi's hat, was driving a four-in-hand down the coal-dock. The launch drifted. Levi stood, holding the sailor hat, resigned to any turn of events. The shout sank to well-bred fury. "Mun!"

Then Levi's hat was on his head again and Mun was leaping wildly to the forward deck, where he was caught by Good Doggie Trimble, who instantly found himself involved in a waltz. Strong hands of dignity seized Mun, manly voices hissed, "For God's sake, Mun," "Damn it, Mun." The boat's whistle fluted, the engine chugged. "Good-bye, Levi," they called kindly, tenderly.

Levi raised his hat, "I hope you all have a nice picnic." He mopped his head. Hey, hey, what a time! Those Worralls sure

were not folks; that Mun would clown it if it was the last act.
And he sure God was the biggest clown of any white man ever
he knew. Not folks, though. Now she was beginning to churn.
Pretty, that boat load, all full of white and colored dresses. Mr.
George was lighting a cigar, up front there; bet every other man
would do it too; always followed Mr. George. That black-eyed
Miss Balso was getting up from her place; going right up front,
among the cigar smoke and the men. Hey, hey. "Good-bye,
Levi"; that was Miss Clara. He waved his hand and bowed.

CHAPTER VIII

FOR some time she had been puzzled by the squawks and metallic bleats and quavers which came from somewhere in the nether regions of the back yards and alleyways behind the house. At first, she had thought that a fishmonger was soliciting customers, but the sounds were stationary and broke out at all hours, sometimes at night, rousing the neighborhood dogs to emulation. Consecutive notes bearing a faint resemblance to French hunting calls began to emerge. It was Levi Mistletoe practising in the stable. His other life in which he wore the blue serge suit and handsome civilian appurtenances, and moved as a social being and an arbiter in the Tenth Ward across the railroad tracks had, seemingly, led him into a band. She remembered on the Fourth of July the Tenth Ward Colored Republican Club and Clambake and Benefit Society marching down River Street with music, frock coats and lavender sashes.

"Levi," she had called back to him, one day when she was driving the spider down the road, "were you practising for the band?"

"What band is that, Miss Clara?"

"The Tenth Ward Republican Band."

"That band! My, no. Just riff-raff, that band. You know who the leader is?"

"No, who?"

"That Frog-eye Jones. Been in jail three times. Ought to be there now. Ain't I told you what he done out at the Good Fortune Firehouse?"

"No, you never did."

"And at the Rise Lazarus euchre party?" A history of Frog-eyed Jones led her away from her first question and held her till they had reached home.

This morning, as, in her shaded bedroom, she drove herself to compose a short and inane answer to a long and inane letter from an old schoolmate from the Misses Wherry's, there was a great creaking of floor boards in the hall. There was a light scratching knock on the door frame. Craning forward turtle-wise and ready instantly to withdraw, Levi's bulk swam into view. He beamed in a deprecating way, then looked back apprehensively. In the house, he always had the air of running Samuel's blockade.

"Miss Clara, could I speak with you? Would that be all right?"

"Why, yes. I hope it's nothing wrong with Norah."

"No, ma'am, nothing wrong with that little thing. It's about my music. Don't seem to me it's right. I do what the book say, but some way it don't sound right to me."

"Is that a fact?"

"Yes, ma'am."

"Well, have you got your book?"

"Yes, ma'am." Levi slid a long, narrow book from under the bottom of his coat and tiptoed into the room. He held the book out. On the dark, flimsy cover, she read, "The Modern Coach Horn." On the first thumbed pages were simple bars, while the last page offered "Annie Laurie" with variations.

"Well," she said, "what seems to be the trouble?"

"Don't seem to sound right."

"These first ones are easy."

"Yes, ma'am, I expect so, if a man knows how to go about it."

"Well, but you can read the notes, can't you?"

"No, ma'am, not exactly. When they go up, I go up, but don't know how far. I thought maybe you could let me know the tune so then I could carry it in my mind."

"Oh, yes, of course. But why didn't you come to me in the first place? I've heard you blowing away for a month."

"I was afraid Mr. George might be after me about it."

"Mr. George! Why, he wouldn't care!"

"Yes, ma'am, he would. He's mighty strict about having it a surprise."

She had a glimpse of George, in his Ascot tie and boutonniere, and Levi rendering instrumental duets, and then, of course, she guessed it. "Has my brother bought a coach?"

"Yes, ma'am, bought a brake."

"Where is it?"

"In the stable."

"When is he going to drive it?"

"Been driving it every night, Miss Clara. Got the big chestnuts in the wheel and the little browns in the lead. They going mighty slick now."

"Oh!" She jumped up. "I want to see the brake."

Levi looked at her. "Please don't do that, Miss Clara."

"Why not?"

"If you don't see the brake, you can say you don't know nothing about it. Then Mr. George, he'll be satisfied. He was mighty strict with me about the secret."

"How long is it going to be a secret?"

"Not long now. I expect he aims to take the folks out in it next week. That's why I'm studying about this music."

She sat down again.

"All right. This is the way the first one goes."

Levi nodded. "Heyo! That sounds like something now."

"All right," she said, "now you whistle."

Thursday, after a night of showers, turned out a cool and clean-washed day. It would, of course. A frown, even from nature, on an enterprise of George's was unthinkable. It was nearly ten, and Clara, in her tan, close-fitting dress and brown suède gloves, stood on the front steps to receive the coaching party. Inevitably, Good Doggie Trimble, his rugged sister and Miss Meta Betts were the first. The sister, a compact monument of gray mohair, tramped up the steps.

"Hello, Clara," she said, "what about this coaching? Pretty elegant. Dangerous, too, I guess. Does George know how to drive it?"

Delicately Meta Betts made sure of the belt of her plaid silk waist. "Quite an exciting innovation for Midian."

Good Doggie grinned down at Clara and crushed her hand smoothly and easily. He wrestled with his disappearing cuffs. "I guess George is up to snuff."

Big Sister confronted Clara. "What if the thing turns over?"

"You open your parasol and jump."

Big Sister thumped her solid hips. "That's all right for you little skinny things."

Good Doggie hauled his cuffs down with a long swing. "What do the men do?" he said.

"They wait till the girls have lit, then they jump on them."

"They won't have time to wait," Big Sister said, "in one of those things."

Good Doggie's hand clamped the fat back of his sister's arm. "They won't have long to wait for you," he said.

"Ow!" Big Sister said. She planted an elbow in Good Doggie's waistcoat without effect.

"Dear, dear," Meta said, "it all sounds very exciting and dangerous, and," she added, "amusing."

From up the street came the sound of a carriage.

"Is that it?" said Big Sister.

Good Doggie continued to grip his sister's arm. "Can't you hear it's just a carriage?"

"Ow!" Big Sister said. "Let go."

"Yes," Meta said, "I imagine a coach sounds more impressive."

"It's Anna Lisle," Good Doggie said, "in the wagonette. Is she asked?"

"Of course she's asked," said Big Sister.

A light wagonette with a pair of cheap horses in the best of harness and a shifty, Irish coachman in the best of liveries stopped well out in the street and made a rough coarse-handed job of backing to the carriage block. Good Doggie hurried down the steps in time to receive the wagonette's final jar, which ejected Anna's thin white muslin figure into his hands.

"Hello, Anna," he said. "Well, you're here."

"Yes," she said, "of course." Anna wrestled decorously to free her hand. "Oh, thank you."

"Would ye mind closing that door, sir?" the coachman said.

Good Doggie gave the wagonette door a resounding slam. The horses jumped into their collars and the coachman's hat tilted sharply back on his head. Good Doggie retrieved his right cuff and offered Anna his arm.

"Mother," Clara called back into the open door, "Anna is here." She looked down the leafy street. "And here is Mrs. Worrall."

"And Mun, too, I suppose." Mrs. Rand's voice sounded cold. "That makes the party. I must send Samuel to tell George." Her voice took on warmth. "George mustn't be kept waiting."

"But," Clara hesitated, "Fitz-Greene Rankin hasn't come."

Mrs. Rand was comfortable. "He'll come along, I suppose. Samuel!" Her handsome black satin surged out into the sunlight.

"Good morning," she said.

"Good morning, Mrs. Rand." The response from all was prompt and dutiful. Mrs. Worrall, in a little brown cape and brown-ribboned bonnet, was moving quietly but briskly toward the steps. Meta plunged toward her.

"Oh, my dear Worrall, how do you do?"

"Good morning, Meta."

Mrs. Rand inclined her head toward Mrs. Worrall. "Well, Emily, it is very good of you to chaperon these children."

Mrs. Worrall came lightly up the steps and accepted Mrs. Rand's gesture of a hand quite casually.

"I was pleased to be asked," she said. She sent a smile around among them, unforced, yet inclusive. She is tiny, thought Clara, yet she commands even in the face of Mother's grandeur. "Next to being wanted as a wife," she said, "the greatest compliment is to be wanted as a chaperon."

Mun Worrall placed his floppy panama against the breast of his checked norfolk jacket. He put his other arm around his mother.

"My girl," he said. "Isn't she wonderful?" He beamed at Mrs. Rand with a sort of inspired idiocy. "Good morning, Mrs. Rand."

"Mun," Mrs. Worrall said, "you are an imbecile."

From the side street down at the corner, a wavering but thrilling blast, the quick tramp of horses, the rumble of wheels, and then the shining manes and brass and steel, the light clink of chains, the red spin of wheels, and, above the little boys running, the long black brake body and George in a gray top-hat and driving apron, and the dark radiance of Levi Mistletoe and Sam, the stable-boy. The tossing manes and browbands swung and straightened out. On the guard's seat, Levi shot the long horn into its case, and began his precarious descent. With a light groan of brakes, they drew up to the curb. The horses sidled, stood still, reaching at their bits while Levi scuttled to their heads.

From the steps they clapped and cheered. George passed the whip and reins to his left hand and raised his hat. His smile was solemn. Mrs. Rand waved her handkerchief and looked like crying. Her George. He was indeed a figure, strong and square, light, quick. His stock was black, the white bone buttons on his boxcloth coat were big as saucers. A red carnation shone on his lapel. His hands inside the brown cape gloves were perfect. He could do anything, and do it well. Hadn't he gone into the Princeton game on an hour's notice and played first base without an error?

"Now, all you little boys," Levi said, "here come the folks."

Young Sam had set up a black iron ladder for the box seat. Above his dark new whipcord livery, the white of his smile met the white of his high collar "Now, all you boys," Levi said, in a strained whisper, "now, you horses."

"Anna," George said, "will you come on the box?"

"Oh, George," Anna flushed delicately.

They all moved down to the pavement. Young Sam steadied the ladder with one hand and with the other made discreet and ineffectual gestures of assistance in Anna's rear.

"Now," George said, "Meta and Sister and Doggie and Mun." Samuel moved the ladder. Meta climbed quickly and modestly.

"Hold on," Doggie said, as his sister started forward. He tested the ladder. Big Sister heaved up manfully; young Samuel turned serious.

"All right," George said, "now Doggie."

Good Doggie squeezed ruggedly past his sister and trampled Meta under foot. He thudded on the boxcloth cushion.

"Well, well," he said, "what do you think about all this?"

"Excuse me," Meta said, "you are sitting on my skirt."

"All right, Mun," George said.

Young Sam promptly stood back from the ladder, while Mun affecting to miss his footing, swung out and came up with flying coat-tails against Big Sister's bulk.

"Mun, I could shake you," she said. "This is no time for fooling. This is dangerous," she said.

"Don't worry, Sister," George said, "I've been working these horses for two weeks."

"Two weeks!" said Sister. "Why, it takes years to teach horses to do this."

"Now," George said, "the rest of you behind. We'll change seats coming home. Oh," he said, "there is no one to help Mrs. Worrall. Go to the wheelers' heads, Sam. I'll get down."

"No, I will," said Mun.

"My dear George," said Mrs. Worrall, "you are absurd. Mun, I forbid you to get off that coach."

And then it was Fitz-Greene Rankin's voice. "Allow me."

"Oh, there you are, Fitz," George said. "Good for you."

"Yes, I stopped for Ellen, but she had gone on." Clara glanced around. Behind her was Ellen in pink tulle, pink tulle a little too fluffy for her pointed nose. She had been there all the time, then, upstairs, she guessed, to be alone to watch George drive up in his glory. Now Mrs. Worrall was up and Fitz-Greene's pongee arm was steadying Ellen. Then his small, handsome features smiled at Clara with faint amusement.

"Ticket, Miss. Only an outside?" His hand, warm and deft as a woman's was steadying her elbow as she climbed.

"I prefer the outside," she said.

He was sitting down beside her. "A democrat at heart."

"All right, everybody?" George said. "All right, Levi?"

"Yes, sir."

"Then let them go."

The brake came off with a light iron thump. With his wrist, George laid a slow, light lash across the leaders' loins. There was a solemn crunch of wheels; the face of Levi Mistletoe came by. She turned to watch his progress. He reached up for the hand strap, he swung on the step; with the latent agility of a bear, he swayed up to the guard's seat. The little boys ran and hollered. She turned to watch the twinkling horses, the new-washed trees, the wide shining river. Behind her, there was a sepulchral hiss, an abortive bleat, and then the thin sweet notes of the Modern Coach Horn, Exercise Number I, were flung around them.

It seemed no time at all till they were between the littered sidewalks and the shacks and tenements of Billy-goat Town. Levi Mistletoe discreetly sheathed his horn, but their tramp and clink and rumble ran before them, a herald of their gay magnificence. Faces were at dirty windows, ragamuffins, the petty enemies of Levi Mistletoe, shot from alleyways. He need not have feared them, the grandeur was too much for them. Their mouths sagged open, they watched the passing coach in stupefaction.

Here was again the river, here were the open country and the first dilapidated fields that hung upon the edge of town. She was riding on the high shining coach to the freedom of the country beside an attractive and amusing, a slightly strange and mystifying young man. Not that he himself was still a mystery.

He belonged to the Aurelian Club at Princeton. And she had overheard her mother speaking of him. Overheard? She had crept behind the curtain and pressed her ear to the door.

"Well," her father said, "what did I tell you? She has no interest in this young Rankin."

"She hasn't?"

"No. I told you before. It would have been better if I hadn't mentioned it to her."

"It certainly would. John, do you know who he is?"

"I told you."

"But who is he, really?"

"I don't know who any one is really."

"He's a nephew of the Passamores. I found out yesterday."

"Well, I guess they're all right. That bank of theirs is small but pretty sound."

"All right? Why, the Passamores about run Philadelphia. It was the Passamores who gave the reception for the Prince of Wales."

"Well, we needn't bother about it one way or the other. She's not interested."

There was no further sound, but pressed against the door, she grinned as she sensed her mother's burning exasperation. Her father remained silent. He was wise. Her mother would never accept excuses from people for her mistakes.

"I suppose you won't tell it to me?" It was Fitz-Greene Rankin.

"Tell what?"

"The joke."

"It was an epigram. I made it by accident."

"Won't you tell it?"

"I couldn't. You have to explain it first or it has no point."

"In that case, I am sorry to have to tell you, it is not an epigram."

"What is it, then?"

"It is a little hard to tell without hearing it."

"It might be harder if you did."

"What have you been doing since the steamboat party?"

"I suppose you ask every girl that."

"Yes," he said, "I do. It's because I want to know."

"Well, then," she said, "let me see. The steamboat party was on Friday, wasn't it? On Saturday morning, we had wheatcakes and maple syrup for breakfast, and oranges, of course, and coffee. I take two lumps and cream. Then I practised for an hour, scales first and then the Barcarolle, you know, tum tum tee tum teedle tee tee, and Ellen came up with the baby and I wrote a letter to a school friend and it was lunchtime. For lunch, we had creamed tomato soup and turkey croquettes. I don't remember what else, I am sorry; and after lunch, I drove up to the farm with my father. It was Saturday, so he didn't have to go to the office. We had supper with the farmer. The next day was Sunday, of course, so we had fried mush and sausage, and baked apples and liver for breakfast. Do I hold your interest?"

"Yes," he said, "but I am a little disappointed."

"I thought you'd soon get bored with the details."

"But that's the trouble," he said, "you're too sketchy. You don't tell what you said and, above all, you don't tell what you thought."

"I don't believe that would add much. What do you think when you are eating sausage and fried mush? You think, I am eating sausage and fried mush."

"I think what a silly performance to stuff myself with great bolusses on Sunday morning and then sit stupefied in church until it is time to come home and stuff myself again. Isn't that what you think, too?"

"Yes, I suppose it is."

"You see, life is never as simple as it appears."

"Sermons in mush," she said, "and God in running brooks." Ahead of them, the pole-chains jingled, thin and musical. "George wouldn't like it if he could hear us."

"What could offend him?"

"I mean, we ought to be talking about the coach. It's sacrilegious to sit here and ignore it."

"I don't know what to say. I have never been on a coach before."

"Why not risk an unprepared comment, then?"

"No," he was serious. "You have to do a thing a good many times before you know what it means."

"Yes," she said, "that's really so."

He nodded his head. "The best thing is just to sit still and roll along."

She sat back and looked out over the gay swaying group, at the river and the tufted islands, at the yellowing wheat fields and a neat stone barn, at the off leader's nervous ears, and the white shade-flecked road ahead.

He, too, had leaned back and crossed his legs.

"That's always the best plan," he said.

Big Sister managed to rotate slightly on the seat in front. She showed the tip of her nose and one puzzled eye.

"Say," she said, "what on earth are you two talking about back there?"

"We were talking," said Fitz-Greene Rankin, "about the best way to enjoy a coach."

Slowly, and completely unsatisfied, Big Sister rotated back again.

Ten miles up the river, where mountains closed in on either hand to form a gap through which the river ran, swift, deep and narrow, they turned off to the right. They heaved up and rumbled over a stone-arch bridge and followed a meandering, dusty road along the base of the enfolding mountain. They were on the way to her father's farm, his pet and pride, his religion, his recreation and his only luxury. It was here that her father was suspected of drinking whiskey with Jacob Heisdick, the farmer, a suspicion not without foundation. But Mrs. Rand was wrong in thinking the whiskey an object in itself. It was merely the seal of their profound and understanding brotherhood. Together they battled with adversity and, undismayed, concocted new systems designed to include that combination of good luck, good sense and science which was the key, they agreed, of agriculture. The systems were good, perhaps as good as any, but John Rand's love of quality in all things physical, a love which showed itself in his desk, his chairs, his boots, his coats, his handkerchiefs, was here his undoing. Everything, from the locust fence-posts to the limestone spring-house must be of the best and must be so maintained. Here he was an artist and a lover and the child of many pioneers, suckled from childhood at the breast of nature. He could not bear that anything in this art, of which he was the inarticulate disciple, any roof, any gate, any wagon-bed or hame strap should be less than perfect. In consequence, he operated at a loss. To account for this, John Rand, normally hard-headed in affairs of business, had evolved a fantastic theory of economic retribution, whereby, at some future date, when all less worthy farmers were ruined, he, the perfectionist, would reap unheard-of profits from his fidelity to the ideal.

Ahead, a short foothill rose up. George laid his thong out under the traces and picked the four up into a short round canter. The brake gathered speed and swayed, talk died to a pleased excited murmur. In a sweeping arc, they crested the little hill. The blinding, whitewashed fences, the sloping fields of John Rand's farm came down to meet them. The horses dropped back to their clockwork trot; with nice, swift accuracy, they swung into a lane through gnarled apple trees. The limestone farmhouse was pointed with white mortar, the parlor shades were drawn. Mr. Heisdick's tufted beard came out the kitchen door. With his hands in his pockets, he surveyed them.

"Hello, Mr. Heisdick," George said.

"Well, well, George," Mr. Heisdick said noncommittally, "that's quite a rig. Better come in," he said, "I guess we got enough to feed you."

"We brought our own lunch. It's in a hamper inside."

"Well, that's all right. No use to set on the grass, though— not with a good house handy."

"We thought we would have some lunch up in the orchard. Much obliged just the same. I would like to get a feed for the horses, though."

"Well, that's all right, George. I'd have to charge for that, though. Your Pop's trying to show a profit again this year."

"All right," George said. "Sam, put up the ladder."

Fitz-Greene Rankin turned to Clara. Let's jump, shall we?"

He dropped lightly off the brake and held up his hands. She soared out and ended with a little run. It was really quite a jump. Above her, Mun was sailing through the air. She heard the thud of Good Doggie on the other side and George's voice, cold and dignified with exasperation.

"Just a moment, please. Sam will bring the ladder."

"We've done the wrong thing," she murmured. George would be unfriendly. Fitz-Greene went to the front of the coach.

"Sorry, old man. I didn't think."

George was appeased. Fitz-Greene came back, looking as far from a man who had acknowledged a mistake as possible.

Mrs. Heisdick's rich, German accent boomed behind her.

"Hello, Clara. When is you and your father coming out again?" Mrs. Heisdick become conscious of the others. "Such good times we have," she explained, "drinking beer and whiskey, and the old man and my old man making jokes, and Clara and me, we get laughing, don't we?"

"Yes," said Clara, faintly.

"Why, Momma," Mr. Heisdick said, "you talk like we was regular booze h'isters."

"Ach, no," said Mrs. Heisdick, "these folks know that. Won't you come in and set down?"

"Oh, no, thank you," Clara said. "We must help now with the picnic things."

She started to follow the hamper swinging between Sam and Levi up through the orchard. Looking back, she saw Fitz-Greene talking with deference to Mr. Heisdick. That's nice of him, she thought. Mun was talking to Mrs. Heisdick. He gave his zany laugh and thrust his thin arm through her fat one. The crazy mountebank! He was going to get a drink out of that old lady.

The hamper gave a muffled clink and rattle as Levi and Sam set it down in the flecked shadow of the apple tree.

"Levi," said Clara, "that horn sounded beautiful. And Sam," she said, "you look just fine in those clothes."

They stole glances at each other. "Yes, ma'am," they said. "Yes, ma'am." They beamed off into space, staring with eyes, unseeing and crinkled by their smiling, at the rolling fields below the winding road, and at the shining streak of river far away. Slowly Levi turned professional.

"Miss Clara, do you reckon this is all right for the basket?"

"Oh, yes," she said, "I am sure it is. This is the best place. Have we got anything to sit on?"

"Sam," Levi said, "you carry up them steamer rugs." He turned to Clara. "I got to look after my horses." He was all business and regretful. "But if you want anything, just holler."

Alone for a moment on the hill, she was tempted to sit on the hamper, but George, who was explaining the art of four-in-hand driving to Mr. Heisdick in front of the barn, might look up. To sit on the lunch hamper might be a breach of coaching etiquette.

And here came the others, wandering up through the trees. Big Sister climbed doggedly, chewing a straw. Mrs. Worrall, neat and brown, stepped lightly through the thick grass in the orchard, resisting the assistance of Meta Betts. Ellen walked beside her mother, observing Meta's efforts with detachment.

Down by the barn, Good Doggie relieved Sam of the steamer rugs and started up the hill. Clara kept looking at the coach. Sam and Levi helped George out of his boxcloth coat. They folded it and put it in the boot. On top of it, they laid George's gray top-hat. Levi Mistletoe closed the door of the boot and locked it with a shiny key, like a handle. He put the key in his pocket. The sacred garments were safe. George took off the coat of his checked suit and threw it over the bracket of the coach lamp; it was the signal for Levi and Sam to do the same. Apostolically solemn, the three shirt-sleeved figures busied themselves with traces, toggle chains, and rein buckles. One by one, the horses were led into the barn, where Mr. Heisdick, who had now disappeared was, no doubt, allowed to throw down some hay for them.

Red from spreading the steamer rugs around the hamper, Good Doggie looked up at her. "Oh," she said, "what was I thinking of? I ought to have helped you. I was watching them put up the horses."

"What are we going to have to eat?" Good Doggie said. He pointed to the rug. "Save that place for Meta. It's got a rock under it. Do her good to have a rock in her——"

"Hush," said Clara. "Here they come."

"What a delightful view, Clara," Meta said. "Your family always has the nicest of everything."

"Whew!" Ellen said. "I'm out of breath."

Big Sister took the straw out of her mouth. "I guess it slows you down to have babies, eh?"

Mrs. Worrall sat down on the steamer rug and laughed. "I didn't need help. I have had babies, too."

Ellen sat down beside her. "And what babies: Mun and me."

Good Doggie's hands swung out and tilted Ellen's hat over her eyes. "Mun's all right," he said.

Ellen's face came up, laughing, but angry. "Don't do that. It ruins my hair. No girl likes that. You never will learn."

Good Doggie looked at the ground, smiling and slightly red.

No girl did like that, but how was it possible to stop? That was the problem, especially if they were nice, and you liked them. "How about lunch?" he said. "Meta, sit there. I saved that place for you."

"Why, Doggie," Meta said, "how sweet of you. You are always doing the kindest things."

"How about starting?" Good Doggie said. "Where is Anna?"

"She'll be along," Big Sister said.

"Well, I know, but she'd better hurry. Where is she?"

"Go ahead, Doggie, and open the hamper," Clara said.

The lid of the hamper creaked. Its under side showed ranks of plates and knives and forks, fitted snugly into little straps. Inside the hamper, nickel boxes lay in a green baize compartment. A tea-kettle sat in its padded hollow. The other end of the hamper was packed with varying tissue-paper bundles.

"What a lovely hamper!" Meta said. "Do let me help."

"Stay where you are, Meta," Good Doggie said. "Clara and I can do it."

"No," Clara said, "I think Ellen and I should set the lunch out." She grinned at Doggie. "You go over there and talk to Meta."

The white-enamelled plates and cups, the nickelled knives and forks and spoons were set out on the plaid steamer rugs. They chatted while the covers of the long nickelled boxes were opened, to show packed rows of sandwiches, lettuce and bacon, chicken and ham, apple butter, cottage cheese, toasted brown bread and marmalade. Plates reverently swathed in napkins, held fried chicken, cold salmon, lobster salad, blanc mange. Fitz-Greene came up the hill, his hands in his trouser pockets, his hat under an elbow. As he walked, the lights and shadows moved over his pongee suit and his tawny hair. Clara looked up.

"Am I safe?" His teeth were uneven, but white and strong.

"Yes," Good Doggie called. "Clara and Ellen are doing all the work. Where is Anna?"

"Oh, hush up, Dog," Big Sister said.

"Well, I know," Doggie said, "but she won't get anything to eat."

"Do you think we ought to start?" Big Sister said. She let out an abrupt roar. "George! Mun!"

Good Doggie roused himself. "Anna!"

Big Sister placed her hands on her hips and studied her brother with resignation. Abruptly, Ellen turned away. "Really," she murmured.

"Oh, well, anyway," Good Doggie said, "let's start." He noticed that Meta was trying to shift her seat and lay down beside her, to block her off. "Chicken," he said, "for me. Lots of chicken."

"Here comes George," Clara said, "and Sam has the water. Now we can make tea."

"Tea?" said Good Doggie. "Good. Three lumps for me."

"Hello, George," they said. "Come on, George. George, that was certainly a lovely drive."

George beamed down on them, as though still on the box. He turned judicial. "Yes," he said, "I thought they went pretty well." He fixed a thoughtful eye on the lobster salad. "Pretty well," he said. "I don't like the way that off leader bears out on the hills, though."

"Oh, George," said Meta, "I thought they were perfect."

George looked at her, gratified but able, professionally, to shake his head. "Where is Mun?" he said. "We don't want to be too long. I don't like to drive these city streets at night." Weighted by responsibility, he sat down by Mrs. Worrall. "Did you like it?"

"I did, indeed, George. I am so glad I was the one to be asked to go with all of you."

George's face lit up. He did have a smile, Clara thought, broad and soft, yet warm and strong. "Who else would we ask?" he said.

They fell to the luncheon, making sure that George was served. Clara stood by the hamper, watching the alcohol flame under the tea-kettle.

"Why don't you let me do that?" Fitz-Greene said. "You've done everything else."

"Oh, no," she said. "You must sit down."

"You're making a great mistake; there never was a better man at watching a flame. Sit down," he said, "and when something happens, tell me what to do."

"When it boils," she said, "bring the kettle to me."

"Oh, there you are." It was Anna's voice. "Am I late?"

"You are just in time," Clara said. "Sit down."

"I was out in the garden," Anna said, "looking at Mrs. Heisdick's flowers." Her thin white figure sank down on the rug.

Good Doggie strove to catch his sister's eye.

"Clara," Good Doggie said, "how about a little more chicken?"

"Thank you, Doggie. I have plenty."

"For me, I mean," Good Doggie said. He inspected the platter. Nothing but wings and drumsticks. He took a wing. "Well, it looks like no lunch for Mun."

"Mun!" they shouted. "Oh, Mun! Doggie is eating all the chicken."

"Save a wing for him," Clara said. "Don't be piggy."

"Not at all, Doggie," Mrs. Worrall said. "He deserves nothing. He's such an idiot."

"Mun! Oh, Mun!" they shouted. "Your mother is giving Doggie all your chicken."

There was a stir in the depths of the farmhouse kitchen doorway. Mr. and Mrs. Heisdick squeezed through with Mun between them, linking arms. Mun's battered panama was perched back on his head. He clung to them, talking and peering up at their mild, red faces. In the sunshine, they came to a halt. Leaning forward at an angle, Mun tried to drag them on.

"George, do go down," Mrs. Worrall said, "and make Mun come. He's trying to get them to come up to lunch."

"I guess they won't come," George said. "They'd rather eat in the house."

Clara leaned forward and watched the group by the kitchen. "I wish they would come," she said. "They're awfully nice."

She heard Fitz-Greene's voice behind her. "I think so too. Here's the tea."

"I am sure they are nice," said Mrs. Worrall, "but Mun shouldn't ask them up."

"Well," said George, "he's not bothering about that any more."

Clara set the teapot down and looked back at the farmhouse. Abandoning his hospitable intentions, Mun was using Mr. and Mrs. Heisdick as a gymnast uses parallel bars. Gripping their arms to his meagre bosom, he kicked wild feet up in front and then behind. They stood firm and red and grinned at him. He let go of them and launched out with a swooping, skating motion. With a short turn he came back, hugged Mrs. Heisdick, squared off and boxed at Mr. Heisdick. They shook with silent laughter. Mrs. Heisdick wiped an eye with a corner of an apron. She shook her apron at him. He broke into a lope, head on one side, arms flapping, like the flight of an idiotic bird. As always with him, his clothes, his checked jacket and wide duck trousers were badly cut, ultra-fashionable and a little too large. He looked as always like a vaudeville performer, shrunken and fragile, but nervous and alive. He flew up to the picnic among the uneasy hush of all the girls. Which one of them would he unpredictably, yet certainly select for his embarrassing attentions? Mrs. Worrall waited calmly, ready to interpose. Instead, he snapped his fingers under their noses.

"That for you," he said. He turned and blew a kiss with both hands at Mrs. Heisdick in the kitchen door.

"Come on, Mun," George said. "We have got to get along."

"Here's your place, Mun," Clara said. "Have some chicken."

With a deep sigh, Mun sat down on the steamer rug.

.   .   .   .   .   .

They were eating their blanc mange. "There's a rig coming up the road," George said.

"Why, that's quite a nice-looking turn-out," Ellen said. "Could it be your father, George?"

George smiled at her with forbearance. "That horse," he said, "is from Simpson's livery."

"Well, who's that driving?"

"I don't know," George said.

Big Sister licked the blanc mange off her spoon. "My land, what a loud blue dress!"

"Why," Meta said, "it's Jeanne Balso."

"Mun," Mrs. Worrall said, "come back. Mun."

With a drumstick in each hand, Mun loped down the orchard. He leaned over the white fence. With flourishes, he stopped the buggy. Good Doggie raised up on his elbow. George shifted his position. Even Fitz-Greene, beside Clara, looked at the road. It was disappointing, she thought, to find a man of his calibre unworthily distracted. Jeanne Balso, of all people! Fitz-Greene Rankin was somewhat less than the person she had taken him to be.

Behind the men's backs the women exchanged glances. "I wonder," Ellen said, "who Jeanne has with her."

"It might be anybody." Anna Lisle cast a hesitant glance over her thin white muslin shoulder.

"Like the livery stable rig," Fitz-Greene suggested. Clara did not smile. The hypocrite; he still kept looking with interest at the buggy.

"Oh, I know who it is," said Meta, brightly informative, "it's that little engineer, Thompson or Johnson. You know, when they put in the new kind of mill."

"Mun will undoubtedly break his neck," said Mrs. Worrall, "climbing the fence with a drumstick in each hand."

"Will you look at that now," said Big Sister. "He's trying to feed the drumstick to the horse."

"Do you know what he is going to do?" Ellen said.

"Yes," Clara said, "I do."

"He's going to ask them up here to the picnic," Ellen said.

"Of course he is," Clara said.

"Oh, but I am sure they won't come." Meta was reluctant to surrender her position of authority. "She knows we have our own party, and no one knows the man she has with her." She smoothed the unexceptionable contours of her plaid silk waist.

Mrs. Worrall smiled. "On the other hand, she does know the men we have with us. On the whole, I don't blame her."

"Shucks," Big Sister said, "she's got Mun already. Look at him climbing in the back of the buggy. Isn't that enough?"

Mrs. Worrall laughed. "I wish I could feel that it was."

The buggy turned in the lane, then came through the gate into the orchard. It climbed, the wheels so muffled by the grass that they could hear the light straining of the harness. Miss Balso, her black hair brushed back, was radiant. She smiled at them, at the sandy little man in eye-glasses who drove, and throwing back her head, and showing her rather short, but fine, full throat, she smiled up at Mun, who stood behind the seat, and waved a benediction with a drumstick.

The buggy stopped, the gentlemen stood up and raised their hats. Mun leaped to the ground and held out his arms.

"Hello," she called out to them. "Hello." Her voice was deep and strong. "Mun, I'm much too heavy. You'd be flat as a pancake." She put a hand on the wheel and jumped down by herself. She was shortbacked and sturdy. She was quick and vivid and tough and warm. "Mun said we must come up. We were on our way to lunch at Hickstown. They say the beer there is awfully good. Thompy is working at night at the mill now, so he's off till six o'clock. You know Thompy? Mr. Thompson, Mrs. Worrall. How do you do, Mrs. Worrall? Miss Betts, Miss Rand, Mrs. Rand, Miss Lisle, and Miss—and Big Sister. Hello, George. You know Thompy, don't you? Doggie, how do you do? Mr. Rankin, I believe. Hello, Fritz. Don't anybody move. We are just on our way. Thompy, tie up the horse. Mun, where is that chicken you promised me?" She turned to Mrs. Worrall. "He'll promise a girl anything." Mun came up thumping his chest. He cocked his hat over one eye and shook down his trouser legs.

"Isn't she gorgeous, my friends? I ask you frankly."

She was unmoved. "No, Mun. It's no use. Where is that chicken?"

"I am afraid," Clara said, "that there is not much chicken left. But we have plenty of sandwiches."

Standing square, but lightly, in her blue dress, Jeanne Balso gave her a quick glance from her dark eyes, a look impudent, but frank and genial. "That'll be fine," she said. She sat down by George. "George, how is the new brake? It certainly looks elegant. Doggie, how about some of those sandwiches before Thompy gets here?"

Clara looked at the others. The girls sat silent with small, fixed smiles, eyeing each other. It was against morality that this girl should come into their party and carry off things unrebuked.

Jeanne Balso looked up from her plate. Her big mouth was full of sandwich. "George," she said, "I hear the brake is elegant. Are you going to ask me for a ride?"

Exchanging swift secret glances, preening themselves for triumph, the girls held their breaths, cocked their ears.

"You bet," George's hearty tone was unbelievable, sickening. "We'll be going out on Saturday, how's that?"

"That's fine," she said, "I'll be there." She sank her voice. "And look here, George. Do you think you could take Thompy? He's a great little fellow. It would just kill him to ride on a brake."

CHAPTER IX

THE life of their crowd now centred around George's brake. There were moonlight drives and supper parties. At times her father joined them in his roadster. Clara loved that. Her father would start an hour after they did; then at suppertime, they would see him coming, in his square-top derby and light driving coat. As impassive, as latently alert as Buddha, between the four tall, spinning wheels, he sat on the narrow, fragile seat, his arms extended, while Lou Belle, 2.28, and Planet, 2.31, stretched their necks and flew together in a maze of blinkers, breechings, spreaders and interfering boots. She had wanted him to let her go with him, but he had said, "No, when there is a young people's party, it wouldn't do. It would damage your reputation, my dear. You would be thought queer, and that wouldn't do. Young men are very shy of a young woman who is queer." He added, "I don't know why they should be. All women are queer."

They had taken a four-day coaching trip to the Indian Warm Springs. Mun had gotten a little tipsy and sworn at the waiters and kissed the girls. Poor Mrs. Worrall! As always, she had pretended not to notice; only, next day, driving home, she had said to Clara, "He is the best son to me that a mother could have. I suppose you find that hard to believe."

In the fall, they drove out to the mountains, chestnutting. They sat on rugs among the rustling leaves, opened the little hedgehog burrs and roasted the bright chestnuts in a fire.

The river froze, black and still. They adopted for themselves a sheltered place between two islands; the men adjusted skates to the girls' preposterous high heels, the black ice cracked, the steel rang, thin and delicate. Jeanne Balso, brilliant in dark red trimmed with white fur, skated with each man in turn, and then cut free to swing off down the shining corridor between the islands, swooping and soaring, almost without movement, light,

quick and strong, deep-bosomed, daring and alone. The little
engineer, bereft, consoled himself with backward leaps, toe-
pointing spins, eye-glasses perched on his impassive face. Big
Sister scuffled and bore heavily on her laboring partners, and
then deciding with exact justice when each had served his term,
slid about alone on curling ankles, with a moist nose and earnest,
puckered brows. Meta and Anna, adequate and undistinguished,
toiled decently along, resisting the menacing rushes of Good
Doggie.

Clara made the last strap fast, stood up drawing on her mittens, thrust out from the bank; it was a moment of bright fantastic glory; the gay yet bitter sky, the flying figures, the laughs,
the speed, the ringing steel, and beneath her own swift blades,
the ice, burnished and taut, faintly resilient like a living thing
which gave to her speed and sped her on. The wind of her flying
nipped her face and pressed against her suit of silver gray. Her
chin was in her otter collar, her hands swung together in her
small otter muff. The ice, the snowy island bank, the black, stark
trees flowed past. Glory of speed and flight and freedom;
when Fitz-Greene found her, as he always did, it was always
something of a blow. No one could help being warmed by his
figure in fur cap and tight, frogged jacket above tight trousers.
But it was a warmth of other things, of pleasure in a handsome
man and in his attendance, a pleasure of vanity, of reality, of
earth, not the delight pure, thin, intense, and other-worldly of
solitude and flying.

Then, as they swung together up the river, where space was
wide, and other skaters few, she seemed with him to enter a new
solitude. Their rhythm, broken at first, became attuned and true,
it stirred and grew in strength. This thing which they had
created had now a life and purpose of its own, a power to lead
them, change them, bind them, almost as if it were their child.
Fantastic thought, and none too creditable for a young girl, well
raised and skating with a young man of family, before the public
gaze. And yet the notion held her. With their arms crossed, they
held each other's fur-gloved hands, surely no very compromising
attitude. The ice was bare and cold, the wind was cutting, the
distant banks were grim with snow and blackened trees, the
distant hills were rigid steely blue and long rigid shadows grew
across the river. A scene to fortify propriety of thought. Yet,

as they flew together, she was aware, not only of his strong, light-moving hands, but through the rhythm which bound them, of every fiber of his body, of every fiber of her own. It was as though the rhythm had caught them up, and blended them into a pure and lovely, yet profound and passionate embrace. Touching together only their mittened hands, they were caught up in speed and flying, and made one.

It was incredible when they returned that the others did not read her glory and her shame. Covertly, she glanced at him. He smiled at her, inscrutable.

But at other times, when he came to dinner, when they went coasting or on sleighing parties, lightly sardonic, cordial but detached, he was, for her, as were all other men, a man of wood, a good companion and a charming figure. She hardly knew whether she wished to skate with him again. What were those moments on the grim river? At worst, perhaps a sort of degradation, at most a dream.

Then there were slush and rain and time for self-improvement and good works. The musicales took on new life and the girls' sewing club, until real spring should come.

They saw a good deal again of Anna Lisle, thin and fragile and graceful, with a thin and fragile voice. And at the girls' sewing club, Big Sister, despair and terror of the skating world, came into her own. She tramped and boomed. She bullied the girls of the lower classes who were being taught to sew, and was tireless in exchanging banalities with them. For them, she was the perfect blend of overlord and boon companion; they adored her.

In the spring, Mun Worrall, who during the winter was given, except for balls and dinner parties, to the strictest hibernation, emerged once more. The little engineer dropped out of sight. And Miss Balso, whose effervescence was less to be trusted, the elder ladies decided, in warm weather, was included only in the larger parties.

Yet under it all, as under the pleasant and impassive house-fronts along the river, something more vital stirred and sometimes even broke the surface. There were not the murders, robberies and public affrays, by which the lower orders managed to enliven the daily papers and their otherwise, no doubt, not too interesting lives; but it was known that Mun Worrall had been to see a doctor in Baltimore and that the doctor, having tapped his chest, had told him he had best devote himself to his mother, to his late father's legal practice and to the preservation of his lungs, and give up whatever idea of marriage he might have. To devote himself to his mother was easy enough for Mun, but as for the legal practice, it became increasingly harder to pretend that he was keeping even the fragments of the Judge's clientele. He sat in the little gray frame office, reading Paul de Koch, propped up behind the Revised Statutes, until he felt that his lack of business would be observed. Then he hurried to the courthouse and around to the other lawyers' offices until it seemed safe to go back to his own again. In the evenings, he played the buffoon and drank a little more.

And what of Anna Lisle and that young man from Richmond, with the face of a wistful, ruined poet, so kind, so clever, and so understanding? He was shut up now in some place where they give salt rubs and well-planned exercises, and the look in Anna Lisle's brown eyes told whether she thought salt rubs would cure what was the matter with him.

Once, in the corridor that led to her father's office, Clara heard an old man's voice. Why, it was nice old Mr. Newson, the head clerk in the counting room. Sharply it rose. "Mr. Rand, Mr. Rand! Give me a chance!" She froze. Her father's voice was charged with the judgment of the ages.

"Get up, sir. You are a scoundrel. You must go."

Meanwhile, Fitz-Greene Rankin was proving a most comfortable companion. He never worried about himself or others. The world was, after all, a slightly ludicrous affair. Once that was understood, it made life easily manageable. And while he was never either earnest or profound, he was amusing and responsive, even to the need for silence, rare gift for an entertaining mind.

It was comfortable, too, to know that he was so acceptable. No man could have possessed a combination of merits better calculated to appeal to the various members of the family. As a member of the Aurelians, he was the object of the critical George's admiration; as a member of the Rankin family of Philadelphia, he was approved by her mother and her father. Her mother knew, as who in the civilized world did not, that the Rankins of Philadelphia were connected with the Passamores;

and her father knew that six generations of Quaker integrity
had made the name of Rankin stand for all that was most solidly
meritorious in the wholesale hardware business. To him, the
name of Rankin on a man was as good as the treasury stamp on
a bar of metal. And while this young Rankin lacked the self-
evident earnestness of purpose which he himself liked to see
young men exhibit, he was bound to admit that most other
young men also lacked it these days, and that young Rankin was
pleasanter company than most.

Ellen Rand, in spite of her second baby and her mounting
church work, was warmed to find a man who did not share the
local theory that neither marriage nor the Ladies' Bible Class
automatically retired a woman from social intercourse. And
among the other in-laws, though their opinions need hardly be
considered, Mrs. Worrall seemed to like his jokes and his habit,
unusual enough in provincial America, of listening to what was
said to him and answering it; while to Mun, Fitz-Greene Rankin
was, to put it simply and imperishably, the man who had gotten
him into the Union League in Philadelphia.

In a word, he was a young man who, from any possible point
of view, including that of Levi Mistletoe, could be asked to drive
with her in the spider. As spring turned into summer, the drive
became a fixture.

But, though pleasantly enlivened by a certain nebulous glow,
an unparticularized light thrill, it was still despite the knowing
glances of the rest, only an amusing interlude. Indeed, those
knowing glances, naïve and slightly vulgar, with which society
in Midian greeted all particular relationships, had some adverse
effect on the affair. They did not change her attitude, but they
hardened it, stiffened it, left it less warmly vague, less natural
and spontaneously charming. There were, no doubt, advantages
to a town as provincial and a group as narrow as this. There
were loyalty, protection, and assistance. But the price that one
must pay for them was far too high: constant surveillance, constant gossip, constant intrusion and advice, the inevitable pressure
to penetrate one's individual spirit, and having done so, to re-
arrange it on the common plan; and having done so, what then?
Why then, to turn from it indifferently and seek other spirits to
re-arrange.

She kept on asking Fitz-Greene Rankin to go driving with

her, and her asking him meant no more to her, or to him as far as she could tell, than at the first. But it was a matter soon of some self-consciousness, some stiffness of determination. The question no longer lay where it belonged, between the two of them. Perhaps the difference was slight, but it was enough to have arrested their relationship.

This morning, when she came down to breakfast, she recognized, beside her plate, his large slanting hand, a hand that had asked her to be his partner at the Mid-winter German and had begged to send her once a copy of "Travels with a Donkey." The broad white paper bore an unobtrusive crest.

My dear Clara: Don't you think it my turn to take you for a drive? If you do, I will call for you with a genuine horse and buggy at four o'clock this afternoon; and if you don't, I will do it just the same. I am assuming that you can obtain the approval of your parents and Levi Mistletoe.

F.-G. R.

Her father, in his golden-oak armchair, was well settled in the financial columns of the morning paper, but as she started on her sliced orange and powdered sugar, she was conscious that her mother was making an effort to appear oblivious.

"It's from Fitz-Greene Rankin," she said. "He wants me to take a drive with him this afternoon."

"That's very kind of him, I am sure." Mrs. Rand affected to busy herself with apricot jam and a Parker-House roll. "Naturally, he wants to repay you for asking him to drive with you."

"He says that he hopes I can obtain the consent of you and Father and Levi Mistletoe."

"Levi Mistletoe! Well, really!" Mrs. Rand debated whether this might be an attempted impertinence or an accepted and legitimate style of humor among the Philadelphia elect. He was an estimable and eligible young man, but let him not presume to treat the Rands of Midian in a manner different from that current among the circles of his home.

There was a rustle of the paper and John Rand emerged like a great sea animal breaking the surface of the water.

"What's that?" he said. "Young Rankin? What's he going to drive?"

"He didn't say, Father. He just said he'd call."

"He has no rig of his own."

"Perhaps he's going to hire one, John." Mrs. Rand's voice was kind and slightly anxious. "He wants to repay Clara for the drives she's taken him."

"Repay her! You can't repay anybody for anything with one of those hired rigs. Dirty, creaky things, iron-mouthed, broken-kneed horses. If he wants a rig, why doesn't he borrow Norah, why doesn't he borrow one of ours?"

"Why, John, that's not the idea."

"And can he drive?"

"Yes," said Clara, "yes, Father. Of course, he can."

"How do you know?"

"He told me so."

"Of course, he did. Did you ever see a man yet that didn't say he knew how to drive?"

"But, John, everybody drives those livery horses."

"Yes, and they get run away with, and upset, too."

"But I am sure Mr. Rankin wouldn't take Clara out with a horse that wasn't gentle."

John Rand gave a deep abdominal snort. He retired behind his paper. As Clara and her mother looked at each other, he emerged for a parting shot over the breastworks.

"Who's spoiling Clara? At least, I try to keep her from breaking her neck."

"Why, John," said Mrs. Rand.

But he had retired behind his paper. They ate in silence. John Rand's consent had not been actually withheld.

He folded his paper with a shake, he heaved on the arms of his chair and rose up steadily. They avoided catching his eye.

"Samuel," he said, "tell Levi to step down the street and tell Mr. Riser I want to see him."

He tramped out of the room. They could hear his steady footfall on the way to the office.

. . . .

She sat in the library at four o'clock, not satisfied in her mind. Outside, while it was still bright enough, the brilliance of midday was past and the trees, the river and the distant hills were softened by a light, still radiant, yet now a little tender. The view was charming, simple, and inexhaustible; and it was

nice of Fitz-Greene to want to take her driving. There was something absurd and a little touching in his insisting on his hired
rig, and she could not help feeling a little proud. Frankly, it
was hard to conceive of his asking any other girl in town. If only
she felt satisfied about her sea-green dress. She looked down at
the skirt, brilliant and billowing in a bar of sunlight. It was a
dress one could not be sure of, too gay and daring for any element
of safety. She stirred one foot. Should she go to the glass again?
It would be useless; really, she could not tell. With a dress like
that, there could be no half-measures. It would be either a dashing success or patently ridiculous. Which of the two it was,
she should be able to tell at a glance, one would suppose; and
at the first glance this afternoon, it now seemed hours ago,
the picture in the mirror had seemed a triumph; but then
she kept on looking, turning and posing. It was too bold,
too bizarre; she had only to think what her mother would say
about this dress to know the truth. Its pattern was simple
enough, a tight smooth-fitting waist with a row of tiny green
buttons up to the narrow collar and a flowing skirt caught up in
a little bustle behind. No one could cavil at the design, least
of all her mother, who had selected it for her from the *Ladies'
Book*. But after selecting the pattern, her mother, reposing confidence in the unassuming browns and grays of other years, had
left the selection of the material to her. And she had commanded
little Mrs. Weinstock, the dressmaker, to send to New York for
newer and more dashing samples; and of those samples, this was
the most dashing of all. Sea-green, it was called. That might
have warned her, but the sample had not prepared her for an
expanse so brilliant yet profound. The fittings had been secret
and today was the first chance to wear it without her mother's
knowledge. Mrs. Rand had gone out to the County Poor House
with the board of lady visitors, and would stay for a specially
prepared supper in order to learn how the poor were being fed.
So she need not worry on that score; if she only knew whether
the dress was a touch of genius or obviously absurd. But it was
not easy—the sublime to the ridiculous, great minds are oft to
madness near allied and all that. Should she run up and change?
It would not take ten minutes; last year's tan habit or the new
white chiffon, both pretty and both safe. It would be the sensible

thing to do. It was easy enough to appear ridiculous to Fitz-Greene Rankin.

No, she would not change; the dress was lovely. If she could not carry it off, that was not its fault, but hers. How could one become distinguished except by daring? And now it was too late: here was Fitz-Greene. What a desolate old horse, and buggy, too; they must have been foaled together; and startling, in the sordid rig, Fitz-Greene's white linen suit; nothing could look more ridiculous than that, or more beautiful. There were other suits of the sort in Midian, but a curse had always lain on them. However starched and ironed, they were shapeless things. But in his white suit, Fitz-Greene looked almost as graceful as a girl. Those blinding suits of his brought out the tint of his slightly ruddy skin, of the latent golden light in his hair. They brought out his fine, small, mocking features and even, she remembered, the microscopic gold hairs on his small-boned wrists and hands.

Nevertheless, she thought, as she went down the steps, in that rig the suit looks absurd. The flash of her sea-green skirt caught her eye. Why, it was blinding. To have the man look ridiculous was small compensation for looking ridiculous oneself. She was on the sidewalk now. She must be erect and bold, yet casual. She waved her hand.

"Hello," he said, "we are both prompt, aren't we?"

"Yes," she said. "I suppose that is due to George's training."

He turned the wheel. She raised the front of her skirt with both hands; and balancing easily, stepped up on the rusty iron step and into the buggy.

"George's function," he said, "is to teach others not to keep each other waiting. Have you any suggestions as to how to start this horse?"

"If we had a piano," she said, "I could play the Barcarolle."

"You are not practical," he said. "If we had a piano, he could not move the buggy." He flourished the whip. "Hold your hat," he said. "Avante! Huzzah, my brave boy! St. George for Merrie England!" He brought the whip down on the horse's rump. 'Never mind the moths," he said. "This is the life." He whacked the horse again. "You can hardly see him for dust. It comes from his coat."

The horse arched his Roman neck with patient dignity and walked up the street. Fitz-Greene Rankin put the whip in the socket, and sat back. "No need for further agitation," he explained. "This is his only gait."

"Oh, well," she said, "we're not trying to get anywhere."

"But that's the point. If you have an objective, speed is no object. Merely getting there is your reward. But if you have no place to go, you must travel fast."

"Why do people take the steam trains, then?"

"There is no other way to travel any more. But does any one imagine they have as much fun as the Canterbury Pilgrims?"

"But the Canterbury Pilgrims would have had as much fun whether they got to Canterbury or not. Anyhow," she said, "I am glad to go slowly and watch the river."

"After all," he said, "that is only fair; because your father is responsible for this horse."

"He is?"

"Yes. You know his confidential man of business, Mr. Riser? I felt very sorry for Mr. Riser, to-day. I suppose I ought not to tell this, but he came to my office. Your father had sent him to interview me on the subject of horses. After all, he is a lawyer and a confidential man of business. But then he is one of these peculiar men who find it painful to discuss something that he does not understand."

"What," she said, "was this all about? Don't let Father sell you a horse."

"No. This was to find out what horse I had hired to take you driving with. I just happened to be able to remember the name." He pointed at the dusty, fur-tufted rump. "It's Alexander."

"I don't believe that," she said.

"Why should I deceive you? It would be useless, once you have seen him."

"All right, then," she said, "go on."

"That's all," he said, "except that I suspect that Mr. Riser was then bound for the livery stable to find out all about Alexander for your father's information. I wish I could have been there with Alexander and Mr. Riser in the livery stable."

"It all sounds silly. Why couldn't Father have trusted you? I told him you know all about horses."

"But he is more astute than you."

"Well, then, why couldn't he have sent to the livery stable? The man would have told him what horse you had hired."

"But that would have been an affront to my honor, to spy on Alexander behind my back." He took up the whip and whacked the unresponsive rump.

"No relation is more sacred," he said, "than that between a man and his horse. Your father showed great delicacy of feeling."

.   .   .   .

Far up the river, where the road abandoned formality and ran through scattered elm trees along the bank, there was a well-worn hitching rail, and beside it, an old stone watering-trough. Alexander veered sedately off the road and plunged his head into the narrow pool.

"Suppose we take a rest," he said. "It is very exhausting to drive so slowly." He handed her the reins and got out of the buggy with a frayed hitching rope in his hand. "Any advice," he said, "will be welcome."

"Do you really mean it?" she said. "I can't believe it. Well, then, the end with the snap-hook goes round his neck. You know that, I suppose."

"No," he said, "it is all news."

"Now snap the hook on the ring. Now, if you want to be very safe, run the other end through the bit-ring. Then you tie it to the hitching rail."

"A wonderful woman," he said. "Thinks just like a man. How's that? Wait. I'll help you."

But she was out of the buggy. "It's all right." She glanced at Alexander's hitching rope. "It's a little long, but it will do."

"I tried to lift his head to make it shorter, but he rolled his eye and made submarine noises."

She laughed. They walked across the road to the park-like grove of trees above the river. Up here, there were no islands, and the water was still deep and swift from the narrow gap in the mountains. There was a dark, tense sheen on it that spoke of power. It had not yet squandered itself in genial expansiveness and many ripples. The hills on the other side were sharper, darker, the bank on this side higher and overhanging.

"Do you know," he said, "you really did something worth while when you bought that dress?"

"Oh, do you like it really?"

"Yes, of course, don't you?"

"I don't know, I want to, but it takes a good deal of conceit to do it."

"Yes," he said. "I suppose you were worried about it."

"You really do understand some things, don't you?"

"I understand everything."

"It sounds a little self-confident."

"I should have said everything except Alexander and myself. Our simplicity is unscrutable."

"Are you trying to tell me that you are a simple person?"

"It's the only fair thing to do."

"I suppose that under all your wit and worldliness beats a heart of gold?"

"Well, not a heart of gold, but something equally simple; just a desire to get what I want."

She looked at him seriously. "Yes, nothing could be simpler than that, if you always know what you want."

"I always do."

"And do you always get it?"

"To get what you want is easy."

"I suppose you wouldn't tell me your great secret?"

"The system is to have great consideration for others."

"That doesn't sound original to me."

"I didn't finish. To have great consideration for others, without any sympathy for them."

"I should think the trouble with your system might be," she said, "that after a while other people would began to notice it."

"What if they do? Why should they object? They are getting what they want from me. What they want, like everybody else, is consideration, not sympathy. Most sympathetic persons are a nuisance. But show me the considerate man who is not welcome everywhere."

"But how can you be considerate if you are not sympathetic? You will have no way of knowing how people wish to be treated or what they want."

"Why, that information," he said, "people are only too glad to give you themselves."

"Have I told you how I want to be treated?"

"No, you are a different customer. I have had to do a great deal of guesswork. Have I made many mistakes?"

"I don't know. I have never thought about it that way."

"Neither have I. If I had, it would have been the greatest mistake of all." He thrust his hands in his pockets and walked off a few steps under the trees, slightly frowning, his eyes on the ground. "With you," he spoke as if he were talking to himself, "I have learned how enormous and exciting selfishness can be." He turned and looked up at her with a quick smile, then looked down again. "I have just wanted to be with you." He started back toward her, still looking at the ground. "Wanting that was all I needed to make me do my best." He arrived in front of her, looked up again, and smiled. "A system was not needed. Give me your hand." Through her glove she felt his warm, slim fingers. She saw his other hand close over hers. Her hand, suddenly enclosed in warmth and strength, almost trembled. He gave it a quick, short shake and let it fall. "Do you believe that?"

"Yes," she said.

He walked away again. "No system whatever," he said. He leaned against a tree. The western sun was on his small, alert, good-looking face. "Now would be the time for the world to stand still, just as it is, the sun, the river, Alexander, you and I."

"But Alexander," she said, in a low voice, "might get hungry."

"His appetite would stand still like everything else."

"But suppose he's hungry now?"

He walked straight back to her. His arm went around her neck a light deft kiss was left on her astonished cheek.

"You are perfectly ridiculous," he said. "Are we going to love each other?"

"I don't know," she said. "I don't know. It's hard to tell."

CHAPTER X

It was three nights later that she was walking home from supper at George's. George and Ellen had been kind. Over the fried chicken and stuffed tomatoes, they had managed to throw a feeling of solidarity and slightly heavy gaiety. There was a touch of the studious in the indifference with which they mentioned Fitz. So the news had spread. But what news was it? She was being tacitly congratulated. It was all too soon, too dubious. Matters were obscure enough, delicate enough, elusive and treacherous enough, without the intrusion of heavy, bland assumptions.

George had offered to walk home with her, but it was, after all, only three blocks, and those the most respectable in Midian. She was pleased to hear the heavy front door jar shut behind her and hurried down the wide granite steps without a look behind for fear that George, no doubt peering at her through the grille, might take it as a chance to join her. She jumped down the last three steps and passed the bulging bay-window of the drawing-room, wondering whether Ellen was observing her from there.

On River Street the new acetylene lights made quite a show. It was only when she reached the field of darkness that lay between them that the street seemed the same. Then on her right a warm glow filtered from curtained drawing-rooms, rich overflow of the elegance within; on her left, the trees were shrouded shadows, and beyond them the river flowed silent, swift, and barely touched with faint reflections of the stars. Far off, on the black shore, small lights of farmhouses showed and behind her, from the darkness, she heard the rumble of a farm team on the covered wooden bridge. Here, beyond reach of the new street-lights' sputtering glare, the town was still the same, still at one with fields and farm teams, the river and the sky.

But then at the next street corner, another light swung to blind and blot out; paradoxical function. Now she was past it and beneath the sky again.

At first, it seemed impossible that it was he, then instantly it was inevitable, and what was going to happen, whatever it was, had been long foreseen. His black, slim shadow stood in front of her.

"Hello," she said. He did not answer. "Where are you going?"

"I'm waiting," he said.

He is waiting, she told herself. Waiting for me? For me. She felt the answer in his shadow.

"Who are you waiting for?" she said.

Again he did not answer.

"I am going home," she said. "From George's. Will you walk along with me?"

He did not move. "Clara," he said.

It was frightening; a voice from strange depths clogged, shaken, not pleasant.

"Walk along with me," she said; then, "where have you been these last few days?" She was saying all the wrong things. He would think she meant to lead him on—while actually—and yet that tall shadow, near and graceful, waiting for her.

"I've kept away," he said. "I've kept away." His shadow was close, in the dim mask of his face his eyes were dark. His hands came to hers, gripped them, hung; the grip of a swimmer sinking in strange depths. Ah, he was trying to hurt her. Did he hate her? The dim mask was set and hostile, the eyes were black.

"Fitz," she said, "that's too hard."

He fell away.

"That hurts," her voice sounded cross.

"Yes," he said. "Do you love me?"

"Fitz," she was serious, "I don't know. I don't know at all."

"Yes," he said, "of course not."

"I like you, of course——"

"I know, I know. Tremendously." He was coming to himself. "You love me very dearly. Only you don't love me."

"Fitz," she said, "have I been unfair?"

"No," he said. He took her arm. "We'll take a walk."

"I can't, Fitz. Truly I can't. Mother would never forgive me."

"Never forgive me, either. That would be worse." He gave her arm a little shake. "Try to think of others, not always of yourself."

She laughed. "Now you are really sweet. I always like you like this."

"Yes," he turned gloomy. "Every one does."

"No, but truly," she said, "I want to be fair. I want to do the right thing. I just don't know. Honestly."

"I know," he said, "I know. Could I speak to your father?"

"Oh, no, not yet. It would just upset him."

"Not yet?" he said.

"Not now."

"Is there any one else?"

"No," she said, "there's no one." Here was the house.

He stopped. Still holding her arm, he looked across the river. It was black, except for the lights of farmhouses on the farther shore.

"Will you come in?" she said.

"Oh, no," he said. "All this has been very foolish. Not like the books," he said. "But I never thought it would be. Are you disappointed? I suppose so."

"Fitz," she said, "can we wait? Can things be just as they were for a while?"

"Yes."

"How can I tell?" she said. "Yet, if I only——"

"Don't let's talk about it," he said. "We can take drives just the same." He took her hand. "It was just an idea of mine," he said. His hand closed on hers; was he going to grip her again? She was alert for that. But it relaxed. "And it always will be," he said. "Good night."

"Good night, Fitz," she said, and pressed his hand. He was a dear, really a dear. She withdrew her hand and started up the steps. Behind her, she heard his footfalls going down the street. It was incredible; she was unmoved. It had seemed unreal, nothing to do with her or anything. Except for the moment when he called her name. That had been disturbing; and unpleasant.

But in the dark vestibule, she fumbled at her pocketbook. The latch key fell tinkling to the floor. He would not follow her: but if he did and called her name again—She rang the bell. Samuel, always to be depended upon in every emergency, must have been passing through the hall, for the door opened instantly.

From the drawing-room, she caught the comfortable babble of ladies' voices and the word "wayward." She heard Mrs. Munkittrick, strident and assured, and little Mrs. Worrall's quiet voice, and old Miss Ba-ba Lamb excitedly agreeing. And there were other voices of obscurer ladies who came to the house only as members of committees. What committee this was, the Ladies' Guild, the Home for the Friendless, the Light of Hope Mission, she could not tell. They were all much the same. But from the word "wayward" she guessed that the familiar band were at the moment functioning as the directors of the Florence Crittenden Home. She started past the door, not looking in, for fear a glance of recognition would oblige her to enter. But her mother had, as usual, taken up a position of surveillance.

"Clara, come in and say 'Good evening' to the ladies."

By the instant hush, she knew that it was, indeed, the Crittenden Home. She stepped through the door into a sort of uneasy vacuum, extemporized by worldly wisdom in honor of her virginity. There was nothing to do but begin methodically with the nearest chair. Mrs. Munkittrick stared at her from under her artificial bang, extended a brief, reluctant hand, and instantly replaced it among the many made-up, magenta bows that rakishly adorned her armored bosom. Dignity so touchy was exhilarating.

Miss Ba-ba Lamb pressed her hand between moist cushions.

"Dear child," she murmured. "Dear child." Poor Miss Ba-ba, fatuous, watery, kind, and sentimental.

There were other obscurer handshakes in obscurer recesses in the room, handshakes where she inspired a little flutter or a touch of beaming reverence. And at the last, Mrs. Worrall, tiny, neat, and brown, sitting, as always, a little apart, her pretty figure very straight in its plain brown velvet, and looking in the red-plush chair, which seemed, as all chairs did, too big for her, like a little girl dressed up for a party. Her thick brown hair went down her temples in beautiful, even scallops. Her cheeks were bright and her bright brown eyes were alert, kindly, penetrating, yet ever so slightly wondering and detached. She was a director of the Crittenden Home as a matter of family policy. With great decorum she supported, when asked, this enterprise of the mother of her son-in-law, although convinced in her heart that moral irregularity was a constitutional privilege of the lower orders and that the only proper outside activity for a lady of quality was the Society of the Colonial Dames. Each year she pinned her medal on and went to Washington, where at the National Convention, with impeccable dignity, she performed prodigies of political chicanery behind the scenes.

"This is nice," she said, "to see a girl for whom I am not responsible."

Clara stopped beside her chair.

"But you are responsible. We are related by marriage."

Mrs. Worrall considered this, as she considered all remarks made to her. It was another facet of her charm.

"The secret of marriage—a secret of marriage," she said, "is responsibility on the part of the man and the woman, and irresponsibility on the part of the in-laws."

The rest had begun to look somewhat askance upon this Socratic dialogue, and Clara was conscious of her mother's commanding glance.

"I didn't mean to interrupt," she said.

"Oh, no," they answered.

"Good night, Mother."

"Good night, my dear."

As she went down the hall, their murmur again was gathering momentum.

She passed beyond the staircase and down the narrow corridor to her father's office. The door was ajar, showing her father, immaculate in his broadcloth and his striped gray trousers. He sat in the upholstered leather chair bent over a book beside the green light of the reading lamp. To signalize the one informal hour of the day, his feet wore red morocco slippers and his hand held a stout glass of whiskey sour. At her step, he set the glass down. He glanced up slowly and picked up the glass again.

"Back early, eh?"

He cocked an ear for the murmur in the library.

"How are the ladies getting on?" he said. "If you shut the door," he said, "you can have some of my whiskey sour."

She shut the door and taking a cane-bottom footstool, sat down beside his knee. It was remarkable how neatly creased his trousers always were. One would think that a single bend of those great smooth joints would bag them irretrievably. The tinkling glass came toward her as though swung by a slow accurate crane.

"It is not very strong. You can have to there." His finger

marked her portion on the glass. "If you hear your mother coming, give it back."

She threw her head around with a quick grin.

"I guess you can hear Mother coming as soon as I can."

"Well, you know," he said, "your mother has her notions, very good ones, too, I suppose they are. How do you like that lemonade?"

"I like it," she said. "It is much better than whiskey straight."

"Good Lord! When have you been drinking whiskey straight?"

"I tried it once," she said, "when I was a little girl."

"Oh, that must have been a long time ago."

"It made me sick," she said.

"Was it my whiskey?"

"Yes," she said. "I'm afraid it was. You forgot to lock it up."

"Well, never mind," he said. "A lady is not supposed to drink straight whiskey."

"I suppose if she does, they send her to the Crittenden Home."

"What's that? What do you know about the Crittenden Home? Is that what they are talking about in there? You shouldn't listen."

"I didn't listen. Everybody knows about the Crittenden Home."

He was not satisfied.

"They mean it well, no doubt, but there are all kinds of women in the world and the less one kind has to do with the other, the better."

"I don't think there is so much difference."

"What! Drink up your lemonade and don't talk nonsense."

She was uncrushed. She smiled to herself. In fact she felt like quite a person, like quite, she almost thought, a man. In a conspiracy she shared her father's manly toddy. "Don't talk nonsense." That was the way he would speak to another man. She buried her faint smile in the glass of whiskey sour.

And had she not just received an offer of marriage? She had often been conscious of possibilities in the past. They were not so frequent as her father or even her mother assumed. There had been many tentative explorations by young men who, while not desiring to risk failure, yet were certainly alert for signs of receptivity. This, then, had been the first.

She paused and stumbled in her thoughts. It had been the first. But now that it had happened she did not know what to

make of it and of herself. She had been numb, passive, and un-
perturbed. Except for that one instant afterward, in which she
had dropped the latch key in the vestibule, she had been unmoved, a sort of shrouded spectator. The moment had wiped
out all her other radiant views of Fitz. He was a strange man
erasing the man she knew.

She was elated; she could surmount a crisis with such ease.
But was it to her credit? Was there a lack in her? She was
old enough for all such matters. In Italy, for instance, she supposed she would by now be set down a spinster; and even here,
she knew of girls who married younger. Were the attitudes of
the Venus Capitolinus and other noted sirens of the past mere
attitudes? Was that posing due, not as she had half-delightedly
expected, to an inner and somewhat disreputable flame, but to
the absence of it? Was it only an effort, grotesque and childish,
of substitution? She drank from the glass, cool, sharp, and
faintly sour. She looked up at her father. His tufted eyebrows
jutted forward, his trim thick beard was haloed in the light;
with faint stertorous breathings he read slowly, carefully. She
dropped her head to read the title on the book's thick back: "A
Report of Geological Formations of Southern Indiana." The moment of comradeship had passed; she was alone. She stood up
and set the glass down on the table. He reached out for it
mechanically. Standing behind his chair, she looked down on
his head. It was round as a baby's; at the crown, the thick gray
hair scrolled neatly in a curlicue like a little boy's. Surely she
could not be wholly lacking in her womanhood to feel such
things about him. She bent and kissed him on his crown.

"Good night," she said, "I liked the drink."

He rumbled deep inside his beard. Mechanically he reached a
hand out and enfolded hers.

On the cavernous stairs, gas lamps, half-turned down, burned
dimly in their green fluted globes. She mounted past her father's
monumental bedroom with its private bath and past the white
door of her mother's boudoir. Across the hall, the New Jerusalem chamber slumbered in its eternal emptiness.

The third floor, especially at night, seemed nowadays somewhat vast and empty. At the back, the old playroom held a
sewing-table and a rocking-horse that still appeared to her colos-
sal. And at the front, across the wide hall from her door, George's

room was, of course, deserted. Nothing remained there of all his odds and ends except a bamboo reclining chair with Yale pillows and on the wall a group—The Signet—in very high collars and flat, very broad-brimmed straw hats.

The matches hung in a pink glass holder just inside her doorway. Automatically, she took one, then put it back. Was he still waiting there beside his tree, waiting there, watching? If so, to turn on the light would be in some way to expose her. Her nightgown would be across the foot of her bed; for once, she could go without brushing her teeth.

She wondered, as she sat in the darkness undressing on the bed, how she would pray when she kneeled down; blessings for those she loved, of course, and thanks for benefits received; but what of herself and for herself? Was she good and fine, or was she cold, deficient? Was there after all in her a little dangerous flame or was what stirred her only fear of the unknown? She could not tell. She only knew that sitting here in the close dark with her stockings in her hand, she could see him under his tree, more sharply than she had seen him then, and clearer even than then, she could hear him say her name. It was not love, she knew, not love; but if she had her latch key in her hand, she would drop it once again.

CHAPTER XI

She was tinkling away at her scales, in the drawing-room. An awful business. Tink, tank, tunk, tonk. Tonk, tunk, tank, tink. If a key would stay down, when it was struck, there might be some satisfaction to it. Some sense of achievement, of finality, like knocking down a nasty little child. But the keys bobbed up again, imperturbably, ready to be struck again. She touched them as lightly as she could. No use to labor unduly at a hopeless task. Tink, tank, tunk, tonk. The faint notes wandered mournfully about the shrouded room. The yellow satin of the gilt chairs was covered with summer slips. The pictures were muffled in cheesecloth; only the yellow and silver wall paper and the black Numidian maid were left to represent the winter glories. The glories, however, such as they were, were not concealed from her. Just as she did in winter she studied, as she played, the dusty tumult of the Thief at the Fair, the sweet vacuity of Bougereau's peasant maid, Jacques' dim, steaming sheepfold, and the stern tumultuous ocean of Moran. "Love still has something of the sea from which her mother rose." I wonder if it has, she thought, and if so why couldn't he have gone on and really written about it. The Moran was the one her father had bought. Her mother had got the others, also the Numidian maid and the Swedish wedding picture with every pin hole painted in the lace; and upstairs, the mother-of-pearl inlaid black furniture, in the guest room, had been her first adventure in beauty and luxury, when they began to be rich. The New Jerusalem chamber, Mun Worrall called it. He said it would be a nice place for God to sleep, after the Day of Judgment. Certainly, no one else slept there. Somehow they never had guests. When one of her father's old canal or railroad cronies came by, he made an excuse to take him out to the farm. Her mother suspected that they put their feet up on chairs and drank whiskey there. She never could get anything out of her father or out of Mr. Heisdick though; men always stuck together. And well they might, thought Clara; she herself would like to stick together with the men. Drink whiskey, too, except that the time she tried it, it made her seasick. Through the wall of the drawing-room she could hear her father, moving about in his office. Soft yet ponderous sounds, the sounds of a big benign bear, in his den.

And all the while, behind the tinkle of the keys, behind the wandering thoughts, behind the sense of the shrouded room, the house, the river, and the town, behind the sense of the great bear, of friends, family, and the world she knew, lay the presence of Fitz-Greene Rankin. In no special moment, a mere tender radiance, diffused and glowing. Now she thought of him; he took shape, sharp and clear. In his linen suit he walked beside the river. "Now would be the time for the world to stand still," he said. Then, "You are perfectly ridiculous. Are we going to love each other?"

She held this picture close against her mind. It was perfect. Her thoughts checked. Why must it be darkened by that strange doomed voice which called her name?

In the depths of the house the front doorbell sounded. She jumped up from the piano bench. Her quick feet ticked on the linen cover of the carpet. She slipped past the bust of the Numidian maid and peered out between the swathed velvet curtains. On the brownstone doorstep, Fitz-Greene presented the back of a dark suit. Not the white linen? It was destructive of the dream. Yet his dark felt hat was slightly cocked, his pose, alert and confident. He was about to turn his head. She hurried back to the piano. Tink, tank, tunk, tonk. She strained an ear for Samuel's stealthy glide. The front door was opened, there was a muffled word or two. She struck the notes more roundly. Samuel must know that she was here.

With his hat hung over a knee, he was sitting on a walnut chair beside the great mirror, inspecting with an air of incredulity the gargantuan herd of cows on the opposite wall.

"Oh, hello," she said. "Are you here?"

He dropped his hat on the marble shelf below the mirror and stood up. "Yes," he said. "You were practising."

"Yes. I'm very poor. Do you play?"

She was flushing furiously. He had kissed her, and she did not even know if he played the piano.

"You can judge." Without a look behind, he walked into the drawing-room.

"Close the door," he said, "there will be trouble if they hear me playing." He struck a chord. "There may be trouble anyway." His fingers ran over the keys. "This is the time," he said, "when all true men should be in their offices. Do you know this song?" With his eyes fixed on the keyboard, he began——

> The lark now leaves its watery nest
> And trembling, shakes its dewy wings—

His voice was light and somewhat husky, his head moved slightly as he played. He sang with his eyes fixed on the keys.

> Awake, awake! The dawn will never rise
> Till she can dress her beauty at your eyes.

"The worst thing about that song," he said, "is that it's already written. It prevents me from being the author myself. If I had written that song myself, you would believe me."

She stood with one arm lying along the top of the piano. "But, Fitz, I do believe you."

"Well, then," he said, "what more can I say? Don't we have fun together? Don't we drive up and down the river? It's nonsense to talk about marrying opposites," he said. "People should be alike."

He reached up and took her hand quietly. "We could be happy," he said, "do you feel that? I do. We can have a life that no one can bother, or even reach. I am not all that you should have, I know," he said, "and certainly I have never before met any one at all like you, but I am not going to come crawling and begging. I respect myself as much as I love you." He looked up at her and smiled, "There is even a way of asking for alms with dignity."

He continued to hold her hand. "I look up to you far more than I have let you guess." His smile was quick and teasing. "It would not have been good for you. But I'm not afraid of myself: I can make you happy."

"I know, Fitz," she said. "I'm the one that's afraid."

"Of course, you are," he said, "what a terrible decision. Here you are," he said, "with a piano and a father and a horse and carriage. Why should you leave them? It sounds like a crazy thing to do."

Inside her something moved ungovernably, against all judgment, against all power of her own. "Fitz," she said in a low voice, "I do love you and if I married you, I would want to make you happy."

"I know," he said, "you would want to do that for any one you married."

"But I don't know how I could leave my father. Does that sound foolish?"

"Oh, no," he said. "I've known about that, of course, and I suppose I should show you that we could take a little house around the corner, and that you would come in here every day to see him, and that everything would be the same. But, of course, that isn't so. Everything would be different."

"I know," she said, "and I can't bear it."

"But think what may happen otherwise," he said. "You will grow old with him, and then some day, you will be left alone. We've both of us seen such lonely women; we always feel sorry for them."

"Perhaps we needn't. They've done what they set out to do." She looked down at him almost disdainfully. "Perhaps I should be satisfied."

"I know, I think perhaps you would; but what about your father? Would he be satisfied to leave you so?" He took both hands in his. "If I could make you happy," he said, "perhaps he might be pleased. Let me ask him," he said. He leaned across the keys and pressed her hands against his cheek, warm and smooth with the light sharp prickle of close-shaved hair. "You must be happy," he said. "Nothing without that. That is understood."

He stood up. But she was master of herself, she thought. She looked at him. Then in a mist of dully glowing hair, warm cheeks, dark eyes, his lips were on her cheek, touch of his lips, quick, firm, strong, steady, shot through with the faint disturbing roughness of the chin. Her hand went around his neck and clung to him as though for support, as though to use him as a shield against disaster.

"I want to love you, Fitz," she muttered, "truly I do. I want to make you happy."

His light quick hand was on her hair. "You are sweet," he said. He stood back.

"Fitz," she said, in a low voice, "you must help me. I mustn't —I—" There were his eyes, his hair, his slimness. It was over; the world was crumbling, she must jump, plunge in a crazed arc into the unknown. His arms were around her, strength and warmth of black irrevocable and sweet disaster.

Then it was not so bad. Arm in arm, they were walking up and down the room; the pace seemed tremendous, and he was talking, laughing and talking tremendously, shaking her arm to emphasize the points. This they would do—that they would do— so, they would live—she was to have a small piano, and a better pair of skates—those skates of hers were worthless, clamp skates were no good. The proper kind of skates were screwed on shoes. Then she was laughing uncontrollably. Here in this shrouded July room skates were the problem. She took his hand. "Oh, Fitz, you are a darling."

"All right," he said, "let's not begin by arguing. Now, about Norah. How would it be if we paid for her board in your father's stable? And we could give Levi a little something every month. Is your father here?" he said.

"He was."

"Then, I must see him right away," he said. "I must speak to him about Norah and other things."

Her heart turned heavy. "Fitz," she said.

"No, no," he said, "now is the time. Right now. It is much the best." He gave her a quick kiss and swung back the door.

In the library she sat down on the armchair beyond the fire-place which half-faced the bay window and half-faced the door. From a low table beside the chair she picked up mechanically a book and turned the pages. Fortunately it was illustrated. "The Port of Horta, Fayal." "A Runaway Donkey." "The Rock of Gibraltar." He was talking to her father now. Was he seated in the upholstered leather chair or in the rattan-seated one with the arms? "The Oracle." What a horrid-looking old man! "Garrison at Malabat." Or was he standing in that graceful pose? "View of a Street in Tangier." "Change for a Napoleon." "Women of Genoa." Pretty veils! If he would just be natural. If he would thrust his hands in his pockets and smile. "Roofs and Spires of Cathedral at Milan." "Central door of Cathedral at Milan." What a stupid book. It was supposed to be funny, too. "Interior of the Cathedral at Milan." Was her mother coming back already? It sounded like her step on the pavement. No, it was Mrs. Munkittrick, in her pongee manteau. But was she coming in here? No, she went on. And her mother would come back in the carriage, of course. But was she coming back for lunch or was she staying for lunch? Wasn't she staying? Hadn't she and her father mentioned it at breakfast? And she herself not been listening? She should have listened. Could she, perhaps, remember? She did remember how it started. "John, I have the Ladies' Circle this month."

"All right, all right."

"We would like you to give—" she could hear her mother's point-blank, authoritative tone, but then it stopped. At that point she had thought of other things. Yet she knew that something had been said about lunch. But what? It was maddening. She had been there when the words were spoken, the sounds had gone into her ears, why could she not hear them? She might ask Samuel. But if the talk was over quickly, was ending just now— she made herself breathe deep and slow—Samuel would be in the room here, and if she went to look for him, she might get back too late.

No, better sit still and breathe slow. She turned the page, "Garden, Lake Como."

On the other hand, it was only ten o'clock. The talk might last till lunchtime. It would be better to settle down to read the book.

We voyaged, by steamer, down the Lago di Lecco, through wild mountain scenery, and by hamlets, and villas, and disembarked at the town of Lecco. They said it was two hours, by carriage, to the ancient city of Bergamo, and that we would arrive there in good season for the railway train. We got an open barouche, and a wild, boisterous driver, and set out. It was delightful. We had a fast team and a perfectly smooth road. There were towering cliffs on our left, and a pretty Lago di Lecco on our right, and every now and then, it rained on us. Just before starting, the driver picked up, in the street, a stump of a cigar, an inch long, and put it in his mouth. When he had carried it thus about an hour, I thought it would be only Christian charity to give him a light. I handed him my cigar which I had just lit, and he put it in his mouth and returned his stump to his pocket. I never saw a more sociable man. At least, I never saw a man who was more sociable on a short acquaintance.

That was funny. What were they saying? How did they look? The great bear square in his chair, no doubt; and he, serious and respectful and engaging in his dark suit. It would be all right. Between them, they would see that nothing happened to her. There was no danger, no dread. He was so charming, so sweet and fine. There need be no dread. But she had agreed to read.

She turned the pages slowly, stopping to read words that meant nothing, glancing at pictures that had no meaning. What was it that lay back of this great happiness of hers, of this pride in the proud, kind, laughing, radiant being that wanted her to be always near him, to listen to him, speak to him, hold his warm hand; what lay back of her glowing tenderness toward him, of her longing to take care of him, his beautiful clothes, his hair? She was raised high on the crested wave of happiness. All was well. She looked out the window. The river flowed, unhurried and interminable, the green, tufted islands seemed serene, indifferent, and very far away.

From the depths, she heard a door closing. The office door. She fixed her eyes on the book. The words meant less than nothing. The book was heavy in her hands. His light, quick step was coming along the hall. She looked up. He was beaming, there was not a swagger, that could never be; but he walked pleased with himself and sure. His hands were out. "Everything's fine," he said. "It's wonderful! A great old gentleman." He bent down toward her.

"Oh, no," she said, "people can see us."

He stood up smiling.

"Let them look."

"Oh, but Fitz."

He patted her. "All right. I know." He nodded at her. "A great old gentleman."

She jumped up. "Is he all right? I must go speak to him."

"Yes, you must. Oh, yes, he's fine, couldn't have been finer."

He walked with her across the room. "I'll wait here." His hand lightly questing, but not insistent, was for an instant around her waist.

Behind her, as she walked down the high, dark hall, she could hear his voice, warm, judicious. "A great old gentleman."

In his chair before the desk, he looked out the window at the river. A long, fresh-lit cigar sent films of smoke above his great firm shoulders and his round gray head.

"Father," she said. He did not turn his head. A puff curled from his cigar. "Father, you mustn't be cross, you know."

His face was impassive, staring at the river, his big cigar was steady in his mouth; tears splattered on his broadcloth waistcoat. "Father!"

He reached for her and pressed his head against her hand.

Her arm went around his head; she held him to her. "I won't do it," she whispered. "I can't. I don't want to leave you. Father, I'm scared. What shall I do?"

From beneath her arm came rumblings. "Here, here," he muttered, "you're choking me." He came up breathing hard. "Whew!" he said, "I can't breathe. You're awfully strong."

"I don't feel strong." She smiled sadly. "Father, what are we to do?"

He had his great silk handkerchief and blew a blast. His firm hand fell on the desk.

"We won't do anything that you don't want to."

"I know, I know. But I don't know what I want. He's sweet. Sweeter than any one but you. And yet I don't know. I'm no good, I guess."

Still looking out the window, he reached his hand up absently and patted her where she sat down. An old habit of his when she was a child. Later, her mother, scandalized, had put a stop to it.

"The no-good girls," he said, "are the ones who marry without a thought. Now then," he said, "let's not worry. Let's not do anything for a while."

"But every one thinks we're engaged already." She blushed. "Even Fitz thinks it, I'm afraid."

He grunted. "I talked to him about that. As for the others, let them think what they like. We'll tell them nothing till we're ready."

But then she saw him, waiting now in the library, so happy and assured, and she saw herself, tall and graceful, going through life with him to the envy of all the world.

"I really do love him," she said. "I just feel hurried; and strange."

"No need to hurry," he said. "He'll wait. Any one would. He's a good boy, first class. I haven't been able to find a thing against him."

"Oh, Father. You've been spying on him."

"Not at all. Naturally, I haven't been asleep these last few months. Any man should be willing to have his record examined. He has a reputation for integrity and sound judgment. He's not the worker that young men were in my time, but no one is. He is being prepared for an important position in Rankin and Company. They are planning to expand all through the Middle West and this will be their headquarters. He has a little income of his own and will come into more. Not that you will be dependent on him. You are suitably provided for in your own right. I'll discuss that with you another time. But naturally you would only want to marry a man who could take care of you."

She shook her head at him. "You have been spying."

"I must take care of you. These are questions that you might possibly not investigate for yourself."

She smiled. "Well, I suppose it's very nice that all that is all right."

"Of course too, he is a charming young man. I can't say I've met any one more agreeable."

"Father, do you really like him a lot? You do, don't you?"

He nodded.

"I do, indeed. A charming young man, with an assured future."

She kissed the top of his head. "You are a dear. I do love you so. And I'm going to love him, too. I know I am." She ruffled the back of his hair.

"Don't do that," he said, "it really does exasperate me."

"Everything's all right," she said, tenderly gaily. "I'm going to love a charming young man." She smoothed his hair and kissed it. "With an assured future."

"Nevertheless," he said gruffly, "such things must be considered."

CHAPTER XII

As she looked back on it, and how often she did, that summer was nothing more and nothing less than a kaleidoscope of bright and ever-changing fragments around a central glow, a kaleidoscope with music that mounted to a crescendo as the brilliant fragments spun; an orchestra that played in colors, a symphony that rose and fell and mounted higher till time and space, the future and the past, were telescoped and rendered negligible, except as they, too, broke into the flying fragments of the dream. Of those fragments, which formed ever-dissolving and never quite remembered patterns, some were mere glowing specks of color, significant only of their own bright beauty and her happiness. Others formed pictures or contained them, pictures, swift, clear, and also instantly dissolved.

But though the pattern might elude her, the pictures which in part composed it, however briefly seen, remained forever and microscopically vivid in her mind. Pictures, of course, of Fitz-Greene, how he looked when he came out in his dark broadcloth from her father's office, graceful, assured, triumphant, walking like a young prince. Then there was the spreading news and all the smiles and looks, the shouts and murmurs; Mun's dance of the Cupids, draped in a bath-towel, with a coat-hanger for a bow; Miss Ba-ba Lamb's moist, fat handclasp, and Mrs. Munkittrick's "Quite a catch, my dear"; George grinning insultingly, "Well, we have an Aurelian man in the family, now," then suddenly, "Sis, you deserve the best. When all is said, you deserve the best"; and those two hands of his that made all horses quiet.

So many hands in those bright patterns, the thin, sorrowful hand of Anna Lisle, Mrs. Worrall's fastidious little fingers, Levi Mistletoe's strange, shy, limp paw, even Gus Ringler's honest meat; so many hands and words and faces flowing together upon her in the centre of the wheel; laughter and little jokes and nods and knowing glances, warm eyes and hungry eyes, and eyes amused and cold. Good will and doglike love from men and boys and ancients; and, from women, envy or hope or bitterness or dreams.

And always the hands of Fitz-Greene Rankin touching her, deftly, lightly, warmly, and his brown eyes, devoted, and amused, and confident. And if, as she now looked back on it, there had been moments when she felt in those eyes a touch of the shadowy and inscrutable, and was vaguely conscious that those hands, however deft, were sometimes charged with mystery and danger, it was only to realize that even in the happiest love, there must be small enigmas and adjustments, and that this leap into the unknown, which she, like all women before her, must make, was robbed of much of its terror by his casual and humorous assurance. The wedding, and all that came before it, became no more than an initiation into the noblest of fraternal orders, an initiation whose buffooneries, designed to awe and frighten, could impose upon only the most ingenuous of neophytes.

But all these were mere sparks and shadows of the central glow. He possessed her, he was always with her. When she brushed her teeth, when she did her hair, when she practised on the piano, he was there; when she spoke to friends or servants, he was a witness who inspired her to bounty and graciousness. It seemed that his actual presence could be no more vivid. Then she would see him coming up the steps, or find him sitting in the library, and feel the instantaneous shock of new delight.

Around this central glow, in which he and she were inextricably mingled, gathered all sorts of smaller happinesses. He was an expert fencer and would give her lessons. He brought his masks and foils. In the upstairs hall, they saluted each other with exquisite gravity and took the first position. He could also play the banjo, and sing the songs from Salisbury's Minstrels. His voice was small and soft, but he could do the Negro dialect. Also in French that shamed her Miss Wherry's Seminary accent he sang "Au Claire de la Lune."

Then she must go to Philadelphia, with all new clothes, and visit his family. They lived in the country and the brownstone house was set in a big park surrounded by a brownstone wall. After all her fears his mother turned out to be small and frightened and very kind. Old Mr. Rankin had died some years before, his two unmarried elder brothers lived at home. They were big, rough men who talked with a country accent, and hunted with the Rosetree Hounds. They used bad language even at the table, and made outrageous jokes about their married sister and her many children. They were gentlemen, without a doubt, she felt that; but she was very proud that Fitz-Greene did not hunt. They took her by the arms and helped her on the train.

"Good-bye, Clara," they said, "thee is a damn good sport. Fitzey's lucky, by God," they said. "The pup." They patted her.

Then it was autumn; the fragments whirled the faster. Little Mrs. Weinstock, her pursed mouth, her hands, her black apron filled with pins, endlessly, nervously, helplessly fitted the wedding dress. It should have been bought in Philadelphia as her mother wanted but that would have been the death blow of Mrs. Weinstock. Pink satin for the bridesmaids, and all their fittings at the house, Anna Lisle's sad, translucent face, and poor Big Sister in front of the tall glass, beneath her blunt indifference hoping against hope that for once she might not look absurd.

Piles of stiff envelopes to be addressed, and smiling visits from the caterer, talks with her mother of chairs and awnings and how the drawing-room should be arranged. Her mother was splendid. She took her stand, and had her way, the captain of a frigate clearing for action. The boxes started coming, silver and linen, Bohemian glass and Wedgwood china, bronzes from legendary New York business friends of her father's, antimacassars and tea cosies from unheard-of cousins up the state, a new top hat and chamois gloves for John Rand, Esq., and for herself, woollen travelling dresses, low-necked dresses of silk, lace and velvet, silk stockings, smooth and limp and heavy, white slips and underwear and nightgowns.

At one time in those confused last days, she had sat seriously in the office with her father and Mr. Riser, soft and alert in his steely gray suit. She was to have money then, an awful lot of money, and it was to keep on coming every year, forever. And if there were children—that was the point, it seemed. Mr. Riser inspected with studious detachment the clasp of his black morocco brief-case; a subject only to be touched on professionally. If there were children, it seemed there were papers to be signed. Mr. Riser unfolded a sheet of foolscap, filled with scrolled aforesaids. He held the pen out to her with one hand and pointed to the blank space at the bottom of the page. It was a tableau; the signing of Magna Charta. Afterwards, he produced a huge nut-cracker and made a round impression beside her name. He wrote "Given this day in the County of Shemingo," "In witness whereof," and many other things, very exact and pleased with himself. So then, little cherubs, still tumbling about in heaven, were being cared for by Mr. Riser, of all people.

There had been that drive with her father up to the farm. The trees showed the first, faint flush of yellow, and pumpkins glowed among the shocks of corn. Lou Belle, 2.28 and Planet, 2.31, to their surprise, had been allowed to walk for miles. Her father's cigar smoke almost drifted with them.

"Young men are different, nowadays," he said, "but I guess he is as good as any that I have seen."

"Father, you're not fair to him."

With a soundless chuckle, he had placed a gloved hand on the lap-robe over her knee. As if to fix and itemize them among her possessions, they had talked about their times together; the day she had cut holes in a silk sock of his, to make a dress for her kitten, and hidden under the stairs while he went roaring over-head; the Christmas morning when she had found a live gray donkey tied to the handle of her bedroom door. Poor "General U. S. Grant," he had died on the farm two years ago.

As though he felt that this drive marked the end of all their days together, he kept on up the river, letting the horses walk, making no effort to turn back.

At last he said, "I guess we might as well go on out to the farm."

"I'd love that," she said.

"I've ordered a new seeder," he explained. "I expect I ought to have a look at it."

"That will be fine," she said. "But I don't suppose you will need it until next spring."

"No," he admitted. "I suppose not. I saw an advertisement in *The Country Gentleman*. It's the very latest thing." He gath-ered up the reins with determination. "We will have to get along if we want to see it before dark."

She smiled to herself. Beneath the demi-god, the small boy with his toy. He was bereft and longed to stretch this drive, perhaps the last, out to some farther limit. To him, the seeder was excuse and consolation. Now they were flying through the lengthening shadows and the light of the low sun that sank beyond the burnished river.

"I expect Mrs. Heisdick can give us supper," he said. He held the reins taut, and knitted his heavy brows against the wind of their speed. "I expect your mother will wonder where we are now." He gave a solemn chuckle. She slid her hand under the green lap-robe and rested it against his massive thigh.

"Yes," she said, "I suppose she will."

In the dusk they stood with Mr. Heisdick, kicking the mud off their shoes against the soapstone kitchen step.

"Ach, never mind the mud," Mrs. Heisdick shouted. Her voice was deep and harsh. "Come in, get warm. It gets dark soon, already." Never mind the dirt in that scrubbed kitchen, its floor boards bleached and ravelled from unending soap and sand! Good Mrs. Heisdick. Friendship and hospitality could go no further.

On the checkered tablecloth the globe of a nickelled lamp glowed, pure and bright. There was a gleam of pots against bright lemon-colored walls. Broad and red, Mrs. Heisdick opened her arms; Clara was flattened against the immense contours of Mrs. Heisdick's gray sprigged gingham. "So, Clara, you get married pretty soon." Still holding her with one fat, firm arm, Mrs. Heisdick turned mechanically to the stove. "Pop," she said, "walk light. We got popovers to-night." She looked up beaming, out of her china-blue eyes. "And the papa, he must walk light too." She gave Clara a little shake. "You want to go in the bed-room and fix up? No? Well, then, take off your things. The papa should take off his things, too. In here it's hot. Pop, take the things and put them in the hall."

Clara looked at the table crowded with thick white plates of sauerkraut and cole slaw, with jars of pickles and brandied apples, with crocks of cottage cheese and apple butter. A fat loaf sat on a bread board beside a cube of pale, fresh butter. Wearing a dark-green coat and a clean white shirt, without a collar, Mr. Heisdick came back from the hall. He slapped the high back of the chair. "Sitzen Sie, Clara. John, set here."

"All right, Jacob," John Rand sat down and clasped his hands together on the red-checkered tablecloth. Mrs. Heisdick turned from the stove and bowed her head. With one gaunt hand wrapped around the other, Jacob Heisdick muttered a German blessing.

When Mrs. Heisdick's "Eat hearty, folks. What have you got, a sickness?" could no longer move them, she carried off the ruins of the meal. For the first time, she sat down. While her husband and John Rand discussed the new seeder over a black bottle, she and Clara confined themselves to thick, squat glasses of Mr. Heisdick's beer. Foamy-lipped, Mrs. Heisdick came up for air.

"And so," she said, "you get married. Well, well, how it goes, the time. Just now, you was a little girl coming out here and didn't know nothing about beer or nothing." She glanced across the table at the men. "And so the papa is alone, now soon."

"Yes, I know," Clara said. "It's going to be awful."

Mrs. Heisdick wrinkled up her eyes and nodded. She opened them very wide. "Maybe you have lots of babies. That will make him happy."

Clara stared at her glass of beer. Suppose she had a baby who became his favorite, a baby, perhaps, just like herself. It would be unbearable, she thought. But why? Was she a monster? Jealous of her own unborn? And what of having children? Was it easy? Was it hard? Was it delightful or frightening and revolting? She knew it was fatiguing, only that. And what of all the rest of it? She knew so little. She had thought of it so little, or if not so little, so differently. It had been but a vague and dreaming other-world, this coming marriage, a world in which she and Fitz-Greene, the handsome, warm and kind, had floated together, thrilled and ecstatic, yet nebulous, cool pure, as they had floated, skating together on the river. Mrs. Heisdick was a kind creature and a true friend. For the first time, she noticed that she was also a little obtuse and gross and tiresome, a sign, perhaps, that she herself was growing up.

They drove down the river fast; the light of the buggy lamps ran swiftly ahead of the trotting horses. She was again contented, protected by her father's bulk, and slightly drowsy from the beer.

Once he had spoken, his voice half lost and muffled in the night.

"If everything isn't entirely all right, come home."

Poor dear. It was the only unpractical proposal he had ever

made. The great bear, for once, was powerless and driven to
refuge in a dream.

And then her interview with her mother. Not the first one
when she had told her of her engagement; that had been easy,
almost too easy. She had been kissed and even wept over, slightly.
But then, the Rankins were well known, almost Passamores, in
fact, and her own grandfather, Michael Snyder, but nevertheless a
distinguished man and a patriot, had served with General Bo-
dine Passamore in the Revolution—a striking coincidence which
would interest the Passamores if they heard of it.

But once she had managed to seize a moment in the midst of
her mother's preparations. It was in the Jerusalem chamber, a
temporary welter of tissue paper and cardboard boxes. It was
the tissue paper and the boxes that had suddenly overwhelmed
her. "Mother," she had said, "sometimes I worry. Will it be all
right, do you think? I can't help worrying sometimes."

"All right? Why, Clara, yes, of course." Her mother still went
on among the boxes. "Think of the thousands of girls who get
married and have happy lives. And, I dare say, not one in a million is as well off as you, in any way. Fitz is the ideal man for
you. You have your own money as well as his, and you have the
most complete trousseau, if I do say, of any girl that has ever
been married in this town. And as for linen and plate and silver
and furnishings, whatever is lacking after we check up the wedding presents, I'm sure your father and I will take care of. You
aren't a good cook, I know, but you won't have to cook, yourself, and you do know how to manage."

Her mother looked up from the boxes quite radiantly. "You
are a dear girl, Clara, and your father and I have been very much
pleased with the way you have taken hold of running this house
since your engagement." Her mother meant to continue smiling
at her, but there were so many boxes. She dropped her eyes. "I
know you will be very happy."

"But mother, I know that. I know all about that. I mean marriage. I can't help worrying."

Her mother kept her eyes fixed on the boxes.

"My dear Clara, you're a perfectly normal, healthy girl. And
Fitz-Greene is a gentleman—very much of a gentleman, indeed.
Most girls would feel themselves very lucky to have such a beau.
Mrs. Munkittrick was saying just the other day that there's not a

girl in town but would give her eye teeth to stand in your shoes to-day. And Mrs. Munkittrick, as you know, is not very free with compliments."

Her mother gave her a look of proud satisfaction and dropped her eyes again.

"But, Mother, will I be all right?" The piles of boxes held her prisoner. These were the wedding presents. It was final. Her voice was a desperate whisper. "Will I know what to do?"

"Of course it will be all right. Now," her mother said crisply, "we must start to make our list of these."

That had been in the Jerusalem chamber where Mr. Edbill, the private detective, now sat like a gnome among mountains of glittering wedding presents. Downstairs the folding chairs rattled, the caterer's men whispered in discreet yet penetrating tones. She sat on the window-seat and looked at the river, already turning bleak under the early autumn sky. Mr. Edbill coughed and creaked in his chair. From the stairs, Amanda smiled at her over a tray of wedding cake in ribboned boxes. The river flowed, gray, slow, inexorable, a steely tide. No retreat from the unknown, from the future, from fate, nameless and unpredictable. Disaster closed her in the trap. But not quite yet. There was still time. There was still a refuge. Downstairs in his office the benign and powerful bear would still hear her, could still save her. She had but to run; somehow the two of them would fly, away, to a safe place, safe from gold and silver plates and little wedding cakes in ribbons, away! away! to safety with a strong kind ruler, the great bear of her universe. Below the light chairs rattled. She sat alone in the tall hall staring at the gray, swift river.

Then many steps on the stairs, many voices, a group of young Aurelians, tried and true and handsome, come to usher. At their head, Fitz-Greene struck up his banjo. They marched down the hall and round and round her singing:

> Clara, the pride of Aurelian,
> Clara, the girl that we love,
> Our musical notes, St. Cecilian,
> Shall praise her to heaven above.

They danced and kissed her. The air was heavy with cloves. They were charming, these friends of Fitz's, and nice, so really nice. She must not be silly.

She had put behind her the sullen river. In front of her were Fitz-Greene and his banjo, and the waistcoats of the Aurelians. They formed a vista down which came the sturdy tweeds of Fitz-Greene's brothers.

"By God, Clara," they said, "thee looks like a prima donna. Is this the chorus?" The tweeds thrust Aurelian broadcloth to one side and gave her potent embraces of sheep's wool, home-made soap and Highspire whiskey.

"I'm glad you came so soon," she said.

"Of course we've come," they said. "There won't be much scent till the weather turns."

The eldest brother, a shade the redder in the face and blacker in the eyebrows, turned to the nearest Aurelian.

"This has been the worst scenting season the Rosetree's ever known," he said impressively.

"Is that so?" murmured the Aurelian. His hobby was Persian enamel ware.

"Well, Fitz," the brothers said, "we've come to keep thee sober."

"Thanks." Fitz-Greene put two fingers in his waistcoat pocket. "Have a clove."

"Tum, tum, te, tum." The orchestra drowned the crowded murmur down below. She had her father's arm, Mrs. Weinstock gave a last clutch at her train, as they started down the stair. In front of her, the pink-satin bridesmaids swayed and rustled. A narrow aisle through faces in the mist, the bright sun in the drawing-room, Doctor Posey's broadcloth against a bank of smilax; ribbons and silver ropes and Fitz-Greene smiling. Kneeling and rising in her satin train, a ring from a waistcoat pocket, murmured words, amen, a burst of loud violins and her mother's proud constricted bosom. Hands and faces, hands and faces, coming by. "Yes, thank you." "How do you do . . ." "Oh, you are sweet . . . "Yes, thank you . . ." "Yes . . ." The Heisdicks' shy perspiring faces above hot clothes and squeaking shoes. "So Clara, always you must come out for beer." "Oh, Mrs. Heisdick, you must give me a kiss." The bosom huge above the creaking stays, the broad face hot and clean. "Na, Clara. Na—Na." A table of pink-satin bridesmaids and the frock coats of Aurelians. "Ladies and gentlemen, allow me to propose . . ." "Hurrah! Hurrah! . . ."

In the upstairs hall, George was on guard before her bedroom door.

"Thought I had better watch your bags. That idiot Mun!"

In the white and silver bedroom, Miranda helped her into the dark-blue travelling dress. "You was beautiful, Miss Clara, oh, so beautiful."

George's voice came through the door. "You're all right, Sis. Best wedding this town's ever seen. Even those Aurelian fellows——"

Above her bed, the infant Samuel raised eyes to heaven, a lamb for the slaughter.

"Don't be too long, Sis. Only twenty minutes. Here come Mother and Father."

"My dear, you were magnificent. I am so proud of you."

"He must be good to you." The great bear took her shoulders. He gave her a shake, as though to wake her. "Otherwise, come home."

She threw herself on him, and broke down. The poor dear bear, abandoned, too, as well as she.

"Only ten minutes, Sis. We ought to go. I'll take the bags, myself. That idiot Mun."

"Good-bye, my darling. Miranda, where is Miss Clara's slipper?"

"Here is. Oh, Miss Clara, much happiness!"

"All right, son, get the bags. Daughter, good-bye."

"Father, I love you so."

"There, there, it's all right."

In the hall below, Fitz-Greene in his brown suit, and the dark coats of the ushers.

"A flying wedge for Clara! Come on, George, you're the centre rush!"

On the stairs, behind the black coats, Fitz-Greene's hand in hers. A roaring storm of rice, the steps, the startled carriage horses; the brougham door slammed shut, pink-satin bridesmaids waving. She flung the door back and threw the slipper. The brougham jumped. Little boys ran. She leaned far forward and looked back at the house. High up in the window of her white and silver room, her father stood alone. She waved and waved. Fitz-Greene's hand touched hers.

"I didn't know," he said, "how much I was asking of you."

She leaned her face against his shoulder. "I'm all right," she muttered. "You are so good to me."

The blast of a coach horn sounded overhead. Had Levi got drunk? Fitz-Greene stuck a furious head out of the window. Another blast.

"Mun, what the devil? Stop, Levi." Fitz-Greene jumped out. A scuffling on the roof. The small boys who had followed were immeasurably rewarded. A thump and Fitz-Greene jumped into the carriage with the bent fragments of a coach horn. The horses dashed ahead. She looked through the little window at the back. Mun, in a streaming frock coat, ran nimbly after them, leaping and blowing kisses. She leaned out the window and blew a kiss to him. He stopped and stood waving to her, with a fixed, unhappy smile.

In a New York hotel bedroom of red plush, she watched the bell boy close the door behind him.

"You are tired," Fitz-Greene said. "So am I. A barbarous affair." He carried his bags into the bathroom. "Just leave the gas burning here," he said. "I am going down to smoke." He picked up his derby hat. "Really a barbarous affair. Try to get a good night's sleep." He smiled at her. "I'll see that no one disturbs you."

In the bathroom, she laid out his dressing case and his night things on a chair.

CHAPTER XIII

SHE sat on the long board porch in front of the hotel. Bright sunlight fell on the spars of gunboats in the roadstead and on the sodded fortress walls. Little boats plied to and fro with officers in capes. On the decks of the gunboats, tiny figures were always moving in unhurried and obscure activity. Muffled by the sodded walls came the stolid sounds of practice of a military band. And over everything lay the warm and bright but tempered autumn sunlight. It was a perfect day, the perfect time, they said, to be at Old Point Comfort.

Here, on the porch, ladies raised small parasols against the sun, busied themselves with fancy work, or simply rocked. Gentlemen cocked tightly trousered legs, and drew reflectively on long cheroots. Elegance and fashion idled in dignified contentment beneath the placid sky of Indian Summer. Well dressed, well fed by Negro cooks and ancient Negro waiters, well mannered and sufficiently well off, they idled in their chairs, cast glances, smiled, caressed mustaches, tapped with bamboo canes, made studiously polite inquiries, told well-phrased, pointless tales, or simply watched the fleet and the waters of the Roads, spread out for their passing entertainment. It gave a sense of well-being touched with a trace of noble elevation to sit there and observe the movements of the tiny figures who busied themselves about the gunboats; to sit there and listen to the labors of the military band, and the tramp of squads on the parade ground. Work was being done and being properly done, one might rest assured; and all to the glory and might of these United States. Fried chicken and rice cakes fortified them strongly. They watched the fleet. Let other nations beware.

Behind her, balls clicked in the billiard room. Fitz-Greene had been playing there a long while now. She heard his light warm voice and the tick of the counters as the marker put up the score. After lunch, he had asked her if she would like to go for a carriage drive or for a sail. He had smiled warmly, but underneath, she had felt, or merely guessed, a small hard nugget of the perfunctory. "Well then," he had said without undue alacrity, "I'll play some billiards."

"That will be fine," she said. "I hope you can find some one."

"That's always easy," he said, "for a man who plays badly and doesn't mind a few small bets."

But now he had been playing there all afternoon, and the barman had been in with many sherry cobblers. She did not mean to spy on him. It was not that. She did not mind the billiards or the cobblers; but she had felt as if unfathomably, suddenly, just to-day, he was conscious of a slight emancipation from her, a slight cancelling of the bond, entitling him to a slight withdrawal. All afternoon a question buffeted her with sharp repeated shocks. Was there some unguessed hardness in his fibre? Not much, of course, it would be absurd to say that, but of a sort to give him, once he had had his way, the faintest tincture of brutality. Such thoughts were monstrous. She would put them from her. She turned to watch with determined interest the ladies and gentlemen along the porch.

But had she not submitted without tears or trembling, submitted firmly, perhaps a little desperately, but also a little warmly, in tenderness for his consideration that first night in the menacing red-plush hotel room in New York? That, it seemed, was a good deal to ask, a good deal to do, for a girl reared to all that was fastidious and fine; to suffer herself to be incredibly devoured by a man who was in that moment incredible and strange. To allow for his sake—and let there be no mistake, for his sake, she did it gladly—this astounding and unpredictable violence to shatter the delicate and fragile radiance of her most lovely dream. Let there be no mistake, she did it gladly. She was strong and firm. She was no prude, she hoped; and, however unbelievably in ignorance, she hoped she was no fool. But such things, lying so utterly beyond her glowing, if nebulous, vision of him, had made immense and most abrupt demands on her. The demands she had met freely and firmly, as one ministers to a dreadful illness in one who is greatly loved. Only last night, again. She bowed her head. She would have thought there might be recognition. Instead, he was glad to be with any chance stranger in the billiard room. He was sweet, he was kind unvaryingly. But sharpened and on edge from her ordeal, she could guess that this was no bond, this sacrifice of hers; that having taken, he was not unwilling to withdraw.

And she had looked on him as godlike, a hero in a vision. For the sake of that vision, she had given all; and he was slightly restive. She had given herself and her vision, too; and all for nothing. All things conceivable and beyond had been asked of her and she had never wavered. Now he was playing billiards. Why, the next time he came smiling to her, she could strike him. She raised her hand to her face—her cheeks were fire. These thoughts were monstrous. She was a monster. She was on edge from her ordeal. Her brain was gnawed by savage and distorted thoughts. She did not know she had such dark and sullen depths. She must stand up; she must walk and seek clear air, out to the jetty between the sunlight and the sea.

Her hurrying heels tapped on the flooring of the porch. Behind her, she heard a rustle and murmur. "There goes the bride," a sweetish, low voice said.

Beyond the end of the hotel, a warm land breeze caught up her muslin skirt and blew it out before her. The little dots of blue, the tiny scattered roses rose and fell. The wind blew out a strand of her hair, provokingly, and pressed against the saucy cocked-up back of her chip hat. And yet it must become her; on the landing stage an officer in a boat-cape turned to watch her as she walked along the wall. The sailors, though, did not turn—that was not their privilege—they sat in the boat staring fixedly astern. But why should they not be allowed to stare? What difference lay between them and that clear-faced young gentleman in the boat-cape whose eyes had followed her? Men were alike it seemed. Under the charm, the grace, the gaiety, under the songs and compliments and tenderness, in each one lay a hard and brutal nugget. All else was only decoration of this inner evil, as a pearl is a decoration of an oyster's deep disease.

But no, she must not go on like this; it was frantic; it could not be true. Here was the jetty, the breeze was gentler now. Below her, the little waves cast shifting planes of light. Far out, they melted into a blue that reached to long green shores. The air was bright with sun, the sea gulls slanted. Here was a world that one could live in cleanly.

A walk of ancient, wave-scoured planks led out the jetty be-

tween great fragments of piled rocks. At the end, there was a
bench and on a pole, a lantern that glowed green every night.

Walking the loose planking between the black chaotic rocks,
she felt like a voyager in a drawing by Doré. She was voyaging
precariously—not very precariously, really—voyaging through a
dark jumble to a good firm seat, to sunny waters, and a chance
to be alone.

The bench bore many carved initials, a few pet names—
"Maudie" and "Flo"—and several large hearts enclosing monograms. The hotel was a favorite one for wedding couples. She
wondered what some of these other girls had thought as they
watched their brisk, new husbands carve their names.

Around her were desolate lost cries. The gulls, it seemed, had
formed some expectation of her. In airy slopes and arches, they
brought small beady eyes to bear on her; grace, charm, and lightness in the service of hard greed. Then they gave up, and with
a last metallic scream, were off to tip around the gunboats lying
at their anchors.

Now everything was calm. The still bay glistened softly; the
distant green shores showed a thread of yellow beach; the sky
was deep and steady. Deep into itself, the bay received the autumn light. Here by the rocks, small shafts of sun were thrusting
down through greens and yellows, through tawny shifting smoke.
In the deep warmth, brown plants waved languidly; a small
fish passed by slowly and was lost in misty shadows. The military band had stopped some time ago; she could see no movement on the gunboats. It was a peaceful moment.

But there was no protection in this solitude. In this soft smiling world of sky and sun and water, she was alone, thrust out,
an alien, on the jetty's end. As far as eye could see, nothing in all
this world had any interest in her; for her in her isolation there
was nothing; except for that momentary hard-eyed expectation
of the gulls.

If she could have her way, this would be her wish: to hear her
father's steady steaming tread on the planks behind her and,
turning, see his ponderous immaculate bulk. He would lower
himself with delicate precision to the bench beside her. Then
they would sit here. Nothing need be said. She would simply
sit here in his warmth, under his shelter, still, silent, and alone
in this charming foreign world, but now supported, sheltered,

and protected. From that safe vantage point she could find comfort in the scene, could find herself, gain ease and gain back self-respect and even confidence. Indeed, just thinking as she did had helped her; the bay and sky were closer to her. They and all life went on, careless perhaps, but unhurried, confident. No single moment in their vast and predetermined progression was a crisis: time healed all things, managed all things, life, in its total and however flawed in detail, must be good.

Behind her, on the planks, she heard the footfalls and knew, at once, that they were Fitz-Greene's. Why, he was running. Reluctantly, she turned her head and realized that, automatically, she smiled. He wore no hat; he was buttoning his short, blue jacket as he ran. For an instant, she feared some unguessable disaster, but he was smiling and pulled up before her with a grin. "Look here," he said, "what did you go away for? I thought that old buffer never would run out his string."

"I thought you wanted to play billiards."

"I did." He sat down on the bench. "There I was, mixing with the boys, drinking sherry cobblers, losing fifteen dollars. Every once in a while, when I looked out the window, I could see you sitting there. Then suddenly, I looked up and you were gone. I saw you come out here. I thought perhaps something was wrong. You know, that fat old dundreary that I was playing with had only nine points to go, and he couldn't make them. The idiot went completely to pieces. I did everything I could, short of taking the balls in my hands and knocking them together for him." He took his cigar case from his pocket. "Good Lord! I thought we'd never finish."

"I didn't know you could even see me."

He shook his head at her. "If I couldn't have seen you, I wouldn't have stayed there all this afternoon."

"I thought," she said, "that you might have had about enough honeymoon for a while."

"What made you think that?"

"I just guessed. I thought," she said slowly, "that after the climax of courtship and marriage, there might be a slight reaction."

"After the climax." He looked away. He was silent. "Yes, of course," he said.

"You see," she said, "I was right."

"Right about what?"

"Fitz," she said, in a tight voice, "you aren't listening."

He turned to her, "Yes, yes, I am listening."

"It isn't easy to talk when you are not listening."

"Well, I am; I just don't quite see what you mean."

"But you agreed with me."

He frowned. "Where are we?"

"I simply said," she said with an effort, "that there was bound to be a reaction I suppose."

"Oh, no!" he said. "Not that."

"But you agreed with me."

"I couldn't have known what you meant."

"And besides," she said, "I could feel it—I could feel it in you to-day."

"I suppose I shouldn't have gone off to play billiards," he said. "You know, my dear, I asked you if you would like to drive or sail; then I thought that if there was nothing you wanted to do, you wouldn't mind. I'm sorry."

"It's not the billiards," she said.

"What else then?"

"It's just something that I feel."

He shot her a strong look, almost a defiant one. "You feel that I am different from what you had a right to expect." He looked out across the bay, his mouth turned set. "I suppose that is something that every one who marries has got to find out."

"Fitz," she said faintly, "what do you mean?"

"Oh, never mind," he said. "All this talk is bad." He swung his eyes on hers, "Clara, you love me, don't you?"

She looked at him. "I think you ought to know—" she felt her color come, and dropped her eyes, "you ought to know."

For a time, he did not answer; then his hand fell on hers. "I know, I know," he said. His hand closed firmly. "We must love each other, we must be patient."

"Yes, yes," she said, "I will be patient."

For a moment he was silent, then he began to pat her hand. "All this talk is bad," he said, "we must just love each other. You know, I think the less said about love, the better." He shook her hand as it lay in her lap. "It's like the theologians and the Holy Ghost. We must just be happy," he said; "not bother about little things or even big things—just love each other and let the details go. All I am going to think," he said, "is how you look in that muslin dress and chip hat, and how you looked in your gray skating dress with the otter collar, and how you looked in your sea-green dress the day we drove with Alexander; and the way you walk, and the way you laugh, and the way you have of raising your hand to your cheek. Do you know," he said, "what I tried to buy you for a wedding present? I tried to buy Alexander."

"Oh!" she said, "poor Alexander. Couldn't you get him?"

"No, he had been sold to a travelling horse trader. I even tried to find the man, but no one knew his name."

"Poor Alexander," she said, "it was sweet of you to think of it."

He smiled at her. "It was, indeed; nothing but my feelings for you could have induced me to put out money for such a perfectly obnoxious animal."

"Oh, no. Poor Alexander."

"Good Lord," he said, "it's time I lit this cigar." From his waistcoat pocket, he brought out a silver match safe and snapped it open. Only two matches showed. "This is serious." He put the cigar in his mouth, took out one match and closed the safe. He studied the match with gravity. "Now, when I strike this, you lean forward and keep the wind off."

She leaned forward; his head, his cupped hands were close to her. Small puffs of smoke arose, the match flamed high. Suddenly, irresistibly, she bent down. Let the hotel look, let the gunboats look, she would touch her lips to his hair.

CHAPTER XIV

It was a pleasant little house on River Street that her father had given them. Two gleaming marble steps in front, a narrow hall beside the drawing-room, and, behind the narrow stairs, a dining room with a bay window on the winter-bleached grass of the back yard. Above the dining room the library, cosy with leather chairs and uniform editions, and in front, the wide bedroom, where she sat knitting a white skating cap for Fitz-Greene and looking at the ice-floes in the river.

She looked out on the black trees, on the ice cakes in the iron water and on the muffled passers-by, from a toy castle of her own. Here she was, safe and firm, mistress of the bright warm castle, to whom her husband, home from the outside world, turned unquestioningly, to whom butchers and cabinetmakers came for orders, to whom Christobel, Mrs. Weinstock's red-haired niece who cooked and dusted and whistled, came for advice about her fellows.

She had taken houses for granted before. This fall on the wedding trip, at Old Point Comfort, meeting the wives of army officers at teas and dances, she had not known what they lacked. They were charming, adroit, assured, and friendly, and there was about them an accommodation and give-and-take which many women lacked, but all these merits seemed a shell about an inner emptiness. That emptiness, she now knew, should have held a house. Even her father's letter, that reached her there, had lacked its full significance. It was delightful enough, as all his letters were. She could recall it now, and the moment when she sat reading it on the wide, board porch in front of the hotel.

My dear Clara:
  I take my pen in hand to advise you that all are well here at home and greatly in hopes that you are the same and enjoying yourself. Your mother has been very active in a difficulty which she and the other ladies of the Board have had with the County Poor Supervisors. I believe that the ladies have carried their point, but needless

to say, I did not allow myself to be drawn into the controversy. George has been obliged to discontinue his coaching parties due to the inclemency of the weather. Ellen reports that her baby has a tooth. Levi Mistletoe has been seriously indisposed with a gathering in the throat. I attribute it to exposure on the coach. Doctor Considine is of the opinion that he will be on duty next week. On threshing, my oats did not come quite up to expectations, so that in spite of a fair price this year, I fear that operations on the farm will not show a profit.

Thinking that on your return here, you and Fitz-Greene would wish to be established in your own home, I have taken the step of purchasing the house at No. 704 River St. You will probably recognize it as the Gilchrist house. Old Mrs. Gilchrist has gone to live with her daughter at Baltimore and the other heirs were anxious to dispose of the property. I doubt if you have ever had an opportunity to inspect it, but you will find that, while the house is small, it is well built and conveniently arranged. The deed will be held here, pending your return. It is made out jointly in your name and Fitz-Greene's, as I consider that this arrangement would be more agreeable to both of you.

My regards to Fitz-Greene, in which your mother joins me. Hoping again that your stay at Old Point Comfort is proving most enjoyable, and that this finds you as it leaves me, I am

Your affectionate father,

JOHN RAND.

Her knitting needles stopped. Was ever a letter so absurd? He always wrote like that and always she felt, beneath the formal words and the neat, formal hand, the heart of the great bear reaching out to her. As he had reached out to her during the wedding journey, even before the letter came. She remembered the comfort she had drawn from the thought of him that day on the jetty. Then came the letter. But even then she had not known how much this house would mean. Now she had the house, and everything was all right.

This room alone was enough to fortify her. The curtains were of lace tied back with blue silk bows, blue bows were on the wide lace counterpane that covered the bed of ebony, picked out with lines of gold. On the bed-table a maroon plush stand held her watch, and the gold brooch from which it hung. Fitz-Greene's bed-stand held a green-shaded night lamp and his cough drops in a silver box. In the top drawer he kept a nickel-plated revolver which he had no idea how to use. A tan and dark-blue Brussels carpet led to the fireplace, whose gas log was flanked by brass-knobbed tongs and shovel. Above the fireplace in a red-cherry frame was a steel engraving of St. Mark's in Venice, and against the yellow chrysanthemums of the wall paper hung a Della Robbia Madonna and a photograph of Fitz-Greene's Aurelians, looking very much like George's Signet except that the hat brims were not quite so wide. Under a gold-framed mirror an ebony bureau was heavy with silver combs and brushes. It was a very pretty room. The highboys and closets were in the dressing-room behind, and beyond that, the tub of the bathroom, boxed in genuine mahogany, had a new zinc lining, and bright brass spigots, and the bowl of the water closet, boxed in mahogany as well, was resplendent with a chaplet of conventional magenta tendrils. Here also Fitz-Greene's walnut shaving-stand, supporting his case of seven razors, his strop, and his immense gilt shaving-mug.

The house had established her not only as its mistress but as the mistress of her life. She found that she drew from this house or from unsuspected resources in herself, powers of foresight, of planning, and of decision. The house was pretty and cosey, nicely kept, without undue formality, and run with economy so easy and genial that even Fitz-Greene did not guess it. Without heat, and certainly without querulousness, she gave strong words to butchers and grocers. Already, she knew, the word had gone around that she was indeed the daughter of old John Rand, and in matters of trade must be treated accordingly. How proud of her the little merchants were, how relieved and pleased that they could not make as much out of her as they had first expected.

Yet, with all this mastery, there was a field that still escaped her, a corner of a field, she should have said, for the field was Fitz-Greene himself. No one could be more open and unreserved. He was also candid and shrewd about himself, his faults and his methods, as candid as he had been that day of spring, now seemingly long distant, when he had driven her in the hired buggy. It would be hard to think of a person of less concealment, and perhaps it was this very openness which sometimes baffled her. Behind his bright and shining presence, one could detect no reservations, one could not even be sure that they existed, yet she felt that somewhere they were there. Yet after all

how much could one expect? Indeed could one expect as much
as he had given? He was so truly kind, so understanding, so
even-tempered, genially oblivious of trivialities, so easy to keep
house for, to have fun with and to love.

To love. She could say it now. Love it seemed must change.
It was not the love that she had felt before their marriage, that
love now seemed naïve and fanciful, a lace valentine. It was now,
she supposed, more the love of a woman for a child, a charming,
irrepressible, and slightly mystifying child. And there was, too,
just a trace now of the love a small girl holds for her protector,
of her love for her father. For Fitz-Greene, child though he might
be in certain phases, was more than able in his affairs; in matters
of finance he was even formidable.

Between these kinds of love she had been changed, her understanding had been enlightened. Now she was willing without
horror to accept those demands that had first dismayed her. And
she knew that what at the first she had in revulsion called Fitz-
Greene's brutality was merely the self-centred contentment of a
satisfied small boy. She no longer resented it. Indeed there was
a certain patient and amused tenderness in spoiling him. She
would lie there afterwards, warmed toward this child, so violent
and incomprehensible, wishing that she could rock him in her
arms.

The early dusk began to fall. In the river down below, the
cakes of ice seemed floating, disembodied, in the night, the
lamplighter came down the street, the light from his torch swaying on his wool cap and ear-muffs. At the distant corner he let
down the acetylene light. She could hear the faint clink of the
pulley. He embraced the glass globe tenderly, the light sprang
up, he hoisted it above the street.

The night fell early now, Fitz-Greene should be coming home.
She watched the sidewalk; only half of it could be seen from
where she sat, and of that half, part ran between the black, frozen
trunks of elms and was never used except by small boys and by
Fitz-Greene. From the first day he came home, he skirted the
trees and kept close to the gutter so that he could easily see her
in the window and so that, he also pointed out, she could easily
see him.

So now he came, a slim silhouette in his black frogged coat
with the astrakhan collar and his rakish broad felt hat. She

stood up and waved her knitting. He lifted a long thin parcel above his head. The white box caught the light.

He came in the front door, held the parcel in front of him like an offering. He bent and kissed her on the mouth. His lips were cold and delicate. She ran her hand around the tight-curled collar.

"I am so glad to see you." She held him by the astrakhan lapels. "You don't look a day older," she said, "than when you left."

"Thank you," he said, "I attribute it to plenty of exercise and clean living." He held out the box. "An offering for the occasion."

"What occasion is that?"

"The week before Christmas," he said. "Except for children, it is a dreary season of harassments and forced contributions. Something should be done to take the curse off it. This is not much, I admit."

He tossed his hat accurately on a hook beside the mirror in the hall. She helped him with his coat. The flimsy lid of the box came off, and showed three lavender orchids on a bed of ferns.

"Oh, Fitz, you are simply crazy, my dear, simply crazy."

"That sounds final," he said.

"I must give them to Christobel," she said. "We will try to keep them till Christmas. I want to wear them to Father and Mother's for Christmas dinner. Now," she said, "there's an hour before dinner. We must do something about our Christmas cards. You know how the mails are."

Arm in arm, they went up the stairs to the library.

"You have the cards?"

"Yes."

"And the stamps?"

"Yes."

"And you will do the writing?"

"Yes."

"And the messages? Then," he said, "we will do something about the Christmas cards. Where are my slippers?"

"Right there," she said, "in front of the fire, and the evening paper, too."

She sat down at the mahogany desk at the corner of the bay window. The brass drawer handles trembled in the firelight.

She heard his shoes drop on the hearthrug and the rustle of the evening paper.

"Remember," he said, "that the great thing is not to disturb me when we are doing something about the Christmas cards."

The list of addresses lay in front of her. Her pen scratched on the heavy white paper of the envelopes.

"Miss Susan Jenkinson," she read. "Do you know Miss Susan Jenkinson that lives in Douglastown, Pennsylvania?"

"No."

"But you must know her," she said.

"This is a free country," he said. "No one is obliged to know Miss Susan Jenkinson. That is the sort of thing," he muttered, "our forefathers fought against in '76."

"But she is on your mother's list, and she sent us a wedding present."

"What did she send?"

"That enamelled Chinese incense burner."

"No card," he answered briefly.

She wrote "Miss Susan Jenkinson, Douglastown, Pennsylvania," on the envelope and stamped it.

Later, she turned in her chair.

"Who is Mr. Duland Sawtelle of Sawtelle, Virginia?"

"He was in my year in Aurelian."

"Is he nice?"

"Not at all. Pompous and disagreeable."

"But you have written his name down here, yourself."

"He always sends me a card. He thinks it's a custom of the Club."

"And do you always send him one?"

"Oh, yes. It's easier to do that than to explain. A terrible fellow."

"And how did he get into Aurelian?"

"In the same way. It was impossible to explain to him that he didn't belong there."

Again she wrote. "What about Mr. Enoch Plimpton at King of Prussia, Pennsylvania?"

"Never heard of him."

"Why, of course you have. He is a cousin of your mother's."

"Well, I've no idea what he is like. What's the use of sending a Christmas card to him? He may be terrible."

"But he's a cousin of your mother's."

"He still may be terrible."

"And he sent us the silver candlelabra. We must send him a card."

"I have an idea that he is terrible. What does it say on the Christmas card?"

"Just Merry Christmas and our names."

"Well, then, cross out the 'Merry.'"

She wrote Mr. Enoch Plimpton on the envelope.

At the end she said, "Why, Fitz, you haven't got Harry Benson on the list. He was the nicest of your ushers."

"I know," he said. "We are great friends."

"But don't you want to send him a card?"

"Certainly not," he said. "He would be very much upset."

"But why?"

"Because he never sends me one. If he did, we wouldn't be such friends." He turned his paper over. "The most friends can do is not to be a burden to each other."

"That's the finish of your part of the list," she said. "Thank you very much for helping with the Christmas cards."

"Have you got a fellow named Randall McClure on your list, from Baltimore?"

"No."

"Well, you can send him a card, if you want. I don't like him very much, either." He folded the paper into a wad, and threw it at her.

CHAPTER XV

It still seemed queer, she thought, as she went up the dark, snow-flecked steps on Fitz-Greene's arm, to be going into her old home from the outside as a stranger. If only she could have kept her place there, and somehow have added Fitz-Greene and the toy castle to her life. Samuel was alert. The front door swung in on brilliance, overpowering warmth, and the voices of the family Christmas party. Samuel wore a dress suit with a black waistcoat. His collar and white tie were immense. In front of the tall mirror, he helped them out of their wraps, with flourishes, and hung their coats with the others. They must be the last.

"Are we the last, Samuel?" she said.

"Well, yes, Miss Clara. Yes, Mr. Fitz-Greene. It just so happens. But it's only seven o'clock. The rest came early."

"Soup ain't ready yet, Miss Clara." It was Levi Mistletoe in a toga-like dress coat. He peeked out from the dining-room door, and beamed on her shyly. His collar and tie were larger than Samuel's.

"Hello, Levi," she said. "You look wonderful."

"Yes, ma'am. You pa give me this after the wedding."

"Did Father get a new dress coat then?"

"Yes, ma'am; said he had to have a new one to entertain his married friends."

Samuel cleared his throat to recall her to the proprieties. "They're all in the library," he said. He led the way back up the hall. At the door, he debated whether to announce them formally. It was a great temptation, but the probabilities of ridicule were strong. He contented himself with a reverberating clearing of the throat and an ushering movement of the hand.

Mrs. Rand, wearing a diamond collar above her tight, creaseless black satin, turned and smiled. She was, indeed, a splendid figure of a woman; but hard to love: like a show-ring horse. Mrs. Worrall, in brown velvet, looking tiny in one of the red woollen chairs, held out her hand.

"Clara, it was nice of you to come to see us this morning. You mustn't feel that you have to."

"But I do feel I have to. I want to make you feel that I am a member of your family. Then you will have to help me."

"Oh, well," said Mrs. Worrall, "if you come for selfish reasons, I have no objection."

"Hello, Ellen," Clara said. "Is little Tommy going to be allowed to come?"

"Oh, yes," Ellen said. "He's here. I hope he won't be bad."

"Merry Christmas, Miss Ba-ba."

Miss Ba-ba, soft and melting inside her lavender and many bows, took both of Clara's hands.

"Clara, dear, may this be a very happy Christmas, the first of many happy Christmases for you and your dear husband."

"Thank you. Hello, Mun, George."

"Hello, Sis. You are almost late."

"Not quite, though. Are you very disappointed?"

"Now, children, children," Mun said. "Clara, aren't you going to give me a kiss just for Christmas?"

"I gave you a kiss this morning, when I came to see your mother. You forgot, I suppose."

"So many other girls have wanted to kiss me, to-day." Mun whirled his coat-tails.

"Miss Ba-ba, I suppose," Clara said in a low voice, "and Mrs. Munkittrick." Mun's spirits wilted.

Her father heaved forward in his chair, his shirt front creaked and billowed. "Daughter, I hope you got a rest this afternoon. All these Christmas visits." Ponderously, he turned slightly in his seat. "Here's your Uncle Linsey. Linsey, here's Clara."

Uncle Linsey, who had been inspecting the pictures and bric-a-brac, with his back to the gathering, and his hands under his thick, wrinkled coat-tails, turned around reluctantly. His sun-burned face looked dark against his black, square beard. He was the brother of her father who still lived on the old place up in Center County. He came down every other Christmas, and went straight home again.

"Well," he said, "I hear you're married."

"Yes, Uncle Linsey. Didn't you get an invitation?"

"Yes. Didn't you get those walnuts?"

Clara laughed. "Yes," she said. "Didn't you get my letter?"

"Where is your husband?" said Uncle Linsey, without smiling. "There he is. I'll call him over."

"Never mind," said Uncle Linsey. "Your father's certainly got a plenty of pictures and things in this house." He turned to inspect the hussar in a red jacket which hung above the mantel-piece.

"Dinner is served," said Samuel.

The long, white tablecloth was encrusted with lighted candles and shining silver dishes, large and small, of nuts, of raisins, of bonbons, of fruits and peppermints and candied ginger. Before the level ranks of gold-rimmed plates and table-ware, stood chased square silver butter plates, silver salt-cellars, and tall silver pepper-pots. On the oak sideboard a little Christmas tree was lighted with miniature wax candles. At the far end Samuel, behind Mrs. Rand's chair, cast baleful looks intended to suppress Levi Mistletoe's genial and unprofessional smile of greeting. In front of each plate a silvery snow man in a paper top-hat held a place card. Between the silver centre dishes there were heaps of col-ored paper crackers. They found their places and sat down. Samuel and Levi and the gentlemen pushed manfully on the ladies' high-backed, ponderous chairs.

"Where's Tommy?" they said.

From under the table came lugubrious squeaks and skirlings. "Tommy, come out," said Ellen. She shook her head across the table. "Mun, I could kill you for giving him those bagpipes."

George, on his mother's right, lifted the heavy tablecloth. "Come out, you rascal. That will do."

There was a dying wail, a shaking of the tablecloth. Tommy's brown curly hair, his big eyes and bright delicate face shot into view. He stood up in his blue sailor suit, electric with excitement and embarrassment, with daring and uncertainty. They laughed. He threw back his head. It was a success, then. He handed the bagpipes to Samuel. They gave a dying moan. He scrambled into his chair beside his mother. In his thin neck, above the open sailor collar, a blue vein pulsed. He was no Rand.

Across the table, he fixed his great eyes on Clara. "Aunt Clara," he said.

"Hush, Tommy," Ellen said.

Beside her at the head of the table, John Rand's shirt front creaked as he bent forward. "Heavenly Father, bless this food to our use and us to Thy service."

"Aunt Clara," Tommy said, "were you surprised? Were you scared?"

"Yes, I was scared."

"What did you think it was?"

"I thought it might be a bear."

"What kind of bear?"

"Oh, a grizzly bear."

"A grizzly bear——"

"Now, Tommy, eat your soup," Ellen said.

"But my soup's not like your soup."

"Will anybody here contribute an oyster to Tommy's soup?" John Rand said. "Then his soup will be like our soup."

"I'll give him one," Clara said.

"I'll give one," said John Rand, "and then if your mother will give one that makes two."

"Three," said Tommy. "Three."

"Good gracious! That's more than I thought." Heavily but delicately, he reached across Ellen on his left and slipped an oyster into Tommy's soup plate.

"Father Rand," Ellen said—if only there were something else that Ellen could call him, Clara thought, but she could think of nothing—"you spoil him terribly."

Her father wiped his mustache with his heavy linen napkin. "I tried not spoiling George," he said, "and it didn't work out."

"Mother made up for it then," Clara said.

"But George isn't spoiled," Ellen said. "Every one says George is spoiled."

Slowly, relentlessly, John Rand pursued the last oyster about his gold-rimmed plate. "Take another case, then." He looked up at Ellen. "You were the most spoiled little girl I ever saw, and look how nice you have turned out to be." Ellen's sharp brown eyes looked pleased. She flushed. Even her small nose seemed to lose its sharpness.

"Oh, but that's different. I am a girl."

John Rand had the oyster. He looked up with one of his rare direct flashes. "A child," he said, "is a sort of girl."

And a girl, thought Clara, is sometimes a sort of boy. I never knew what it was, then, but now that I am married, I know that when I was with him, I was a Greek boy.

"How did your father make out with his farm this year?" With his napkin, Uncle Linsey was just completing a very thorough job on his beard. "Lost money, I suppose."

Clara turned. "I suppose he did," she said, in a low voice. "He generally does, but not very much this year. Hardly any, I think."

Uncle Linsey was far from satisfied. "What did he raise this year? Corn and oats, I suppose. And wheat? How much wheat? Well, then, how many bushels did he make to the acre? Fifty? He certainly ought to have made fifty. No reason why he should not have made fifty-five. This year is a good wheat year. All right, then." With his fork, Uncle Linsey proceeded to make some calculations on the tablecloth. "Thirty-one hundred bushels. Should have been more. What did he get? Don't suppose he held off till the top. I thought not. He sold at seventy-eight when he should have held out for eighty-two. He dropped four cents a bushel on thirty-one hundred bushels."

Clara looked down the table at her mother, at the foot, in front of the fireplace. Undoubtedly, Uncle Linsey was about to do some more calculations on the best linen tablecloth.

But Uncle Linsey was interested in discovering not what his brother had done, but what he had not done. And having demonstrated that his crop was short, and his price low, he was satisfied.

"You can't farm that way," he said, with intense conviction. "A man's got to tend to business, if he wants to farm. I've told him that."

"But, Uncle Linsey, Father just does it on the side, for fun." She tried to sound genial. "He's got all his other business."

Uncle Linsey picked up his soup plate and handed it to the startled Samuel. "You can't farm that way." He turned to Miss Ba-ba Lamb on the other side. "Ever get up around Center County?"

"Why, no, Mr. Rand," said Miss Ba-ba in a very responsive and social voice. "I don't believe I do."

"Well, you'd find it very interesting. We've got one valley there, the Wyomensing, that grows more wheat per acre than any section east of Illinois."

"That sounds very interesting," Miss Ba-ba said, "Mr. Rand."

"What do you do about ensilage around here?"

"About what?"

"Ensilage. What do you do about it?"

Miss Ba-ba lost her remnant of assurance. "I am afraid I don't do anything about it. Do you think I should?"

Uncle Linsey's laugh was explosive and reluctant.

"Not a farmer, eh?"

Miss Ba-ba was on firm ground. She was sure that she was not a farmer. Uncle Linsey attacked a plate of salted almonds.

The preposterous and exasperating old nuisance! He came every other year, just when she had got over him; and always she was put next to him at Christmas dinner. And always he acted as if he were the original and authentic Rand and her father were a strayed sheep who had lost caste and sunk into an almost contemptible estate. He had taken this attitude when her father had set him up in the wholesale hardware business, and when he had set him up in the wholesale grocery business; and when he was in the retail grocery business, it had been the same. And now that he was retired, to the farm with an allowance from her father, Clara suspected, it seemed that all his suspicions about her father were confirmed. She was grown up and married now. Her position should confer some privileges; one of them ought to be that she should never have to sit next to Uncle Linsey at Christmas dinner again.

Across the table, Fitz-Greene was talking to Mrs. Worrall. Fitz-Greene bent his smooth, tawny head and grinned and whispered confidentially. He really was charming. He treated all women alike, with freedom, deference, and intelligence, almost, one might say, with a light but genuine affection; and all women blossomed in his presence. He really was charming. How nice, Clara thought, to have him to look at and feel her own, when she had got angry with Uncle Linsey. She smiled to herself. Marriage, besides its central happiness, brought all sorts of minor compensations. Compensations? Compensations for what? What loss was there? Was it not pure gain? Yet no, there was her father, untouched, it might seem, by her desertion, as she too, seemed almost untouched. But had he not given his old tail-coat to Levi and bought a new one, because she now would dine here as a guest?

Beyond Miss Ba-ba, and next to her mother, Mun was beginning to show signs of activity. Clara remembered the aroma which enfolded her when she shook hands with him, and guessed that he had prepared so extensively for a Christmas dinner without wine that, on arrival, he had found that for the present his only refuge was reserve. But now with two courses safely stowed as ballast, he was ready to risk a more spontaneous demeanor. With most ornate politeness, he tried to get the watchful Mrs. Rand to pull a paper cracker with him. He cracked a joke with the uneasy Levi Mistletoe. He greeted Fitz-Greene as a fellow member of the Union League, and invited George to join that institution, for the sake of its terrapin and its social advantages. Meeting with small success in these directions, he fixed on Miss Ba-ba as his proper field. For Miss Ba-ba Lamb, resigned to the colorless life of a sort of poor relation of the world, Mun's bizarre and unpredictable advances exercised a horrid fascination. Under their very eyes, she was rapt away, a pavid kid in the clutches of the Hyrcanian lion. Stupefied by terror and embarrassed delight, she pulled firecrackers from whose exploded remains a leaden wedding ring was disembowelled, to be presented to her, together with amorous verses read aloud. She pulled again, with eyes tight shut and a plump finger placed to a plump ear, and found herself crowned with a green cocked hat before the formal and unresponsive smiles of the dinner party. Only little Tommy gave full support to Mun's program of conviviality. His big eyes shone, he clapped and cheered in his high treble, and when Mun danced around the table and placed a paper shako on his head, his joy was perfect.

"Look, Mother, look!"

As Ellen looked reluctantly, a clown's hat descended on her own neat, chestnut head.

"Go away, Mun," she cried. "Mother, make Mun sit down. Tommy will never finish his dinner."

Mrs. Worrall looked away from Fitz-Greene. "Mun, dear, sit down," she said.

Very sedately and quite steadily, Mun returned around the table, pausing only to place a paper sunbonnet on the outraged Uncle Linsey. John Rand looked down at his plate with a long soundless chuckle. He carefully wiped his eyes with his napkin.

In the drawing-room, after dinner, every gas jet in the crystal chandelier was blazing. The ladies sat on gilt chairs beneath the dark oil paintings in their wide gold frames. On the sofa with Mrs. Rand, Miss Ba-ba Lamb attended the recitation of a victory in the interest of good works. Mrs. Worrall and Ellen sat watching Tommy pretend to be a locomotive travelling the curving pattern of the rug. They were both in brown, and Mrs. Worrall, like so many women after talking with Fitz-Greene Rankin, looked particularly young and delightful. They seemed like twin mothers, as they sat beside each other, watching the little boy. And as it was so often when they were together, Mrs. Worrall seemed wordlessly to urge her daughter, so neat, responsible and assured, to be young and delightful, too.

"Tommy," said Clara, "do you want me to sing a little song for you?"

"Oh, yes," he said, "toot, toot, whang, whang!" He steamed up to the piano bench. He stood for a moment breathing deep, locomotive breaths. "Pahhh, pahhh . . . pahhh, pahhh." He climbed on the piano bench, his narrow feet hung down in their patent leather pumps. She played "Three Blind Mice."

"Now," she said, "you sing, too."

Eerie, she thought, the treble of a little boy; disembodied, almost phantom, quite different from the voices of little girls. Those were human, this somehow purer, more universal.

The gentlemen, having, out of consideration for little Tommy, made haste with their cigars, and, no doubt, with some of her father's Old Overholt rye, filed into the room. They must have been drinking rye, Mun was reduced to dignity again.

"Well, Grandson," her father said, "what shall we play?"

The blue sailor suit bounded from the piano bench. "Squeak!" he said, "let's play Squeak!"

"All right, then get my cane."

John Rand drew a white silk handkerchief from his tail pocket and folded it into a bandage. Mrs. Worrall and Ellen jumped up eagerly.

"George, we must take this table out of the way."

George lifted the silver vase of yellow roses from the marble-top table, and carried it to the piano. He grinned at Clara. "Orchids, by George! You certainly married above your station."

"Fitz really is crazy," she said. "He gave me these last week, of all times." Clara placed a hand on the piano bench, still warm from Tommy's small posterior. "George," she said, "I think Tommy is the nicest little boy I ever saw."

George grinned enormously, looking, at the same time, as if he were going to cry. "He really isn't a bad kid," he said. He came around behind her, and thumped her lightly twice on the ribs with his big delicate hand. He walked off down the room, without a glance behind. Suddenly she knew that she looked beautiful in her pale-blue satin gown, with the three orchids below her slender breasts.

"Who's It, Grandfather?" Tommy held out his grandfather's gold-headed cane.

"You can say."

"Could I be It?"

"All right, turn round. I'll put the blindfold on."

The small blue sailor suit held still in front of John Rand's bulk, while the folded handkerchief was tied around his eyes. Beneath the handkerchief, the mouth and the delicate chin looked pure and steady and intent.

"I like to be It," he murmured, "because it's dark and queer. Grandfather, give me the cane."

The others tiptoed and rustled, smiling, about the room. The boy stood still for a moment, holding the gold-headed cane. He looked like a precocious and delicate magician. Then he whirled and thrust the cane out like a fencer. The point stopped in front of John Rand's white waistcoat. Her father took it and looked intently at the boy. The boy gave the cane a little shake.

"Squeak!" he said.

John Rand's beard bristled as he closed his lips; he emitted a most natural and unmistakable grunt.

"It's Grandfather!" the boy cried. He pulled the blindfold off, and looked at his grandfather, flushed and smiling. He had come back from his enchanted world. Only the cane, held by the ends between them, remained as a souvenir.

He shook his head. "Grandfather, you are so poor at Squeak."

"I know," said John Rand. "I suppose I'm It, now. Get on this chair and tie the blindfold on me."

"But wait till we play Going to Jerusalem," he muttered, under the silk handkerchief, "and then we'll see what happens to you."

"I'm going to sit down first," Tommy said.

"If you do, I'll sit on top of you."

"I don't care. Father sat on a tree-toad once, and when he got up, the tree-toad got up and sang."

Later, Miss Ba-ba Lamb, blindfolded, poking unsteadily about the room, her little mouth intently pursed, brought the wavering cane to rest in front of John Rand.

"It's no use," he whispered. He thrust his hands behind his coat-tails. "They always get me."

Mrs. Rand, massive and handsome in her satin and diamond collar, stood beside him. She had not been caught all evening. John Rand, with a quick movement, thrust the end of the cane in her hands and tiptoed away.

Miss Ba-ba shook the cane, "Squeak!" she said. She stood with her head cocked like a pug dog in front of a mouse hole. Mrs. Rand raised two impeccable fingers and placed them in her mouth. Their ears were split by a knife-edged whistle. Miss Ba-ba sprang back, the blindfold fell around her neck. Distracted and incredulous, she stared at Mrs. Rand.

Mrs. Rand surveyed them, calmly pleased. "I learned to do it when I was a girl. I used to help my brothers with the shepherd dogs."

Tommy bounced on the sofa, swinging wild feet. "Do it again, Grandmother." He put his fingers in his mouth, and blew a soundless hiss. His fingers came out dripping. Ellen searched him for a handkerchief.

"Don't do it again," John Rand said. "Whew! That's terrible." He took hold of his ears and vibrated them tenderly. Miss Ba-ba continued to stare at Clara's mother, as though all these years together had suddenly come to naught.

Ellen looked up from wiping Tommy's fingers. "I think that ought to be the finish. It's after nine. If we are playing Going to Jerusalem, don't you think we ought to start now?"

"That's right," said George. "This boy of ours has had quite a day."

"Father, I'm not tired."

"Wait till to-morrow and see how disagreeable you are."

"He won't be disagreeable," Ellen said. "He'll just be tired."

"Clara," Mrs. Rand said, "you play the piano. George, set out the chairs." The chairs were set in a line facing opposite ways, down the centre of the room. Clara struck up the Barcarolle. They marched around the chairs in single file, her mother stately and alert, Tommy keyed up, making false starts and dashes in front of Ellen. Fitz-Greene, graceful and casual, was saying

something to Mrs. Worrall in front of him. George greatly disturbed Miss Ba-Ba by creeping scientifically from chair to chair
immediately behind her. Mun bringing up the rear showed signs
of sinking.

Clara stopped on a note. There was a scuffle and a dive which
Mun declined to enter. With stately melancholy, he removed a
chair from the row. He sank into great dejection against the wall.
Clara struck up the Barcarolle again. Her mother, marching
round, kept glancing at her. Should she be playing faster, slower?
Not that it made much difference. She tried both without effect.
She stopped in the middle of a bar. Their flurry left Mrs. Worrall
stranded on her father's lap. "Why, bless my soul," he said, "you
don't weigh anything." Mother won't like that, Clara thought.
Whatever is wrong about my playing will be worse now.

Mrs. Worrall stood up. "John, you seem very large," she said,
and went to sit down beside Mun.

During the next round, Mrs. Rand's glances continued. Best
simply to ignore them; the problem was insoluble. When Clara
stopped, George vaulted over a chair to reach an empty seat.
There were loud outcries and passionate debates. In the end,
Fitz-Greene and her father ruled that a violation of the higher
ethics of Going to Jerusalem had occurred. To Tommy's rapture
George was disqualified and led off, digging in his heels and
howling, by Ellen and Fitz-Greene. The march began again.
At this stop, Mrs. Rand made no pretense of trying for a chair.
She made a stately rush for the piano.

"E flat," she said.

"What?" said Clara.

"E flat. How can you play E natural over and over again?"

"E flat where?" Clara said.

"Never mind, never mind. Let me play. This last round
doesn't count," she called out. "Clara takes my place. Start now."

As Clara, crestfallen, joined the marchers, the music of the
Darktown Races filled the room.

> The Darktown ladies sing this song,
>   Doo dah, doo dah,
> The Darktown racetrack five miles long,
>   Oh, doo dah day.

Then came the trills and ripples.

> Gwine to run all night,
> Gwine to run all day,
> Bet my money on a bob-tailed nag,
> And somebody bet on the bay.

The chorus again with variations; it stopped. No one was ready. They had been caught up, swung along keyed up to march all night. Then before John Rand had taken his chair to the wall, the tune was Jingle Bells, tinkling bells running up and down the keys. John Rand sat tramping silently, and tapped his fingers on his knees. Fitz-Greene began to sing.

> A day or two ago,
> I went out for a ride,
> And soon Miss Fanny Bright
> Was seated by my side.

"Bang, Bong . . . Bang, Bong!" George made booming bells with his bass.

At last one chair was left. Clara and Tommy crept around it, lynx-like and tense.

> Soft o'er the fountain,
> Lingering falls the southern moon,
> While on the mountain,
> Breaks the day——

Tommy leaped, and Clara sat down on him. Underneath her, he squeaked and wriggled. His pumps flew out beside her blue satin gown. She got up and laughed. "You felt just like the tree-toad," she said. He bounced into the air.

"I won, I won." The clapping stopped. He eyed her, breathing hard. "Did you really try?" he said.

"Yes," she said, "I really tried."

"I suppose you could do better," he said, "without those skirts."

George came in from the hall, with Tommy's sailor cap and reefer jacket. Tommy went to the piano. "Good night, Grandmother." He kissed her on tiptoe. On the way back, he stopped in front of his grandfather's chair. "Good night, Grandfather," he said. "I'm sorry you got put out so soon."

CHAPTER XVI

IN her home now she had whom she wished come to see her, and no one else. There had been, of course, the calls of her mother's friends and the return of them, when she sat in marmoreal drawing-rooms and talked of the Monday morning musicales and of Doctor Posey's sermon on "Calling and Election." And, of course, one asked in others for many reasons; Good Doggie and Meta, to 'try to help them make up their minds. Why should they be so stupid? Otherwise they were perfectly suited to each other. Each was so nice and, no doubt, deserved something better. Of course, George and Ellen came in; Ellen perhaps a little sniffish because Clara's house, while not so large or handsome as her own, was actually on River Street, but soon mollified by the slightly mocking but delightful attentions of Fitz-Greene, and George, full of cheer and a new kind of comradeship. Her marriage, it seemed, had raised her, in his estimation, to a sort of honorary membership in the Aurelian Club. The problem of Big Sister was not an easy one. The first step, of course, was to eliminate the well-meant but blighting influence of her brother, Good Doggie. It was the second step that had required thought. She had finally hit on the little skating engineer from the foundry. It required some effort to recall his name. Thompson or Johnson, but when found, he accepted with alacrity and, no doubt, some surprise. He turned out, even deprived of his skates, to be pleasant company, easy and self-contained, with a good mind of a simple pattern. She had hoped that his solid worth would respond to the solid worth of Big Sister; but after several attempts, she was beginning to feel that when the young engineer was given a chance to explore the higher reaches of society, solid worth was the last thing he was looking for. He had, apparently, had too much of it where he came from. It was a pity. She wondered whether to ask him to dinner any more. But why not? There was poor Anna Lisle.

144

And so, as the winter passed, she gave small dinners at which young persons in the heyday of their lives were afforded notable opportunities to discover each other's merits. Fitz was the perfect host. One would, of course, expect him to entertain the ladies to perfection. And with the men he was equally successful. It is true that he had no fanatical interest in the matter of the Bessemer process or of Good Doggie's stamp collection, but he liked to see how a man thought and talked when properly encouraged; and, however incisive he might be in the open, in his own home he enjoyed intensely the spectacle of a man having a good time.

When they were alone, he talked during supper to her and to Christobel as she came in with the dishes. At first, it had seemed rather an odd party, and she had been afraid that Christobel, whose notions of private service were rudimentary, would attempt to carry the arrangement into the evenings when they had guests. But, in any case, there was nothing to be done about it. He was a man who simply could not refuse to talk to any woman present. To do that would seem to him, as Clara saw, not precisely like a rudeness, but like a breach, almost monstrous, of the natural order. And as far as the formal dinner parties were concerned, she soon found that Christobel understood that those were occasions on which Mr. Fitz-Greene, herself, and, as an afterthought, Clara, entered into an amiable conspiracy, a masquerade, a game whose object was to impress the visitors with their own knowledge of the rules.

After supper, they sat upstairs in the library; the two red-leather chairs which they had christened Darby and Joan were drawn up to the fire. In his dark blue smoking jacket with braided cuffs, he leaned back against the dark, red leather and smoked a long, thin cigar. Each of their rôles was understood. She supplied for his consideration the gossip and small talk of the town, while he, enthroned on the red-leather chair and wreathed in the smoke of the havana, offered comments, footnotes, ribaldry, and judgment. From time to time, he leaned forward with his legs still crossed, and tapped his cigar against the toe of his slipper; the ash flew neatly into the fireplace; he leaned back, pleased with himself but not deceived; it was a compensation to her to see crumbs of news from her petty world consumed by clouds of fine havana smoke and flashes of derision.

For after all, it was desirable that a husband should be a demi-god, and if one could not be a demi-god among men, one might, at least, be a demi-god among gossip.

When the cigar was smoked, he took up his volume of Gibbon's "Decline and Fall of the Roman Empire," and she lifted the lid of the sewing table beside her chair and brought out the doily she was working on. Without much conviction she was making a set to give to her mother next Christmas. The linen, stretched over a small wooden hoop, showed a design of pine boughs and cones. She had picked it because of its straight lines and simple colors. From time to time, Fitz-Greene would read aloud to her some detail of interest, or one of Mr. Gibbon's more suggestive footnotes.

"One of the finest things about a virtuous woman," he remarked, "is her wholesome enjoyment of an impropriety. There is nothing so clean and refreshing as the way a nice girl laughs at an improper story. Men who laugh like that are rare."

"How do you laugh?" she said.

"I am afraid I laugh both ways. I am amused, but I have a man's child-like morbid interest, as well. I suppose the reason," he ventured, "that women are purely amused, is that they are realists and that words mean so little to them. We men are so mixed up between ideas and the actual, that for us an equivocal story takes on the scandalous fascination of an adventure."

"I suppose," she said, "that scandalous adventures have a great fascination for men."

"Yes," he said, slowly, "I suppose they do."

"Is that because they are muddle-headed, do you think?"

"Yes," he said, "in a sense. We think that there is more in life than actually exists, and we try to find it, restlessly, in religion, and in art, and even in business, and above all in various forms of love. I think," he said, "that women know better what they expect of life, then when they get it, they are satisfied, or when they don't get it, they are resigned, because they know that there is no substitute for what they missed."

"Are you satisfied, Fitz?"

He put his volume of the Roman Empire on the table. "Clara, dear, we were speaking in general terms." He smiled at her. "I imagine that you, as a realist, feel whether I am satisfied better than I can tell you."

"Still I like to hear it," she answered. "I suppose the way a miser likes to count his money."

For a second he stared at the fire. His look was sad. Then he stood up, smiling, and kissed her on top of the head. He sat down and fell to reading his book again.

But for the most part he was cheerful. Spring came and there were drives with Norah up the river. Levi was now, of course, superfluous. She borrowed the buggy from her father and took great pains in teaching Fitz to drive. There was pleasure in his incompetence and in her skill. Unlike most men, most husbands at least, she imagined, he was not resentful; he took her teaching with amusement, but also with interest. He had no particular feeling for horses, even for Norah, but mechanically he was deft, and a ready learner. Norah soon went well for him but without great sympathy. They would go flying along the river road between the river and the bright green fields of spring. When they passed the watering trough where he had driven her with Alexander, he always raised his hat. One morning—it was Decoration Day—they dared the covered bridge. After all forebodings, Norah faced the darkness and the thunder, the sudden flashes of light and the narrow glimpses, through cracks, of the river far below, with equanimity. On the other shore, they turned upstream between short hills, green with winter oats. They ate their picnic lunch at the top of a long pasture field above the river. Behind them Norah, tied to a buggy wheel, jiggled her feed-bag for the last grain of oats. Below them ran the river. And between two islands they could see the River Street houses, diminutive yet sharp and clear in the bright spring air, like the houses of a cardboard town. The faint pulse of bands came across the water, and moving slowly in front of the cardboard houses, they could see the glint of the fire engines and the red flash of the Epworth League Zouaves.

When summer came, she went with the other wives to the Indian Warm Springs. The old wooden hotel was breathlessly located in a densely wooded pocket. The food was indifferent; the proprietor congenitally hostile to the human race, and the famed waters slightly nauseating. But it had always been the place where people went in the summer, and its shortcomings were actually its assets—they supplied a field of conversation to ladies marooned alone throughout the week. And for Clara herself, there was the added thrill of being, as a married woman, entitled to live in a hotel without a chaperon. Her summer stay was almost over before it dawned on her that at the Indian Warm Springs, there was actually little that one could do with this new-found freedom. In the meantime, with the other men, Fitz came up on the cars each Saturday. There were card parties, croquet tournaments, cotillions; and she was once again the envy of the world of women. He moved among them like a prince, she told herself. His words, his clothes, his gestures made her proud. She must not be a silly, or an ingrate. Surely for her good fortune, the night was not too much to give him.

Yet, when the last breakfast of weak coffee, tepid cakes, and watered maple syrup had been eaten, and she was back in her little house again, after the glow of her first return to her own home, old thoughts—or the memory of old thoughts—besieged her. He was everything to her, and she—she thought she had the right to say it—was everything to him. Why, then, was he not more warmly grateful? Why, then, with all his candor, was he not wholly candid? What was the fastness into which, only at times, but unmistakably, he seemed withdrawn?

CHAPTER XVII

In her nightgown she leaned far out the window; the October morning frost was in the air and in the yellowing trees. Her nightgown, as she leaned, stretched taut across her breasts. Below her she could see him putting on his hat. The front door had just closed, she had sprung up from her warm nest and her warm dream. His slim dark figure moved away, straight, easy, beautiful. Could she keep from calling shamelessly? But then he turned, looked up. His eyes were dark, his teeth were white against his face, ruddy in the sharp fall air. She felt herself cave in; she pressed herself against the window sill. Her bare arm went out to him. His hat was off; he stood there, holding it between his hands, unsmiling, like a man transfixed. She wanted to run, to fly, the wind of her speed pressing her nightgown flat against her body; to run, to fly until her body pressed itself to his. She was shameless. She would not care. His face was there turned up to hers.

Like a man waking, he put his hat on uncertainly. Abruptly, he walked down the street. She strained to follow him. At the corner he looked back, stopped. Was he coming back to her again? Impossible. And just then Senator Beaver emerged from his house and greeted Fitz-Greene with a heavy morning salutation. He raised his hat to the Senator and was gone hurriedly. She threw herself into the warm tumbled bed and lay there shaking. The room was strange and far away. She was alone and shaking in the warmth where he had lain.

Outside the sky was pure and cool. Beside the window the maple leaves were yellow, and through the paling locust leaves across the street she could see the river, blue with the cool and solemn blueness of the sky. Below her, invisible feet stamped lightly on the sidewalk, a double team drove by, travelling quite fast in the crisp morning air. Steadiness returned, languor, and, underneath, a deep unbroken glow. So this was what it was meant to be. This was the true god. There was nothing that she would not do for him; no act of violence or of daring. If he would wish it, she would run after him in her nightgown down the street and throw ecstatic arms about him to the stupefaction of the burghers. She would be glad and proud.

A delicate light trembled and moved lightly on the ceiling; the soft reflection of the maple leaves. The sun must be quite high by now. Let it rise. She would stay here and drain this moment to the last.

What had suddenly come to her to enlighten and transport her? He had been away to Philadelphia for several days. But then, he had been away to Philadelphia often before. Yet this time he had been gone longer and when he came back, there was something pitiful about him. All his warmth and tenderness were there and more than ever an eagerness to please. But under all lay a hint of loneliness, almost of despair. Back of the gay and charming front stood a lost child, unyielding, but haunted by visions of some obscure abyss. Suddenly, profound, ungovernable pity had stirred her. And he had answered to her stirring. And she, in a swiftly mounting, inconceivable moment, had been translated in chariots of fire. Instantly; rapt, whirled, carried away. To a new world. She would never be the same again. To-day, this morning, as she lay here, she was irrevocably changed, she was as different from yesterday as steel from iron.

However much in pity she might have begun, all that was changed, too. She may have thought of him as a child, and so she had, first as a brutal child, then a spoiled child, last night as a lonely child. But she never would think of him so again.

And what of him this time, this long time, it almost seemed, since they had been married? For her, these moments with him that had just passed had been a revelation. But for him? She began to see it now. It was something that he had long hoped for in vain, hoped for almost despairingly, almost with bitterness. She began to see it now. What a ninny, what a worthless stick she had been; what a prig, ignorant, supercilious, and conceited. She had looked on herself, in her passivity, as conferring an inestimable boon upon him. And she had looked on him, at worst almost with hatred, at most with tolerance, as unworthy of that boon. And all the time, desolate, baffled, but patient, he had been waiting and hoping for that moment, to him inexplicably delayed, when she would be able to see and feel and seize their common joy. In those perilous, those high and desperate first

days when in the innocence and ignorance which was considered
the exquisite prerogative of nice young girls, her dreams, her
silly dreams, had trembled on the abyss of nameless fears, of
bloody threats, of dangers, of vague yet anguished horrors of impending mutilation, had he not comforted her mind and, indeed,
her frightened coward's body? She looked out at the river. If
there were nothing else, surely a woman could worship a man
for that. Surely a woman was lucky above all others to find a
man so. There must be many other kinds of men.

What she had blamed him for so bitterly then, or later learned
to tolerate with condescension, was but a faint yet uncontrollable
reflection in his eyes of her own unguessed lack. Poor Fitz!
Poor Fitz! All her life long, she would make it up to him.

She would start now. She must rouse herself. She smiled. She
would give him the best lunch when he came home from the
office, the best lunch that a man ever had.

Into her consciousness the room began to drift: the yellow
chrysanthemums of the wall paper, the dome of St. Mark's in
Venice above the square where pigeons fed, the twinkle of brass
knobs about the fireplace and of silver on the bureau in front of
the tall mirror beside the Della Robbia. The Aurelians in their
wide straw hats and stand-up collars eyed her in a well-bred
cluster. Let them look, she did not care. They belonged to another
world; they had no meaning for her. Even Fitz, standing among
them in the Aurelian hat-band and wide four-in-hand, was, there,
a stranger. He was not her Fitz. Her Fitz was some one that
no one but she would ever guess or know.

There was a gentle tapping at the door. "Come in," she said.
There was a gentle clink of china; the door swung open. Christobel stood there with the tray; above the tray her face was fiery.

"I got some breakfast."

"Why, Christobel, that would be fine," she said. "You make
me feel like a baby. You know, I have never had breakfast in
bed in my life, except when I was sick."

Christobel checked a shy, swift smile. Still very red, she
tramped hastily from the room.

"Christobel," she called out, "do you think we might have
brook trout for lunch?"

Christobel's receding voice came down the narrow corridor.
"Yes, ma'am, I ordered them."

CHAPTER XVIII

In the bedroom the gas lamps had been lit an hour, but it was not time for supper yet. Seated at the window she knitted steadily on a brilliant scarlet glove for Fitz; the gas log muttered, the needles twinkled, the scarlet worsted caught the light; in her lap the ball of yarn stirred. She had no time to lose, Christmas was almost here again, it was incredible. What a swift, perfect autumn it had been. Let poets write of spring; for her, autumn, this autumn, would stand as the time of beauty, love, and wonder. On Saturdays and holidays the coach had rolled down flaming country roads, past heaps of winter apples scattered through low-spread orchards, past glowing pumpkins among the shocks; the hard, clear air was filled with the clink of toggle chains, the wink of brass, the mingled staccato of the trotting horses. High aloft, gently swaying as they rolled, she had sat beside Fitz-Greene, felt his warmth and strength as they rolled through autumn. They had driven Norah too—in the buggy given her by her father in recognition of her married status—close to each other on the narrow seat, flying along, well muffled, in the light narrow body, sometimes until a sharp, thin sickle moon had warned them home.

Her eye fell on a brown chrysanthemum which stood on her bureau still, though long since withered on its stalk. That, too, had been a day to be remembered: the football game. Breakfasting here in the dark and the trip in the cars and college friends of Fitz's getting on at nearly every stop. At last the stretch of docks and endless buildings as they crossed on the ferry. And then the coach-load of Aurelians driving up Fifth Avenue. They waved their orange flags, the coach-horn sounded, people turned, smiled, cheered, "Hurrah for Princeton!" "Hurrah for Yale!" Other coaches overtaking, being passed, orange coaches cheering; blue coaches jeering—she was furious.

The crowds stamped on the wooden bleachers, canvas jackets plunged, canvas bodies thudded: the mud-stained pile which

152

toppled and fell. Then Fitz-Greene throwing his hat clear into the field and all the Aurelians hugging her. Those nice Aurelians. A horrid little boy had run away with Fitz-Greene's hat, she had seen him but didn't care.

All the way home, she had slept on his shoulder. Levi had driven them from the station through the dark silent town; and Fitz-Greene, still explaining about the game, had undressed her and put her to bed.

"It was that tackle-play that did it," he kept saying.

"Yes," she murmured.

"They never knew when it was coming."

"Never know." She felt like the dormouse in "Alice in Wonderland."

"The score was on an end play. But that's because those tackle plays had pulled the end in. It was smart."

"Treacle, treacle, treacle."

His face was against the hollow of her neck. When he laughed, it tickled her insanely.

"Oh, dear," she moaned.

"You are so cunning," he said. "You're sound asleep." His arm came under her knees, the other around her. She was rolled into a deft bundle, rolled into bed. She clung to him happily.

"Oh, dear, oh, dear," she said. "I do love you so."

Though it was almost Christmas now, she kept the big chrysanthemum in a narrow vase on her bureau.

That had been Thanksgiving: immediately, it seemed, they went sleighing, stinging faces above their soft, warm, fur-bundled bodies, slightly swaying to the sleigh's light-balanced motion. Thin bells and streaming backs and balls from flying hoofs; black trees, white ·banks, the icy river. And now, again, they skated between the islands, and almost all the men asked her to skate with them just as they had before she married, but not with the same mysterious and seductive dash of fervor. She was a married woman and her relationship with men, reaching its peak on her wedding day when they had crowded on the dock, so to speak, loving and moist of eye and somewhat fortified with rum, to wave her a tender adieu, had dropped abruptly to something wooden and lifeless, to a mere shell of that which had departed. It was too bad, she should like to have had them still feel loving toward her. Why should they not continue? But her dethronement in accordance with the customs of the country was a minor point. She had Fitz-Greene, that was the major point and all other points besides. Yet it was just because she had him that she wished the other men would still be thrilled by her. She would have thought that if a man was at all stirred by a woman, he would be doubly stirred by the sight of her in love, by the thought of her possessed. But men's minds, or, at all events, the minds of young American gentlemen, did not work that way, and she was bound to admit that from the point of view of peace and civic order, the system had advantages. Yet she could have wished for a continuance of their affection as a tribute to Fitz-Greene in a sense, and in another sense, even more obscure, as a satisfaction to her awakened and inexhaustible radiance.

Her needles paused. She looked out the window into the dark for the yellow lights and the black, rumbling shape of a public cab. Fitz-Greene had left that morning before daylight to see his brothers in Philadelphia on business. Now it was after six o'clock, his train should be coming in. She could see in her mind the plume of steam and the line of bright car windows, weaving among switch-lights, bright rails and patches of dirty snow. She could see the trickle of people from the car doors, and Fitz-Greene, tall and dark in his fur-collared overcoat, giving his bag to the old colored porter. She could see him striding through the small inconsequential people of the waiting room, who would be impressed by this flash of beauty across their gray horizon. Now he had a word for the cab driver, another word went with the quarter to the old colored man. Now the cab, a humble and unpretentious beetle, freighted for once with rare distinction, was rumbling across the Belgian blocks of the station plaza, up the business street, past lighted shop fronts and trolley cars, through the snow-dusted city square. Now it should be turning on to River Street. It did not come. The dejected slave between the shafts could not keep pace with her thoughts. In spite of the cold wind of the river, she raised the window slightly. Before she could see it, she could hear. And so she did. What a disgraceful horse! No wonder he had not kept up with her. The silhouette appeared around the corner. She hid the glove in the drawer of the bed-table. He was here, but what a disgraceful horse! She ran from the room and down the narrow stairs.

He came in, smiling, on the wind, as she opened the door. Her

arms went round his neck. It was so long since he had slipped
out of her warm, sleepy bed. It seemed as though he stiffened
slightly and slightly strained away from her. When he kissed
her, he only brushed her cheek. She gave his collar a light pat
and let him go. Poor boy! he must be tired. What an awful
day! Riding and riding in cold, drafty cars, talking and talking
to hard-mouthed brothers, who were never satisfied. She was no
sentimental ninny. A man who was tired had no desire to be
clung to. No Christmas cards to-night. Nothing for him, but
warmth, and food and freedom from bother. He was out of his
coat now, she could see his face. He still held his smile, but it
was empty, glassy. Poor dear, why need he try? He must not
feel he had to. "Would you like a bath and a change before
supper?"

"Yes," he said, heavily, "I think I would."

"Go upstairs, then," she said. "I'll tell Christobel to keep back
supper until we are ready."

On the way to the dining room, she did not look back at him.
That was important. And she had not said "Would you like a
nice bath?" If she had, he would have said "No." His footfall
on the carpeted stair sounded light enough. Already, the warmth
of home had heartened him, that or relief that he did not have
to battle with indifference or exacting solicitude. And then, perhaps, he was glad to see her again. But a woman must not count
too much on that, when a man is tired.

What had exhausted him so much this time? He went to
Philadelphia often, and generally his return was something like
a festival. His brothers were harsh, but he was adroit and
laughed at them, and every one said this branch of his was the
best that the business had. Had there been bad news, or was he
catching cold? Here was the kitchen; a chair rail and dressers of
pine stained to look like cherry, blue plates, bright pots, and a
stove whose nickel ornaments surpassed, as Fitz-Greene said, a
masonic Negro's coffin.

"Christobel," she said, "Mr. Rankin seems pretty tired to-night.
Do you think we could put back supper till he has a bath?"

Christobel raised a pretty hand to the freckles on her dead
white cheek. Under her red hair, her eyes were an icy blue. "Say,
that's too bad," she said. "You don't think he's sick, do you?"

"No, I don't think so. It's just the long trip."

"You don't think he'd like an omelet instead of those veal
cutlets?"

"Well, I don't know."

"The cutlets are nice," Christobel said, "but an omelet sets
lighter on your stomach."

"I know," said Clara.

"Why don't you ask him?" Christobel said.

"I don't like to bother him when he is tired."

Christobel looked at her with some respect. "Well, I guess
that's good policy. I'll tell you what. If he don't take a cutlet,
I'll be fixed to make the omelet before he finishes his vegetables.
He eats so slow, you know, and then he talks a lot. But then,
maybe, he won't talk to-night. If he don't talk, I guess he's sick.
Now, I'll be ready with the eggs. You can holler down the speaking tube, when he's ready for his supper."

She stood on the narrow landing in front of the library. She
could hear him, most comforting and child-like of sounds, splashing in his tub.

"I'll be in the library, when you're ready," she called. "No
hurry, though."

"All right." His voice sounded cheerful enough, but she wished
she could see his face.

At supper, he seemed to rouse himself to talk to Christobel.
It was, perhaps, natural enough. A brakeman friend of hers had
been on the train. Yet Clara could not help feeling it was not
quite the result she had looked for from her good judgment.

Upstairs, in the library, he lighted his cigar. He crushed the
cigar out on an ash receiver and took up his book. She kept on
with her embroidery. She should be working on the scarlet
glove. Christmas was almost here. But the gloves were to be a
surprise.

She was conscious that for a long time no leaf had turned. She
looked up. Quickly, he looked down at his book. She had caught
an echo of his eyes on her, a gaze, fixed, pitying and tragic, a
look, heart-broken, suddenly old, and the look too, of a horror-
ridden child. With a breast constricted and leaden, she was beside him on the footstool. She took his hand and laid it on her
cheek.

"I love you, dear," she said.

Almost quickly, he drew away. She looked up to read his

meaning. Now, for an instant, he was smiling at her as he always did. Then he glanced away.

He stood up. Sitting on the footstool, staring at the fire, she heard him pacing the room.

"From now on," he stopped, turned, walked away, "I'll have to go to Philadelphia all the time, two or three times a week." He seemed to wait, looking out the window into the blank night. "It's not fair to you to be rousing you out at all hours of the morning. I think the best plan would be for me to use the little upstairs bedroom."

"On the nights you have to be leaving early?"

"Well, it's hardly worth while to keep moving."

"Oh, but I don't mind."

He did not speak. "Fitz——" she said. She waited. He did not move.

She looked in the fire, as still as an animal. There was nothing to say. But she was not an animal. There was a game of smiling fortitude to play.

"Would you like your things moved now?" she said.

"Oh, that's all right," he stood up quickly, "I can do it myself." His voice sounded strange and hard and far away.

"Oh, no, I'll do it."

With a stiff half-smile, she rose. She forced herself to throw him a friendly glance as she left the room. He tramped the floor with his eyes on the carpet.

In the bedroom the light was dim. Beside the folded green-satin quilt his dressing-gown lay on the bed, broad-striped dark blue, and his linen night shirt, white and fine, heavy as she picked it up. She laid the dressing-gown on top of it across her arm. She stooped for his brown leather slippers and seized them violently. What was it? What had happened? She would go back to him where he tramped in the library, demand an explanation, that was her right. To leave her this way, without a word, after all that lay between them, withdraw at his pleasure as —the slippers shook in her hand—as he would leave a bad woman when the morning came! Everything lay between them, everything, there could not have been more. They had been happy, what could he ask for more? Had he then been half pretending, nursing all the time a secret grievance, or some secret of another sort? If so, he had wronged her unbearably, had

violated her, defiled her. She would not bear it. She had rights.
The right to be told, to understand.

Still holding his dressing-gown and slippers she sat down on
the bed in the dark room. But if she asked, what would she
learn? Would her asking make things better? What she learned
might be no help to her. Rights might be talked about but with
a woman what was gained by claiming them? She knew that
much. A woman's only means to happiness were patience, understanding, love. She would not be like her mother, exacting,
firmly reasonable. Her thoughts flew back to Fitz tramping the
room. This trouble was not hers alone; he, too, was caught. But
then ought she not to know, to help him? No, that was self-
deceit. Her mother was always helping people and could never
learn that help must first be wanted. Fitz would perhaps call on
her for help. Then she would be ready.

Swift sleigh bells passed outside. Beyond dim snowy branches
at the window, lay the river, dim, silvery, underneath a crescent
moon.

What was love if it was not faith? If all were set out clearly,
explained, agreed upon; there was not merit, no mystery or glory.
But to venture all without a question—"love is not love which
alters when it alteration finds—ah, no, it is an ever fixèd mark
which looks on tempests and is never shaken."

Still he was tramping. She could hear him. He had been
patient long with her. She could be patient now. She stood up
resolutely: sadly she almost smiled. She need not make too great
a virtue of it, for there was also her pride.

CHAPTER XIX

WAS ever a winter so interminable? Why, even the Christmas dinner, which now seemed years ago, had seemed to last a year: smiling and talking to awful Uncle Linsey; smiling and meeting squarely her father's benign proud glances; smiling at George and at George's little Tommy. And ever since, through the long weeks, the long little dinners, the long skating parties, smiling, chatting, smiling and being gay.

She would not speak. It was necessary to play the farce with unwavering conviction. Once only she had given way. It was on the landing, they were going upstairs for the night. She had reached out across to him, to feel his body stiffen, his face turn set. Since then an instinct as inviolable as the freezing of a rabbit in the face of danger obliged her to face the catastrophe with perfect firmness, perfect naturalness; no hint, no sign that could be taken for self-pity or a plea. And it was as vital to her being that no one outside should guess the rôle that had been so suddenly assigned and was so immeasurably exacting.

In the library, she let him brush her cheek, then went to bed, exhausted. She wondered whether time would make it less of a sickening drain to maintain the pose of undisturbed acceptance, self-reliance and good cheer. Most forlorn of all hopes. She dared not look ahead and feel that it would be the only boon which time would bring her.

Curiously, she had never slept more heavily. It was not, indeed, a good sleep. It was as though the unnatural and morbid quality of her rôle generated each day in her a poison, a toxin which left her not only exhausted but also stupefied. Going to bed alone beneath the infant Samuel, she sank instantly into a dark and sometimes troubled trance.

In the morning she woke unrested and still half-stunned, yet not so stunned but that she could, at those hours of low resistance and unnatural creeping chill, when the mind is clear and swift, but timorous and sickly, revolve with demented and sterile impotence the causes of her grief. She searched her own conduct for a clew. Spurred by the crisis, she was meticulous and merciless; yet all her little errors put together made no sum total that would give the answer. And while, as she knew, of all errors in marriage little errors were the worst, yet one would expect their effect to be gradual. But this had happened in an instant, in that one day, when he had gone to Philadelphia. And it did not seem to be for him a withdrawal from her as a person. Indeed, he appeared even now to be devoted. He was infinitely considerate, though that was, of course, no sign, or, if any, an evil one; but he also clung to her with a new intensity in a way both frightened and dependent.

It seemed rather a case of physical revulsion. He rarely touched her. When he kissed her, he only brushed her cheek, and she could see that soon he would kiss her no longer. Had she never really appealed to him? Had he been deceived by her shyness, thinking it covered a latent power to respond, and when that shyness passed, had he then found himself deceived? She wished she knew more of other women and their loves to measure her deficiency. Fantastic notions seized her. She would degrade herself, would spy in unspeakable hidden precincts in order to learn the secrets of the art. She was abashed, but not at her distorted thoughts. There she was hardy and shameless. It was, rather, that in her body or in her spirit, in which, it seemed, she had been inordinately confident, she lacked some element that should have been her woman's portion. If this were so, might he not have found another, and suddenly then, by contrast, have been brought face to face with all her own deficiencies, and, while still devoted to her as the good companion, have suddenly found physical contact a violation of nature? Perhaps that could have happened without another, merely by the operation of his own instinct, which, like a steel rod, at a given point tolerated distortion no longer but sprang back to the normal. She hoped that this was not the case. Her thought perhaps was wicked; but if it had to come, she hoped that there was some one else. Her harried mind ran on, seeing him with women of a hundred different kinds, and sometimes, in its misery, by an instinct of despairing self-mutilation, going on to draw sharp details of extravagant and vivid scenes. It was no easy task to face the picture of him with another. But there was sharper anguish in the thought that she had been deserted without a rival, simply on her own account. That was indeed a degradation.

These pacings of her prisoned mind were ended each morning, by the sound of Fitz-Greene upstairs, getting out of bed. From the bathroom, he called "Good morning" to her. She heard his razor on the strop and afterward, the water in the basin. His slippers sounded on the narrow stairs as he went back to his room to dress. Nothing of his remained here in the bedroom, except the picture of him in his wide straw hat and stand-up collar, surrounded by other straw hats and stand-up collars of the Aurelians. She had thought for a while that he might rather breakfast alone, it could be done without arousing suspicion among the family or the town. But she had found that he seemed disappointed; a bitter paradox. So now, her mind still drugged with sleep and yet on edge, she turned back the green-satin quilt, a wedding gift made by Miss Ba-ba Lamb herself and presented by her shyly, archly. She thrust her long narrow feet into the white rabbits' fur on her red slippers and put on the gray silk dressing-gown with white fur around the sleeves and neck and even around the bottom, that she had bought for her wedding journey.

A slant of morning sun came in the small bay window and brightened the silver coffee-pot above the thin blue flame of alcohol. Across the circle of white linen they faced each other, fortified with sugary baked apples, with deep brown strips of liver, and enfolded between the busy little fire and the morning sun. It sometimes seemed that real disaster could never penetrate to two so snugly protected; catastrophe would be powerless in the face of such warmth, such neat and cosey shining, such coffee and fried liver. A new day lay ahead; truth with its beauty would come to its own again. She would feel his hands upon her. He was cheerful, almost loving, even now.

But then, one morning, he was staring at her. He dropped his eyes as she looked up, but again there was the echo of fear and horror. She turned to stone. After all this time, this monstrous and bizarre eternity, there had been no gain. No gain.

" You don't look well," he said. His voice was small and tight. "Are you well?"

"Oh, yes," she said. "I have a headache sometimes in the morning."

"A headache?" he said. "A headache?" She could hear him breathing. "Have you been to see the doctor?"

"Oh, no," she said. "It is nothing. Just a headache, and a little sore throat. I suppose I ought to take a little calomel."

For a long time, he did not speak. "You must go to see Doctor Hartman," he said, in a loud voice, "this morning."

"Doctor Hartman?" she said. "Doctor Hartman? But we have always had Doctor Considine."

"Doctor Hartman is the best." He was harsh. "Clara, will you please go to Doctor Hartman this morning?"

"I will," she said, "if you want me to. But I think it is silly."

"I know," he said. He spoke rapidly. "There's a lot in what you say. We might all be better off if we never went near them. But I think there is only one of two things to do; either stay away from them altogether, or else pick the best man and go to him at the earliest possible moment."

"At the earliest possible moment?" she said.

"I mean whenever we are not feeling well, go right away. If a doctor can do good, it stands to reason that the sooner he starts, the better it will be. Or if it's nothing, you have lost nothing but the fee. So you will go to Doctor Hartman then, this morning? Better go early. His office gets crowded. Shall I tell him that you are coming? Oh, well, all right then. Well, I must be getting down to the office. I won't be back for lunch. I'll have it at the hotel. There are some men there that I want to see. Hartman's hours are nine to twelve. You had better be there at nine."

Back from the river front, on the street that led to the town square, two cast-iron Negro jockeys held rings for hitching horses. A gate in a white picket fence along the sidewalk stood always open. A flagged path, flanked by blighted gladioli, led to a tall brick house, sickly brown with tall and very narrow windows. The wooden front steps were uncomfortably steep. The panelled brown front doors were formidable and sad. Beside the doorway, another cast-iron Negro spread his arms to receive umbrellas below the shinning, gold letters on the black sanded ground, *Peter Hartman, M.D.*

Passing through the hallway, where a narrow stair toiled up under a monumental balustrade, she pushed back a double door and saw black wicker chairs and a black walnut table.

In the corner of the room, an old gentleman in a snuff-colored overcoat watched her take a seat with unconcealed interest and satisfaction. Having made note of her smart, blue costume and high, buttoned shoes, smooth and blackly shining, of her beaver muff and fur piece and small, round, blue hat, he drew from his overcoat pocket, hand over hand, a vast silk handkerchief and blew a blast that filled the room with twinkling lights. The crystal pendants of the chandelier were trembling. Peering at her over the folds of the handkerchief, the old gentleman blew again. Scarlet, he emerged, breathing hard, cleared his throat with a resounding gargle and rolled his handkerchief into a bundle, which he thrust back into his pocket. He gave a final glance at her, then picked up a flimsy country newspaper and began to read. He had done what he could to interest and astonish her. On the wall, a be-ribboned parchment announced, in Latin, the confidence of the University of Pennsylvania in the medical attainments of Peterus Hartmannus, while above the fluted paper of the empty fireplace, a steel engraving had caught President Chester A. Arthur in an effort to look distinguished. On the walnut table, bound in black imitation morocco and heavily tooled in gold, lay a "Trip to the Centennial Exhibition" and "Shemingo County in the War of the Rebellion."

The door at the back of the room opened, a tall young woman led out a muffled child in a reefer jacket. From the office came a thick, breathless voice.

"How long since you have been spanked, Laura?"

The woman turned. "Since I was spanked, Doctor? Why, not since I was nine years old."

"Well, then, if that child is not in bed and kept there, you will be spanked again."

He came into the doorway, a round, short, little man with a tuft of white beard on his smooth, pink chin and creased eyes behind his gold spectacles. His hair was limp and silvery. He waved a hand at Clara and the old gentleman. "Witnesses," he said. "To-morrow you will be spanked. Now, go along, and keep his mouth inside his muffler. Who's next?"

"Right here," said the old man promptly. He thought better of it. "After the lady," he said.

The doctor raised a plump hand and made the tuft on his chin wiggle.

"Are you a patient?"

"Well, yes and no," the old gentleman said.

"Insurance?" the doctor said.

"No."

"Subscriptions, books, lightning rods?"

"No," the old man said. "Just a little matter. I can wait."

Still looking at the old man, the doctor beckoned to Clara, as though she were a child.

His desk before the window was piled high with papers, books, and publications, with bottles and flasks. A light burned in a bull's-eye lantern on a swinging bracket above a chair and stool. The top of a narrow table was padded in leather. Below glass jars on shelves, a tap dripped in a marble sink and a stained marble top carried a pestle and a mortar.

He pointed to the chair across the desk. "Well, Clara, sit down." He spoke as though she had been coming there for years.

He sat down, gave his own chair a backward thrust, and leaned forward with his clean, fat hands on his wrinkled knees. "How is Fitz-Greene?" he said. "Nice young fellow. Awful nice young fellow. And what seems to be the trouble?"

"Really, Doctor, there isn't anything the trouble."

"Good. No trouble."

"I just mentioned to my husband that I had a headache."

"And he insisted that you come to see me. Good. That's fine. He's one of my best patients. Hold out your tongue. An awful nice young fellow. That will do. How are your bowels? Any soreness in the joints? Let me feel your pulse." His warm finger tips settled lightly on her wrist. An immense gold watch came out of his waistcoat pocket and opened with a tiny click. His shirt front creaked to his thick breathing. The watch ticked loudly. He wore an old-fashioned, full-bosomed shirt with a stand-up collar attached, badly laundered, though very clean. His wrinkled, low-cut waistcoat and the ends of his black string tie rose and fell. The watch clicked shut. "Stand up, please." The silvery head came against her chest. A hand gripped her. "Inhale. Exhale." He crept around her, taking soundings and tickling her with his pink ear until she almost giggled. She held her breath manfully. It would be scandalous. She heard him heave up behind her. His hand came against her back. He tapped it shortly with the other fingers. Tunk, tunk . . . tunk, tunk. He worked around her like a cooper around a cask, with one ear cocked, gleaming and breathing hard.

"Sound as a nut," he said. "Clear as a bell. Any discomfort after eating? Nausea? Wind on the stomach? Wind on the bowels? Fitz-Greene had quite a case of jaundice when he first came. An awful nice fellow. No feeling of chilliness or heat? No rash, no pimples? You've had your eyes examined? Look right in the light." With a thumb and forefinger, he opened one eye wide.

"You make me feel like a horse," she said.

"Well, you ought to feel like a horse. Sound as a nut. Have any trouble sleeping? Lost your appetite? He was one of the worst cases I ever saw. That was before you knew him. Took a fancy to him right off. It seems you did, too. What about your inner workings? Think you might be starting to have a baby?"

"No," she said. "No, I don't suppose so."

"All right, just as well. Plenty of time. *Carpe diem*. First years of marriage only come once. Other years come over and over again. No night sweats, I suppose? All right, take a seat." He sat down and locking his hands in front of his mouth, began to play a tune on his teeth with his thumb-nail. "Can't find a thing organically wrong," he said. "Sound as a nut. Wish I had your bronchi and lungs. Liver and lights, too. But you don't look quite right, and that's a fact. He's not asking too much of you? These young men nowadays have no sense, you know. Oh, I was sure of that. Awful nice young fellow. Nothing else on your mind, is there? Well, I'll tell you what. You are probably just a little run-down. Everybody is, this time of year. I'll make you up a little tonic. My boy will bring it around this morning. A wineglass full three times a day before meals." He stood up smiling. "If you don't feel better," he said, "come back. And if you do, pour it down the sink." He patted her slim blue shoulder. "Nothing to worry about," he said. "Sound as a nut."

He watched her go out the door. What a nice pretty girl. A fine young woman. But her smile was still unsatisfied. Queer things, these young creatures. If I had a set of vitals like that, I'd turn cartwheels down the street and drink a quart of burgundy for dinner. Perhaps she's merely shy. She's always gone to Considine, that windy ignoramus. He'll throw a fit when he finds he's lost a patient. Awful nice young fellow, that Fitz-Greene.

The man in the snuff-colored overcoat stood up. "Doctor," he said, "you got a few minutes?"

"If you have anything to sell, I can't see you now. These hours are reserved for my patients." Confound the patients! Why couldn't some of them be here when they were wanted?

"I come from the northern part of the county," the old man said, "near Bowman and my wife's got a goitre." The old man looked at him severely. "They tell me you can cure goitre."

"Who does?"

"Well, the hotel man up there says a travelling man told him." The old man plunged his hands in his trouser pockets. "Now what I want to know is, is it a fact?"

"No, it is not a fact. Sometimes we can help, and then sometimes we can cure it. It all depends."

"Well, that's the first point," the old man said. "Now here's the next point. How much does it cost?"

"Well, friend, there's no way in the world of telling that. I don't even know what shape she is in."

"Well, if you saw her, could you tell?"

"Why, no. Even then you wouldn't know how long it might take."

"In other words, you don't know what you can do or what it will cost, whether you do it or not."

"Yes, that's about the size of it."

The old man remained planted. "Well, how in time is a man to do business with you that way?"

"Confound it, nobody has to do business. But it's all I can say. What's the use of promising to cure your wife when I don't know? And if I don't know what I can do, how can I tell what it will cost?"

The old man stopped chewing his beard. "That's what you tell 'em all, eh? Take that young woman that just come out. Did you tell her what it would cost?"

"I didn't have to. Everybody knows my charges. Two dollars for a visit."

"Does that include the medicine?"

"No, that's extra."

"Did you tell her whether the medicine would cure her?"

"I guess she'll be all right. There's nothing much the matter with her."

The old man gave a snort of triumph. "What way of business is that? Selling them medicine when there's nothing the matter with them."

"Who the devil do you think you are, coming down here and telling me how to run my business?"

The old man put on his hat. "Tell you how to run your business? Nobody can run your business better than that. Selling medicine to well people." The old man started back toward the door. "Don't you hit me. I'm leaving. If they're well already," he called back over his shoulder, "you cure them; if they ain't well, you don't." The front door slammed behind him.

The reception room swam before the doctor's furious eyes. He started back for the office. A little spirits of ammonia. That asthmatic heart of his.

There was a tap on the window-pane. The old man peered in, flourishing his handkerchief. "That's why you have to see them first," he shouted. He could hear him blowing his nose furiously on the garden path and his parting shout, "To see if they're well!"

He drank the cloudy spirits of ammonia. Nasty drink! Confound these old-time farmers! Mule-headed and ignorant. Good riddance anyhow. They never paid their bills. The damned old fool! Too bad, though. Maybe he could have done something for that wife of his. Poor woman! Too bad.

"Doctor Hartman." The voice was low and tight. He wheeled. Fitz-Greene's eyes were on him. His face was pale and his voice hadn't sounded like his own. What was the matter with this young couple?

"Well," he said, "what do you want?" Confound people, walking in the office, without a by your leave. A man couldn't even drink a sedative in peace.

"Have you seen Clara?"

"Yes, yes, of course."

"Well, what did you find?"

"Little run-down condition." Confound the fellow, charging into his office.

"A little run-down condition." Fitz-Greene spoke slowly and still looked aside. "What do you mean by that?"

"Damn it, young man! I mean just what I say. It's plain

enough, isn't it? A little run-down condition. What else do you want, for God's sake? Do you want me to tell you she has tuberculosis and cancer?"

"You mean there is nothing seriously wrong with her?"

"Of course, I mean that. It's plain enough, isn't it? If there was something wrong with her, I'd tell you. I mean just what I say."

"You're sure, absolutely sure?"

"If you're not satisfied with my opinion, what did you send her here for? Send her to Considine. I'm not accustomed to having my opinions questioned by a layman. Don't think because I took a fancy to you that I can be insulted. Here, here, let go of me."

The young man had him by the shoulders. He was talking fast. "You don't understand. I didn't put it well. I made a regular mess of it. I am awfully sorry. You musn't think that. I wouldn't have you. You are the finest doctor I ever saw, absolutely the finest. Absolutely! And a real friend. Shake hands and say it's all right." The young man had him by the hand. "Clara and I would never think of having any one but you." He let go the doctor's hand. "I feel as if you'd saved my life."

"Nonsense, you were never in the least danger."

Fitz-Greene thrust out a finger with impudence. "In that case, why aren't you more grateful to me?" He put his hat on at an angle, and marched out of the office. Evidently, he was himself again.

CHAPTER XX

SITTING in the bedroom, talking with Christobel about the supper party, she heard the front door close. Christobel leaned easily against the bed post.

"Now about those salted nuts. Do you want the almonds and the walnuts in separate dishes?" She had on a starched blue gingham. Her face was rosy from the oven. Small copper strands of hair lay damply on her forehead. "Or do you want them mixed up like?"

He was hanging up his hat and coat; he was on the stair; he was running, two steps at a time. "Hello," he said. "Hello, Christobel. You certainly look nice in that blue dress. Next time I run into that brakeman, I am going to ask him if he ever saw you in that dress."

"Oh, sugar," she said, "I'm a sight. I'm all hot from the oven and these are just my work clothes."

"Clara," he said, "I hope you didn't mind my sending round the note about the others. I thought as long as we were having people in, we might as well have a party. You sure you feel up to it?'

"Yes," she said. "I think Doctor Hartman has cured me already."

"Didn't you like him? I went in afterwards to make sure you were all right."

"You did?"

"Yes, I'm afraid I did. I didn't trust you. I know you wouldn't tell me anything you thought would worry me."

"I don't suppose you'd tell me, either." That was a mistake. She kept smiling cheerfully to try to cover it. But he was oblivious.

"Of course, I wouldn't. Now about the party. I thought we really ought to have Jeanne Balso. It's no use asking Thompson with Big Sister all the time. After all, if you are going to entertain a man, you must entertain him as a human being and not as a filler to take care of a wallflower." He remembered Christobel. "Big Sister's the finest person of all the girls in town. I know that. But it's Thompson we've got to think of."

"I was having Anna Lisle," Clara said.

"She's great, but George always likes to talk to her. She's fragile and soulful, and he's so big and strong. That leaves me and Ellen, and that's all right."

"And me and Doggie, and that's all right, too," she said.

He laughed. "Put Thompson on the other side."

"All right," she said. "Go and dress. Christobel and I must finish."

"All right," he said. "Will you wear that light-blue satin?"

"Oh, I couldn't," she said. "I couldn't. It's much too grand for such a dinner. It would look silly."

"It sure is a elegant gown, though," ventured Christobel. "Tell you what you ought to do. Take off the lace festoons on the skirt and have it kind of simple. It wouldn't take a minute."

"Good for you, Christobel," Fitz-Greene said, as he went out the door.

"A wonderful girl, Christobel," he said, as he came in the drawing-room. "I do like that blue satin."

She felt herself stir under the shining gown. "I feel perfectly absurd," she said. "I don't know why I am wearing it."

He walked over to the marble mantel and studied the bronze clock between the crystal brackets. "I don't know, either."

She gazed around the room, small, but formal and seldom used, green-velvet cushions on the slim gilt chairs, old Rands and Rankins in heavy oval frames against the French gray wall. There had been no gain. When he had come springing up the stair, she had wished that they were to be alone to-night. Now it was just as well.

The doorbell rang. Fitz-Greene went out.

From the doorway, Mun peered at her in indignation. "Great Governor! What a night!" He slapped his beaver gloves together and stamped his arctics. His pale eyes and thin aristocratic nose were moist. "It's bitter, bitter." He struggled out of his bearskin-collared coat and unwound a long white muffler.

Clara laughed. "You think anything below forty is bitter. Mun. It's been thawing all day."

"All right," said Mun. He was on one leg wrestling with an arctic. "Stick your nose out. A heavy freeze, by Jupiter."

The arctic came off, with Mun's pump inside it. "You ought to go to Samoa, Mun, where it's warm and there are lots of beautiful girls."

Mun had his pump in his hand by now, and pointed it at her. "If there were a good hotel there, damned if I wouldn't go." He balanced again, and put his pump on. He wore heavy woollen socks with white toes and heels. "Everything is cold in this country, climate, women, railroad cars. It's a life of misery."

"The question is," said Fitz-Greene, from the hall, "whether in Samoa, the climate makes the women, or the women make the climate."

Mun hopped around, pulling at the other arctic. "It's no good, Fitz," he said. "I know Oscar Wilde."

"Well, if you know Oscar Wilde, you ought to know that it's as good as anything can be."

"Never mind. The main thing is, are we going to have terrapin?"

"No," Clara called. "It's too expensive."

Mun came in the room. His dinner clothes were dashingly cut and slightly too large. "Well, then, what about that Château Lafitte? Are you going to have some more of that?"

"You must ask Fitz-Greene about that," Clara said. "He has the keys to the cellar."

Mun shook Clara absently by the hand. "Do you mean you haven't gotten the wine up yet? On a night like this? It'll be much too cold. Look here, Fitz-Greene, we will have to do something about this."

"About what?"

"About the wine. What are you going to have?"

"Oh, I don't know. I hadn't thought."

"You hadn't thought. Well, what's your meat course?"

"It's really just a supper," Clara said. "We are having sweetbreads en casserole."

"Well, then, that's all right. Château Lafitte would go with sweetbreads en casserole."

Fitz-Greene came into the room, grinning. "We've got it up, Mun. Don't you worry."

"You have? The Château Lafitte, eh? Worry? Well, then,

no. I should say not. Clara, my old sweetheart, you look perfectly delicious to-night."

"We've had it on the back of the stove for two hours," Fitz-Greene said.

Mun whirled around. "On the back of the stove! On the back of the stove!" He jingled the cluster of seals on his meagre stomach, and whistled between his teeth. "Not at all funny," he said. "Clara, you ought to make him take these things more seriously. I was talking to a fellow in the Union League the other day. Everybody likes Fitz there, you know, can't help it, but they just don't understand him."

The doorbell rang again. Fitz-Greene started from the room. "Well, that's a pretty good sign, there's something wrong with me," he said.

Good Doggie and Big Sister entered in a compact mass. "Wow, Fitz," she said, "it's cold."

In front of the fire Mun spread his coat-tails. "You see," he said to Clara.

Good Doggie beamed down on Fitz. "Yes," he said, "it certainly is cold, by gum!"

"You see," said Mun to Clara.

Beaming kindly and thoughtfully at Fitz-Greene, Doggie reached up and clamped Fitz's ears between two snowy mittens.

Big Sister jammed an elbow against Doggie's ribs. "Let him alone, Doggie. Here, Fitz, I'll wipe the snow off. Ow!" she said. "If you do that again, Doggie, I'll jump on your feet."

Big Sister's face was flaming above an incredible magenta gown. A loose tuft of hair sticking out of her top-knot gave her the effect of a Chinese strong man. She tramped up to Clara and shook her hand. She sat down massively and cocked up a large slipper.

"Where did you get this chair?" she said·

"It was a wedding present. I think it came from Wanamaker's in Philadelphia."

"Well," Big Sister said, "it's all right. I like a well-made chair."

Good Doggie, with a pleased grin, was prowling toward Mun. "You would," he said.

Mun edged off, fumbling uneasily at his thin mustache.

"Keep away from me, Doggie. I don't feel well. I have a cold."

Good Doggie brooded genially over Mun and pretended to spit

on his hands. "Listen, Doggie," Mun said, hurriedly, "we are going to have Château Lafitte for supper. What do you think of that?"

"That's fine," Doggie said. "Are we going to have much of it? What is it?"

"It's a sort of corn whiskey," Fitz-Greene volunteered. "They make it in the South."

"There goes the bell, Fitz," Clara said.

"It's Jeanne Balso." Mun started for the door. "I can hear her laugh." He was checked by Doggie's grip on his coat-tails. Mun's light-blue eyes struck fire. "Let go, damn it. You'll tear my coat." He plunged on for the door.

"Mun, darling!" Jeanne Balso's voice was rich and teasing. "Where have you been, my beautiful boy? Hello, Fitz. Johnny, help me with these things."

Big Sister stared at Clara and grunted.

"Doggie," Clara said, "you mustn't tease Mun so. Really you mustn't."

Good Doggie, looking like a small boy in outgrown clothes, sat down beside her and dropped a big hand on her arm. "All right, I won't," he said, "the damn fool."

"Look here," Big Sister said, judicially. "You can't call Clara's brother's brother-in-law a damn fool to her face. That's no way to act."

"Oh, yes, he can," Clara said, "if he wants to."

"Everybody is a damn fool," observed Good Doggie.

"Well, I like that," said Big Sister.

"Does that mean me too?" Clara asked.

"Everybody else, though."

"Well, I like that," Big Sister said.

In a burst of crimson velvet, Jeanne Balso came in. It was as though she were flying down hill on skis. Her sturdy but rich figure leaned forward, her black hair was dashed back from her brilliant face. The three men trailed behind.

"Hello, hello," she said, "everybody."

She nodded to Clara, as one invited guest to another. Good Doggie stood up. "Have a chair."

"No, I'll stand in front of the fire." She took a pose, her fine firm legs apart, her bare arms locked behind her. "That feels good," she said.

"How do you do, Mrs. Rankin?" Mr. Thompson bowed. A

small sandy man, he seemed to be made of one piece from the
waist up and another from the waist down. He straightened up
and adjusted his eye-glasses. Then he became one piece from head
to foot. He was the prettiest figure skater in town, but this was
his social manner. He bowed to Big Sister. His neck had no
more modelling than a piece of wood. No wonder his collar
failed to fit it.

"Good evening, Miss Trimble," he said. Good heavens, they
thought, that's Big Sister's name.

"Well," said Big Sister, "been skating lately?"

"Yes," said Mr. Thompson. "I was hoping to see you."

"Like fun you were," said Big Sister.

"Why, Miss Trimble." Mr. Thompson removed his eye-glasses,
blew on them, and joined the men, who flanked Miss Balso at
the fire.

"Look," Clara said, "it looks like a scene in an operetta." She
nodded at Miss Balso. "You ought to sing something, and the
men ought to kneel down and hold out their arms."

Still straddling in front of the fireplace, Jeanne Balso slightly
opened her smiling mouth.

"When love is kind,"

Her voice was low and deep and dead true,

"Faithful and free,
Love's sure to find
Welcome from me."

Mun bent over her solicitously, and pretended to strum a
guitar.

"But when I see
Love given to rove,"

his eyes fixed on the ceiling, Fitz-Greene dropped in with a light,
impersonal tenor,

"To two or three,
Then good-bye, love."

Good Doggie came over to Clara, and sat down. Mr. Thompson
looked respectfully at Miss Balso, and continued to beat time
with his head.

"The damn fools!" Good Doggie said.

Miss Balso smiled at him provokingly. "Now I must turn round and warm the other side."

"Wait." Mun took her by the arm. "You'd better let me see whether this side's done." He winked at Mr. Thompson, who smiled uneasily and looked carefully away. Poor Mun, Clara thought, why did he always have to be a little out of key? There was a pounding on the front door and muffled cries.

"Good Lord!" said Fitz. "That's George. I suppose we didn't hear him ring."

Ellen's plain white silk was most becoming, Clara thought with satisfaction. She, herself, had persuaded her to get it. Its straight lines made her seem taller, its whiteness left the field clear for her bright brown eyes and blended in its girlish effect with her small pointed nose. She came up to Clara's chair.

"Are we late?" she said. "I am afraid it is my fault."

"Ellen, you're wonderful," Clara said. "But why don't you save that for people who don't know George?"

She looked up. Fitz-Greene was leading Anna Lisle into the room, tall in her close-fitting pink chiffon, fragile and exquisitely slender, with keen, sad eyes, under a weight of mouse-colored hair. They were a striking pair, Clara thought with a pang. How was it Fitz-Green always seemed to form a couple of himself and any woman he happened to be with? Always there seemed at the moment to be a subtle bond between them, between him and every woman, except herself.

"Anna, hello," she said. "It's nice to see you."

"Hello, Clara." Anna's voice was low and toneless. "Hello," she said, with a half glance around. George was coming through the door. She turned on him a look of sombre, child-like admiration. She was a simpleton for all her shrewdness, or was it that since the young man from Richmond, she no longer cared what people thought? George would look silly if she kept it up, though. He looked so now, broad-faced and beaming under Anna's eye. Ellen could not be blamed if she were angry; not on account of jealousy, there was no cause for that, but it was exasperating to have one's husband made to look so silly. Fitz-Greene was extraordinary. The girls were all foolish about him, but never made him seem absurd.

"I bet I can tell you just what George did to make you late for dinner."

"You can't," Ellen said.

"He got home late," Clara said, "because he stopped at Father's stable to talk to Levi about the horses, and when he got home, you told him to hurry. Hello, George. We're talking about you." George crossed to the corner of the room, and sat down beside Anna Lisle. "Then," Clara said, "he played with Tommy. Then when you wanted him to come up and see the baby, he said he didn't have time, because he had to dress for dinner. Then he sat down in the library and read the evening paper till dinner-time."

Ellen glanced at George and Anna in the corner. "Some of it is true," she said, "but you wouldn't guess what really happened. When I was nearly dressed I went down to see why he didn't come or even answer. What do you suppose he was doing? He had a whole set of harness on four chairs. You couldn't get in the library, and he was sitting there with that book on coaching in his lap, practising with the reins. That was at five minutes of seven. He would have been there yet. Do you think Anna Lisle is pretty?"

"Yes, I do. Did you arrange to call for her to-night?"

"Yes. She pretends she doesn't like to go out alone."

"Did George know you were calling for her?"

"Oh, yes. George is the one she asked."

"Well, then, I wouldn't worry," Clara said. "It doesn't look as though he was giving much thought to her, does it? He'd rather practise with the reins."

"With any other man," Ellen said, "you might think that, but George was always late when he was courting me."

The little dining room could barely hold them. They were crowded close together. With the third bottle of Château Lafitte the din had become extraordinary. At the other end of the table, Fitz-Greene, his fine head slightly inclined, was making Ellen happy. Close in front of Clara, George and Doggie leaned their heads together across the board.

"You can't have a football team without a line," George said. "We've never had a line since I left college."

"That's right," Doggie said. "What about a little more of that wine?" He turned to Anna Lisle. "Anna, do you like this wine?"

"Oh, yes," she said, looking at George.

Mr. Thompson, beyond Anna, bent forward stiffly. "What I call an excellent wine," he said in a loud voice, and sat back in his chair with an air of finality.

"What there is of it," Doggie observed. He turned to Clara. "Doesn't seem to be any more wine."

Big Sister's voice boomed down the table. "Doggie, hush up!" Doggie hitched forward in his chair. His knees caused the tableware to rattle, the candles to sway wildly. "Hello, Sis." He beamed at her with a mouth slightly open. "I can't hear what you say."

"What's this?" Fitz-Greene jumped up. "No wine?" he smiled down at Ellen. "Ellen, that's your fault. I never noticed."

He hurried into the hall, and down the steps beneath the narrow stairs.

"No, Fitz," Ellen called. "Every one's had plenty. Fitz, every one——"

"Suppress her," George called. "Mr. Thompson, suppress my wife."

Mun sprang up. "My good woman, what does this mean?"

"Sit down," Big Sister thundered.

Jeanne Balso, beyond George, passed her napkin about Mun's waist. She held him firmly, laughing.

Fitz-Greene came through the door, bearing two more of the sacred bottles, tenderly.

They sipped it tenderly until at last, amid the peppermints and salted nuts, they sat around the table, singing.

> "Sing a song of cities,
> Roll that cotton bale,
> Nigger ain't half so happy
> As when he's out of jail."

The noise was terrific. The gentlemen's cigar smoke curled and wavered.

> "Savannah for its rice and corn,
> But for niggers New Orleans."

George rapped his coffee-spoon against a glass. "Hold on. Let's sing that over and get it right. Everybody hold the chord on 'corn.' Then Fitz comes down two notes and I come up one with the bass. Anna, could you keep Doggie on the key?"

"I'll try to," Anna said.

"Sing right in his ear. Doggie, listen to Anna."

"What about Sister?" Doggie said. "She's worse than I am."

"Fitz," George called out, "sing right in Sister's ear."

"But I'm singing tenor," Fitz said.

Big Sister knitted her brows and frowned at him. "That's what puts me off," she said.

"Well, Mun," George said, "you're singing air, aren't you?"

"How can you ask?" Jeanne Balso said. "He's deafening."

"George wouldn't know," Ellen said. "He never hears any one when he's singing bass. He goes into a stupor."

"Congratulations, George," Fitz-Greene raised his glass. "Some people have all the luck."

"All right now," George said. "Mun, you sing in Big Sister's ear."

"No, you don't," Big Sister said, "you screeching idiot."

Good Doggie hitched his chair forward, and shook the table. "Throw her out," he said. Jeanne Balso smiled at him and let her big deep voice come welling up.

"Sing a song of cities"

Mr. Thompson drew in his neck like a puff adder. Mun raised a threatening fist above Big Sister's head. His thin, sharp voice cut through the others. Anna leaned dutifully forward and sang in Doggie's ear.

"Go along," he said. "I can do it." He turned and sang at her loudly. She looked appealingly at George. But George's chin was in his collar, his eyes were lost above her head.

With the fifth bottle they called for solos. George stood up by request, and with heavy strainings of the shirt front, gave them "Scos wha hae." Having pitched it a trifle low, the deeper notes came out as little more than abdominal gargles, but he made up lost ground in the middle register and sat down to great applause.

"Now, Anna must sing something." Ellen's voice was hearty, she turned her sharp childish face to Anna. "Anna, can't we have that solo you gave at the Monday evening musicale?"

Clara looked at Ellen with respect. It was the Mad Song from "Lucia di Lammermoor." What could be more inappropriate?

"I have no accompanist," Anna said.

"Never mind," they cried.

"Come on, Anna," George said, "let's hear it."

Anna stood up.

Her voice was finished, but small and artificial. They could not understand the words. But she was an actress. The effect of madness suffused her frail, nervous figure and her violet eyes so close to theirs. It cast a chill on them. They watched her uneasily and looked away. She sat down amid forced murmurs and clapping led by Ellen, amid the distaste of the herd for the abnormal, tinged with the faint contempt of the amateur for the perfection of technique. Jeanne Balso sang "Blow the man down" with a great swing and everybody on the chorus many times repeated. And, of course, Fitz-Greene was called on. He leaned his elbows on the table, and looked down at his plate. His voice was only moderate, but they all liked him.

> "The lark now leaves his watery nest
>   And climbing shakes his dewy wings,
> He takes this window for the east,
>   And to implore your light he sings,
> Awake, awake! the morn will never rise
> Till she can dress her beauty at your eyes."

He looked down at his plate and raised one hand as though to shield his eyes from the light. Clara could see only his mouth moving beneath his curving hand. Perhaps he was smiling. She could hardly tell. If so, it was the smile of a singer, blind and lost. At the end, he did not raise his eyes. He kept them on his plate and lifted up his glass of wine.

The gathering was simmering down. The time had come for "Good Night, Ladies," and for wrestling with coats and arctics in the narrow hall.

"Don't stand here, Clara," they called. "It's cold. Good night. We had a lovely time."

In the green and gold drawing-room, she stood alone in front of the dying embers.

"Good night, Fitz. Good night, old man." The door closed. He came into the room. He was smiling; his face was dark, his eyes were dark from wine and heat and singing.

"It was a nice evening, wasn't it?" she said. "I think they all had a good time. Mun was in elegant form. He didn't take too much and he was so nice about being next to Big Sister. But then he had Jeanne Balso on the other side."

He stood before her, looked at her intently, as if what she said was of the utmost significance. "Awake," he said, "awake! The morn will never rise, till she can dress her beauty at your eyes." He took her hand and gazed on it. She gripped the mantel with her other hand. "Fitz," she said in a low voice, "do you love me," she said, "at all?" He shuddered lightly. "Oh, you're cold," she said. "Come by the fire. I'll get a stick of wood." He raised her hand to his face. She was touching his face again, so smooth, so dark, so warm and quick. She left the mantel, she flowed toward him, toward his arms and breast, and fibre. Here were power and weakness, thunder of blood and warm swift flowing. Here was her lover and her child. She would make him happy. His lips were in the first curve of her shoulder, he held her up and clung to her. She bent her cheek against his hair. "We must love each other," she said, in a strangled voice, "always. Couldn't we?"

He trembled violently, and pushed at her. She felt the mantel-piece against her shoulder. He thrust his hands in his pockets and started tramping. She leaned against the mantel, looking at the floor. His feet passed now and then. So it was over then. It had come to nothing. Let this time, then, be final. If she were sure of that, she could almost be glad. No more of this. She could rest then, numb and empty for ever. His feet still crossed the floor in front of her unseeing eyes. A dreadful peace came on her. The peace of death. She was about to die. And would even that change her?

"Fitz," her voice sounded far away but loud and clear. "I will never change toward you."

The feet stopped. "And I will never change toward you."

"We must go on like this then?" She seemed to ask the question of herself.

His voice was high and harsh. "Yes, if we can."

His footsteps left the room, tramped up the stair, up to the second floor, then on and up. There was the closing of the distant door.

CHAPTER XXI

IT was late when she woke. She lay, stunned and dazed in her warm bed. Was it the unaccustomed wine or was it the heavy blow which left her numb? Thin, weak sunlight lay across the carpet. Beyond black branches, ice floes in the river were clotting together in the cold. On the islands, and on the farther shore, bare trees raised an iron mist above black earth and patches of frozen snow.

Just outside the window an English sparrow, withdrawn into a desolate bundle, stared fixedly into the room. His gray claws on the frozen twig must be frozen to the marrow of their tiny bones. No wonder he looked with longing at the shelter of her room. How could he know that she would be the happy one, if it could be arranged to change her place with him? He had better fly away and be content. If he stayed there, something might happen to him. His wishes might be granted; then he could never be merely a cold and hungry sparrow again. When she went downstairs, she would get him some bread and see if Christobel had any suet. She would do him a good turn out of the bounty of her despair. There was the bounty of happiness, that she knew; the summer of her engagement, she had been fantastic and probably absurd in the eagerness with which she had squandered inappropriate benevolence. But that had been a mere sportive ornamentation of her happiness, a form for her exhilaration. Was misery about to raise good deeds from a luxury to an anodyne, indispensable to her tormented state? Either that, or else, perhaps, she might turn savage like a lioness robbed of her cub, to injure all things living in a brutal world. For was not happiness her lawful child born of love and nurtured by her care? Who had a right to steal this gift away? She had done no wrong.

And who had stolen it away? Not Fitz-Greene. That answer was too easy, and it carried no conviction. Surely it should. She loved him, and it seemed he did not love her. Therefore, he was

181

to blame. The demonstration was perfect, and left her perfectly unmoved.

Who, then, was to blame? Was it herself? Even by raking up each least item of her conduct, that could not be demonstrated, and even if it could, that demonstration also would leave her unconvinced.

No, she felt that not only was she held powerless in a trap but that he was, too. She did not believe, she would never believe, that he wished to leave her. In some curious way he longed to love her, or even did love her still. The two of them were caught in a labyrinth, certainly not of their own design, whose nature and extent, she, at least, could not understand. What then became of her notions of an ordered universe, a universe where love, sincerity, good sense, forbearance, all the appropriate virtues, brought their own reward; where marriage, based on character, with love, of course, to weld the two divergent personalities, was justly predestined to succeed? But what, then, were these other forces, which wrecked her simple and admirable scheme of things, and how could these forces be met? She was intelligent, she thought, more so than most girls. But now, in her dilemma, where she should call up, and where she had tried desperately to call up her resources, she could think of nothing better than to feed a sparrow crumbs.

Here in the bathroom it was dark. She lit the gas light beside the washstand and threw the match in the water-closet. Too late, she remembered that he had told her she must break them in two. Otherwise, they would stop up the pipes, he said. She had always disposed of matches so, without accident, but undoubtedly he was right. He was very clever about practical affairs. She fished the match out, a horrid task, although the water was quite clear. Then she washed her hands thoroughly, and used the scrubbing brush. There was plenty of hot water and there would be all morning. Christobel would need it in cleaning up after last night's party.

The windows were open in the dining room, but a coal fire was burning and the air was not unbearable. The room was neat and fresh again with everything in order. At the sound of the window sliding down, Christobel came to the pantry door. Her sleeves were rolled up to her shoulders.

"Hello," she said. "You look like you'd had a good sleep."

"My, that was a nice party, Christobel," Clara said.

"It was all right," Christobel said. "You know, they had me kind of worried about that soufflé."

"It was the men," Clara said.

"Sure, it was the men. They get drinking that wine and talking. I thought they'd never get through."

"Men are like that," Clara said. "They never think."

"Sure they never think. But what was I to do? She was ready to go flat on me."

"You shouldn't have waited."

"In the end, I didn't wait. One or two of them give me a kind of a look when I taken their plates away from them, half full."

"Oh, I don't think they noticed."

"Not notice them sweetbreads? Sure they noticed. But it was no time for foolishness. I suppose you want some breakfast."

"Well, anyhow," Clara said, "they had a wonderful time. I just want some coffee."

"You bet they had a time. Couldn't I hear them singing all night long? The whole neighborhood's talking about it this morning. The Middlecooper's girl asked me this morning whether we was running a joint here. I bet it's all over town by now. You better have some oatmeal too." Christobel left both pantry doors open when she went back to the kitchen. Her voice was loud. "The boss sure was having a time last night."

"Who?"

"Mr. Rankin. He's the greatest man I ever saw to make folks enjoy themselves." Amid the clink of dishes on the stove, her voice ran on. "Everybody takes to him, don't they, though?" A stove lid rattled. "Yes, sir, last night, he was on a regular high horse."

"Did he get some breakfast?" Clara said.

"I never saw him. I just seen that his hat and coat was gone." Christobel came in with an orange and a bowl of oatmeal. "I guess he'll get something at the station. Well, there's one thing about those station places. They have good coffee. I'll get the sugar. Yes, sir, wherever there's railroad men, there's good coffee. This friend of mine on the B. and O. says you can't run a railroad without coffee any more than without coal. Here's the sugar. I'll get the cream. All the same, I'd been ready for him, if I'd known he was leaving early."

"I suppose he thought you would be tired."

"Say, what's he take me for?" She was out on the porch at the ice-box now, and shouting loudly. "He worries too much about other folk's feelings. That's the trouble with him." Her footsteps came back in the kitchen.

"Christobel," Clara said, "have you got any suet?"

"Suet? No."

"There's a sparrow outside my window that looks half frozen and starved."

"No suet. Here's some stale bread if you want it, though."

After breakfast, she helped Christobel clean the pantry and put the mound of last night's dishes in the pantry cupboards and in the fluted racks above the sideboard in the dining room. The smoke of battle still hung about Christobel. She accepted Clara as a shipmate who had weathered with her a victorious engagement. Clara learned a great deal of unsuspected news about her neighbors' doings and the customs and habits of brakemen on the B. and O.

"Well, that's everything," she said, hanging up the dish pan. "I guess you'll be alone for lunch."

"Yes," Clara said, "I guess so."

Upstairs, in the library, she sat down at her desk. What would she do with the day, and with other days to follow? She had never been much of a person to visit around at the houses of the others. Her house had always been the capitol. If she suddenly came calling, it would cause surprise. Perhaps some of them would drop in. But was that to be desired? So far, she had carried things along without a flaw, but now, if she met them, her secret might be guessed. A warmth sprang up in her. She knew what she would like to do. She would like to go for a drive with her father. The weather was ridiculous. Still, he drove in all weathers, when he had the notion. But might he not read her secret in her face? More likely than any one else; beneath his firm stolidity the bear was astute. She looked at her desk. Meanwhile, there were some letters and the household bills.

The rows of figures occupied her morning. She checked each bill and added it. She spread the big check-book with its marbled cardboard cover on the desk, and wrote out checks for all the bills and one for Christobel. She had her pass book and the monthly balance from the bank. It showed a discrepancy with her check-book of one dollar and ten cents. She attacked the problem. She verified all the entries on the stubs, pausing only to wonder crossly why check-books were bound so that the stub pages flew back as if on springs, and had to be held down by fists or paper-weights. She verified her addition and found an error of ten cents. There was still a dollar to account for. She allowed herself a fantastic hope that the bank had made an error. She checked the addition in her pass book and then each entry, item by item, against the cancelled checks. All was correct. With resignation, she turned to her check-book again. In the end, she found a place where in carrying a balance forward to the head of the next page, she had simply written it incorrectly. A mere mistake in posting and no reflection on her arithmetic. Still, the bank was always right; a disappointment. At any rate, the small adventure had helped to get through the morning, and there was still the account book to make up. It was a formidable affair, a tall heavy ledger, whose columns, lined with pale blue, were neatly labelled according to a system of Fitz-Green's devising: a column for meat, for groceries, for household supplies, a column for repairs, for fuel and water. There was a column labelled wages, a stately blank, except for the single monthly entry under the head of Christobel Kammernich. When she had finished, she got out a smaller check-book and went over her personal accounts, but with less care. The way the money was piling up was quite appalling. Each month a check came in, accompanied by a formal statement bound in heavy, blue paper, the whole enclosed in a letter from Mr. Riser, written as though he had never heard of her before. The statements were piled in a pigeonhole of the desk. She rarely looked at them. They gave her a headache, with their Great Northern Equipment 6's, Nos. 29702-29712, their Shemingo County Gold Debenture $3\frac{1}{2}$'s, and Baltimore Johnston Turnpike Company first 4's, due 1902. As if any one cared what was going to happen in 1902. She liked making up her check-book and her accounts. There was a mastery and perfection in dealing with the figures and in getting the correct result. Already, this morning, she felt better for her work and for the neat "Balance, correct with bank," that crowned it. But these higher finances simply puzzled her. She had asked her father once what was the difference between a Gold Debenture 4 and a First 4.

"Never you mind about that," he had said. "You keep your check-book posted and balanced, and use your good sense in what you buy, and we'll tend to the income."

Her father had his firm ideas. He did not mind her taking a drink of his whiskey sour, but to learn about gold debentures would be to carry the hoyden too far. As for Fitz-Greene, he would have told her, no doubt, but it would have been at the cost of some respect. Not that he felt as did her father that a knowledge of debentures would constitute a diminution of her woman's virtue, but simply that, while good enough himself in business, he looked upon the whole apparatus of commerce as immensely tedious. While it was necessary for a man to suffer this tedium as a sort of penance which justified his otherwise amusing existence, he would not respect or understand a person who, without necessity, insisted on venturing upon these arid wastes. And so from mysterious and complex sources, and ushered by Mr. Riser's comical formality, the money came in every month, five or six hundred dollars; more than she could spend. Already, her balance inspired uneasiness and awe; over two thousand dollars. To have a sum like this lying loose in the bank, or however it did lie in the bank, was, in some fashion, to violate the proprieties and the moral code. Certainly it was to invite disaster. It was not likely that a woman so gorged with undeserved affluence could long escape the watchful eye of fate. She supposed she should give it away or buy jewellery. Thus, she would cease to be a target. It might be a good idea to consult her father. She would go up there after lunch.

Lunch itself was a heavy chore. With the closing of her check-books, the fervor of her mathematics died. In the dining room, the sun was thin and pale. She was alone, abandoned to the bitter sky. The sardines on toast, the baked sweet potatoes were tasteless and dry. She knew that the pumpkin pie, left over from two nights before, would be dry too.

"What's the matter?" Christobel said. "No appetite?"

"Oh, yes," she said, and took a drink of water.

"Maybe that wine didn't set so good," Christobel said. "I know when I drink beer——"

"I'm all right," Clara said. "You know I haven't been feeling so well. You know Doctor Hartman gave me that tonic."

"Don't I, though," Christobel said. "I smelled of it the other day. There's one thing about that tonic. If a person can swallow it, they can swallow anything. Do you want some? It says a wineglass full after meals on the bottle."

"Yes, I know it does," Clara said. "No, I don't think I do."

She went upstairs to look at her hair before going out. The crumbs on the window sill were gone. As far as the day went, that was a point gained. She got her beaver coat out of the closet. It would do her good to wear it. Her father and mother had given it to her for Christmas. No one knew how much it cost. From top to bottom, it was solid, deep, thick golden beaver, the most beautiful and the nicest coat she ever knew. But then she could hardly wear this old house dress. She must put on the cherry-colored broadcloth. But then she must hurry. Her father would have left and gone downtown to the office. Her gray-blue house dress slipped to the floor, the cherry-colored broadcloth slipped over her head. Her hands squeezed through the narrow sleeves. Could she do up the side and the shoulder by herself?

"Christobel!" she called.

She gave her hair a pat and put on her beaver hat. Down in the hall, Christobel met her and did the hooks and eyes. At the doorway, with a freckled hand she smoothed the beaver. She stood on the marble doorstep, watching Clara up the street.

"Go in!" Clara called. "You'll freeze."

Christobel wrapped her hands in her apron. She kept on looking.

It was hard to be nice to Samuel in the hallway. Why did he have to be always so cheerful? Was he never unhappy himself? Could he not guess that sometimes people felt less than radiant? He must be an imbecile.

"Thank you, Samuel, I'll keep my coat on." She would not have him ecstatically wrestling with her beaver.

"Your mother's in the library, Miss Clara."

"Oh! Well, where is Father?"

"I think he's gone out. I'll make sure."

"Oh," she said. Why need he have gone already just to-day? He hardly ever did. Always he smoked his cigar first in his private office. Why should he have left early this one day? In the library, her mother looked up from the alcove desk beneath the Martha Washington. "Clara, dear." She raised a cheek round and firm under its microscopic wrinkles. "Take off your coat," she said. "If you leave your coat on in the house, then you catch cold when you go out afterward."

"Where's Father?" Clara said.

"He left early with George. They're going to look at some property along the railroad."

"Oh, I thought perhaps he'd like to take a drive." She took the coat off and laid it on a chair. She stared hard out the bay window at the frozen river.

"A drive? Why, my dear child, it's bitter."

She heard the scratching of her mother's pen. It turned her furious. "Father's driving, isn't he?"

"But, my dear, your father is a man. He has his business. And besides, they took Levi and the station wagon. There would be no one to go with you."

Now she was obstinate. She would batter down the world, and have her drive, a freezing, joyless drive, but she would have it. "I'll take Sam," she said.

"My dear, that wouldn't do at all. Young Sam's just an ignorant colored boy."

"Norah's my horse," Clara said.

"But she's not been out for weeks, and it's too slippery. I heard your father tell Levi to have the pair rough shod this morning."

"I'll look at Norah's shoes myself," Clara said.

Her mother laid down her pen. "Clara, what's got into you? No one would want to drive on a day like this. In an open carriage, it would be absurd."

She kept staring out at the bitter weather. "Well, it's what I want to do," she said.

"You're a married woman, now," her mother's voice was cold, "and I suppose if your husband wishes it, you have a right to take the horse out. But I am your mother, and I cannot allow such a thing unless Fitz-Greene insists. Does he know what you want to do?"

"He's gone to Philadelphia," Clara muttered.

"Well, then," her mother's voice was firm and satisfied, "I

couldn't dream of allowing any such thing. Let's talk of something else."

She felt her mouth turn to a bitter slit. Let's talk of something else. She stared at the river. A delicate way to change the subject.

"I have been talking to some of the ladies," her mother said, "about the Crittenden Home. They felt that we should have some one from among the younger people on the Board. Naturally, it should be a married woman, some one who knows the— who knows the meaning of life. Without any solicitation on my part," Mrs. Rand was congratulatory and triumphant, "the ladies have suggested your name."

Clara stood up and threw on her coat. "You'll have to ask Fitz-Greene," she said. "Whatever I know about the meaning of life, I learned from him."

Out in the cold air of the street, her passion cooled. That was a stupid thing to have said. Her mother would guess. The visit was disastrous. If she could have found her father! She had added and subtracted her way through the morning and if she could have found him, she would have made a day of it. Now, there was nothing but the empty house.

She was hailed from a side street. Big Sister in a rusty, man-like overcoat was tramping beside Jeanne Balso in bright orange. What terrific colors that girl wore, and how well they became her.

"Hi," they said. "Well, how do you feel?"

"I feel all right." Her grimace must be ghastly. They laughed together. Incredible, they did not notice it.

"That was an elegant time we had last night," Jeanne Balso said.

"It was all right," Big Sister said. She gave a hitch to a paper bundle. "I'm not much for singing myself, but it was all right. My, Doggie was terrible this morning."

"He was terrible last night," Jeanne said.

"He had the most awful headache," Big Sister said, "and he kept trying to tell me it was something he had eaten. 'Yes,' I said, 'I suppose it was the sweetbreads. They give them to invalids, because they're so indigestible.' That's what I said. 'And who was the one who kept asking for more wine? I was ashamed of you,' I said. 'It serves you right.'"

Jeanne Balso laughed. "Hoist by his own petard. Poor Doggie."

"Hoist by what?" Big Sister said. "Poor Doggie nothing. It serves him right. How is Fitz this morning?"

"I didn't see him," Clara said. "He left early to go to Philadelphia."

"He would be all right," Jeanne Balso's nod was admiring. "Fitz can hold his wine."

"Well, Doggie can hold whiskey," said Big Sister, stoutly. "I will say that for him. He just never fools with wine. You set Doggie to drink whiskey," she said.

"Well," Jeanne said, "Fitz can drink whiskey, too, can't he, Clara?"

"I don't know," Clara said. "He never drinks much."

"You know, Clara," Jeanne said, "I thought Mun did pretty well. He generally can't hold anything. Poor Mun!"

"Pretty well!" Big Sister said. "If you could have heard him screeching in my ear. I was almost sick myself this morning."

"I wish some of Big Sister's working girls could have seen her last night," Jeanne Balso said.

Big Sister was unabashed. "You bet they'd have been all for it," she said. "They do the same, only it's beer."

"Come on with us," they said. "Where are you going?"

"I'm going home," Clara said.

"Oh, come on."

"No," she said. "Honestly, I've got lots to do."

"Well," they said, reluctantly, "it was a great party. Good-bye."

"Let's have another," Big Sister called back, "without the singing."

"Look at the river," Jeanne called. "We'll have skating soon."

With an effort, Clara raised her hand and waved to them.

CHAPTER XXII

SHE hesitated now to ask her father to go driving with her. Snow fell again, sleigh bells ran up and down the street and the light bump of runners over ruts. Then it turned warm and melting, languor and restlessness were in the air. It would have been fun to go sloshing up the river road under the dripping trees and the soft unnatural sun. But beyond a doubt her mother had told him how she had flung out at her, and above all, how she had demanded Norah and the spider on the bitterest of days. Warned as he would be that something might be amiss, he would surely begin to feel and guess her trouble, if she were alone with him.

It was necessary to dine there quite often now that Fitz-Greene was gone, but there was the protection of the servants and of the house's accumulated and established formality. When no guests were present, the three of them sat in the library till it was time for Levi to escort her home.

But this was not the only front on which she must defend herself. She had supposed when Fitz-Greene's letters first began to come, putting off from day to day his return, that her rôle would now be easier; the hardest part had been to carry it off in front of him. The relief should have been enormous. But as the days went on and his letters, brief but kind, kept coming, she felt that she was faced by new exactions. He was well, the business was taking longer than he thought, but everything was going well, the hunting, thank God, had been stopped by frost, his brothers sent their regards, his mother sent her love. He would have her come to Philadelphia but it was hardly worth while. He would be home now any day. Would she like to move up to her father's or have Doggie and Big Sister come to stay with her? Sister could have a bed in the dressing-room and Doggie could sleep upstairs in his room. Would she need any money for her household accounts? She could make a transfer from her own funds, whose magnitude he suspected she concealed, and when he got home he would make her a refund.

She did not want to go back to her father's but she did consider asking Sister and Doggie to keep her company. An audience a little more exacting than Christobel might help her to sustain her rôle.

It was fortunate, she thought, looking back on it, that she had not given way to this first impulse. For she was becoming conscious that her rôle had, suddenly, somehow, ceased to convince. What had happened? Surely the bearing which she presented to them all was no less poised except for that single little outbreak with her mother, and naturally that would not be known in town. But just, as she remembered dimly from a visiting lecturer at the Misses Wherry's, a jar of chemical might stand for so long a time, then swiftly change, so some unknown element in the group she knew had suddenly crystallized suspicion. Was it merely that their curiosity and instinctive morbid nosiness had led them to form and circulate a guess which happened to be right? An unusual triumph of their itch for scandal and disaster, an itch not ill-meant, curiously enough, merely mechanical and unappeasable. Or had Fitz-Greene's mere absence, prolonged from day to day, been sufficient to start their investigations in motion, and led to a more critical examination, which had detected flaws in her performance? Or did they deserve no credit, after all? Had her fancies of Fitz with another been prophecies and, now that he had been this time so long in Philadelphia where that other doubtless was and where also, so she heard, little that one did escaped detection, had the history of this other life been learned and spread abroad?

If this were so, then all her defenses had been vain, the wearing, ceaseless watch upon herself had gained her nothing. She was like an army, which, inflexibly defending a position against assault, awakes, weary but determined in a bleak dawn, to find that the position has been taken from the rear.

And like that army, she felt in the débâcle a certain satisfaction, a cowed and contemptible but unmistakable relief. All had been lost save honor, she was able to say smugly, and honor, all being lost, could ask no more of her. The struggle was over, she was entitled in the eyes of all to lay down her arms.

In the eyes of all, that is, except herself; for after the first flush of bitter, but nourishing relief, she asked herself at once, has the defense been of no avail? How would I now stand with myself if I had not attempted it? She saw that while a failure in point of its result, in essence it had stood a defense of herself as much as of the position. As such it had protected her from her own weakness and despair and also from the degradation of inquisitive approaches. Even now, no one by a word or look had dared to hint of guesses or of knowledge. Whatever she had gathered, she had gathered by instinct. If she had assigned herself a rôle, she had compelled them to accept rôles for themselves. The whole became a species of farce, yet a farce, which, like all farces worthy to be played, concealed an inner truth and was being enacted in accordance with certain universal laws.

And so instead of finding herself relieved of further dissimulation, she knew that from now on, whatever happened, she must, as strongly as ever, maintain her pitiful hypothesis. Only so could she save whatever of herself was left for saving. And that there was something to be saved, she knew. Her love for him was desperate and unchanging. The blow was mortal. But no more than mortal. Love of the quality she bore him sprang from some quality within her which also could not be destroyed.

She was not then like an army which has been flanked out of its position. An army could be forced to surrender, or could be destroyed, and once that were done, the episode was unquestionably concluded. But she could not be captured or destroyed. The loss of the position did not, therefore, relieve her from maintaining, so to speak, her own formation.

At the end of the third week, Christobel met her in the front hall with a telegram. Night was falling, the hall was dark. She carried the flimsy envelope up to the library. What shock was to come? In the dark library, she fumbled for a match. The gas light sprang up. She tore the envelope. "Home to-night. Well. Love. F.-G." She sank into a chair beside the fire, smiling tremulously. Here was the reward of honor. Yet how much was there of reward? No more than permission to go on, hopeless and futile as in the past. But that was something. The thread of life remained unbroken. While they both lived, while they were together, she did not give up. Give up? Not then, or maybe even, afterward.

And now, she had not long to wait. She stood up. She would change to a pretty dress, and sit beside the window in her bedroom.

The cab horse came clumping through the snow as always. What varying loads must he haul about in his daily toil, oblivious, indifferent, focussed dimly only on his own dejection, indifferent to lovers, mourners, rascals, hypocrites, to virtue, merriment, greed, and cruelty, and to all other varied and unpredictable cargoes that rested behind him on the musty cushions. But of all cargoes, none could differ more than Fitz-Greene as he first had brought him home, eager and warm and radiant, and Fitz-Greene, as he brought him now.

The cab door opened, the bundled driver turned stiffly. Fitz-Greene's tall, narrow figure showed in the light of the downstairs windows. She stood up; then she sat down. At all costs, one must not press in upon him.

His step was on the stair. She leaned forward, listening. Let her prepare herself. He might go straight on to his upstairs room. No, he was coming down the hall. He was at the door. She looked up, smiling.

His face was terrible; old, pale, and haunted. "Clara." His voice was low and strained. "Clara." He was across the room and down in front of her, his face was in her hands.

Her heart stood still with fear and joy, "Fitz, dear," she said, "what is it?" She bent toward his bright head. At her touch, he stood up quickly. He smiled through his pallor. He touched her shoulder and withdrew his hand.

"I'm glad to be back," he said, and looked away. His voice was sad. He forced himself to look at her. "How have you been?"

"Oh, I've been fine," she said. She must not seem to study him. "You got my letters?"

"Oh, yes," he said. "I'm afraid mine were very poor. I was busy every minute. Still, they always are. It was lucky we were never separated when I was courting you." He thrust his hands in his pockets and took on some assurance. "It must be a shock to get a letter like mine from a brilliant conversationalist. I suppose it's time for supper?"

"Oh, well," she said, "we can have it when you like. We always do, you know."

"Yes," he said, "you always do. I won't change," he said. "I'll just put on another shirt and my old coat. You can call me when you're ready."

"Yes," she said. "I will."

She watched him leave the room. His jauntiness was labored. Even so, was there any other figure in the world so gallant and engaging? Poor child, poor child! Lost and forlorn in a mystery. What must she do for him? What should she say to him? nothing, perhaps, as little as possible; be patient now, stand firm and quiet. For he was coming back to her. Be quiet, hold firm.

She went out through the bathroom, where she lit the gas, and filled the basin with hot water.

He was slow to answer when she called from the dining room. She had gone there to make sure that everything was as it should be. She heard him coming down from his room. His light footsteps on the carpet dropped like small plummets down the stairway. He was stopping on the second floor.

"I'm here," she called out, "in the dining room."

The footfalls left the stair and moved along the hallway toward her bedroom at the front. Fantastic notions swept her. He was bringing down his dressing-gown; he was bringing a present to put beneath her pillow. The footsteps came back down the hall and down the stairs. His face now had a trace of color and he was smiling, but his movements, while not heavy, seemed slow and muffled.

He stood at his place, looking down at the tall narrow cup beside his plate. "Hot chocolate," he said. "That will be nice."

"I thought you might want something warm."

"Yes," he said, "I do." He spread out his napkin, looking at it attentively.

"All right, Christobel," she called out. She hoped it was not a shout, too loud, too happy.

"Hello," said Christobel. "How you been? That so? Well, it don't look like they fed you right up there." She held out to him a platter of turkey hash, girdled with vegetables and browned potatoes. He took a little of everything politely. He was polite to Christobel, but absent. His attention seemed to be on the things immediately about him, on the heavy silverware, the cut-glass tumbler. Christobel went out.

"Were you lonely?" he said, without looking up.

"Yes," she said, "I was."

"You should have gotten Big Sister or Jeanne Balso. I wrote you, you know."

"Yes," she said, "I know. I didn't want any one else."

"Any one else? You're satisfied with poor company."

"I never said I was satisfied." Better a light note. "It's just the ill I know of." She smiled at him.

He stared at his plate.

"And to be alone is an ill you know of, too." He looked up and managed to lighten his tone. "I see you are prepared to defend yourself to the last."

"To defend myself?"

"Yes." He still kept looking at her and still smiled, keeping both light and casual. "I noticed the pistol was gone from my bedstand. I happened," he added, "to be looking for those tablets of mine."

"Oh, yes," she said. "It was a silly idea. I just took it down to my bedroom. It's in the drawer of my bedstand."

"Yes," he said, "I found it."

"I took the bullets out," she said. "I was afraid of them. I just thought if a burglar came I would wave it at him."

"But if he waved back with a loaded pistol, he would have the advantage of the salutation. No," he said, "that was foolish. It's better either to shoot or to snore. Preferably snore."

"But what are you doing with a pistol then?"

"That," he said, "is the question. It's supposed to be an attribute of manhood."

"I locked the bullets up in my desk," she said. "I was afraid they might explode."

"The cartridges?" He flashed her a warm look. "You are perfectly ridiculous."

"Well, but they could explode if they fell down, couldn't they?"

"Not likely," he said. "Practically impossible."

"Well, if they fell into the fire, they could explode then, couldn't they?"

He was looking at his plate again. "Yes," he said, "they could then."

She was going to cry: "There you see!" He had started to eat doggedly and listlessly. She was checked. He had gone then to her room to find his pistol. Only that. There was no gift of his for her. No thought of her had sent him. She looked at him

covertly. But what thought had he? It was a risk to look at him
so. But what thought had he?

The food and the cocoa, however perfunctorily swallowed,
brought his color back. In the end, he sat up and told her news
of Philadelphia. He was amusing, as he always was, about his
brothers. "The Infant Samuel in the lion's den," he said. "My
nonentity is what saves me. Being lions, they can't imagine that
anything so small is edible. And what's going on in town?"

"Not much," she said, "there was skating and then it thawed.
And now there is good ice again. They're having a bonfire on
the island to-night."

"To-night?" he said. He looked about the room. "There
ought to be a moon."

"Yes," she said, "I think there is."

"There won't be much skating any more this winter," he said.

"No," she said.

"Have you been?"

"No, I haven't gone since you left."

"You should have," he said. "That's absurd. Would you like
to go to-night?"

"To-night?" she said. "*That's* absurd. You're worn out."

"I haven't had any exercise, that's my trouble. Let's go for a
little while. It will do me good."

"Oh," she said, "but it won't."

"I know myself," he said. "It will." He looked at her warmly.
"Wouldn't you like to go? It may be our last chance. Come
on," he said.

"I don't know," she said. "I just want to do what is best
for you."

"I know that," he got up from the table, "better than anything." He came behind her chair and put his hands lightly on
her head. "Come on," he said.

CHAPTER XXIII

SHE stopped for a moment in front of her mirror. The gas jets which flanked it were half-turned down, but she was content with the dimmer light; it made her look like an old master. The round dark fur cap of otter, pressed down on her forehead, gave her an air at once child-like and wild. Its lower edge melted into the dark line of her eyebrows. She was a young Cossack or a girl of the Stone Age. The steel-gray suit was cut on slender racing lines, and the otter collar, thrown back, showed the bright edge of her chamois vest. In her hand were her beautiful, black skating boots and the shining blades. She raised them up; the blades clicked together. Fitz had given her them last Christmas. Never again with swelling, senseless fingers would she have to fumble at straps and screws and levers.

How well she looked, slender and tall and easy. Her cheeks were delicately but deeply colored. Her mouth and her lean chin were strong enough to carry those ridiculous, great eyes of hers that now peered out under the otter fur like the eyes of an astonished and observant animal. She buttoned up her collar and turned away. She should be ashamed.

But she had not had on her skating things for weeks. She had forgotten how well they became her. It was pardonable to be grateful for such a delightful surprise. And perhaps the picture in the mirror was a prophecy, a charming promise of happiness to come. Surely, as she looked just now, she should be formidable to a rival. A great beauty would, of course, surpass her; but the great beauties were likely, she understood, to be spoiled and silly. Certainly that should count for something.

She sat down on the bed and let the skates hang down between her knees. But did it? Or for that matter, did beauty, or did anything? Her rival, for all she knew, might be grotesque and mean. There was no limit to a man's capacity for self-delusion. There was small credit, when you came to think of it, in holding a man's love. But that was not the question. Who wanted credit? The question was to hold it.

She brightened. To-night, amid all that was inscrutable and obscure, there were signs that he was coming back to her.

His door closed overhead. She stood up and took a breath. The skates clicked together. Let her be happy and love him patiently; he was coming back. She almost forgot to turn out the gas.

Her wool-lined arctics made no sound as she went down the stairs. He was standing in the hallway, peering into the dimly lit drawing-room.

"What are you looking for?" she said.

He turned quickly. "Just looking things over," he said. He put on a white-knitted skating cap, the one that she had made. "I feel as if I had been away for months. I had forgotten how nice things look."

He took her beaver coat off the hook and held it out for her. She slid into its warm embrace, feeling his hands close over her shoulders. It was hard not to delay. She would have been content simply to stay there in the beaver coat with his hands on her shoulders. She turned and faced him, buttoning up the big fur-tufted buttons, and dropped her chin into the soft beaver. He watched her hands. "Where are your gloves?" he said.

"Oh," she said, "I am stupid. They are in my inside pocket. Never mind. I'll get them when I take my coat off."

"You ought to put them on," he said. "You can't walk down to the river with your hands in your pockets. It's too slippery."

She unbuttoned a button and tugged at her pocket. The suède gloves lined with rabbit's fur came out.

"Will you be warm enough?" he said. "What about a muffler?"

"I can't wear another thing. I've got the fur of every animal in the world on me now, poor things. Otter and beaver and my chamois vest, and wool; I suppose that counts as fur."

"And rabbit fur," he said, "inside your gloves, and muskrat outside mine."

"Yes," she said, "and your coonskin coat. Isn't it dreadful? All those animals."

"Yes," he said, "I suppose it is." He put on his coonskin coat.

She allowed herself to give a little hoist to the collar. "Thanks,"
he said, and picked his skates up from the bench.

The night air met them like a solid bulk. She felt the tiny
hairs in her nostrils prickle and stiffen. The arc lights glared on
the frozen ruts. Beyond the black trunks of the locust trees, the
river's bank dropped into a black void. Out on the island, the
bonfire glowed ruddily and sent a ruddy path across the ice to
them. A swift black figure crossed this path and faded into
darkness. Around the bonfire, high lights and shadows moved.
The crowd was there.

They walked down the street, past the congealed, impassive
house-fronts and the glow of curtained windows. At the corner,
they crossed the roadway and crunched through frozen snow
patches to a flight of wooden steps.

"Let me look," he said. "All right. God's in his heaven; some
one's put ashes on them."

They stopped on the snowy bank. "Do you think you can see,"
he said, "to put your skates on?"

"I can in a minute," she said.

He sat down. "Here, sit on the edge of my coat."

She kicked off an arctic, and straining in her swaddlings,
stretched forward and thrust her toe into the shoe. Already the
leather was cold as iron. The laces slid taut without much help.
She wrapped them twice around her ankles and tied them
quickly. Then she tucked her hands into the front of her coat
against her chamois vest, and kicked her skate-heel against the
ground to warm her foot.

"All right," he said, when she had finished, "you get up first.
You're on my coat. I'll take your arctics. Look out for that
rough ice by the bank."

Holding hands, they crossed the snowy ice with short steps.
In the darkness, there were sounds, shouts and a girl who
laughed, and the swish of blades; there was the sense of dim,
swift figures. The ice smoothed out, they swung together and
started up the path of light to the bonfire on the island.

Jeanne Balso swooped at them; her fur-trimmed skirt was flattened in the wind; she poised like a tight-rope walker and came
curving up beside them.

"Hello, Clara," she said. "Good for you."

"Hello, Jeanne," Fitz-Greene said.

"Hello," she said, "you're back."

"He just got back to-night," Clara said, "and here he is. How's that for the sporting instinct?"

"You're being asked to admire me, Jeanne," Fitz-Greene said, "but you needn't answer." He skated on ahead.

"Is everybody here?" Clara said.

"Yes," Jeanne said. "And guess who's here. Anna Lisle."

"Anna Lisle! Why, I didn't know she skated."

"Neither did Ellen," said Jeanne. "She's so disappointed." She gave a deep, sweet laugh.

Mr. Thompson, his elbows neatly crooked, was gliding slowly backward on one foot. His other toe was pointed out behind him. The firelight shone on his eye-glasses.

"Hello," Clara called out.

"How do you do?" he answered, absently.

"Clara is the name," Jeanne called.

"Mrs. Rankin," he murmured.

"He goes into a trance," Jeanne said, "when he does that backward roll. I have had to put Mun off the ice."

"My goodness! What's Mun doing here?"

"He kept coming out with little straws and putting them down on the ice behind Thompy when he wasn't looking. Thompy would have killed him, if he had found out what it was."

"But what's Mun doing here?"

"I told him I'd give him a kiss if he'd come on the party. Poor Mun!"

"Why; aren't you going to do it?"

"Oh, yes, but he's already decided that it isn't worth it. Look at him."

Utterly withdrawn into his many wraps, Mun stood beside the fire. Only his pale, dejected eyes showed between the swathings of his muffler and his ridiculous toboggan cap. Beside him, rocking on her skates, Big Sister boomed and slammed her hands together.

On the bank, Fitz-Greene rolled their arctics into his coonskin coat. Good Doggie, skating furiously with Ellen, dashed out of the darkness. In a spurt of ice, he stopped, spread-legged. Ellen spun like a top. Her feet flew up. Calmly, Good Doggie clasped her to his bosom, and set her down.

"Hello, Clara," he said, "why didn't you come sooner? Did they tell you about the ice?"

"No," she said, "what?"

"Don't go between the islands," he said, "the rest of the river's all right." His mackinaw, too tight for him, made his legs look immensely long. His shadow, stretching across the ice, was lost in the darkness.

Fitz-Greene glided up. "I'll take your coat," he said. "Hello, Doggie, hello, Ellen."

"Let's crack the whip," Doggie said.

"We'll get warm first," they said. "Yes," they said, "let's." They stood in a row and spread their hands behind them to the fire.

A figure came out of the darkness into the first dim zone of the fire's light, a stout little man in a derby hat and ear-muffs. His old-fashioned Dutch skates curled over the toes. With slow scuttling strokes and a chopping swing of arms he wound his way toward them among their long, tangled shadows on the ice. His frosted mustache curled over a scrubby chin. He toed in, bandy-legged, and came to a scraping halt. "Hello, fellows," he said. He blew on his hands and stuffed them inside the waistband of his trousers.

"Hello," they said.

He looked at them, alert and impassive. "Got a fire, I see."

"Yes," they said. "Do you want to get warm?"

"Me? No." He undulated in order to ease his hands inside his waistband. "Pretty good ice to-night."

"Yes," they said. "It's lovely."

"Yes," he said. "It's all right. Who's that fellow cutting capers out there?"

"His name is Thompson."

"Thompson, eh? He's all right. Say, you need more wood, don't you?"

"I suppose we will," Good Doggie said. "There's lots of driftwood on the island."

The stout little man skated away into the night.

"Who's your friend, Jeanne?" said Ellen.

"He's not mine," Jeanne said. "He's Mun's; from the Union League in Philadelphia."

Mun's muffled eyes gave her a baleful look.

Mr. Thompson sailed slowly up. "Good evening, Mrs. Rankin. Hello, Fitz," he said. He rocked up on his toes and stepped up the bank to the fire.

"Hello, there," Fitz-Greene said. "How are you?"

"I'm finely, thank you." He held out his hands to the blaze.

"Cold?" Big Sister said. "I guess it's cold work, that fancy stuff."

Mr. Thompson withdrew his muffled hands. "Not at all," he said. "There's more to figure skating than you would suppose."

"I guess it's pretty hard work, really," Big Sister said.

Mr. Thompson looked at her. "Not that either," he said. "Miss Jeanne, would you like to skate?"

"I want to get warm," Jeanne said. "You skate with Ellen."

"That would be a pleasure," Mr. Thompson said, with great reluctance. He stepped down on the ice.

"I'm sure you don't want to," Ellen said.

"Oh, but I do." They moved off sedately.

A muffled voice came from Mun's muffled figure. "A woman's intuition." He sank his head lower into his muffler and watched his sister out of sight.

"Hello," Jeanne said. "Here comes Hans Brinker."

The stout little man came back with a large armful of driftwood. "Here," he said, "I guess this is what you need. Give me some room now. Look out, I'm going to throw it down. Look out there, ladies." He crouched over the fire. "What you need is a couple of real good logs set together like." He looked up at Mun. "Say, fellow," he said, "you ain't doing nothing. How about you and me getting a couple of logs? There's some at the end of the island."

Mun rolled his eyes at him. "I haven't got skates," he said, "and I'm going home."

The man in the derby hat stood up. "No skates?" he said. "Well, that's the heck of a thing. I got an extra pair at home, if I'd knowed."

"Come on," Fitz-Greene said. "I'll help you get those logs." They disappeared together, Fitz-Greene with long sweeping strokes, the little man working his elbows and industriously scuffling his curved Dutch skates.

"You see," Jeanne said. "He's in the Union League. They always lend each other skates." She tiptoed up to Mun and threw her arms about him dramatically. "Now you can go home," she said.

Mun shook off Jeanne with dignity. "I'll go home when I want to," he said.

Unrebuffed, she took his arm. "No, but really, Mun, it's silly. Come along with me. I'll go over to the bank with you."

"I don't need help," Mun said.

"I know you don't, silly. I just meant for company. If you don't, I'll go home by myself, right now. Really, I will."

"Come on, Mun," they said. "We are all going home soon, now."

Mun was led down the bank. With Jeanne gliding slowly beside him, his muffled figure moved with short and apprehensive steps across the ice. Good Doggie moved away from the fire.

"Doggie," said Big Sister, instantly alert, "let him alone now." Her ankles bent as she made a clutch at him. "Doggie!"

Swinging his long arms, Doggie vanished. They heard his long, deep whoop and Mun's exasperated curses. Jeanne Balso called out fiercely, "Doggie, you ass. I'll kick you with my skate." With long, trailing whoops, Good Doggie skated furiously away.

Fitz-Greene and Hans Brinker came back heaving two short, stout logs between them. "All right," the little man said. "Set still, ladies. We'll make this fire up good." He squatted down and poked the fire together with a stick. Without looking up, he held out a hand. "All right, Fitz, let's have one of them logs. The great thing in a fire," he said, "is a couple of good stout logs. With that old fire," he said, "we'd have been carrying trash all night, and then we wouldn't have had nothing." He held out his hand for the other log. He was strong as a little ox. He stood up, dusting his hands together, his face red, his black eyes bright. "Now," he said, "we're fixed." He blew through his frosted mustache and threw a glance at Clara. "You're his wife, I suppose? Thought so." He looked at Big Sister. "Lady, I ain't seen you stirring around much."

Big Sister grinned at him. "I'm a poor skater."

"Aw," he said, "come on. I'll show you how. There's nothing to it."

"I don't know," Big Sister said. "I fall down."

He bent his arm. "Feel that," he said.

"Yes," Big Sister said, "you've got the muscle."

"You bet," he said. "Come on." Big Sister continued to grin at him under beetling brows, but made no move. "Look here," he said, "I'm a widower, I live with my married daughter, and I guess you'd call me pretty settled in my ways." He held out his hands and led her stumbling across the ice.

The fire shot up between the logs, shone on high overhanging branches and then was lost. It touched the nearest tree trunks and laid a circle of light out on the ice. Its brightness blanketed the stars. Fitz-Greene and Clara seemed to sit in a small cave of light, hollowed out of the night. Through the darkness shadows fled with faint, slicing sounds of speed; but they were of another world. She and Fitz-Greene sat in the cave of light, warm, sheltered and alone.

"I thought you said there was a moon," he said.

"I'm afraid I did. Are you disappointed?"

"No, I like this better."

Ellen and Mr. Thompson crossed the path of light. They were stopping, turning, coming to the fire. No, they kept on. They swayed together into the darkness. She and Fitz-Greene were again alone.

She stared into the night, thinking, "We are here together and alone. I did not expect that much when we came skating." Now he was looking at her, studious and intent. But she would not take any notice. That would be best. All in good time. Be steady.

"You should always keep that dress," he said.

She laughed and raised a mitten to her face. "It's worn already." She stretched an arm out. "Look at the fur around the wrist."

"Then you should get another," he said. "The cap will last."

"Yes, she said. "I suppose it will last all my life."

"Ah," he said. "I hope so."

"But I can't go on dressing the same forever," she said.

"Why not?"

"Well, it would be too unoriginal."

"Who else does it?" he said. "It would be original." He took her wrist, examined the fur, his head bent. He brushed the dark fur with his fingers.

"You must always have a dress like this," he said.

"You know," she said, "it's quite an idea. If every one did it, it would be interesting. A tremendous jumble. Crinolines, and manteaux and riding habits, and fancy-dress costumes, I suppose, all mixed up together, whatever in each one's whole life had looked the best. But then when we got together—" She was staring at the ice, picturing the motley gathering, the astonished gentlemen. She heard him jump up.

"Some one's coming." He was urgent. Their hands were together, they were swinging into the darkness. Behind her, she heard George's voice. "Hi! . . . Clara!" She felt Fitz-Greene stride out and swung herself with him. "Hello, George!" she called. Her voice was snatched away.

Their long distorted shadows swayed in front of them, reducing the charm of their two figures to slightly sinister absurdity. The darkness closed behind them, the ice, mere phosphorescent flecks and scratches on a bottomless black floor, seemed to slope away. Their blades bit in together and came up faintly ringing. The white flecks flew under them, the black vault and the stars, now dimly felt, turned above.

With their momentum, they gained rhythm. They no longer seemed to skate. There was no act, no volition. Their light, firm clasping hands and bending bodies swung in a rhythm, easy, light and free, yet perfected and inviolable, a rhythm which, creating first itself, went on to create more, so that they flew without thought, weight or effort, caught up, sustained and carried by the magic flowing from their swaying hands. Ruddy house lights from the river's bank swung in their distant orbit, faint sleigh bells mingled with the wind of their speed. Stars, sharp and reserved in the great cold night, touched the immediate ice with misty silver that ran ahead of them. The world was turning under them. They felt the roll of that gigantic ball.

The etchings on the ice were few, not many skaters had been down so far. "Fitz." She had almost to shout. "Do you think we ought to go here?"

"What?" he said.

"Do you think we've gone too far?"

"We're all right," he said.

He must know. Or if not, they were together and flying fast. The lights of town were left behind. There were no skate marks on the ice. They swam over perfect blackness. No marks of man; no lights on shore. Only the night and the ice. They flew.

His hands broke the beat. They stood up, rigid, and swung a circle. Then they stopped.

"No one has ever skated here before," he said.

"I know," she said. "No one." She felt the vapor of her voice against her cheek. "It feels different," she said. " 'We were the first that ever burst.' "

He gave her hand a shaking. "It must be tantalizing," he said, "to have a great fund of inappropriate quotations."

"Well," she said, "you know the feeling."

He held her hands against him, peering down at her in the night, his face dark beneath his white-knitted cap. "Let's go back," he said. "This was a foolish thing to do."

"Yes," she said, contentedly. "I suppose it was. But it's only bad between the islands, I guess." He did not answer. "Doggie says there's an air-hole between the islands," she said. "Where the current runs."

He held out his hands. They struck out together. The journey back was not so swift. They met their skate marks—made just now. The ice, then, and the night were no longer quite the same. They had been here before and left their trail, spoiling the new ice by that, even for themselves.

They could see the others gathered around the fire. The little man in the derby threw on sticks; the flames blazed up and showed George's square figure and Anna Lisle, looking cold and white beside the fire.

Good Doggie left the fire and came flailing down to them. He made an awkward, rapid turn alongside. "Hello, where've you been? We want to crack the whip."

"Oh, Doggie, I couldn't just yet," she said. "I'm tired."

"Well, then, let's have a little skate."

"Oh, I don't think I could," she said. "We've been miles."

"Just a little skate," Doggie said.

"Well," she said, "I'll skate just back to the lower end of the island, then."

Good Doggie's big hands seized hers.

"Yes," Fitz-Greene said, "then come back to the fire."

Good Doggie lunged out. She looked back as she flew away. "I will," she called. He stood still in the dimness of the firelight's edge, looking after her.

CHAPTER XXIV

SHE let Doggie propel her down the dark, wooded shore marked by the faint white gleam of snowy banks. It was useless to try to follow his powerful, ill-judged thrusts. She allowed herself to be jerked along. This was a very different kind of skating; but it would soon be over. The island ended here. Doggie stopped, pigeon-toed, and swung her around. Unflagging, he toiled back toward the firelight. Was it a mistake to have come with him? What thoughts had been in Fitz-Greene's mind as he stood looking after her? But he seemed pleased to have her go. He was never one for petty jealousy, even when he—even before. He had been proud of any least attention to her, had taken it to himself as well as to her for a well-deserved compliment. "I'd make the ideal cuckold," he had once observed. She remembered that he had been a trifle disappointed at having to explain the meaning of the word. And she must not seem to hang upon him. For he was coming back.

There was the fire. Good Doggie put on a burst. The speed was not great, but the sense of power was enormous. It was like being caught up in some great aimless convulsion of nature.

As Doggie rushed upon the group around the fire, there was a resigned scattering; Big Sister scuttled with furious, fixed eye, Jeanne Balso raised her fists defensively. Good Doggie lunged up on the bank. The group re-formed. The little man looked up from the fire. "Hey, fellow," he said, "look out how you do. You'll scare the ladies."

"How are you making out?" Good Doggie said. "Do you need any wood?"

"No," the little man said. "That fellow Fitz and me, we got plenty." With a stick, he shepherded a coal back into the fire. Clara sat down beside him on Fitz-Greene's coonskin coat. Across the fire, Anna Lisle, looking fragile and bizarre in white wool skirt and jacket, was talking to Ellen. Ellen was probably trying to persuade her to sing the Mad Song from "Lucia di Lammermoor." An industrious and resourceful fighter for her rights, was Ellen. Below them, Jeanne Balso had sat up, and was paying no attention to a long discourse of Mr. Thompson's. She was probably trying to hear what Ellen was saying. George, draped in his coonskin coat, stood on the ice. He took a stout cigar from his mouth and looked at it.

"Didn't you hear me holler?" he said.

"Yes," Clara said. "I called back, but Fitz wouldn't stop."

George put his cigar in his mouth. "Doggie," he said, "have a cigar?"

"No, thanks," Doggie said. "We're going to crack the whip as soon as Clara gets warm."

"We ought to wait for Fitz," Clara said. "He loves it."

Doggie was gruff. "He'll come when he hears us start." He was a man to be put off no longer from his project.

The little man squatted down on his heels. "Well," he said, "did you have a good skate?"

"Oh, yes," she said. "We just went to the end of the island."

"I mean the first time, with him."

"With my husband? Oh, yes."

"He skates awful good," he said, "and so do you, too."

"Well," she said, "we've skated a lot together."

"I'm always glad when winter comes," he said, "then I can skate. My daughter says that if we had winter the year round, I'd be the easiest man in the world to live with."

"I guess you're pretty easy, anyhow."

"Well, in the summer, I get kind of restless, now that I don't work no more. I fool around with a truck patch in the back yard, but it don't seem like I could take no interest in it. I do pretty good with it, too. Sometimes, I think maybe I'll get a job again. I don't have to work, though."

"What did you use to do?"

"When I quit, I was a trimmer in the rolling mill. I've had other good jobs, too. Never lost a job in my life; walked out on them, but never was fired. I guess not everybody can say that."

"No, I guess not. You must be a pretty good workman."

"The whole thing," he said, "is for a man to learn a job and then to do it. If a man will do that, he don't never need to look for work." He added two sticks to the fire. "If a man will take

some satisfaction and interest in his work, he will be all right.
I guess that's what I miss since I quit."

"Yes," she said, "I suppose every man that amounts to anything
is lost without a job."

"That's a fact," he said. "What's he do?"

"Who? My husband? He's in the wholesale hardware business."

"Well," he said, "I guess that's a pretty good job. There ought
to be money in that."

"I think there must be some," she said. "He doesn't tell me
much about it, but he seems to be making out all right."

The little man brought out a small white ball of handkerchief
from his hip pocket, and rubbed his nose hard. "That's a smart
fellow, and awful nice. Took a fancy to him, right off."

"I think he's nice."

The little man concentrated on injecting the handkerchief into
the pocket of his skin-tight trousers. "Yes, sir," he murmured,
"he's all right."

Good Doggie stamped his skates on the ice. "Now then, what
about it?"

They rose stiffly and reluctantly, Mr. Thompson held out a
hand to Jeanne, who got up without it. "What about Fitz-
Greene?" he said. "We need him for an anchor."

"He'll be along," said Doggie.

The little man stood up. "Here," he nodded at Good Doggie,
"let this big fellow be the anchor and me come next." He
clumped down toward the ice. "We'll swing them."

George threw his coat on the ice. "All right. We'll put Big
Sister at the end."

"You will not," Big Sister said. "I go on the inside, or I
don't go."

"Why, lady," said the little man, "you were doing fine out
there. Just keep your ankles stiff-like. You're all right."

"Come on, Clara," Jeanne said. "We'll take Big Sister between
us."

Mr. Thompson took off his eye-glasses and snapped them into
their case. He smiled jauntily to conceal his opinion of this
form of sport.

They joined hands and started. Bearing Big Sister's wobbling
weight between them, she and Jeanne Balso skated hard. They

felt the line check at the other end and the taut stretch of the curve. They stood up straight and flew. "Wow!" said Big Sister. The tension snapped; they sailed away.

"That was Anna," Jeanne called. "She let go."

Ellen was with them. "I know she did," she said. "I tried to hold on."

"Why couldn't she hold on?" said Jeanne. "We missed half of it."

They stopped in a group. Big Sister glowered at them and grinned. "Wow," she said. "It was enough."

The others were calling. Their voices rang in the cold night. "Come on! Come on, you. Let's hold it this time."

"All right," Jeanne called. "We're coming."

"I'm going to look for Fitz," Clara said.

"Who's going to hold me up then?" Big Sister said.

"Don't go chasing after Fitz," Jeanne said. "He'll come when he's ready. They always do."

Good Doggie's voice came through the darkness. "Come on. What's the matter there?"

As she skated away, she heard their voices behind her near the fire. "She's gone to look for Fitz" . . . "to look for Fitz? oh, sugar!"

She turned first toward the lights of town. She passed dim figures in couples and some little boys and reached the bank at the foot of the wooden stairs. He must have turned upstream. She struck off for the middle of the river. The ice here had been used by many skaters. It was scarred and powdered, all its freshness gone. Ahead of her, dim trails of skaters formed and divided, passing around rough ice cakes embedded in the river.

There were skaters now, people, she supposed, from the upper end of town. There were silent couples, and a group of girls who laughed. Whenever she saw a single figure she swung over to it. Sometimes it was a girl, and once it was a man who said, "Hello, there, sister. What's your hurry?"

She guessed by the look of the bank and by the lay of the islands that she had come as far as Billy-goat Town. That was a long way, she thought suddenly, a long way. The river here was deserted. She skated on, straining to look across the dim, starlit ice.

All skate marks ended. It would be crazy to go on. "Fitz!"

she called, then louder, more urgent, "Fitz!" She listened; her pulse rustled in her ears. She called again. Far off from under the dark, overhanging houses, the bad little boys of Billy-goat Town sent her a mocking answer, faint whoops and a long falsetto.

She was skating down the river fast. Still she kept calling, screening her ear with her hand to listen. The lights of town crept slowly by, the stars wheeled overhead. Skaters slowed up, stopped, turned to look at her as she passed through them, calling.

The bonfire lay ahead. He might be there now, waiting for her. She dropped her head and flew. "Fitz!" she called. "Fitz!"

A figure spun out of the night. "Oh, George!" she said. "Oh, George!"

He took her by the arms. "We can't find him." His voice sounded small and furiously angry.

She tugged at him. "Where is he?" she said. "I must look."

He gripped her arms. "No, we're doing everything."

"I must look," she said. She thrust at his chest with her fist. "I'm not a baby."

He was running like a sprinter to keep up with her. His words came in short bursts. "We saw the skate marks between the islands there . . . right to open water. May not be his . . . We made a rope of belts and mufflers. . . . Doggie's been in and that old fellow. . . . They could get their skates off quicker." She squeezed his hand. Poor George, he wanted to be first.

Between the islands Big Sister held a blazing branch high, her face a set mask under her heavy brows. There were logs laid on the ice and crouching figures. Their faces turned toward her and looked at her as though from far away. Ellen came up. "Clara," she said, "we don't know if it's him." She did not try to touch her. Anna Lisle came skating with two more blazing sticks. The flames flew back like small flags, the front of her white dress was marked with charcoal and she was crying. Big Sister took a stick from her. "Stop crying," she said, in a loud, fierce whisper.

"Here," said George's voice, "Clara, you can't go out there till Doggie comes in." He looked up from the shoe he tugged at. "Watch her, Ellen."

"It will only hold one, Clara," Ellen said.

Good Doggie's dark silhouette lay stretched out on the ice. Behind him, another silhouette lay holding him by the legs.

"Did Jeanne go for the firemen?" said George's voice.

"Yes." The second silhouette answered. It was Mr. Thompson. "I gave her my knife," he said, "to cut her shoe laces."

"All right," George said. The other shoe dropped on the ice. "Come on with that rope."

She turned. "George," she said. Her voice was tight and small, "don't go." George did not answer. "How long has it been?" she said.

"Twelve minutes since we got here," Mr. Johnson said.

"It is no use," she said. "It's no——"

"Clara," Ellen's voice was quick and clear. "George wants to go."

Stocking feet thudded on the ice. The little man came up. His frozen clothing crackled and shone. His face was white and set and he was dancing to keep warm. He bent over close behind George and passed the end of the line of knotted mufflers under George's arms. "Now, listen, fellow," he said. "There's a gnarly root about twelve feet downstream. Keep to the right of that now. We've tried the other side."

George nodded. "Give me a minute and a half," he said. "I can do it easy."

Mr. Thompson backed in from the hole. "A minute and a half," he said. He stood up and handed his watch to Big Sister.

Good Doggie backed in and stood up. His clothing crackled as he shivered. "Everybody keep wide apart," he said. He chattered wildly. He looked at Clara. "You go away." She shook her head.

George crawled out on the ice. "Tommy," he said. "You'll have to hold the rope. You're the only man with skates."

"I'll hold it," Doggie said. "My stockings stick to the ice."

There was a gentle splash and George was gone. Paying the rope out, Doggie crept nearer the hole.

"Ten seconds," Big Sister said.

"He's on the bottom now," Good Doggie said. He crawled ahead on hands and knees.

"He's under the ice on the other side of the hole. He's about at the end of the rope," Good Doggie said. He lay down on the ice.

"I gave it two jerks to let him know!" he said.

"He understood," he said. "He's not going any further."

Big Sister studied the watch. "Twenty seconds," she said.

The little man stamped his stocking feet. "Look here, fellows, this is foolishness. Give him a minute." He hugged himself. "That's plenty long enough down there." He looked at Ellen and Clara and shook his head. "Trouble enough already," he said.

"I'll give him a minute," Good Doggie said in an angry, chattering voice, "and a damned short one, too."

"Could he have got out the other side, Ellen?" She was shocked at the steady quietness of her voice.

"We looked. No marks. And he'd have called."

"Yes," she said.

They stood silent. At long intervals, Big Sister called the time. Far across the ice, they heard the ringing of a fire bell. "That's Jeanne," Mr. Thompson said. "She's quick." Up the river, a skater shouted, a long, high, shaking cry.

"Fifty seconds."

Good Doggie began to pull. "Can you make it, fellow?" the little man said.

When there was a free end to the rope, Mr. Thompson skated quickly in and seized it. Good Doggie backed away. Together they pulled. The others watched the water-hole.

George's head came up and drifted toward the ice. "All right," the little man said. "Hold him there." On stocking feet he ran forward and lay down on the sticks. His head was close to George's as he clutched him. "Nothin', he says," he called out in a loud voice. "Nothin' at all." He wrestled with George. "Folks, I can't make it," he said. "I keep slipping."

She was skating forward, she was on her knees. She stretched out and grasped the icy stockings of the little man. She could not hold them. She inched ahead and seized the edges of his trousers. She felt some one grasp her ankles.

Breathing hard and splashing water, George crawled by her on all fours.

"All right, all right," the little man said, impatiently. "Let go my legs." She backed away.

Big Sister's hand came under her arm. She stood up. Big Sister's voice was booming slowly, quietly. "You come with me.

We'll go back to the house. All right," she called to murmuring voices, "she'll come with me. Get those men home and make them run. Make them run. Clara," she said, "you must come."

"Yes, Clara." The voice was Anna Lisle's.

"Go on, Anna," Big Sister said. "Go on away. Clara, you must come. The boys have done everything. They'll get the firemen and planks and ice saws now. There's no use to wait, Clara," she said, "they're going to do everything."

"I'll come," she said. "I'll come." She took a long, hard breath. "Fitz!" she cried in a loud voice. She listened. Back in the town another fire bell was ringing.

Once there were sled marks on the dark ice. It was foolish, she thought to let children come out there with sleds. She stumbled on the bank. There were the whites of Levi Mistletoe's eyes. Levi and she climbed the wooden stairs, crowded together. Her skates made the cinders crackle. At the top of the stairs stood the great bulk of her father. She fell against it. So then Fitz-Greene was dead.

In the night she woke, heavy with the drugged drink of Doctor Considine. Why, this was her own old room of white and silver. She sat up in her bed. Lights were reflected on the ceiling. She looked out the window and fell back, strangled. All among the islands, there were torches.

CHAPTER XXV

SHE sat at her desk in the upstairs library. The window beside her was open to let in the first authentic day of spring. Birds were busy in the back yards. Sunlight fell across her desk. Above the blank brick wall of the next house was a patch of intense blue sky and a frivolous white cloud. In front of the house snow water, she knew, filled the gutters. Buds of the locust trees were swelling. The last ice cakes were drifting down the river, white and slowly turning in the bright, blue water. On the islands the mist of tangled branches showed faint pink and yellow. Spring had come early this year, they said. To her it did not seem so.

Her arms in black, ribbed silk with cuffs of white linen lay across the check-book on her desk. She ought, she supposed, to get on with her accounts. She wished that she had come to the end of this check-book and could start another. On these stubs that were for ever flying up, there were too many entries to remind her. "Three skeins white wstd." That was for his skating cap. They had never found it. "One pr. fur gloves; six pr. men's white dress gloves," and below that, sounding most unbusinesslike, "for Fitz Xmas." And then, of course, there were all the entries of last month, for flowers and carriages and extra chairs and for the men at the cemetery. The bill had not yet come from the man who made the gravestone. George had attended to that and had gone out to see that it was properly set up. She, herself, did not want to go there any more. She would be expected to go at least each anniversary and lay flowers on the grave. It was the custom. But she would not do it. That was a scene of the farce beyond her power to play; it was too much to ask her pride. The others did not know, of course. They spoke of the accident. They argued endlessly, she knew, among themselves, how he had failed to be warned about the ice, how it was no one's fault and yet they all must share the

blame. But she knew. Let them think what they would. Before
his death and since, she had done all that could be asked of her.
Now as time passed she saw things clearly. It should not be
asked of her to bring flowers to one who preferred death to
another day with her.

And yet. And yet, one must bring flowers somewhere, and
where else could she bring them, now or ever? Her head sank
on her arms. Below she heard the front doorbell ring. She sat
up bitterly. All these people! She was not even free to cry.

She heard Christobel murmur at the front door and then her
mother's voice. "Clara, may I come up?"

"Oh, yes," she said. Her mother was punctilious, but what
would she do, if she had called down "no" to her? She wiped
her eyes with her black-edged handkerchief, and blew her nose
as silently as possible. She tried to see herself in the silver top
of the inkwell. In that grotesque reflection, her nose was enormous, but not red. She could not tell about her eyes. They were
tiny and far away, and close together like a ferret's.

Her mother swam into the room. Her fine figure in its tight
black satin looked as though it had been cast in gunmetal.
From the landing, Christobel, her arms akimbo, peered into the
room. She nodded once, and vanished. She felt reluctant awe
of Mrs. Rand.

Dutifully, Clara stood up. Her mother kissed her on the forehead. "My dear," she said, "how are you to-day?"

"I'm fine, Mother."

"You have been crying," her mother said.

"No, I haven't."

"My poor child! You should be out on a day like this. You
mustn't stay in the house and mope."

"I'm not moping," she said. "I'm doing my accounts."

"It's hard, I know," her mother said, "but what's done is done.
. . . It's God's will," she added with the detached conviction
of one who states a mathematical axiom.

"Sit down, Mother," Clara said.

"I mustn't stay," her mother said, as she always did. She sat
down in the leather chair in front of the cold fireplace. "I suppose you've written to every one who sent flowers by this time,"
she said. "Sit down, my dear." She pointed to the other armchair.

"Yes," Clara said, "I have, and answered all the letters. A few still keep coming from his college friends in the West."

"The letters are comparatively simple," her mother said. Comparatively simple, Clara thought. "After all, one can hardly mislay a letter, but the flowers——" Her mother opened her reticule of black velvet. The silver clasp was enormous. "I know you made a list," she said, "but things are so disturbed at such a time."

"Mr. Riser made the list," Clara said.

Her mother drew a paper from the reticule. "Well, of course, he's an excellent man, very careful and painstaking. I thought the arrangements were admirable. But one can never depend entirely on other people." She opened the paper. "This," she said, "is a list that I made out myself. I thought we might compare it with your list. Then if any one has been left out——"

Clara leaned forward and stretched out her hand. "Thank you, Mother. I'll check it over with my list." She was heartless, she supposed, to deprive her mother of the pleasure; but she would go over no more lists with her.

"Be sure you do it," her mother said. "If we get the list checked, that will be everything. The marker is being put up to-day, George tells me. He will go out to-morrow to look at it. I think it would please him if you went too. George has worked very hard over it. It would please him to feel that you were interested."

Clara nodded and kept her lips closed tightly. It would be terrible to laugh.

"Your father has sent money to the fire companies," her mother said, "and to the men down the river who——"

"Yes," Clara said quickly, "I know."

"He sent fifty dollars to the Hope company and fifty to the Four Leaf Clover, and a hundred to the Superbas. They had the most men out. Of course, it all came to nothing, but I must say they were all very active."

She felt her mother's speculative eye. "Clara, I'm sure it isn't good for you to live here by yourself."

"Oh, but I want to stay here, Mother. I feel as if this house were my own."

"At home you could have the whole top floor," her mother said. "George's room could be turned into a sitting-room. You could entertain your friends there and if you wanted a meal on a tray at times, that could be managed." That was indeed a concession. "Your father and I have talked it over," her mother said. "We could even make the playroom into a library. And your father says that a dumb-waiter could be built. It would be almost like a house of your own."

The poor, dear bear! Pottering about the back of the house with his ruler, making drawings of the dumb-waiter that was to bring her home. But this house was hers, this and no other. And it was all she had to show for her love and for her marriage. Once she had left it, there would be nothing. And it was small, and cosey, and charming. She must cling to it.

"It's sweet of you to want to do all that," she said. "You mustn't think I'm ungrateful."

"Indeed not," her mother said. "You have always been most grateful for everything your father and I have done."

"But I must stay here."

"Very well," her mother said. "We will do everything to see that you are well looked after. I will stop in every day." She rose.

"Thank you, Mother."

"Don't come down," her mother said. "I just stopped in." She paused on the landing and turned. "Perhaps it might be well to engage a companion for you. It would give you company."

"A companion," she said. "That would be horrible." Her mother went down the stairs.

That evening there was a little fire in the grate of the library. She sat in her accustomed chair and opposite her, George smoked his pipe. By some instinct, he had started to push up a chair from another part of the room, but she had said, "No, George." So he had sat down in the dark red-leather chair where Fitz had always sat. He had not put on mourning, but he wore a dark suit and a black-satin tie. His square chin dropped down in the opening of his wing collar. His bushy eyebrows jutted over his blue child-like eyes. He had grown, she thought, to look more like his father.

"Ellen stayed home with the children," he said. "She'll be in to-morrow." He took the pipe out of his mouth and smoothed the bowl with an immaculate thumb.

"I went out there to-day," he said.

"Oh, did you?" she said. "Mother was here this morning. She said you were going to-morrow."

"No, I went to-day. It's all finished. The workmen were still there. I made them put a spirit level on the stone. It's set square and it's well down below frost line, two feet six. The lettering is all right. It's all very nice and simple, just right."

"Mother thought I ought to go out with you."

"What for?" he said. "A man can do that kind of thing the best. You know how it is. These workmen will always pay more attention to a man."

She smiled a little. "Yes, that's so, I suppose."

He thrust the straight stem of the pipe at her. "Anything you want done," he said, "you come to me." He thrust his pipe in his mouth hastily, and assured himself that it was still alight.

"Yes," she said. "I will. You don't mind my not going with you?"

He gave her a slow, impudent smile. "Didn't even notice it, Sis."

Heavily she answered his smile. "I knew you wouldn't. Mother thought you would be insulted."

He puffed on his pipe. "Never was insulted in my life, or if I have been it's gone by me. I suppose that amounts to the same thing."

"Pretty nearly, I guess," she said. "Poor Mun Worrall, for instance."

He hoisted himself in the chair with enthusiasm. "Yes, look at Mun. Always being insulted—waiters, railroad conductors, cab drivers, acquaintances, friends, enemies, everybody. There never was such a fellow for getting insulted. And the funny thing is, he seems proud of it."

"Oh, no," she said, "he's proud of the answers he gives. That's what he always tells you about: how he set them down where they belonged."

"Well, I suppose if a man wanted to be proud of that kind of thing, he'd better be proud of not having to set them down instead of having to do it."

"You don't understand Mun," she said.

"Yes, I do. He's all the time playing the clown and exasperating other people, and if any one bothers him, he's furious. I don't see what he's done in the world that's so important."

"That's it," she said. "He's never done anything. It makes him sensitive."

"Do you mean to say," he demanded, "that if he made a million dollars he'd be different? He'd be terrible."

"He's been wonderfully nice these past weeks, fussy, of course, but kind and sweet. That means a lot to a woman. Too much, perhaps." She stopped.

"Yes," he said, slowly, "I guess it does. And it should, too, I suppose." He was silent.

"George," she said, after a while, "do you think I need ever go out there?"

"Do what?" he said. "Oh, go out there. Why, no, I suppose not. Not if you don't want to."

"I don't," she said, "ever." She was looking in the fire. She felt that his eyes were on her. She looked up. He was inspecting his pipe.

"Well," he said, "there's no reason why you should. Not at the present. Everything is in good shape. Excellent."

"I don't want to, ever," she said.

"Well," he said. "I certainly wouldn't go now. It's hard enough to pull yourself together. No use to tear things up inside for no reason. Some people seem to like to do it, but I'm with you." He puffed on his pipe. "In a way I'm sorry about that provision in the will. Otherwise he could have been buried in Philadelphia. It would have been the natural thing."

"Yes," she said.

"Well, never mind," he said. "Let's never talk about any of it, again."

"Oh, but," she said, "I don't mind that. Nobody ever seems to want to talk about it."

"I know."

"It's almost a conspiracy. And that seems queer." She clasped her hands together. "Because, you know, I think there was something fine and wonderful about that night. Does that sound morbid?"

"Oh, I don't know," he said.

She stared in the fire. "The way every one worked and did their best, and you and Doggie and that little man, and Jeanne Balso running in her stocking feet through town."

"You know," he said, "that old fellow wouldn't take a thing.

I got him two hundred cigars, though. Sent to New York for them. The best that can be bought. He probably won't like them."

"I wrote," she said, "and asked him to come and see me some time."

"That was nice," he said, "but won't it be too hard on you?"

"Oh, no," she said. "I tell you that everything about that night seems wonderful to me. The way you went in under that ice even when there was really no chance left. I suppose I should have stopped you, but Ellen said you must go. She was magnificent."

"Ellen," he said, "was pretty good. I ought to have been the first, but those fellows had clamp skates. They simply beat me, and there was no time to argue. As it turned out, of course, none of it made any difference."

"It made a difference to me," she said, "and it always will."

He looked at her with a small, modest grin. "You know, I guess a minute and a half must be pretty near a record for that kind of work."

She smiled back at him, warmly, and nodded. "Yes, I guess it is."

"I only mean that doing it sort of makes up a little for having been the last. You know how a person sometimes feels." She leaned far forward, and touched his big hand resting on his knee. This he allowed for a moment, then put it in his pocket. "You know," he said, "what haunts me? I suppose I oughtn't to say this."

"You can say anything," she said.

"If I hadn't been off like a damned fool with Anna Lisle, I'd have told him about that ice. Doggie says he mentioned it, but now he can't be sure he heard. I'm not blaming any one, you know. I'm just awfully particular about things like that, just happen to be made that way. If I had been there, I think I would have made it plain. Instead of that, I was—" He smoked. "I wake up in the night," he said. He put the pipe down on his knee. The thread of smoke wavered and failed. It was going out. He did not notice.

She was standing over him. "He knew," she said. The pipe in his hand came up, dropped again on his knee. His face was turned toward hers.

"He knew?"

"I told him when we were off together."

"Why, then—" he said. He looked away from her.

"Yes," she said, "I was ashamed to tell." Her voice was calm and low. "I loved him and he couldn't—" A black flood rushed on her. She was whirling down. George's arm was round her, his deft hand held her shoulder, delicate and firm.

The last sob rent her and was gone. With distant, faint reverberations, his pipe dropped to the floor.

"Now then," he said. "Now then. Never you mind." He held her in his lap in the leather chair. He stroked her shoulder. "Now, then, never you mind."

She sat up. He brought a huge, white handkerchief from a breast pocket. She buried her nose in it and blew. The sound was tremendous. She could not help a sad little giggle. He looked at her. His child-like eyes were misty and dreadfully concerned.

A weight pressed on her. "I suppose we must tell Good Doggie," she said, sorrowfully. "Poor Doggie!"

"Never mind about that now," he said. He allowed her to put the handkerchief back in his pocket. "Look here," he said, "I'll tell you what I'll do. I'll just go back and get my things. I'll take the upstairs room. How would that do?" She stood up and brushed back her hair. He got up slowly, staring into the fire. "Have you got a tin pot?" he said.

"Why, yes, I guess so."

"Well, then," he said, "I'll tell you what I'll do. I'll make you some tea, right on this fire." He looked at her and smiled. "I'll show you the way we used to do it in the Adirondacks."

It was late, the town was asleep. They still sat before the dying fire, the teacups on the table between them. George's hand rustled in a tin of ginger snaps. He munched slowly.

"We ought to go to bed," she said, "and yet I hate to."

"Is it bad then?"

"Oh, no," she said, "no worse. But this has been nice, just sitting here. I wish it could go on."

"A cup of tea," George said, "is a great thing. You take coaching, for instance. Sometimes, when I get in at night, I'm really tired, especially in the fall. Driving through the dark, you know,

responsible for all those people, and half the time the farmers
never carry lights, and then it's cold. But if I can have a cup of
tea when I get home, in five minutes I'm ready to do it all over
again."

"Yes," she said, "it must be a strain. I don't think people
realize it."

"No," he said, "they roll along, having a good time, just like
the passengers on a ship."

Yes, she thought, they were passengers and they could not
have been in better hands. Never was a man more competent
in all affairs.

"George," she said, "I wonder if you could tell me something."

"What's that?"

"I wonder if you could explain it."

"Well," he said, in a quiet, sure voice, "I'll try."

"I feel ignorant," she said, "I keep asking myself things over
and over."

"I know," he said, "a person sometimes does. Go ahead."

"All during the last winter, I tried to puzzle it out without
letting any one know. And since he has been dead, I have
thought I might be able to understand it, because now that life
seems long ago. It seems as if it belonged to some one else. I
thought at first I might be able to get a better view and understand it." George's hand was rustling in the tin. She locked her
fingers together. "He really left me last fall." George's hand
stopped. He sat very still.

"Oh," he said, "did he?"

"Yes," she said, "it was all a farce, last winter. It was hard to
keep people from finding out. I was afraid they would."

"Yes," he said. "It must have been."

"And all that time," she said, in a low voice, "I kept asking
myself what had happened, and why it had happened, and what
I ought to do. I suppose I ought to know more about such
things," she said. "It all came very suddenly. There was no
drifting apart, just one night when he got back from Philadelphia."

His hands were clasped in front of him. He was listening
closely. "If it had happened sooner," she said, "it would have
been easier to understand, or anyhow, I would not have felt so
shamed. Because," she said, "I was very bad when we were first
married."

"You were bad?" he said.

"Yes," she said. "I didn't know anything and I was afraid, afraid as I could be; for a long time. I can see," she said, "how he might have thought then that I did not love him."

She steeled herself and went on. "But between that time and the other, there was a time when, it seemed to me, we were very happy, both of us, in every way.

"What I thought, when he left me, of course," she said, "was that some one else had come along. But still I thought that he would come back, and I thought so more just before the end than at any time. I was wrong, I know now, of course, but it seemed so then.

"And now," she said, "I am not even sure there was another person. That is what makes me bitter."

"It does?" he said.

"Yes," she said. "In the time when we were happy, I used to look back on those first months when I was just a silly, frightened child, and think how wonderful he had been. I loved him, I think, as much for that as for anything."

"Well," he said, slowly, "I suppose nothing can change that anyhow."

"But it can," she said, "because now it seems as though all of it had been a part of the trick."

"What trick?" he said.

"The trick," she said, in a low voice, "to win me. It must have been a game for him. And when he had won his point, he had no further interest." Her voice tightened. "He was always kind and always charming, but he had no further interest. Then at last he got sick of it, so sick of it that he skated——"

"Hold on," he said. "You don't know why he did it."

"Tell me another reason," she said. "His business was all right. At the funeral, his brothers did nothing but talk of how well he'd done. They thought it would please me to know there was no chance that he had killed himself for business reasons."

"They didn't know that he had done it," he said. "Nobody knows but you and I, and even we cannot be sure. You know how some fellows are. If you tell them a place is dangerous they want to go and have a look at it. It was dark there."

"He'd skated all his life," she said. "You could feel the ice thinning out, and you could see the hole. It's no use to try to fool me. I can't even fool myself."

"Whether he did it or not," he said, "a man like that wasn't worth your little finger. It's a hard thing to say, but however it happened, it happened for the best. It's too close yet, but some day I think you'll see it. He fooled us all," he said, "and we're all to blame, all except you."

She shook her head. "It's no use, George. Do you know what I feel like? I feel like a kitchen maid that's been dazzled and dragged down and laughed at."

"I wish he'd died," George said, heavily, "before you ever saw him."

She was on her feet. "Don't say that," she whispered, softly. "He was—" She was shaking. She sat down in her chair and gripped the arms. "Don't say that," she said.

He was patting her and muttering phrases. Poor George! There was no more help in him.

CHAPTER XXVI

ALWAYS people kept coming in. It was well-meant and she was grateful; but they seemed to feel that they must assiduously whittle down her hours of loneliness by staying long, although they had nothing to say; singularly little indeed. For herself, of course, knowing what she did, there was nothing to say. But to them it must seem an accident which had ended a happy marriage. And yet, they mentioned Fitz-Greene seldom, a form of delicacy, no doubt. Yet it was strange that some of them, at least, should have had no customary words of praise for the departed. Not that she wanted them; she was happy enough to escape the mockery. But she wondered why they were not forthcoming. Did they, after all, suspect the manner of his death? She must, she thought, concoct with George some message that would ease Good Doggie's mind. Or had their rodent instinct led them to facts or to clever guesses which ended in a secret and a different estimate of him? They were kind, these people, and they were loyal to her with an almost savage loyalty. There was nothing, she knew, that they would not do for her, nothing. On every side, she was buttressed by their devotion, buttressed and constrained. She was glad of an arrangement of her father's that took her driving every afternoon. Punctiliously, they alternated according to his plan. One day, he drove her with Lou Belle and Planet in the light roadster. The next, she drove him with Norah in the spider.

To-day it was her turn. In her bedroom, before the mirror, she buttoned a long black coat across the front of her black-silk dress. She wore a straw sailor, low and broad-brimmed, almost a duplicate in black of the straw hat Fitz-Greene wore, standing, in the photograph on the wall, among the other straw hats of handsome and decorously jaunty Aurelians.

From her bureau drawer, she took her old pair of brown cape driving gloves. They were one of the minor satisfactions of the

227

whole arrangement. Every other day, she wore them, when it was her turn to take the spider. Brown gloves with mourning and, above all, on a recent and peculiarly tragic widow had caused, she knew, some comment in the town. But to wear black gloves for driving was unthinkable, though hardly more so, to her notion, than to wear them for any other purpose. Black gloves were one more of the minor tragedies that followed in the wake of the great disaster. They were morbid, creeping things, and when, as in proper mourning, they were not suède, but slick and shiny, she felt that they made the wearer an object of loathing to beholders and to herself. She drew on the brown driving gloves. Why could not the desolate be permitted to make shift to assuage their sorrow with gloves as warmly ruddy, as richly grained, as these?

The afternoon sun lay deep across the bedroom floor. It was a pity the drive must come just at that time of day. The yellow wall paper was bright; on the bed the green counterpane shone. Across the street, under the glow of faintly greening trees, boys were shooting marbles, black silhouettes against the wide sheen of the river. On the bricks of the sidewalk, the light roll of a baby carriage sounded. She went to the window and looked down. It was Ellen, all in gray. The window was open, she started to call and wave. As she raised her hand there was a flash of a crimson jersey from behind a tree; Tommy crept up behind his mother swiftly, stealthily. His eyes, his face were bright, he slapped his hand against his serious open mouth, "Hooo!" he said, "Indians." Ellen made as if to raise a gun, "Bang!" she said fiercely; but he had slipped behind another tree.

She was thrusting back into the room, a knife against her throat. She must not let him see her, he would call to her, would laugh, would want to play. She stood inside the room, staring at nothing. She did not hate him, she could never say that, but at the sight of him a horror filled her. And now as she stood, like a sick dumb animal, another horror followed. She had played with him since his babyhood, had caught birds for him, told him stories, and at the Opera House she had, to the later scandal of the town, let him ride on the trained bear. Now she had come to this. It could not be true. She made herself look out again. And, truly, that small crimson figure, light, live and eager, now distant and removed from any chance of speaking to her, did soften her and warm her, however sadly, as it crept from tree to tree.

In front of the old, pressed-brick house of John Rand, she pulled up Norah and turned the wheel. The spider sprang up as Levi Mistletoe stepped down from the dickey. But before he could go to the door, it opened ponderously, and her father came down the brownstone steps. He removed his cigar and raised his square-topped derby. Levi went to Norah's head, he turned toward her father's dark, majestic figure and touched his hat. At the same time, he grinned to offset the formality of the effect. In answer, John Rand twinkled on him and raised a gloved hand almost imperceptibly. "Hello, Clara," he said, as she threw back the lap-robe. The spider sank beneath him. He bent forward ponderously and tucked the robe around him.

"All right, Levi," Clara said.

Levi came back, pausing to give the robe an added tuck around her father's shining congress boots. They must be nearly of an age, Clara thought. It was curious to couple them together in that fashion. Yet starting from origins so different, they had become alike, so that now, as Levi seriously tucked the robe in under John Rand's feet, it was really one stout old gentleman taking care of another.

Her father waved his cigar in his gloved hand. "That will do, Levi, thank you." Once more, the spider settled lower as Levi took his seat behind.

As they moved up the river, people on the sidewalk bowed or raised their hats with solemnity. The town was pleased to elevate the daily drive to a ritual. They saluted the young widow's weeds with conscious reverence. The spider might have been the hearse itself. Even Mrs. Munkittrick, who was always on the street—"just like a police on his beat," she remembered a song learned from Levi in the harness room, when she was a little girl—even Mrs. Munkittrick had bowed to her with courteous distinction. In a word, the daily journey was an ironic and petty royal progress through the domain of mistaken reverence for her bereavement. The phases of the farce were infinite, but here, at least, the rôle was not exacting. She had merely to bow gravely in return. Even the little boys of Billy-goat Town stood round-eyed in the littered gutter to watch them pass. There was good in everything, if one only looked for it, she had been told. In this case, obviously, the benefits of the disaster had descended on Levi and clothed him in immunity from his tormentors.

The country opened up, winter wheat showed in black fields, the first hint of spring sunlight lay on her face and on the melting ice floes of the river. She must not be bitter. The people who had greeted her and her father could not know what she knew. Let them alone then, they meant her well. Light, fluffy clouds swam in blue brilliance overhead. Full-bellied robins bounced on the damp, warm earth under the trees; somewhere a cow was lowing; in a field a man on a wooden roller shouted to his team. She must not resent the success of her imposture. She must not be unreasonable or silly. She must not be bitter.

Four light, swift wheels behind them; Gus Ringler's two black trotters in their interfering boots and blinkers, and Gus Ringler's wide red face and red mustache under the little derby hat. He gave a pull with his widespread, meaty hands. The reinloops trembled.

"Heyo, Clara," he said. "Well, John, here's where I get a chance to beat you on the road."

Her father waved his cigar with detached benignity. "Maybe you couldn't," he said, "if Levi weren't so heavy."

Gus Ringler's red mustaches lifted in a grin. "I guess that's right," he said. "She's a cute little mare, she is. Heyo, Levi." The black team moved ahead. Gus Ringler's fat back vanished up the road.

"A plain sort of fellow, Ringler," her father said, "good-hearted, though, and an excellent business man. I remember there was some little discussion with your mother about inviting him—" Her father stopped.

"To my wedding? Yes."

"Do you remember how he put on Samuel's apron and helped to serve? Your mother was quite upset."

"I remember," she said lifelessly, "he was very funny."

"And the German song he sang? Oh, I guess that was afterward."

"After Fitz and I had gone? I wish I'd heard it."

"What became of the wedding present he and Mrs. Ringler sent you?"

"I sent it to the bank," she said. "It's too valuable. It's solid gold."

"Of course it is," he said. "Must be worth three thousand dollars, that vase, if it is a vase."

"Yes," she said, "I guess it's a vase. Fitz-Greene used to say it looked like a prize for the wrestling championship of the world. There's nothing you can do with it in a house like mine."

"Clara," he said. "I don't feel comfortable about you living there alone."

"Oh, I'm all right."

"You have some valuable plate." He raised his cigar to his mouth and drew on it. "It would be feasible to arrange the top floor at home as an apartment," he said. "It would be feasible to install a dumb-waiter." He waited for her to speak, inspecting his cigar. "Naturally," he said, "you are a grown woman and would wish to have your own friends and all that. I understand that; so does your mother."

"I know," she said. "But I love that little house. It has all my things."

"Yes, yes," he said. "I know. You would want to keep them, of course."

"But I want to keep the house."

"You could certainly do that, too," he said, "then if, at any time, you wished to occupy it——"

"But I want to occupy it now. I want to live there always."

"I know," he said. "It has happy memories for you, of course, my dear."

"It has all kinds of memories," she said slowly.

Her father allowed his cigar to rest upon his knee and turned to make sure that the curtain shut them off from Levi Mistletoe. "Clara," he was very serious, "he did not use you well?"

"Oh, yes," she said, "he was kind."

"Of course," he said, "there are the adjustments of married life. We know that." She did not answer. "I might tell you now, I think," he said. He studied his cigar. "At the time of your engagement, I took the step of sending Riser to Philadelphia for a week to make all proper inquiries."

"Oh, and what did Mr. Riser find out?"

"Nothing but good, naturally, only what we all know. Before coming here, Fitz-Greene had been three years in the home office with his brothers and had given an excellent account of himself. He did not gamble, he had no debts, and as a member of the Rankin family, naturally he was received everywhere."

"That was all?"

"In effect, yes. Riser's report was detailed, of course. If you would care to see it, I will show it to you. But most of it is of a financial nature, and would hardly interest you."

"No," she said.

He looked ahead at the trotting, shiny Norah. "Daughter," he said, "you are unhappy. Come home. You are my daughter," he said firmly, "and must be protected."

Her hands trembled on the reins. "Protected?" she cried. "I've always been protected and look what it's brought me to."

The patting hand on her knee fell dead. She turned toward him. Heavily he stared ahead. "Father," she said, "why did I say that? You are good to me and I am bad." She felt the hand begin to pat her knee again.

"Perhaps you'd like a trip abroad," he said after a time. "Rome and Paris and all that.

"It could be arranged," he said. "Easily. It would be very interesting."

Her throat closed. "Oh, no," she cried in a choked voice. "I only want to live here in my house."

CHAPTER XXVII

In the library, Big Sister cocked a long and shapeless foot on the fender of the fireplace. Opposite her, Jeanne Balso, a flash of black hair, high color and brilliant blue, lay back lazily in the red-leather chair and watched her with amused respect. Clara in her black ribbed-silk sat between them on a rocking-chair whose sleigh-like runners moved slowly to and fro. The emptied teacups were before her on the table. Big Sister drew her chin down on her large gold horseshoe pin, further crushing what was meant to be a military collar. She frowned heavily under her brows at her shoe.

"Well," she said, "that was a nice tea. I wouldn't be surprised if that marble cake made me sick."

"It's not heavy," Clara said. "It's just the name."

"This was," Big Sister said. "It was good, though." She fetched a handkerchief from the side pocket of her brown jacket and wiped her downy chops. "There's something I wanted to say." She heaved sidewise and thrust the handkerchief back. "Maybe it is too soon, but it's got to be said some time, I guess."

"Oh," Clara said. Her rocker stopped, hung suspended.

"You can't go on this way," Big Sister said, angrily.

"Why not?"

"You'll make yourself sick."

"You think I ought not to live by myself?" Clara smiled, weary but relieved. So that was it.

"No, sir. I do not. Of course, Doggie's all right but I have often thought if I could just have a house of my own." So that was not it, then. She waited alert. "What you need," Big Sister said, "is something to occupy your mind."

"Well," Clara said, "I have the house."

"If you were dumb," Big Sister said, "that would do. But you can run this house on an hour a day. I do mine."

"It takes me most of my time to do it," Clara said.

Big Sister's foot came down. "Look here," she said. "You

233

know you're not a dummy. You've got tremendous brains. Hasn't she, Jeanne?"

Jeanne sat glowing in the red chair. Her smooth close bodice was a vivid blue, her skin was warmly dark against the crisp white ruching that stood against her neck. "Oh, yes," she said.

"What do you want me to do?" Clara said.

"My girls," Big Sister said.

"But I don't like good works. I truly don't."

"Oh, come on," Big Sister said, "you ought to give them a try."

"The more you dislike them, the more credit it will be to you," observed Jeanne Balso.

"It might be a credit to me," Clara said, "but it would be of no use to any one else."

Jeanne Balso stirred the triple flounces on her skirt.

"You might learn to enjoy them," she said. "I did."

"Yes," Big Sister said, "look at Jeanne. She was much worse than you."

"I was much worse," Jeanne said. "I used to hold hands with every man I met."

"She still does," Big Sister wriggled her eyebrows in scared pleasure. "It's one of her strong points with the girls."

"It's one of my weak points with the men," Jeanne said.

"But," Clara said, "I don't care about sewing, either."

"Never mind the sewing," Big Sister said.

"But it's not in me."

"You'd be the best of all, I'm afraid," Jeanne Balso said. "You have my charm and Big Sister's ideals."

Clara smiled.

"Yes," said Big Sister, seriously, "and brains too. Well, anyway," she said, "you're missing a lot. You'd be surprised at the things they say when they find out you don't mind anything."

Clara shook her head. Those girls of Big Sister's were splendid, no doubt, but they belonged to another world. It was a better world than hers, she guessed, and from her isolation she envied them. But it was useless to pretend to bridge the gap between them. Big Sister might succeed with her girls, though even there she suspected it was for both sides a mere pretense, an amiable and half-unconscious conspiracy of self-delusion, lacking reality. Though what life's reality was was also a question. Her love for Fitz-Greene had been real, and where was it now?

Even her love for her father had suffered mutation, something that had been withdrawn from it for Fitz-Greene was lost and could not be returned or even found. It would never again be central and all-sufficient. The great bear, poor dear, had diminished in size and potency. He was again, as he had been before, the first love of her life. But no longer did he hold safety and all wisdom. He, too, was mortal and ultimately helpless in the toils of circumstance. In the vast cavern of the universe, all men were mortal. And each, she had learned, was ringed at birth with fundamental isolation. It took extremity to disclose this gulf; and once perceived, life never could be the same again. That was the dark, the almost unbearable secret of maturity. No one could help another; all men were mortal and alone.

Big Sister was speaking to her. "I know you don't want to work with the girls. We didn't mean to bother you. We just think about you." She knitted her brows, crossly. "You know."

Jeanne Balso stirred. "That's it," she said. "To think that some one like you should be so sad," her voice was low, "when nothing ever happens to me."

"Oh, sugar, Jeanne," Big Sister said. "You're not so bad."

"Before I came here," Jeanne raised her black eyes in conscious recklessness, "I was engaged to three men at the same time. Twice," she said, "and they were all different men."

Clara smiled.

Big Sister pursed her lips in a soundless whistle. "Well, I guess that's bad, all right," she said, "but I kind of envy you."

Christobel's voice came from the landing. "There's a man down here that wants to see you."

Big Sister and Jeanne stood up. "We must go," they said.

"Oh, no," she said. "It will probably only be a minute."

She followed them down the narrow stairs. "I do like this house," Jeanne Balso said. "It's like a doll's house."

"I wish I had a house like this," Big Sister said, "but Doggie would break everything."

In the hall, they paused for a covert glance into the little drawing-room. They glanced at each other. "Good-bye," they said. "We had a lovely time."

He looked like a gnome among the gilt and crystal of the drawing-room. She hardly recognized the little man who had been with them on that night, Hans Brinker, they had called him. Mr. Twilliger, his name had turned out to be. His suit of shepherd's plaid was too tight in the body and too long in the sleeves. Only his knobby fingers peeped out below the cuffs. He sat rigid on a gold chair tapping one blunt knee, while the other hand made sure that his green, ready-tied necktie was still attached to the collar button. The tightness of his coat across his barrel chest threw into high relief George's cigars in his waistcoat pockets. His hair, well damped, was scrolled across his forehead to one eyebrow. His thick-soled shoes were freshly blacked. He sat in patient, exquisite discomfort, obviously slicked up and turned out with final instructions by his daughter.

There was talk of the weather and of his truck garden in his daughter's back yard. There was talk of his daughter and of her children's progress through the grades in public school and through the diseases common to their age and station in life. There was talk of her husband's position in the Royal Eagle Laundry. All reference to that night was laboriously avoided. Unbuttoning the straining buttons of his coat, from his ruby-colored crocheted waistcoat he produced a cigar for Clara's inspection.

"George gave me these," he said. "I didn't want to take them."

"But he would have been terribly disappointed if you hadn't," she said.

"Well," he said, "that's about what I figured. He kept after me one way and another, and at last, I says to my daughter, 'I guess I'll have to do something about it to ease off that young fellow's mind.'"

"Well, I'm glad you did," she said, "George was pleased."

"Well," he said, "so was I. As long as he knew I wasn't looking for nothing."

"Oh, but he knew that. We all did," she said. "We were all just grateful and wanted to show it."

"Well," he said, "a fellow can never be too careful, though." He shook the cigar at her. "Take a look at that. Go on. Take it. Smell it."

"It certainly smells very good," she said.

"Good! I guess it does. What do you think a cigar like that costs?"

"I don't know," she said.

"Well, I don't, either, although I seen George on the

street the other day, but I didn't like to ask him. But there's
a fellow on our block that used to be with the cigar factory when
they had it. He says these cigars can't be sold for less than thirty
cents apiece. That's the minimum. Might run anywhere up to
fifty." He took out another cigar and squeezed it between his
fingers. "So what I do is call it a forty-cent cigar. 'Here you
are,' I says, when I meet a fellow, 'a forty-cent cigar.' Sometimes,
they're scared to light up. Think the cigar will explode or smell
bad or something. You know those trick cigars." He smiled at
her under his sweeping mustaches. "Then they find it's the
genuine article. You ought to see their faces."

"It must be fun," Clara still held the cigar, "to hand cigars
around like that."

"Well," he said, "it is, for a fact. Of course, I smoke one
myself, now and again, but I've been smoking Sweet Dreams
for twenty years now, maybe more. That's a three for a dime
cigar, a little strong for some people, but it just suits me. No,"
he said, "keep it. Probably be a friend of yours in some time."

"Thank you," she said. She put the cigar on the mantel.

"You know," she said, "it all seems queer giving you cigars,
even the best, for what you did."

"It was nothing," he said, "none of us did nothing. We failed,
didn't we?"

"That was not your fault," she said. "If any one could have
succeeded, you men would have. That is the way I feel about it."

"Well," he said, "I guess we did as good as most fellows could
when you come down to it. I guess maybe that does some good,
makes you feel more like it was something that had to happen.
In my wife's time," he said, "we lost three children, and, of
course, we felt mighty bad about each one. But the second one
died of croup, one night when I couldn't find a doctor. I went
to four places before I could get hold of one. Then it was too
late. Seems like that child, Harriet her name was, preyed more
on my wife's mind than the other two put together. And on
mine, too, I guess. It seemed like something that needn't have
happened."

"Yes," she said, "that must have been awful for you."

"Well," he said, "it was. My wife never really got over it,
although we raised five others."

"What grieved her so," he said, "was that in the end all these doctors got my messages and come around. We had four doctors to the house, with all their tools and everything to save her, within an hour after she was dead. My wife used to say that it seemed like the devil was playing a prank on us. But then later on when the other children growed up and turned out good, she got over such notions, but it always grieved her."

"I know," she said. "Poor woman. I am glad that I can never feel that way."

He made sure of his necktie. "Oh, well," he said, "everybody was glad to do his best, and I was just as glad as the ones that knew him."

"I know you were," she said. "You were splendid."

He waved her aside. "Fact is," he said, "I felt like I did know him. I like young folks, kind of miss them since all mine has moved away. But I never taken to a fellow like I did to him. All I did," he said, "was to go up to the end of the island for a couple of logs with him. We talked along. He said that if he had a pair of the right kind of shoes, he'd like to try my skates. Fact is, we fixed it up to try them, the next night. Well, you know, most of the young fellows kind of look down on them old skates.

"Yes, sir," he said, "I felt like him and me had been together a long time. I'll always feel that way.

"Look here, I oughtn't to be going on like this," he said. "My daughter told me— Why Lady—" he said, "Lady, you must excuse me. I didn't go to make you feel so bad. I just got talking."

"Oh, no," she said, "I'm glad you did. You must come again."

CHAPTER XXVIII

Spring night had fallen on the river. She sat at her bedroom window, looking out. Beyond the black trees there were only swift gleams on the water and misty silver distances. Far away were pinpoint lights from farmhouses on the dark shore. Down below town a late team rumbled on the bridge. Even at night, she felt the river growing warm and fragrant in the air of spring. Young water rats were coming out to play, wild ducks on their northward flight were feeding in the rushes. Along the shores, the birds were nesting and squirrels and rabbits peeped out of holes.

But as she sat there, holding back from going, as at last she must, to the dark prison of her bed, pictures of Mr. Twilliger, of George, of Mun, and the rest besieged her. The faint praise or deprecation of those who knew Fitz-Greene best would never convince her now. The truth about him lay in the praise of strangers, a truth so blinding and so final that nothing the future held could ever diminish the magnitude of her disaster. He was lovable and she loved him still. And he had spurned her and chosen the unknown depths rather than any more of life with her. Her head sank down. That was a rival she had never counted on. But such was the truth and nothing could ever abate a single letter of its condemnation. She loved him and he, kind and gracious to the last, had gone to the uttermost lengths to cast her off. This was the message spring, the looked-for healer, had brought to her.

And spring by now was almost gone. In the back yard, the snowdrops had showed their frail white beads and let them fall. Crocuses had pushed up through the grass, had swelled their tight buds and flung them open to the sun. Flatboats, hauled down from sandy beaches, puffed flatly up the river to anchor in the stream and dredge for sand and coal. By daylight, the island thickets showed a mist of green, the distant hills had turned from gray and brown to blue. It was the time she had been waiting for. She had felt that if she could hold out till spring, then she could manage. It was like recovery from a dreadful operation. First, there had been numbness and a sort of stunned, uneasy peace; then came the first sharp hints of pain which mounted in recurrent waves. They in turn blended into a steady flood, where there were no more shocks or unpredicted thrusts, only one steady tide of misery. It was under this endless pressure that her laborious and pitiful defenses had gone down.

She had tried to think that as long as he had felt that way about her, it was better so. She had tried to think that, unable to give her love, he had meant to show by this last gesture a touch, at least, of loyalty, choosing annihilation rather than to flout her openly. She had tried to think that she had been delivered from a finally and eternally impossible dilemma. And to reinforce the weaknesses of these structures in her mind, she had tried to think of the will of God, of His wisdom and good- ness, each alike inscrutable. She had told herself that the first part of her life with Fitz-Greene was the delusion, the last alone was the reality in which his true colors for the first time could be seen. With the fatuous and demented persistence of a sickened mind—she told herself—she had been hugging to herself the image of a man who never was. As if this last device had brought its retribution, the whole ingenious, meretricious struc- ture had given away. With a crash and whirling fragments, the flood had burst its bounds and swept her down. She was over- whelmed and lost forever in the knowledge that she loved him.

What then had been left? Only to wait for spring, to hold on blindly, clinging to life until that time when life in all things would be renewed. It was as though this operation which had cut all that was best of her away, severing the taproot of her soul, had left her hanging between life and death, her being suspended in the balance, while within her there went on a race between dissolution and the healing of her dreadful wound. If she could hold till spring, when all things quickened, the wound might close in time to save her. She would then survive, go on living, in some sense, and be able at last, though maimed and forever crippled, to take a place in the world of living men.

Among the elements which ended by bringing her to face the completeness of her disaster, she could count as foremost the efforts of those who wished to help her. Dear people they had been, desperately loyal, thoughtful and generous; all of them, each in his way, suffused and made beautiful by the fastidious delicacy with which they tried to show the strength of their affection.

George, for example, was another man, a sort of new-found friend. He came in every day, to eat uncounted ginger snaps, but never to stay too long. His talks were on coaching and from them an impressive idea slowly emerged. As soon as the proprieties allowed, he was to let her drive the four-in-hand. It might jeopardize the schooling of horses that were just becoming perfect in their work. He made that clear. And certainly it was an honor that he would accord no other man or woman; but she was to do it, and he made it also clear that the concession was not on any grounds of blood or sentiment, but in recognition of her hands and level head. Already he had deposited "Coaching" by Howlett on her library table, together with four short lengths of rein which he had had made by the saddler. With this equipment, he explained the diagrams in the book, and particularly some small improvements on Howlett of his own invention.

Good Doggie, on the other hand, came only when she asked him, but he was always ready. Once, flouting convention, the proprieties, she had asked him in to supper. She had heard from her mother on that score, there had been murmurs in town. She did not care. Doggie seemed pleased to come. But then she found out he had given up a three-day fishing trip, carefully planned and laboriously arranged for with the bank where he worked.

"Doggie, that was a silly thing to do," she said. "The spring fishing is the best of all."

"Look here, who told you?" He knitted his sandy brows, a little like Big Sister. "Ah," he said, "Mun, the damn fool."

When she told him that Fitz-Greene knew about the open hole between the islands, it should have been a moment of release for him. For from the night of the tragedy till then, he had spoken to no one about his thoughts, he had offered no explanation and looked for no reassurance. He had simply withdrawn and sat alone, regarding himself as a murderer. To hear what she had to tell him was a complete reprieve. It should have meant everything to a mind like his, slow and simple, yet inexorable and sensitive. Instead he only stared at his big-knuckled fingers.

"Clara, I'm sorry," he said. "I'm awfully sorry. That makes it all the worse for you." He seemed to wrestle with the problem. "I guess we'll have to call him crazy," he said.

"He was a smart fellow, all right," he said, "but there were queer things about him. I guess they got the upper hand. Must have," he concluded. "Nobody does a thing like that unless he's crazy.

"You take animals. Animals never do it. It's because they're never crazy. And animals have their troubles too." He roused himself to complete the chain of thought. "All the same," he said, "I'm sorry."

He had sat for a long time smoking Mr. Twilliger's cigar. "Well," he said, "it's late, I'd better go." He dropped the cigar in the grate. "I suppose the town will talk about my being here alone for supper." He stood up with a grin. "Good night," he said. "The nosey pups."

Mun, on the other hand, was full of comment, especially when fortified by a few glasses of Château Lafitte. He then became dramatic and somewhat tearful. He took the highest grounds upon every subject and particularly in regard to Clara and her grief.

"I know you are unhappy," he would say, "terribly unhappy, God knows. It is only natural. You are a wonderful woman. No, now, I say this to every one. Every one knows it. Why shouldn't I say it to you? You are. Certainly that's nothing to be ashamed of, is it? Well then." He leaned forward on the table and eyed her furiously. "Let us face the facts. It all seems terrible to you now, and that is as it should be. No one can take exception to that. But remember that you have many years before you and that what has been done cannot be undone. And remember this." He took a drink of Château Lafitte, inspected the glass and set it down. "Speaking as a man of the world, I know and many other people who know life know that, while Fitz-Greene was the most delightful fellow in the world, and without the least idea of criticizing one who was so highly regarded in the best circles in Philadelphia and at the Union League and everywhere else, he was simply, through no fault of his and with all due respect to his memory," here Mun's eyes were suffused, "he was simply not up to you, my dear girl, in any sense of the word. He was simply——" Poor Mun! she should not have turned on him. He had looked quite scared, poor dear, and been unable to speak as a man of the world the rest of the evening.

Even Mrs. Worrall, to whom she turned in one of her tormented efforts to escape, could offer only wisdom. In her brown-panelled reception room, distinguished from others of the town by an easy disorder and rows of books meant to be read, she sat, a neat, small figure, withdrawn from the light of the green-shaded lamp, and looked at Clara with her firm, brown eyes.

"People say we have no right to despair," she said, "because we cannot know the future. That, of course, is true, and, especially when one is young, the future may hold anything. But I feel that we have no right to despair unless we claim to know what would have been life's other possible alternatives, unless we can surely say that the life we are leading is worse than any other life we might have led, if matters had turned out differently at any time in the past. You love Fitz-Greene, and I know how terrible the loss of love is to a woman, either," she said, slowly, "through the death of the one we love, or through any other cause. But while you may grieve, you cannot despair unless you can say that had he lived, your life would have been happier. You think it would, and I am sure that I can guess the kind of dreams which haunt you. But you do not know what other kind of fate might have been in store for you or for him or for your children. This thing which has come to you may be, I know, an unalloyed disaster or again it may be a bitter sort of mercy, to one or both of you. That is something that no one can tell, and that is why you cannot despair.

"Let me tell you something about myself. If Judge Worrall had died when the children were babies instead of four years ago, I should have felt that I had suffered a desperate wrong. And yet I know now that my life and his would have been happier.

"What I am going to say may sound trivial, but I think you know how men sometimes are about such things. The Judge was a successful and distinguished man as such things go, but his heart was set on getting to the Senate. In his later years, all that ambition and singleness of purpose that had raised him from a poor boy to a leader in the state were centred on that. When he was defeated, it broke his spirit and it also changed him. I think that most men and perhaps many women go through a change in marriage, a phase of restlessness and discontent, but if a marriage is a good one, all that passes and leaves things often more perfect than before. When the Judge was beaten, it seemed to render him distracted. He became toward me a different man and a strange one. I knew not only that he had left me, but that whatever I could do he would not return."

Mrs. Worrall, still sitting very straight, had raised her eyes from her small hands to Clara's face. "So you see," she said, "one never can be sure."

That was what Mrs. Worrall had said. It had seemed wise then. Now it did not. One could be sure of misery that was not worth bearing.

It was late, nothing was now astir. The night was warm. Dark and close-knit. In the night and silence the river seemed to run the faster.

She looked out at the shivering patches, at the dim silver mist. Life, warm and stirring, had now renewed itself along this river down which he had rolled. What an immense and relentless stolidity went to make up the basis of this world. Even for those who knew him, there were loving and dining, the new story, the latest song. Like the owls and the river rats, they were going about their business. No doubt, it was a merciful arrangement, which enabled the world, blindly and dumbly, but somehow, to go on. But if that were so, why could not some slight portion of that mercy have been granted to her? And what of him, now that he had escaped her? Did he still exist, if not in a heaven or hell as outlined by her Bible teachings, at least in some vague refuge of the spirit, perhaps beyond those farthest stars? If so, was he triumphant or was he merely grateful and at peace? Was he regretful, or, worst of all, was he desolate or frightened? The starlight trembled and seemed to glide along the gliding river. Beyond the dark shore of that nearest island was the spot where he had stepped out of the known world, closing behind him the iron door. If she were to take the path which he had followed, what would she find? Nothing perhaps? Only oblivion? That would not be bad. Or would she find him, to plague him and defeat him, leaving him with no further refuge even in the unknown? Or would he then feel differently toward her and know why she had come? Would she perhaps be welcome? She stared at the broad river, swift, dark, inscrutable. There was a place not far uptown where one could rent a boat, twenty-five cents, the sign said. That was not much to pay for a glimpse beyond the iron door, for even the least chance of escape from destiny.

She sprang up from her chair and groped through the darkened room. Where were the matches? Could she ever light one with those shivering hands? The gas jet flared. She stood at the mirror, breathing hard, and looked at her white face as though at a ghost come back from another world.

CHAPTER XXIX

SEATED in Fitz-Greene's chair in front of the now empty fireplace, George finished his cigar. She sat in her accustomed chair, feeling stunned and slightly nauseated, as she often did now after forcing herself to eat food always dry and tasteless, and watched the window curtain. She sat still, watching the ruffle of the muslin window curtain move in the spring air that came in through the slightly opened window. All movement, great or small, was becoming meaningless to her, almost an offense. What was the sense of that idle nervous swaying or of the wandering breeze that caused it to sway? If only all things could once and forever be still; entranced, as in the fairy story, through the ages until the hour of their extinction, when they would dissolve in dust like mummies. Or, at least, entranced until they should be awakened to some new existence, happier and more rational. Long ago, how long ago it seemed, she had wished that a moment of her good fortune and highest hope might be fixed by a stroke of magic and stand unchanged forever. Now, in her despair, she wished almost the same. But if she were wishing, why not wish for better fortune and be done with it? Impossible! Even in wishing, there must be some relation with what might be conceivable. Good fortune of any sort lay beyond her horizon. But extinction of one sort, if not another, was easy, dangerously easy, for her to picture.

George, who had busied himself in tamping out the light of his cigar on Fitz-Greene's bronze ash-tray, stood up. His gray flannel suit fell into well-cut lines. His black-satin tie flowed smoothly into his white-piqué waistcoat.

Her heart, at least, was not so dead but that it could contract as she looked at him. So he was going home early. Another lonely evening; and the river, whether she looked at it or not, running by.

He smiled at her. What kind and assured obliviousness to all that was going on inside her mind. "I brought something for you," he said. "I'll get it." He went down the stairs to the hall.

She only wondered whether what he had brought was meant to solace her for his leaving early, whether, having given it to her, he was going home, leaving her here alone beside the running river, inside this house that now seemed no stronger to hold her than the world outside. She had thought of the house as the one small treasure which she had salvaged from the wreck. But it was beginning, here, now, before her eyes, to go the way of all the other things that once had held meaning for her.

Yet where else could she go? Certainly not home with him. Yet that, perhaps, was what she wished for. She wished that both of them were still children in their innocence, and that she could go with him and creep in bed beside him, to lie safe in the shelter of his strong simple bulk. Her harried thoughts checked. Was this a vile idea? Or was it—her heart turned slowly over—a mad one? Was she being crushed and harried out of her natural instincts, out of the possession of her mind?

His foot was on the stair. She sank back in the chair. He must not see her rigid pose.

He held out a narrow parcel as he came across the room. She fumbled ineptly with the wrappings. "I got you these," she heard him say, "for coaching. You need an extra heavy glove, extra large too."

"Oh, thank you," she said, dully.

"Try one on," he said. "I found a pair of your gloves in the hall, and got the next size larger."

The buff-colored glove, heavy and stiff, but soft, slid on, smooth and cool. He settled it firmly between her fingers. He felt the palm and the loose welted back. He pinched the tips of the fingers. "It's all right," he said. "The size is right. You'll like them when they get broken in. Now what I thought," he said, "is that it would be a good idea to wear them when we practise here. That way, you break them in and get used to them, too. Don't take it off," he said. "I thought we might do a little work on the driving to-night."

He was not leaving then. "Oh, thank you, George," she said. "They're beautiful."

"What I want," he said, as he went across the room, "is to get you in such shape before you start—" he found the practice reins, "before you start, that when you are up there, I'll never have to touch the reins. There is no reason why you shouldn't do it." He came back across the room pulling two Windsor chairs. "You've got good hands and a good level head. And if you get the theory right, before you start—" he was strapping the reins to the backs of the chairs, "the trouble with most people is they won't spend any time in preparation. They want to climb up on the box and drive. No wonder they get in trouble. Where's that Howlett?"

"George," she said, "thank you so much."

"What for?"

"For the gloves. They're beautiful."

"Oh, they're all right," he said. "Where's Howlett?"

"Over there," she said, "on the shelf beside the dictionary."

He swung around Fitz-Greene's leather chair. Mechanically, she stepped up on the seat and sat on the broad back. She was glad to have him stay at any price. Serious and satisfied, he handed her the practice reins. "Where's that cane," he said, "that we use for a whip?"

She was content, she thought, to have him stay at any price.

But in the middle of the lesson, at a moment when he had stopped to peer into Howlett, abruptly she saw herself. She saw herself, most desolate and doomed of all mankind, perched like an ape or an infant on the high back of a chair and wrestling solemnly, endlessly with a game of make-believe. What if she learned to manage these reins attached to silly wooden spindles? It was a ghastly farce, the antics of a demented corpse that should long ago have been hidden away. And to what end? To fit her for other antics on the coach, equally grotesque and meaningless.

"Now," George said, "here it is. For a right turn, you take up the whip and the off-side leader's rein in your right hand. That's your point, of course. But as you do it, with one motion you make a four-inch loop with the near side wheeler's rein over your thumb. Otherwise——"

She slid down the leather chair back and sat bolt upright, staring stupidly at the Windsor chairs and the tangle of practice reins on the floor. She heard the book close and his voice, "What's the matter? Had enough?" His tone changed. "What are you looking at?" He had her by the shoulders. His voice seemed like a shout. "Clara!"

"I don't care," she said. "Not about anything."

"Clara," he said, "old lady."

"He hated me," she said.

His hands were light on her shoulders. "No, he didn't," he said. "He never did."

She looked beyond him at the tangled reins along the floor. "Go away, George," she said, "and let me alone."

He took his hands from her shoulders. His footfalls sounded. So he was going away, too. And now it made no difference. Nothing made any difference except the sound of flowing water in her ears.

The footfalls came back. They passed her by and turned again. He was walking up and down.

On the carpet, his firm, light footfalls sounded. To and fro, in a slow, unbroken rhythm.

Why did he not go home? It made no difference, his being here. They were no longer together, not remotely. She sat alone in her cold, uttermost pit, walled in and buried, lost forever to the world of warmth and light. And he, helpless, too, and utterly at a loss, tramped aimlessly an endless road that turned forever on itself and led back whence it came. However grieved for her, he still was in the land of living men and from that bright and lovely world so far above her, he never could reach down to her abyss.

Yet in the end, his tramping eased her tension. She felt the lassitude which follows the immense and horrible excitement of despair. She sank back in the chair.

He kept on walking. The sound of his footsteps slowly eased her. She was lost to him and to all other beings; but in that world above, from which she had been harried, his footsteps never ceased in their unhappy search for her.

From her cold prison she must try to reach him while there yet was time, before his search had ceased, before she lost the will, before whatever lay ahead of her might put it beyond the power of her to speak or of him to hear.

"George," she said. "Where is he now, do you think?"

The footsteps ceased. "I don't know," he said, "but I think he's all right. Absolutely."

"Do you think I'll ever see him again?"

"Yes," he said, "I think that, too."

"If I did, do you think he might feel differently toward me, if he knew why I had come? Would a man ever do that, do you think?" She stopped.

His eyes were on her. "Had come—?" his voice was low. "You love him still then."

She nodded. "I suppose I ought to feel ashamed." She clasped her hands to keep them steady. "I don't know what I'll do."

"There's nothing you can do. Nothing." His look was kindly but official. "Try to forget. Be brave."

"Be brave!" she said. "What for? If he were here there would be something to be brave for. Why should I be brave? Why should I even stay here?"

"Stay here?"

"Yes, why should I? Can't there be that much freedom?" Her voice turned sad, "Can't there be that much freedom?"

He was tramping again. Fast. Now his eyes were on her. He stopped in front of her.

"He loved you."

He started walking.

"Please, George," she said. "Remember I told you everything, here in this room, the night you made the tea."

"You don't think I've forgotten? Only I thought that things were better so."

"Better so?"

"Well, it was over and done with and if you thought what you did, it might make things easier. You see," he said, "we sort of agreed he wasn't much and that it was for the best."

"Yes," she said, "I know, and I got a little angry. Now you can say what you like about him, and I wouldn't mind. It would be too small a thing to make a difference." She shook her head sadly. "It would be nothing."

"I wouldn't say anything against him now," he said.

"You forgive him then? I am glad."

"Yes," he said heavily, "I forgive him. Because he loved you."

"You keep on saying that," she said, sharply. "Do you think it makes me happy to be treated like a child? Nothing can make me happy," she said, "but I should be treated like a woman."

Queerly, because of this trivial offense against her dignity, she began to cry. He came and sat down on the arm of the chair and took her cold, heavy hand. "I guess that's right," he said. He stood up and fell to walking again. "Do you know what really happened," he said, "at all?"

"I told you," she said.

"That's all you know?"

"What more is there?"

"There's more," he said.

"If there's some one else," she said, "I don't want to hear about her."

"There was no one else," he said. "Ever. No one ever; but you."

"This is what happened," he said. "I have found it out, piece by piece." His footsteps quickened. "When you were first married, things didn't go so well, for a while. You told me that."

"Yes," she said sadly, "I know, I know."

"Well, he took it hard. I guess he didn't understand."

"I was the one who didn't understand. It was my fault."

"No. Things take time. He didn't understand."

"I know; but that was at first. Things changed. I changed. I thought we were very happy. In every way. I thought he was happy."

"So he was. Completely happy. That's what made it so bad."

"What are you saying to me?"

"I'm trying to say what I found out."

"Go on," she said. "I don't mind what you say."

"I found out that, once when things weren't going well, he was in Philadelphia and he got to drinking at the club. Some of the fellows there told me about it. I had a hard time to get them to talk."

"Go on," she said. "You can say anything."

"He drank too much and then he talked too much. He had the idea that you didn't care for him in the way he did for you. He talked too much. Then suddenly he stopped and after that he left the club. The next time any one saw him was next morning. He showed up at his mother's still in his dress clothes and still drunk."

"When was this?"

"In October. He came home next day."

"In October. That was the beginning of our happiness. He seemed so sad when he got back. It made me love him. Then we were happy. He was happy, I thought."

"And so he was. Remember that. And so he was. But the next thing I found out was from the doctors."

"From the doctors?"

"Yes. From some doctors in Philadelphia no one had ever heard of. He had come to see them, about Christmas time, several different ones, under a false name."

"So he was sick. But he should have told me. He should have gone to Doctor Hartman."

"He was ashamed. That night had done for him."

"Well, but I don't see——"

He turned, red and almost brutal. He almost shouted. "He had been—with God knows who. Anybody—they hang around the clubs—" He dropped his voice. "Then two months later, or so, he found that— That was when he went to the doctors. And all last winter he was going to them. Frantically. And all the time he was getting worse. He got it in his head his mind was going to be affected. In a sense, perhaps, it was. In the end, he couldn't stand it. He loved you so."

He pressed his hand against his face. "Well," he said, "I guess that's all."

She was across the room and had him by the shoulders. "George," she said, "is that true?"

"Yes," he said. "It's exactly true."

Her arms went round his shoulders. She fixed him with her eyes. "So then he loved me."

He nodded. Heavily he cleared his throat. "Ah," he said.

"Poor Fitz," she said. "Oh, Fitz." Then suddenly, "Why didn't some one tell me?"

"No one knew."

"Right at the start. I wouldn't have cared."

"Clara, no one knew."

"Why didn't he tell me? I wouldn't have cared."

"Now then," he said. "Poor old lady." He took her hand in his. "That would have been impossible."

CHAPTER XXX

In the sunny dining room, Christobel, her hair and freckles bright copper above her light-blue dress, her arms akimbo, surveyed what was left of the fried mush and syrup.

"I haven't seen you eat like that since—in a long time." She flushed. "I guess though, it just kind of wears itself out, and then one day you find you're a little better. More coffee? Starving don't help trouble."

"I know," Clara said, "you always say that."

"But you don't listen."

"Christobel," Clara said, "you have been wonderful to me. You have been."

"Oh, shucks," Christobel said. "I never had any trouble with you, excusing about this eating," she paused unhappily, "since the trouble came. And I don't blame you for that. Honestly I ain't eating right myself.

"That fellow of mine," Christobel said, "wants me to go to dances and all such, and he thinks there's something wrong with me, I guess. And if I told him what it was, that wouldn't help either. He'd think there was something wrong with me for sure."

"Oh, but you ought to have a good time."

Christobel looked at her gravely. "Sure I ought to," she said. "But how am I to do it?"

"Pull up a chair, Christobel," Clara said, "and have a cup of coffee."

From the wall, Christobel pushed up a chair. "Well," she muttered, "I guess no one will come in."

Turning in her seat, Clara reached a cup and saucer from the sideboard. "What if they do?" she said. "You take two lumps?"

In her front bedroom, after breakfast, she did not need to look out at the familiar sound of Norah's trot. As she buttoned up her long black coat before the mirror, she heard the wheel of the spider scrape against the curb and stop. Putting on her gloves, she went to the window and looked down on the fringed canopy and on Norah's neat, fat, shining back, on the brass terrets, check-rein, hook and brow-band, twinkling in the morning sun. Levi Mistletoe, in his massive mourning band, stood at her head, allowing her to nibble at the straining buttons of his steel-gray coat.

She stopped in the dining room to get two lumps of sugar from the white, rose-circled bowl on the sideboard. With her gloves on, she had to tip the bowl to get the small square lumps out. From the dining-room table she took a long, narrow cardboard box.

"Good morning, Levi," she said, as she stepped out on the wet and freshly scrubbed marble doorstep. He touched his hat.

"Miss Clara," he said, with a sad smile, "it's a mighty nice morning."

"Yes," she said, "it is, Levi."

She handed him the box. Norah tossed her tufted forelock; she nickered soundlessly and stretched out her small, slim neck. Her little muzzle, very black against the bright bay of her head, ran swiftly over Clara's coat, wavered, hung at the pocket, then nudged her earnestly. Her mouse-like ears were pricked, her eyes were fixed in soft intensity. Clara pulled out a lump of sugar. It was deftly picked off the palm of her hand.

Levi stowed the box under the seat. Walking sedately on his wide, lumpy shoes, he came back to Norah's head. "Now, then," he said, "don't you slobber your juice on me." He smoothed a stray hair on the shining, even wave of Norah's mane. Norah shook her mane impatiently, leaving matters worse than before. "Once she get her sugar," Levi said, "she don't care about nobody."

"I know," Clara said, "she's a little pig."

"No, she ain't, Miss Clara," Levi said. "She's the smartest, most pleasant little horse I ever had. We going up the river this morning, Miss Clara?" Levi now looked forward to parading before the little boys of Billy-goat Town.

"No, Levi," she said. "To-day I am going to the cemetery."

Levi lowered his eyes. "Yes, ma'am," he said, "yes, Miss Clara."

As Clara went back to the spider, Norah gently but firmly thrust Levi's bulk aside and turned to look at her.

The light damp of morning still lay on the dust of the road. Two blocks up the street, they turned from the wide, shining river into the light tracery made by the young spring leaves on

Poplar Street. They passed, set back in its narrow yard of old hydrangea bushes, the little house painted bilious brown, where Fitz-Greene used to board. It was on that porch that he had sat the day they went on the canal steamboat picnic. In his suit of light pongee, he had leaned back on the porch seat, his long legs crossed, inspecting his thin cigar. The sun lay golden on his hair. She had been a little afraid of him then and a little suspicious of his grateful, amused perfection. The spider's wheels bumped lightly across the rails of the horse-car line. Here they had met Good Doggie and Big Sister.

The street of commonplace respectability ended with the tree that was encased in wire against the nibbling of the corner grocer's horse. Then came the block of railroad men, all black except for the noble gold and red of the bock beer sign.

At the end of the street, the old figure with his dirty flag still kept watch over the railroad crossing. It seemed incredible that he could have survived her disaster. What was it Fitz-Greene had said? "A salute to the flag." She believed that she remembered every word that he had spoken, every look and gesture. It was hard not to imagine that they were crossing the railroad tracks now. "Nothing ever happens to the man who salutes all flags." "Don't you want anything to happen to you?" "Not at a railroad crossing." Big Sister trudged beside her. George was with Ellen. Levi and the picnic basket came behind. It was not hard to imagine all of them. The feat was to imagine that Levi was behind her on the dickey, that she was driving Norah; that Fitz-Greene was dead.

The road turned off before it reached the blackened coal dock from which they had set out that day—how dreadful Mun had been with Levi and the hats. It ran beside the dark still water, then swung and humped abruptly over the canal. As Norah's small, goat-like feet thumped on the wooden planking, Clara remembered that the man in charge of the steamboat had tilted back the smokestack, passing under here.

They passed a scattering of chaotic and amorphous houses of people who lived neither in the country nor in the town, but had created an ambiguous world that was deficient in everything, even in reality. The color of the houses, once evidently painted, was indeterminate and their structure, lacking the bizarre and disorderly distinction of Billy-goat Town, was merely commonplace and uniform. It was even difficult, amid the dilapidation of the yards and porches, to tell which houses were inhabited; though pale children staring at her with thumbs in dirty mouths, gave evidence that this unhappy and exiled race not only existed, but was capable of reproducing its kind.

With the mounting of the road, the limbo ceased abruptly. The road was purified; it led, bright-red and lightly dusty, up a long hill between grave oaks. The harness creaked, Norah's stout little back bent to the task.

At the top of the hill, white marble spectres showed among the farthest trunks. She came to an old board fence, loaded with vines of honeysuckle that had lost its bloom. A wooden gate leaned open. She turned off through it into a grassy lane.

The trees were left behind and far below her. Creaking softly, the spider moved through the long field of marble fragments. Cherubs and crosses crowned enormous deep-cut names. Polished granite raised urns and angels to the impassive sky. Fences of iron and of stone and padlocked gates continued to protect the wealthiest inhabitants in their possessions. Here and there flowers withered in glass jars and little cotton flags, already faded, awaited renewing on next Decoration Day. In the distance, an ancient figure with a rake moved slowly through the stony chaos. If he saw them, he made no sign.

Near the far end, where beside the caretaker's chapel-like stone house the proper road came in, she halted. That was the road by which she and the long train of dark carriages had come before.

"All right, Levi," she said. "This will do."

Treading delicately, Levi went to Norah's head. His hat was in his hand. She stepped out on the grass. Lifting the weighted curtain that hung under the seat, she took the cardboard box. She walked down a grassy path, between stone fragments, great and small, that strove with mottoes and devices against oblivion.

Where the hill began to fall away, old Rands, disdaining the generality, maintained their accustomed solidarity and distinction by slabs of deep red granite. Just beyond, the hill dropped off steeply. She went down three rough stone steps to a narrow terrace.

The stone was simply a low square of marble, still new, and sparkling in the sunlight. There was no mound—George had agreed to that—merely a pale oblong in the sod where many little blades of grass were pushing through the tawny earth. In the centre lay a withered sheaf of stalks. She picked them up and laid them to one side against the low retaining wall. She opened the cardboard box. The golden tulips glowed. She put them in the centre of the young spring grass and straightened up. This was folly. He was not here. Wherever he was, he was not here, and what was here would not bear thinking of.

Some of the tulips had fallen awry. She took her gloves off slowly and stooped again. With her fingers, she altered and straightened them so that all lay in a wide and level sheaf. Each one showed bright above its pale smooth leaves.

It was this act that brought her to her knees. The graveyard; the hill, the known world were swallowed in the mist. With demented and endless persistence, she knelt in the damp earth arranging the tulips in his honor, utterly alone.

She rose up stiffly and sat down on the low retaining wall. The cardboard box lay upturned and incongruous beside the grave. And on the grave itself, her blinded efforts had only left the tulips askew. She must straighten them before she left.

Below her, the tops of the nearest oaks reached almost to where she sat. She looked down over them at the spires of the town and at the roofs making planes of light and shadow among the tufted trees. Beyond them, the river gleamed under the low, blue hills against the sky. She sat beside his grave and looked down on the world she knew. This pleasant town, these hills, this broad, bright river, had seen her beginning and some day would see her end. There in that shallow bowl, she had been a child. She had spun tops and paddled in shoal water under the eye of a nurse long dead and half forgotten. She must have been a nice and gay child. Then she had been a girl, of course, and, it seems, had stayed a girl too long. Into her life of shyly curious dreams, of unconscious waiting, of trance-like seclusion, he had flashed; like the story of the Sleeping Beauty. Only she had not wakened wholly, or had wakened too late. That, not the trance, was the curse that had been laid upon her.

Perhaps a different mother might have prepared her. Even a different father might have done so, somehow, at least a little. There was no reason why a father should not help his child, especially when he was omniscient. But now the poor dear bear's omniscience had departed. He was still loved, but now she seemed the elder, and he, an adorable sweet-natured child, wise at the little games at which he played, but at a loss in the larger fields which she had travelled. And somehow even his shining, too, had been dimmed by traces of blame for her disaster. Though when it came to blame, the inescapable bulk fell on herself. More courage, less fastidious and naïve disdain of the strong earth in us, in our hearts and in our loins; more courage would have saved her, and him. It had come, at last, but, as it turned out, not in time. She had been punished, she would say it here among the dead, or on any other consecrated ground, out of all reason, for her fault. And yet it was the fault that brought the punishment. She looked down at the yellow tulips.

And so it was with him. Not with him here, with what this well-constructed coffin held, and what must be—she would not think of it—but with his bright spirit, which still lovely, unblemished, tender, graceful, existed somewhere, if only in her heart. What iron vengeance had been dealt to him. They were two children in the vast inscrutable universe, whose little blunders of ignorance and weakness had brought down the lightning.

Why could he not have told her? Why must he hide his shame? What was love for if not for a refuge in all possible disaster? Why could he not have told her? But then why could she not have guessed? Ignorant to the last, always to the last too weak, inadequate for each succeeding crisis. But stop. She would not let herself be caught in this tormented futile round. She would not be weak.

Against an oak tree, rising down below her, a flicker rapped incisively. Head cocked, he listened, rapped again. From deeper in the wood a song sparrow raised his delicate, brief notes. Pure, fragile clouds sailed slowly overhead; beside her feet the ants were busy. And, in between, the sunlight filled the soft mild air. The world fulfilled itself, went on, lovely, mysterious, unhurried, alert and sentient, yet blind, and blind yet undismayed. She would not be weak.

And she would not be bitter. Not bitter—she must remember her dark night and then look on this summer day. For she, against all hope, had been given back from beyond the grave her lover. She clasped her hands against her breasts. Poor dear, poor sweet, once lost and maimed and harried to despair, she had him now within her, shining and lovely and safe from harm.

CHAPTER XXXI

Against the hospital window, the granite block of night showed the first faint traces of deterioration. Only the merest dimming of its polished density. But soon the black would come to fade, and then the gray, in turn, dissolve before the first unearthly premonition of the sun. It was the death-like hour, the hour when night had lost its vigor and day was not yet born; the hour when things that were doomed and failing died, and when all things living, if asleep, lay suspended in a scarcely breathing trance, and if awake, were touched by desolation and fears, and by dim intimations of outer darkness.

And yet, for him, lying in the tall stiff bed on rubber wheels, the hour held no threat. Perhaps the fate which now enveloped him conferred immunity to any petty fears or dangers. Most likely, though, the story which he had told himself and which had unrolled itself so lucidly, so beautifully, so swiftly in his mind, had carried him to some safe haven, vaguely defined perhaps, and enigmatic, but giving a sense of shelter and of hope.

Even if the haven in which he found comfort were illusory, nothing could take from him the stimulation of the voyage. Embarking dubiously, as he had, on scarcely charted seas, he had found his course undeviating. Picked up in fragments from different sources, he had reconstructed the story of his Aunt Clara; the early story, at least. There was more to come; for now he, so far only a child who hid under the Christmas table with his bagpipes, would be on the scene. From now on, what he had to tell himself would be first hand. He could not say that it would offer any answer. It would not go far toward telling him what principle controlled the ever-flowing stream of life or the ever-elusive mystery beyond. But it would show that he was able, or that some power was able, to provide material of a kind that might lead to some sort of discovery.

The gray outside his window soon would turn to green. He was tired and relaxed, content with what the night had brought him. In a few hours now, authority would see to it that he shaved and brushed his teeth. The hospital was utterly quiet. He turned on his side and laid his head on his outstretched arm. Poor Clara; Fitz-Greene, gay and doomed; Grandfather Rand, obtuse and all-providing; and others of that older generation, once solemnly revered and now long dead; he had them here with him, seen now as brave and touching children, to comfort him and give him courage.

BOOK TWO

TOWARD MORNING

CHAPTER XXXII

DURING the day, there had been no change. No change at least, so far as he was aware, in himself. The change, if there was any, lay in authority, in whose competent and fundamentally indifferent hands he was drifting. The news, which his body had told the doctor the day before, apparently had spread. Another doctor, a shy enigmatic doctor with a very black mustache against a white face had come in during the morning, and made elaborate soundings with a stethoscope around the region of his heart. He, himself, had been called on to breathe deeply, breathe not so deeply, breathe naturally, and to say ninety-nine. Deftly looping up his stethoscope, and remarking, "Good, very good," the strange doctor had departed with his enigmatic smile. In all this there was nothing portentous. The whole procedure might have happened to any one. The change was, rather, in the attitude of the familiar ministrants; of his special nurse; of the orderly, a pimpled youth who bore shrouded bedpans with a decorous piety worthy of a sacrament; of the floor superintendent's starched majesty, and of the ancient, lame ex-jockey who brought the morning and evening papers. Beneath their accustomed and mechanical attitude, he detected a trace of what might best be called professional reverence to which, it was agreed, the state into which he had entered entitled him.

This, after all, was as it should be. Authority could not be expected to expend emotion on every instance of an endlessly repeated phenomenon. And even if it could, such sympathy from strangers, hired for another purpose, would be only embarrassing.

He lay now, once again, in the cave of night, secure and safe and free. Again the silence of the hospital was broken only rarely by light, impersonal footfalls on the corridor's rubber floor. Once the creeping wagon's rubber wheels had gone by.

Inside the room, the crack of light from the door, held just ajar, was enough to show, as a blur in the easy chair, the white skirt and cap, and between them the dark cloak of Miss—who?

263

Miss Wesson, was it? Not that it made the slightest difference. When she first came on, this evening, he had resented her. He wanted no night nurse to destroy his privacy. He thought he had made that sufficiently clear to her; but, to his annoyance, she had, professionally or otherwise, remained oblivious to his hostility. In fact, she had unbent sufficiently to tell him about her brother who had scored the touchdown for Atlantic Christian against Wofford last year. In the end, they were beaten fifty-eight to six, but it had been years since Atlantic Christian had scored on Wofford at all. All this, it turned out, was in South Carolina.

So, then, he was about to be launched into Eternity knowing, of all things, the score of last year's Atlantic Christian-Wofford game. A pity Heaven was not as he had conceived it as a child. In that case, he would have counted on getting in with the old Atlantic Christian men.

But now, after a certain hour when all the big lights in the hospital went out, her function was merely to sit there. She was a mere outpost of authority who, like all authority, had intrinsically nothing to do with him. During these hours, according to the rules, she was at liberty to think about her brother at Atlantic Christian, or about any other matters; but she was not allowed to mention them to him. And he, on his side, was granted the night's immunity from interference, granted the freedom, if he were able to achieve it, of his own mind.

CHAPTER XXXIII

His own life, of course, began with the moment when his Aunt Clara had held out her leghorn hat with the baby sparrow motionless in its depths. Then came the other scenes with her; the drive in the buggy, the splashing water of the river, the story of the page boys' escape from the papier maché castle, the ride, caverned in night and solitude and power, on the tufted shuffling bear. Once, a toy soldier he was melting over a gas jet had exploded and a splash of lead had fallen on his finger and burned it to the bone. The pain had seared and jarred him, but not so much so as the terror. He had done wrong. He had hurt himself. He would be found out and scolded. And so it was. If it were light in this room he could see the oval scar, a symbol like a memory of an event, now incredibly distant, that could never return. Once, he had thrown a snowball through a neighbor's window and run home desperately pursued by the footsteps of imaginary cops, in through the wooden gate, along a narrow alley-way; the dirty gray back porch, the yellow kitchen cabinets flashed by. Making the turn in the front hall, he almost fell on the skidding rug. He was home now, but he could not stop running. In the library of many books and one wide bay window, he found his mother. She wept, and said he had disgraced her. He must go to his room and stay there. That was the last he ever heard of the affair. He imagined that it had taken him a long while to realize that the incident was closed; he remembered sitting on his window-seat that afternoon watching for the cops, a child of seven, perhaps, with brownish somewhat curly hair above a thin blue-veined neck, and big gray eyes, credulous and shamed, peering out between the muslin curtains.

From then on, for years, nothing seemed to happen. It was as though he had spent them all watching for the cops.

Once, in a great crowd, he had sat on a hot and flimsy board holding Levi Mistletoe's fat hand. Crouched figures in bright jerseys flashed by on racing bicycles, and came in view again against a distant high board fence whose lettering he still could see: "Wise Buyers Buy Barnes White Fliers." Once in the night, he had heard a solemn thrilling rumble, and run to the window of his room. At first, all had seemed dark, but hanging far out in his canton flannel nightrobe, high above the street, he had seen under the corner arc light, paling before the dawn, the shapes of circus wagons rolling up the river road.

Behind these episodes stood as the one firm element of his life Susan Tarr from Fauquier County, Virginia; old and pretty and almost white, with rimless spectacles that she was forever breathing on and wiping, and a sweet, clear voice, soft but ringing. She used to tell how her father worked in the tanyard for Mr. Harrison and brought home boots with red tops for all her brothers. And she had one song she used to sing:

> "Two little niggers upstairs in bed.
> One turned round to the other and said,
> 'How 'bout that shortening bread.
> How 'bout that shortening bread?'"

She would pat him lightly while she sang. "You're my baby," she would say. "You certainly are my baby." She thought that everything he did was perfect and that everything his father and mother did was perfect. And when he and his father and mother disagreed she could not explain it.

Then one day he was sitting at his seat in the row of empty desks. He should have been able to remember his first day at school, but he did not. This was long after. Miss Bletchley was talking to him. It was a warm, rich day of spring and he had been kept in. Outside children were playing hopscotch and shad flies crawled across the mellow bricks. The echo of Miss Bletchley's English adenoids was in his ears. She wore pince-nez and a shapeless, colorless waist of flannel. A gold chain led from her pince-nez to a little black pill box on the front of this waist. When she took off her pince-nez the pill box, reeling in the chain, held the glasses dangling in front of her flat chest. He was being kept in because he had not learned the county towns of England. But Miss Bletchley was talking about Deric. Deric had been her private pupil before she had come out to the States. Afterwards he had gone on and won the silver cricket bat. Out here the marmalade was horrid and men wore pot hats with morning coats; and no one, not even he, knew the county towns of England.

Those county towns came into it again. He had learned them in the end. And then one morning in the dining room with all the golden-oak spindles and spiral columns over the mantelpiece, his father had given the paper a shake, and fixed him with his eye. "What's the capital of Illinois?"

"It's Chicago." Covertly he searched his father's face. "I don't know," he whispered.

"Don't know? What do you learn at school? It costs two hundred dollars to send you there."

"I know the county towns."

"County towns! What county towns?"

"The county towns of England."

The paper came down with a slap. "Good——"

"Now, George," his mother said, "the boy must learn what he is taught."

His father had stuck the folded paper under his arm and marched from the room. There were sounds of a whisk-broom on a derby hat in the front hall. His father's voice came in the room. "He's ten years old, and doesn't know the capital of Illinois."

"It's Springfield, dear," his mother whispered.

He steadied his voice. "Springfield!" he called out. The front door closed behind his father with a solemn bang.

He was perhaps ten years old then, yet he did not remember his mother much before this moment when she had defended him against that august presence and that heavy banging door. At that moment he could see her in her neat brown serge with puffed sleeves, her sharp, yet child-like nose pointed down at her plate, her firm small mouth compressed inscrutably, but her brown eyes filled with swift protecting anger in his behalf. He had always been conscious of her as a voice, a disembodied presence, a central abstraction of the cosmos, but only that. There was no loneliness or sense of deprivation, he accepted his isolation as in the natural order and did not need to explain it as he explained it now by recalling that in this time a younger sister had been born, had lived three years and died.

On Friday evenings, he used to put on his Eton collar and his plaid necktie. With plenty of water, Susan Tarr slicked down his hair. "Now you look elegant. A fine little gentleman." He walked to the corner, then down the river front to the dove-gray house on whose white door a silver nameplate bore the name 'Rankin.' He pulled the silver bell handle. The brilliance of the marble step reminded him to scrape his feet. Generally Aunt Clara, herself, would open the door. "Hello there," she would say in a high ringing voice just like another boy. She would stand smiling, very tall and slender. After supper in the upstairs library, he sat across the checkerboard from her, his well-filled stomach pressing tight against the inside of his clothes. Then he lay on the floor turning over the pages of bound "Harper's Weeklies." Little engines puffed over trestles; a paddle steamer labored in a gale; buckskin men chased buffalo. But for the most part, level lines of small soldiers in cape coats all ran in step together. Their guns all slanted evenly; a flag waved in the middle; in the sky neat puffs of smoke made cotton balls. It was a thrilling, beautiful and orderly affair. What happened next, he hardly visualized; but apparently all was simple and triumphant. Aunt Clara, where requested, read the captions: "Union Troops Carrying the Rebel Lines at Spottsylvania Court House." "Union Troops Assaulting the Rebel Position at Vicksburg."

Sometimes he would be asked not only for supper, but to spend the night.

Up in the bedroom where the eaves sloped back from the sides of the dormer window he unpacked his small black satchel, laid his flannel pajamas on the pink quilt and his hair brush on the bureau under the oval mirror beside the military brushes, whose black backs bore the letters 'F.-G. R.' They had been Uncle Fitz-Greene's; that smiling figure already fading in his mind, but standing for jokes and teasing and Christmas dinners; another boy, like his Aunt Clara and himself.

Under the eaves he thought about Uncle Fitz. He, himself, was not allowed to go out alone on the frozen winter river like the other boys. He could only go when young Sam could get off and go with him. And so even when he went he had no standing with the other boys. "Hey, fellows," they hollered, "here comes Percy with his valet." And all because his uncle Fitz-Greene had been drowned between the islands. Only once on the river had there been a satisfying moment. The boy had had a white face and separated teeth above his red-wool tippet. He had

swooped at him—"Hey, Percy!" and knocked him down heavily.
"Hey, Percy!" they had shouted, "Clear the track!" The white-
faced boy had swooped at him again. What he had done he did
not know—stooped down somehow and made a grab; sharp
skates struck on his chest, the boy's head bounced and rang along
the ice. He came up sick and breathless—there lay the white-
faced boy. A spasm gripped his heart; what had he done? But
then the boy began to blink. A great wave lifted him. "Clear
the track!" he shouted insanely, "Clear the track!" With savage
yells the other boys closed in. Luckily here came young Sam.
Though that too was frightening. Young Sam's eyes rolled, he
jabbered from a trembling mouth; the boys went spinning or fled
away. All the way home he and Sam skated slowly, hand in
hand, disdaining the cat-calls and cries, "Percy, the Punk!" "Black
ape, black ape!" Back in the house Sam still was jabbering,
"Ninth Ward white trash, Alley cats." But Susan Tarr, putting
witch-hazel bandages on the two enormous bruises on his veined,
narrow chest, lashed out. "You Sam. Look what you done. Let
them 'buse my baby." Behind the spectacles, the gentle eyes
caught fire. "What you for, man?" It had been scaring, this
glimpse of Sam and Susan. So then, unguessed violence and wild
passionate life crouched beneath the smooth crust that he lived on.

In the end his mother heard of the adventure. She was sad.
To fight was not truly Christian. He must promise not to. His
chest was hurting now; he promised, feeling pure and noble.
He had thrown down a bigger boy; it might not turn out that
way next time. He had better be a Christian now and stay away
from the river for a while. There was, it seemed, much wickedness and sadness in the world and he would do well to prepare
for it and for unknown distant judgments and rewards. For
Uncle Fitz with his jokes, his quick eyes and bright head had
been carried to the cemetery one wet, raw winter day. He, himself, had sat beside his black-swathed mother on the damp, rank
carriage cushions. He had stood in the cluster of umbrellas among
the wet, white stones and wet, dark earth and watched the box,
where Uncle Fitz now lay beneath flowers, creep slowly down
into the dark abyss. It had been a solemn moment but beyond
reality. Far more actual had been the spell which seemed to fall
upon his aunt. He saw her seldom and only at a distance; her
dress was black, her face was white and cold; if she saw him she

made no sign. One day, though, in the spring when he was playing in front of his house she had come to him and put a little
cast iron locomotive in his hand and smiled; that portion of his
world was bright again.

And then their own house had been hushed, and on the
stairs he had heard the thick, deep whispers of Dr. Hartman
and of Dr. Considine and, aimless, helpless and unending, his
baby sister's feeble cry. Susan Tarr had packed his satchel
and he had been brought over at night to this room at his
Aunt Clara's and had lain as he lay now, his eyes fixed on
the ghostly ceiling sloping over his bed, frightened and solemn
and also sustained by a horrible elation. That little bundle, ever
since she came, had been the centre of the universe. He had not
minded much, in fact, he had discovered that indifference to himself, desolating enough at first, had practical advantages. But
now the bundle held the centre to some good purpose. A rustling
nurse in eye-glasses was in the house, and on Linden Street, in
front of their door, straw was laid down dramatically for all the
world to see. At school he was a person of distinction and
teachers treated him with great gentleness. When a doctor in a
black frock coat came from Philadelphia on the fast express, it
raised him to a height from which he never fell until he saw his
mother's dreadful face and his father staring at him with working
lips.

Again the train of hacks moved to the stone-crowned hill
behind the town; again the people stood around the hole, and a
box, this time a small one, drifted out of sight. His mother
shockingly, incredibly, began to babble like a child and people
closed in swiftly on her with hushed, firm words and shut her
off from him.

That day in spring, among the marble fragments on the hill,
had wrought its changes, dimly felt at first. The jingling coach
no longer made the sharp turn into Linden Street, a burst of
unbelievable glory from the narrow alleyway. His father never
wore his gray top hat, his white, long coat and leather-strapped,
tan apron. His father did not sit in the library on Sunday afternoons reading the Sunday papers and throwing the big sheets,
one by one, on the floor where he lay studying the pictures of
battleships and dressed-up ladies, of floods and fires and baseball
teams; instead, his father went with his mother down to the

church on the city square and he, himself, labored all afternoon with Susan Tarr over Bible verses and the Shorter Catechism. All magazines and books were put away. For entertainment, there were the stories from the "Lesson Illustrator" and "McKay of Uganda," given him by his mother, a book wherein a good old gentleman had brought the savage blacks to a knowledge of God with far less incident than might be reasonably expected. The book, which was a disappointment to him, was also, surprisingly, an offense to Susan Tarr. She declined to help him read it or even to look at the pictures of the grass-girdled black men surrounding the intrepid missionary.

By dint of his determination he formed a confused, though solemn, notion of the world. There were the heathen whose only hope lay in rescue by Dr. McKay. There were Catholics, mostly found in ignorant and backward places, unscrupulous in method and idolaters. There were Episcopalians whose amiable frivolity and dependence on tasteful ritual and polite forms debarred them from serious consideration. There were also Methodists and Baptists, but they, in general, were found entrenched in the less desirable sections of the town. They were prone, besides, to allow emotional excesses to take the place of hard, straight thinking.

This hard, straight thinking whose monopoly lay most fortunately with his own family and their church, was unable to prevent extreme confusion in his mind. They alone were the elect—that much was clear—he and his father and mother and the other Presbyterians. Within this hierarchy his Grandfather Rand, he gathered, occupied a somewhat dubious ground. His Grandfather had been baptized a Presbyterian but had, in a sense, let it go at that. He contributed to the church and rented a pew, but only on condition, apparently, that except on certain high occasions he should not be required to go there.

For the most part, however, their position was assured. But what that position was often puzzled him. There was Jesus, meek and mild, Who taught that one must have no traffic with the world, no riches, no impulse to resist. If one believed on Him and followed Him, salvation was assured; and after death one dwelt, enrobed, in a city of luxurious magnificence whose jeweled gates and minarets and golden streets bordered a river swifter, deeper, purer than that which flowed along the banks of River Street.

But Jesus, Himself, was the Son of a God of a very different temper—a God of judgments, One of wrath, a God Who led His faithful into war and by His miracles destroyed their enemies horribly, a God Who set great bears to rend and eat the little boys who mocked Elijah. The picture of that scene dwelt in his mind and, as with the pictures of his "Slovenly Peter," from time to time he reverted to feed on it with a sickening, yet unappeasable, hunger. Great, shaggy shoulders came from the dark wood; small evil eyes were fixed and mouths were open. The little boys fled screaming. The prophet walked away indifferent.

So then, this God of bears and plagues and battles must also be worshipped too. In fact, He, together with a Personage, far more obscure and vaguely terrifying, Whose name, the Holy Ghost, conveyed a vision which more than offset the effect of His other name, the Comforter, were both at one with Jesus—were, in fact, identical.

All this, however, must be believed if he were to reach the Holy City and see his Uncle Fitz and his baby sister again. Otherwise, down in the bowels there was Hell where, amid smoke and flames and tortured nakedness, forever rose the wailing and the gnashing of teeth. It was this last thought which consoled him when, on summer afternoons toiling over his Shorter Catechism beside the open window, he heard the shouts of Catholic boys, of Episcopalian boys and of unsaved boys in general as they swam in the river.

From all these doctrinal anomalies little comfort was at best derived. Comfort and pleasure came from ideas of his own. He found that they, however fragmentary, were more palatable and more sustaining than anything offered by authority. Visions of hell for the unregenerate and mother-of-pearl minarets for himself were well enough as solaces for life's minor irritations. But for refuge against the profound and irreparable tragedies of his intense, ever-confident, yet ever-baffled life within, his best defenses were his dreams. There were many thrusts to parry. Each day at best was an anticlimax, could not help but be; what day could satisfy his hopes as he woke up and saw the sun through the muslin curtains or lay close in warmth and safety, hearing the rain impotent on the armor of black and shining slates? What day could offer the color and adventure that would match his waking hopes? There were moments; the day when he launched his new sled on the sparkling crest, the day when the new boy across the street brought over his engine that would run, the Christmas morning when he opened the basket and the puppy looked at him through tangled hair and wriggled joyfully. Up on the farm too, with Aunt Clara there were many moments; his fishing line went under fiercely, he tugged and hollered, but before young Sam could come there was a white shape in the air and on the bank lay the biggest catfish man had ever seen; and the steamboat made by his grandfather's Samuel, who stood beside him utterly disguised in sleeve garters and a hard straw hat; the alcohol burned blue and for a long time nothing happened, then there was a wheezy tapping, the paddle wheel turned, the flatboat teetered slowly out into the pond. Even on less eventful days great happiness was about to be his. It was only by evening that the passage of the day was seen to be irrevocable and that he must admit that nothing worthy of his morning's hopes had happened. Night in his bed, between the saying of his prayers beside his mother and the coming of sleep, was apt to be a time of sadness.

Then, far surpassing life's monotonous inadequacy, were the abrupt and piercing strokes of fate; the morning radiant with cowboys and Indians and the street parade, the storm at lunch that quenched the promised trip with young Sam to Buffalo Bill's Wild West Show. The day that he had, utterly incredibly, found the puppy stiff and blank-eyed in its basket. They had offered him another puppy, but even then he knew that that could never be the answer. In fact, their offer, so preposterous in its incomprehension, had grown slowly in his mind as the first true desolation of his life. These two, all-wise and all-protecting, were powerless to help and knew him not at all. Once his father and mother had gone to Philadelphia and had promised him a popgun rifle and a patent-leather cartridge box when they came back that evening. A patent-leather cartridge box with a golden eagle on the flap. All afternoon he watched from his window-seat. Just before suppertime he heard the clopping of a horse and saw the black roof of the cab. Down he rushed; there was no cab before the door; on River Street the clopping died away. They had come back next day and brought the rifle and the cartridge box, both perfect, both magnificent; and yet that night of desolation could never be effaced. And there were other griefs. His allowance was fifty cents a week, but before he received it he must present his account book, properly balanced for the week gone by. He had found it simpler to make up items that would balance. For months the result had been happy. Then in one of his unpredictable swoops his father had asked to see the "marbles 25c.," of the past week. There were no marbles. He was, it seemed, no better than a thief. Men had been sent to jail— all was blackness.

Against these disasters his mind spun refuges and revenges. He went away to war, led charges, and returned under arches and massed flags. He stopped the runaway team. He flagged the train. He drove through death to triumph in the Vanderbilt Cup Race. And when his wrongs had bitten him most deeply, he returned from achievement, burly and poised, to tell his father, his teachers, the Ninth Ward boys what he thought of them. From his august and measured indictment only Susan and his Aunt Clara would escape, possibly young Sam, too; his mother was, of course, immune, as being of another world.

In Aunt Clara's upstairs room his mind began to tumble into sleepiness beneath the shadowy gray loom of the eaves. His last thought was he was here in his Aunt Clara's house and that he would be here when he woke in the morning.

As he woke there was an instant when the sloping ceiling, papered white with minute silver stars and lighted by the morning sun, slowly dawned on him. Then with the exciting feeling of the unaccustomed bed came the joyful surge of knowing that he was at Aunt Clara's, had spent the night there in manly freedom, would eat his breakfast there alone with her. When he went down to the bathroom to wash and to brush his teeth, she would always hear him and call, "Hello, there," from her bedroom. Her hair lay in big waves on the counterpane. She would rise up on one elbow and throw back the covers. Sometimes they would lie in the big bed talking about school and the other boys and things until they heard the vigorous tinkle of the breakfast bell. "Oh, golly!" she would say, "there is Christobel."

CHAPTER XXXIV

IN the summer, the locust trees along the river turned dusty; he played on the bank with boys of all degrees, but was never one of them. After the tops came marbles and then one-o'-cat with a ball hard as a rock from going in the river. He conceived of himself as potentially skillful and once or twice made brilliant catches, but was regarded as, fundamentally, a player of no value.

Pushing his two-wheeled cart, the Frozen Idea man came by. "Frozen Idees . . . Frozen Idees!" His voice came high and sharp from inside his beard of dirty wool. The Frozen Idea man's small black eyes met his. "Frozen Idee, Bub?" The cart stopped, tilting forward onto the small leg that stuck out in front. Keeping his bright black eyes on him, the old man mechanically raised the cover of the cart and dipped a grimy hand in. He held up a cube of soft, sweet gray ice-cream wrapped in wet, gray paper. "Frozen Idee?" They were forbidden, these dripping sweets, as being the unsanitary product of a dirty old man. "Bub?" The old man's eyes, alert, impersonal, smiled at him. "Yes," he said.

Sometimes to square himself with God and raise himself in popular esteem, he bought Frozen Ideas for the others as well, and once he bought two for a red-headed boy named Dicey, who was the mascot of The Superba Hose Company and had promised to show him how the stalls flew open and the harness dropped down over the horses. That was the last he ever saw of the red-headed boy. It took him a long time to realize that this boy, glamorous, perfect figure, was not going to keep his promise. Perhaps it was a punishment for buying Frozen Ideas.

These grave speculations and the tedium of summer heat were suddenly and gloriously shattered by good news. In the already shrouded dining room, his mother peered at him around the percolator, her eyes sharp but benign, her mouth pursed for an announcement of high import. "Your Aunt Clara," she said, "has very kindly invited you to spend two weeks up at the farm."

His mouth flew open; he licked at the egg that was running down his chin. "Oh, golly!" he said.

"Now your father and I want you to remember——"

"When do I go?" he said.

His father cleared his throat. "Here," he said, "you're interrupting your mother."

"He didn't mean to interrupt," his mother said. "He was just excited, weren't you, son?"

"Yes, Mother. When do I go?"

"Your grandfather," his father said, "will come by for you at four o'clock this afternoon. I want you to be ready, waiting on the steps, bag packed and everything."

"Golly!" he said. "Do you think grandpa will be driving the trotters?"

"Did you hear what I said?" his father said.

"Yes, Father."

"Yes," his father said, "I think he will be driving them; he always does; but the point is you must be on time."

"He must have a bath," his mother said, "and get out all his crash suits and underwear and I think I'll take him to Dr. Hartman this morning."

"What for?" his father said.

"Well, anyway," his mother said, "he oughtn't to play baseball on the bank this morning."

"The trouble with him," his father said, "is that he will not keep his eye on the ball. He tries to throw it before he catches it."

"But, Father," he said, "a boy knocked a long fly and I——"

"Oh, I know," his father said, "sometimes you do but you'll never make a player until you keep your eye on the ball. I've——"

"Well, never mind that, George," his mother said, "he won't be playing now 'til he comes back."

"I've told him a thousand times," his father said. "He'd better take his ball and glove up to the farm."

"But he can't play by himself, George."

"There may be boys up there. You can never tell who Clara is going to have around. Anyhow, I'll be up Saturday and we can practise. Another thing, I don't want you to fool around that millpond unless your Aunt Clara is with you. Has he got

his bathing suit? When I'm up there Saturday I can teach him
how to dive. The great thing in diving," his father said, "is to
keep your legs straight and close together."

"Never mind that now, George," his mother said, "you can tell
him that on Saturday."

"Well," his father said, "he can be thinking about it."

Flying up the river road, he sat stiff and clean in his crash
suit, squeezed in on the narrow buggy seat beside his grandfather's warm, placid bulk. His grandfather's tan duster fluttered;
on the taut reins the pigskin fingers of the gloves moved delicately; the level, slightly trembling backs of the black pair
stretched out ahead and sped along. In the midst of this dangerous
light swiftness, this dust, these whirling trees and fences, his
grandfather sat imperturbable and even talked with detachment
of large affairs. "That place on the right," he said, "is the
Maurer's place, about two hundred and thirty acres. It used to be
one of the best farms in the country, but then young Maurer married a foolish wife and milked it dry. You can't get more out of
land than you put in."

He, too, turned grave and imperturbable and sat back firmly.
"Yes, Grandpa," he said, "that's a fact." Against his thin frame
he felt his grandfather's soundless chuckle.

They turned in from the river, the rubber-tired wheels gripping
and skidding on the powdered limestone road. Hot, sunny farms
flashed by; a humpbacked stone-arch bridge heaved up under
them. The trotters' dripping loins tightened as they climbed the
winding hill; and then they saw against the mountains the white
plank fences and the mares and colts, brown, red and chestnut
dots against the dusty grass.

"Some real good-looking foals your Aunt Clara's got this
year," his grandfather said as they coasted down a slope. "Too
soon to tell yet." He laid a slow light lash along the off horse's
flank. "But she seems to know what she's about."

Still travelling fast they turned down the apple-bordered lane
and passed the hammocks on the wide verandah, the stone flank
of the house and the open kitchen door where Mrs. Heisdick's
face glowed in the depths. As they slowed up her voice resounded after them. "Ha!" she said. "The papa and the little
one."

Behind the house the ground rose gently to the great red hill-side barn, between whose stone ends a heavy side jutted out to form a dark cave underneath, where colts with gleaming eyes looked out of shaded half doors, and chickens picked at straw between enormous posts of whitewashed oak.

There was the tap of small hoofs in the depths, and Aunt Clara, bareheaded and in a light-blue, belted dress, led out a dark bay two-year-old.

"Hello," she said, "I heard you coming."

The buggy seat rocked slightly as his grandfather heaved out his thick gold watch. "Forty-seven minutes," he said, "from George's house." He looked at the horses. The sweat, dripping from their bellies, threw up little puffs of dust.

"Where's Jacob?" he said. "These horses will have to be cooled out under sheets."

"Jacob!" she shouted; her voice was high and piercing like a boy's. In the silence, Aunt Clara's colt shook his halter, reached down and scattered the chickens with his sharp muzzle. From deep in the barn came a furious growling roar.

"He hears me," Aunt Clara said. "Now, Tommy, jump down and we'll take your bag to the house."

"You better put up that colt," his grandfather said.

Aunt Clara unsnapped the halter rope. "Oh!" she said, "he follows me everywhere."

The colt came up to Tommy; his tender muzzle ran swiftly, delicately over the crash suit; his soft eyes gazed intently into vacancy.

"Aunt Clara, look!" he said; "he's smelling me all over; he's smelling my bag. What's his name?"

"His registered name," Aunt Clara said, "is 'Arab Sentinel,' but I call him 'Geranium,' because he eats up all the geraniums," she laughed, "right out of the window boxes on the porch."

"Geranium," he said. He reached a hand out slowly.

"That's right," his grandfather said, "never make quick moves around a colt." The colt examined his hand and thrust it firmly aside.

He laughed with excitement and delight. "Look at him, Aunt Clara."

"Come on to the house," she said, "he'll come with us."

Behind him he heard Mr. Heisdick's hobnails on the cobbles

of the covered way, and his broad voice. "So, John. What did you make it in?"

"Jacob." His grandfather said tranquilly. "Forty-seven minutes."

The colt's head swung between them as he walked with his Aunt Clara; his mouse-like ears were pricked and his forelock stirred.

"He's coming along just like a dog," he said, "isn't he, Aunt Clara?"

"Yes," she said, "he's just like a puppy. Maybe when you get to know him you can ride him. Would you like that?

"I said would you like that?" Aunt Clara looked at him. She smiled. "Well, that's all right then; you can ride him."

Every day then he rode Geranium while Aunt Clara walked beside him with a lead rein. He sat in the soft buckskin saddle, feeling underneath his thighs the strange excitement of a live thing moving, of lightness, warmth and strength. Geranium tossed his small mane, but not alarmingly, and now and then reached back his small head to take the scuffed toe of Tommy's shoe in his mouth and held it firmly. "Hey," he giggled, uneasy but delighted. "He's biting me. Will he bite?"

"No, he won't bite," Aunt Clara said; "he's just an awful tease. How do you feel up there?"

"Oh, golly," he said. "I guess this is an awful good horse."

"Oh, yes; he's fine."

"I guess I'm doing pretty good, don't you think?"

"You're doing fine," she said. "Do you think you could try to trot a little?"

"Oh, sure," he said. "I could do that all right."

"We can't go far," Aunt Clara said, "it's too hot to run. Hold on to the front of the saddle so you won't pull him. Watch his shoulder here; when it goes forward you go up; when it goes back you sit down. Come on, Geranium."

A bounce or two and he was doing it. "That's fine," Aunt Clara panted, trotting through the dust. He grinned and kept his eye fastened on the colt's shoulder.

"Whoa, colt!" Aunt Clara said. "Hold on. Whew!" she said, "that's hard work." She looked at him. "Why, you're remarkable; you've got your grandmother's sense of time."

He kept his eye fixed on the colt. "Yes, I guess that was pretty good all right; let's do it again."

Later Aunt Clara rode beside him on an old brown mare, and in the end she took the lead rein off and let him loose, but she would not let him ride alone; a feminine precaution which irked his budding manhood until the morning that a chicken flopped out from among the cannas by the porch and he was instantly among squashed cannas and old chicken feathers on his stomach, while the colt looked down on him with detached astonishment. One day it rained; a warm, unceasing, heavy rain. He went up to the barn with Mr. Heisdick. "To-day we move some hay," Mr. Heisdick said, "and I think maybe there is rats. Do you want to see my Fritz catch rats? Fritz!" he said to the brilliant yellow, pug-faced little dog with a tight-curled tail, "come here! Ach! such a dog for rats he is." Among the dark hay mountains under the barn he climbed; he leapt off precipices and slid down slopes and lay concealed behind high peaks, while close above him sparrows twittered disconsolately among rafters, and the rain drummed down on the vast roof. It was a world huge, mournful, dim, but solemnly delightful until the moment that Fritz found a nest of baby rats and ate them horribly with conscious self-approval.

That night the memory of that grinning, crunching, yellow Fritz came back to haunt him in the attic room above Aunt Clara's bedroom in the new wing. A wet half-moon was out now and against the whitewashed walls the pictures of St. Simon and Arundel and Eclipse were dim black squares. But nothing in these shadows and this silver mist was half as real as the picture of Fritz and those small, pink wrigglers.

His door creaked; against the lamplight of the stairway he saw Aunt Clara in her dressing-gown.

"Hey, there," she said, "are you still awake? How's everything? All right?"

In the end she sat down on the bed. "I know," she said, "it's dreadful. My goodness! but the thing is, all you can ask of animals is to do what they think is right. Fritz knows that he is meant to catch rats and that he's helping us. And you know," she said, "we couldn't keep these horses here, Geranium or anything, if we let the rats have their own way. There would soon be thousands and they would eat up all the feed and run over the colts at night and scare and worry them. But you can't teach Fritz

the difference between a big rat and a little one, and even if you
could I don't know which is best. When rats are so small they
don't know anything; they don't know what's happened to
them."

"I guess that's so. And anyhow," he said, "you couldn't have
rats running over that colt."

On Saturday, when his father and mother came up in the
hired surrey, he was almost sorry, but he had a pretty good time.
He and his father passed baseball on the lawn in front of the
porch while his grandfather, in a linen coat and wide straw hat,
sat under a locust tree and watched them with a whiskey sour
in his hand. His father was full of tricks and jokes to-day. He
caught the ball behind him and threw it back under his leg.
"Hey, pop," he said, "here you go." He tossed the ball at Grandfather Rand. His grandfather caught it deftly. "Here, here!" he
said, "you'll spill my glass." He threw the ball back.

"Why, pop, you're a ball player," his father said.

His grandfather jiggled the ice in the glass. "We used to call
it rounders."

After the baseball, he and his father with bathing suits rolled
in towels under their arms, walked past the barn along the lane
where weeds pushed through the gravel. Below, and to their
right, a big white-fenced field of mares and foals stretched down
to the county road, and to the left the pallid green of an oat field
which rose to the wavy fringes of the mountain forest, was turning yellow where it caught the earliest sun. Ahead he heard a
steady tramping rumble; the mill was running. And then they
saw the level stretch of close, green grass through which the road
ran, and between the two big butternuts, high and narrow, the
weathered siding of the mill. Mr. Heisdick, disguised as a
miller in flour-dusted cap and denims, came out on the lofty loading platform as though carried from within on the volume of
sound. He stood looking down at them. "George!" he shouted
above the rumble, "Twilliger is here." He stuck his head in the
door and howled with gestures. Bandy-legged and sturdy, Mr.
Twilliger came out on the loading platform swinging an enormous monkey wrench; he wore a short-sleeved undershirt and an
old, derby hat. "George!" he said. "So that's the boy. How old
is he now?"

"He's twelve."

"Buddy!" Mr. Twilliger shouted. "What do you like to do?" Behind him the roaring mill was shaking dust down from the lintel of the door. "He like to skate?"

"Yes, he can skate."

Mr. Twilliger thrust his monkey wrench toward the dark, silent millpond. "Dandy ice here, I bet."

"That's right, but we've got to fill the ice-house."

Mr. Twilliger looked at the towels and bathing suits. "Can he swim?"

"Some. I'm going to teach him to dive."

"Well," Mr. Twilliger said, "I guess that's a good thing to know." He went inside the mill. His face immediately reappeared; he imbibed a large portion of his gray mustache and blew it out again. "Got a little trouble here." He flourished the monkey wrench and disappeared. As his father and he went up across the grass toward the alders, the rumble of the mill was pierced by tremendous sounds of hammering.

When he was brushing his damp hair in the attic room, he heard his father's voice down on the porch below. He left the steel-framed mirror and opened the casement window cautiously.

"I can't make it out," his father said. "I tell him and show him——"

"But, George dear," his mother's voice was anxious. "He's not like you."

"He'll never make an athlete," his father said.

"He takes after my side of the family. Look at Mun. And father never could do anything with his hands. Whenever he went to a banquet, mother had to tie his tie. You ask her. On my side of the family," his mother said, "it all seems to go to brains."

"Brains?" his father said. "He still don't know the capital of Illinois."

"But, George dear, the boy has got to learn what he's taught."

"The sooner he goes away to school, the better," his father said. "He'd get some coaching there too."

"George Rand! You ought to be ashamed. He's a wonderful boy. Why, every night you ought to get down on your knees and thank your God for giving you a son like that."

Hanging far out the casement window, Tommy Rand glowed and gave a silent cheer.

"Well, that's all right, I guess," his father said. "I guess he's a better boy than I was at his age."

"All I meant," his father said, "was that he'd never make an athlete."

CHAPTER XXXV

HE sat in his chair between his father and his mother in the
Pullman parlor car, whose nickeled lamps above the aisle looked
ominously stately even in the day. The plush arms clutched at
his hands, the cherry panelling creaked, the stained glass glowed
above the window, past which the fields and brown, wooded
ridges and stone farms ran. His father wore his dark box coat,
his mother, a purple suit with puffed sleeves and a hat with a
startled purple bird among black flowers. His small new glad-
stone bag was beside his knees, his canvas-covered trunk was in
the baggage car. But his father and mother had no baggage;
they would be coming back that night. That night they would
pass again these hills and fields, these farms where people then
would all be safely in the house, and come that night back to
the house in Midian, to the hall, the dining room, the library, to
young Sam and to Susan. Only he, himself, among all these
people would be lost and desolate—small and strange and exiled
in the unknown.

His father and mother talked to him. His father sat square in
the parlor-car seat and tapped a knee with his square tipped
finger. He, himself, had only gone to the Midian Free Academy
and then straight to Yale. Now Tommy was going to a boarding
school where they had a gymnasium and a swimming pool and a
football team, probably the best prep-school team in the country.
And a fine atmosphere, his mother said; her sharp brown eyes
that seemed so competent were now fixed on him softly, as
though they wanted to hold him to her, and she smiled eagerly;
probably the finest atmosphere in the country. It was a wonderful school, they told him; they were making a real effort to send
him there; they would miss him and it was expensive. He should
be glad, they said.

At the station where they got off there were other boys and
other parents, an alien and horribly indifferent world where, over

his head and the heads of other small but passionate doomed souls, the elders exchanged bland glances, salutations, incredibly at ease, amused and casual.

Between his mother and his father, he drove in a hack up an ugly village street and through a brownstone gate. The hack horse dug his toes in and dropped his sad bony head, the gravel crunched slowly; on the summit the chocolate buildings were enormous and very sad, and around them, in the three-sided quadrangle on the steep lawn in front, the figures of other boys and parents seemed unnatural, aimless, hopeless, static.

In a dark hall a gust overwhelmed him. A turmoil of people was governed by a swarthy, frog-like man. "Heyo! Ha-ha! Howdy do. Here's dear old Bill." The man swung toward them. He clapped his father on the shoulder; "Mr. Rand?" he said. "Well, well, Mr. Rand." He hugged his father's elbow to his paunch. His bow to his mother was a flourish. "Well, well," he said, "so this is the boy. And what do they call you? Tommy? Very good. Well, Tommy, I suppose you want to start your studies right this afternoon. Ha! Ha! Percy!"

A smooth negro in a page's uniform stood before them. His sky-blue chest was filled with rows of small brass buttons. His ushering gesture was modulated, yet assured. They followed him up the stairs and down the hall where a glass door gave a glimpse of a ponderous, elegant study. The colored page walked with stout assurance in his tight, short jacket. His posterior in the tight pants was agile and expressive. Across the end of the hall was a great oak door. He flung the door back. Before them stretched a long bare corridor.

Standing on the gravel, he watched the hack go down the hill; he could not see his father or his mother, nothing but the black leather curtains and the old, sad horse. At the foot of the hill, the hack passed between the gateposts and was gone. Gone! He turned to face the square of enormous chocolate buildings. His heavy numb feet must move, his heart must beat, his leaden lungs must breathe. Laboriously he passed by boys who laughed and hailed each other, by the tall chocolate wing where other parents lingered but not his. He came to an arched door and climbed a dark stair; at the top his throat was rigid, he was breathing hard.

Back in his room, standing on the other bed, a boy was nailing
a large Yale banner to the wall. He was small, but wore long
trousers. He looked over his shoulder; his yellow hair was
bushy, his face was pink and confident. "Hello," he spoke around
a mouthful of thumb tacks. "Are you the kid in here?" He
pointed a shoe-tree at him. He turned and went to hammering a
nail. With his eyes on this boy, he sat down on the bed. Above
him hung the brown and fuzzy-haired Sir Galahad which his
father and mother had hung there. At the foot of the bed, his
table held a student lamp and, between two bronze heads of
"Dante," his "Red-Letter Testament," "Daily Strength for Daily
Needs," and a Latin dictionary. In the bureau beyond, lay his
shirts and underwear and socks neatly put away by his mother,
and each, according to the rules, marked with a white label into
which was woven, "Thomas Rand."

"So you're Thomas Rand," the other boy said.

"Yes."

"I was looking over your stuff. D'ye want to trade that blue
striped necktie for a knitted one?"

"I don't know. I guess so."

He watched the boy drive the last nail with a tremendous
whack of the shoe-tree and jump down from the bed. With his
hands on his hips and his legs apart, the boy looked at the banner.
"How's that," he said. "Class."

"Yes! My father went to Yale; I am going there too."

"My uncle was Buffer Molloy."

"Oh!"

"Ever hear of him?"

"No, I guess I didn't."

"Never heard of Buffer Molloy?" The boy swung around and
gave him a crooked, pitying smile. "He was on Walter Camp's
All-American three years. The greatest guard Yale ever had," he
said; "that's all he was. They call me 'Buffer' too."

"Oh!"

"Your father play football?"

"I don't know."

"Well, if he did, sure you'd know all right. What are you
going out for?"

"I don't know."

"Go out for football. It's the only thing that gets you anywhere; even if you're no good they'll put you on the kids' team."

"Oh. What team do you play on?"

"I guess I'll be on the third team." He threw the shoe-tree under the bed. "I'm a quarterback," he said. He thrust his hands into the pockets of his long trousers and stared at Tommy with minute attention. Tommy looked down at his hands. "Now then," he heard the Buffer saying, "have you got your schedule, yet?"

Tommy shook his head.

"Say, you better get busy. Hey! What's the matter with you? Judas priest, you haven't got all day. You know how to do it, don't you? Ah, for Pete's sake. You go down to the registrar, first, see. That's the mug that has his office downstairs right where you go into the dining room. While you're there, get your notebooks and pencils and all that stuff. He sells them and charges them to your old man. Then you come back up here and go to the study hall. You can see the door at the end of the corridor. It's got a bulletin board with the class schedules and time for physical examinations and study hours and all that duck crap."

Tommy stood up, blushing. Duck crap. "Thank you very much," he said. "Can I do anything for you?" He was conscious that the Buffer was grinning at him with insupportable delight.

"No, I got a kid working on that for me already."

It was several days before he discovered that the Buffer was a new boy, too.

At six o'clock, small, sharp electric bells rang everywhere. On wood and concrete and gravel, feet were tramping in from all directions. He was swept by a great strange crowd of boys that laughed and joked in a frightening, thrilling way, into the dining room. When he had found the napkin ring that he had brought from home and sat down in front of it, an electric buzzer checked the noise. The Doctor stood up and asked the blessing; his rich, thick whisper was very moving. Tommy felt his sickness coming on him stronger. The talk broke out, and thick white plates were being passed along the tables. All around him was loud talk and jokes that he could not understand. He laughed heartily. "Hey!" they said; "what are you laughing at?" In silence, he tried with his tongue to get the pale dry-mashed potatoes out of his mouth.

From far away he heard the Buffer calling, "You're all right, kid. Don't let them kid you." But the Buffer was laughing at him, too.

After supper, the pine rafters in the study hall were very high, white-plaster busts stood on high brackets between the windows. Ahead of him, he saw the backs of two hundred boys' heads. Each boy was seated at his desk except the Sixth Form that sat up front on benches. The yellow-oak organ sounded; they sang, "Oh, Come All Ye Faithful." Then the Doctor stood up at a yellow-oak reading desk and talked about what Wyomensing meant to every fellow in this room. It meant cleanness and high purpose, decency, and doing a fellow's best on the football field, win or lose. It meant earnestness and the things that were worth while.

And it meant it not only here at Wyomensing, which we all love, but it meant something that a fellow carried with him wherever he was. It was the Wyomensing spirit. And not only here but in the larger life beyond. Wyomensing boys stood for the things in life that counted. There was dear old Alfred Smithers, who was doing such a wonderful work for Christ at New Haven. All the old boys knew it, but for the benefit of the new boys, he would say that Alfred Smithers was President of Dwight Hall, and the first man tapped for Bones last year. And there was no one in this room who did not know the touchdown against Harvard last year had been scored by a Wyomensing boy, dear old Pete Mulbaur. And everywhere you went you found that the things that counted were being done by Wyomensing boys; and if a fellow wanted to know the reason, the answer would always be the same—the Wyomensing spirit. And to the new boys who were just about to learn what Wyomensing stood for in a fellow's life, he would simply say— Here the Doctor's rich whisper sank so low that Tommy and the other new boys, who all sat at the back of the room, were unable to hear him. But they could see his fat finger stabbing at them over the top of the golden-oak desk. They could see the tremble of the chops that fell over the immaculate collar and the solemn stare of his suffused, protruding eyes. The silence was intense. They were Wyomensing boys; and when, at the end, the sixth former jumped up on the platform, "Now, fellows, three long Wyo's for Doctor!" they fixed their eyes on him and screamed.

The Doctor, mopping his brow, rocked down the aisle. The seals on his gold watch chain were enormous. With dignity, the Sixth Form filed out. With the Wyomensing spirit still upon him, he opened the lid of his desk and took out his Latin grammar. On the fly-leaf he wrote, "Thomas Rand, Second Form, Wyomensing."

But in the night, his face against the flat, strange-smelling pillow, he heard the creaking of the Buffer's bed and then his voice, "What's the matter, kid, crying?"

He turned his face to the wall. "No," he said.

"Ah," the Buffer said. "Forget it; you're all right," he said. "Don't let them kid you."

Between that first day at Wyomensing and his last, the memories were confused. Each year he and the Buffer, who looked on him with a sort of contemptuous and amused admiration, were moved with the rest of the form to a corridor of greater dignity. Under the Buffer's guidance, he passed through the necktie swapping phase, the odd-or-even mania that swept the school, the craze for making watch fobs of interwoven leather shoe laces. With the Buffer, he had run an agency for chewing gum, and taken his strangled turn in leading the Y. M. C. A. meeting in prayer. One year their room was over an archway, and they had filled paper bags and dropped them on the passers-by below. That must have been before they joined the Y. M. C. A. Certainly the affair of the sparrows was. That was the Buffer's notion. He, himself, had done nothing but keep watch. That spring they had discovered a nest of young sparrows in the eaves outside their window, and these the Buffer had secured and adorned in accordance with his purpose. After evening prayers, the study hall had settled down to work; hundreds of bent figures, hundreds of student lamps, and Mr. Merkle, a regular sneak and a stinker, in charge. A boy opened a desk. There was a whir and a tinkle, then a vast ecstatic murmur as a sparrow, streaming ribbons and many little bells, soared wildly round their heads. In the end, the sparrow perched on a rafter. A semblance of order was restored. Heroically he fixed his eyes on his book; his diaphragm was caving in ungovernable spasms. Another whir and tinkle as another desk was opened. This time there was a cheer.

When the third bird whizzed out, the riot broke. Boys bowed

their faces on their knees and moaned. They whistled, shrieked, yodelled. Little boys bounced on their seats and screamed like demons. The Doctor arrived to find Mr. Merkle having a sort of epileptic fit. He sometimes thought that that had been the happiest moment of his life.

Then as sixth formers, they put behind them all such childishness. The Buffer was captain of the football team, and therefore was the leader of the Y. M. C. A. He, himself, used to write out for the Buffer what he was to say at the meetings. The Buffer, he was glad to say, had cut out saying "duck crap" and any smutty talk. It looked as if he were going to be a big man when he got to New Haven.

And he, himself, was conscious of notable development. When he first came to Wyomensing, things had been pretty bad. There seemed to be no means by which he could fit in with this distinguished and admirable life. His efforts to be rugged and haughty, like the rest, led only to outbursts of unnatural and frightened insolence, which mystified and astounded him as much as they exasperated the old boys and the masters. When Newt Bonney, the fat sixth former who played tackle on the football team, and Mr. Twigart, the manual training teacher with lanky hair and a blue jowl, had stood up to sing a duet at the school entertainment in the study hall, he had heard a whisper—his own piercing whisper—announce "The Walrus and the Carpenter." A delighted titter had run through the room. The names had stuck to Newt and Mr. Twigart ever since; but he, himself, had been visited that evening by a solemn delegation of the big men in the school. In the darkness they had sat in a row on his creaking bed. "Pretty fresh for a new kid," they had said. "This time we're just telling you, but one more crack and you go in the pond." Heavily they filed out.

Late that night the Buffer stirred. "Ah, what the deuce!" he said. "Forget it. You're a good kid," he said, "only you talk too much; that's all. See?"

For a time then he kept quiet, only he never was quite trusted, and every once in a while the frantic, hearty fit would come on him and he would say something terrible; but they never threw him in the pond. The intervals were long enough for that.

As he grew, the frantic fits subsided. The life of the school no longer seemed one where he must make passionate and dramatic contacts, or else from which he must escape entirely. He no longer felt caged by the close, yet alien world beyond which lay horizons toward which he longed to run, or, failing that, within which something must be done to give life to the laughter, joy and eagerness that tugged inside him and that were forever baffled by the stolid days, until in numb despair he used simply to hang on, hugging to himself the thought of night when he could lie in bed, secure in the freedom of his dreams.

Those dreams themselves became, in time, more allied to reality; a sign, he took it, of maturity and a potent solvent of his childish bewilderment and sense of hope betrayed.

At night he no longer pictured strange adventures with birds and deer and railroad locomotives, with trappers, farmers and damsels in distress among the wooded hills that lay beyond the bounds of Wyomensing. Instead he conceived that it might be possible, all things considered, that next year he would be chosen on the Sixth Form Committee, whose wisdom governed the school in matters of freshness and of hazing, each of whom wore on their waistcoats a special pin which combined the head of Minerva with the Wyomensing seal. They also had the privilege of wearing panama hats instead of hard straw hats in the spring. This dream, in fact, emerged to the surface and became a subject of a lecture by the Buffer. The Buffer was of the opinion he would make the Sixth Form Committee if he made the Track Team. It was conceded that in all games of skill, Tommy Rand was impotent; but in the class athletic meet he had almost won the mile. Greatly encouraged, the Buffer had made a thorough study of the situation with a borrowed stop-watch. He announced with satisfaction that there was a dearth of even passable milers in the school and no prospects coming on. The Buffer believed that with proper diet, which he immediately set himself to supervise, and with proper training, which he also supervised, seated on a Wyomensing pillow in the middle of the track, Tommy Rand would make the Sixth Form Committee his last year.

In the end the scheme had borne fruit on the day when, in front of the huge, packed stands at Franklin Field, he had lined up, sick and white, among the jerseys of the large and burly boys of Mercersburg and Hill and Lawrenceville. The pistol cracked, his legs moved in a fuzz of terror. The great crowd murmured like the sea. He strained to stride out firmer, longer. The burly jerseys swung away. Consistently he fell behind. "Last quarter, last quarter," a huge voice shouted. In the end through a mist of sweat, he saw the leaders swing on round the oval. And then, amid frantic shouting, the two last men in front of him went on through the straight-away. His mind, at least, still worked. He could not be worse off if he followed them. Then the coach and the Wyomensing team were all round him with bathrobes and sponges and a bucket for him to vomit in. He had placed third in the mile and won his W. Years afterward, cleaning out old files for his father, he had found a yellow clipping. Far down the column of events he read, "One-mile Championship, Preparatory Schools. First, Mackey, Haverford; second, Diller, Tome; third, Rand, Wyomensing." He had showed the clipping to his father with a laugh. Unsmiling, his father had folded the yellowed paper carefully and put it in his pocket-book

From then on his position was secure. He had become, somewhat to his embarrassed surprise, a symbol of what Wyomensing stood for—hard work, high purpose, earnest effort. He had also become the demonstration of what Wyomensing believed, that these qualities were, in the nature of the universe, destined for concrete, practical reward. The next year there were twenty boys out for the mile, each convinced that if he practised hard enough some day the other faster runners would turn wrong.

He, himself, was simply happy that now he fitted into a system which had proved its worth. Wyomensing was the best school and had changed him from a dreamy, frightened, yet impudent sissy, into a member of the Sixth Form Committee who wore the Sixth Form Committee pin on his vest and had his picture in the Year Book, a boy of purpose, ideals and straight thinking; he could say it without conceit, for he owed it all to Wyomensing.

He owed it all to Wyomensing. That knowledge reached its zenith, diffusing grave elation and warm gratitude, on that warm day in June when he was standing, a sixth former, nervous but assured and masterly, on the commencement platform. Standing in his blue coat, white flannels and gunmetal leather pumps on the very spot where, for five years, the Doctor had been making his addresses on the Wyomensing spirit. Now it was his turn. He made a bow and tried to clear the dryness from his throat. From the blur of fathers and mothers and pretty girls in front of him, came a rustle of applause. "Education and character," he said. An illimitable silence loomed around him. "Ladies and gentlemen," he said in a tight, piping voice, "and fellow class-mates." He turned to the triple row behind him, sitting alien and wooden in their blue serge coats, white trousers and gun-metal leather pumps. He revolved slowly to face again the blur of colored dresses and sack suits. "I have chosen as my subject for the Class Day oration the subject, 'Education and Character.'" That was wrong. He felt a crimson flood raise the hairs on his neck. "I have chosen 'Education and Character'; for one, we must agree, is valueless without the other. What do we mean by education? A wise man once observed—" He was on the right track now. His voice rose, the first gesture came automatically. He advanced the right foot and made a short sweep with his hand.

And now the words stood printed in his mind. He rolled along. "We must admit then that education is not simply knowl-edge; it is more than knowledge." His voice rose on the 'more.' "It is," he paused—one—two—"knowing how to use knowledge. "But how can we use knowledge wisely without character? What do we mean by character? By character, we mean——"

From the crowd in front of him, his father's face emerged. He sat in his dark, sack suit, his ascot tie and boutonnière, solemn and perfectly expressionless.

His gestures and words flowed on. He was sweating slightly and felt a sense of power. He clenched his fist and raised it higher than his shoulder. "And that is what we mean when we sing the song we love so well, 'Old Wyomensing, Maker of Men.' We mean that here in this school we love so well," he swept both hands back from his chest, "we have learned that not only—" His voice rang out; he stabbed a finger at the audience. "We have learned that not alone—" This was the part that Mr. Tussman, the rhetoric teacher, had written. It was certainly fine. "—but that to all this must be added—" He clasped his hands before him. "—so that while we shall live, and whatever fortune shall bring, we shall bear ourselves worthily, even, let us hope nobly, as sons of old Wyomensing."

He bowed: he saw the Doctor banging his clean, fat hands to-gether and heard the Doctor's voice above the tumult, "Ha! dear old Tommy!" He turned and swam through waves of receding

clapping to his seat between the Buffer and a certain Stink
Sheetz who was going to Lehigh. "By the holy cats!" the Buffer
said. "Thomas, you're a spouter." Stink looked on him around
the corner of his steel-rimmed glasses. "Congratulations," he
said. "That was excellent."

CHAPTER XXXVI

WITH soft wooden creakings like the cabin of a ship, the parlor car swung round the curves and straightened out to lay its running squares of light along dim snowy fields and white-capped fences. Black trees were turned to wavering gold and in the farther darkness mild farmhouse lights passed slowly and stars stood steady overhead. He sat in his dark suit, his high, close, turn-down collar and rich, black, knitted silk tie, with his Christmas parcels beside his seat, a junior at Yale returning to his heritage.

Three days ago, he and a group of the best men in their class had marched with an air into the Manhattan Bar, just off the train from New Haven. Their dark overcoats had black-velvet collars, most of them wore small diamond horseshoes in their dark, knitted silk ties; all wore gold watch chains in their upper waistcoat pockets. He had confined himself to a couple of sherry flips. Then they had moved in a group through the lobby, ignoring the several unattached ladies in their exaggerated hobble skirts. With arms held low, they had shaken each other's hands, genial yet dignified; and so had broken up. He had gone to spend a couple of days with the Buffer in the Bronx. The Buffer's father, of course, was a great old fellow, and the Buffer's mother was formidably motherly. She did a good deal of the work around the house. And the Buffer's older brother who had gone from Fordham into the contracting business was dark and thin and serious and polite. But the house itself: bright blue limestone with a red-tile roof, and, inside, the Wallace Nutting photographs and the mottoes. And the younger children were fun, but when they talked, as they did tremendously, you could not help thinking of the actors who took the part of crooks in "Alias Jimmy Valentine." The family had a wonderful time together, and the way they laughed at the Priest when he came in to dinner was something new to him in the way of religious experience. He was glad that he had gone there; it was a good example of what was meant by Yale democracy.

Across the wide black window of the parlor car, among the reflections of its ceiling lights and of his narrow darkly shadowed face, a snowy road ran, ghastly bluish white, between dull furrowed fields. He saw a team and on the long box body of the sled a muffled figure crouched beside a lantern.

Certainly it was about time he visited the Buffer, after all these years together. And especially since they had been at New Haven, so near by. With the Buffer as his friend, he had come a long way these last two years. He remembered his first day at Yale. Number 242 York Street was a grim, Byzantine fortress of dingy brick. There was nothing particularly inviting about its clumsy, round-headed windows and peaked slate roof; but by the time he had hung up his Yale banner and his imitation-bronze Wyomensing seal in the downstairs front room, he realized that as usual the Buffer had known exactly what he was about. The Buffer himself had not arrived; he would appear at precisely the right moment. At the foot of the other bed, stood a trunk addressed to "Mr. Francis X. Molloy, 242 York Street, New Haven, Connecticut," and on top of it, a suitcase well sprinkled with the green and gold labels of the Wyomensing football team. Other trunks bumped overhead, and other freshmen passed the open door. Some parents were in the house also. Without exception they were very smart people.

Beyond a doubt the Buffer knew what he was about: this was the best freshman house. They had two of the big men from Exeter and about half of the Andover football team, while just above him were a couple of boys from Groton to give the place a little tone. When the others asked him where he was from he said, "Wyomensing. So's my roommate; he was captain of the team last year. Buffer Molloy."

"Buffer Molloy?" they said. "Any relation to *the* Buffer Molloy?"

"Yes," he made it casual, "he was his uncle."

"Gosh!" they said. "Well, what Yale needs is another Buffer Molloy." Then, "How good is he?"

"Well," he said judicially, "he's pretty good. He's small though."

"Oh!" they said. "Why, the Buffer Molloy weighed two hundred and ten"—"Two hundred and ten? A hundred and ninety; that was all he weighed"—"A hundred and ninety? I'll bet you"—"I won't bet, I know. My old man was a substitute on his team"—"Well, anyhow, he weighed plenty"—"Sure he weighed plenty, and he was fast and rangy." They turned on him. "What's this fellow weigh?"

"A hundred and forty-five. He's fast though."

"Oh," they said. "Well, old Buffer Molloy was fast and he weighed a hundred and ninety." One of the big men from Exeter shook his head. "A good big man will beat a good little man," he said. They filed out of his room.

A carriage stopped out front. In an open barouche, the Buffer wore a checked vest and smoked a big cigar. The angle of his straw hat was gay. Three bags were up beside the driver, but he had taken the Wyomensing labels off them. The Buffer was smart. He gave a look at the house.

With leisure he descended and shook down his trouser legs. He drew a dollar from his lower waistcoat pocket. He was wearing a watch chain across the upper pockets—that must be the new thing then. The driver put the dollar in his hat. The Buffer reached a hand up toward him. "Now, then, Commissioner," he said, "just hand down that stuff." With his quick, wide-legged gait, the Buffer mounted the steps. "Hello, Thomas. How are we fixed?" He shook his head. "Sure it's the best house. Just give me a hand with these bags."

"Commissioner!" he shouted. Far down the street, the hack driver turned around. "Take care of yourself!" The hack driver grinned.

Inside the room he flipped the ash off the cigar. "Well, Thomas," he said, "how do you like the stogie? Bronxville's best," he said. "Been passing them out for the old man. Election's in November." He sat down on his bed and looked at the cigar. "This is the last though. Beginning this evening, the Buffer goes in training. How's that?"

"That's all right."

"Sure it's all right." He made a gesture with his cigar. "Next year," he said, "I'm going to be in there with the Varsity." He nodded his head. "Take it or leave it," he said, "that's my bet."

He stuck his cigar in his mouth, he jumped up, squared off; he crinkled his left eye up against the smoke. "What do you say, Thomas, am I right?"

Therefore next year, the Buffer, playing regular quarterback, was not the least surprised. "It's nothing to be proud of," he said, "who else would they get now? Between ourselves there's no one out there but Miller. He's a good Yale quarterback, just only that. He does nothing wrong and he wouldn't fool a bunch of boys from grade school. After the first five minutes the other team know the plays he'll call as good as we do. And the rest are bigger chumps than him, or else they fumble or they're brittle or they lose track of the plays. They're all good boys except Delane who is a stuck-up, dressed-up, handsome millionaire, and yellow too." He cocked a knee and clasped his hands around it. "Ah," he said, "they're all good boys. Did you notice my pass this year? I put it there just like on the end of a bamboo pole, and then sometimes they drop it. Do you know what's behind it? Last summer I found a young fellow at the Young Democratic Club. He was an old pro basketball player. So then every evening he gave me a workout in the park. That's where I got my quick kick going right too. Ah," he said, "they talk about Wally and his tackle slants, but it was the quick kick that broke up Princeton this year." He nodded seriously. "This is between us. The boys might think I had the big head or something. Now what about this Dr. Johnson for the test to-morrow?"

"Well, what about him?"

"I mean was he the fellow that wrote the book about the dog?"

"You mean the dog, Harvey?"

"No, that wasn't his name. He was a Scotchman, wasn't he?"

"You mean Dr. Johnson?"

"Sure. Didn't he write a dog book?"

"Not that I ever heard of."

"There was a dog book at school. I saw a kid reading it. It was about some dog and his friends."

"Good Lord, Buffer, you don't mean 'Rab and His Friends'?"

"That's it," the Buffer said. "I knew it was that."

"But that's by Dr. John Brown."

"Ah!" said the Buffer. "I knew it was something like that. Now then," he said, "let's do a little workout with the books."

The parlor car swung past the switch points of the yards. "Coming into Midian, sir," the porter said. "Brush you off?" Switch lights and tower lights went by in colored flashes; and a shuffling figure with a naked torch. "Now, sir, your shoes. Just set down here."

At the top of the steps in the train shed, the ticket taker raised a flipper. "Hello, Thomas. Back from school?"

"Hello, Mr. Heisman. Yes, back from college."

"Kind of late, ain't you?"

"Well, I stayed in New York for a couple of days."

"Oh, boy!"

The red-cap held back the door of the waiting room for him. "Mistletoe's here," he said, "with your grandpa's carriage."

The harness fittings and the smooth side of the brougham shone at him under the arc light. Levi rolled his eyes above his turned-up collar, he raised his whip to the brim of his squat silk hat. "Mr. Tommy, they been expecting you."

"Hello, Levi, how's everybody?"

"All fine, sir; all fine." The horse stamped on the thin snow.

In Centre Street the lights of the gay store windows fell on Christmas shoppers. There were wreaths and stacks of narrow furry Christmas trees, and in the bright display windows skates and dolls, and silverware and a stuffed Santa Claus in a chimney. Wrapped in a fur-lined robe, he rode looking out at the cheery Christmas street, elated, happy and conscious of comfort and distinction.

The lights of Centre Street and of the city square dropped behind him leaving only their faint reflections on the brougham's hammercloth. Here was the silent frozen river, the night of stars, the chaste cold house-fronts behind stark trees. The brougham turned down Linden Street. Ahead he saw the rich glow of the big bay window. Their wheels were grating on the curb. Young Sam in flapping coat-tails was coming down the steps.

"Well, Sam, how's everybody?"

"Just fine, sir. Everybody. I'll get the bags." Sam coughed, "Mister Mistletoe, would you please to hand down them bags?"

His father stood in the open door with the evening paper in his hand. In silhouette, he looked like an athlete still, a young

sturdy athlete. From the side you could see that his head was
beginning to drop forward like Grandfather Rand's, and his
waist was thickening up. "Well, son." He gave a little half-
smile. His still child-like face lit up when he smiled that way
at him; Tommy always felt for the moment as if they really
were great friends. "Ellen," he called out, "here he is."

His mother's black dress had quite a few pink bows; her
curled hair had turned grayer even since last fall. "Tommy," she
said, and put her arms around him in a quick hard hug. "Open
your coat. Oh!" she said. Her brown eyes were fine. She had
a touch of color. "You do look elegant."

His father looked at the high, close turned-down collar and the
small tight knot at the very bottom of the opening. He looked at
the elevated watch chain. "I suppose that's what they're wearing
now," he said. "I see it in the theatrical advertisements."

"Go wash up," his mother said. "We're having a cold supper.
It's prayer-meeting night, you know."

"I washed on the train," he said. "Yes, of course; it's Wednesday. But look here," he said, "it's the dance to-night, isn't it?"

She walked through the corner of the heavy hall into the
dining room; the oak table was well filled with plates of sandwiches and salads, with iced gingerbread, an Edam cheese and
fruit cups and, on a lazy Susan in the middle, jam and butter.
Their family had been almost the first in Midian to serve meals
without a tablecloth.

As they sat down in the square oak chairs, they heard young
Sam tramping upstairs with the bags. His father asked the blessing. "Yes," his mother said, "a lot of people in town think it's
very queer that the Thompsons couldn't have picked another
evening, even if they are Episcopalians."

"The Thompsons," his father reached for the Edam cheese,
"are not interested in the Church; not even in their own."

"Well, of course, if I were an Episcopalian," his mother said,
"I wouldn't see much there to be interested in. It all seems so
sort of light, their church life. Still," she said, "if a person is in a
church, whatever church it is, I always say they ought to be
interested in it. I have lots more respect for an Episcopalian who
is interested in their church life than I do for some people I
could name in our own."

"All right, Mother," his father said; his mouth was full of

Edam cheese, "Tom wants to know about the dance. I'll have a little of that buttermilk, please."

"I know, George, you always cut me off; but it's the truth and you know it. Pass your father the buttermilk. Your father and I," her voice turned serious and slightly artificial, "have been talking it over. We don't approve of the idea of holding a dance on prayer-meeting night and we don't want any one to think that we do, but Mrs. Thompson is an old friend of your Aunt Clara; and, of course, the dance is for young Jeanne. It's not Jeanne's fault, I'm sure. At least, I wouldn't blame her without knowing. It would hurt her very much if you didn't go. It would really be a terrible slap, coming from us that way, on account of the family connection and all." Mechanically she passed the potato salad to his father. "So your father and I have decided that after prayer-meeting, it would be all right for you to come back here and change. Susan can have your things laid out. You won't be very late."

He stared down at his plate. Two nights ago he had been drinking sherry flips in the Manhattan Bar. "Oh, all right," he said.

They moved along the snowy sidewalks under the arc lights and the thin shadows of bare branches. Their breath rose up and slowly trailed behind them. "Look out here," his father said. "Tom, take your mother's arm."

"Some one ought to speak to the Chessmans," his mother said. "They never put cinders in front of their house. Never. George, you ought to do it."

"Some day, some one's going to break a leg," his father said, "and then the Chessmans are going to have a fine suit for damages on their hands."

"It would serve them right," his mother said. "I almost fell here yesterday myself."

"Well, we'll soon be on Clara's," his father said. "You can always count on her to keep her walk in order."

The white door, the silver nameplate, the marble step shone in the winter night. He turned to his mother. "Gosh, Mother, I'd like to step in and say hello."

"We've no time. She's probably up at the farm."

"But I saw a light," he said.

"Well," his father said, "how's your friend Molloy?"

"Oh, he's all right."

"Did you enjoy your visit?" his mother said.

"He's a real quarterback," his father said. "I wish I could have gotten up to the Harvard game."

"Your father was on the committee to raise funds for the new church organ. That Saturday was the last day of the Drive."

"The Buffer was good in the Harvard game," he said. "They all talk about Wally White, but it was really the Buffer's quick kicks that broke them up."

"That's what I figured," his father said, "even from the newspaper account." His voice was almost cordial. "I have always claimed that the quick kick has never been properly developed; it's not understood."

"I know, Father, but it's hard to find fellows who can get the ball off fast enough and get the distance too."

"You can find them," his father said. "You can find men for anything if you want them enough." They crunched along over the cinders and the snow. "They don't understand the quick kick," he said. "The quick kick——"

"George," his mother said. "George, we're getting near the church. Those are the McElwaines right in front of us."

The tall stone face of the church was dark. "I wish you could see the organ," his mother said, "but it's locked up."

At the end of a narrow passageway, a gas light trembled. Ahead of them the McElwaines cast long shadows and went in through a low door.

The basement parlor was a blaze of light. There was a scatter of heads and bonnets among the rows of chairs, a scatter of overshoes, dark coats and limp silk mufflers along the benches at the side. The steam heat met them like a wall.

A seat near the door would be an advantage, but his mother steered down the aisle. He slid his arms out of his overcoat's rich silk-lined sleeves and followed her. He thought there was a slight stir among the chairs. At the harmonica Miss Ba-ba Lamb peered at him through thick lenses and nodded almost imperceptibly.

They sat in the stunning heat. Twice more the door opened and there was a stir as they took note of who came in.

On the low platform, Mr. Stellwagon, the leading elder, gingerly patted the lock across the baldness of his head and poured himself a modest glass of water. He ran a thin finger around his low, standup collar and made sure of his ready-tied, black four-in-hand; he took his watch from his sagging vest and laid it on the table. With a last glance at the door, he stood up and fixed his lidless eyes on interstellar space. "We will open our meeting," he said, "by singing hymn number fifty-two, 'Oh Lamb of God.' 'Oh Lamb of God' "—Miss Ba-ba suppressed a premature bleat from the organ—"hymn number fifty-two."

The watch which Mr. Stellwagon had laid out on the table proved an empty gesture, once Mr. Stellwagon had uncurled the roll of foolscap and addressed himself to deciphering its closely written pages, "Prayer should be inspirational. . . . Prayer should be frequent. . . . Prayer should be purposive. . . . Prayer should be practical . . ." there was nothing to do except to try to guess the number of pages which remained. Then, after the closing hymn, there was the lifeless but insistent greeting of auditors stupefied by steam heat and fifty minutes of Mr. Stellwagon. It was after nine o'clock when he hurried on alone up the snowy sidewalk along River Street. There was a light in his Aunt Clara's upstairs window. He whistled and paused briefly. Half relieved, he hurried on.

CHAPTER XXXVII

UPSTAIRS his dress clothes lay spread out on his bed, magnificent against the background of his boyhood books. As he struggled with his immaculate shirt bosom, "Hans Brinker," "The Lion of St. Mark," "The Dog of Flanders," and "Eric," or "Little By Little" watched him. There was a perilous moment with his white tie; one more mistake and it would have to be discarded. Then he was on River Street again, his chin sunk into his white-silk muffler, his fingers in his pocket against the tissue paper around his white-kid gloves. He had been tempted to borrow a stick of his father's from the stand in the front hall, and he wished that he had dared to buy an opera hat and wear it here in Midian.

As it was, when he hurried around the dancing couples in the Thompsons' downstairs rooms, he was sufficiently content. There were men from the State University with dinner coats and gray silk ties, and a some one with a soft silk shirt and a black tie with white edging. According to the etiquette, he was supposed to pass unseen through the gathering and up the stairs to the men's cloakroom. But there was a rustling movement among the waltzing couples, the burst of a somewhat straining bright red dress, of high color and black hair. Mrs. Thompson had his shoulders between her strong hands. Her eyes were black and bright, in the centre of her brushed-back, gleaming hair was a single narrow flash of gray.

"Well," she said, "where've you been? The town is in an uproar." He cast about for a worldly phrase. "Jeanne," she called without stopping, "here's your Yale boy."

At once young Jeanne was bearing down on him. She also wore a dress of red that crashed a horrible discord beside her mother's. She, too, had black hair and bright color in her dark smiling face, but she was quick and slim although her—although for a young girl her front was somewhat startlingly mature.

"Hello, Bulldog, where've you been?" She took his arm and hugged it. These two were the greatest women for getting their hands on a man.

"Bulldog!" Mrs. Thompson said. "Why, he looks like William Gillette."

"He does," Jeanne said. "Like my beautiful William. I have his picture in my bedroom."

Fortunately the music stopped. A group formed around him. He extended a low hand and well-poised greetings.

"Go up and take off your things," Mrs. Thompson said. "The next dance is a Paul Jones."

"Ah," he said, "Jeanne, may I have it with you?"

Jeanne nodded hard. "You're bright," she said. "In a Paul Jones a man is never stuck for long."

As he mounted the stairs Mrs. Thompson called to him. "Tell Thompy to come down. He's up there doing something about the drinks." She was a fine woman, Mrs. Thompson, and Jeanne too, of course, was fundamentally all right, but what a way to speak of your husband.

Mr. Thompson crouched among the mounds of overcoats. He looked up distractedly over his eye-glasses. "Oh, how do you do? You're looking finely." He crouched again. "How is the party going on?" He spoke as one asking news of a distant land.

"It's going on splendidly, Mr. Thompson. Mrs. Thompson and Jeanne are looking well."

"Oh, yes," Mr. Thompson muttered, "they're both finely, thank you. I can't do anything with this cork. You see," he said, "it's rotten; it comes out in pieces." He held the bottle up. "Some of it's fallen into the wine, I'm afraid. The punch bowl's in the bathroom." He held the bottle up between his eye and the electric chandelier. "I don't like to leave things downstairs with these caterer's men in the house. Yes," he said, "there is cork in it. Have you got a knife?

"All right," Mr. Thompson said, "we'll cut it out. Then if there's any left we'll skim it off the punch bowl." They were in the bathroom now. The bathroom, too, had electricity. "This is really the simplest," he said. "That's got the most of it. Now we'll pour it in. It's Château Lafitte," he said. "It's really a mistake to put it in punch, I suppose. You know the first time I ever tasted Château Lafitte was at your Aunt Clara's years ago.

Your Uncle Fitz-Greene was alive, of course. I wonder if you remember him?"

"Oh, yes."

"Now we can take these teaspoons and go after the cork. He was a charming man; probably the most charming man I ever met. And he always served Château Lafitte."

Downstairs the music started. "Mr. Thompson, I'm afraid I have to go; I have this dance with Jeanne."

"Oh, yes," said Mr. Thompson. "Yes, of course. Well, I hope every one's having a good time."

He descended the walnut stairs toward the field of couples moving in light and music against the background of red curtains and palms in tubs. As he buttoned his white-kid gloves, he could feel the set of his well-cut coat across his shoulders. His pumps gleamed on the dark carpet of the stairs. Jeanne fending off two obscure importunates was frankly waiting for him at the bottom. His hand, compressed and lightly muffled in the kid glove, gave a delicate pull to the bottom of his piqué waistcoat. He smiled at Jeanne. With assumed nonchalance the importunates fell away.

"Talk about prinking," she said, "why I could get dressed and everything quicker than that."

"I was helping your father."

"Is he prinking too?"

"With the punch."

"Oh, how's it coming?"

"It's about ready."

"Good. Some of the boys are getting gloomy." A whistle sounded, the music stopped. Jeanne gave his shoulder a farewell pat. In the middle of the room Bill McGuire, freckled and gangling, took the whistle out of his big mouth and grinned at them. He crinkled up his light-blue eyes.

"Grand chain," he said in a stately emotional voice. "All take hands." The grand chain stretched out into the drawing-room, through the double doors, and came back again across the front of the big hall stairs.

"Isn't Bill sweet?" Jeanne said. "He's leader of the Cornell Glee Club this year."

"Oh, yes, Bill's a peach. Hello, Bill, glad to see you."

"Thomas," Bill said, "a real pleasure. Now, gents, hand the ladies round." He blew his whistle.

Jeanne threw back her head as she passed him. "Good-bye," she said. Good Lord! What a girl. Yet fundamentally—"Hello, Nora." Why must Nora wear all that tulle with eye-glasses—A stranger with a shy, quick smile—Sturdy Ann Emory rocking along and beaming—Right hand, left hand, the girls came by.

She was all in white. Her thin face was translucent. "Why, Julia," he said, "where've you been?" The whistle sounded, they glided across the floor. Her gray eyes were serious under firm straight brows. Her gloved hand barely rested on his shoulder. She was intangible but she did dance well. Tall and light, her bones must be smaller than a bird's. Perhaps he had been a little naïve and exuberant in his greeting.

"Have you been here long?" He was able to make it stately yet kind. She raised her gray eyes briefly to him and looked away.

With a faint fixed smile she shook her head.

"Neither have I," he said. "Where have you been?"

"Ah!" she said.

The whistle sounded. As they stopped, she seemed to elude him and be standing, light and ethereal, and vaguely smiling. And now Bill McGuire's voice was stately. "Ladies in the middle, gents upon the outside."

At the end of the dance there was a stir and brightness on the stairs. Carefully holding the silver punch bowl between them, by its handles Jeanne and her father descended, step by step. Two State boys raised a college cheer, there was a clapping of gloved hands. Mr. Thompson's face was pink, his eye-glasses trembled. Jeanne raised a strong arm cautiously and waved it at them. Down an admiring aisle, they marched into the dining room and set the punch bowl on the tablecloth among the rows of twinkling glasses. They all trooped in behind. He stopped to snatch a dance card from the table beneath the stairs.

Among the crowd around the punch bowl, he could see, a little taller than the other girls, Julia's ash-blonde head. He was an adept at penetrating such a gathering. With delicate ruthlessness, he made his way among them. "Sorry—Do you mind?"

—Just a moment please—Oh, thanks—Excuse me. Julia, may I have the supper dance?"

"I think so." She glanced down at her escort. "Porky has my dance card."

Porky's ruddy face swung up to them, his light-blue eyes came slowly to focus. "Card? Certainly. Julia, have a little punch. No? Well then—" The stout, straining back of Porky's dress coat burrowed away toward the punch bowl.

He smiled at her. "Those Princeton boys like their liquor."

"You know," she said, "it's a shame. I think he had something to drink before he came here. He's been terribly attentive."

He laughed. "That's no proof."

"It's a shame," she said, "and he really is a nice boy."

"Hello," he said, "Porky's been at work on your dance card, I see."

"Oh! What's he done? Let me see?"

"Never mind," he said, "I'll get you another. Let's get out of this." He folded up the dance card firmly. He had saved her from seeing that on her card Porky's name was followed by Elijah Dowie, Casanova, Moody, Heliogabalus, Sankey, and the Marquis de Sade.

In the meagre shelter of potted palms, they sat against the wall.

"You were going to tell me where you've been."

"I really wasn't."

"Is it a secret?"

"No," she steeled herself. "I've been to prayer-meeting."

"That's tough," he said. "So have I."

"Oh," she said, "but I suppose people can do their duty and have fun, too."

"Duty!" he said. "At the First Church we look on prayer as a privilege and a joy."

She colored slightly but she smiled.

"You know," he said, "I've hardly seen you since you were a pigtailed girl at school. You were always very shy and very clean."

"Well," she said, "I'm still very clean."

"Are Farmington girls so bold then?"

"Oh, no," she said; "but I think as you grow up you outgrow shyness, don't you? You were shy, too, when you were a little boy."

"You know," he said, "I think shyness is a form of conceit."

"Oh," she said, "I don't think I was ever conceited; just shy."

"It comes from imagining every one else must be thinking as much about you as you are yourself. After a while it dawned on me that no one was paying much attention to me."

"That's certainly a modest way of explaining self-assurance."

"Do you think I am self-assured?"

"Well, yes."

"Really, it's just a trick, I guess. When you go around with people, you learn what to do and how to do it. After that you fit in and there's nothing to worry about."

"Just the same," she said, "I think it would be nicer if people weren't so conventional."

"What would you do?"

"I wouldn't do anything; but people would be more sincere."

"You would remain the same and other people would be more disagreeable. I don't think much of that."

"Oh, no," she said. "I think there's a lot of good in everybody."

"Of course there's good in everybody; but a lot of people would be sort of uncouth."

"But a lot of good people are uncouth, don't you think?"

"Of course they are. What I mean——"

"What I mean," she said with great earnestness, "is that you oughtn't to hold it against them."

A shadow loomed. "What I mean," it was Bill McGuire, "is that this is my dance. Hold what against who?" he said.

"Julia and I were just talking." He rose meticulously.

"Well," Bill said, "it looked like big stuff." He dropped into the vacant chair. "So it goes," he said to Julia. "One girl's meat is another girl's poison. And vice versa. Now all I can do is yodel; and yet, every once in a while, I find a girl that loves it." He looked up at Tommy. "Oh," he said, "your uncle was looking for you."

"He was? Where was he?"

Bill gave his wide, freckled grin. "Well, he seemed to be more or less in the den behind the dining room."

Cautiously he opened the door into the den. There was a burst of talk and dense smoke above black coats. Wrought-iron wall brackets strove against the darkness of the fumed-oak wall.

He moved among the Morris chairs, shaking hands with older men, toward where his Uncle Mun, in the lee of Mr. Trimble, stood stroking his drooping gray mustache, his small frame lost behind the pleatings of his white silk shirt. He turned his narrow, high-bridged nose. "There he is." He raised a highball glass from the dressed-hide cover of the table. "Tommy, my boy, a health to you."

"Uncle Mun," he said.

Uncle Mun was wearing a white stock like some old actor, his slack white waistcoat was dragged down by an enormous watch and fob, his thin hand shot out. "So you're back, my boy. Shake hands with Mr. Trimble."

Mr. Trimble dropped his bald head, he wrinkled his sandy eyebrows and brooded over him. "Hell of an uncle, don't you think so, Tommy?"

"Well, now my boy," Uncle Mun said, "how about you and me having just a little drink?"

"Thanks, Uncle Mun, but I've just had some punch."

"Punch?" Mr. Trimble said. "That's awful. Don't any of you boys drink whiskey?"

"Of course they do," Uncle Mun said, "but the boy just said he started on punch. He should stick to punch then. Well, my boy," he said, "I see you are breaking hearts already."

"Who was it?" said Mr. Trimble.

"Doggie," Uncle Mun said, "never ask such things. She was a dream. Ah, exquisite! Personally I have a weakness for opulence; but if you like them ethereal, by God, sir——"

Mr. Trimble's hand dropped on Uncle Mun's narrow shoulder, "Mun," he said, "you give me a pain in——"

"Here, Doggie," Uncle Mun said, "that hurts. You will ruin my coat."

"Pass the decanter," Mr. Trimble said.

"Well, my boy," Uncle Mun said, "how are things going at New Haven? I understand you boys have some pretty gay times since they built that Taft hotel." He smiled behind a hand on his mustache and winked a pale-blue eye.

"Some of them do," he said. "How are all the family?"

"Very well," he said. "Your grandfather has his gout, of course. I don't suppose you've seen your Aunt Clara yet."

"No," he said. "I'll go to-morrow."

"You must make a point of that, my boy. She thinks the world of you. Absolutely the world. A wonderful woman, absolutely. Isn't she, Doggie?"

"Look here," Mr. Trimble said, "I hear you room with that new quarterback they've got up there."

"Oh, yes," Uncle Mun said. "He's right in with the football crowd. I understand," he said, "that the football crowd practically run things at Yale."

"Well, I'm not in with them much. I just happened to be a friend of Buffer Molloy's at school."

"Well," Uncle Mun said, "all the better. I always say that a man can choose any one he wants for a friend, of course, but it never does him any harm to have them the right people. For instance, it doesn't do any harm to have it known that I am a personal friend of the Division Superintendent's," he said. "No, sir, it's Mr. Worrall this, and Mr. Worrall that, as soon as I get on the train." He held out his hand. "I hear the music. Those charmers would never forgive me."

"Good-bye, Uncle Mun."

"Good-bye, my boy."

As he made his way through the Morris chairs, he heard his Uncle Mun's voice behind him. "A damn fine figure of a young man."

As he stood at the edge of the field of dancing couples a bridling voice accosted him. "Well, Tommy, don't you recognize your old friends any more?" He turned. Under her gray pompadour Mrs. Trimble smiled at him rigidly. Her gloved hand stroked the front of her dove-gray silk. She carried herself as one unconscious that the glories of her figure had diminished.

"Why, Mrs. Trimble," he said, "how do you do?"

She allowed his extended hand to hang in air a moment; her hand then touched it with marked impersonality. "So we meet at last," she said.

"Yes, indeed, Mrs. Trimble. It certainly is a pleasure. I was just——"

"You passed me several times this evening. I thought perhaps you didn't know me."

"Oh, no, indeed," he said vaguely. "I was just talking to Mr. Trimble in the den."

"So he's in there, is he? What's he doing?"

"Well, he seemed to be—he was just talking with my Uncle Mun."

"Was he drinking? What have they got to drink in there?"

"I really don't know, Mrs. Trimble."

"You don't know whether he was drinking?"

"I mean to say I don't know what they have to drink. I didn't have any."

"I should hope not. You know my husband's been in there ever since we came. You know," she said, "I'm afraid a good deal of the old courtesy has gone. Perhaps," her smile turned arch, "you have found it again in the younger generation."

"Oh, I don't know," he said uneasily.

"I adore dancing," she said, "and I've hardly danced all evening."

He roused himself with a burst of passionate vitality. "Oh, that's too bad, Mrs. Trimble. I'll tell you what I'll do, I'll see what Mr. Trimble's doing now. Just a minute, please." Instantly he was wending his way among the Morris chairs and outstretched legs of the den, conscious, however, that Mrs. Trimble's glance still followed him.

"Good God!" Uncle Mun said, "no luck?"

He could not help but grin. "No luck," he said.

Uncle Mun brought his eyes on the decanter. Slowly and accurately he reached out his thin hand. "A touch of solace?"

"Thanks, Uncle Mun; I had some punch."

"Never mind the punch." Uncle Mun busied himself with the tall glass and the decanter. " 'If, of herself she cannot love, nothing can make her. . . . The devil take her.' "

"Mr. Trimble," he said, "Mrs. Trimble seemed to be looking for you. That's really why I came in here."

"Looking for me? What's the trouble?"

"Oh, no trouble."

"Good! Well, tell her I'll be along." He stared at Tommy firmly over the frosted glass. "Tell her to enjoy herself."

"Oh! All right, Mr. Trimble," he said uneasily.

"Hold on," Mr. Trimble said. "Never mind. Don't tell her anything." He eyed his highball glass in disapprobation. "Mun," he said, "pass the decanter."

He perched on the edge of the table from where he could steal swift, casual glances through the half-opened door. Between times he stared at the burnt-leather likeness of Sitting Bull on the antelope hide over the empty fireplace and listened to the discourse of Mr. Trimble and his Uncle Mun.

"I don't mind swearing. After all, I am a man of the world. But there's swearing and swearing, and what I say is that if a man can't swear like a gentleman, he ought not to swear at all."

"Well," Mr. Trimble said, "I don't mind what language a man uses if he only uses it enough. Then it don't mean anything. Pass the decanter."

"Doggie," Uncle Mun said, "you always were more broad-minded than I am. I'd be the first to admit that," he added in a tone of great satisfaction. "Here, easy on that rye! Anyhow, it's a delicate point. Great Governor!" Uncle Mun said, "you half filled my glass. Doggie, my old friend, this is a punishing evening. A punishing evening. But we mustn't go too hard a pace with this Old Pepper, we must show some consideration for our host."

"Where is Thompy?" Mr. Trimble said. "Haven't seen him all night. Let's get him in here and give him a drink. Thompy's all right."

"Absolutely," Uncle Mun said, "an excellent fellow. Really very much of a gentleman, in his way, and I think we must all admit that he's made a very faithful husband for Jeanne."

"Certainly," Mr. Trimble said. "I'll admit it. Why not? It's something nobody can prove. Here, you! Mind you bring back that decanter."

Through the maze of tobacco smoke and outstretched legs, he wandered to the door. In the dining room, the punch bowl and all the little glasses stood alone on the big, stained tablecloth; beyond them were the dancers and the palms, the tall, red curtains and the sounds of music. In the heart of this confusion, Jeanne Thompson's scarlet dress clove through the black coats which surrounded her. Her black hair seemed blown back from her impudent, yet not unfriendly, face. Her gown seemed blown back against her small, but ample figure. She raised a bare arm toward him with exaggeration. "Hi, Bulldog, where have you been?" She came up to him where he stood beside the table, her black eyes mocking him above her big, half-smiling mouth. "In with the heavy drinkers, eh? How are they coming on in there?" She leaned back against the table and locked her arms sturdily across her front. The attitude caused something of a display. He cast his glance aside.

"What's it like in there?" she said; "do you think I'm missing anything?"

"Not a thing, Jeanne," he said.

"Oh, go on," she said. "What do they talk about? Let's have it."

"Here, have a little punch," he said.

"Why, certainly," she said. "Now what do they talk about? Do they talk about us?"

"Oh, Lord, no," he said. "They wouldn't do that."

"Just rough stories. But why wouldn't they? We talk about them. What do you think about our punch?"

"It's great stuff."

"The idea is to compete with the boys' club in there. It keeps them out here on the floor where they can do some good."

"It works," he said, "except with the real old whiskey drinkers."

"It hasn't worked with you, though. What goes on in there?"

"It's terrible. I've been talking with Mr. Trimble and Uncle Mun."

"Getting an earful of chivalry. But you know I love Uncle Mun. He's so gallant and at the same time he always makes me feel so potentially degraded." She licked the punch off her lips with relish. "You can't expect more than that from any one man. Well, why did you stay there then?"

"Do you really want to know?"

She waved a hand again. "Just a clean-cut young Eli," she said, "impressive but obtuse. They turn them out by thousands." She took his arm and hugged it to her. "Listen, my Bulldog," she said, "I really want to know, in fact, I've been asking."

He could not help but grin at her, but slightly uneasily, conscious that the tableau was intimate and that many people watched it.

"I am obtuse," he said. "I can't believe that you are so nosey." With her arm in his, she laughed, throwing back her head and still holding his somewhat rigid arm.

And now the covert observation was brought to an awkward

focus by the figure of Porky Montross that wove across the open double doorway. He came to a stop and made a flourish toward them.

"Our last number of the evening," he said. "The Temptation of Saint Anthony." He studied them attentively. "Perhaps a shade more sense of struggle, Mr. Rand." Seriously he wavered out of sight amid the giggles.

"Isn't he wonderful?" she said. "He's always that way when he comes, and all night long he never changes, no matter what he drinks."

"Oh, yes," he said; "Porky's quite a sketch. Well," he said, "I went in there to get away from Mrs. Trimble."

"Oh, golly!" she said; "there's more things going on in this town. But what's the matter with Meta? Her heart's in the right place, and most of the rest of her anatomy."

"Anyhow," he said, "it has the look of having used-to-have-been."

"Complicated," she said, "but true."

"Whose anatomy?" Bill McGuire grinned down at them and mopped the freckles on his brow. "The word anatomy will bring me every time."

Jeanne took his arm. "Have a seat on the table, Bill," she said. "Mrs. Trimble's anatomy."

Bill rammed his handkerchief into his breast pocket. "Oh." he said.

"Well, then," Jeanne said, "we'll talk about anybody's anatomy you want."

Bill brightened. "A fair, businesslike offer," he said; "we'll talk about yours."

The music had started again. Leaning against the table with Jeanne's hand still in the crook of his arm, as she leaned away from him and laughed with Bill, he watched the crowded floor. Then he was on his feet: in the heart of the dancers, the tight, fat back of Porky Montross was bouncing about eccentrically and, above it, the dignified, set face of Julia Wilton.

"Wait, Tommy," he heard Jeanne say; "you're missing something."

He hovered for a moment on the edge of the floor. The two came by. Porky bounced and pushed, industriously attempting to animate Julia's floating dignity, while at the same time he turned a red face up to her unresponsive mask and shouted above the music.

From his place between the palms, he stepped forward and laid a hand on Porky's arm. "May I cut in, please?" Porky continued to bounce assiduously. He was obliged to follow him. He closed his hand. "May I cut in, please?" The bouncing subsided to a gentle rocking.

Slowly Porky peered over his shoulder. "Hey, what the deuce?" he said.

"Come on, Porky," he was firm and genial, "don't you cut in at Princeton, yet?"

"Absolutely!" He rotated slowly. "Well, it's up to Julia."

The light color rose in her pale fragile face. "That would be lovely," she said. She turned to Tommy. "Thank you, Porky."

Porky made a gesture of demonstration with a bursting glove. "The Lily Maid of Astolat," he said.

As they wound among the dancers, she let her hand rest on his shoulder. "Thank you, Tommy, that was nice of you."

CHAPTER XXXVIII

No direct sunlight could penetrate the golden-oak dining room, but a gas log glowed and muttered in the fireplace, and bright electric bulbs protruded from the fluted pearl shades of the brass chandelier. Under his hands the linen tablecloth felt cool and deep. The voice of young Sam was in his ear. "Good morning, Mr. Tommy. How you feel to-day?"

"I'm fine, Sam."

"You mother say save everything hot on the stove. You like that shaddock first?"

On the table lay the *Morning Messenger* and the *Midian Daily Times*. He glanced at the headlines: "Samuel Schmall Out For Sheriff . . . Unrest in Barcelona . . . Oddfellows Convene . . . Sewer Mooted For Duck Creek Extension." The *Messenger* was about the same, except that instead of the mooted sewer they had a headline: "Tot a Heroine." It seemed that Vida Enschmingle, six-year-old daughter of Mr. and Mrs. Ovid Enschmingle of 1597 Huckleberry Boulevard, seeing her little brother, Royall Enschmingle, on fire, had run out onto the street and smashed the glass of a fire alarm. This timely action had attracted the attention of neighbors who had then saved Royall before the fire company arrived. An ambulance was summoned by Patrolman Harry S. Smith and Roundsman Cassius Delahanty who had also responded to the alarm and the babe removed to the Midian General Hospital, where he was treated for burns by Dr. Ralph W. Pottfield who pronounced him out of danger. At a late hour the child was able to leave the hospital in charge of his father, Mr. Ovid Enschmingle, the well-known and popular steam stationary engineer connected with the Little Jewel Sanitary Mattress Company.

The grapefruit slid into view, and Sam's alpaca sleeve and long gray palm. "Hear they had mighty fine times up there last night, Mr. Tommy."

"Yes, it was a fine party."

"They tell me they had music from Baltimore. Nine pieces."

"Yes, I guess there were nine. They were pretty good. Who told you?"

"Well, Mr. Levi, he said something about it. He was up there helping out, opening oysters for the supper and all such."

"Didn't you go up there, yourself, Sam?"

"Well, yes, I was up there a little while. I didn't get into the big room though. Didn't have my clawhammer on. I was just kind of helping Mr. Levi with the oysters. Just kind of helping out. How you like your eggs to-day?"

Over the scrambled eggs he looked at the social column: "Mr. Thomas Rand, a student at Yale University, has returned for the holidays where he is the house guest of his parents, Mr. and Mrs. George Rand, 7 East Linden Street. . . . Mr. and Mrs. W. J. Z. Thompson honor their daughter with an elaborate entertainment —Among those present Mr. Harry Yawkley, Mr. Fordyce Montross, Mr. Thomas Rand," he raised his eyes up the column, "Mr. and Mrs. M. M. Trimble, Mr. and Mrs. Ulysses Sockman . . . also the Misses Lou Ella Pastor, Imogen Ronthaler, Sarah Westwood, Julia Wilton." . . . He laid the paper down and finished his scrambled eggs, his eyes fixed unseeing on the sea bass in the still life on the opposite wall.

"Good morning, dear."

He rose, hastily wiping at his mouth. "Good morning, Mother."

He wished she would not wear that dove-gray. It was too old for her bright eyes and little pointed nose.

She gave him her quick hard hug. "Did you sleep well? I told them to keep breakfast hot. Go on and finish. Your father left an hour ago. Did you have a good time? Who did you see? Who did you dance with?"

"Well, I saw Uncle Mun."

"Your Uncle Mun? He will keep going to those parties for younger people."

"Well, Mr. Trimble was there, too, and several other older gentlemen."

"Who did you dance with?"

"Well, I danced with Jeanne, of course."

"Oh, yes, of course. Jeanne's very like her mother. Was Julia Wilton there?"

"Yes," he said, "I danced with her. She'd been to prayer-meeting too, and then came afterwards."

"Julia is a very fine girl," she said, "and very popular. You see, people can do their duty and have a good time too. That's what I always say."

He smiled at her perched on the arm of the dining-room chair looking down on him with watchful vigor. "Well, we had a good time, Mother."

"You see?" she was triumphant.

"Everybody had a good time."

"Oh," she said. She rallied. "Have you any things to be pressed? I have been looking at your socks. Isn't there any one at New Haven who can mend them for you? It seems to me that they ought to have some one at these colleges that can do things like that."

"I have been letting them all go until I got home," he said.

"Of course that's really the best, but then you ought to have more socks."

"All right," he said, "I'll get them."

"Oh, no," she said, "you mustn't do that."

"Well, but——"

"Just wait," she said, "you wait and see."

"Oh, all right, Mother. Merry Christmas!"

She compressed her lips and affected to ignore him. "I don't want to hurry you, but I really think it would be well to call on your grandparents and your Grandmother Worrall."

"All right," he said, "and I must go to see Aunt Clara."

"Oh, yes, of course. That will be everybody. You saw your Uncle Mun last night."

"Yes," he said, "I saw him."

At the front door she smoothed the white silk muffler around his neck and the black velvet collar of his coat. "Don't stay too long," she said, "just a call, you know."

"All right, Mother."

"Wait!" she said. She looked behind her and sank her voice. "Have you——"

"What?" He stopped on the step.

She peered out the door. "Have you been to——?" Her voice died away, her face turned crimson. "It's very important for your health, you know."

With a grin, he reached a hand in through the door and patted her gray hair. "That's right, Mother. It's all right." Chuckling and glowing he ran down the steps. On the sidewalk he took off his derby hat and waved it at her.

As he reached the corner, the river and the snowy islands were blinding in the winter sunlight. Skaters' black figures wound among the frozen cakes, little boys coasted down the bank and shot far out across the ice. Behind him as he walked up the street, sounded the sparse sleigh bells of a farm team on the wooden bridge.

He passed by the pressed-brick front and tall brownstone steps of Grandfather Rand's and crossed the rutted snow where Maple Street came out on the river. He was in sight of Grandmother Worrall's bay window when the front door opened to emit a sort of mustard-colored glow; the enormous wide-shouldered collegiate overcoat of Uncle Mun gingerly descended the two front steps. A green Homburg hat rakishly cocked-up in front accentuated the dejected pallor of his face. His feet and trousers were encased in arctics which disappeared under his voluminous low-hanging overcoat whose bilious brilliance was embellished by wide checks of green.

"Good morning, Uncle Mun."

Uncle Mun shuffled toward him precariously along the snowy walk. "Well, what are you up to?"

"I was coming up to see Grandmother."

Uncle Mun gave a short sardonic laugh which ended in a slight display of flatulence. "Your grandmother? She's gone out an hour ago." He shuffled past without a glance. "You'll never find your grandmother in at this hour of the day."

"Well, then, I'll go down and see Grandfather Rand." He caught up with Uncle Mun.

"Don't wait for me," Uncle Mun said. "Go on and break your neck." He walked patiently beside Uncle Mun. "Go on," Uncle Mun said. "Well, what is it? By gad, look at these sidewalks. If I were mayor of this town—Look here," he said, "take a tip from me, I'm an older man; never mix round with fellows like that Thompson. He's simply not our kind. If it weren't for Jeanne and her mother—What I say is if a man doesn't want to entertain, he doesn't have to. But to serve absolutely green undrinkable refreshments is an insult. Look out for this ice. It's just the same as if I were to ask a gentleman to my house and slap his face. You're going in here, I suppose. Give my regards to your grandfather and grandmother. I can't stop, I've a lot of business waiting for me at the office." Without a look behind him he shuffled steadily down the street.

He pressed on the mug-like handle beside the big oak door. This house was really incredible, these pink tiles on the floor of the vestibule, the fanciful brass grilles in the little windows in the door, windows, themselves, shut off by pink silk curtains; and up above, the pressed-brick face, the unpalatable brownstone trim, the red and blue and yellow slates of the mansard roof with its spiked iron railing to keep the birds from falling off it. His grandfather, quiet, strong and simple, did not belong in a house like this. The old man should build a house in the style of Vanderbilt Hall at New Haven. Inside there could be Morris chairs and fumed-oak panelling like Mr. Thompson's den.

There was a heavy tread on the walk behind him and the slap of unbuttoned arctics. He had a glimpse of the large and formless figure of Miss Trimble, and shrank back in the vestibule. One of the families' inexplicable friends, uncouth, incredible, beetle-browed, downy-faced, and ruthless. Would Samuel never come? The door swung open. Ignoring Miss Trimble's booming, "Hey, there!" he stepped into the hall and Samuel's inevitable embrace.

"Well, I declare," Samuel said, "you are a regular young gentleman." Holding him by the elbows, Samuel swayed back to survey him.

"Hello, Samuel. Well, I try to be."

"It's a great pleasure to have you back, Thomas." He felt the shake of Samuel's warm white hand. "Your grandfather and grandmother will be delighted. Your father and mother are delighted too, I'm sure."

"Well, it's nice to be back."

"And now let me take your coat and hat. Your grandmother is out at a meeting, The Ladies' Auxiliary, but your grandfather is in his private office."

With a flourish Samuel had his hat and coat hung up beside the enormous mirror opposite the cows. His wide-cut collar showed an expanse of white, fat throat which quivered as he cleared it in preparation for resuming office. "Now, sir," he spoke if he had never seen Tommy in his life before, "just step this way."

A thread of cigar smoke hung about the strong white head, the firm dark figure. He was leaning forward toward Levi Mistletoe who knelt in the shadows at his feet among a collection of boots and shoes.

"Mr. Thomas Rand," Samuel said in a loud voice, and vanished with a bow.

"Well, T," his grandfather tramped slowly around in his stocking feet, revolving his swivel chair.

"Hello, Grandfather. How are you?" His hand was enfolded in the big hand with its liver spots and white square immaculate nails.

Heavily, Levi Mistletoe struggled to his feet and bowed beamingly with a congress boot in each hand.

"Sit down," his grandfather said. "Levi, get Mr. Thomas a chair."

He sat down, guarding the creases of his trousers, and fingered the small knot of his necktie and his diamond horseshoe pin. His grandfather's dark-blue tie was not knotted, it passed through a gold ring and then fell smoothly to his broadcloth waistcoat.

"I'm glad you came in," his grandfather said. "I was just going out. Now, Levi, we'll try on that other pair. Have a cigar? Well, then, smoke a pipe if you like."

As he brought his pipe out he wished it was a little older. It had a small "Y" in silver on the bowl and looked quite new. "How is grandmother?" he said.

"She's well, thank you. Very well indeed. She has her indigestion, of course." He reached slowly back to the desk for his lighted cigar. "Don't know how she'd get along without it. Don't know how Considine would either." He gave his soundless chuckle. "Well," he said, "does them both good. She's very fond of Considine."

"Well," he said, "I suppose Dr. Considine is a very good doctor. He must be getting old, though."

"Old? Nonsense. He's younger than I am."

"Well, how are you, Grandfather?"

"Oh, I'm all right; if only I could get proper shoes." He tapped his cigar against the big bronze ash-tray. "You know, they don't seem to know how to make shoes any more." He pointed his cigar at Tommy's cherry-colored cordovan shoes with their sharp toes. "Take those shoes," he said, "the material's all right, I imagine, but I couldn't wear shoes like that. Whew! Levi," he said, "that's too tight. Let's try another pair. Well," he said, "I hear you had quite a party last night."

"Yes, we did, Grandfather. Who told you?"

"Levi. He's the only person who ever tells me anything."

"Well, I guess Levi knows all about it. He was up there."

"What!" his grandfather said. "Were you up there, Levi?"

Levi dropped his head among the shoes. "Well, sir, I was just up there kind of helping round for a little while. The butler up there he talked like he needed a little help with the oysters."

"So you were up there," his grandfather said. "Well, why didn't you tell me that?"

"Young Sam was up there, too," Tommy said.

"Everybody was there." His grandfather chuckled. "Yes, I expect there were a lot of people ringing bells around town last night without getting much result. If you wanted any service last night you had to go up to the Thompsons', I expect. Who was there?"

"Oh, everybody was there, Grandfather."

"Come, come," his grandfather said.

He grinned. "Well, I danced with Jeanne Thompson and Lou Ella Pastor and Sarah Westwood and Imogen Ronthaler, and I had supper with Julia Wilton."

"Oh, yes," his grandfather said, "a pale girl. Lives uptown. Very nice girl, they tell me. Well, how is Jeanne?"

"Oh, she was fine."

"Lots of life, that girl," his grandfather said. "So had her mother, still has too. Good-hearted girls, too, both of them. Your mother was always a little down on her though."

"Oh, but I thought she was a friend of mother's."

"Your grandmother, I mean. I don't know about your mother, I suppose they are friends. Well, what else went on?"

"Well, Uncle Mun was there."

"Mun? I expect he doesn't feel so well to-day."

"No. I saw him on the street. He seemed a little bit gloomy."

"Ah! Well, who else?"

"Well, Mr. Trimble and Mrs. Trimble, and a fellow I know named Porky Montross."

"Who?"

"Fordyce Montross, his real name is."

"Oh, yes, of course. I know the family. Well, what was he up to?"

"He was all right. He really had a little too much to drink, I think."

"Too much to drink, eh? Well, he didn't make himself disagreeable, did he?"

"Oh, no."

"Well, that's all right then. Very good people, the Montrosses. Levi, I think we'd better go back to the old ones. How are you getting on with your studies?"

"What's that, sir?" Levi said.

"I was talking to Mr. Thomas."

"I guess I'm all right, Grandfather. We don't have exams till February."

"Examinations, eh? Well, how about finances?"

"I guess I'm going to make it, Grandfather. Of course, there are a good many expenses junior year."

"No doubt. Well, here; this will keep you going till Christmas anyhow." His grandfather slowly reached in his waistcoat pocket and drew out a twenty-dollar gold piece.

"Great Scott, Grandfather, that's an awful lot!'

"Well," his grandfather said, "it's twenty dollars. We can all agree on that. Just ring for Samuel, will you?"

"Thanks, very much, Grandfather. I certainly am much obliged."

"Levi," his grandfather said, "we'll need a little more of that talcum powder."

Samuel's stealthy tread sounded in the hall. "Samuel," his grandfather called out.

"Yes, sir."

"Bring me my hat and coat."

"Yes, sir."

"And another twenty-dollar gold piece." He clamped the arms of his chair and pushed himself up. "Yes," he said, "these old shoes are the best. It's a funny thing they can't make them any more." He took a slow experimental step toward the table and crushed out his cigar on the ash-tray. "I must be off," he said, "I want to see your father down at the office." He looked out steadily at the river. "I suppose you'll go skating to-day." He kept on gazing at the river. "Look out for air holes between the islands."

The light ring of sleigh bells came nearer. "There goes Gus Ringler," he said. "I'm glad somebody still keeps a good horse in this town."

Levi's voice came from among the boots. "That horse got a spavin."

"Well, he travels sound."

"Got a spavin just the same."

His grandfather chuckled.

Samuel came in with the overcoat and square-topped derby hat on his arm. His grandfather turned slowly round. As he did so, Samuel made a sort of respectful magician's pass at him. His grandfather raised his hand and tapped the new gold piece in his waistcoat pocket.

His heavy shoulders rocked and strained as he got into his overcoat. With a flourish the hat was held inverted before him. "Gloves?" he said.

"In the overcoat pocket, sir."

"What about a muffler, Grandfather?"

"Muffler? Good gracious! I never wore a muffler in my life." Very deliberately his grandfather buttoned his coat of dark melton. "Samuel, you might get me my stick with the steel point." He turned to Tommy, "Half the people in this town neglect the sidewalks. A man ought to be rough-shod like a horse. Those automobiles get stuck. The wheels go around b-z-z-z."

"They can put on chains though, Grandfather."

"Yes. Whang, whang, whang. They're good things in summer though. I think I'll get one. Do you know anything about them?"

"A little bit. Father's Apperson is awfully good."

"Yes, it's all right. He takes me out in it. It's too flashy though, black body, red wheels. That's well enough for a coach."

Samuel brought in the stick, his grandfather got under way.

"Would you like me to go with you, Grandfather?"

"To the office? No. You wait here; your mother—your grandmother will be home any minute." Samuel and Levi fell in behind, and he started to follow. His grandfather's voice came back from the corridor. "You can wait here in my office."

He turned back and sat down in his grandfather's swivel chair. Everything, the cutglass inkwell, the agate paper weight, the ivory paper knife, was enormous. In front of him through the double window was the snow-dusted iron stag, the low brick wall, the river where black specks of skaters moved against the shining ice. A light sleigh came by, and the mumbling runners of a long farm sled. There was a Reo with curtains flapping, and the eerie silence of a Stanly steamer.

At his right, on the desk, stood the nickel-plated telephone, and hanging from a hook, the flimsy telephone book, its gray cover bearing advertisements of the Midian Grain and Feed Company, and Moller's, The One-Price Store.

Was it too early to call her? He pulled his thin watch from his upper waistcoat pocket. Ten o'clock. The thin chain swung in his hand. That was not too early, but was it too soon, right the morning after? A little soon, but he ought to be able to make it casual. A man his age, a Junior at college; and here was a chance to telephone in private. Levi was in the stable, Samuel was in the pantry.

He opened the telephone book on the desk. "H." . . . "M" . . . "W." . . . "Wilton, Mr. and Mrs. Edward F., 1232 River Street." He stared intently at the type. What would he say? "Hello, Julia. How do you feel after the prayer-meeting last night?" Then she would say, "Who is this?" "This is your conscience." For a moment he smiled. But then it didn't seem so funny; though, of course, you could never be sure. And she might not take it well, especially about prayer-meeting. After all a girl's ideals ought to be respected, and besides she might not say, "Who is this?"

"Julia, I just called up to see how you were feeling. I thought you looked tired last night. I wondered if you were doing anything this afternoon." But that would sort of let him in pretty deep, a girl might take that as having a good deal of meaning. And that part about looking tired at the dance. Gosh! That was no thing to say at all.

He slapped the book shut. He was a man, let him plunge in, rely on his resources. That was the way these fellows that the girls were crazy about did; spun it along without a thought, and it all came out all right. Why certainly! He reached his hand out and ground the handle of the box.

"Number, please."

"Oh. Just a minute. Excuse me." He tried to find the place with one hand. The book flopped perversely on its back. "Messersmith, Coal and Wood."

"Number, please."

He laid the receiver on the desk. Williams. Williamson. Wilson. Wilton. He seized the receiver. "Seven-one-J," he said. There was no response. The telephone emitted a hum and a dry cackle. He ground the handle. "Seven-one-J, please."

"Hello, Julia, is that you?"

"Hello, hello," the voice was faint and sweet.

"Julia, is that you?"

The voice came now, distinct but far off, tiny. "This is the maid."

"Oh. Well, I want to speak to Miss Wilton, Miss Julia Wilton."

"Miss Julia's gone out."

"Gone out? Well, when will she be back?"

"I don't know. I don't know at all."

"Where has she gone?"

"I don't know. She's gone sleigh-riding."

"Sleigh-riding? When did she go?"

There was a pause at the other end, and then a conference and distant shouted words. The telephone hummed and cackled. "About ten o'clock. She went out with Mr. McGuire."

"Well, don't you know when she will be back? Will she be back to lunch?"

But now there was only the steady, vacant hum. Slowly he hung up the receiver. He stared at the skaters on the river. His grandmother might be back any moment now. He hoped he could get out of the house without Samuel hearing him.

But Samuel's step was in the corridor; his moonlike face was at the door. "A lady wishes to speak to you."

He jumped up. "A lady! Who is it?"

"I did not inquire, sir."

"What's she look like?"

"It is on the telephone."

He sat down again. For an instant he stared at the nickelled telephone. Was there such a thing as mental telepathy? He picked up the receiver.

"Hello," he said, "hello!"

A delicate, mincing voice came through the humming. "Hello."

"Hello," he said, "is that you? Who's that?"

The voice was low. "It's Meta."

His heart sank. "Oh. Why Mrs. Trimble," he said, with uneasy heartiness, "good morning. How are you?"

"When can I see you for a moment, Tommy?"

"Why, Mrs. Trimble, is it important?"

"To me it is," the voice was mournful, "Tommy, dear."

"Why, Mrs. Trimble," he said. The receiver spluttered faintly. "Who's that?" he said. "Jeanne, you goat!"

"Bulldog," she said, "I've been chasing you all over town by telephone. What are you doing this morning?"

"Oh, I don't know," he said.

"We're going to have a hockey game at eleven o'clock."

"All right," he said, "I might do that."

"You might as well; your girl is gone."

"What girl?"

"With Bill McGuire," she said, "sleigh-riding. See you at eleven. Oh, say," she said, "have you got any extra sticks?" Affecting not to hear her, he hung up the receiver.

On the snowy street he stepped along briskly. He had a happy thought. He had not given his name when he called up Julia. So then he could call up again at lunchtime. A funny thing, her going sleighing with Bill McGuire. Bill was all right, but just a diamond in the rough when you came down to it. And who would expect that Bill would be attracted to her. Not that any one wouldn't, but you'd think that Bill would feel that she was too fine a type for him. He'd probably feel more at home with girls more ordinary.

When you came to think of it, it was a funny thing the way bums and roughnecks made a beeline for her. Take Porky, for instance. It was a lucky thing that he had been there himself.

He slackened his swift pace. Moving ahead of him with an air of carrying a figure was the tight-waisted, lavender coat of Mrs. Trimble. He inched along, looking at the skaters and the boys on sleds, and stopping once to watch a Cadillac one-lunger steam, pounding, out of sight. Caught between Mrs. Trimble and the indifferent humming telephone, he saw the world as something less than radiant. The skaters shouted and gyrated with exaggerated gusto, and as for the pleased expressions bumping along in the Cadillac, they were fatuous.

Here was Linden Street, but he didn't care to go back home. A lonely figure; he was in no mood for mothering. He crept along in the wake of Mrs. Trimble. At the moment, he was suspended in a void.

Then he remembered he was to go and see Aunt Clara. And she would say, "Hello, there," and be full of laughter. Before he knew it, he had gained on Mrs. Trimble dangerously.

His Aunt Clara was coming down the narrow stairs at the back of the narrow hall. Her black silhouette was slim and quick. "Hello, there," she said. He almost laughed. She gave his hand a quick firm shake. Except for the crow's feet around her eyes, her face was like a strong but sensitive young man's. "I've got a fire upstairs in the library."

"I was afraid you might be up at the farm," he said as he mounted the stairs behind her.

"Oh, no," she called back. "I suppose I oughtn't to say it, but I was hoping you'd come in." In the library she turned and gave him her faint smile. "Here, take your Uncle Fitz-Greene's chair."

With a quick careless movement she smoothed her dark-blue skirt and sat back. One pointed slipper lay far out in front of her. "Do you want to smoke?"

"Thanks." With a slight heave he brought his pipe out and examined it professionally. "What about the farm?" he said.

"I'm having a great time. Father thinks I'm crazy."

He knocked his pipe out against the fireplace. "Why," he said seriously, "what's the trouble?"

"I've got a French stallion," she said. "I had a terrible time with Mr. Heisdick too. He's a real Dutchman; and anyway," she said, "I'm always just a little girl to him."

"Yes," he said, "I guess that's so. What's grandfather say?"

"Oh, he's dubious; but, you see, he's a trotting-horse man. Anyhow," she said, "I've got Mr. Heisdick. He's always been wonderful with any stock on the place. He has the touch. But when I mentioned bringing a horse from France, he said the most terrible things to me."

"What!" he said. "He did? Well, by gosh!"

"No, no," she said. "He's just a Dutchman; you can't change them."

"Never mind," he said. "I'll bet you make a success of it."

She laughed. "That isn't even a compliment. There's too much luck in it. But look here," she said, "what about you?"

"Oh, I'm fine."

"Of course you're fine. I mean what are you doing? How's the Buffer? What's going on at New Haven? What about last night?"

"I went to prayer-meeting first with father and mother."

"Yes, yes, I know."

"It was a dandy party. It really was."

"How's young Jeanne?"

"She was fine. The life of the party."

"She always is, and I believe there's more to her than just that too."

"Yes," he said.

"Who did you have supper with?"

"With Julia Wilton."

"Oh," she said. "I don't know her. Every one says she's a nice girl."

"Oh, yes," he said. "But I'll tell you. You know there's a funny thing about her. I can't figure it out. She's an awfully fine girl, she really is. And yet, all the roughnecks and fellows that have a little edge on all make a bee-line for her."

"Does she encourage them?"

"Oh, my goodness, no! But they just stick to it. It's a funny thing. Julia," he added, "wouldn't encourage any one. She's not that kind."

"I'm sure she's not," she said. "Sometimes the kind that do encourage men are nice girls too."

"Oh, yes," his voice was perfunctory and worldly wise. "I suppose you never can tell." His hand, negligently in his pocket, touched the twenty-dollar gold piece. "What do you think," he said, "what do you think grandfather gave me just now?"

She laughed. "He would be apt to give you anything."

"A twenty-dollar gold piece. And then what do you think he did?"

"Then I think he sent Samuel for another one."

"Shucks!" he said. "You know everything."

"I ought to know that," she said, "it's been like that for years. Didn't you ever hear about the time that father got on the B. and O. without his pocketbook?"

"No," he said.

"The conductor came along and he had no money. Since then Samuel keeps a supply of twenty-dollar gold pieces and puts one in father's waistcoat pocket every morning when he lays out his clothes, so it can never happen again."

"I should think grandfather could have told the conductor who he was. Gosh!" he said, "they didn't put him off the train, did they?"

"Put him off the train! Why, the conductor had known your grandfather for years. He gave him a ticket and loaned him money too."

"Well, then——"

"It was just the idea of it; the idea, I suppose, of not being able to meet an obligation when it was due. He never got over it."

"Well, I'll be darned," he said. "I never heard of that."

"You ought to have been told," she said, "because you must never speak of it to him."

"All right, I won't." He grinned. "I've got to go; we're going to have a hockey game at eleven o'clock." He stood up. "Come on out," he said, "and get in it."

She flushed with pleasure. "I'll get my skates and come out and watch," she said.

On the shining ice the dark figures dodged; hockey sticks cracked and rattled; the puck slid to and fro and rapped against the sticks; figures sprinted, turned and stopped in spurts of ice flakes. They bumped and shouted good advice and eager adjurations.

Along the side lines, his Aunt Clara, a slim figure in her steel gray suit, moved with easy grace; and also, slim and graceful in warm brown, Julia stood among the small boys and little girls with sleds, and watched the game. It seemed that Jeanne had also gotten word to Bill McGuire who, at the moment, in shirt sleeves and brown felt hat, leaned intertwined and locked in a rigid pose with Mr. Trimble down at the other end.

Skating slowly toward them in his Wyomensing sweater, he joined in the passionate exclamations, "Stick to it, Bill!" "Don't let him get it!" The locked pose broke. The puck was wobbling across the ice. He bit his skates in and swung toward it. From another angle, Jeanne's orange sweater was also flashing toward the puck; it was a close race. He leaned ahead and felt his legs fly after him. As he reached for the puck, the shock of her sturdy body met his hip; he seemed to rotate slowly, then faster and with this speed to rise like a pinwheel and hover gyroscopically. There was a stunning thump when he came down and a far-away thin ringing in his ears. Far down the ice, he saw the orange sweater and the waving sticks and heard them shouting, "Goal!"

CHAPTER XXXIX

It was the Sunday after New Year's, his last day at home. The morning was fine and mild, and the sidewalks were clear; and according to custom, the worshippers of the better sort were parading River Street after the morning services. There were Episcopalians from St. Vincent's and Presbyterians from the First Church and from Hancock Square, and there was Captain Mottley who stayed at home and read Colonel Bob Ingersoll but always turned out in time for the Sunday parade. He said it was the only religious ceremony that had any value. The strict Sectarians thought it regrettable there was no legal way of preventing Captain Mottley from participating. But it was even impossible to refrain from reasonably cordial greetings, for a direct ancestor of Captain Mottley's had been scalped by Indians on this very river bank in the year that Midian was founded.

He came along now among the scattering of well-dressed pedestrians on the undulating bricks; his pointed nose was dripping, and his narrow chin, though much scarred by the razor, was only partly shaved. He waved his silver-headed oak stick in salutation, causing his rusty black raincoat to flap. Under cover of this general camaraderie he kept a pale, but sharp eye out for any young girls with charm.

Tommy Rand, neatly swathed in his Kresge suit, his high collar and his black overcoat, and working industriously at raising his well-brushed derby hat, felt his mother's glove tighten on his arm. "Goodness!" she said. "Look at Captain Mottley now."

Looking ahead among the slowly moving people he made out Captain Mottley's tall frame and incurably rumpled brown felt hat. He was bending over in a predatory attitude and grinning with insufferable assurance. In front of him, Julia Wilton, lovely in a gray tailored suit with black fox, was serious, well-bred and slightly flushed. Beside her stood her tall parents, politely restive.

"I declare!" his mother said. "That old man! . . . Good morning, Mrs. Munkittrick. Wasn't it a lovely sermon?"

Mrs. Munkittrick shook her ostrich plumes. "Well, Ellen, you may think so."

"It certainly was the Gospel, though," his mother said.

"There was no elegance to it," Mrs. Munkittrick said. "My father never preached a sermon," she said, "without at least five classical allusions. It was the one unvarying rule of his life. In his day a minister of the Gospel was supposed to be a scholar. A sermon!" she said. "It might do for the Mission at the lower end of town."

"But, Mrs. Munkittrick——"

"I don't know where the Church gets its ministers these days. The Foundling Home, perhaps."

"Why, Mrs. Munkittrick!"

"If it keeps up, we'll be no better off than Rome."

Captain Mottley was talking away, shifting on his long thin feet; and every shift brought him closer to Julia Wilton. He felt his mother's hand on his arm. "Aren't you, dear?"

"I beg your pardon, Mother."

"I said you are interested in church work. He's very active in the Y. M. C. A. up there."

"Dwight Hall," he said.

"Yes," his mother said. "They sent eight boys to the Foreign Field from there. Sometimes," she said, "I think, perhaps Thomas may feel the call." He looked at her astounded. She was trying to impress.

"What!" said Mrs. Munkittrick. "And go to some outlandish place?" She clutched her ruffled taffeta cloak around her. "Ellen, you're crazy." Her plumes nodded away.

"Poor Mrs. Munkittrick," his mother said in an angry voice. "You have to humor her." The Wiltons had started moving on ahead and Captain Mottley, unabashed, was walking beside Julia. Good God! He was taking her arm. The old— "She's been like that for thirty years," his mother said. "I don't see how she stands it. She's always furious. A woman that age. Why, I can remember when Dr. Flowers introduced individual communion cups; and she's been awful to your father about the new church organ. It got so bad that finally, one day, I made up my mind.

I said to her— Why son! What's the hurry?" His mother's
sharp face broke into softness. "You run along then."

To catch up with Mr. and Mrs. Wilton and with Julia was
not easy. He strolled as fast as he dared, slowed down passing groups to raise his hat nonchalantly. But the Wiltons, at the
same time, were attempting to walk away from Captain Mottley.
Their speed was unbelievable, yet unavailing. With ease the flapping figure maintained its grip on Julia.

Worse still, as he strode along uptown, he passed the limits of
the First Church beat. His pursuit became increasingly conspic-
uous. Up here the communicants of Hancock Square would
mark him well.

Luckily, at Sycamore Street they halted. There was a sound of
bells, the scrape of runners on bare ground. Gus Ringler's double
sleigh came out from the side street. His fat shiny wife sat beside
him, his fat half-grown children beamed over the buffalo robe
behind. "Hello, folks," Mr. Ringler waved his whip. "Whoa,
horses." His thick loud voice engaged the Wiltons on the curb.

He looked up, waved his whip. "Hello, Tommy. What are
you doing up at this end of town?"

All turned. "Good morning, Thomas." Julia dropped her eyes.

Captain Mottley still had her arm. "Just a little constitutional,"
he ventured. He hid his small sardonic grin with a rawhide
mitten.

"Come on, Papa," Mrs. Ringler said, "you keep everybody
waiting."

Gus Ringler waved his whip above the 2.40 trotters. "Come
up, mules." Silently beaming, Mrs. Ringler was borne away.

With his mitten Captain Mottley gestured after them. "Look
at that," he said. "Even the Catholics are better off than you
are. At least their notions don't spoil their fun."

Mrs. Wilton turned her pale aristocratic face. "Captain Mottley,
if you please, let us talk of something else."

The dilapidated face showed no discomfiture. "What else is
there to talk about on Sunday?" Calmly he led off the proces-
sion, still holding Julia's arm. "Why, when I was a boy, I used
to be whipped and sent to bed for talking about anything but
religious subjects on the Sabbath."

Mr. Wilton brushed at his brown mustache. "Captain, you're

a great joker," he said in a cultivated voice. "Tommy," he said,
"did you have a good sermon this morning down your way?"

"Every one seemed to like it but Mrs. Munkittrick."

Mr. Wilton smiled faintly. "Yes, we hear up our way that she's
a little hard to please."

Mrs. Wilton shook her head gently at Tommy. "One person
like that in a church will often cause a great deal of dissen-
sion."

"They often cause a great deal of harmony," Captain Mottley
called back without turning his head. "Every one else unites
against them." He looked back at them, malicious and proud.
"I'll bet I've done more than any one man in this town to bring
the churches together. Hello, Tommy. Come up and join us."

As he drew alongside, he could have seized Julia's other arm
and pulled her away.

"You're a great joker, Captain Mottley," Mr. Wilton said.

"I have my beliefs, too," Captain Mottley said, "but I only
believe what I can prove."

"How pretty the river looks in the sun," Mrs. Wilton said.

"I believe, for instance," Captain Mottley said, "that Julia is the
prettiest girl in town."

"I'm sure that Julia appreciates the compliment," Mrs. Wilton
said. "Here we are. I'd ask you in, but we only have cold lunch
on Sundays."

"Otherwise," Captain Mottley grinned, "you'd be delighted.
Good-bye, my dear." He raised his battered hat; his waving
stick, his flapping raincoat went back down the street.

After an exchange of perfectly expressionless glances with
Mrs. Wilton, Mr. Wilton mounted the steps of the quietly, but
elegantly hideous house of yellow pressed brick. It was a little
far uptown, but Mrs. Wilton had been a Lisle, a cousin of Miss
Anna Lisle; and Mr. Wilton, though not a Midian man, came
from a very good family in Cincinnati, and had been to Yale.

"Thomas," Mrs. Wilton said, "I wish I could ask you in, but
we only have cold lunch; and then, of course, we have our
Sunday School at two-thirty."

"I know, Mrs. Wilton," he said. "We have ours at three."

"Yes," she said, "I know. I should think it would make you
late with your Sunday dinner."

"Well," he said, "we don't have ours till five."

"Oh," she said, "we have ours at four-thirty. I suppose you are going back to college?"

"Yes," he said. "To-morrow. It's been a fine vacation."

"Yes," she said, "the weather has been good. Julia goes back on Wednesday."

In the black mouth of the opened door, Mr. Wilton waited. "I must go," Mrs. Wilton said. "Good-bye, Thomas. I hope you have a successful term at college."

"Good-bye, Thomas," Mr. Wilton said. "I may get up to New Haven this spring."

"Oh, that would be fine, Mr. Wilton. Look me up, I'm in Fayerweather Hall. Anyhow," he added, "I guess I'll see you at Eastertime."

"Oh, yes," Mr. Wilton said. "Of course."

Mrs. Wilton paused beside him. "Lunch is ready, Julia," she said.

He hung suspended. Firmly he stared at the river, bright with melting ice, and at the distant mottled banks of wet earth and of snow.

"All right, Mother." What a sweet lovely voice she had. "I'll come in just a minute." Her voice was sweet and lovely, yet how firm, how determined. The front door closed. He could have capered there right on the street.

"Gosh!" he said. "It certainly got my goat to see that old fool, Captain Mottley——"

"Oh," she said, "Captain Mottley."

"It would do him good if somebody took a poke at him."

"Oh," she said, "it's just his way."

"I know it's his way," he said, "and I don't like it."

"Oh," she said, "I didn't mean that. I meant that he doesn't mean anything by it. I am just a little girl to him."

"Like fun you are."

"Why, Captain Mottley must be seventy."

"Well, why doesn't he make up to little girls until they're—I mean, if he's so fond of little girls, why doesn't he make up to children?"

"I really don't think he means anything. And, anyhow, it's so hard to know what to do. After all he's an old gentleman."

"Old gentleman! If he's a gentleman, I'm a port-mahon baboon."

"You're a what?" she said seriously.

"It's a sea term. Do you read Masefield? Well, you ought to, it's great stuff. I tell you what I'll do, I'll send you a copy. Just Farmington, I suppose."

"Oh, thank you. I'll love to read it. You must put Miss Porter's School."

"Oh, yes, that's right. I forgot. I'll send it as soon as I get back to New Haven."

Over the top of her black fox, she gave him her sweet serious smile. "Thank you ever so much, Tommy. And thank you for everything else this Christmas, the skating and the dances and all." She held out her gray-gloved hand.

At its fragile touch something surged within him. "Look here," he was saying, "I was meaning to ask you. That's what I wanted to see you about to-day. Will you come up to the Junior Prom this year?"

"Oh, Tommy," her hand lingered, "it's sweet of you." He thrilled, the hand was withdrawn. "But they wouldn't think of letting us do that at Farmington. It wouldn't even do any good to ask. It would just make me unpopular with the teachers. I'm awfully sorry."

"So am I."

"It's dreadful. But I know you understand. Thank you ever so much, just the same."

A shadow paused at the thick lace curtains. "I must really go," she said. "Good-bye, Tommy." Mounting the steps she looked back over her black fox, pale and sweet. "I hope I'll see you at Eastertime."

His hat was in his hands. "Good-bye, Julia. You certainly will."

As he was striding down River Street, breathing in the mild, yet sparkling tonic of the air, he was hailed from behind. "Hey, student, where are you bound?" "Hey, Tommy!" He turned reluctantly. Bill McGuire wore a fawn-colored paddock coat and derby hat, and Porky, a pyramidal raglan of worn tweed. "Or rather," Porky said, "where have you been?"

"Don't tell," Bill said. "We know. Is Julia home?"

"She's having lunch."

"That's tough," Porky said.

Bill nodded. "Ain't it the truth, though? She'll miss seeing us.

Well then, we'll walk along with Thomas." They fell in on either side of him. "This is the last day of the inter-collegiate team," he said. "I do the sprints and Porky does the distances. No girl escapes. I overwhelm them and Porky grows on them."

"The only trouble," Porky said, "is that they grow on me faster than I do on them. It's a defect in the system that no one has been able to account for."

"The trouble is," Bill said, "that the liquor grows on Porky faster than Porky grows on the girl. He tends to fade on the home stretch."

"I don't fade," Porky said. "I just fly right out over the rail."

"You lose," Bill said. "That's what counts."

"It's not the rum though," Porky said, "it's my cultivated mind. If I were as ignorant as you, Bill, I'd be even more successful."

"It's funny," Bill said, "how all girls love a civil engineer. That's a fact, but still it's the liquor with you, Porky. Two drinks and you have to display your erudition. It kills you with them all. Even Julia. And look how serious-minded she is. Look how you stand with her. Out. Absolutely out."

"Oh, I wouldn't say that, Bill," Porky said, "she still speaks to me."

Bill thrust his hand against Tommy Rand's ribs. "You see," he said, "for him that is a triumph."

"But nobody gets anywhere with Julia," Porky said.

"Oh, yes, they do," Bill said. "Who did we see just coming down from Julia's and stepping like a hackney stallion? No less than our Thomas."

"Oh, for Pete's sake, Bill," Tommy said.

"That's what I say," Porky added. "Your simile is most unfortunate." He puffed along, his mouth puckered, his light-blue eyes looking at nothing. "And that, by the way, is why you have never gotten anywhere with Julia, Bill. Your coarseness repels her. Now Tommy and I have our failings, but we are always genteel."

"Well, anyhow," Bill said, "I think Tommy ought to tell us his method."

"Oh, for Pete's sake," Tommy said.

"His secret," Porky said, "is earnestness of purpose."

"Well," Bill said, "I'm earnest."

"You are," Porky said, "but your purpose is a low one. Now

my purpose is high, but I lack earnestness. Julia," he said, "is very quick to notice a thing like that."

"I'm sorry fellows," Tommy said, "but I have got to turn in here."

"Come on," they said, "what about Jeanne Thompson's for a stand-up lunch?"

"No," he said, "I can't do it. I'm sorry."

They stopped, their grins were genial and insulting. "Good-bye, old man." They shook his hand. "See you at Easter."

In the dining room his father looked up from his plate of potato salad. "Well," he said, "where have you been?"

His mother looked at his father. "He just went for a walk up the river, George."

His father pushed back his plate. "Ellen," he said, "where are those notes for the Bible lesson? I've only got half an hour."

"They're on your desk, George."

Heavily, but swiftly his father walked out of the room.

"Your father is a little upset, dear," she said. "Have some cold consommé? Sunday is always a very hard day on him, and then one of the notes in the new organ has gone wrong. Did you notice it?"

"No," he said, "I didn't."

"I didn't either, but your father always notices everything." She sank her voice. "Were you able to catch up with the Wiltons?"

"Yes," he said, "but you know Captain Mottley walked with them all the way up to the house." He put down his cup. "He's a terrible old man."

"Oh, yes, he is," his mother said absently. "You know," she said, "I think there's a lot of good in Captain Mottley."

"A lot of good?"

"If he could be converted I think we'd all feel very differently toward him. I was talking to Miss Ba-ba Lamb when he came back down the street. He insisted on walking back to the house with me."

"He did? Why——"

"He teased me about being out on the street alone. Just joking, you know. Your father had stayed to see about the organ. It was awfully silly, of course, but I couldn't help laughing."

"Did you tell father?"

"Yes, of course. I always tell your father everything; just the way he does me."

He gave her a grin in the manner of Captain Mottley himself. "Well, it didn't seem to cheer him up much, did it?"

"Tommy," she said, "I don't know what to make of you. When I was your age, I would no more have dreamed of speaking to my mother, or about my father that way."

"All right, Mother, if you want me to, I can be respectful."

"I didn't mean that. I think a child and his parents should be companions."

"All right," he said, "I'll be a respectful companion."

She smiled at him. "Now you're trying to tangle me up, but you know what I mean." She passed him the potato salad and the cold rolls. She looked out the window at the blank wall next door.

"How was Julia?" she said.

"She was all right." He busied himself with the roll. "I don't suppose I could run up there this evening," he said.

"The Wiltons would never understand," she said. "Besides, they'd be at church. And then," she said, "we have our own church too."

"Yes," he said, "of course."

"I know some people call on Sunday," she said.

"Yes," he said, "I just came down the street with Bill McGuire and Porky Montross."

"Oh," she said, "those two.

He ate his roll. "Well," he said, "I'll drop in after church this evening and say good-bye to Aunt Clara. I guess that will be all right."

"Yes," she said lifelessly, "your Aunt Clara wouldn't mind."

"Ellen," his father shouted from the library, "where's that red ink and my loose-leaf notebook?"

CHAPTER XL

HE SAT surrounded by the steins and pennants of their room in Fayerweather Hall with the letter in his hand. At the desk the Buffer's shoulders hunched forward aggressively; with his elbows flanking a book, he knuckled his fists into his tufted hair and moved his lips. He, himself, was in the Morris chair under the student lamp. Outside, the lights of dormitory windows made patterns in the night. Voices called, there were whistles, and somewhere far away, a phonograph. He looked at the letter with the young, firm handwriting . . . "feel badly" . . . "honor." He read it once again.

DEAR TOMMY:

I suppose it is very fresh to write you, and now that I have started, I don't know what to say. You may not like it at all, and if so, I hope you will forgive me. But on the other hand, I can't help hoping that you will understand.

I have already thanked you once for the Masefield poems, so I will only say that I have read them and like them very much. Thank you again.

What I wanted to say is that I have just seen in the "New York Times" about the elections on Tap Day. I suppose it is very fresh of me to write about this, and perhaps it is not the thing that a girl ought to do, but you have been so nice to me that when I read about the Tap Day, I thought you might feel badly on account of your father. And so I thought I would write and tell you, just as a friend, that I hope you do not feel badly on any other account, because I think that it is what a man is that counts, and not what honors he has. Those things must be a good deal of luck anyway. My father is the finest man I ever knew, and he was not elected; and I remember his saying that as time went on, those things made less and less difference, and how a good many of the men who were elected had not amounted to anything. I don't mean that it was not a great honor for your father to belong and that he should be proud of it, but then he was a baseball player and that makes all the difference.

I am afraid I have not put it very well. I just wanted to say that if you feel badly, I send you my sympathy; although I think you ought not to, and that I value our friendship just as much as ever, and hope you will always feel the same towards me.

Yours sincerely,

JULIA WILTON.

He let the letter hang down in his hand. The Buffer turned his head. "Well, now," he said, "what about a little work-out with the books? Look here," he said, "what about this Gresham's Law?"

"Well," he said, "can't you remember it?"

"Sure, I can remember it. There was one of the Poes at Princeton named Gresham. But what's it mean?" The Buffer gave a nod. "Why don't you get to work?" he said. "Then I could get my lesson done, too. Look here, Tommy," he said, "must I tell it to you all again? It's all just a trick, don't you see? If a man can kick a ball, or write a speech, or, God forgive me, make a prayer, he's in, do you see? It means nothing; ten years from now we'll laugh at it. Why, ten years from now," he said, "you'll be the biggest man in Midian, and my crowd will be passing the hat to keep me out of the poorhouse." He grinned. "Although there is a fund, they tell me. Perhaps that's why they let me in."

"Oh, forget it, Buffer," he said. "It makes no difference to you or me, does it?"

"By God, it does not."

"Well, then, forget it. I was thinking of something else. Here," he said, "look at this."

The Buffer spread the letter carefully on the desk. He hunched himself forward, his lips began to move. At the end, he sat back and nodded at the letter. "That's class," he said. "Class all over it." He tapped the letter. "There's the girl for you." He looked up. "Mind you, I've seen her picture too. You never see a Molloy taking anything on faith." He clamped his hands on his blunt knees. "Now, do you see what I mean? Here I am among the brethren, and will I ever get a letter like that?" He shook his head. "Mind you," he said, "I don't say that Kitty and the rest of them down in the Bronx are not good girls too." He leaned back and looked up at the ceiling. "Ah, well, Tommy, you know what I mean.

"And now," the Buffer said with a wave at Fetter's "Economics," "what about all this?"

"I'll be with you in just a minute." He stood up. "I just want to get off a letter." He sat down at his own desk and turned on the hooded light. He stared at the sheet of paper on which there was nothing so far except "Yale University" in neat blue lettering. He got up from his chair. "I guess I'd better have another look at that letter."

The Buffer held the letter out to him. "You should know it by now," he said.

Back at his desk, he rapped the handle of his pen against his teeth. By opening his mouth he could make the scale; also the Whiffenpoof's song.

The Buffer rocked in his chair. "Oh, for God's sake!" he said. "Can't you think without playing the jew's-harp on your teeth?" He buried his head in his knuckles. "What's it matter what you say?" he said. "It's just a line from you, she wants."

With a handkerchief he wiped off the handle of his pen.

DEAR JULIA:

Of course I don't think it was fresh of you to write; I think it was very fine of you, and I appreciate it more than I can tell. I know that there are other things in life, and that the serious part lies ahead of me; and I hope that I will be able to do my part and always be worthy of your friendship. I will not say any more about your letter except that I will always keep it, and remember your kindness; and I think it was an awfully nice thing to do.

I guess it's too far to look ahead, but next year you will be through school, and I have been wondering if you would like to come up to the Princeton game. We play them here next year, and I think we are going to have a wonderful team. My roommate is Buffer Molloy, the quarterback, and he can get us good seats. I will get one for your mother too.

It's a long time off, of course (I'm sorry to say) and, of course, I'll see you at Easter (I'm glad to say) but I didn't want any one to get ahead of me; your old dancing partner, Porky Montross, for instance. (Yea!) You will be out next year and, I suppose, doing something every minute."

I am glad you liked the Masefield. It's great stuff, and I think very few people really appreciate him. I liked the one beginning, "I must down to the sea again" the best of all. In fact, I memorized it. I think it is a great thing to memorize poetry. In that way, you really get to know it.

Well, I really just started to say thank you for your nice letter, and as I must close I will say it once again, and send you my best wishes.

THOMAS RAND.

He read the letter over once, then twice more. On the whole it was good; serious and friendly and with a light touch here and there. He only wished that it had just a little more style, but if he gave it more style, it might sound literary; like Porky Montross, for instance.

But was he really worthy of her friendship? He ought to be, he meant to be. But of late, strange and unsuspected impulses had sometimes raised their heads. Just last week that girl on Chapel Street. He would see her now, walking down Chapel Street ahead of him with a driving wind behind that flattened her green dress. And sometimes in the night he saw her. His face burned. Was there something wrong about him after all? Why no, it was impossible. His friends were the best men in the class, men who stood for the right things. They looked on him as one of them. And did he not instinctively recoil from those unsavory catch-basins of the class where vulgar rounders bummed their way through Yale, contemptuous of decency and all the things Yale stood for, perversely parading their own love of nastiness. Don Juans of Savon Rock or at best Bustanoby's. He remembered Professor Filley, clever, but evil under all his cleverness, in the Shakespeare course last year, "The position is ridiculous, and it always gives me a headache." There had been snorts and snickers, but, in himself, only a little rending horror.

"Well," it was the Buffer, "you've signed your name, haven't you?"

"All right," he said, "all right. Buffer, have you got a special delivery stamp?"

"I have." He tossed a dime to the Buffer. The Buffer rustled in his drawer. "You're making a mistake," he said. "Just take it natural. That's the best way. And then, maybe, too, when they see it's a special delivery, the teachers will want to read it."

"Farmington's no convent."

"They're all alike, those places for young girls."

He watched the Buffer bring out a sheet of stamps. "I notice you use plenty of them."

"I do. But then I'm only jollying, I don't mean anything." He held up the stamp. "Here it is, if you want it; but you've my advice. On the other hand," he said, "if a man don't mean anything, a special delivery stamp will go a great ways to make up for it."

.   .   .   .   .   .

On the morning of the Princeton game, his senior year, he thrust his way through the crowds that drifted out of the squat New Haven station, through the taxis and vendors of blue and yellow pennants, of chrysanthemums and violets. The day was almost too warm for his new coonskin coat, but he had it on. His father who had seemed much more friendly ever since Tap Day last year had given it to him. At the taxi-stand he put into effect a scheme of the Buffer's. He tore a dollar bill in two, and held out half of it. "Look here," he said, "I'm meeting some people on the ten-fifty. You wait for me and I'll give you the other half and the fare beside."

"Yeah! And if you don't show up, where am I?"

"Well, I lose my dollar, don't I?"

"Sure you lose it." The driver looked at his coonskin coat. "You can stand it."

He reached inside his coonskin coat; with great presence of mind he tore another dollar bill in two.

"Well," the driver said, "I'll wait a little while." He started for the station. "Hey, Mac!" the driver called. He turned. "Make it snappy!" He continued on his way with dignity.

In the milling waiting room, the second feature of the Buffer's plan came into effect. He had bought a ticket to New London. While many undergraduates and several casually recognized acquaintances waited like cattle at the gate, he marched through to the train shed. Afterward he would redeem the ticket.

"Train number six! New London, Providence and Boston!" The blunt-nosed engine was rolling silently along the rails, the train bent round the curve and straightened out. There was a monstrous clank of steel, an express messenger with a shotgun at an open door, the smooth sides of the Pullmans and the light groan of air brakes coming on.

He saw her and her tall mother above the crowd, the gray hair and the blonde. She wore a gray fur coat and a flaring collar turned up behind. Her mother's coat was sable and very smart too. "Hello," he said. "Hello, Mrs. Wilton. Here, let me take those rugs."

"Tommy, it's nice to see you."

"Thomas, how do you do? We thought we'd better take them, and I remembered this shawl carrier of my father's. I hope it's the proper thing. Mr. Wilton said——"

"Of course," he said insincerely. "Come on, I have got a taxi waiting."

"Oh," Mrs. Wilton said, "we've lots of time. We made a point of getting the early train."

"I know," he said, "that's fine, but it's hard to hold a taxi on these big game days."

"I cannot hurry on these steps," Mrs. Wilton said. "I daresay another cab will be along directly."

The instant they emerged, the taxi driver's hawk-like eye was on him. He took Mrs. Wilton's arm. "There he is," he said, "right over there."

Mrs. Wilton set herself. "Tell him to drive over here," she said.

"It's just a step, Mother," Julia said.

"With all those automobiles?" Mrs. Wilton said. She continued to stand rigid on the platform. "This is much the best."

Reluctantly, Tommy signalled to the driver. The driver's head dropped down as he threw off the brake, and his lips formed the word which Professor Filley said was the one word no gentleman ever used. The cab came to the platform with a swirl, stopped with a jolt. Mrs. Wilton got in with deliberation and sat down next to the door. Julia stepped over her. "Vanderbilt Hall," he said. He got in, the door slammed. He was shot on top of Mrs. Wilton's sable coat.

On the centre table of his room were two white cardboard boxes, and on the lids, inscribed in gold was the name "Small's, Fifth Avenue." He opened a box. Under the oil paper the purple and green was veiled in gray. He laid it back. "Mrs. Wilton, these are for you."

"Why, Thomas," she said, "these are very nice." Very nice, he thought. Right straight from Small's this morning. These were no street vendor's violets. "But the Yale color," Mrs. Wilton said, "is really blue."

"I know," he said, "but they wear violets at the game."

"Why, Tommy," Julia said, "aren't they beautiful? They're enormous," she said, "and just as fresh. You must have sent away for them."

"They came from Small's," he said.

"The name is on the lid," Mrs. Wilton said.

Julia looked up at him from over the bunch of violets. "From Small's? Aren't you swell?"

"So this is your room," Mrs. Wilton said. "Isn't it very dark for studying?" She started on an inspection of the pictures and the banners.

"Well, we mostly study at night," he said, "so it doesn't make much difference."

Mrs. Wilton continued her inspection. "I should think you'd want more light and air. I suppose there are other rooms with bigger windows."

"There are a little bigger windows in Connecticut," he said, "but most of my crowd lives here."

"But aren't we in Connecticut?"

"No, this is Vanderbilt."

"Connecticut, Mother, is the name of a college building."

"I see. Have you another student that lives with you?"

"Why, Mother, you know his roommate is Buffer Molloy, the quarterback."

"But he's not much of a student," he said. "Won't you sit down?"

Reluctantly Mrs. Wilton gave up an attempt to peer beyond his bedroom door. She sat down in the Morris chair, and Julia sat down on the striped divan in the corner. She looked tall and graceful, tall and graceful and clean and fine. He was cleansed and inspired sitting here with her in her narrow gray skirt with the violets against the gray fur of her coat, and a little wave of ash-blonde hair under the dark blue of her hat.

"I thought we'd have lunch in the rooms," he said. "It's much the easiest, if you don't mind cold lunch. I've had some put up. There'll be coffee, of course."

"Oh, no, I don't mind," Mrs. Wilton said, "but I never take coffee except at breakfast; and then only a thimbleful in hot milk."

"I can get milk," he said, "or tea, if I can find another thermos bottle."

"Oh, no," Julia said, "Mother just drinks water at lunch."

"We ought to have some water," Mrs. Wilton said, "to put these violets in."

"We could do that," he said, "but they are in silver foil; and anyway we'll be going in an hour."

"In an hour?" Mrs. Wilton said. "But that will be only half-past twelve."

"The game's at two," he said, "and we ought to have lots of time. That's one thing you learn in four years at Yale. I'll get the lunch. Oh, hello, Buffer," he said. "Here's the Buffer. Mrs. Wilton, Mr. Molloy. And Julia."

Standing square, his legs slightly spread in front of the divan, the Buffer made a serious and minute inspection. "Ah," he said, "so you're Julia?"

"Yes," she said, "I'm afraid I am."

"Ah, well," he said, "it's nothing to worry about. I heard you were coming and just stopped in to say hello. Tommy, did you get the tickets?"

"Yes, Buffer. Thanks."

Mrs. Wilton turned to Tommy. "Perhaps your friend would join us for lunch."

"He couldn't. He's got to eat at the training table."

"I should think the college authorities would let him off," Mrs. Wilton said. "Especially on a day like this."

The Buffer rubbed his knuckles nervously against his back hair and grinned. "Thank you just the same though. Well, I've got to go. Pleased to have met you."

Julia held out her hand. "I'm glad to have met you, Mr. Molloy. Good luck in the game."

"Thanks. Will you bring them back afterward, Tommy? Good!"

Outside in the narrow entry he took the Buffer's iron arm. "Good luck, Buffer," he said. "Tear 'em up, fellow."

"Sure," the Buffer said. "We'll take them." He had a solemn hand on Tommy's elbow, he gave a solemn nod back toward the room. "Class," he said. "Class all over."

The roaring stands rose up as the blue squad shot into the field. White-sweatered cheer leaders raised megaphones and semaphored. "What are they getting up for?" Mrs. Wilton said.

"There's the Buffer," he said, "calling signals! There he is, taking the pass from center."

"They all look alike," Mrs. Wilton said. "And where are the other boys against them?"

"They're just warming up."

Julia touched his arm. "I see him," she said, "but he looks bigger."

"That's the shoulder pads."

"I think he's awfully nice," she said.

"They say he's the best quarterback Yale's had in fifteen years."

"You must be awfully proud to room with him."

"It's not that; he's just a great little fellow, that's all. And wait until you see him play." His mouth flew open. "Come on, Yale!" he shouted.

Then in a vast confusion of bands and cheers and singing and of waving flags and sudden rumbling surges of the stands the game drifted maddeningly up and down the field. At that great distance the puppets seemed small and moved apparently with ease but no great speed. There was no hint of impact or strain. It was an unreal puppet-show whose drama, nevertheless, meant everything to him; perhaps to Julia. She began to cheer.

Then suddenly it happened with all the slow precision of a dream; unbelievable, yet foreordained. The Buffer caught a punt and dodged a tackler, another tackler seemed to touch him lightly, and then, an apparition, the ball was rolling on the ground. The Buffer ran; the loathesome, ring-striped jerseys ran; the ball rolled slowly on ahead. And then a jersey dove and cut the Buffer down. There was nothing left to do but sit there, utterly incredulous, while the other jersey scooped the ball up and ran down the field.

. . . . . .

Back in the room, the early November dusk was falling. Out on the street the straggling sons of Princeton passed by with vulgar and outlandish cries. "Well," Mrs. Wilton said, "that was very exciting, wasn't it?"

"It was terrible," he said. "I never saw the Buffer fumble a ball before. It was just bad luck," he said. "He played three years at school and four years here, that makes seven, and I never saw him fumble a ball before."

"We must go," Mrs. Wilton said. "We have seats on that train."

"You have lots of time," he said, "and you're not going back to Midian until the late train, I suppose. There'll be lots of trains."

"Tommy, I wish you'd come down with us," Julia said.

"Gosh," he said, "I'd like to. We could get dinner on the train and catch a show."

"Do what?" Mrs. Wilton said.

"Go to the theatre."

"Thank you very much," Mrs. Wilton said, "but Julia doesn't go to the theatre, unless we know about the performance. Most of the plays nowadays."

"We could have a late dinner, then," he said, "and I could put you on the train."

"Thank you very much," Mrs. Wilton said, "but an uncle of Julia's is going to do that. He's not really an uncle; actually he's a cousin of Mr. Wilton's. He has some position with the railroad, so I wrote and asked him. He lives in Hackensack. I never met the family. I understand he has seven children."

"Oh, Tommy," Julia said, "do."

"By golly," he said, "I will. Mrs. Wilton," he said, "you can wire Julia's uncle not to bother; he doesn't want to come way in from Hackensack."

"Oh, I'm sure he wouldn't think that was too much to do for a cousin's relatives," Mrs. Wilton said. "And besides being in the railroad, it makes me feel much more comfortable about that train."

"But, Mother, people make trains all the time without anybody in the railroad to help them."

Mrs. Wilton stiffened. "No, my dear, I think this is the best."

"Well, anyhow, Tommy, you'll come," Julia said.

"Me? Sure I'll come." The game and the ring-striped jerseys were forgotten. He was warm and bold and happy and talking like the Buffer.

"In any case," Mrs. Wilton said, "we should make a start."

Under his window he heard the Buffer's step and a stranger's voice, "Hello, Buffer. Hard luck, old man."

He was out the door. Swinging sturdily, the Buffer came in the entry. There was a raw mark across the bridge of his short nose. "Hello, Buffer," he said, "that was tough."

"Ah," the Buffer said, "it was nothing. Are they in there?"

"Yes," he said, "they're just leaving. I thought maybe I'd——"

"Good! I'll have a chance to tell them good-bye, then."

"Good evening, Mr. Molloy," Mrs. Wilton said. "We saw you out there on the field. But it took the longest time before I could tell which one you were."

The Buffer started to whistle between his teeth and checked himself. "Well, you know now," he said.

Julia looked up from the divan, that steady assured look of gray eyes. "What a shame that we lost."

The Buffer jerked a thumb. "Do you get that, Tommy? We! She's a real Yale girl."

"Of course I am," Julia said.

The Buffer stared at the drawing of a girl by Harrison Fisher. She had a pompadour and a ruffled skirt, and was patting a horse's head that came from nowhere. "We were the best team," he said.

"And I always will be," Julia said. "I really mean that."

Tommy grinned at her with confidence. "What about if Porky asks you down to Princeton?"

"He never would."

"Of course he would. He will. What'll you bet?"

"I'll bet you——"

"Julia doesn't bet," Mrs. Wilton said.

"Anyhow," Julia said, "I don't think much of girls who are always for whatever college they're at. Mr. Molloy," she said, "won't you sit down here on the divan? You must be tired."

Gingerly the Buffer sat down on the divan. He leaned forward, his elbows on his widespread knees, his knuckles clamped together. He was hard and tight inside his smooth dark suit. "We were the best team," he said, "by three touchdowns. We were down at their end all the time. They had no offense, Princeton never has. Why," he said, "they weren't a football team. Just a bunch of lucky gamblers. I handed them a touchdown, but we should have made a dozen of our own. We never got going," he said, "we never clicked. I don't know what got into the boys," he said, "and that's always just when you get the breaks against you. Why," he said, "they had nobody on that Princeton team. They had one man; that man Monahan, backing up the line. Anyhow, he's an Irishman, thank God. Every time the interference took him out, we'd make our distance; only they wouldn't take him out. Why, I can tell you three times when we ought to have scored. The first was when they got off that short kick from behind their goal. We had the ball then——"

Outside the window there was a yodelling cry of "Tommy Rand," and then a chorus of strange voices. "Thomas! Thomas Rand! Mr. Rand!" He hurried out.

In the light of the entry Porky Montross stumbled forward in his ample coonskin coat, his derby hat was pushed way back from his smooth pink brow. "My fellow townsman," he said. He waved his hand. "These men are from the Bureau of Standards in Washington."

A hatless youth in horn-rimmed glasses eyed him solemnly. "We're making tests for the Department of Internal Revenue."

"And as big-hearted tigers," Porky said, "we ask you to join us."

"Do you consider that offer fair?" the tall youth said. "Restrict your answer to five hundred words."

"Gosh, Porky," he said, "I'd love to, I ought to show you around New Haven myself, but I'm leaving for New York in a minute; and I've got some people in there."

"Not Julia?" Porky said.

"Well, yes. Julia and Mrs. Wilton."

"My Julia," Porky said. He swayed forward, firmly followed by the horn-rimmed spectacles. The others also started to move with murmured "Julias."

"Hold on, Porky," he said, "my roommate's in there."

"Well, what the—!" they said. "Who is your roommate?"

"A very sacred relationship at Yale." They were in the entry now.

"Buffer Molloy."

"Oh," they said. "Well, so long." Silently they wandered away. From the darkness there was one plaintive wavering cry, "My Julia."

In the room Mrs. Wilton was standing up and drawing on her gloves. "Thomas, we must go. We really must go. I insist. Mr.

Molloy," she said, "it was a most enjoyable afternoon; very interesting."

The Buffer stood up and rocked his shoulders, pulling down his coat behind. "Good-bye, Mrs. Wilton." He held out his hand. "Good-bye, Julia. I'm glad I met you."

Julia stood up, tall and straight. "And I'm glad I met you. Tommy talks so much about you."

"Ah," he said. "Tommy, I hear you're going to town. Will you go up and stay at the house? Just walk in and take the bed you had before."

"Thanks, Buffer," he said. "Maybe I'll telephone, anyhow, when I get there."

Julia turned in the door. "Good-bye."

The Buffer grinned at her. "Come up to Cambridge next Saturday," he said. "We'll take Harvard sure."

In the waiting room Mrs. Wilton sat with her eyes on the station clock. "Well," she said, "this has been an interesting experience; very fatiguing."

"Tommy," Julia said, "you've been perfectly sweet. I hope the Buffer doesn't feel badly."

"Why should he," Mrs. Wilton said, "over a game? He was very cheerful. He seemed to think that some of the other players had not done well."

"Julia," he said in a low voice, "will you be angry at me? I think I ought to stay here with the Buffer. No one else will come to see him, they'll think it looks like sympathy. He'll be alone."

For a moment she didn't answer; she looked anything but happy. "Yes," she said slowly, "I can see what you mean. If you think it's the right thing to do, of course, you ought to do it."

"It's not what I want to do; you understand that, Julia, but I think I ought to."

"Well, then," she said, "that's settled. Mother," she said, "Tommy thinks he won't go down with us."

Mrs. Wilton kept her eyes on the clock. "I thought that was the wisest from the start," she said.

"Julia," he said, "you really do understand, don't you?"

Her face was pale and tired, but she gave him a brave smile. "Of course I do. I always think a girl has more respect for a man who does the right thing," she added firmly.

Back in the room, the Buffer, in his shirt sleeves, wrote a letter under his desk light. "Forget something?" he said. "You've missed your train."

"I gave it up," he said. "They decided to go on back to Midian to-night." He threw his hat and coat on the divan.

The Buffer looked at him grimly. "Well, didn't you know that when you started?"

"I—well, it's one of those things that look good at first, then you change your mind."

"That's no way to court a girl." The Buffer's tone was brutal. He whirled. "Here, what's come into you?"

"I just decided to come back, that's all."

"You leave a place where you're wanted, and come back where you're not—where you're not needed."

"Don't you worry," he said, "I think I'll go down to Mory's."

The Buffer turned back to his letter. "Now you talk sense," he said.

CHAPTER XLI

In his small glass-closed office he drew triangles on a sheet that bore the letterhead, "John Rand & Son, Wholesale Coal." Then he drew shadows for each letter making them all stand out in high relief. Through the partition he could see the general office; at the far end, under the map of West Virginia, was the high desk where the old bookkeepers in their alpaca coats still sat on high stools and wielded different colored inks and hard rubber rulers; on the main floor, among the rows of men who worked the typewriters, were two girls in shirtwaists, the latest innovation in the staff; and opposite the entrance door on the right was the large denuded desk and the small denuded head of Mr. Wherrill, the office manager.

To look at this long dingy room, its tan walls, dingy and featureless except for the map of West Virginia and the large faded photo of Tipple Number One of the Minnehaha Coal Company, the dirty tan paint flaking off the pressed tin ceiling, no one would ever think that probably half a million dollars had been made right there. Of course, it had not been made there; it had been made, he supposed, back in the inner office behind him where for long years, long before he himself was born, his grandfather had hatched his schemes. His grandfather's roll-top desk still stood there with its big brass inkwell, its black-bristled pen-wiper, its paper weights of carved polished coal. But his grandfather seldom used it. The old gentleman came in from time to time and sat down on the desk chair in his hat and coat, resting his clean, liver-spotted hands on top of his stick, and listening to problems brought up by his father, by old Mr. Riser, by Mr. Wherrill. At the end he would nod, heave up, and steam away in silence. From the window of his cubby hole, Tommy could sometimes see him climb into the station wagon as Levi touched his hat.

From his window he could also see the paper-littered Square; on the other side, the brownstone columns of the courthouse and the new electric sign on the top of the Midian "Messenger" building; and nearer, the gold of the saloon, the bright varied colors of the grocery store, and the huge plate-glass window in the lobby of the Atlantic Hotel.

Toward the other office workers, ever since he came, he had been polite and modest; and they, on the whole, had received him well. "In theory," his father had said, "you ought to go in at the bottom and work up. In practice, the office people would just look on you as a spy. It's better for you to keep clear of them and learn the business answering inquiries outside my door." It had been a disappointment. He had wanted to join the office force, had pictured himself as rising early, arriving promptly at eight with the other office workers, putting on his alpaca jacket, sharing the office jokes, a college boy among the toilers. But this way was really more sensible, he could see that; and he was learning more important things than bookkeeping.

Just now he had been assigned by his father the job of making a report on the advisability of substituting wire fencing on their properties as the old wooden fencing gave out. He would tackle it and do it well. But spring clouds were overhead, the sparrows chased each other in the city square. For a moment he would take his ease and look out the large dingy window at a gayer and more tender world. Then he would write the American Fence Company and also get the names of other fence companies to write to for estimates. From them he would also try to get the names of some of their largest customers, and from the largest customers he would try to get a report on the service the fence gave and its approximate depreciation. At the same time he would write the superintendents of their own properties for a report on the cost of the wooden fences and their approximate depreciation. Perhaps he could get the cost off the books right here in the office. When all the material was assembled he would write a report with paragraph headings in red ink; and perhaps a graph or two, showing the relative merits of the two propositions, although he was not sure he knew how to draw one. He remembered having to make some graphs in Senior Economics at New Haven, but that was two years ago, and anyhow he had gotten some one to show him how.

In his dark striped suit and dark striped tie, his father came to the office door and stopped. "Have you started that report yet?"

"I was just figuring about it. I'll have it out as soon as I get the replies."

"Better write to the American Fence Company."

"I was going to."

"Better write to the others too. You can get their names from a wholesale hardware catalogue."

"Yes," he said, "I was going to."

"At the same time," his father said, "you'd better write our superintendents about the old wooden fences." His father's voice ran on ". . . initial cost . . . maintenance . . . depreciation."

"Yes, Father, I was going to do all that."

His father turned away before replying. "Let me see those letters before they go out," he said as he went back to his desk.

The telephone rang. "John Rand and Son?" a smooth voice said. "This is Mr. Riddick, representing the Mutual. Could I speak to Mr. George Rand, please?"

"My father is busy just now. Could you talk to me?"

"Well, then, I'll probably call him later. We have been making a check-over of your portfolio and find that in your coal yard at Roysterstown you could make a material saving in your rate by improving your fire protection. The proposition is this——"

A shadow loomed over him. "Who's that?" his father's voice said.

"It's Mr. Riddick of the Mutual."

His father took the phone from him. "Hello, Riddick. . . . Yes. . . . No. . . . No. . . . Well, you ought to give us that rate anyhow. We have been talking to the Liverpool and Globe. . . . You don't? Well, I can't help that, that's the way I feel about it. . . . Good-bye." His father tramped back to his office.

He continued to look out the window. There was no hour of the day when he was free, hardly an hour of the night without its consciousness of supervision, of his father's intense and slightly exasperated interest, an interest which managed to combine a vague general pride in him with instinctive disapproval and suspicion of every detail of his life. At home this close surveillance was reinforced by his mother's love, by her passionate belief that he was destined to remain a mere enlargement of the small boy of whose perfection she was now convinced; not that there was in him anything fundamental that would disillusion her, simply that those perfections were so minutely specified that there was no moment of his days when it was not tacitly and proudly understood how he would act. There were no chains or barriers that he could point to; there was simply an atmospheric pressure that made it hard for him to breathe.

To-night he would get out of the house, walk alone up the river bank, alone with the stars and with Masefield's rugged, ringing words; and where would that walk lead him? He thought he knew; he could at least go by her house and see if she were there. For she was fine and true; her slim, cool pose suggested delicate, immaculate nobility; there was about her none of that blatant physical hardihood that made Jeanne Thompson almost, at times, embarrassing; and she had none of Jeanne's irreverent mockery, bent on reducing beliefs and standards to a rowdy farce.

"Hi, Bulldog," Jeanne always said, with a dry wide smile, really a grin. And she was always taking his arm and pressing it, sometimes against it he could feel—it was almost embarrassing. Certainly it was irritating. If a girl wanted to be provocative that was one thing; there were such girls and, though they weren't his style, he had no personal grudge against them; they went their way, he, his. But when a girl acted like that and at the same time seemed to laugh at him—she needn't expect anything else from him; either was unpleasant: and both together—

At times, also, to his anger, he was, against his will, in a surprising and undesired moment, swiftly and deeply troubled by her: such warmth and vigor so displayed. It left him furious, contemptuous, uneasy. That was no way to feel about a girl, no way for such a girl to try to make one feel.

But Julia—it was almost sacrilege to think of her in this same instant. When he was with Julia, all the finest that was in him seemed to flower. Beside her, other girls were scrubbred, cheap and earthy, of this world. The contrast was almost pitiful. He was not the only one who found it so, not by any means; there was not a man in Midian, of high or low degree, who did not recognize her fineness. Men had come from New York and from Baltimore to see her; big men, too, some of them; the captain of the Princeton track team, and a Harvard man. Among the girls and women also she was regarded as an honor to her sex. Some might dislike her; she was too perfect for their little, nibbling souls; but try as they would, they could not find a word of criticism. In Farmington, too, a girl once told him she was outstanding in her fine, true character. That was among the picked girls of the nation. And she, incredible as it might be, seemed almost to look up to him. He must be wrong in thinking so; the very notion made him humble and ashamed; yet when he was with her, he felt the thrill of latent powers within himself, a sense of manhood and of freedom, a strengthened and confident desire to accomplish the things that he and the rest of Midian believed in.

"Well," his father's voice came ringing from the inner office, "have you started on those letters?"

That evening he left his father under the onyx library lamp, settled for the evening with the *Midian News,* "The Strenuous Life," and "The Sunday School Lesson Illustrator."

His mother met him at the door. "Where are you going, dear?"

"Just for a walk."

"Don't stay out late, dear, it upsets your father. And, then, you're not fresh for the office next day."

His mother looked away from him. "Isn't there some one you could call on? It would do you good."

"Oh, I don't know," he said, "I may drop in somewhere."

"We could have some young people in some night," his mother ventured, "and give them ice-cream and cake. Your father wouldn't mind."

He gave a short laugh. His mother's face turned puzzled and distressed. Why, she was growing old. He patted her shoulder. "No, Mother, that's all right."

She followed him to the door. "Are you all right, dear? You don't read your books any more. Do you remember," she said seriously, "when you were always reading 'Lorna Doone'? If you could just have that book," she said, "you were perfectly happy to stay home all day."

He gave a wide, unhappy grin. "I'm all right, Mother; honestly."

Along the river the electric street lights' glow was intersected by the beams of acetylene headlights as motor cars chugged slowly up and down, their occupants enjoying the spring night. Buggies passed, a man and girl in each; and across, under the locust trees along the river banks, other dim figures, two and two, moved slowly, or stood still. Beyond them the river seemed to tremble underneath the moon, to tremble and stretch away to dark banks, and distant farm lights on the other shore. Behind him other motor headlights slid along the new steel highway bridge; and farther down there was a rumble on the trestle, and the glow of the locomotive's stack against the pulsing clouds of smoke.

He hurried past his Grandmother Rand's firm silhouette in the big bay window, and up the street past the neat, narrow front where Uncle Mun and Grandmother Worrall kept their home. Then he slacked off; he had escaped. He was free. Far above the street-lights' glow, the stars looked down, remote, mysterious, and imperturbable. The moon was bland and coldly radiant. The river ran in silver silence. Beyond, the shore was shrouded and remote. They were remote, all features of this world, remote and lovely; a refuge from the thick, unsavory compression of his life. Here, for the moment, he was free. He had escaped his cage, but not his chain. This moment of release was a delusion. To-night, this same starry, silvery night, would see him back again, surrounded by love, by care, by duty, and by watchful guidance. What he wanted, he did not know. Nothing, he had no doubt, that he had not been taught to reverence and believe in. What he wanted then, was still to reverence and believe in them, to live them too, he hoped, but under his own power. A hard wave of anger rose against all the love of which he was the fruit, against all the care and planning and good judgment of which he was the product. He wanted to be a man.

As though the Fates had listened to his angry prayer, alone on a straw mat on the brownstone steps, Julia Wilton was sitting.

"Is that you, Tommy?" she said. "I thought I knew your step. Isn't it a lovely night?"

"Go in and get a mat," she said.

"I'll sit down on the mat beside you."

"But won't it be rather crowded?"

He felt her slim tall frame against him. Instantly she moved away.

"Yes," he said tonelessly, "it's a lovely night."

"I love to look at the stars," she said. "Do you?"

"I don't know," he said, "they made me sort of angry coming up the river."

"Angry?"

"They make me feel so little and tied down."

"Oh," she said, "you mustn't feel that way. We all have our petty duties. Is that what you mean?"

"But I have nothing else."

"But I suppose we do them and in that way we are ready when the bigger things come along."

"But then if they don't come, it would be as if Aunt Clara bred and raised a colt, and trained him and got him fit, and then locked him up in a box-stall till he died." She didn't answer. "I want to amount to something," he said.

"But you will, Tommy. You do. I don't know any one—" she paused, "I think you do," she said.

Then it was coming, he felt it coming; a wave of power and purpose, cool and clean. In the dark he saw her hand and took it. It was fine and cool.

"Julia," he said, "could you ever—" He stumbled, he was clinging to her hand. "I think with you I could amount to something."

"Tommy," her voice was low, "you will amount to something anyway. You amount to lots now."

"I don't."

"Why," she said, "ever since I was a little girl, I have always thought you were the nicest boy I knew."

"Oh, no," he blundered on, "that's foolish."

"I have," she put her other hand on his. "I have."

Blindly he leaned forward, her hair was on his mouth. Awkwardly he bent still further, his trembling reverent lips touched her white cheek.

The hour was scandalous when he walked down the river bank again. House lights were out, the streets were empty. When he got to Linden Street he still was striding strongly. Not home just yet. He kept on down the river.

His thoughts were strange and tumbling. Now he could see ahead, sense, scope and freedom. Now he would have a home and be the master, not master, but the sharer of a new incomparably finer life. Share it with the finest girl in Midian. In

Midian? With the finest girl that he had ever known, ever would know. With the girl whose noble and divine high qualities showed in her tall and quiet beauty.

She had chosen him, he had been chosen. A man of no distinction, not yet, at least, but now he felt that time might tell a different story. There were leaders in his class, real leaders, Skull and Bones, voted most likely to succeed, who had already married. And some of the girls they had married, he remembered from Proms and football games. Those girls of theirs! It was laughable. Well, they had had their moment at New Haven, those leaders of the class, while he had remained obscure. Now he could picture their respectful eyes when he said, "Why, hello! I want you to know my wife." He could picture their wives' exaggerated gush to hide their envy.

He looked ahead along the dark house-fronts and the silent street. This town of his would be his field, and in it he would be acknowledged. He had been chosen by the finest of all women. All that was fine in life, now lay ahead of him.

The light of some late watcher, showing in an upstairs window, brought him to himself. Here was the familiar block, here was Aunt Clara's house. The light was hers. She, of all the world, was still awake to hear his triumph. He whistled. No shadows moved against the light reflected on her ceiling. In the darkness he fumbled in the gutter for small pebbles.

The pebbles clicked against the pane, a shadow moved. Her silhouette stood in the glowing square. He watched her. Seen so, she might have been as young as Julia. She raised the window. "Tommy?" she called, "Hello, there."

"Aunt Clara, I want to see you."

Her voice changed. "Oh, what's wrong?"

"Nothing. Nothing at all. It's something different."

"Fine!" she said and vanished with a gesture.

In the dark hall she greeted him, a softly padding wraith. "I never can find the light," she said.

"Never mind," he said. "Go ahead."

"All right," she said. "Can you see me?"

"Yes," he said, "I can see you."

"Here are the stairs."

"All right," he said, "all right."

"When you get up here," she said, "you can see the light from my bedroom."

Along the hall she was again a silhouette against her lighted bedroom door, a tall and graceful silhouette in her ruffled dressing-gown.

"I'm going to get into bed," she called back. "My legs are cold." She gave a little jump like a boy, and pulled the covers over her. "You can sit over there," she said.

"I'll sit on the bed," he said.

"All right," she said. "Now what?" She leaned forward and locked her arms around her cocked-up knees. Her face, bent on his, was warm, alive and delicately humorous. Over the faint high color it was warmly tanned, and lines were around the firm warm eyes. It was the face of a young man who had seen all kinds of weather.

"Aunt Clara," he said, "I've asked a girl to marry me. I think I'm engaged; I guess I am. I wanted to tell somebody, I wanted to tell you."

Her smile turned slightly set, but her voice was ringing. "Why, Tommy, my dear. Oh, Tommy." Her hands flew up to him.

"It's Julia Wilton," he said.

"The lucky girl," she said. "I thought it would be."

"She's wonderful," he said. "I never knew how wonderful it would be." Eagerly he shook her hands up and down. "Wait till you get to know her."

"Oh, yes," she said. "I hear she's very fine." Her dark eyes searched him. "But all I want is that you should be happy." There was a tremor on her lips. "You must be happy," she whispered.

Her lips turned firm. Her smile turned rigid, her face was a dreadful smiling mask. And then it broke, broke horribly. She dropped it down between her knees.

He jumped up in distress and terror. "Aunt Clara!" he said. "Aunt Clara!" She reached blind hands up to him through her shaking.

In the end she sat up with a small crooked smile. "Oh, dear," she said, "I'm terrible. I'm so ashamed." She brushed her hair from her heavy eyes. "I'm just a sentimental goat. Look here," she said, "there's one thing. Your mother would be terribly hurt if she knew you'd been here."

"I know," he said, "but mother's been asleep for hours."

"It makes no difference," she said. "Don't be stupid. To-morrow you must come and tell me."

"All right, I will." He nodded. "You're wonderful."

"Oh, no," she said, "I'm not. You must go."

Sadness and pity weighed him down. In that instant a mist of desolation seemed to lie ahead of him.

"Yes," he said dully. He put out a hand which she took mechanically He stood up; the hand which he still held was cold and dead; he was alone; he felt the chill and shadow of his loneliness. "Aunt Clara."

"Yes," she said.

"Are you all right?"

"Yes," she said. "Oh, yes."

He still stood alone, holding her hand and reaching out to her. "I must go," he said.

He felt her hand stir, come to life, her face came up, soft, strong and faintly smiling. "Good night," she said.

Between those two strong hands of hers his hand was shaken once, hard almost fiercely.

CHAPTER XLII

HE HAD borrowed his father's Apperson and driven Julia up the river to a hill near his Aunt Clara's farm, a round knoll crowned by a gnarled and abandoned apple orchard. Behind it, the rough-coated green shoulders of the mountains; below it, the shining river and the low blue hills beyond. Through the trees they could see the twinkle of sunlight on the brass of the Apperson where it stood hub-deep in orchard grass, a magnificent and alien visitor. Far down the road Aunt Clara's mares moved, grazing inside the tall white fences. Their legs, their heads, their necks looked fragile in contrast to their swollen bellies. A farm team rumbled under dust; the mares stopped nibbling and pricked up mouse-like ears.

"You know," he said, "there's something kind of touching about a mare in foal." He kept watching them. She didn't answer. "Don't you think so?" He turned, her face was flushed.

"I suppose." She spoke with an effort. She put on a brighter manner. "Aren't those clouds pretty? You can see them reflected in the river."

"Yes," he said, "they're beautiful. I wonder if the fish like it when the clouds are in the river?"

"What an idea!" She smiled faintly. "But I don't suppose the fish notice. Anyhow," she said, "we just see the reflection here. If you were in the water you wouldn't see it at all. It's an illusion."

"Yes," he said slowly, "I know it is."

"It's very pretty though. And, then, you can see their shadows on the fields."

"Yes," he said. "Don't you think this is the nicest view you ever saw?"

"It is very pretty."

"All right," he said. "Now what do you think of this idea?" He paused for emphasis. "We can buy this place. Cheap, too."

"This place? Buy it? What for?"

366

"We could build a little house here."

"A house? A house?"

She was incredulous. But he must keep on. "I could get a little car and drive down to the office every day; it wouldn't take more than twenty minutes," he said. "And so, instead of being stuffed up in town, you could be out here in the country."

"But I would be alone."

"Oh, but we'll have a servant of course. And Aunt Clara's right there at the farm practically every day." She didn't answer. "And then some day," he tried to make it light, "there may be more than two of us."

For a long time she did not speak. Then she said with an effort, "But the housekeeping, have you thought of that?"

"Of course I have." His voice was warm and self-congratulatory. "You can get most things at the grocery store at the corner where this road comes out on the river. And meats and anything else, I could get in town."

"But winter?" she said.

"We could go in, then, and live with father and mother. You see?" He looked at her and was instantly without conviction. "Oh, well," he said, "it was just an idea. I guess it wouldn't work."

But somehow, this idea, so fragile, fanciful and secretly broached, was spread about the town. "Look here," his father said, "what's this notion of your leaving Midian?"

"It was just an idea, Father. It was not serious."

"Well, I should hope not," his father said. "Automobiles are all right in their way, but a man can't depend on them to get to his office on time."

"And then, too," his mother said, "the strain of driving so far every day."

Mrs. Wilton had been prompt to send for him. "Thomas, I'm sure you wouldn't think of leaving our little Julia up there all alone."

"Oh, no," he said. "It was just an idea, Mrs. Wilton."

Uncle Mun had accosted him on the street. "Look here, what's this talk I hear about your turning yourself into a countryman?"

"It was just an idea," he said. "I sometimes think the automobile is going to change things, but I guess it's too soon."

"The automobile won't change human nature. And let me tell

you one thing; I'm an older man; half of the business in this town is done by social contacts in the evening. If a man wants to leave Midian, that's all right, I suppose; but if he wants to live in Midian, he's got to live in Midian. Notice me," Uncle Mun said, "I never miss a social gathering. And the other evenings, I exchange civilities; or perhaps I give a little dinner, have some terrapin sent down from the Union League Club, and a bottle of sound wine. No sir," he said, "things like that never do any harm."

With a sagacious nod, Uncle Mun departed for the little two-room wooden office where he sat all day reading de Maupassant and "Tales of Oriental Love" under the portrait of old Judge Worrall and the steel engraving of the Shemingo County Bar Association.

In his private office, beside the terrestrial globe, his grandfather had sat and looked at him with a friendly grin beneath his neat white beard. "Well, Tommy, what's all this about?"

"It's nothing, Grandfather. I was just looking at that Mowry place up near the farm, but Julia didn't like the idea, so I dropped it."

His grandfather looked out the window. "Yes," he said, "the women don't like to be alone. They like to have their little gatherings. What's Mowry want for it?"

"Twenty-six hundred dollars."

"Ah," his grandfather said. "Well, that would have been a good buy. A good buy at any time. And let me tell you something, these automobiles, don't like them much myself, wham-wham! bounce-bounce! but they're going to change values. Have you got a firm price?"

"Gruber, the agent, got a letter. I kept my name out. Everybody seems to know about it in town, but I don't think Mowry knows out there."

"I know," his grandfather said. "He lives at Myersburg."

"That's right. He's not on the place; no one is."

"Well, now," his grandfather said, "maybe we can do a little business together. We get an option, then we will see if we can't rent the farm to Clara for extra pasture. If it goes through, we will buy it together. I'll take your personal note for your half-interest." By tugging on his watch chain, his grandfather produced a gold penknife. With the blade he proceeded to attend to a slight roughness on one of his broad, clean fingernails. "In that way," he said, "Clara gets a new pasture cheap, and we have a nice little property that is carrying itself."

Thereafter, when people made their inquiries, he was able to say, "Oh, no. Just a little business venture." And about that time a rumor started that the choir of the First Church were going to be made to wear vestments; whereupon all interest in him ceased, not to be revived until his wedding.

During this lull his father, after a perfunctory and somewhat impatient consultation with Julia and himself, had bought a house that was at least precisely what Julia wanted. He was surprised at how quickly his father had lined up with Julia. The house was somewhat far up the river, farther even than Mr. and Mrs. Wilton's yellow-brick façade; but it was old and had a charm of a simple red-brick sort, and a narrow garden at one side. Undoubtedly, too, the town was growing that way. That is to say, persons of distinction were now buying houses in the district formerly occupied by persons of no distinction. The population of Midian, either actual, or as annually over-estimated, remained about the same.

With this house practically her own, new and charming talents of Julia's came into play. A new door with a fan light was installed, and solid blinds were hung, painted soft blue. With the white picket fence in front, and the imitation flagstones in the garden path, it looked like an illustration in the "House Beautiful" in whose pages Julia had, in fact, been preparing herself for just this opportunity.

Of the wedding, he remembered only the yellow oak and the astounding stained glass of the Hancock Square Church edifice, and his distracted and barely successful efforts to keep the Buffer who had struck up a passionate friendship with Uncle Mun, presentable. And of the honeymoon at Spring Lake, New Jersey, he retained, still more curiously, only a picture of the ocean, the boardwalk, the bright fragile houses, and a sense of listlessness and strain. The time from the night when he had taken Julia's hand on her front doorstep seemed incredibly short until the night when she had come to him in the square library of their new home. He was sitting surrounded by white trim and flowered wall paper and the reproductions of Maxfield Parrish, and reading John Masefield.

"Tommy," she said.

"Yes." He read on '—and all I ask is a tall ship and a star to steer her by.'

"You're not listening."

"Yes I am." '—I must down to the sea again, to the call of the running tide.'

"I went to see Dr. Hartman to-day." He shut the book. She spoke in a toneless voice like a little girl reciting. "He says I'm going to have a baby."

He was on his feet. "Oh, gosh!" he said. "Julia!" He had her hands. "Julia," he said, "isn't that wonderful?"

She did not seem to hear him. For all her height and fineness, she seemed like a desolate little girl.

"Julia," he said, "I know you'll be all right. Isn't it wonderful?"

"Yes," she said slowly. She roused herself. "I think these women that don't want children are most unnatural."

"Why, yes," he said awkwardly. "I guess that's so."

And then, immediately, it seemed, he was sitting, bound in iron chains of discipline, on a bench in the hospital corridor. His mother was bustling somewhere in the distance. His father was calling every fifteen minutes from the office. His grandfather, to the chief surgeon's irritation, had sent down Levi Mistletoe with the carriage to be available in case the hospital lacked anything. The door of her private room had opened. Between the nurse and the thin, white-coated interne, she had crept out. He had sprung up, but her face was deathly, her eyes were sightless. He fell back. Bent and crooked in her pink silk dressing-gown, she had shuffled down the corridor toward the unknown.

And then his mother, trim and tiny in the long hall, was scuttling toward him and calling, "It's all right, it's all right. It's a boy!" And he was telephoning, gnawing at the inside of his cheek to keep his voice steady. Somewhere down the corridor he could hear a microscopic bleating, mechanical, inhuman, unreasonable, persistent, and, frankly, damned exasperating.

To feel that way about the child, George Rand II, and to admit, even to himself, his feeling had been the first shock, certainly the first illumination, of his life. Not that he did not have in high degree the pride ascribed to fathers by convention. He was proud of his own manhood, proud of the idea of a son, proud of the thought that the Rands were going on; but the actual baby was hard to warm to. A denuded and almost idiotic troglodyte blinking fretfully in the unaccustomed light of day, a sinister memento from the primeval depths whence man, according to godless Science, had crawled. Only in sleep, and rarely, did a fleeting expression, passing over his tiny and amorphous features like a light breeze over water, give a faint, yet lingering forecast of his humanity.

And just as Cupid, the beautiful child, united lovers, so did this gnome-like infant, wizened and ancient, yet horribly incomplete, divide him from Julia. She was weary and prepossessed; had been for months before the coming of the gnome. And though their life together from the first had been conducted on a plane of the utmost delicacy and temperance, it was a trial to have it cease. It was no consolation to know that this change was no deprivation to his wife, either before the coming of the baby, or afterward. But for the time being he consoled himself. It was to be expected. It represented, after all, the difference in their feelings from the first; a difference which undoubtedly existed between the sexes, at least in the case of all women who were fine.

In other fields, however, the child had served him better. It had, together of course with his marriage to Julia, set a seal upon him which established his position in the family and in the town. He was allowed to listen to discussions between his father and his grandfather on questions of policy. His grandfather, while radical and almost visionary in his forecasts of human achievements—he spoke with almost alarming casualness of steel and concrete highways for automobile trucks, and even of flying machines as common conveyances—was immovably reactionary in regard to the coal business. At least, so Tommy gathered, his grandfather felt that while daring ventures might have been proper to himself in the heyday of his youth, now that the business was virtually in his father's hands, routine conservatism offered the only safeguard against disaster. His father, on the other hand, had notions of a heyday of his own. These notions took the form of controlling the business from its source, the mines. To acquire them would mean increase in profits, and more important still, security from the whims of mine owners who might at present see fit at any time to select another broker, or even set up a sales organization of their own. He, himself, was given charge of the old customers' accounts, at least of the accounts of such old customers as could be relied on to remain attached to John Rand and Son under any conditions. He ushered at the First Church and was elected a trustee of the Midian Boy's Club. Yet from time to time, sitting in the library of their home up River Street, while upstairs Julia kept her eternal watch over the baby, he seemed to himself, for a man who had a wife and child, not to mention parents, grandparents, an aunt and uncle, a roommate, college friends, and boys and girls of his own age in Midian, unexpectedly, inexplicably alone. Friends came in; Bill McGuire, fresh from a big day in the Midian Sheet and Tube Company, Porky Montross, just out of the Harvard Law School. Always they asked for Julia and nearly always Julia was too occupied to see them more than briefly; so then they sat and smoked, and he felt beyond their unspoken longing for a drink that they sensed that he was of another world, a higher world perhaps, but, for them, uninhabitable. Even Aunt Clara when she came up with her cheer and all her meaty satisfying talk of mares and foals and farming, of Mr. and Mrs. Heisdick and their bad son, Fritz, who was writing for money from British Honduras; even Aunt Clara stayed but a little while, then seemed to retire in favor of Julia. He had been promoted, it seemed, or, possibly by his own exertions, had attained to a solitary world.

So then he was alone again in the library whose gray entwined foliage ran between the neat white baseboard and the neat white picture moulding, looking at the colonial brass and the red-brick fireplace and at the boy above, who blew his bubbles against a bright, unchanging sky. In such moments, once or twice, a picture drifted through his mind like a question faintly asked and quite irrelevant. It had happened long ago, it now seemed, before his marriage. It was two days after his engagement; still in a state of high excitement, he was trotting smartly up River Street in his grandfather's buggy to take Julia for a drive. It was after five, a bright, low, level light was on the river, on the rigid cardboard house-fronts, on the locust trees' new fern-like leaves. His horse shied at a brilliant flash of yellow on the pavement.

"Oh, Jeanne," he said as he pulled up—what clothes that girl wore—"I'm glad I saw you. I wanted to tell you——"

"Yes," she said, "I know."

"I can't shake hands," he said. "This horse is foolish."

"No," she said, "we can't shake hands."

Still smiling she looked at him.

"When did you hear?" he said at last.

"Oh, I don't know. I've known a long time."

"A long time? Why, I only got engaged—well, really, yester-day."

Under the shelter of her smile, he felt her eyes were searching him. "I know," she said. "I guess I guessed it."

"Well," he said, "you were right. You ought to get a prize.

"Of course," he said, "I know Julia will want you to be brides-maid."

And still she smiled. Good Lord, could she do nothing but smile?

"That will be fine," she said.

"I must be getting along, I guess. This horse don't like to stand."

"Good-bye, Tommy."

He drove on. He felt that her eyes still followed him and her smile. Why, she had never congratulated him.

And yet, as now, long after, the scene came back to him, her looks seemed lightly, but sharply tinged with mockery and pain.

With mockery and pain; surely that was unlikely, it was in-credible; always she had been his enemy, an uncomfortable girl. She could not help, of course, the marked degree with which she had been endowed with what Uncle Mun referred to as a woman's charms; but she need not have sought, by her clothes and bearing, to have capitalized them. To do so, merely de-feated its own purpose as far as men like himself were con-cerned; and certainly she need not have always seemed to be laughing at him. Not that he minded; he could say that he took it in good part and even that he was amused. He could afford to be; he had his own ideas about life and she had hers, and he had no doubt that she was entitled to them; only, if she insisted upon making a point of them, she need not expect that people of a different point of view would be attracted to her.

And yet, since that day when he, driving up the river road, had met her he could not help the feeling that she, in spite of her

ineptitude, had had for him a feeling— He roused himself impatiently; this was no way to let his thoughts run.

In any case, there need be no regrets for her. Such matters, if
this might be called an instance of them, clearly worked themselves out for the best. Long since, she had gone away to Baltimore where she was studying to be some sort of hospital tech-
nician. Undoubtedly she would be happy in the work and make
a great success of it. She had her father's scientific mind; the
discipline would settle her down. Under the vellum-shaded
lamp, he searched the volumes on the table for something to
distract him. Undoubtedly she would succeed; it was just the
sort of thing for her; she was really a fine girl, Jeanne, but,
frankly, she was a materialist at heart.

And yet he saw her standing there, in that canary-yellow dress,
her color high, her black hair dashed behind her ears, vital and
bold and teasing, her figure thrusting through the close-cut brilliant jacket, as she thrust through life, as though assured and
conscious of its power. And yet in her black eyes, on her large,
daring mouth that smiled at him, there was a shadow that softened them, showed depths and a glimpse of touching sweetness.
He roused himself. He had not seen this. He had imagined it in
the glance which followed after him—a glance like an echo, an
echo of a sound unheard, unguessed.

CHAPTER XLIII

As he entered his grandfather's office under Samuel's guidance he knew that it was a solemn moment, for beside his grandfather sat his father looking at him, chin down, over his wide wing collar. "Your grandfather wished to see you," he said.

His thoughts flew back, fluttered nervously: was it that mistake in the carload rate for the Maysville Power and Light Company? that was the only one of moment that he had made, and even so he had corrected it and got the order.

"We both did," his grandfather said. "Sit down, T. Just close that door."

"T," his grandfather said, "your father and I have been watching your work since you came with us. Of course," he said, "I have not the opportunities to observe that he has, but what he tells me confirms my own impression."

"Yes, sir."

"He tells me that you have shown great industry and fidelity, that you pay good attention to detail, and exhibit willingness to learn, and, above all, good judgment. He feels as I do, gratified that you have shown yourself to be an excellent young business man."

His father turned to his grandfather hastily. "Hold on, Father," he said, "that's putting it too strong."

His grandfather did not even return his father's glance. "Those were precisely your words," he said with his eyes still fixed on Tommy. "In consequence," he said, "your father and I feel that it is an appropriate time to make some change in our organization. As you are aware, the principal conduct of the business is now in the hands of your father. Under the circumstances, I have decided that I am not justified in retaining my full interest. It is a business which I built up in my younger days, but I feel that I have already been amply rewarded for the part that I played. My interest now stands at seventy-five per cent; your

375

father's, of course, at the remaining twenty-five. While this dis-
parity, as far as income is concerned, has been largely offset of
late years by my assigning to him my salary as president, I feel
that the time is suitable to make some changes in the capital interests of this business so that they should more accurately represent the actualities of its present administration."

Unhurried, yet unhesitating, his grandfather's words fell
clearly, firmly, beautifully chiselled. There was a thrill to hearing them. It was a sort of poetry, at least it had the stirring and
endearing quality of all perfection.

"I have therefore divided my interest into three equal parts:
one part I shall retain, perhaps for reasons of sentiment." His
grandfather did not pause or otherwise lay emphasis. "It will
pass to your father at my death. One part goes to your father
now, giving him, with what he already holds, a half-interest in
the business; and one part goes to you."

His grandfather's great firm arm had lain along the table. The
hand now closed on a long manilla envelope.

"For purposes of business convenience this firm is represented
by one hundred shares of stock. This envelope contains twenty-
five shares assigned by me to you. I wish you to check them
over, and when you have satisfied yourself, to sign the enclosed
receipt prepared by Mr. Riser who, as you may know, acts
as the secretary, not only of the firm, but of our formal meetings."

The envelope swung toward him. "Grandfather," he said, "I
didn't expect this." He stood up, grinning uncertainly. "Not
yet, anyhow."

"These shares," his grandfather said, "are of no par value.
They are never to be offered for sale except by agreement of all
living partners, nor are they to be otherwise transferred except to
another partner. I suggest that you allow Mr. Riser to add a
codicil to your will."

"Oh, yes, of course I will. I suppose I should leave them to
Father in case he survives me."

"That would be the proper arrangement," his grandfather
said. "You can, of course, assign your share of the earnings of
the business to your wife or child."

"Yes, yes. I'll see Mr. Riser right away. I'll sign the receipt."

"You have not counted the certificates."

He sat down on the edge of the desk. "All right, grandfather, I will." He opened the envelope. "It seems not very courteous though, especially when you're giving them to me."

His grandfather's slow smile stirred his beard. "There need be no implication of fraud," he said, "but mistakes are always possible."

He was counting the certificates. "Did you ever make one, Grandfather?"

"No, I never did.

"One word more," his grandfather looked out the window at the islands and the slow bright river. "We have in the course of our history perhaps shown some skill and rendered some acceptable service, but in the last analysis our only asset is our integrity." His voice was slow, unhurried; he chiselled each word out unerringly. "To some persons, integrity is a relative term. With us its meaning is absolute. All bills, if correct, are paid on the day received, all deliveries are made on the date specified. It is a frequent temptation to others in this line of business, when confronted by the necessity to deliver at a loss, to delay, hoping that the price of coal will change to their advantage. We not only do not delay, we invariably allow from two to three extra days for transportation. In consequence, we have never missed delivery except once, that was in 1889, after the Johnstown flood in Pennsylvania."

There was silence. His grandfather continued to look out on the river. His father cleared his throat. "He might have my office perhaps."

"Yes," his grandfather said. "Then you will have mine." The river was bright and flowing slowly but strongly, high in its banks. "It is no longer necessary that I should have an office there."

For a year or two then he sat at what had been his father's desk in charge of all accounts and all new business, dictating, checking orders, making terms, learning how with unhurried and masterly precision to wade through the welter of letters, carbon copies, statements, memoranda, of telegrams, long distance calls and visitors, leaving order in his wake. During this period, as though to reinforce him in his steady, sure advance, another child was born, a daughter. Perhaps because of her sex, perhaps because the troglodyte himself had now developed into a personality, of barbaric impulse it is true, but also of a most pleasing charm, the baby from the start was dear to him.

In fact he seemed at times to cling to her. It was as though her tiny helplessness were his support. Not that Julia was not magnificent. She was, he told himself, a girl without a flaw. Of even temper, thoughtful, planning well ahead, dignified, considerate, reasonable in the sense that she had reasons for everything she did. When he heard jokes about the failings of the sex he felt a small glow of superiority. Let the other husbands wrestle with their problems. Of course Julia was well dressed and liked nice clothes and she had, unconsciously, as you might say, a very good figure in a quiet way. But there was no feminine nonsense about Julia.

But about the baby, Jane, there was feminine nonsense already. She rolled her brown eyes at him in an almost revolting travesty of more sophisticated wiles. She clung, she wept, she pleaded. She was in one instant enraged, caressing. And yet he found that it was on her that he had focussed. It was an anomaly. He had small instinctive leanings toward babies, even his own, and yet that little bundle, so formless, so almost imbecile and yet so live, so preternaturally knowing and alert, stirred him as nothing rational had ever done. He sat on the floor of the living room, his hands locked over his knees and watched this strange small animal, at once delicate and clumsy, this half-divine inhabitant of a nebulous, a distant world, both simpler and more mysterious. When she was put to bed the day seemed over for him. He read or talked to Julia about the doings of their friends, about the Church, the Boy's Club, the latest movements in Child Training. No gossip, however, and no business; that was understood. And if the conversation flagged and she, as often, did not care to settle to a book, he found that she never tired of Double Canfield. It was a peaceful life on a fine simple plane and she was perfectly content.

But in the spring nights when the locust trees were soft and warm and the moonlight ran along the running river, just before bed he would take a turn along the river bank.

And once walking alone and restlessly in the warm darkness, he had sensed a couple in the deeper shadows, lost to shame. His first impulse had been to call for the police, but as he hurried away shocked, angry, and civically aroused, he was swept by a succeeding wave of lawless sympathy. Of lawless sympathy and worse. As he walked, he shuddered ungovernably. He walked and walked, and when he got back home he treated Julia's pleasant inquiries almost with rudeness. Fierce, brutal thoughts struck at him. There sat his wife, so calm, so sure, so perfect. He had two children that was true. But as his wild thoughts drained away and left him empty, the children and their mother seemed synthetic, the products of high purpose and of chemistry, flawless and admirable and utterly without significance.

Fortunately, not long afterward, events became kaleidoscopic. In what seemed like a single, unreal, but terrifying instant, all Europe went to war. The stock exchange was closed, for three days John Rand and Son would accept no orders. Then came cautious resumption, and after that the dawn of realization, slow at first, then accelerating, that this catastrophe was making business hum. Afterward the old business men had laughed at their first fears. It seemed that the magnitude of the affair in Europe had blinded them for the moment to the axiom that there is no fertilizer for quick profits like the blood of men. As for him, he was too busy to generalize or even, in any real sense, to think. The orders crowded in on him; there were wires, and long distance calls and strangers always waiting in the outer office, pleaders, threateners; there were cables, and two terrific little men from Italy. It was necessary to sublet the floor above from their own tenant, the law firm of Beaver, Merrivale, Mulvaney, and Beaver, at a painful advance, and bring in a lot of girl stenographers.

Then slowly the drift began. From the East it came first, where traditions were the strongest and respect for culture, and where Allied officers were appearing on obscure and momentous missions to be entertained and listened to by social leaders of the better sort. And then out here in this middle ground, above the great mass of indifference, the older families and those who, like himself, had had the advantage of going to one of the great institutions began to grasp the import of the struggle. From the first they had known by instinct and through the endless columns of the press that English gentlemen and the children of Lafayette had drawn the sword against barbarian atrocity The realization grew that these Allies, despite inspiring aims and greater heroism, were not accomplishing the quick results which would please every man of honor and good breeding, as well as an inscrutable but undoubtedly passionately interested God. In the press the Allies continued to pile up victories against fearful odds, and even when the victories were not geographically demonstrable, they continued in every action to decimate the Germans by virtue of their superior intelligence and morale. There were minor episodes. Kut-el Mara and the Dardanelles could not be put down as tactical successes however much they might contribute, as it was explained, to the grand and recondite strategy of the cause seen as a whole. And on the misty Eastern Front, the Russian steam roller rumbled obscurely hither and yon achieving fabulous advances and equally fabulous retreats. The real mystery was, however, how in the main theatre of war in France the superior qualities and the almost unbroken series of victories of the Allies had brought them slowly and inexorably to what began to look like irretrievable disaster. The feeling grew among the men and women known to Tommy Rand that it would not do to stand by and see the children of Lafayette and the English gentlemen go under. And among the business men of larger calibre, whom he sometimes met, there was a sense that if, contrary to all decent sentiment, the Marseillaise, the buff cord breeches and impeccable field boots went under, the mounting obligations which were due America would undoubtedly go under too. This flood tide rose sharply with the sinking of the *Lusitania,* and gathered force as, under the gun-fire of German submarines, American cargoes of arms to Germany's enemies went down. Then came the days of tension and of ultimatum; and then the sombre ringing words, the trumpet call, the organ music expressing the great heart of America and consecrating her serried phalanxes and all her solemn, eager power to the freedom of the world.

The town broke out in posters, extra editions were always on the street, torchlights filled the City Square and wavered on Senator Beaver, old and ponderous, fragrant with sentiment and Highspire rye. He swayed there, his thick cracked voice still able to resound, and told how, under him as captain, the boys of Midian had answered the call and saved the Union in '61. At the end he put his arm around an old house-painter, originally from Western Maryland, who wore the long gray coat of the

Confederacy. Under the roar the band of the Midian Fencibles was thumping. The roaring died, the band blared out: it was the new song, "Over There."

On the way uptown, River Street was crowded with dark figures drifting back from the meeting in the Square. He walked among them, strong and straight.

> "Johnny, get your gun, get your gun, get your gun,
> Get it on the run, on the run, on the run——"

Incredibly, the people on the sidewalk idled along, laughed, whistled, talked of the mass meeting as though it had been a show.

"Wonderful how the old Senator holds up, ain't it?" "Yeah, he sure has got outside of a heap of liquor in his time." "You bet! Still does." And, even more preposterous, a young man's voice called, "Hey, Dicey! How about the White Sox to-day? See what they done?"

He left the sidewalk and stepped out on the street where he could have more scope.

> "The Yanks are coming, the Yanks are coming,
> The drums drum drumming everywhere——"

Uptown the crowd thinned out, he was back on the sidewalk walking almost alone, the tune ran in his head, and back in town the band thumped faintly on its way back to the Armory. The Fencibles would be the first to go. They looked like high school boys, most of them lost between their baggy, khaki uniforms and broad-brimmed campaign hats. They *were* high school boys; some of them he knew; he had seen them at the Boys' Club, at the entertainments, sleight-of-hand men, travelogues.

> "Over there, over there,
> Send the word, send the word
> Over there——"

Just high school boys, and how the crowd cheered them, cheered them in their uneven ranks and baggy, khaki uniforms. And Dr. Millspaugh, that ridiculous dentist from downtown, how had he gotten to be the captain? Yet, they would probably be the first to go.

His house stood dark and solitary except for a dim light in

the hall that Julia had left burning for him. As he turned in the path, in the darkness of the front steps two cigarettes made points of light. They moved and two dark forms rose up.

"Hello, Tommy."

"Why, hello, Bill!" he said in a low voice. "Hello, Porky."

"Still marching to the band, I see," Porky said.

"Boy," Bill said in his big, resonant voice, "a stately tread. We could hear you coming a mile."

From the upstairs window, Julia's voice floated down. "Tommy, why don't you go inside? You'll wake the children."

"Gosh!" Bill said, "I guess we were all making a noise."

"Come in," he said, "Julia has gone to bed early."

In the living room, he pushed two cretonne-covered chairs up for them. "There's cigarettes in that box. I'm sorry I haven't anything to drink."

"Oh, that's all right." Bill's voice resounded through the house. "We've just come from Porky's."

"I've been down to the meeting," he said.

"Oh, that!" they said. "We left there early. How was it?"

"What you'd expect," he said, "kind of ridiculous and yet kind of stirring."

"It was the band," Bill said. "You certainly were marching."

"It was the Senator," Porky said. "How was the Senator?"

"The Senator was the same; ridiculous and kind of stirring."

"I don't blame you," Porky said. "The Senator gets me too."

"That drunken, old snake-charmer," Bill said.

"No," Porky said, "the Senator is a great man. He has faith in the imbecility of the human race."

"What's great there?" Bill said. "I have faith in your imbecility."

"But just blind faith: you just feel the imbecility is there. But the Senator knows how to reach it and bring it out. That's genius." Porky pursed up his small, round mouth and blew three perfect smoke rings. "It's the difference," he said, "between a believer and a prophet."

"He's just a cock-eyed, old snake-charmer."

"William," Porky said, "doesn't he get you too?"

Bill's cigarette rose under his eye with his wide grin. "Yes," he said. He and Porky looked at him.

Porky made a gesture. "You see," he turned. "So it's nothing to be ashamed of, Thomas."

"Anyhow," he said, "to-night was different. He couldn't go wrong. The war is something every one believes in."

Porky fixed his round, small eyes on the Maxfield Parrish boy on the mantelpiece. "That's what we came about," he said, and stopped.

"You see," Bill said, "it's this way." He stopped.

"I can't put it as well as Bill has," Porky said, "but the idea is this. The Fencibles have just got orders to recruit up to three hundred men, and Bill and I, over a little jug, have been talking about going in."

"The idea is this," Bill said, "to go in on the ground floor, like everybody else, and see what we can do."

"In a word," Porky said, "not to avail ourselves of our prestige. We may have to change our names."

Bill frowned. "This way we can be together."

Porky brought his eyes down from the picture. "Your position is altogether different."

"Of course it is," Bill said, "you'd be a fool to go right now anyhow."

"But if the situation ever changes, just keep it in mind that we'd like to have you with us."

He felt most juvenile flushes rising to his face. "I had no idea you fellows—Of course, we've always known each other, but I certainly do——"

Porky stood up. "We were hoping," he said, "to be spared all that." He pulled his coat down over his neat, stout figure.

CHAPTER XLIV

AMONG the paper barracks stretched out in straight rows on the plain, the men in khaki swarmed. Beyond the plain were trees and house-roofs, a towering spire, and the white block of a big hotel. And far away, on cloudless days, he could see, incredibly aloft above the ground-haze, vague points of brightness, the monstrous towers of Manhattan.

The khaki figures were forever moving, forever falling in between the barracks, forever forming lines and columns on the open plain. Far off they broke up into single specks and, to the sound of whistles, like dogs or like obedient ants, advanced in open order. Farther off still, all day there was the sound of firing. Down on the stone roads where the lines of barracks ended there was the wink of harness and the sombre rumble of caissons and of guns; and at the other end, inside the guarded gate, there stood a widespread building, painted green, where beautiful young ladies forever poured out coffee and forever smiled.

He walked alone between the paper barracks and the plain. The sun was sinking, and on the plain a regiment was marching in column, was swinging into front by companies; he saw the guides run out and bring their rifles down. His shoulders were set square under the new gold bars; his arm was going automatically, yet with a conscious pride, in answer to salutes.

A month ago, when his commission had come through, he had gotten a three-day leave for the purpose of buying boots and an officer's uniform; and so arrived on the following morning in Midian, rigidly outfitted as a second lieutenant of infantry and wearing boots of a brilliant yellow that caused his feet to burn. The family were standing in a phalanx on the station platform. The color had come to Julia's pale, translucent face, and little Tad's bare legs had galloped in one spot, and he had hollered, "Hey, Daddy! Hey, Hey, Hey!" To mark the contrast with Julia's reserved greeting, his mother, wearing an American flag in the lapel of her long, brown-satin coat had thrown her arms around him a shade theatrically, and his father had turned quite pink, and grinned, "Well, Lieutenant, how did you get elected?" In the offing there was a hushed, but tense, altercation between young Sam and Levi Mistletoe for the possession of his single bag. As a special privilege and an evidence of his standing with the railroad, Uncle Mun, who had bought himself a light tan waterproof of military cut, insisted that they should all ascend with some discomfort and danger in the baggage elevator, a slow-moving, unclean platform devoid of sides.

In an old linen suit of clothes, he had sat for the day on the river bank across from his house. Beside him Tad made mud forts and Julia, saying little, watched the baby carriage. Hot sunlight lay on the burnished river; the fine-leaved locust trees were a tired, dusty green; a little breeze came down along the bank moving slowly with the stream. But it did not seem hot to him. His shirt was open and inside his old duck trousers his legs felt free and cool. "Hush, baby," Julia said. She waved her hand against a fly. "I suppose my mother will be up soon," she said.

"Oh, yes," he said. "How is she?"

"She's fine. Father sent word that he would try to get around this evening. He's on the Draft Board, you know, and," she said, "then the mill is working night and day."

"War orders, I suppose."

"Wheel spokes for artillery. Tom," she said, "do you think it would be all right if I went back to Hancock Square while you're away?"

"To church?"

"Yes. Dr. Alwine has been so wonderful. Last Sunday he preached on the text, 'The Sword of the Lord and of Gideon.' I couldn't help but feel proud. It was just as if he was preaching about you."

"Nonsense," he said. "There was no reason why I shouldn't go. No reason, I mean, except you and the children."

"We ought not to be a reason," she said. "It's a question of saving the world. I should think some of these women would be ashamed."

"Well, I guess some of them need the weekly pay envelope. We don't."

"But I don't see how they can respect their husbands. I couldn't."

"Maybe they don't. Maybe they just want them 'round."

"But don't you think all real love is founded on respect?"

"I guess so."

"I don't think I could love you if I didn't respect you."

"No. But that's us. Every case is special." He grinned at her. "In general I guess the only thing to say is that all real love is founded on love."

She flushed; her eyes filled. "Do you think it's easy for me to let you go?"

"Why Julia," he said, "Julia. What makes you say that?" He took her cold hand. "We were just talking."

On the street they heard the big noise of his father's Locomobile. He jumped up as the black touring car stopped beside the trees. His father sat square at the wheel in his dark-gray flannel suit and nodded at him seriously. His mother, in the pongee duster and purple veil, descended with alacrity.

"Hello, dear! How are you to-day? Did you sleep well?" Her voice turned formal. "Julia," she said.

"Hello, Father," he said. "Where did you get the polo shirt? You look like quite a sport."

"I think you'd better come down to the office to-day," his father said. "There are a few matters and I've had the First National prepare a Letter of Credit for you. It's just as well to have one."

"Yes," he said, "that's right."

"And then for smaller amounts," his father said, "you can have some American Express checks. The time your mother and I went abroad we found that worked out very well."

"That's fine," he said, "but right now it doesn't look as if we were going abroad."

"Do you think you will be familiar with the duties of an officer?" his father said. "I don't see how you've had time to learn them."

"I don't know much," he said, "but neither does anybody else."

"There must be books that you can study."

"Yes, I had to study them in Training Camp for my examination."

"I should think it would be well," his father said, "to employ some older, more experienced men to teach you in your spare time."

"The trouble is the experienced men have got more than they can do already."

"Well," his father said, "all I know is that in any other business there is always a way for a man to learn his job if he is sufficiently determined." His father stepped on the accelerator. The Locomobile snorted. "I'll send the car back for your mother; after that you can have it if you want it."

"Thanks, Father, but we have the Ford."

His father put his big, gloved hands on the wheel. "You can leave the Ford for me in front of my house. This is a better car."

Beneath the locust tree, Julia, tall and cool in white muslin with a wide fichu, and his mother, a short, trim pongee figure under the purple veil, looked into the hooded depths of the baby carriage. The baby was crying. She had settled down to it without haste but relentlessly—wawa—wawa—as regular as clockwork. Slowly, inevitably, his mother's small, gray-gloved hand stole forward. It rested on the edge of the baby carriage. The carriage began to rock almost imperceptibly. The baby's cries diminished. "Well, Tommy," she said, her voice was gay and artificial, "what do you think of your little daughter?—a dear little thing, a darling little thing." Under cover of this small talk, the rocking increased. The baby's cries diminished. Julia fixed a firm eye on the baby; as though casually, she placed a hand on the baby carriage to steady it. Mrs. Rand was still able, however, to agitate her side. Entranced by this singular and novel motion, the baby's cries died away in bubbles. It lay there underneath the mosquito netting, goggle-eyed and beaming fatuously.

"Mother Rand," Julia said. His mother's smile dissolved. "I've just been talking to Tom about Hancock Square. He thinks it would be all right if I went back to church there while he's away."

His mother looked into space across the water. "Well, I am sure," she said in a distant voice, "that that is a question for you and Tommy to decide."

"I think I would like to," Julia said. "Dr. Alwine is preaching such wonderful sermons about the war."

"Well, I am sure," Mrs. Rand's voice took on life, "that no one could be more patriotic than Dr. Flowers. Dr. Flowers is, perhaps, not as oratorical as Dr. Alwine——"

"Why, Mother Rand. Dr. Alwine is the most sincere person——"

"But in his way, Dr. Flowers is doing as much for the war as any person in this town. Dr. Flowers is, of course, the studious type. I suppose you saw the editorial in *The Messenger* about his sermon on the causes of the war." She turned to Tommy. "*The Messenger* said that if Dr. Flowers had not devoted himself to the service of the church he would have been one of the great thinkers of this age. What's that?" she said with some asperity, as he laughed. "And besides," she said, "Dr. Flowers gives every minute of his time working for the Cause in other ways. He has practically given up his pastoral work to be the chairman of the Governor's Educational Committee on the Causes of the War."

"Hey, Dad!" Tad looked up from the fort, "make me a gun."

" 'Make me a gun,' Tad?" Julia said. "Haven't you forgotten something?" Tad stood up; solemnly, decorously he marched behind a tree where, with heavy puffings, he proceeded to take down his brown linen overalls.

"Good heavens!" Julia murmured, "not here."

"Oh, let him go," he said. He took her hand. The three of them sat on the bench, warmed and drawn together by their noiseless giggles.

That evening, his field boots had come back dark and soft and shiny. All afternoon in the furnace room, Levi Mistletoe and Sam, having composed their differences, had been at work with saddle soap, with cloths and brushes and Meltonian Cream. In his uniform he had driven Julia down through the soft, pink twilight to his grandfather's for supper. Susan had been sent up by his mother to stand watch over the children for the evening. She had stood in the white-trimmed living room underneath the Maxfield Parrish picture, breathing on her spectacles and wiping them. When she put them on, he was obliged to stand up, show himself, walk away, rotate slowly. In the end she came up to him. Her step was feeble but still graceful; her smile was hesitant but warm; she raised her brown eyes to his face. Under the guise of seeing how this fine new uniform fitted him, her delicate, brown hands ran over him as though to take possession of an image of him and carry it away forever.

The headlights made small progress through the twilight. The dusky house-fronts and the lighted windows flowed past and the dusky, shrouded trees along the bank; through the twilight, under an opalescent sky, he was flowing with the lavender-bright river.

"Do you really think it's all right," Julia said, "if I go back to Hancock Square?"

"Oh, yes," he said, "of course. Yes, yes." He took a hand off the wheel and closed on hers strongly. "Julia," he said, "we must love each other."

He felt her pat his hand consolingly. "Why, Tom, dear," she said, "of course we must."

Here were the big, wide, brownstone steps; the two bay windows; and, motionless on its staff among the shadows, a big American flag above the door. He swung the car abruptly in a circle and pulled up at the curb.

In the hallway Samuel pumped his hand and beamed. "Thomas!" He wiped his moist palm on the edge of his alpaca coat and shook hands again. "You are an officer. Yes, indeed," he said, "the only proper thing."

"Samuel," he said, "you're looking fine." He started for the library door.

"One moment, sir," Samuel said, and stepped quickly ahead of him. At the door he paused. "Lieutenant Thomas Rand," he said.

"Good Lord," he thought, "they've asked a crowd for dinner."

But in the library was no one but his grandmother in white muslin, seated as always at her writing desk; her short sleeves showed her still well-rounded arms. She placed a ringed hand, still firm and competent, on the pile of papers as she turned. When she took off the ribboned eye-glasses that she had just begun to wear she looked much less severe.

"You're prompt," she said. "I suppose that's the army." Her hand just lingered in his. "Your father was never prompt."

"I think it's Julia, Grandmother."

"Oh, yes. Julia," she said without looking at her, "good evening." She kept her eyes on him. "I'm just trying to finish up"; she tapped the papers, "you've no idea." Masterfully she gave him facts and figures. It seemed that a development of the war which he had failed to give thought to was a serious overcrowding of the Crittendon Home for Wayward Girls, complicated, she added without quite making it clear, by a disposition on the part of the wayward girls already well established in the home, to disappear.

"And now," she said, "I must finish this letter to the Governor's Committee on Delinquency. Your grandfather is in his office; Julia, those are the new magazines on the table."

Under the shaded amber light his grandfather's thick, close-cut hair and beard looked almost dark above his starched white linen. He sat back in the tufted leather chair, holding a tall glass in his hand. Above in the darkness, the wooden paddles of a fan moved slowly. Without turning his head, he held his hand out shoulder high.

"T," he said. "That's you."

The big hand closed firmly, softly, hung for an instant, then shook the hand it held slowly from side to side. And still his grandfather did not look up. Under his bushy eyebrows he looked out the open window past the street light on the river bank to the last faint band of crimson and the farm lights just beginning to show on the dark, distant shore. He did not speak or turn. Like Susan Tarr, he seemed to want to take this strange, beloved elusive being through his hand alone, as though by that means, and by that means only, there would be something that he could know and hold. And so they remained; his grandfather in his chair, he standing, both looking out at the river and the fading day, held together by the slow rock of their hands.

With the unhurried promptness of an animal that knows when it has drunk its fill, the hand released him.

"Sit down," his grandfather said. "No. Ring for Samuel. A whiskey sour, a mild one, is good in this hot weather."

He made the ice rotate in his glass, then looked up slightly frowning. "Those people," he said, "are not reasonable, not at all. They want it all," he said. "Samuel, a sour for Mr. Thomas. There is nothing to do but to control them, but it will be bad for business. In the end, prosperity cannot come from destruction. But those people are unreasonable," he said, "they must be controlled. The world must either do that or else give in to them. We are right in principle. Only," he said, "there is too much talk. All nonsense, these preachers and orators and women."

"I know, grandfather," he said, "some of it is pretty bad. I know," he said, "a lot of this war stuff makes you tired but under the nonsense you can feel the real spirit of the people; you can feel it in the army. It's been a great experience; I guess the biggest experience in my life."

His grandfather inspected his tall glass and nodded. At the sound of Samuel's footsteps in the corridor, he looked up. "Yes, yes, of course," he said, "here comes your whiskey sour."

A great old gentleman, he thought, as he walked along between the barracks and the plain. He could see him now looking out at the last light on the river, making the ice revolve slowly in his glass. A great old gentleman.

Into his consciousness came faint bellows and on the parade ground the running rustle of rifles coming up from order arms; the band burst out, he brought his heels together and his hand to the brim of his new campaign hat. On the tall mast in front of headquarters, the flag trembled and crept slowly down. Farther along the path, two prisoners in blue denim had set down a G. I. can and faced the flag with folded arms; and everywhere along the path among the barracks, the khaki ants had stopped their endless movement and, turning toward the magnet, stood motionless at the salute. It was a noble world.

The music stopped, his hand came smartly down. On the plain the regiment was moving. Everywhere men were moving again. His arm resumed saluting as he walked along. His thoughts flew back to that last day at home.

After supper, he had sat on the straw mat on the brownstone railing of the front steps. His father and mother and his grandmother were in the big bay window where they could observe what went on. In the night and silence he could hear the faint puff of a belated flatboat in the river, and around the corner of the house a murmur from the office where his grandfather sat talking to his Aunt Clara; a murmur low and quiet with long intervals. Two dark figures paused below the steps.

Then Mrs. Thompson in a tremendously flowered dress was holding his hand and pressing it to her; a vivid and dramatic figure against the background of Mr. Thompson's eye-glasses and bows. "Tommy, my dear boy, why, you look magnificent! We ought to have more light," she said. "How are you?"

"I'm fine," he said. "How's Jeanne?"

"Haven't you heard?" she said. "Jeanne's been sent for."

"Been sent for?"

"She's gone to France. They sent for her by name."

"That's wonderful."

"Isn't it wonderful? There's a doctor in the hospital at Neuilly that Jeanne worked with in Baltimore. She went two weeks ago."

His mother had come out. "Good evening, Jeanne." she said.

Mrs. Thompson looked up. "Ellen, you didn't tell Tommy about Jeanne."

"I know," she said. "We haven't said half the things we want to, have we, son? Won't you come in?"

"Thank you, Ellen," Mr. Thompson said. He looked at the bay window. "Good evening, Mrs. Rand. Good evening, George." His father leaned out the window. "Hello, Thompy. You and Jeanne come in."

Mr. Thompson raised his voice. "I'm on my way down to the mill. There's something wrong with that night shift. Our number three furnace is not holding heat. We lost a run yesterday. Thank you, just the same."

"Thompy is wonderful," Mrs. Thompson said. "Do you know what he's doing? With all his regular work, he's working on a machine to make bandages by electricity. An electric machine," she said. "I know it's going to work."

"But, Thompy," his mother said, from the top step, "what will all of us women do then?"

"Jeanne shouldn't talk like that." Mr. Thompson was disturbed. "Why," he said, "it's only in the blue-print stage. I haven't even made a model. At the same time," he said, "we must recognize that the present way of making bandages is highly inefficient."

"You know," his mother said, when they had left, "I often wonder how they get along together. There is something inhuman about him. It would drive me crazy."

"They say he's a fine metallurgist."

"You know," his mother said, "I don't see why they should be sending girls to France. Jeanne's just a young girl. Anyhow, I should think they would send soldiers."

"Well, I guess our turn will come."

"Oh, no," she said, "oh, no, don't talk that way." She took his hand. "Don't talk that way." They sat together silent. "But it's all nonsense," she said, "sending those young girls."

For a moment the river bank was silent. There was no sound, no motion, except far downstream below them where headlights flashed and twinkled on the state highway bridge.

"Son," she said, "there is something I would like you to do for me. Will you promise?"

His mind took stock of possibilities. He had his Testament and read it on occasion; he always went to hear the chaplain preach on Sundays; he smoked a good many cigarettes now and sometimes he swore, but nothing to compare with what he heard around him; and last Saturday night in the hotel in Mineola he had found himself feeling bold and friendly on the mixture which Porky Montross called "duck soup." But of these matters surely his mother knew nothing. "I don't know," he said, "what is it, Mother?"

"Won't you promise your mother just one thing?"

"Oh, all right," he said. "Shoot."

"Shoot!" Her voice was warm and proud. "What a way! Your own mother!" she cleared her throat, "I have made an appointment for you with Dr. Hartman."

"With Dr. Hartman! Good Lord, what for?"

"Tommy, dear"; her voice turned earnest, "I love you and I think you are the most wonderful son that any mother ever had, but I don't like you using such language. I know they do it in the army, but it's not right. The Bible tells us——"

He pulled himself together; he was able to sound serious. "All right, I won't. What about Dr. Hartman?"

"I think you ought to see him."

"What's the matter with him?"

"Now you are not being serious."

"What's the matter with me then?"

His mother cleared her throat. "I made the appointment for nine o'clock to-morrow. That will be plenty of time before your train leaves. Dr. Hartman can give you a tonic. I know people think he is old-fashioned, but he makes his own medicines and there is nothing like a good tonic to have with you. You never can tell when you are going to get a little run down. I remember that summer after you were born," his mother struggled with herself, "and then that winter after we lost our dear little baby."

"All right, Mother," he said quickly. "All right, I'll go." He made his voice loud. "Nine o'clock to-morrow."

She had him by both hands. Her hands were plump but the skin was dry and thin. "Be sure and always keep it with you."

On the sidewalk there was the sound of a massed formation. Heavily tramping, Mr. Doggie Trimble and Big Sister marched toward the steps. In dove gray, Mrs. Trimble was borne along between them.

"Hello, Ellen," they said loudly. "Well, you've got your kid back. Hello, Tommy." Their two big hands wrung his. Mrs. Trimble smoothed her dove-gray torso. "I suppose we should call you Lieutenant now."

"Come in," his mother said.

"Yes, indeed," Mrs. Trimble said, "I must say good evening to dear Mrs. Rand." She bowed to the bay window. "Good evening, Mrs. Rand. I'm coming in to say good evening to you." Her figure, consciously carried with an air, moved in through the hall. Mr. Trimble and Miss Trimble grinned down on him, their arms akimbo. "So you're an officer," they said, "well, well."

"He got the highest mark at Training Camp," his mother said.

"No, I didn't."

"You got the highest mark in the company."

"No, I didn't, Mother."

"Well, you got the highest mark in something." He was silent. "What was it you got the highest mark in?"

"It was nothing. It was signalling."

"You see," his mother said, "I told you."

They still grinned down at him. "Signalling!" they said. "What do you know about signalling?"

"I don't know a thing."

"Why, Tommy," his mother said.

"And, anyhow," Good Doggie said, "the Signal Corps does all that stuff."

"Hello there, folks!" The thick rich voice from the sidewalk was Mr. Gus Ringler's. "Is this here the new lieutenant?"

"Hello, Mr. Ringler," he said. "Come up." Mr. Ringler shifted his coat to his other arm, and took a blow through his gray mustache.

"Well, there, Lieutenant." His hand was fat and hot. "You look elegant. Well, folks!"

"Mr. Ringler," his mother said, without enthusiasm, "you

must excuse us. We are just going in for some iced coffee and cake."

"Go right ahead," Mr. Ringler said. "I'll be along." He held Tommy's arm till Mrs. Rand had gone in the house. "Just a little matter"; he said. "How are our boys getting along back there? Do you think they'd like some beer?"

"They'd like it all right, Mr. Ringler, but it's not allowed on the reservation."

"Well, ain't there somewhere around? I thought I'd send about six barrels. We been closed down; no more malt, but we got our stock, so the other day I says to mama: 'What the hell,' I says, 'Let's send our boys some real good beer.'"

"That's certainly nice of you, Mr. Ringler."

"Gus, you're all right," Mr. Trimble said.

"Now, I tell you what," Mr. Ringler said. "When you get back, you send me the name of some good, reliable fellow outside the camp grounds, and so I send the beer and you get the notification."

"That's fine, Mr. Ringler; the boys will certainly appreciate it. Come on in the house."

"It's nothing," Mr. Ringler said, as he rocked through the door tugging on his coat. "We can't make beer no more."

As he started to follow Mr. Ringler, he was seized and turned around. Mr. Trimble wrinkled his eyebrows down at him. "Say," he said, "what's the matter with the damned army? I went to the Second Training Camp," he said, "and I stood seventh in the Company in all the tests. And on the hikes, I could walk the damned pants off those college boys. And after a month they sent me home. 'Too old,' they said; 'new regulations.'"

"Gosh, Mr. Trimble, that's certainly tough. There's no sense to it. It's certainly——"

Mr. Trimble loosed his grip on him and marched through the door abruptly. "The damned fools," he said.

"Mr. Trimble," he called in a low voice; "grandfather has some Scotch in the office." Mr. Trimble did not answer, but he deviated sharply from the library and kept on toward the back of the house.

He looked around him as he walked. The regiment had left the plain. Far off among the distant barracks the tramping companies were lost to sight and sound. Here by the officers' quarters there were few enlisted men and it was necessary in the dusk to keep alert for his superiors.

He went up wooden steps and past glass doors and clicking typewriters, and climbed the stairs to the long, dark hall of narrow doors and fire buckets. He passed the door marked "Captain Biron P. Millspaugh," and stopped at the door which bore the cardboard sign, "First Lieutenant Fordyce B. Montross."

In the narrow room the recumbent sandy hair and freckles of Bill McGuire stood out sharply under the shaded drop-light. He lay on Porky's Gold Medal cot, his blouse unbuttoned, and a copy of *The Motion Picture Classic* propped up on his chest.

"Hello, Bill." He sat down on the single chair. "How did it go to-day?"

Bill's eyes stayed on the magazine. "Have you seen this?" he muttered, "some pumpkin, that Theda Bara. Zowie!" he said. "Some pumpkin." Slowly his eyes left the page. "Oh, I forget," he said, "our Benedict. Well, Thomas, how goes it?"

"It was all right, I guess. I got my rifle apart and got it together again, but I couldn't remember the names of all the pieces."

"Good!" Bill said. "It will make you less valuable to the Germans if you're taken prisoner."

"I made the men put all their parts on their shelter-halves but Feibleman lost his firing-pin."

"Charge him with it," Bill said. "You know this Edith Taliaferro is a cute little piece of fluff. Have you seen this copy?"

"Bill," he said, "what did you do to-day?"

"You know what I hate about extended order," Bill said, "is holding the whistle in my mouth. I am developing a self-bailing whistle. Like the lifeboats the Coast Guard uses."

He grinned at Bill. "Yes," he said, "that's pretty tough, making you blow a whistle while all the men have to do is to run forward and flop down under full packs."

"Combat packs." Bill said. "By gosh; it says Elsie Janis is going to open in a new show. Here's her picture," he said. "Boy, what a smile!" He inspected Tommy. "Go wash the cosmoline off your hands and I'll let you look at it."

"I was looking for Porky," he said.

"They sent for him at Brigade Headquarters, all Regimental and Battalion Adjutants. C. O.'s too, I suppose. Yes," he said, "our Porky is rising into higher and higher circles of paper work."

A step came down the hall and entered the next room. Feet shuffled on the planks, a soft high voice began to hum.

> "Catfish, catfish, swimmin' up stream.
> Catfish, catfish, where you been?
> Grab that catfish by the snout
> Pull that catfish inside out.

"Our military man," Bill pounded on the wall. "Hey, Single-tarry!"

"Hey there, brother." The feet came out in the hall.

He was long and dark and slender with the face of a precocious and unnatural child, his eyes were brown, and his close hair fitted him like a tight fur cap. "Gentlemen," he said, "how you all? McGuire, what you got there?"

"This is very interesting," Bill said. "Here's an advertisement that for ten cents in stamps——"

"Never buy any of those plain-cover books," Singletarry said. "If you want the real thing, there's a man in New Orleans. Postcards too."

"For ten cents," Bill said, "they will send you full information as to how to become a railway postal clerk."

"My lord, McGuire," Singletarry said, "give me that book."

Bill handed up the magazines. "You can get Masonic watch charms and ear phones," he said.

"I'll take the charm," Tommy said.

"You know," Bill said, "they say it's great stuff if you get captured. The Masons over there take care of you."

"We're not going over there to get captured," Tommy said.

"Even so," Bill said, "they say it don't hurt any when it comes to promotion. All the high-ranking officers are in it."

"I don't believe that. We've got along without it so far, haven't we?"

"They was a man down home," Singletarry said, "Randall Du-bose. When they come to him to join the Masons he asked what was the advantage. 'Well,' they said, 'if you go to Jackson or New Orleans and get broke or in jail or anything, the other Masons are naturally bound to help you out.' 'Well, gentlemen,' he said 'if a Mason gets broke or in jail here in Charterain, am I bound to help him out?' So they said, 'yes.' 'Well, gentlemen,' old man Randall said, 'I appreciate the honor, but I believe that is more liable to occur.'" He turned over another leaf. "Why, damn my soul! This book is quite an aphrodisiac."

Still looking at the magazine and making a noise like a saxophone between his small petulant lips, he went back to his room.

Bill grinned at him. "Thomas," he said, "how you all?" From under Porky's pillow, he extracted *The Motion Picture Classic*. "Got to always keep one in reserve," he said, "with that bird around, also clothing, cash, everything."

He grinned back and turned serious. "Bill," he said, "how do you really think we are coming on?"

"We're coming on fine," Bill murmured from within the pages of *The Motion Picture Classic*. "What's the matter with us?"

"The men are all right and some of the officers, but sometimes I feel as if we didn't know a thing. There's too much to learn."

"The men can shoot," Bill said, "and they really want to fight. What more do you want?"

"I know," he said, "but I've run a business. It drives me crazy to see how things are going."

Bill looked up. "Shut the door," he said. "Now," he said, "sit down here where you can whisper." He punched a finger at the wall. "I wouldn't trust that Mississippi bird," he said. "What's on your mind?"

"Nothing," he said, "I just wish we were getting on faster."

"We'll be all right," Bill said. "Six months from now we'll probably look like quite an army."

"Some things are getting better," he said. "I thought our regimental dress parade last night was pretty good."

"Sure it was good. Try to remember the first one when we got here."

"How did my platoon look when we passed in review? Could you see them?"

Bill dropped his eyes to the page. "They were all right. There was one man out of step."

"That's Feibleman. I don't know what to do about him. There's no way to get him in step. You watch him; he's got some kind of hock action. If his feet are in step, his knees are out; and if his knees are in, his feet are out."

"Make him a Company clerk."

"He practically can't read."

"Do you know what?" Bill said. "When you come right down to it, Lina Cavalieri's got them all beat." He held the magazine off critically. "They can say what they like, but I bet she'd make a wonderful wife if the right man ever came along." He turned the magazine. "Look at that face!" he said.

"I know, Bill," he said, "she's beautiful all right."

"You bet," Bill said. He studied the magazine. "Who's the most beautiful woman that you ever saw?"

"Come on," Bill said, "let's have it."

"I don't know; I guess my aunt is. How's that for romance?"

"It's all right with me," Bill said; "it's perfectly all right with me." He shook the magazine at him with great solemnity. "I've always had a theory that if she had gone into the Pictures she'd have made mugs out of them all." Serious and satisfied, Bill went back to the pages of the magazine.

Outside, the stars showed through thin, fast-moving clouds; low down the light from the corner of the barracks faded into the night where, on the gravel, the feet of men were always crunching. The feet of men, of twenty thousand men, that moved in groups, or singly, and never ceased—even at night the feet of sentries moved—and, on occasions, the feet all moved together to thunder into rhythm. They were always with him now, these feet of twenty thousand, and he was with them. It was a new world, and a brave and strong one; that was what his Aunt Clara had known the last night on the brownstone steps when all the rest had gone. "How is it?" she had said, sitting a dim, white figure on the step, her knee cocked up between her long, locked hands; "How does it really seem; how does it feel?"

"It's wonderful," he said. "I've never been so— It's great," he said.

"I thought it would be; all those men together," she said; "I would like to see them march."

"You must come for a Divisional Review. I'll wire you."

"I suppose some are homesick and some are scared and some just hate it all."

"A few," he said, "not many."

"For most of them it must be fine to have life simple and direct, and to be with all the others doing something that they know is right. We would nearly all be happy if our lives were like that."

"Yes," he said, "that's the way it is; that's the way I feel."

"I envy you," she said, "whatever happens will be better than not to have had this happiness."

"I know; that's the way I feel."

"Of course you do," she said, "I always knew you would, but I wasn't sure that I would feel that way about you." In the darkness, she turned her eyes on him; her voice was firm and warm. "I would miss you more than I ever have any one except your Uncle Fitz-Greene."

"You know," he said, "a funny thing; since I've been in the army I seem to remember Uncle Fitz more."

"Do you?" she said. "I'm glad; that's because you're happy. Good night, my dear, fine boy," she said. "You must take Julia home."

His thoughts jumped ahead to next day. As the train had left the family group on the station platform, his father, in his dark-gray flannel suit, had swung aboard. "I thought I'd ride up the line as far as Myersburg; I can have a look at the coal yard there."

"But, Father," he said, "that yard's been closed."

"Porter," his father said, "get us two chairs together."

As the Pullman wound among the fields and hills that he had first seen when, as a little boy he was on his way to school at Wyomensing, his father settled down to check up on the duties of an officer. It was necessary, with pencil and paper, and in the face of many interruptions, to explain to him the service rifle, the theory of fire control and of command in combat, company paper work, close-order drill and the construction and use of Mills bombs, hand grenades, trench mortars and Lewis guns; also Browning machine guns, French machine guns and automatic rifles.

"What about German machine guns?" his father said.

"We've not been given anything on that."

"You'd better speak about that to your Commanding Officer." He managed not to smile. His father did not smile.

"When our men capture a German machine gun, they should know how to use it."

"Coming into Myersburg!" the porter said.

His father sat back stiffly on his spine and stared out the window. "There's one thing I thought I'd mention," he said. "Our Shipping Department gets a good deal of confidential information. We're going to move troops over fast from now on."

"Do you think we'll go soon?"

"All troops that are ready will go."

"Brush you off, sir," the porter said. His father did not answer. There was a rattle of dirty backyard fences and of loading platforms past the window.

"Myersburg, Myersburg!" the porter said.

"Father," he said, "here we are; Myersburg."

His father stood up. "Don't get off the train."

"I'll just come out to the vestibule."

In the vestibule, his father turned. The porter, on the ground below them, was wiping off the hand-hold with a rag. "I want you to do your duty as an officer," his father said, "but I want you to use good judgment. Remember that no one can win this war by himself. This war," he said angrily, "is a scientific proposition." Suddenly, instantaneously, his father's firm, grave, child-like face turned deadly white. "I don't want you to do anything foolish." His face was a rigid mask. Painfully he opened his lips. "Do you understand me?" He wheeled and stumbled down the steps.

"Look out there, boss!" the porter said. "Watch you' step!"

"Father!" he called. He started to follow. But as his father passed the people on the platform, they were turning, with grave surprise, to look at him.

He went back in the car and sat down heavily.

"All 'board! . . . 'board!" Steel doors slammed. He kept his eyes on the floor till the last house in Myersburg had clattered past.

Outside the barracks, feet still crunched beneath the stars and the high fast clouds; far off a mess-call raised its cheerful nagging notes. Behind him, feet came down the corridor, short, quick steps.

The door flew open. Porky's face was pink, his neck bulged out above his straining uniform.

"Attention, men!" Bill said without moving. "Our Adjutant."

Tommy stood up and saluted with a smile. "Porky," he said.

Bill rose up slowly and raised a hand to his freckled brow. "Porcellus."

Porky fixed on them his mild, but short-sighted eyes.

"You want us to get out?" Tommy said.

"You heard the question," Bill said. "Speak up like a man, Pork."

"You're among friends, Porky," Tommy said.

"And your rank protects you," Bill said. "Singletarry's got your magazine."

"We've got our orders," Porky said.

"What?"

Porky strained at his breast pocket and pulled out folded, flimsy sheets of copy paper. They seized them and huddled together under the light, straining to read the blurred words against the pale-gray background. ". . . and . . . Company commanders will turn in all Government property to the Post Quartermaster, obtaining receipts therefor except as follows. . . .

"Company commanders will draw supplies as follows for each commissioned officer, non-commissioned officer, and enlisted man present for duty:

ticks, bed	one
caps, overseas	one
helmets, trench	one
disks, identification	two."

"Porky," they said, "what about it? Does it mean anything?"

"This does," Porky said. He thrust another carbon copy toward them. "Special Order Number Three."

"Move over, Bill," Tommy said. "I can't read."

"I'll read it. 'The battalion to fall in with full field equipment at two-fifteen p.m.

'The battalion will then proceed to the railway yards, Track Number Seven, where it will remain in ranks awaiting further orders.' "

"Is that all?"

"More here," Porky said. " 'All men not present for duty transfer out to casuals; all Companies filled to strength by transfer from casuals; medical inspection by Companies to-morrow morning; all grades above seventeen draw thirty-two rounds of service automatic ammunition; inspection of packs; regular inspection; Company officers limited to one hundred pounds baggage.' It's all been sent down to the Companies. I've got to get along; a full night's work."

"You'd better get down to your Company," Porky said. "Hear that?"

Outside in the quickly falling darkness they heard hard running feet and a wild, long-drawn cry. A babble of voices rose and formed itself into a great round ball of cheering; and then all over camp, there was the flat, quick crack of service rifles firing at the sky. M.P.'s whistles sounded, the firing stopped, the ball of cheering rolled up and down between the barracks.

CHAPTER XLV

The damp and cavernous French kitchen seemed to be lighted only by reflections from the copper pans beside the open fireplace and by the minute glow of a thin log of wood whose other end stretched out into the room. Over the fire a deep pot simmered feebly. He set his writing case down on the flags and stood up. With his field boot he gave a cautious thrust to the cold end of the log. Madame Valleton took sharp note of how fast her logs were fed into the fire.

His hobs clicked on the flags as he walked to the stone mullioned window. Through the wet dusk he could see the tall heap of manure, faintly smoking in the raw air, and the branched shafts of the carts protruding from the shed. The great wooden gate in the stone wall was open on the street of cobbles, forever dripping between the close-built iron houses.

Across the opening in the gate, like weary supers in a play, in groups or singly the men in khaki moved. On the wet cobbles their steel-shod, clumsy feet made sharp but mournful sounds. The sounds took on a pattern. A sergeant and a detail with side arms and scarlet M. P. brassards moved across the opening. He looked at his wrist watch through the nickel guard across the face, and went back to the low straight-backed chair beside the fire.

The small board on his knee was covered with blotting paper, the turned-back flaps were filled with flimsy sheets of notepaper and flimsy envelopes lined with purple. He stretched out a stiff hand to the little fire, and when he felt it come to life he drew it back again.

"Somewhere in France." The pencil moved in jerks across the paper. He breathed on his fingers and bent them straight against his knees.

Dear Julia:

We are here in a little sort of village farmhouse and very comfortable. We give our rations to the old French lady and it's wonderful to see what she can make of them. I thought I never wanted to see gold-fish again, but she adds olive oil and herbs to it and cooks it up in little cakes. She makes French toast out of our army bread. Porky calls it the miracle of the loaves and fishes.

He paused to rub out the last sentence.

The men are billeted in the houses around us and they are splendid. Ever since the brigade did that two weeks in a quiet sector, they have been restless. As I wrote you, nothing much happened and they were disappointed. I think we all were, although it is probably just as well to have a chance to get used to things in that way for a starter, but now they want to get back to the Front. After all, that's what we're here for. It's a great experience to be a part of this Division, over twenty thousand men from all over America, and to feel their spirit and comradeship and courage, and to feel, too, that it is in a cause that we can all be proud of and believe in, the people at home, as well as us over here. I wouldn't have missed this for anything. All of us here are the lucky ones. I feel like King Henry IV, in a speech we learned at school,

> "And gentlemen in England now abed
> Shall deem themselves accurst they were not here
> And hold their manhoods cheap whiles any speaks
> That fought with us upon St. Crispins Day."

Does that sound too theatrical? It wouldn't if you were here too, and could feel the spirit of these men.

The tap of sabots came along the passage. The heavy battened door creaked. He looked up from his writing pad. "Hello, Madame," he said, "Ça va?"

Her cap clamped her hair, tight-drawn from her leather face, her dark skirts hooped out below her formless waist. "Oui, ça va." She kept her sharp black eyes fixed on the fire, as she rocked across the room. Her shadow fell across the writing paper. "Mon lieutenant," her silhouette shook its peaked head at him. "Faut pas gâcher le bois."

"That's right, Madame." He grinned at her and nodded. "Je paie un supplement. How's that?"

She took him up quickly. "C'est entendu." In two clumps she was beside the pot. Her voice turned toneless. "Faut pas gâcher. . . . C'est pas bien. . . . On n'a pas l'habitude chez nous." Her bulging skirts cocked up behind as she bent to peer beneath the lid of the marmite. . . . "C'est des mauvaises façons. Pourquoi faire comme ça? Je vous demande."

"But Madame," he said, "je vous dis je paie supplement."

She stood up stiffly and fixed her wrists on her bulging hips. "C'est entendu. C'est de la gâche quand même. Ça gâche votre solde." She made for the door. "Les Americains," she said, "ça gâche tout." The door groaned, her footsteps clicked along the passage. He went back to his letter.

I haven't heard from you lately, but we are expecting to get mail in a day or so. Meanwhile I read the Testament you gave me. And even oftener, I think of you and the children as I last saw you. How did you find out we had got our orders? And how did you get there in time? As long as I live, I will never forget seeing you and Tad and Jane standing there against the ropes as we marched by. And then the dock gates shut and you were gone, and perhaps it was just as well.

I suppose I ought to stop mentioning this is in every letter, but it is always in my thoughts.

Give great hugs to the children for me and tell them I'll be back after while, and we will all have fun and go for a picnic up to the farm. I send you my best love, my dear, and I know that you are good and brave.

Your affectionate husband,

Том.

He folded the letter and licked the sweet edge of the envelope. He moistened the tip of the indelible pencil with his tongue, and wrote the address, wet and purple, and in the upper left-hand corner, "Censored by 2nd Lieut. Thomas Rand, Company D, 192nd Inf." He unbuttoned the flap of a side pocket and slid the letter in. In a little while, two weeks perhaps, this letter, this very envelope, would be in Midian. It would probably come in the morning mail, Julia would read it at the breakfast table, seated behind the percolator between Tad, in front of the fluted silver porridge bowl his grandfather had given him, and Jane in her high-chair, well smeared with cream of wheat. Maybe a winter sun would be coming through the many little panes and falling on the ice floes in the river and on the distant snowy banks.

That was a distant land now, far away and long ago. Sometimes it seemed as though nothing of it remained a part of him except that one brief unbelievable instant when they marched down on the dock. The column stretched ahead among the warehouses, it turned and vanished in a black resounding cavern. He was marching on the flank of his platoon. "Column left," the command came back. The mouth of the cavern was upon them. On each side M. P.'s held long ropes. Behind the ropes a fringe of people watched them. "Good luck, boys." "Over the top." "Go get 'em, Yanks." "Good luck, boys." "Harry! Harry! Harry Meisler! Here's mama. Wave, mama. There he is, there's Harry! Wave!"

He picked her out because of her tallness. She wore the dark-gray tailored suit. Jane in her tiny overcoat was a bright blue bundle in her arms. Beside her, Tad stood square in his reefer jacket; his eyes were sombre, puzzled, and remote; he gave one frightened, short, excited shout, then clutched his flag. Her lips were white and firm. Against her bosom Jane waved her little flag unseeingly. Beside the marching column he passed into darkness and the rumble of the docks.

The darkness of the docks had merged into the darkness of the transport, as in single file, crouching beneath their packs, they climbed the cleated gangplank and stepped over the high sill of the door in the ship's side. There, in rank darkness, voices herded them; his men were taken away from him and cast into blacker, fouler depths, while the attendant voices elevated him to a tiny, inside cabin packed with four narrow bunks.

That night, on the faintly throbbing deck, they watched the mountainous lights of New York City fall away; they crept past distant rows of lights along the beaches and then they drifted to a gently rocking halt, while out of the darkness a little steamer came to rock beside them for an instant and throw a gangplank down. The gangplank scraped away from them. There was a long, sad cry. Under his feet the decks began to tremble; the water rustled far below; blind and alone, they entered the dark ocean.

The morning showed a double column of ships that trudged and wallowed, and two gray razor blades that circled around them, white numbers on their bows and, above the canvas on the bridge, small naval caps and faces that were always watching.

For days then he walked the dirty, crowded deck or at night sat behind the deadeyes in the packed saloon. In the cabin

Bill McGuire lay on his bunk and read the magazines, and the vague, old face of Mercer Vrooman was bent over endless letters that he was writing home. Only Porky Montross was happy. A seasoned traveller, he came down late each afternoon to make rum tea on his Sterno stove and serve it in collapsible cups, together with Huntley and Palmer biscuits. Mercer Vrooman continued to write on, but Bill McGuire would blossom and tell about the night in Midian when he had given Ethel Barrymore a lift down to the theatre.

"She's a wonderful girl," Bill said. "She'd make a wonderful wife for some one; of course, he'd have to be the right man."

"Why, Bill," Porky said, "she's married."

"What do you know about it?" Bill said. "Didn't I drive her all the way from Hickory Avenue down to the Lyceum. There they were at Hickory and Twentieth and the chauffeur working on a flat——"

"Yes, yes," Porky said, "from that point on we know it." He lifted the lid of the kettle and peered in. "Lieutenant Rand," he said, "what was the date of the meeting between Mr. William McGuire and Miss Ethel Barrymore?"

"September twenty-third, 1915."

"Correct. Ask me one."

"When Miss Barrymore," he said, "asked McGuire if he lived here in Midian, what was McGuire's reply?"

"He said 'Yes.' Am I right?" He turned to Bill. "You see?"

"If you fellows make so much noise," Mercer Vrooman said, "I can't write my letter."

The rest of the time Porky spent in an office on the upper deck, where to his great contentment, paper work still went on. Single-tarry had vanished into an endless bridge game in the Major's cabin. Bill lay prone in his upper bunk with all his magazines, and he, himself, tramped the dirty decks or tried to find a place where he could study the "Manual of Interior Guard Duty" and "Lettres de mon Moulin" with glossary.

On the ninth day, two other dingier razor blades came out to meet them. Briefly they broke out British flags and signals and then in low, fast running wallows they clove circles and cast back lumps of smoke that rolled down the gray seas. Inside the magic circles the double column stumbled on, changed course, coughed smoke and hurried. That night all lights were out in passageways and saloons, and on the deck M. P.'s stood every twenty feet to grab the man who struck a match.

At dawn, smooth, long, round hills loomed dead ahead and, in a cleft, a crowd of masts and funnels. They passed the end of a breakwater where a light still burned palely, and a short man in a blue tam o'shanter waved at them, and shouted. Then they were in a narrow gut of shipping below a steep town, all crowded together against the background of the long, smooth, peaceful hills, treeless and neatly striped with bands of greens and browns.

They left the docks, echoing to the whirling truck-wheels and the long, wild cries of negro roustabouts in khaki, and climbed in column a steep and narrow street where sad, old houses leaned above them and sad, old figures stood motionless, and sometimes, in answer to their shouts and laughter, took off hats.

Behind the town they came out on a sodden plain of tents and paper barracks, where the tops of big Pierce Arrow trucks were swaying, wallowing, and where men 'n khaki lined the duckboards, looking at the straggling column as it passed. "What's the matter, boys?" they said. "Pick up those feet." "Pick up them feet, guys!" "Keep moving." "Now she feels it!"

For a time it seemed as though the great adventure was going to stall and disintegrate right there in mud and the chaos of muddled, conflicting orders and endless, aimless waiting. At night down in the town they fought with French civilians, with American sailors and negro roustabouts. They spent enormous sums in bistros and other institutions without achieving happiness or the least popularity, and trudged back out to camp, morosely drunk, to form long queues under the blue light of the hospital tent beside the entrance gate. It was a happy day when they piled into little third-class carriages and rattled off across the rain-soaked fields of France. To those wet fields and to the slow, old figures that moved among them; to the close-built iron towns and the impersonal, straight popular-bordered roads, there was a severe, reserved and mournful beauty which might have moved him deeply, if it had not been for the harassments of his men. They were genial and respectful, but nothing could exceed their ingenuity in getting drunk in what would seem most unfavorable conditions; and nothing could make them take these French trains seriously; they were children with a new toy. Be-

tween the stations they swarmed the running-boards and climbed
up on the roofs. When they detrained next morning in a driving
rain, he had one killed, three injured and seventeen prisoners
under guard in the baggage car. It had been the low point of
the war. Left behind with the detail to wait till trucks came for
their heavy baggage, he had slumped down in the station's
waiting room and listened to the rain on the wet slates. Through
the heavy drip from the eaves that fell across the window, he
could see a file of ducks and a row of houses, dark gray in the
wet; from a narrow door, a girl appeared and strode away, wide-
legged and clumsy in her wooden shoes, her apron wrapped
around her head.

Behind him, the station door flew open; two heavy feet stamped
hard on the floor; a big, red sergeant shook himself like a dog;
he took his tin hat off and swung it; the drops of water flew; he
wrestled with his short overcoat; he had the chevrons of a Master
Engineer Sergeant. With his helmet and his overcoat on his arm,
he saluted; then he spread his coat out on the bench opposite,
sat down and wiped his red and smiling face with a big hand.

"Sergeant Major?"

"Yes, sir."

"Is it always like this here?"

"Can't say, sir. I'm on my way back from the front." The
Sergeant took his hand down and showed big, white teeth and
little copper hairs in his big nostrils. "And am I happy!"

"It's pretty tough up there, eh?"

"No, sir. It's all right; we're building narrow gauge."

"Well, I guess we'll be going up ourselves pretty soon. We
just moved up from Brest for training."

"Yes, sir. Do you know a town down that way called Rennes?
That's where I'm bound. I got a three-day leave."

"You've got some friends there?"

"Yes, sir; I'll say I have. There's a house up town there where
I used to go and when we came to leave, you know what they
did? They gave me a dinner; just the old lady and the girls,
wouldn't let me pay a cent. Of course, afterward I bought
champagne and the madame made a speech about me, a good
speech too; so the last thing I promised was when I got leave
I'd come back and give a party to them. Yes, sir," the Master
Engineer Sergeant said, "by this time to-night I'll be there. I

ain't sent them word; I'll just walk through the door; it'll be a surprise." A shadow crossed his face; "I hope they're all there, all the same ones." He thrust a foot at his musette. "I got twenty pounds of sugar here and two dozen chocolate bars. I didn't know how things would be in the S. O. S."

"You can get plenty," he said coldly. This was not the purpose for which sugar was being rationed back home.

"All the better," the Sergeant said, "they've treated me right; I'm going to treat them right."

Outside, two Mack trucks splashed along the stony street. As he went out the door to meet the trucks, the Sergeant stood up and saluted. "Goodbye, Lieutenant." The red and happy face followed him out of sight.

Here in the stone-flagged room of Madame Valleton, he stretched a foot out to the feeble fire. At the time, he had been coldly angry and contemptuous; these old-time regular noncoms were pretty low. It still was a view of life quite alien to him, but that brief moment with the Master Engineer Sergeant in the station waiting-room was long ago, and now he sometimes wondered whether the Sergeant's attitude were any more absurd than his had been.

The door banged open, steel hobs rapped on the flags. "The curtain rises, Singletarry," Bill McGuire said, "disclosing Mr. Rand in thought. Tom, have you heard the news about our Captain?"

Singletarry spread his legs and projected his meagre posterior into the fireplace. "Transferred," he said, "toe Base Hospital Numbo Nine."

"What's the matter? Is he sick?"

Bill rubbed his hands together in front of the fire and looked at Tommy over his shoulder. "The incurable optimist," he said. "No, this is a transfer to the Dental Corps. Suppose we have a touch of cognac. Where's Madame?"

"I'll call her," he said. "I'm going to put my writing pad away."

In the stone-paved passageway a flicker of light came from the kitchen door. "Madame!" he called, "trois verres cognac, s'il vous plait."

"Mais pourquoi pas quatre?" The voice was Porky's. "Ah, there, mon vieux! I take it you've heard the news."

"You bet."

Porky's pink face shone in the light from the kitchen door. He peered up earnestly. "A great piece of work, the damned old f——"

"Whoa," he said. "Singletarry's in there."

"No doubt. He's everywhere, he's around headquarters all the time since he made that trip to Nancy with the Major."

"How did he get to be a first lieutenant, you suppose?"

"That is a delicate question."

"Millspaugh was down on him, though."

"Millspaugh recommended him. I saw the papers when they came through."

"Pardon, messieurs." Madame's fragile grandniece thrust them firmly aside and went down the passageway with a bottle and glasses on a tray.

Seated beside the fireplace, Singletarry waved his glass at Tommy. "Brother," he said, "shove that log in some. Looks like we never could get warm here."

"I shoved it in a while ago, and Madame accused me of wasting wood."

"That ole sister," Singletarry said. "Why, these folks don't want to keep us warm enough to save their country."

Bill McGuire shoved his foot into the fireplace. "We haven't saved much of it yet."

"Well, sir, we ain't found much of it worth the saving."

"That is a larger question," Porky said. "The question is, does the mess pay for the wood?"

"I told her yes," Tommy said.

"I guess that satisfied her," Bill said.

Porky screwed up his eye. "My guess is that it didn't."

"That's right," Tommy said.

"You see?" Porky said. "With them, it's a principle. A penny saved is two pennies earned. Well, here's to Captain Millspaugh."

"To hell with that, Pork," Bill said. "You didn't have to serve under him."

"Why, gentlemen," Singletarry said, "the captain always treated me mighty nice. What is the matter with the captain?"

"He balled up all his paper work," Bill said, "he looked like a suet dumpling, and he always blew in a crisis."

"He treated you mighty nice, indeed, Singletarry," Porky said. "How did you get him to recommend you for promotion?"

"Well, brother," Singletarry said, "you see, I'd had my training at the A. and M. That gives a man a big advantage; not that you gentlemen aren't good officers too."

"When does the captain leave?" Bill asked.

"He's gone," Porky said. "There was a camion went down to-night. Singletarry, how did you get to be a first lieutenant?"

"Come on, Singletarry," Bill said, "Millspaugh's gone."

Singletarry reached forward and filled the small thick glass. "Gentlemen," he said, "I was conscious of being at a disadvantage being among Yankees, where ideas are different and my family is not known, so naturally I reckon I just paid particular attention to duty." He emptied the glass. "Probably, if any one of you all had been down in Mississippi, you would have done the same way."

"This cognac," Porky said, "is hideous. How about another drink all around?"

"I don't think this cognac is so bad," Bill said. "It's the quantity, not the quality that bothers me. You can't drink enough to get a feeler before you have had enough to make you sick."

Tommy Rand felt the hot raw trickle down the front of his spine. His boldness rose. "Singletarry," he said, "how did you get to be promoted?"

"Quite so," Porky said. "That is our topic for the evening."

"Gentlemen," Singletarry said, "I know you all mean well, but where I come from that kind of talk would be liable to be resented."

"In fact," Bill said, "Singletarry doesn't know but what he does resent it. He's just trying to make up his mind. Let's make this drink the last."

The door creaked open. Zéline, Madame's grandniece, stood in the door. "Servi, messieurs," she called in a loud impersonal voice.

CHAPTER XLVI

In the kitchen Madame held a small oil lamp beside him, while he studied the long columns of accounts, pale purple items in Madame's old-fashioned hand.

"Seems to be all right," he said. He pulled out his wallet from his hip pocket. "C'est correct."

"Oui, c'est correct," she said. "Merci, monsieur"; her hand closed on the paper notes. "Mais je n'ai pas de petite monnaie. Faut attendre une petite minute."

"Never mind," he said. "No time. Pas de temps. Keep the change. Donnez à Zéline." He shot his arm out and looked at his wrist watch. "Partons toute suite."

The curtained feather bed loomed large in the tiny bedroom above the kitchen. The little oil lamp on the mantel illuminated the faded photograph of the late M. Valleton in a dragoon pea jacket and ponderous mustache, his firm hand on the shoulder of his bride, starched and corseted and crowned with flowers. Flowers also adorned the bowl and pitcher on the washstand's marble top, and faded flowers hung over the colored lithograph of the Virgin by the bed. At the foot of the bed, his bedding roll was piled up on his trunk, his equipment hung from wooden pegs beside the door. He unbuttoned his shoulder strap and, sliding out of his Sam Browne belt, rolled it up neatly and put it in the top of his duffle bag that leaned against his bedding roll. He buckled on his web belt, heavy with ammunition and the forty-four, and tied the holster to his leg with the rawhide thongs. He hooked his water bottle to the eyelets in his belt, then he slung on his map case and his packed musette and buttoned up his shoulder straps again. He had forgotten his helmet. He had to unbutton his left shoulder strap and sling his helmet back over his shoulder by the chin strap.

That was all then. He had been ready since two o'clock this afternoon.

There were stumbling footsteps on the stone stair, and a knock on the door.

"All right. Come in."

The man saluted, crab-like. In his shapeless overseas cap and leather jerkin he looked like a mediæval serf. "Escort wagon, sir," he said.

"All right," he said, "there it is." He pointed to the duffle bag. "Have you seen any men from Headquarters Company for heavy baggage?"

The man had the bag on his shoulder. "Yes, sir. They're working right behind me."

"I'm going down," he said, "I'll give you a light."

The man went down the stairs ahead of him. "Yes, sir," he said. "Much obliged, Lieutenant."

He still stood on the top step with the lamp in his hand. Through the open door he could see the narrow freezing room, so neat, so dainty, so eternally cold. If it weren't for that brick on the hearth in front of the sealed-up grate, that brick that Madame heated and put into his bed at night, he believed he'd find more comfort at the Front.

In the narrow passageway Madame was waiting. "Au revoir, monsieur. Vous êtes bien aimable. Vos camarades aussi."

Zéline came clacking to the door. It was incredible that the child could manage those big sabots. "Au revoir, mon lieutenant," she said. "Je vous remercie beaucoup."

He took her thin cold calloused hand. "Oh, that's all right," he said. "Avec nos compliments." He patted her shoulder. "Good-bye, Zéline." The bone felt sharp against his palm.

Madame took his hand between her two hard paws. "Bonne chance," she said.

"Good luck," he said. "We hate to leave. Nous—au revoir," he said. "Merci beaucoup."

As he walked down the courtyard they stood in the passage looking after him. He waved. "Good-bye!"

They stood immobile. "Bonne chance!" they called together, the high voice and the cracked one. They turned then, promptly, and went back to their work.

All over town the sergeants' whistles sounded. As he came out the gate the men were falling in in front of him. The ranks of other Companies wound out of sight far down the dim-lit street.

The sergeants' voices echoed up and down the street. "Attention. . . . Right dress. . . . Right dress. . . . Front. . . . Count off. . . . Count off. . . ."

In front of him Sergeant Miller called the roll. "Corporals Anson; Brightmire; Simpson; Zinder. Privates Ables; Anstruther; Arnhiem; Asbury; Burman; Bishop; Black, E.; Black, J.; Blakely; Bowerman; Bowsley. . . ." Against the din of many other voices, the voices of his men stood out. One by one their rifle butts came down in quick succession and rang on the wet cobblestones. Sergeant Miller thrust his little book, which he had never looked at, in his pocket. He about faced and saluted. "Third Platooon present or accounted for." He himself faced about. Where was their new captain, Singletarry? Another minute and that Mississippi cavalier would be in trouble. Precisely at that instant, Singletarry sidled out the estaminet beside the farmhouse wall. Unhurried he took his post at the centre of the Company. "Repo't," he said.

On the right, Lieutenant Mercer Vrooman's voice was high and nervous, then Bill McGuire sang out strong. Quickly he brought his hand to the salute. "Third Platoon present or accounted for." Major Offburg's puffy distant shout was heard, "Report." Captain Singletarry was able to about face and await his turn. "D Company," he sang out smartly, "present o' accounted fo'."

Then the commands were coming down the line. "Squads right." "Squads right." "Squads right." "Squads right. . . ." "March." "March." Rifles came up and the tramping started.

He fell in step and swung along. Madame's old farmhouse, where he had lived, fell behind him, the dim-lit town where silent figures watched the column would soon fall behind him, would soon fall far behind to join his home in Midian, his early life, his office, to join the house fronts and the running river, all now far behind him as he marched beside three thousand men into the unknown.

. . . .

The dugout still held the smell of Frenchmen and their incredible tobacco, by which the single candle on the box between his bunk and Bill McGuire's seemed oppressed. It burned low in the raw thick air and cast light only on lines of moisture on

the walls and on Bill McGuire's ruffled sandy hair. Bill lay like
a stone crusader on his bunk, his eyes on the sheet-iron ceiling.
"You know," he said, "I'd say this was a quiet sector if it hadn't
been for that stuff we passed coming in here."

"That's a fact, Bill."

He looked up slowly from the thin page of the Testament.
The words hung in his mind. 'Whatsoever things are of good
report, whatsoever things are true—' "Yes," he said slowly,
"those guns are hub to hub back there."

"You're damn right they are," Bill said. "We ought to have
some help to-morrow." Without moving he rolled his eyes at
Tommy. "Oh," he said, "excuse me. Didn't notice what you
were doing."

He shut the Testament. "That's all right, Bill," he said. "I
guess I know it pretty nearly by heart anyway."

"Yes," Bill said, "I guess you do. A darned good thing to
know."

"Yes," he said, "it's a good thing."

"They tried it on me when I was a kid," Bill said, "but it
didn't take. Maybe some day I'll wish it had."

"It didn't take with me either, not the way I was taught. But
even so it's a help."

"It is, I guess. But what gets my goat are some of those God-
hoppers back in Midian, and over here too; especially here."

"Well," he said, "there're all kinds."

"Look at that little horse's neck that ran the Y back there in
Sommerance. He was too damned lazy to keep the canteen open
when the men could get off duty; and when I spoke to him
about it, he tried to square himself by offering me first crack at
the new supplies. The slimy little bastard."

"I know, Bill. He was pretty bad. They've got to take anybody
they can get, I guess."

"Well, what about the chaplains? They're regular preachers.
They come over here with Sam Browne belts and bedding rolls
and eat at the Regimental mess, and then on Sunday they preach
clean living to the boys."

"A lot of them are pretty old," he said, "they couldn't stand it."

"Well, what would happen then? If they couldn't stand it
they'd die. Is that so out of the way in war?" He raised himself

on an elbow. "Look at those priests in that French Division in
the Vosges. Stretcher bearers and enlisted men. They made our
Sam Browne bishops look like monkeys."

"They're all kinds of people in the Church. Always have been,
I suppose. Don't seem to be any way to beat it."

"And they're all kinds of people in the army, but an army can
only stand so many duds. Oh hell!" he said. "This is no time to
start an argument. Not with you, Thomas." He glanced down
at his foot. "Look here," he said angrily, "just let me look at that
Book, will you?"

"Sure. Help yourself. I think I'll take a turn along my trench."

He pushed aside the gas curtain, the night air struck him cold
and clean. His hobnails sounded on the wet log steps, then on
the duck boards between the two black solid walls of earth. At
intervals a silhouette stood on the fire-step, the butt of the rifle
face-high in its wooden rest, and peered into nothingness ahead.
Far off on each horizon there was a flicker like heat lightning
and faint erratic thunder. On the trench's other wall, the blackness of the earth was punctured by openings blacker still. From
one of these a gleam came out. He rapped on the lintel above
the door. "Who's in charge here?"

There was a pause. "Corporal Zinder."

"Put out that candle and come out here."

The light went out. A gray face crept up from the narrow
door. "What are your orders about showing lights?"

"Why, Lieutenant, we ain't supposed to show no lights."

"You know what showing a light at the Front means in this
man's army?"

There was a pause. "Lieutenant, I didn't——"

"You're one of my best men, always have been. To-morrow I
want to see that squad of yours do something. That's all."

He came to the last of his sentries, a little man whose short-
ened coat stuck out behind him like a bustle as he leaned forward
against the parapet.

"Is that you, Ables?"

"Yes, sir."

"Seen anything out there?"

"No, sir. Not a God—no, sir."

"Let's have a look." He mounted the fire-step. With his cheek
against the cold butt of the rifle, he peered between the sandbags.

Against the flickering horizon there was nothing but low black foreground and above it, near at hand, a tangle of enormous wire.

He stepped back. "All right," he said. "What're your orders?"

"Our working parties are coming through at nine o'clock to cut our wire."

"That's right. You can catch their helmets against the sky. If the Boche were coming, they'd be creeping. Good night," he said.

"Good night, Lieutenant."

Back in the dugout, quietly he hung his helmet, his equipment, his overcoat and blouse on pegs above the chicken-wire bunk. There were boards nailed below the pegs to keep things from the wet wall. He sat down on the bunk: to-night he'd better not take off his trench boots. He looked for something to scrape them with before he rolled into the blankets. He didn't want to disturb Bill, who still read the Book. Finally he scraped them gently on the leg of the bunk. A sharp sardonic laugh astonished him.

"By God!" Bill said, his eyes still on the Book, "He certainly made monkeys of those Pharisees." He read on with a fixed, delighted grin. He closed the Testament. "Yes, sir, I'd give a lot to see Him with our Regimental chaplain."

.   .   .   .

He stumbled over the tangled legs and rifle butts. Above him the barrage rumbled and the whole sky glowed and flickered. "Gangway," low voices said, "here's the lieutenant." With Bill McGuire behind him he reached the P.C. on the right of his platoon and went down through the curtain.

Captain Singletarry sat on his bunk and pulled a trench boot on by the candlelight. He paused to sip at a cup of coffee on the candle box.

"Gentlemen," he said, "where's Vrooman? Check up on your watches. I've got fo'-fo'ty-eight. Well, Vrooman, you decided to join us after all? Check up your watch. I've got fo'-fifty."

Lieutenant Mercer Vrooman pursed his lips nervously.

"Captain, I seem to be four men short, Withers and Jones and——"

"You seem to be?"

"Well, I'm afraid I am."

"Christ, Lieutenant, what difference does that make to an old militia officeh? Unless you goin' to miss them socially?"

"But what ought I to do?"

"Do? Why, Lieutenant, you don't need to do a thing. They'll do it all fo' you in Blois. You'll probably make a right good janitor in some nigro regiment's canteen. Sergeant Major?"

"Yes, sir." The gas curtain swung aside. The Sergeant Major was tall and dark and sad. He had been a freight conductor on the B. and O.

"You take the fo'th platoon," Singletarry said, buttoning up his blouse. "Squads in columns of files at six pace intervals. Keep you' automatic rifles on the flanks."

"Now listen, you all," he stood up and slung on his harness, "you've got you' rifles, but don't go to using them. They just to keep the Germans from spotting you. Keep you' eye on the men, and if any man turns back, let him have it."

They stood there while he strapped his helmet down. "Well?" he said, "well? Ain't that enough? Do you want me to hold you' hands and pray with you?"

Out in the crowded trench, they stumbled along. The sky was fiercely flickering, a thousand trains roared on their unseen trestles overhead. They crouched, still safe, inside the roaring dome.

"Vrooman!" he shouted. He pulled at the trench coat half a step in front of him. The trench coat stopped. He took Vrooman's arm. He put his face close to the bowed trench helmet. "Never mind, Vrooman. He didn't mean it." Vrooman's long pale face, obtuse and middle-aged, remained bent on the ground. "He was just nervous, Vrooman." He shook Vrooman's arm. "To hell with it."

Vrooman nodded slowly.

He was pushed from behind. "Go on there. What the hell!" Bill McGuire shouted. The three moved on.

On his platoon's left flank, he stopped. Vrooman, head still bent, went on and disappeared around an angle.

Bill put his face down close to his. "Vrooman feel bad?" His voice came low and harsh above the rumble. "That's tough," he said, "but what can you do for a bird like that? In ten minutes he could have reported them missing in action."

"Cigarette?" Bill said. "We can smoke now." He looked at Tommy above the match. "Well, fellow, how do you feel?"

The cigarette smoke seemed to flow through him, light, sharp and strong. "I must be crazy," he said, "but I never felt as good in all my life."

The tip of Bill's cigarette glowed on his wide firm mouth, his eyes were shaded by his helmet. "Good boy," he said. He thrust out a hand. "Good luck." Still holding Tommy's hand, he looked away. He let go quickly. His big loose, back crossed with the straps of holster and of map case, swayed with gangling strides down the dark trench, vanished.

He walked along his platoon, crowded against the fire-step and parapet, showing his cigarette to them. Some grinned and reached for packets in breast pockets, some fixed their eyes on him with inscrutable distant longing, a look of lost and homeless things; some men never moved. A young boy made as if to take his arm. From the shadow of his helmet his eyes peered out with frenzy. "Lieutenant, what're we going to do to 'm, heh? What're we going to do to 'm?"

"Take it easy, son," he said. "We're going through 'em all right, Pelley."

The kid's high voice ran on behind him. "You hear that, fellows? Hear what he says? We're going through 'm by the living, —ing, —ing Jesus."

At the end of his platoon, the sergeant met him, square and pig-headed in the flickering light.

"Sergeant, everything set?"

The sergeant's short jaw tipped up at him. "Yes, sir."

"You'll take this flank, and I'll take the right. We'll go ahead of them and make them spread out when they've passed the wire. Then I'll come back to the centre if you want me. How're the men?"

"They're all right," the sergeant said reluctantly. "They were wanting a real fight, now they'll get it.'

He looked at his wrist watch. "Call in the squad leaders and the first aid." In the violent darkness helmets turned as the message passed along the trench.

When the group of harnessed bundles stood in front of him, he raised his voice and shouted.

"Our first objective is the crest straight ahead, not where the

German trenches are, but the big one back of it. You can see it against the sky. We're due there at seven:ten. Our barrage will go right in ahead of us." He cleared his throat. "When we get there, we'll see a little town down in the valley; you can't miss it; that's our second objective. We're due to take it at ten: thirty-five.

"Now get this," he shouted; "we go right through the German front-line trenches, don't stop. The second wave will clean them up. The main thing is," he shook his fist gently, "to keep touch with our flank platoons, don't leave a gap. Each squad will advance in columns of files at six-yard intervals. As soon as you get through our wire, you must extend. Don't let the men bunch up in front of the opening. Any questions?"

"What about the First Aid Station, Lieutenant?"

"You ought to know that, Corporal, you passed it coming in. It's at the end of our communication trench but no man can go back there until he's been tagged by Martin here." He pointed to the dim white brassard with the Red Cross on it. "If he does, they'll try him. Anything else?" The bundles stood silent in the flickering light and stared at him from the shadows of their helmets. "Good luck, then," he said, "let's get them. Take your posts."

"Good luck, Lieutenant." The sergeant's voice was abrupt, impersonal.

He hurried back along the trench. "All right, boys," he kept on saying, "let's get set. All right, boys, let's get set. Get set." He felt them rising up behind him.

All the great trains that had rumbled overhead, abruptly stopped. There was a moment's intense, incredible silence. He heard a bayonet scabbard tap against a coat.

"Corporal Zinder!"

"Yes, sir."

"Right in behind me." His voice sounded tremendous, the-atrical, silly. "Gangway ahead there," he said in a lower tone. The men edged off the fire-step in front of him. Then the dome of sound clapped down on them. The field in front of them burst into heaving flame; all down the trench, the whistles sounded. He put his hands up on the ladder and jumped up on the naked, shaking earth.

CHAPTER XLVII

Across the gray churned earth they trudged, the little groups in single file, weighed down with their equipment, bent forward and crouching down a little in the cave that had been hollowed out for them in the great bursting world of death. Ahead of them a spouting field of fire trudged as well. In its wake they passed the relics of the German wire. Lumberingly they climbed across the chaos of the German trenches. Some men looked back at him with longing, but he waved them on. It was hard to leave behind those furrows in the jellied earth. Then too, there might be white and shaken Germans still lurking in their pits below the ground; but they were the affair of others who would come behind them. He waved them on.

They were walking on level earth again, behind the churning fire. Here, in this cave, this steadily advancing cave which authority had established for them, they were safe. Daylight had come; the sky, the earth were wet and gray. As far as he could see, to right and left, the little groups were trudging. All was designed, precise and orderly; all was progressing according to the plan. He trudged along, alert and stiffened by a sort of solemn firm elation, swinging his face from right to left to watch the little squads that wound along among the wet gray clods and furrows.

Under his eyes, a man made a slow stumble. He watched to see him right himself. The man went slowly down, he sagged on all fours like a beaten horse, then started sinking.

He looked ahead. His skin moved with fear and horror and rage. He started running. They were loathsome, those beetle-headed lice that rose up in the back-wash of the bursting shells and pointed rifles below white staring faces. His mouth filled with foul water, his trench boots struggled desperately across the mire. The beetles climbed up from their lair to meet him.

There was a scattering of his men beside him; grotesquely they and the staring beetles danced around each other with shouts

423

and gestures. A rifle went off by his ear, a beetle caved down backwards. With naked teeth above the scrub a little German thrust at him. He knocked the gun aside and thrust back wildly. Around him khaki men were swarming now. One jumped behind the German; the bare teeth flew wide open; his eyes came out, his endless groan was buried in the mud. They stepped across gray bodies and went on, their faces set, wild and incredulous, looking for other men to kill.

And now the ground rose up, and they were trudging harder. He kept his eye for Germans. He'd get his own next time. He wanted to seize the toiling squads and push them forward. Instead, on the right, they were falling behind. Those damned men with the automatic rifle! He blew his whistle and waved at them. They trudged on stolidly. He started running toward them, clumping and slipping over the harrowed ground.

"Here! What's the matter here? Corporal Zinder!"

Corporal Zinder screwed up his bony face. "Them ammunition bearers can't keep up."

"You've got to keep alignment. Take one musette," he said, "and get up with that gun. Here, give me one." Without a word the tall, sallow man in the rear unslung one of his big canvas bags and held it for him to put his head through the web strap.

"Now, come on."

The ammunition bag beat on his hip as he jogged unevenly across the clinging ground. The strap cut on his shoulder, his feet were slipping. Behind him they scuffled heavily.

"Now, you're up," he said. "Keep going. Here, take this." He tried to keep from panting. "That's your objective on the crest." He was jogging back to the centre of the platoon. The sweat was in his eyes, his heart was pounding. He wasn't looking for Germans any more. A man couldn't fight the whole war by himself. That Zinder wasn't worth a whoop in hell, and never had been. Ahead, the plunging fire vanished over the crest and seemed to die away, leaving it gray and still against the pale gray of the sky.

From somewhere far ahead there was an invisible slow tapping. On his right a squad keeled slowly over. The tapping came toward him like a blind man with a cane. He was in a shallow shell hole and spurts of earth were falling on his back. The tapping, unhurried, inexorable, moved on. He pulled his helmet over his eyes and raised a cautious head. Among the furrows and the shell holes, flat brown patches hugged the ground. The tapping stopped. Against the background of distant thunder there was a pall of silence and of solitude.

He searched the crest. Nothing but level gray and a few sparse withered bushes slightly trembling in the wind. He dropped down into the wet cone and took his glasses from their leather case. Two hundred yards, perhaps, to the crest. Turning the milled screw, he tried to guess at the adjustment. The first thing to do was to find that Maxim gun.

Ever so slowly he raised his head again. All was still deserted and still silent except for a faint, choked crying from on his right. He raised his glasses and pressed them to his eyes.

At first there was only a milky gray. He turned the screw. The bushes on the crest jumped into vision, withered and shredded, their pale leaves close to him now, and slightly trembling in the wind. As he watched them, the tapping started, that slow searching tapping. He curled back in the hole, but no bullets kicked up little clods of mud; the tapping this time was not meant for him. With the glasses to his eyes he raised his head. Inside the double ring of milky blue, the bushes wavered in the wind. He ran his glass along them slowly. On the left, the dead leaves trembled violently; and as he watched, one fell and flew along the ground. "Bowerman!" he shouted.

From another shell hole a faint subterranean voice answered him.

"Can you hear me?"

"Yes, sir." Bowerman's voice was disconsolate and far away.

"Tell Corporal Zinder on the right flank that that machine gun is in the bushes on the crest at the left. Tell him to keep them down with his automatic rifle. I'm going ahead with the bombers as soon as I hear him open. Have you got that?"

"Yes, sir."

"Well, repeat it, man. Repeat it."

The subterranean voice chanted the message in a monotone.

"All right. Get going!"

He saw the top of Bowerman's neat compact figure leap up and vanish toward the rear. It was his turn now. He put the glasses back into the case and snapped the catch. He grasped the

unaccustomed and detested rifle at the balance and drew his
feet up under him. With a heave he jumped out of the hole and
ran hard, eyeing the churned ground for an opening. As he
slammed himself down in the muddy hollow cone, he heard the
tapping up ahead. He watched the flecks of mud fly over him.
Snug, but impatient, he lay in the greasy earth. Another rush
would bring him to those bombers.

The tapping stopped. And then, ahead of him, he heard the
muffled grunt of a rifle grenade and a clanging explosion on the
crest. The bomber was at work then. He was up and running.
On the crest a cloud of brown smoke curled and eddied, and
little fragments still fell back to earth. But that was too far to
the right. He saw three khaki backs and flung himself among
them.

The hole was deep and the bomber squatted in the bottom,
the butt of his rifle in the earth, its funnelled muzzle pointing
to the sky; the ammunition bearers hugged the side against the
Germans. He slid to the bottom. "That's the stuff, Wendig; but
you're too far to the right."

The blue-jawed bomber didn't answer. Squatting beside his
elevated rifle, he seemed to listen like a man in a trance, except
for his eyes, which were full of hate.

"Load her up, Wendig," he said to the bomber as though to
arouse him. "I'll give you the line." Mechanically the bomber
shot his rifle bolt back with a muddy hand, and lowered the
funnelled muzzle toward the ammunition bearers.

"For Christ's sake, Wendig," their voices were harsh and
furious, "keep that thing away from us."

He crawled up to the edge of the hole. Without his glasses
the bushes seemed far away. With his finger, he made a quick
mark in the mud, and slid back hastily. "There's your line of
fire. About a hundred and eighty yards."

Still without hearing him apparently, Wendig raised the
muzzle of his rifle, now heavy with the fat, protruding bomb.
The ammunition bearers and Tommy squatted in the mud like
apes, their eyes fixed on the swollen muzzle. The rifle coughed,
the bomb vanished as a small gray wraith that flickered away.

He jumped to the top of the hole in time to see a jet of fire
and smoke in front of the nearest bushes.

"Load her up. You're on the line, twenty yards short. Come

on, keep crowding it." His voice was high, almost singing. To complete his joy, he heard the automatic rifle from Zinder on the right.

He lay there, confident and eager, his eyes above the shell-hole's rim. The gray bombs travelled overhead and burst among the bushes. And drawn by their devastation, the khaki figures of his men leap-frogged from hole to hole, frantically hurried and ludicrous, but drawing nearer to the crest. They were leaving him behind. "Keep it up, Wendig," he shouted, "until you see us rush the gun."

He was on his way over the bare earth, toward the bursting bombs and the bushes, cut and flying from Zinder's automatic rifle.

Just then to the right and left slow tapping started. His khaki men spun, plunged, turned round. They vanished as he flattened in another hole. He lay there listening to the sobs and the frantic angry voices. "First aid . . . first aid!"

And there he lay while a sickish, feeble sun crawled up the sky, while the sobbing died away except for a distant childish voice that endlessly reiterated in a tight, high puzzled tone. "Oh, Billy, shoot me! Oh, Billy, shoot me! Oh, Billy, shoot me!" That was Pelley, the Chippewa kid. His hackles stirred. If they could take that gun!

Ahead, he heard the bursting of grenades to right and left, and raised his head. He made a quick jump forward. The gun in the bushes opened on him, but he was down in time. Behind him the high voice trailed away. "Oh, Billy, shoot me." He heard the grunt of Wendig's rifle. A bomb burst on the crest.

In the end, it was a crazy rush by six of them. Among a heap of empty shells and tumbled helmets, the smoking Maxim pointed to the sky, and waist-deep in the earth, one German with a bloody face raised two blunt black hands to the sky, then went down silent, clutching at the bayonets.

Crouching and squatting on the top, they looked down a gentle slope of sparse gray grass, to a gray-walled village, half a mile away, where a house burned brightly underneath a curling pall of smoke. Except for that, in all that gray flat landscape there was no life or sound. Behind him other men came up. "Jesus!" they said, "look what we done to that gun."

"Look what who done?"

"Who took the gun?"

"The Third Squad and the Louie."

"Was he there?"

"Yeah, he was there."

He turned. "Here, what goes on? You corporals take the men ahead thirty yards down the slope and then dig in at three-yard intervals."

"Hold on," he said. "Can anybody work this gun?"

"Sure," they all said. "Yeah, we can work it."

The squat figure of Sergeant Miller came clumping up the slope.

"Sergeant," he called out, "who's a good mechanic here?"

The sergeant ran a cold eye over them.

"Mackintosh was a mechanic in that garage on Fourth Street."

"Give him two men and see if he can work this gun. The men are to dig in thirty yards down the hill at three-yard intervals."

"Yes, sir," the sergeant said. "Now then, what the Jesus is biting you birds? You heard the order. Get going. You, Mackintosh, and Jones, and Septak, reverse that gun and elevate it before you fire," the sergeant said. "Then you don't hurt nobody. See?"

The three men moved slowly toward the tumble of dreary German tunics around the gun.

"Well, shake it up," the sergeant said. Septak's bandy legs moved faster. "Come, guys," he said, "we got to move dead mans." He bent down. "So."

"Well, Sergeant," he dropped on one knee and reached behind for his binoculars, "we've done pretty well so far."

"Yes, sir. So far."

"How are the men on your flank?"

"After the second machine gun opened, they wouldn't come out of the ground."

"If Mackintosh can work that gun," he said, "they'll have to dig a new emplacement. The Germans'll have this spotted."

"That's right," the sergeant said, "but I don't tell Mackintosh that till he's got it working."

He grinned. "O.K., Sergeant."

He raised his glasses. After the first blur, the village roofs of straw and tile and the blazing house shot into view. He searched the street. As he watched, a clumsy, iron-hooded figure showed darkly as it crept along a wall. As he stared, a rifle cracked almost beneath his feet, and a spurt of dust flew from the wall beside the German's head. The clumsy figure seemed to dive, feet first, into the earth.

His glasses came down. "Who was that, Sergeant?"

"That was Gregory. Did he get him?"

"Just missed him. Go down the line and tell the men to keep their eyes on that town and see that we're joined up with the flank platoons."

He stood up stiffly and walked back over the crest. The long flat slope up which they had trudged and crawled was now quite populous with other trudgers, two skirmish lines in extended order, and back of them small knots who tramped ahead with stretchers, with sacks and picks and shovels and coils of wire.

He jumped at the sound of the Maxim gun behind him. Above the emplacement rose Septak's dog-like grin. "God damn, Lieutenant, we got 'em work!"

"All right," he said impatiently. "All right. Mackintosh!"

Mackintosh's long sad nose came round to him.

"Get that gun out of there. Take it up to the far end of the bushes and dig an emplacement just like this one."

"My God, Lieutenant, we ain't got no tools!"

"Use your bayonets and mess kits. I'll get tools if I can."

Septak's smile vanished. He formed the last of the dreary group that staggered under gun and tripod and ammunition boxes up the brushy hill.

There was a brief, high whistle, an instantaneous bang; a muddy fountain shot up on his left; and in the smoky silence, little clods pattered down. Flat on the ground, he watched the line of men down the hill. They had been sitting up to chat and throwing a perfunctory mess-kit cover of earth ahead of them from time to time. Now their shoulders were down and working. The earth was coming up in short wide jets. Another whistle, a quick plunging explosion. Down the slope ahead of him, the mess kits and the bayonets flew faster.

Immediately there was a long approaching train of cars. In a blinding whirl of earth and noise and smoke and flashes, he was jumping for the machine-gun emplacement. He crouched against the back and tried to dig a hole out with his hands while the shell-fire plowed the German corpses overhead. Then he had his mess kit out. With its cover, he carved away at the cheesy earth. Clumsily he stabbed earth loose with the handle. In the end he was underground, half buried alive in the shaking earth. There was nothing to do but stay there while it shook to pieces. Inside that hole he cowered, no better than the meanest grub or worm, no more heroic, no less ignorant of what was going on in the world above. He'd heard tales of how immaculate British officers walked about under fire encouraging their men. It must have been some other war.

Like a gigantic team and wagon the shaking rolled away. He crawled out blinking and stood up. There was a moment of vast calm, of deep relief. He started a long, slow breath, which instantly was cut in two. It was incredible, those two slow, solid blocks of Germans running clumsily, opening their mouths. They were coming up at him. Two solid blocks of Germans running clumsily. They were coming, nothing was stopping them. Fixed in a cold trance, he pulled out his automatic. Where were his men? All gone? No, there ahead were two. They rose up from the ruined earth without their rifles and passed below him, running with fixed grins. Another came by, his mouth stretched open. "Halt!" he shouted and jumped out of the hole. He struck at him with the butt of his automatic; the blow glanced off the shoulder. The man dodged over the crest. He shot a cartridge into the chamber. He'd rather get the next man that ran back than all the Germans in the world.

And all the time the two small blocks of running men were coming up the slope. He stood alone in a bare, ruined world without fear, without hope, a dead man, cold and rigid, in the shroud of fate.

Then in the squares of Germans some running men went tumbling as sparse rifles cracked along the line; and then—a sound of joy and wonder—he heard slow tapping up the hill. Beneath his eye, the nearest square broke into fragments, stopped and streamed back down the slope. Now the crackling ran along the line and other crackling lines came up behind him and dinned about his ears, and a loud voice, "Jesus Christ, Lieutenant, get away from there!" Beneath this crackling, the other square had melted and was drifting down the fierce stream of their fire.

Emptying his automatic as he ran, he got among the fox holes of his men. There were fragments, and there were shrunken bodies half buried, face down, on the ground; but here and there, under the tin hats, close to the churned earth, eyes rolled up at him. He ran among them, his dry mouth open wide. "Come on, you buggers, come on! Are you going to let the second wave go through you?"

CHAPTER XLVIII

It HAD always seemed like a dream, those days in the Base Hospital. He sometimes used to wonder if they were true. Lewis Carroll himself could not have thought of more fantastic imbecilities. And, yet, they must be true; confused, perhaps, in detail and in sequence, they stood out sharply in his mind. The long gray flimsy room, forever cold, with its Sibley stove whose stack ran out a window at the farther end; the iron cots on which the men looked dark against the sheets and pillows. And on his right, that most unmilitary man, the gentle brown-eyed little captain from West Point, always dishevelled, always mislaying his possessions, who used to borrow inappropriate odd clothing and shyly play the clown up and down the aisle between his fits of vomiting. The captain had been with the British in a regiment of American Railroad Engineers. How he had gotten there, he didn't seem to know. "I am, by profession, a calvaryman and something of a soft-shoe dancer." He made his borrowed slippers patter on the floor, accompanying himself by gestures with his voluminously hidden hands. "However, there we were, building a railroad for the Limeys' plum and apple jam; a peaceful scene. But who should come over the hill but the Limey army at great speed. They were throwing their rifles high in air, also tin hats, haversacks, packs, tunics, loose change, keyrings, keepsakes; in a word, all dead weight. Quite a barrage, in fact. It was a dangerous spot. Our men gave way, and I placed myself at the head of them. We made for our work train, but the Limey engine driver, as they call them, was just a shade too smart for us. He cut the train out and disappeared with his engine. Then here came the Germans. There was nothing to do but pick up rifles and play rat-in-the-corner. It was weeks," he said, "before we found out we were heroes. And that," he said, "is how I came to eat the bully beef with gas on it." He placed a flopping sleeve against the front of his dressing-gown. "Feel that," he said. "That's how chronic nausea can build up the stomach muscles. Captain," he called out in a soft solicitous voice, "how about that Gillette of yours? I'm expecting to be decorated some time to-day."

Three times a day the orderlies, recruited from obscure and filthy races of the Orient, brought them their beans and slabs of bread and oleo. And morning and evening, Miss Heston showed her radiant teeth and cried out, "Well, boys, give us the old smile."

The rest of the time, he lay and thought about the action. On the triangle paper that the Y supplied them, he wrote short notes to Tad and Jane and Julia. He wrote a letter to Aunt Clara and a note to his mother and to Grandfather Rand. His notes were cheerful and unreal. Just a little whiff of gas, he said. Now he was feeling fine and would be out soon. Let no one worry, they were well taken care of over here.

But though he wrote, he didn't think about those people. "Those people," he called them to himself. To reach them, his letters must pass through not only vast space, but through, it seemed, uncounted years of time. The space, if he survived, he would himself pass through some day again. The time moved on; would he ever find his way back through it to where they were and be at one with them again? For he hardly ever thought of them in this new time where he existed closely surrounded by other homeless spirits, yet coldly alone; and, yet again, not alone, or, if alone, somehow in his isolation united with a bleak and vast but not wholly hostile universe which he had never guessed. What this universe signified, this universe of fathomless suffering, fortitude and courage, of sentimentality, indifference, cowardice and greed, what all this signified, this fantastic, heroic, senseless, endless agony, he did not know. He knew only that he stood naked and unashamed before the mystery; naked and un-ashamed, having travelled far the dangerous road which led from the river bank in Midian. Before this mystery, he, the denuded worm, might be unshaken, but he had no power. To his interrogation, came no answer. Only the false news in the daily papers and the unending tramp of stretcher bearers along the endless wooden corridors. No answer. His mind recoiled and drifted always to the action.

There, much might have been ordered differently. They should never have advanced, to start with, in columns of files under

machine-gun fire. But that was not his fault, they had their
orders. The taking of the gun was good, but should he have
ordered it out of the emplacement? If he had let it stay there,
Mackintosh might not have been killed, or Jones. In that case,
Septak would not have manned the gun and won the D. S. C.
and he, himself, would not have been expected to write a letter
to Mrs. Mackintosh in Midian, and Mrs. Jones in Bowman, con-
doling with them on their sons, dead by his order.

From then on they hadn't done badly. Purged by death and
by desertion, what was left of them had all day crept and burrowed toward the blazing town. That night they had hugged a
road embankment and gnawed their iron rations. And all next
day they had lain there fighting the flies and nursing their
canteens. That night he had sent men back with all their water
bottles, and one of them had gotten lost or run away. Mellick
had run away, and Seaver besides. There were only twenty of
them left. He was glad to see a battalion runner come creeping to his fox-hole, his pale and greasy face illumined by the
flashes low down in the sky. They had done enough, it was clear
that they were to be relieved. Battalion orders, the runner said:
they were to attack again at dawn.

At dawn then, they rose up. A blast of tapping burst out from
the town. Bowerman went straight up in the air and came down
snapping. And one man walked in circles with blood whirling
between the fingers pressed against his face. They dragged him
and the others back to their holes again.

And then the second wave came through them proudly and
climbed between the fox-holes up to the bank above. The tapping
started, and soon the dead men and the wounded men and all the
other men were tumbling down the bank again. Their satisfaction was complete. They bared their dry encrusted teeth. "Get
the hell out of here!" they said to the second wave. "Go back to
the rear where you belong." From then on, no other men
deserted, though he had an idea Wilson shot himself in the hand
on purpose. The rest of the day, they lay there fighting flies and
sniffing the dead Germans ripening in the sun.

That night they brought up coffee and bread and karo and a
marmite can of hot slum slung on a pole. Bearers came up, with
stumbles and hushed curses, carrying ammunition boxes and
hand grenades and bombs.

By the next day their scrubby beards gave them the look of

starved explorers, or of obscene wild animals at bay in filthy lairs. Their own dead joined the Germans now in fouling the damp, sunlit air.

And yet that night a sort of peace came over them, a change mysterious and unreal, yet comforting; it was as though their translation from the world of living men had been, through various and degraded stages, made complete, that now, with irrevocable finality, they found themselves condemned to a cold pit in inter-stellar space where, lost to all things that they had ever known, they must dwell forever. Once they had grasped their situation, it was not so bad. With unbelievable adaptability, they proceeded to bivouac in their limbo; to make themselves somewhat at ease in outer darkness and utter desolation; the smells of dead men ceased to trouble them; their own encrusted, greasy filth ceased to trouble them; their fox-holes were their natural homes and any food that came to them was good.

At dusk they came out of their holes and stretched themselves. He got up from his hole and watched the men as they sat down, brown formless shapes, on the embankment.

"Don't bunch up," he said. "Pass the word." He heard the murmur, "The lieutenant says—he says."

"My God, Feibleman!" he said, "where did you get that cigar?"

Feibleman's sad, brown eyes were anxious. "I got some more, Lieutenant. I got plenty. You like a cigar?"

"Much obliged," he said, "there won't be time to smoke. It will be dark."

"That's right, Lieutenant. For me; just a dry smoke." He held the cigar out to show that it was unlighted. "Tastes good, though."

The blue-jowled bomber moved his cud. "Feibleman," he said, "why don't you answer the lieutenant?"

"Answer!" Feibleman swung his big nose around. "I ask you. Ain't I answered?"

"The lieutenant says where did you get them cigars?" The bomber turned from Feibleman. "A fellow give him them cigars in Bar-le-duc for giving him a knockdown to his girl."

"To whose girl? Why should I fool with girls? There's plenty else to keep busy in this man's army, if a man wants to make a soldier."

"Feibleman had this girl," the bomber said.

"All he asked," Feibleman said, "was would I speak for him in French. So then he was so pleased."

"If he give you a box of cigars, Feibleman, he must have give her a house and lot."

"Wendig," Feibleman said, "what was that red-headed girl uptown you used to go with?"

"What's it to you?" Wendig said, "That little tramp."

"Lieutenant, Wendig met this girl at the I. O. A. M. picnic, and he give her a diamond ring."

"Never did," Wendig said. "Lieutenant, don't listen."

"And when he come to find out, Lieutenant, she was nothing but a hustler down on Centre Street; ha! and so there went the diamond ring."

"The hell it did," the bomber said.

"What's that?" Feibleman said.

"I got it back."

"Wendig, you ain't never got it back. How did you get it back?"

"Easy. You know Joe Garver on the Force? Well, I know him, so Joe told her that if I don't get back my ring, there ain't nothing doing for her on Centre Street no more."

"So you got it back," Feibleman looked satisfied and happy. "Well, well, ain't that a business?"

A single shell passed overhead with a swift, high rustle. It burst on the dark ridge far behind them. Feibleman straightened up again and pushed his tin hat back from over his eyes. "Ha!" he said, "Well, they say you never hear the one that hits you."

"What good would that be?" Wendig said. "What good would that be to hear the one that hit you?"

"Ain't you dumb?" Feibleman said. "It means if you hear it, it ain't going to hit you."

"Who's dumb? What good is that? What I want is to hear the one that's going to hit me."

"I don't see no good to that either," Feibleman said.

"Who's dumb?" Wendig said, "then I can move."

The two of them looked at him as though he were a referee. He felt his face crack into a grin. "Wendig's right," he said, "that would certainly be an improvement on the system."

Next morning after dawn, along the embankment another animal was crawling. The long soft figure of Captain Singletarry moved swiftly, peaking up behind. His sullen, girlish face was prematurely aged. There were pink rings around his eyes, the pale fuzz on his chin was dirty from the chin strap of his helmet. "Lieutenant," he said, "can you get these yearth worms of yo's to move?"

"They'll go where any troops can."

Captain Singletarry lit a cigarette, affecting not to hear him. "We going to take this town."

"Not without artillery support."

"The guns are up. Eleven-twenty we start. Check your watch." He rubbed his cigarette out in the earth. "You want to have plenty of grenades and bombs whenever you get in that town." On hands and knees Captain Singletarry ambled along until his delicate posterior had disappeared around a bend in the embankment. He never knew until the end that Captain Singletarry was going on to have a look at the Second Platoon, who were without an officer owing to the loss of Second Lieutenant William S. McGuire, killed in action.

In his cot, he stirred to move back from the pain that thrust against him. Bill McGuire gone forever, into the vast unknown. Lost, and perhaps forever lost, in time and space, yet nearer to him still than people living back in Midian. His Testament beside his bed contained the page that Bill had touched, had read the night before they trudged their separate ways toward the inscrutable. "Good luck," Bill had said. And now, what could be said about him? What ever could be said that would make him live, except in the memories of some few of those who knew him? That he was brave and honest and of a simple, ready wit, a big smiler with freckles and sandy hair and the best Glee Club leader that Cornell ever had? And then you had said nothing. It all had vanished as the touch of Bill's fingers on the leaves of this New Testament had vanished. Life had now no more to do with Bill McGuire than had this Testament.

And this Testament, he sometimes thought, had little more to do with life, with living men, than it now had to do with Bill. Certainly this Testament had little to do with what went on that last day in the burning town. They had fought with bombs and rifles and grenades in windows and doorways and back yards; and into cellars they had hurled explosions that silenced all the cries. And everywhere they went Singletarry with red eyes like a ferret's and a foul acid tongue that never stopped had led and driven them until at the last when he, himself, went down in blinding light and sweetish fumes, it was Singletarry, so they told him, who had crawled out and put the gas mask on him.

He smiled. He had written Singletarry from this hospital to thank him, and Singletarry had answered promptly to ask a loan of seven thousand francs. He had sent the money. It was not much to pay for the life of even a second lieutenant; and besides, no one else in the regiment, perhaps in the A. E. F., would lend Singletarry money any more.

So now Bill was dead. He, himself, was in hospital. Vrooman, trying doubtless to be killed or wounded, instead of being sent to Blois, had received the Croix de Guerre with Palm. He grinned. As always, Vrooman's plans miscarried. And Single-tarry was under charges brought by a hairy and most uninviting little girl who used to do their laundry in Médaux.

In the hospital the coughing started, the screens went up around the beds and forms were carried out by heavy-footed men. Three times a day, there was a sound of solemn field music outside the window. It moved away and paused, then sounded Last Post. Beside him the West Point captain lay with his brown eyes sunk back in his head, his bony cheeks burned bright.

The next time Miss Heston flashed her teeth, he beckoned to her. She came down toward him; her lips closed over her teeth in a straight hard line.

"Look here," he said, "aren't you going to do anything for the captain here? He's pretty bad."

Her teeth were flashing again, her heavy hand patted his. "Now don't you worry, big boy. We'll take care of him."

Once, a medical officer in horn-rimmed glasses and breeches that bagged out behind came by. "Doctor," he said.

"Well, well," the doctor said, "what is it?"

"This man here is in bad shape."

"Hm," the doctor said. He looked at the board that hung at the foot of the West Point captain's bed. "This is not my line."

"But, Doctor——"

"He'll be taken care of."

And so he was. Two nights later, when the little West Point captain began to whistle through his teeth, a medical captain came in and held his pulse until it was time to go out for the screen and the orderlies and the long white sheet.

One of the orderlies came back to turn the mattress. Sitting up in his bed, he reached beneath his pillow for his wallet. The French notes rustled as, in the darkness, he pulled out three. "Orderly." He tore the notes across. "There's three hundred francs. Bring me my outfit and you get the other halves."

"Can't do it," the orderly whispered. "Get in bad."

"What's that music up at headquarters?"

"Maybe I try," the orderly said. "Big dance."

CHAPTER XLIX

THE starlight shone dimly on the mud-encrusted boardwalks and on the endless paper roofs. Up on the hill, the windows showed cracks of light and a jazz band pulsed with rapid, sad insistence. There was the hollow, mournful knocking of coconuts; the saxophones' inhuman, mirthless laughter—wha, wha, wha. Down the hill, small blue lights marked the switch points in the yard and a small French locomotive moved with stealthy silence; and farther still, headlights showed on the highway, and he could hear the rigid rattle of a camion.

He moved his soft and aimless legs along the boardwalk that led down the hill. Even to do this much caused his chest to tighten and his heart to run wild—to stall and then turn slowly over. A caped nurse was approaching on the boardwalk. He kept on, steady but unhurried. "Good evening, Doctor." He took a breath. "Good evening, Miss," he replied in a tone both stately and benevolent.

Before the boardwalk entered the long corridor, he left it and, through black holding mud, worked round the end of the receiving ward, now dark and empty. The hobbled soles of his trench boots became enormous, like the boots of deep-sea divers. He paused to listen to the driving of his heart before he stepped down to the cinders of the railroad yard. Among the small blue lights the little engine breathed, moved delicately, and little cars whose white paint glowed a faint blue underneath the stars moved lightly, slowly on the sidings and lightly bumped together. The yards were not big. If there was no fence on the other side he would make the highway.

"Hey, you! Come back here." He turned and paused and steadied himself.

"Are you the M. P. on this post?" he called out sharply. He stood still, holding himself erect—his back already had begun to break in two. A man came crunching over the cinders. He made his voice hard. "You heard me." The man saluted. "Yes, sir. My orders are——"

"I want you to keep an eye on these hospital cars. These French will steal the fittings out as quick as look at you."

"Yes, sir."

He turned and walked on firmly. The footsteps of the M. P. followed him, then moved off to the left and headed for the siding. He sat down on a windlass by the tracks and hung there sweating.

Below the railroad yards it was a battle with mud and deep grass that seemed like some sort of rushes, and with old tin cans.

Then he was on the highway and feeling rather light and sprightly. He sat down on a round stone guidepost and lit a cigarette. He held the match between his knees and read the guidepost upside down—"Orleans, 110 K."

Far down the road he heard the roar of a Pierce Arrow truck. He jumped up and stepped off the road. As the great behemoth came closer, it slowed down. He stepped in behind its headlights, seized the tailgate chain and, locking his teeth, crawled up into the empty body. He moved up forward into the blackness and sat down panting. The truck swung around the corner. Then it swung again, slowed down. For a moment he could not believe it—then it was so—above the engine he heard the wha-wha of the saxophones. He was over the tailgate and on the ground where he almost fell.

Beside the building where feet scraped to the saxophones, there was a scattering of staff cars. The drivers' cigarettes were clustered underneath the window. He crept between two cars and sat down on the running board. So far it was a circular escape. He wondered, as a problem of mathematical interest, how many other possible destinations for that Pierce Arrow truck there might have been besides this hospital.

After a long time there were voices and feet on the gravel where the cars were parked.

"Sure it's a dud here. Didn't I tell you? Let's go up to Orleans."

"We've got no passes." The voices were young and eager and full of noble, alcoholic refreshment.

"Use our Italian passes."

"Let's do. Brophy!" A cigarette moved from the ring of drivers.

He got up off the running board.

"Did you fellows say you were going to Orleans?"

They tried to make him out in the half light. "No, sir," they said. "No, sir. Not seriously."

"That's tough," he said. "I just came in on a camion. I'm trying to get to my outfit at the front. I thought if I could get a lift——"

They had him by the arms. "Signor Tenente." They said, "Old-timer, not another word." They led him forward between them. On the black body of the Dodge, he read in large, white letters the words "Excercito Americano."

"How do you like our motto?" the short one said. "If you turn it over, it means bath-mat in Welsh." The door gave a tinny slam behind them; the motor started. The two still had his arms.

"Andiamo," they said. "Here we go." The tall one fumbled ponderously in the breast of his trench coat. "Tenente," he said sternly wrestling with himself. "How do you feel about the wine of Burgundy?"

The night wind made the curtains of the Dodge flap as they rolled along. From time to time, the headlights of passing cars lit up the back seat.

"I see you are first lieutenants," he said. "I suppose——"

"In the sight of Burgundy," the tall one said, "all men are equal. Another touch?"

"Don't spare it," the small one said. "We are just using it temporarily."

"Just as a stop gap," the tall one said.

"A jurymast, a stepney wheel."

"Actually we are looking for Ponte Nero. We are searching France. Do you know the wine, Ponte Nero?"

"A wine of Italy. Viva L'Italia."

"E il Presidente Veelson."

They raised a chorus, " 'eep, 'eep 'oorah!"

"Do you remember Smith?" they said to each other. . . . "At the Municipal banquet? Why not? . . . 'Fellow Citizens of Genoa: I only regret that I have but one liver to give for my country.' " They turned to Tommy; "We have saved Italy from the caterers," they said; "but can we save France from the Germans?"

Inside him he had felt the warm rays of the Burgundy expanding. He felt soft and light, bold and assured, yet drowsy. Their voices came to him from far away. . . . "A wonderful people, the Italians; the finest army in the world; the best artillery; the best engineers; and . . . on Monte Grappa . . . best military roads—old ladies sprinkle and sweep them every day; a wonderful people—nothing can check them except fighting."

"Well," he said, "fighting can check anybody if they get enough of it."

"How true that is!" they said. "My grandfather was the first man to reach Washington after Bull Run."

"A relative hero," the tall one said. "My grandfather was the first man to reach Baltimore."

He tilted up the bottle. The Burgundy was warm and rich and smooth. "My grandfather," he said, "was the first man to reach Boston." Through his drowsiness he felt them hug his arms. "A typical Italian," they said; "he will say anything to attract notice."

An ancient Frenchman with sateen sleeves was standing over him. There were long windows on an iron balcony and much of the paper was off the wall. "Monsieur désire?" The Frenchman kept his eyes fixed on the legs in muddy field boots, lying on the counterpane.

It was, it seemed, the Hotel de L'Universe. The town was Cortenay. There had apparently been a change of plan.

After a shave and a half-bath, standing astride a cracked bowl on the floor, his mind conceived the picture of a champagne cocktail and of what such a precious article might do for him. The corridor was dark and carpetless. The stairs were narrow and once on another darkened corridor a door swung open and a tousled woman's head peeped out at him.

On the walls of the front hall, Marshal Joffre sat, stolidly benign, beneath a flag, and a lady received an honorable proposal within a bower. An open door showed the linen of the dining room, another the corner of a small zinc bar. In the bar there were also American voices and the cheerful sound

of glassware. By the door two local dignitaries sat at a table
sipping their horrid Quinquina, and at the next table there
were American uniforms and faces that turned to look at him.

"Bon jour, Madame," he said to the large black silk bosom,
"un champagne cocktail."

"Look here," a voice said, "didn't you go to New Haven?"
Slowly he swung around. The conventionally clean-cut officer
wore captain's bars and some obscure insignia on his collar. He
couldn't make it out. They were getting out all sorts of trick
services now. The two men with the captain were looking at
him too.

"Weren't you in '12?" the captain said. "I was in '14. You
wouldn't remember me. This," he said, "is a regular Yale town.
I suppose you know your R. T. O. here. He was in '12. Buffer
Molloy—played quarterback. Gosh! I'll never forget the time he
dropped that punt. My name's Harris. Won't you join us?"

"Thanks," he said. "Madame, quatre champagne cocktails."

Down the narrow street he came out on the square of perfectly
expressionless stone houses, broken only by the awning of a small
café. To his right, the station squatted beside its iron fence
through whose black bars he saw some peasants and their bundles
on the platform, and farther off across the tracks a man in
corduroy who labored with a windlass and a long rope, shifting
cars.

Under the café awning, shaded from the pale sunlight, a
well-preserved young man in enormous stand-up collar, gray
gloves, and a straw hat, sat like an effigy. Deep inside, the waiter
flicked his big apron at a fly.

The champagne cocktails, brioche and café au lait were dying
on him fast. He felt the chill of this late summer weather.
Hardy animals these French flies—French café sitters too.

The walk in front of the station was paved in hexagonal
granite blocks on which his slowly moving hobnails clicked. He
pushed on the worn brass handle of the waiting-room door and
entered the despondent, squalid atmosphere of railway travel in
this foreign nation. Those condemned to be transported sat immobile on the benches—a French poilu who carried his wine in
two long paper bundles; two nuns; a peasant woman; a man in a
velours hat, a braided morning coat and high-heeled canvas

shoes; and two American enlisted men who sat with their rifle butts and packs between their legs, their eyes, like all the rest, fixed on the shut window of the ticket office. Beside a door on the other wall, a white sign, strangely immaculate, bore the letters "R. T. O."

The office was tiny. There was nothing there except the Buffer in his chair and the sheafs of orders on the table. The Buffer's tufted head was down between his hands, his elbows on the table. He was fat.

"Hello, Buffer," he said.

The Buffer shut the book. His face was red and old and furious. Then he shouted; his empty chair flew backward—"Thomas, my lad. Why, by God, Thomas! Now where in hell—" He stood there red and happy. "Ah, Thomas, sit down." His eyes were puffy, his breath was like a dragon's.

As Tommy stooped to right the chair, he caught the flash of the book as Buffer shoved it underneath the pile of orders.

"Put your musette bag in the corner, Thomas. I'll sit on the table; you take the chair." The Buffer carefully explored a table drawer and brought out a small zinc bottle. "A little snifter? I'll get this train off and then we'll go to the café across the square. Meanwhile, you don't mind if I spot myself a little one to go on. Just kick that door shut with your foot.

The Buffer screwed the cap back on the small zinc bottle and tasted his wet, heavy lips. "And now, me lad," he said, "what are you doing here? How did you find me out?"

"I ran into an Eli that knew you or knew about you anyhow."

The Buffer's face lost all expression. "Ah," he said.

"It was up at the Hotel de L'Universe. I spent the night there."

"You did? At the Hotel de Universe? Ha," he said, "and what were you doing there, a married man like you?"

"I didn't know a thing about it till this morning," the Buffer grinned. "Believe it or not, you dirty-minded bum. Two ambulance fellows from Italy gave me a lift. They had a quart of Burgundy," he said.

"Thomas," the Buffer said, "you've changed on me and not for the better."

"It crept up on me, Buffer. Never happened like that before. I wasn't in shape, I guess."

The Buffer continued to grin at him. "Ah," he said, "that's the way it always happens. It never happens any other way."

"But this is straight. I just got out of hospital."

The Buffer brought his feet down. "What!" he said, "were you wounded? Are you all right?"

"Sure I'm all right. Just a touch of gas on the Vesle. Buffer," he said, "they're dying in rows back there. The Flu is knocking them. The man beside me passed out and half the others. So last night I gave the orderly three hundred francs to get me my outfit."

"That's a lot," the Buffer said. "They'll cross you up as soon as look at you, those hospital cooties, and you have no comeback."

"You know," he said, "I remembered something you told me once. I tore the notes in two and kept my half 'til I got the outfit in my hands."

"That's the play," the Buffer said. "Did I tell you that?"

"Yes; that time that Julia came up to the game."

"Ah," the Buffer said. There was a silence. He made an effort. "How's she?"

"Julia? She's fine."

"And how did you get in town without your orders?"

"I don't know a thing about it. I told you about those Italian fellows. I think they had Italian passes."

"I know. They've been fooling some of our fellows with those wop passes. Those damned fellows."

He fumbled in the drawer in search of the zinc bottle. "How about a little snifter?" He brought the bottle out and took a swallow. He studied it slowly. He screwed the cap on, put the bottle back. "Well," he said, "where do you want to go?"

"Back to my outfit."

"Where are they now?"

"In the same sector, I guess."

"Never mind; I'll find out from G 2."

"Look here, Buffer, don't get me mixed up with any head-quarters."

"You'll not be in it." The Buffer began to fumble through the sheaf of papers on his desk, still keeping the book hidden. "I've got a travel order somewhere that we took off a bird who was wanted for a shortage in his Company funds." His thick fingers moved heavily among the papers. "Here it is," he said. "Now all we need is the French word for ink eradicator?"

"Hold on, Buffer, you'd better not pull any of that; that's dynamite, you'll get in wrong."

The Buffer continued to study the order. "By Jesus, that would be a pity." He looked up sombrely. "What do you think I was when I was sent here? You know what I started with?"

"You were with the 69th, but, hell, Buffer, a man can't stay with combat troops forever."

"He can stay awhile. That horse's neck of a major was down on me to start with. The very first time he caught me having a bit of fun, do you know what he says to me? I was no worse than the others, but he called me out and he says: 'Mr. Molloy, we can't have any punts dropped over here.' So after that I didn't care—and the next time out I go." His face turned crimson. "There's twenty fellows in the regiment that wasn't half the officer that I was."

"I know," he said, "it's hell when a C. O. starts to ride you. But, Buffer," he said, "why don't you ease off on the cognac and make a job of it here? The way they are doing we'll soon be needing combat officers again."

"Ah, what do you know about it?" the Buffer said. "You and your Boy Scout advice."

"Oh, go to hell, Buffer."

The Buffer looked down at his blunt locked hands unhappily. "Tommy," he said, "forget it. That's out." He looked up sadly. "I've no one to talk to," he said, "so now I let fly." He looked down at the ground. "For two seasons and all but one minute of a third," he said in a low voice, "I was just as good a quarterback as Yale ever had, in our time anyhow. I used to pack 'em in for even the Brown and Dartmouth games. My mother's got a book that big of clippings, and what has it all come down to? I'm marked for life as the man who booted away the Princeton game."

"Buffer, you're nuts. We're not in college now. That's prepschool stuff. Nobody thinks of it but you."

"They all try not to show what they think and some of them are pretty good, but I always know. That's why a few good snifters come in handy."

"Do you know what's the matter with you?" Tommy said.

"You won't grow up. Have you ever noticed kids? I've got two of my own. They can't think or talk about anything except themselves and they have got the notion that every one is just as interested as they are. Buffer," he said, "in this man's army, nobody gives a damn about you or me or anybody. They've got themselves to look out for."

"That's a good line," the Buffer said, "the best so far." He grinned and then turned sober. "Do you know a funny thing? That Princeton end, Milliken, that picked up the ball, was in the regiment. He was all right but nothing special. But he got a captaincy and his men would do anything for him. And why? Because he picked up a loose ball and stepped across the line." The Buffer slammed a foot down on the floor. "For Christ's sake, what else was there for him to do?"

CHAPTER L

THE light truck turned off the straggling village street through carved stone gateposts and circled toward the little pink château. It came to a swinging stop with locked wheels skidding over the Belgian blocks.

"Wait here," he said to the driver already lounging over the side in an attitude expressing dissociation with all that might occur while this truck of his was not in motion.

"Yes, sir."

On the top step the sentry's rifle with fixed bayonet came smartly to present.

Mechanically he started to salute. "My God, Feibleman! they've made a soldier of you. As you were." He held out his hand. "How's the old platoon?"

"Lieutenant, the boys will certainly be glad you're back."

"Well, Feibleman, I'll be glad to see them. I guess there's some of the old crowd left."

"They give us a new officer. You hear now what he done last week? He give Blackie ten days K. P. For what? For having his first aid packet upside down on Saturday inspection. So it was in the pouch and everything, only that little ring like was on the bottom." Feibleman searched his face with sad, dark, earnest eyes. "Ten days," he said. "Lieutenant, it's like that all the time."

He grinned at Feibleman. "Well, Feibleman, he sounds like a soldier."

Feibleman hung upon his rifle in dejection. "Lieutenant, the boys will certainly be glad you're back."

In the vast hall, half of a double door was open. Inside beyond the clicking typewriters, Porky sat stout and pink and earnest. There was a heavy plaster cornice in the tall bare room, and gilded valences over the tops of the two high windows.

"Second Lieutenant Thomas Rand," he said, saluting, "reporting for duty. Porky."

449

Porky's light blue eyes swung around to him. His little mouth curled in a smile. He turned quite pink. "Tommy," he said. His stout, clean hand shot out. He knitted his faint brows. "You make things difficult for me," he said. "These hospitals are hopeless on their paper work. It would have been more considerate if you had stayed away until your orders came through."

"Well, Porky, you see, I'll tell you how it was." He told Porky how it was.

"Hm," Porky said. "Did I say you make things difficult? You will agree that I was not exaggerating. Are there any other circumstances? Forgery? Assaulting an officer in the discharge of his duty? Rape?"

"I understand there's been a touch of that around here since I left."

Porky lowered his voice. "Remember that girl that did our laundry in Médaux?"

"The Shetland Pony."

"Last month she caught up with You All."

"Beaucoup francs, eh?"

"To her consternation, no. They send him down to Chaumont to stand charges." Porky shook his head in resignation. "And he comes back a major."

"Can you beat that bird?"

"We've given up trying. We confine ourselves to not lending him money. But still he gets it."

"Well, anyhow, he's brave. You've got to give him that."

"Certainly nothing disturbs him. But now what am I going to do with you? Do you want a sick leave?"

"I want to stay with the outfit. Ever since I heard about Bill——"

Porky's small mouth fell into heavy lines. "Oh, yes," he said, "Bill."

"I heard it in the hospital. I wish I hadn't heard it there."

"I didn't know that. You know back home I always thought that you felt Bill——"

"Back home. Yes, that's what gets me now."

"Look here, who started this?" Porky said. "I've got a bed for you upstairs. Stop first and see the doctor. Orderly!"

At the end of the tall hall, on the handsome panelled double door was nailed a sign "Bn. Med. Off." The orderly knocked;

there was no response. While they stood and waited they could see through the soiled glass of French windows a ruined garden, a distant pale pink wall of brick against which pear trees, shaped like candelabra, were impaled; and, in the center of pallid paths' and hedges' half-obliterated geometry, a stone child who wrestled with a dolphin in an empty fountain filled with yellow leaves.

"Is it Captain Gorell still?" he said.

"Yes, sir." The orderly knocked again.

A rising wind stirred the fountain's yellow leaves and made the twigs of the untrimmed hedges tremble. As though the shadow of a cloud passed over him, he felt a chill of faint, but piercing, terror and despair. It was just so that the twigs had trembled in the clump of bushes that had held that German gun. He kept looking at the bushes; now that he knew the source from which the shadow came, it vanished; nothing remained except the peaceful sadness of the wet, gray, ruined garden.

"All right!" an ancient voice, hardy and impatient, rang through the panels. "All right! Whut is it?" The orderly opened the door.

In the tiny, but lofty, box-like room, there was nothing but a newspaper being held spread wide, from under which the stout legs and the papery, unpolished gaiters of Captain Gorell protruded, cocked up on a table.

"Captain Gorell," he said, "this is Lieutenant Rand reporting for duty. The Adjutant——"

"Tawm!" The voice rose up behind the paper. "We heard that you were daid."

"No, sir, not yet."

The paper came down with a crumple. "Boy! let me show you something." Captain Gorell, dropping his scrubby chin on his crushed collar and pushing his gold spectacles into the sparse fuzz of his crown, looked at him with solemn satisfaction. He twisted his wide mouth until his red-veined cheeks rose up in knobs. "Let me show you something." He whirled the paper around and pointed with a stubby finger. "Read that, Tawm."

He looked at the headline, "Doctor Mamby Passes."

"Read it aloud," the captain said.

" 'Doctor Mamby Passes,' " he said. " 'Flu carries off leading practitioner. The many friends and acquaintances of Doctor

Cassoway W. P. Mamby will be shocked to learn—" the paper
was removed.

"That's too bad, Captain," he said. "Was the doctor a friend
of yours? '

"Tawm," he said. Carefully he folded the paper so that the
obituary notices showed. "Son," he said, "there's a lesson hyer."
He fumbled in his sparse fuzz for his glasses. "Hyer was a
man wasn't satisfied with whut he had." He settled his glasses on
his nose. "No, sir." He cocked the narrow wad of paper on his
paunch and studied it. "Not unless he could get my practice
away from me; he never did though; only he tried. Pshaw!" he
said, "I never had to fret about him. No sir." His finger moved
along the lines of print; his lips moved with it; he looked up
with solemn brightness. "Yes, sir, there it is. Well, when the
war come on, did he do his duty? Tawm; he stayed right home,
a younger man than me and whenever I was gone in the army,
right then he started in to toll my patients away, just like they
was hogs. My wife wrote me all about it." He nodded, gravely
radiant. "So look what happens." He slapped the paper on his
knee. "Daid as a nit! And hyer I am."

"Well, Captain," he said, "that certainly is fine."

"Tawm," he said, "there's mo' to this mortal world than man
has knowledge of. You boys nowadays don't pay no attention to
getting right with God, but let me tell you something. They is
nary thing can happen on this earth that escapes His eye." He
pushed his glasses up again and planted his hands on his baggy
knees. "Let a man do right," he said, "and then he has no
cause to worry. You boys remember that. Now, Son, what ails
you?"

"Well, Captain, I had a touch of gas."

"That's a fact; I heard about that."

"Well, I came out of the hospital maybe sooner than I should,
so the adjutant said to get looked over."

"What seems to be the trouble, Son?"

"I'm all right; a little weak but I'm pretty lucky, I didn't get
the Flu."

"Have they got that back there?"

"Yes, sir; they've got plenty."

The captain shook his head. "Well, that's too bad. Don't seem
right to have that over here. So you feel weak?"

"Yes, sir, and my heart goes sometimes."

The captain's eyes stole to the newspaper.

"Do you want me to take off my coat, Captain?"

Captain Gorell looked up. "Oh, no," he said, "just hand me that pad."

With the pad cocked on his knee and breathing hard, the captain wrote.

"I've diagnosed you; low blood pressure and mild chronic inflammation of the bronchi. Light duty," he said. "Come back to-morrow." He looked up benevolently and scratched his nose with his pencil. "Did you ever take Poole's Pectoral Compound?"

"No, sir, I never did."

"It would probably do you good," the captain said, "if a man could get it."

.   .   .   .   .   .

They sat at the window in the upstairs room between the two four-poster beds. Their feet were on the window sill, his big field service shoes and Porky's English polo boots. Together they watched the feeble sunset over the gray and dark red roofs.

"A little more champagne," Porky said. "Doctor's orders."

"This is great stuff, Porky."

"Naturally."

"It's a shame to drink it in these tumblers."

"Thomas, we must try to get you up a better war."

"Oh, go kiss yourself, Porky," he said. "I've no complaint."

"No complaint." Porky pursed his lips judicially. "Do you mind if I have that read out in orders? It would do much to encourage the men. He comes back on a forged order and unfit for duty. I get him a new set of papers, a soft job in charge of the battalion's Allen's Foot Ease, a dog robber, a king's mistress' bed, and a quart of Veuve Cliquot 1904, and he announces that he has no complaint. It makes me so happy."

"Porky," he said, "what's going to happen next?"

"How do I know? This is the lull before the storm, I suppose. Have you seen the new C. O. of your platoon?"

"No."

"He has the boys all pretty well at sea. He's an old man almost and a West Pointer: and a second lieutenant. Can you guess the answer?"

"Been out of the service, I suppose. But even so——"

"No, he had a regiment in the Champagne this spring. He left a lot of German machine guns behind him and got cut to pieces and so they sent him down to Blois. They were going to reclassify him and give him an area in the S. O. S. These West Point boys beat Skull and Bones for sticking by each other. But that's where the fight started. Our hero wouldn't play; in the end he got his way and here he is, a second lieutenant, but with combat troops again."

"Well, I'll be damned. How did you find that out?"

"I find things out."

"I'll say you do. You always have. It's your nature, Pork."

"In any one except an adjutant it is perhaps a vice."

"What's this bird like?"

"A little old man, quiet and polite, the perfect soldier and a great grief to that old platoon of yours. Your children suffer." He raised himself by his elbows and peered out the window. "Hello," he said, "here comes Jaclard." A trim small figure in French blue was crossing the courtyard. "Probably coming to see me," Porky said. "You know him?"

"I remember him back there at Mills, but he was at Regimental. I never met him."

"Jaclard and I have gotten pretty thick. A great little fellow." He brought his polo boots down and leaned out the window. "Hank!"

"Allo, Porky!"

"Come up."

Porky leaned back deeply satisfied. "A great little fellow," he said. "Up there on the Vesle, where you got your whiff of gas, the back areas were pretty hot. Counter barrage and all that. The colonel decided to move up Regimental anyhow. There was nothing for Jaclard to do up there, of course, so the colonel told him to go back to the echelon. The fellows said those two little spots in Hank's cheeks got red-hot. He did his little French salute and asked the colonel's permission to ask a question. 'How long, sir, have I been with this regiment?' he said.

" 'Hell, I don't know,' the colonel said. 'Ever since we were formed at Mills. Six months, I guess.'

" 'Precisely, sir,' Hank said. 'I have been with this regiment six months; and I ask you, sir, to say as a soldier whether this is not a very peculiar moment to be leaving it?' So after that he went along. He even came up to our battalion with a message when the wires were cut. That's how we got so thick. I'd managed to bring a couple of bottles of Château Margaux with me, and, of course, they hadn't anything like that at Regimental."

There were light heel taps in the hall, and a light knock at the door. The Frenchman's eyes were small and black beside his fine sharp nose. His black mustache was clipped short over his small tight mouth.

"Captain Jaclard," Porky said, "Lieutenant Rand."

Tommy saluted and took the small gloved hand. The white cuff was immaculate. The blue stock above the tall blue collar was starched and neatly folded.

"Champagne in the afternoon?" he said. "You are luxuriant."

"Hank," Porky said, "I beg you not to assume surprise. I'll get another glass. Here, take my chair."

He came back from the washstand with a tumbler. "Hank," he said, "has the infallible ear for champagne corks. He would be better than all the flash and sound ranging sections put together if the Germans would fight with champagne bottles."

Captain Jaclard held out the glass. "A fine suggestion," he said. "It would be a very immense improvement in technique."

"Not 'very immense,' Hank," Porky said. "You can't have anything bigger than immense."

"Not among Americans?" the captain answered placidly.

Porky filled the tumbler. "Hank has the French mind," he observed. "He does not learn our language, but daily he acquires greater skill in justifying his mistakes."

The captain smiled at Porky. "Perhaps we should speak French then."

"At least, when I speak French, I recognize my limitations."

"You should not deceive yourself, Porky. You recognize the limitations of those who attempt to understand you. If you recognized your own, perhaps you would select some other medium."

"The Indian sign language, perhaps," Tommy ventured. "I used to know the word for antelope. I learned it from a book my aunt had." He formed a fist and stuck out his two outside fingers. "Then with the other hand, you show how many there are."

Porky sat down on the bed, his short stout legs dangled above the floor. "This is extremely useful information."

"In Italy," the Captain observed, "it would also protect you against the Evil Eye."

"It was a couple of Italian fellows that got me out of the hospital," Tommy said.

"Italian officers?" the Frenchman said.

"No, they were Americans; just been transferred to France from the Italian front."

"That will be an anti-climax," the captain remarked incisively. "However, war sometimes is." He turned to Tommy. "So you are all right now, I hope?"

"I'm feeling better, thanks." He took a sip of champagne. "Moment by moment I feel better."

"It was gas, I think I heard."

"A gas shell. It was too quick for me."

The captain smiled. "There is no discredit; they are sometimes quick. And you contributed indirectly to the decoration of your brother officer."

"The Mississippi Bubble."

Porky bounced on the bed. "Wonderful!" he said, "when did you think of that?"

"Just now," he said, "Porky. Just like that."

"I can appreciate it also," the captain said. "In our school books we, too, learn of the Mississippi Bubble."

"In your school books," Porky said, "you learn everything. Every Frenchman knows everything. It is a matter of principle. In our schools, we learn nothing. A matter of principle, too. Hence, our superiority. From birth we are thrown on our own resources."

"And our own initiative, Porky. We have not been educated to recognize impossibilities."

"It is conceivable," the captain ventured, "that that might sometimes lead to a mistake."

"It is conceivable, Hank," Porky said, "that the French system may lead to mistakes also. Man is creative." He waved his glass. "If you set the recognition of impossibilities as his goal, he will not stop there; he will go on to create more for himself."

"Porky," the Frenchman said, "you illustrate a difference between the races. A Frenchman is at his best when discussing his special subject. An American is at his best when discussing something that he does not understand."

"What it comes down to," Tommy said, "is that we are a race of illiterate enthusiasts, while you are a race of educated fatalists."

The captain smiled at him not unkindly. "You, too, are ingenious; but as far as France goes, I can only suggest that the question is not simple."

Porky raised the champagne bottle to the light. "There's just one more little touch all around," he said. "I was telling Tommy about what you said to the colonel up on the Vesle."

The captain held out his glass. "I am glad you told him. It is an admirable example for every young soldier."

Tommy stared at him. The captain met the look with firmness.

"In war," he said, "there is no great question of courage. All men are brave enough if properly equipped and trained and led, but an added value can be given normal courage by communicating it in a sufficiently telling manner. On the spur of the moment, my remarks were the best that I could do. I have since thought of several points at which I could have made them more effective. But even so, they gave a little buoyancy to the colonel and the staff; in fact, we all went up together in an excellent mind."

Porky glowered at him over the top of his tumbler. "Henri, I'm damned if you don't talk sometimes like an Englishman."

The captain turned to Tommy. "A dangerous type, this Porky." He gave his tight and clever smile. "The wine makes him seek quarrels." He stood up smartly and bowed to Porky. "Nevertheless, that was a delightful refreshment. Will you dine with me to-morrow night?"

"Fine," Porky said. "Where?"

"At the Mess," Captain Jaclard answered firmly. "Then afterward we go to my quarters for biscuits and a wine of my country."

"All right, Hank, I'll be there."

"And your friend." He turned precisely and spoke to Tommy. "You, too, Monsieur; I hope you will accept."

When his light, accurate footfalls had died away, they sat back in their chairs and waited till they saw his foreshortened figure, dim now in the faded light, march briskly through the court-yard and out the stone-crowned gates.

"A great little fellow," Porky said, "not strong, perhaps, at entertaining in a big way, but then that's not the custom."

"Do you think he knew we'd opened this bottle?"

"If he had, he wouldn't have come."

"He liked the champagne."

"He liked the champagne, but the general idea was a secret grief to him. Champagne, for no reason, in the afternoon; he finds it hard to forgive me. In fact, the only thing that per-suades him to forgive me is the champagne."

"Like Madame Valleton and the firewood."

"Like her. Every Frenchman is a peasant at heart."

"It makes them difficult."

"Difficult," Porky said. "And practically indestructible. How about another bottle of champagne?"

"No, thanks."

Porky stood up and bending stoutly inspected the sheen on his English polo boots. "I'll just go down and check up on the paper work."

"Porky, if I'm going to stay here, we'd better go fifty-fifty on the expenses."

"It is a matter of no interest."

"We'll do it then."

"Sentimentally, I approve." He started toward the door. "I had a letter from our old playmate, Jeanne."

"From Jeanne?"

"She's still at Neuilly; she sent you her love." The door closed on the sound of Porky's stumping footfalls and creaky English boots. His voice came back from down the corridor. "A figure of speech."

Outside, now, it was almost dark; small sparks flew up from scattered chimneys; down below there were dim lights, the faint click of steel hobs on stone and the sense of many men. High above and far removed, the first faint stars showed through the evening mist.

CHAPTER LI

INTO the long dark shed the French train stole. "Gare St. Lazare!" a whining voice came down the corridor, "Gare St. Lazare!" Already the gentleman in whiskers and pince-nez and the two over-stuffed but firm ladies were reaching down their portmanteaux, their paper parcels, carryalls, net bags full of seashells, their rugs in shawl straps, umbrellas, parasols, and light malacca canes, and edging with determination toward a position of advantage at the door. Firmly blotting him out with their massed bundles they cast on him a look of cold and distant satisfaction. This was their revenge for the altercation about the window. Undoubtedly he would have small chance of a porter or a taxi now. As he took down from the rack his two musettes, his trench coat and his overcoat, he smiled to himself. In some ways the French made him feel that he belonged to a far older race. The three proceeded with apparent inattention to make it difficult for him to get his coat on—he stepped out into the corridor.

In the compartment they had now dropped the disputed window open wide, and leaning out in a compact mass addressed imperious adjurations to the skirmish line of ancient porters whose unresponsive faces passed slowly by. The porters, however, evidently appraised these adjurations by some infallible system. In the end, he descended with leisure, shouldered his musettes, and walked away with well-concealed elation, leaving his travelling companions still stranded among their flotsam.

The iron grille at the end of the huge mournful train shed was well defended. American M. P.'s with scarlet brassards, fortyfours and nightsticks; French poilus wearing their blue coats buttoned back and their long thin bayonets fixed on their rifles; British M. P.'s with buttons shined and boots greased, the acme of self-conscious rectitude; and a long Australian in Norfolk jacket and felt hat cocked up at one side. There were also other

459

more obscure officials who might be station masters, Cook's guides, or Portuguese naval attachés. It was evident that if the Germans ever reached Paris it would not be via the Gare St. Lazare.

Behind this first line of defense a small crowd waited. It was a moment before, among them, he made out Jeanne. She was no taller than the French, and her blue serge uniform blended with the black that France was wearing now. And then she raised her hand just as she had on the stairs when she and her father carried down the punch bowl—why, that was years ago—and then outrageously she bounced up and down and hollered. Suddenly he felt happy.

Her strong hands had his elbows, her strong small body just touched his, then leaned away. "Oh, Tommy!" she said. "My dear." Her eyes were black and bright, her big mouth was delicate and tender.

"Jeanne," he said, "how are you?"

"You got my letter?" she said.

"You got my telegram?"

She threw her head back, laughing richly like her mother. "Otherwise," she said, "this is quite a coincidence."

"Jeanne," he said, "how are you?"

"The question is," she said, "how are you? I heard about you on the Vesle. That was when I wrote."

"I didn't get it for months," he said. "They lost my record in the hospital."

"I heard about your record."

He glowed.

"Jeanne," he said, "how are you?"

"I've got the afternoon and evening," she said, "we can do anything you want. How do you feel?"

"That's great! Oh, I'm all right," he said. "That's great. How do you feel?"

And all the while a distant voice was in his ear. "Sir . . . sir. . . ."

"What's that?" he said. "What is it, sergeant?"

"Sir, the Lieutenant will please to pass through the Provost Marshal's office to have the Lieutenant's travel orders stamped."

The taxicab lurched and quacked down the steep driveway and out the station gates. He leaned back on the bounding cushions and smiled at Jeanne. "This is the life," he said. "Where are we bound?"

"I'll tell you what I did," she said. "I took a room for you at the Continental. Was that too bold? They're hard to get though. You can give it up if you know a better hole."

"It sounds fine. I don't know anything."

"Then we might drive a little first." She leaned forward speaking to the driver, cordial, quick, and fluent. The ancient nodded over a humped shoulder.

"Is this too cold?" she said. "I had the top let down, I thought you'd like to have a look at Paris."

"It's fine," he said. "I would."

"This is not much," she said, "right here, but wait a little."

The taxi quacked and bumped along among the other quacking taxicabs, the spindly torpedoes, the chunky little camions, the wildly weaving bicycles.

The great humped back of the Opéra loomed ahead. They crept around it and broke out in the open. Jeanne said nothing then except to give brief answer to his questions. She sat beside him silent. For an hour they jolted by boulevards, broad embankments, wooded avenues, through wide expanses of charming graceful splendor.

.   .   .   .

At seven o'clock he sat in the plush lounge where officers passed hurriedly, indifferently, sat stolid or alert, gathered at little tables or crowded in the bar; and where elaborate ladies, half reclining in corners or sweeping slowly by, trailed slow cold eyes across his face. There was one, however, with a slightly ruddy face and an almost merry smile. She was sturdy, like a little horse; and as she passed, she searched him with a humorous quick eye. "Behold us, monsieur," she seemed to say, "you and I, in this absurd situation. But what can one do? Nothing, then for each of us, but to make the best of it." She was not like the others, that little horse. He followed her warmly with his eyes, only to discover that her humorous and intimate glance had not been particularly reserved for him. He left off watching her abruptly. This was a fine time and place, and he was a fine person to be entertaining such cheap notions.

Across the lounge the pavement of the glass-enclosed courtyard ꞏhowed dimly under the light beside the archway where the porter had his desk. Through this archway always the silhouettes came and went, the officers, and sometimes a top hat, and the elegant women often two by two.

Diagonally across the courtyard bright lights marked the hotel desk and lobby where even now, amid heaped baggage on the floor, belated majors strove in vain for favors from the suave and soulless frock coat.

He turned the stem of the cocktail glass between his thumb and finger. Just to watch those majors was enough to make an evening. This particular evening, it was an added touch to what was already practically perfect. Practically perfect; he jumped up; she was coming along the corridor, a strong, yet graceful figure in her plain black-satin gown. The officers at the tables were turning to look at her with the distinguished and unconscious vulgarity of the Continental male. He was hurrying forward, "Hello," he said. Angrily he turned to glare at the little tables. But in accordance with the code, their glances had been withdrawn. There was nothing to do but walk beside her scornfully.

"They're holding a table," he said. "Jeanne, you look simply swell." He wished it might have been better put. "Simply swell," he said.

"I feel simply swell. I suppose you think I do this every night."

"I don't think anything about it," he said, "I just think about myself."

"That is the simplest plan." She gave him a teasing sidewise smile.

"Simplest and best; I am simply having a good time."

The high gold ceiling, the crowded tables swallowed them. Behind her he was wafted across the room on a bridge of waiters' bows. She gave him a look of respectful amusement as they took their seats. "That was quite a triumphal entry. You've evidently treated all the boys here right."

"Well," he said, "you might as well have a good time. I mean I might as well have one."

"Go right ahead," she said, "it's all good clean fun for me, too. You know, I haven't been outside the hospital in forty days; exactly forty days—I counted them."

"Just like the Ark," he said. "But why not?"

"Work," she said. "But let's not drift into that; I only mentioned it to prove that all this plush is quite a little treat."

A waiter hovered; large *cartes du jour* were slipped into their hands. He ran an eye down the serried ranks. "There seems to be a choice," he said. "Why don't you order for us both?"

"All right," she said. "Soup?"

"Anything," he said, "that doesn't interrupt the conversation. No shad."

"No shad," she said. With a quick finger on the big card, she won from the waiter an inclination of respect.

Along the arcade underneath their table window many feet sounded, and beyond the pillars many dim-lit taxis chugged along the dimly lighted streets. The *carte du jour* was deftly extricated from his hands.

"I'm living for the time," he heard her say, "when Paris is lighted up again. I've never seen it any way but this."

"When it's lighted up," he said, "I'll get a real leave and we'll have dinner somewhere high where we can see it."

"The Savoyard," she said, "on the Butte. I'll meet you there."

"That's a date," he said. "The Savoyard."

"Yes. You know 'Louise'?"

"Louise who?"

"The opera."

"No," he said, "no music."

"There's a French girl at the hospital that told me about the Savoyard; one of the scenes in 'Louise' is laid there. It has a glass terrace high up on the mountain; you can have dinner by the window. The city gets dark and smoky, and then the lights begin. A few faint lights, and then, as the night gets black, more lights by hundreds and all the lights becoming brighter until there is nothing but millions of lights as far as you can see."

He looked at her face. "We ought not to go," he said; "it will never be as beautiful as you see it now."

She turned on him with a sort of vehement gravity. "Never say that," she said. She paused, and went on quietly. "We should be able to get pleasure from things as they are."

"From everything?"

"Oh, no," she said slowly, "not from everything; but what pleasure we get should be from things as they are. Then it's real and lasting." She smiled at him. "It's hardy."

"That's right," he said, "I can see that. But how are things? Who can tell? What proof is there?"

Again there was hovering and a large silver chain. "Will you order the wine?" he said. Outside, feet moved on the arcade and the dim slow taxis passed beyond the arches.

"In the hospital," she said, "there are girls who live in a sentimental haze, and there are other ones who seem just numb and stolid; but I think the ones who get the most happiness from their work are the ones who see themselves and their jobs just as they are and still believe in them."

"You're happy then?"

"Not always," she said, "sometimes, not at all. But what happiness I have, I think I'll keep."

"Yes," he said, "I can see that. I think you will."

"Sometimes, I am miserable," she said. "All I do is sit, month after month, making sections and cultures. When I think about it, it makes me miserable."

A bottle was presented, he nodded absently. "I suppose there are twenty million girls at home that would give their souls to have your job; to be in France with the army and with real work to do. To them, you can't be anything but a heroine."

"They're far away," she said. "When you get close you know that nothing but death and suffering gives any one the right to belong. There's no difference between me and a salesgirl in the five-and-ten in Midian."

"There's quite a difference," he said, "and what you have just been saying shows it."

The pale pure Graves slid into the thin glasses. Firmly she shook her head. "Never mind," she said, "we mustn't fuss about ourselves." Her black eyes looked at him, her big mouth gave its tender half-smile. "In our hearts we know that we belong on the side of the people that are doing the best they can." She raised her glass.

The light cool tang of the wine ran through him. "Good wine," he said. He set his glass down. "Finding happiness in reality," he said. "Just now I feel as though I could see that clearly."

Now she was laughing at him. "As through a glass, clearly," she said.

.   .   .   .

The Place de la Concorde lay wet and dimly shining in the raw still night; the statues stood, black bundles of lashed sand bags. It was perhaps absurd to have the taxi open. He pulled up the collar of his overcoat and, leaning back in the corner, watched the dim mask-like outline of her face. But not absurd for Jeanne; it would be hard to think of her in any taxi but an open one.

Up the dark, wide and slow ascent, straight, between darker trees, they followed their feeble creeping light to where the Arc de Triomphe brooded. Then they slid down by boulevards, still straight and wide, still bordered by dark trees and faint gray house-fronts level as a wall. He curled his hands in his flannel pockets. They were flying, the two of them, through darkness and through silence; the world was shrouded and mysterious; the city of shadows through which they voyaged was grave and beautiful and utterly withdrawn. They were alone, they should be going hand in hand. "This is beautiful," he said. "A beautiful city."

"Yes," she said, "it is much the most beautiful city in the world."

"Have you seen many others?"

"No, but I know it is."

"Yes," he said, "I believe you do."

"Just the way that you know, even in the dark, that it is beautiful along here."

"I suppose I know," he said, "I hope it is."

"Oh, yes, it is," she said. "It is. Nothing dramatic, just small town houses side by side, but all so decorous and well arranged; and then, of course, all the horse chestnut trees."

"Does it ever seem to you queer to be over here?" she said.

"It did at first," he said, "but I can hardly remember that. Now this seems real and everything else before, a sort of dream. Does it seem that way to you?"

"It did," she said, "but now this seems like a dream. It seems so queer that two people from Midian should be driving to Neuilly in the middle of a war. Who would have thought it?"

"We never thought it when we used to play hockey together on the river."

"No," she said, "we never did."

"You were the best hockey player I ever saw."

"For a girl," she said.

"Well, yes; for a girl. You used to make me furious."

"Was that what made you furious?"

"Well, you know I had the new kind of tubular skates and I thought I was pretty good."

"But was that what made you furious? There was something."

"Why no," he said, "I always thought we had great times together."

"So then we are back in Midian," she said, "and talking just the way they talk there."

"Well, then," he said, "I had no sense; I was a prig and I was scared of you."

"That all sounds reasonable," she said, "except that you were scared. You had the perfect Yale assurance."

"I know," he said, "that's what assurance is for, but I was scared."

"What of?" she said. "I never guessed it."

"I was scared of your warmth and vigor." He took a breath. "I was scared of your torso."

She laughed, and fell silent. "I never guessed it," she said. "I was scared of you."

"You?"

"Yes; it was dog bluff dog. You know," she said, "how they walk around each other stiff-legged with their hair on end and their teeth bared? And all the time," she said, "their poor little hearts are going pit-a-pat."

"I never noticed your heart going pit-a-pat."

"That was because my hair was on end." She laughed. "And my hair was on end also because I was scared. You were so impressive. You really were."

"Such an impressive young horse's neck," he ventured.

"No, you really were. I thought if I could tease you, you might collapse; and then you would be no better than me. A worthy purpose."

"Like the time old man Eschelmann was in the gutter and the other drunk came by. 'Partner, I can't raise you up, but I'll lay down beside you.'"

She laughed. "We do remember some things from Midian."

"Yes," he said, "but they're not the things we're expected to."

"And sometimes," he said, "not the things we want to. I wish we could play those hockey games over again, and I could go to the dance at your house. I would try to be less—" He paused.

"Never mind," she said, "I would try to be more——"

"Hush," he said.

"More obviously scared," she said.

His hand was out of his pocket and starting to search for hers, but instantly he felt that she remained unmoved. In fact, she turned quite rigid. He reached in his breast pocket and brought out cigarettes.

"No, thanks," she said.

He lighted his without looking at her.

At the last when they swung and teetered through the iron gates up toward the big white pile, it was she who reached a hand to him. "It has been a lovely evening, truly lovely." As the darkness of the portico fell on them, with quick precision she stepped from the cab. He followed hastily, but she was going up the steps.

"Jeanne," he said. "Jeanne. Good night," he said. "Good-bye."

She turned, "Good-bye." She gave his hand a quick firm shake and climbed the steps again.

.   .   .   .   .   .

It was midnight by the time the taxicab had brought him back from Neuilly. The lights were dim in the lounge that just now had been so gay, and an old, old man made gestures with a mop. He set the mop against a table and shuffled toward the lift. Once in the slow ascent there was the sound of American singing, which trailed away below them as they rose, "—at the k-k-k-kitchen door." "On s'amuse," the old man said, and shook his head.

But all these things were happening in the distance; around him certainly, and, no doubt, now; yet far beyond that quick sturdy figure in the close black-satin gown; far, far beyond the big firm tender mouth, the neat black hair, the quick black eyes. And when at last, in his pajamas, on the window sill, he looked across dim house-tops to the dimmer vaster bulk of the column in the Place Vendôme, it dissolved, all things dissolved into the silent vastness of the night; nothing remained, except the vague vast night and that sharp glowing figure. If there were sometimes feeble lights that moved, or errant taxi horns that honked, they were lost.

But no more lost than he, in this immeasurable mysterious darkness; no more lost than he, fantastic and demented in the

night. The notions that came to him were incredible. He could
dress himself, find a taxi; back then to Neuilly through the night,
to the white silent hospital among the trees. His mind leaped
like a bell struck, like a deer shot. To Neuilly; she was there.

Why should he sit here on this window sill? It should be
possible to leap, to fly, to drive through night to where—he knew
it now—he ought to be.

He paused; he was two hundred feet above the concrete street
and felt that he should fly. Was that the cause of lovers' deaths?
Not always suicide, by any means.

And all the time, she was before him. She walked along the
lounge in her small strength and fullness; she lit a cigarette; he
saw the laboratory stains on her quick hands; she blew the
smoke; she laughed and talked—her voice was in his ears—she
raised a hand to a satin shoulder strap; her full strong bosom
showed. On the window sill he fell to shaking. Two hundred
feet above the street. This, too, might be another cause of a
lover's ending. In the darkened room he fumbled for his overcoat. When it closed around him he shuddered wildly.

He did not wish to turn the light on in that room, but in the
bathroom he turned it on and took a drink of whiskey straight
from his silver flask. As he screwed down the hinged stopper
his fingers steadied. He turned the light out and went back
through the darkness to his window.

In the sky now a motor droned. The beam of a searchlight
travelled slowly, erasing the faint scattered stars. The drone of
the motor, far and high, moved off into outer darkness; the beam
withdrew its finger. Just now, in all this night, there was no
sound or movement.

What was this that had struck him down, robbed him of his
senses? Was it the war that lowered men to brutes? Was it that
gas shell that had shaken him off balance; left him a nervous
idiot, devoid of judgment?

And what state was he in? What did he intend? Till now he
had not stopped to think, he only knew that, in a world of his
own making, he would go to Neuilly; now; at once; fast as an
arrow, and there, would find her, be with her.

Yes, and what then? Let this demented mind of his, that was
proposing blindly, go on then. Let it go on and tell the story.
What next, mind; what next, hurrying heart? What happens

then? The whiskey warmed and cleared and hardened him. "What happens then," he said. "Be tough," he said. "Do you just want to sleep with her? Is that what you have come to? But then why pick on her?—the town is full of girls. In this town the girls are always ready."

His mouth turned bitter. No other girl would do.

No other girl would do. So what did that mean then? Did it mean that if he survived he would marry her? That he would go back home to Julia and tell her the outcome of her years of faithfulness and loyalty, of this past year of patient, solitary waiting, and tell the children that he was leaving them—no fault of theirs, of course; he was simply leaving them? He saw those three as he had seen them last; standing like silent captives behind the ropes, watching the regiment and him march by and vanish in the dark resounding cavern of the docks. He saw the baby's heavy weight in Julia's arms and Tad's flag waving. It was impossible.

And was it even love? What, then, was love? He did not know. If only he could see her, at least from time to time; if only he could have her for his friend. For his friend? Let him be tough. They must be lovers.

He must be more than half demented. He sat here, the husband of the finest girl in Midian, the father of two children, and the Trustee of the Midian Boys' Club, proposing to himself that he and the daughter of two old friends of his family, Mr. and Mrs. A. C. Thompson, 718 River Street, Midian, should bed together. Put so, it almost made him laugh.

And what about Jeanne's side of it? Perhaps it might make her laugh too. In fact, it would not be amiss to remember that she might have something to say about the whole affair if she ever knew. If she ever knew. Certainly she did not know now. There had been nothing in the evening to violate the tradition of the clean-cut home-town boy. Right to the very last, when in front of the hospital, he had saluted, genial, polite, and kind, and exchanged with her the warm but uncharged handshake of old friends.

And yet, one never knew. Sometimes this evening, he had felt that her warm body was stirring toward him under the satin gown. He should know more, by God; a man his age! And certainly long years ago she had seemed to favor him; even now he sometimes recalled that day when, driving up the river, he had told her of his engagement and driven on feeling that he was followed by eyes of mocking despair.

The present case was different; irrevocably, illimitably different. Could he now come to her, having made his bed elsewhere and on a higher plane, to ask her to fill in the chinks in it? He had a notion that Jeanne was capable of making a man look foolish. Here was plenty of material to work on.

He got up from the window sill. So much had been accomplished, the situation was clear and was impossible; the frenzy of a night in Paris after too long service.

But in his bed she came to him again. Here in this room, this very evening, she had changed her dress. Here, while like a fool he had waited down below, she had— He switched the light on angrily and fumbled for a cigarette. What had come over him? By God, at heart he was a horse's neck like Singletarry.

CHAPTER LII

WITH a gentle running roll the transport slipped along through sunlight and soft seas. Locked shoulder to shoulder with the other officers he leaned on the railing of the upper deck and looked ahead at the horizon's bright yet tender mist. Below him the forward deck was crowded with the brown of men who also stared and formed in groups to pass around the gray-green field glasses brought back as souvenirs from Germany. On that placid deliberate tub there was no need for any lookout to report when she raised land.

Her faint smoke drifted off to starboard, a solitary gull dropped in astern of them. Far off to port an American tanker, outward bound, wallowed slowly in the smooth seas. "Oil Can!" they shouted, "How's everything at home?" And then a high voice, "How's my sweetie in Omaha?"

The sun shone bright; the big ship rolled; America lay just ahead below the shining shoulder of the sea. To-night, maybe, they would be in their own country. He looked down at the swarming men in khaki on the forward deck. They were coming to the land that they had left; but could they ever go back to where they started? Were they not changed? Certainly some he had seen changed in a flash to a splash of blood and hash on the stones of that old burning town; and others had been changed, in less abrupt progression, to meat, to carrion, to worms, to bones, and having been spitefully kicked around the battle-fields as a stench, a horror, a curse, a nuisance, were now being sacked up in the form of black and leering effigies and accorded proper honors. The pomp of war had broken down; it could no longer be managed, even for the dead. There was no one, so far as he knew, who lay like a warrior taking his rest with his martial cloak around him. When last seen, most of them had been merely shrunken dirty bundles; some lying rug-like; and others twisted into humble or comic postures. And some had unavoidably remained until their faces turned to slightly moist bluish-yellow balloons, quite slick and smooth except for a tiny mouth like the mouth of something dredged from the deepest sea; becoming briefly once again monsters, perhaps like those from which, a billion years ago, the race had sprung. And then sometimes the balloons would— He pushed back from the railing and walked along the dirty deck. From the crowded rail faces were turned to him. "Hey, Tommy boy!" they said. "It won't be long now."

Astern, more gulls were following the ship; her smoke lay in a faint long arc; the wake spread fantail across the bright slow water. On the afterdeck, men watched that too.

And these, the living, were not the same; with them there had been changes, less obvious, but as profound. Not with all, by any means; of some, nothing could break the iron nugget of stolidity. In death one would expect them to remain the same, simply to ossify as they, in fact, were doing now. Nor had the worthless changed; they had simply, if clever, enlarged and adapted their dubious talents. But they, in fact, were few; and every one else, he imagined, would not be quite the same again. Certainly not himself; not quite, nor anything like it. He remembered, as a child, he had been taken to the Indian Warm Springs; he had formed beforehand a vivid picture of it in his mind, but it had turned out to be different; and he never could remember afterward—though he often tried—what he had thought the Indian Warm Springs looked like before he saw them. So now he hardly knew what he had seemed to himself to be before he went to war. Perhaps he did not know, either, what he was like now. Undoubtedly there was much that one never knew, the greater part perhaps was hidden. Yet certainly he saw himself with greater candor; and certainly he saw life with a more rugged and realistic eye.

He had, it is true, manfully resisted in Paris the temptation to overstay his leave and see Jeanne again. He had indeed; and why? Fear of humiliation, of her mockery; fear of disgrace in the army, of disgrace and complications at home. There had perhaps been a touch of decent feeling, of sense of duty, of honesty toward Julia to make the mixture barely potable, but not enough to give him any grounds for pride or to prevent his seeing that a man of different merits, merits probably far greater than his own, might well have taken another course.

It had been just as well; he might have missed the great attack above Varennes. He paused; he also might have missed the sight of Porky lying in the big red pool that leeched the blood from his pink face and the light from his unseeing eyes. And so he would have missed the madness that came on him and brought him, not in line of duty, with the second wave over that last crest that lead straight onward to the Armistice; a madness now ironically symbolized by the narrow strip of blue and yellow ribbon on his tunic, and by the letter from Porky in his trunk below. Porky was now at Nice, the wine was good, his cork foot a success except with polo boots. For a moment he had been a little proud when, in Coblenz, he stood in front of his regiment while the Generals pinned the medal on him. And his old platoon had taken great credit to themselves for the affair. It was pleasant to have it of record that he was not afraid to go where men were dying; better still to know it for his own satisfaction. It was no rare virtue in a man—the nations had proved that— still it was worth having.

But on the military side there was a touch of the farcical. The men in the regiment who were dead, were as dead as any heroes; and the men who had been brave were as brave as heroes too. But now that the smoke had cleared away he began to see that his division had met, for the most part, half-strength battalions of pasty German boys and weary old men of the war. The French were weary, too, and the British; and the fresh divisions, full of fight, had smashed the deadlock of the war. That was the game, of course; to overwhelm the enemy, and no questions asked. But in this case it was nothing for the victors to get sentimental over; let the triumphant warriors reserve emotions for the families of the dead. What was done had had to be done, and it was well done. There had been no politics and no dishonesty; at least compared to other wars of candid American history. The discipline was good; the training as good as the time allowed; and behind the lines the mushroom organization had surpassed all hopes and all beliefs. With trackage, docks and warehouses, with depots, plants and training schools, from St. Nazaire to Chaumont they had built in steel and concrete Germany's despair. It was well done, but it was done, now; let them turn their faces to the making of a world to live in.

For him, from now on, life must be freer, more candid,

more genial; it must be gay, not with the senseless, frantic, gaiety of the Armistice, rather, profoundly, warmly full of fun, open to friendship and open talk forever found among all men and women who, like himself, were eager for a fuller life and were newly free. There were such men and women everywhere, such men at least. Now, on the afterdeck, he could see Sergeant Miller, Wendig, Feibleman, men who, for twenty years, had lived a block or two away from him in Midian and never a word between himself and them of understanding, of knowledge; moving, as they had, forever parallel; he, a River Street dude, and they, in the little drama of his narrow life, anonymous supers from the back part of town. But now with these men he had lived in filth and naked misery, had conquered fear and the slow palsy of despair. He knew their fortitude, their latent resourcefulness, their inexplicable fidelity, and if their views on drinking and on women, even on property outside the sacred precincts of the Company, were somewhat at variance with his tradition, he knew how small a fraction of the whole man such views were. They, in turn, felt that there was something to him besides a job and money, both inherited, and a high-class education superficially applied. What had happened between him and these men was happening to other thousands everywhere. They had learned how widely manhood is diffused, in what unlikely and unlooked-for corners it can flower; and toward mankind they could there-fore, to their good fortune, never be the same again.

About women also something had been learned; by himself at least: the natural genial brutality of the rank and file perhaps had less need of further illumination. He had made the discovery, possibly belated for any one except an American of the better class, that women also might profitably be regarded as human beings. He had learned in the hospital to hate some women, and with great benefit to himself and possibly to them, to tell them roundly what he thought of them. That would have been in the old days an unbelievable violation of their sanctity. But now it seemed natural: women were not ex officio divine. Once you knew that, you got so much more happiness from them, and they, in turn, were relieved, he had no doubt. After all, they had not asked for such an exalted, bloodless rôle.

Might that not have been the secret of the night when he loved Jeanne? That his eyes were open to her humanity? And might it not be the secret of his life with Julia: that he, in the artificial, lifeless virtue of his rearing, had only asked of her to stand as the symbol of his emasculate ideals? Woman's intrinsic weakness had made her wise even in America where her spoiled life had atrophied her cunning. Might it not be that Julia's instinct told her that she would do violence to his pallid virtue were she to appear in any guise save that of the worthy mate of a worthy young man of Midian, the apotheosis, as far as marriage was concerned, of River Street, of Yale, of Wyomensing.

If, that dark starry night in Paris, it had been Julia he dined with, might it not have been the same? For Julia was beautiful, willowy and soft with long smooth legs that shone in their silk stockings, with a quick light flush that almost escaped notice, and straight gray eyes that might hide depths that he, in his smug obtuseness, had never found the way to.

And about women he had learned in other ways. His thoughts ran back to that other world, strange, rigid and complete, that he had caught a glimpse of after the Armistice. He saw the first-class compartment and on the opposite seat, Jaclard's trim figure under the rackful of musettes.

"We arrive." Jaclard had pointed a gloved finger out the train window at the flat and heavy fields whose pattern of furrows rose almost imperceptibly from the willow-fringed canal. Among the willows' gray and motionless reflections a barge moved slowly, a miracle of shining black hull and neat white and red where a woman in a shawl was knitting. Ahead, along the towpath, fat horses leaned into their furry high-peaked collars. Then the engine's smoke and steam shut down across the view. There was nothing to be seen but a swift-moving bank and then the printed admonitions, "Defense de se pencher dehors." "Beware to lean out the window." An indomitable race, the French, he thought; they had written that English notice on ten thousand car windows and always got it wrong. The steam rolled back, beyond the canal the fields now mounted slightly to the gray sky.

"Over there," Jaclard said, "is our château. You will be disappointed." He stood up and started putting on his gray-blue overcoat with its flaming golden bombs of the artillery against the dark-red collar tabs.

"Why?"

"The word château," he raised his chin as he buttoned under

it. "You think of Blois and Chenonceaux. But we are at most petite noblesse. Allow me."

"Much obliged," he said. It was something to be helped on with his overcoat by even the smallest of nobility.

The stop was smooth and silent, a few gray houses and roofs of tile or thatch slid by and there were heavily burdened market women on the stone platform and an old porter with his strap and blouse who wrestled with their compartment door and raised his hat ceremoniously as he spoke Jaclard's name. With their bags suspended about him, he waddled crabwise behind them, retailing the village news.

Beyond the station of pink and yellow brick, a shining high-wheeled cart stood in the dreary stone-built village square. Its leather top was folded back and on the high seat a stout ruddy old man wore a square-topped derby and gaiters. He was stout and ruddy but as he touched his hat to Jaclard he was severe.

"Robert," Jaclard said. "Ça va? Ici un de mes amis, Monsieur Rand."

"Bo' jour, mon lieutenant." Robert touched his hat. With their luggage stowed behind, they sat in a row on the high seat. "Hooo!" Robert said. "Blaise! Va-t-en." His whip cracked like a twenty-two. The big sleek bay whisked his docked tail and bent to his work. They rattled on the narrow stone street between the stiff stone houses and the tiny shops, the archaic-looking citizens and little boys in belted black blouses. Jaclard was always speaking, saluting, hats were always coming off. They passed the sad, naked plane trees in front of the hotel de ville, a bistro, some farm-like buildings, and then their tires melted into the quiet of a country road. The poplars stretched ahead until their bare limbs made a gray mist on the distant crest. The narrow strips of plough and fallow made patterns running toward the low gray sky. A countryside at first glance without distinction, yet growing with slow potency, with elusive mournful beauty.

All the while Robert's voice rumbled, "jour de naissance . . . jour de naissance . . . Ça n'est pas bien fait, mon capitaine . . . du tout, du tout."

"He is scolding me," Jaclard said. "He feels the birthday present I sent my sister lacks elegance." He answered the coachman vigorously. The coachman's grumble rose, slowly died away and

then as they kept on down the road of naked poplars it broke
out in bursts, implacable iterations.

Over the rise, beyond a group of thatched farm buildings a
brick wall ended in stone posts and funereal urns. Blaise turned
in down a gravelled drive which showed at the end a rigid gray
façade whose black slate mansard rose above the clipped trees
of the avenue. Tall white French windows flanked the entrance
and above them other windows, also tall, gave onto minute iron
balconies; a dolphin fountain stood in the leafy circle that swung
the drive up to the low stone steps.

A thin little man in sideburns, sleeved waistcoat and green
baize apron, talking quietly but fast, helped them off with their
overcoats in the darkened marble hall. As he went back for the
bags Jaclard glanced at himself in the tall dusky mirror, and
smoothed his polished hair. "You, too, look very smart," he said.
"Now I present you to my mother. This way."

As the double door swung back the first effect was one of lofty
dignity; pilasters, tall windows, long curtains of crimson damask
But the high salon held a sediment of strange disorder. The gold
and damask chairs were littered with paper-covered books, with
gloves and garden tools and knitting; on an inlaid table a radio
set disgorged its contents; on a fragile tapestry sofa an ancient
pug rose up and barked.

In the centre of this flotsam he made out a small black-silk
figure in a high-back chair; her hair was pulled back under her
white cap, her dark, carved face was shrewd. Behind her the
sportive cherubs of the mantle looked enormous.

Jaclard's trim figure wound among chairs, footstools, tabouret
with skill. The pug came waddling toward him with rheumy
joy, a tiny bell on his brass collar tinkled. "Cher Maman," Jaclard bowed and kissed her hand and then bent down as her
arm passed around his neck. He straightened up. "Pardon—
mon ami, Lieutenant Rand." Madame Jaclard held out her hand.
He advanced to take it, encumbered by the suspicions of the pug
who sniffed his gaiters wheezily. He took the jewelled claw, he
had prepared himself for this moment. "Enchanté, Madame."
he said, "vous êtes bien aimable. . . ."

The small carved face smiled at him, the teeth beneath the dark
shrewd downy lip were white and pointed. Her black eyes
snapped, a burst of words overwhelmed him. Standing helpless

and awkward in front of the small black figure, erect and rigid and alive, he tried to grasp their meaning. Could this be French? Could it be Magyar or Polish? He found no clue. She stopped and nodded once at him with vigor and finality. He inclined his head with what he hoped was also vigor and finality. The big doors at the back end of the room swung open.

The first effect of Monsieur Jaclard was one of whiskers, of redness and of precarious crooked pince-nez. As he came down the room there was an ample stand-up collar, a ribbon in the broadcloth coat lapel, a pair of green long trousers stuffed into pigskin shooting gaiters. Behind him a pale mouse-like girl in black looked down as she walked and raised a slim hand to a bang of mouse-colored hair.

Under cover of Jaclard's talk he shook their hands. The father puffed and grunted, the daughter, a jeune fille of probably mature years, said "How do you do?" in precise school-girl English and let fall her cold hand.

"I explain," Jaclard said, "that you are not like other Americans." The girl smiled faintly.

"Is that good news or bad?"

"For them it is good. They have only known one other here. He did not leave a fortunate impression."

Monsieur Jaclard brushed up his beard, spoke briefly to his son, tilted his precarious pince-nez and glanced with fierce interrogation at this American.

"My father," Jaclard said, "inquired if you knew how to repair the radio." He pointed to the litter on the inlaid table. "He struggles with it."

"I'm afraid I don't, Hank. Please tell him."

"I will. But do not expect him to believe you." He gave his swift sharp grin. "You are an American."

Monsieur Jaclard was indeed unconvinced. He retired to the tapestry sofa where with hoarse mutters, "Loulou—mon vieux— mon bon petit vieux—Loulou—" he caressed the snuffling pug. The girl still faintly smiling sat down with a hoop of embroidery.

Among the ruins of the radio, Jaclard talked in a low voice. "Each time he dissembles this machine he has more that will not go back. Soon he will have two radios, but it would be preferable to have one that worked."

"I don't know a thing about them, Hank. Maybe he ought to

have new tubes." He lowered his voice. "I don't think I understood your mother. Is she French?"

"Completely, but she was speaking English."

"Oh." He paused. "That puts me out on a limb; don't it?"

"You are not resourceful," Jaclard said, "you must answer her in French."

The ship ran onward with a swift faint roll, a mere sense of silent sturdy speed whose level rocking was hardly felt or noticed except when he looked at the clean sharp horizon where a tail of smoke hung motionless, left by a vanished steamer making down the coast. The brown men on the lower deck, the officers locked in close rows on the rail watched it. They were now in the coastwise zone. They were coming home. The tail of smoke paled almost imperceptibly.

That afternoon the Jaclard's salon had held a group, old ladies in plumes and scarfs and narrow chiffon ruffles round the neck, old gentlemen in toga-like coats and dark gloves, a slim girl in tweeds who spoke to him in fluent English accents almost as difficult to catch as French, a pale boy incredibly too tall for his short trousers and little socks. In the centre Monsieur Jaclard's eldest brother, the head of the family, sat by the tea-table, still wearing his gray silk muffler whose fringed ends he used to wipe his shrewd but watery eyes and to dust the crumbs of cake from his explosive brown-dyed beard.

"And now, Thomas," Jaclard touched his elbow, "let me show you the garden. We shall go through the hall and get our hats."

They should have gotten their overcoats as well, he thought, as in the gray damp they walked among the vacant formal beds, the gravel paths, the terrace steps and balustrades and benches of the wet gray garden. He looked at Jaclard's trim blue figure, his narrow ruddy cheeks and high-bridged nose; a hardy race these French.

"Hank," he said, "you can stand it but I'm damned cold out here." He had also been damned cold in the salon but all the family relatives were beginning to warm it up.

"Five minutes more," Jaclard said. "Then we return."

"All right," he said. "But what's the idea?"

"A family conference."

"Oh," he said. "But oughtn't you to be there?"

"I? No. I know you already." He grinned. "They confer regarding you."

"Well, what the hell?" he said.

"In this case," Jaclard said, "a mere formality. You are an American and not subject to human laws."

"But what about this other bird that was here before?"

"It will have no effect. You come as a friend. But you would be interested to hear of him." Jaclard pointed to a moist wooden bench slightly sheltered by bare lilac bushes from the wind. "Here," he said, "we can be comfortable. A cigarette?"

"He was an older man in the Red Cross." He snapped his lighter shut. "He came here to convalesce. We have a Norman church, important, I believe, but little known, that he had heard about. He lived *en pension* just outside the village with a lady and her daughter, of good family. We know them well."

"So he made a pass at the girl, I suppose, on the strength of *La Vie Parisienne.*"

"By no means," Jaclard waved negation with his cigarette and flashed a smile. "He was a man of honor. It was that," he added, "that made him so incomprehensible to the people here."

"They fell in love, each with the other," he said. "She was a widow, her husband was killed in the Champagne, a captain in the chasseurs, I knew him. She was young and charming. She was intelligent, gracious, sincere. A type of young French woman. The American also was charming," he said, "but an older man, an architect. He was also honest. At the start he told her that at home he had a wife who for some years had meant little to him. He had four children." Jaclard paused, looked up, inviting comment.

"That's a tough situation, Hank," he said, "but I still don't see where he was to blame."

"It was his next proposal. There had been between them no, as you say, no affair. So then when his leave was up he came to her with an air of triumph and told her he had made up his mind. He could get a divorce and marry her." Jaclard paused again.

"Well, Hank," he said. "Go on. What did he do wrong there? Of course it's hard on the children. I always think that."

"You say that," Jaclard said, "and I esteem you to that extent. But are you capable of guessing what she told him? She told him that she loved him and that she would have been honored to be his mistress. She said she had supposed that he loved her and set a value on her character. But now it seemed he considered her a woman capable of breaking up his children's home, a mere adventuress, self-seeking and ruthless.

"And so," Jaclard said, "they parted, he horrified and she—" his hard, sharp face showed a swift and light, but profound flash of pity. "My mother says that she sits looking out the window." He glanced at the wrist watch under his white cuff. "We may return." On the gravel walk he took his arm. "And so," he said, "I tell my family that they must not misjudge you." His small dark mustache bristled in a half-smile. "I assure them you are a man of honor incapable of proposing anything but a liaison."

In the salon he felt that as he entered, without seeming to do so, they all turned toward him.

"Vous avez eu une jolie promenade, monsieur?" they said.

"Oui, merci, c'est jolie, le jardin." They understood him. That was pretty good.

The elder Monsieur Jaclard tightened the scarf around his bulging neck. "Vous nous donnerez beaucoup de plaisir, monsieur," he said, "si vous dinerez chez nous, le mardi, à sept heures."

He attempted a bow and wondered whether he was grinning. "Merci, Monsieur Jaclard. Avec plaisir."

On the deck of the transport behind him, he heard a murmur, then cheering. Below him the brown men made a surge and hung three-deep out on the rail. "It's Long Island," they said. "It's Long Beach." "It's Coney Island." "It's Rockaway." "See them big hotels?" "The old U. S.," they said. "Oh, baby!" "Oh, boy, oh boy, oh boy, oh boy!"

Out in the well-remembered Midian freight yards the train slowed down. Through the compartment door, he could see in the main body of the car the men slinging on their packs; under the dense tobacco smoke some still slapped cards down playing setback, and in the aisle, a gang were finishing a bottle.

"Sergeant Miller."

"Yes, sir," the sergeant's square dogged face was in the doorway.

"Come in," he said. Littered back yards and the railroad
Y. M. C. A. crept by. "Well, Sergeant," he said, "this about
winds it up, I guess."

"That's right, sir," the sergeant said.

"We march straight to the Armory," he said, "and turn in our
property."

"Yes, sir."

"Are any of the men too drunk to march?"

"No, sir; not exactly."

He looked out the window impatiently. There were the gold
letters of O'Hara's saloon, and the dingy lace curtains of the
Bon Ton Hotel.

"What's the matter with this train?" he said. "Good Lord!
Listen to that."

Ahead there was an immense, inextricable conflict of brass
bands and a swelling roar. "Good Lord!" He grinned at the
sergeant sheepishly. "Here, help me to get this window open."

The train-shed was a mad, resounding bedlam through which
the engine slowly ploughed. Then under the window, wild hands
were reaching up to him; wild mouths seemed to shout without
a sound. There was a jumble of Templars' ostrich plumes, of
flags, of fire helmets, and the red pants of the Epworth Zouaves.
In their gray shirts, state cops sweated and grinned and pushed
to no avail. And all the time the hands were running under his
and clinging and the bands were tangling in the roar.

As he climbed down the car steps, his father's dark-gray flannel
suit was butting through the crowd, his panama knocked askew.
Why, he was getting bald.

"Father!" he shouted. The crowd gave ground and flung the
two of them together.

His father hung to him and studied him.

"How are you, Father?" he shouted. "How's every one? Are
they all right?"

His father nodded. On his lapel he wore a large red, white
and blue rosette and a long white streamer with "Marshal"
printed on it. A portion of the crowd surrounded them with
great appreciation. "Well, Mr. Rand," they said, "how's it seem
to have the boy back?" "Pretty good, hey?" "I'll say it's pretty
good."

"We've got to get out of here," his father shouted. "Mr.

Trimble will show you." He pointed to where Mr. Good Doggie Trimble in the dark uniform of a home guard captain was flailing industriously through the press, tall, red and absurd under his stiff new campaign hat.

Mr. Trimble came up and struck Tommy's shoulder a blow. "By God," he said, "Tommy." He jerked a thumb. "You'll be the first unit, of course. Right across the tracks and up the ramp for the express wagons."

"All right, sir." He nodded, grinned, saluted Captain Trimble solemnly. "Sergeant!"

From the heart of an immense number of stout, elderly women Sergeant Miller emerged. "Yes, sir."

"Form the company." He was solemn and military. "Form the company" was good; a second lieutenant and half a platoon, all that was left of the boys from Midian.

The sergeant's whistle sounded, the roar of the crowd subsided to respectful murmurs.

"Fall in," the sergeant said. "Take off them rifle covers."

Up in the blinding sunlight in the street it really seemed incredible; they marched between the roaring sidewalks under flags. The Omar Temple band in front of them competed with the fife-and-drum corps of the Moose's Orphanage that followed close behind; and farther back there was the white of Templar's plumes, the glint of fire engines and the blare of other bands that burst into music as they turned the corner from the railroad station into Center Street. Along the sidewalks, names were shouted and handkerchiefs were waving and hats were coming off in honor of the flag, the old flag of the Midian Fencibles that was being carried before them by a detail from the depot company. Overhead, banners, violently inscribed, were passing by. OUR HEROES, MIDIAN WELCOMES YOU . . . THIS IS MIDIAN'S DAY . . . OUR CONQUERING HEROES. Behind them the fifes of the Moose's orphans shrieked, on the sidewalks girls squealed and jumped and yodelled, men and boys were howling. Another banner passed. THE FENCIBLES—FIRST IN WAR. From crowded office windows paper was coming down, klaxons were breaking loose in side streets. And on both sides of him the faces made a wall; faces grinning, beaming, nodding, laughing, shouting with great glee, proud, stupid faces of old men, the sullen and appraising eyes of high school boys, fat women wallowing in emotion, and the faces of girls bobbing like painted egg-shells on a stream. What did they know, these faces? How could they understand? He searched them for a sign. The wall of faces stretched ahead unbroken. There was nothing to do but march ahead through this frenzied and pathetic farce.

Their shouts were in his ears. " Hey, boys!" "Hey, boys!" "Didn't you give them hell though?" "Hey there, Lieutenant!" "I guess we showed 'em something, hey?" "So long, Kaiser Bill."

A monstrous thought took hold of him. Suppose they were to say to all these faces, he and the line of men behind him, "Hey, folks, hello yourself. Yes, folks, here we are, and here's the way it was if you want to know. Here's the way it was, folks. Here it is." And then the rifles would begin to crack and hand gre- nades would slowly tumble into smoke and flame. A monstrous thought. He looked surreptitiously back at the line behind him. No, they were lapping it up, marching well, but carelessly, and grinning over their rifle stocks. Another banner overhead: The bravest of the brave.

Out on River Street, the crowds were thinner; the people merely clapped and shouted. Moored in the stream, the flatboats, elaborately bedecked, tooted their peanut whistles.

Here was the narrow gray front of his Aunt Clara's. Of his Aunt Clara's. Evil thoughts vanished. He searched the windows through the maple leaves, but there was only Christobel's red hair and freckled face. He caught her eye and smiled. The two flags in her hands were agitated wildly.

Passing Linden Street, he saw the bulge of the bay window and hoped for a sight of young Sam and of Susan Tarr.

At first the high stone steps before his grandfather's seeemed simply a mass of colors and of waving flags, and then he saw them all. Julia, tall, white, and still against the doorway holding the waistband of a boy who stood on the balustrade, a grown-up, grave little boy whose eyes looked into his. Under her arm, his little daughter bounced. Beside them, Uncle Mun, in voluminous pongee, was wrestling with his mother who was struggling fiercely to get down the steps where Miss Trimble and Mrs. Trimble and Miss Ba-ba Lamb stood waving exultant flags. In the shaded vestibule his grandfather reached a hand to Sam- uel; he heaved up from his chair and stood with his straw hat pressed against his dark coat and the sunlight on his thick neat iron hair.

Then they were gone, leaving him deeply stirred, and yet still distant, as though by a strongly moving tableau, by a deep but ancient memory. He marched behind the colors in front of the platoon, the shouts of friends on the sidewalk in his ears. Was he so hardened then, so numb?

.   .   .   .   .   .

He was perched on the twin bed nearest to the window. The white room's pale yellow wall paper was shaded except for where a shaft of sun came through half-closed blinds. Through this crack he could see Tad and Jane and the nurse, a new one, peaceful and almost motionless on the bank under the locust trees. Beyond the trees he could see the river, peaceful, too, and shining blue under the bold June sky, and the little farmhouses, white and sharp among the bright greens of the hills of the farther shore. This was a beautiful town, a beautiful river.

His polished leggings and tight khaki knees stretched in front of him. With a hand on the brass rod of the foot, he hung high-perched and languid on the narrow bed. His feet were tired from marching on the unaccustomed asphalt; his hand was tired from shaking many triumphant impassioned hands; and all the rest of him was weary from the beating of their questions, of their proprietary and self-congratulatory interest. The war was over now for him, its end was signallized by this inept and well-meant carnival; a carnival whose very inappropriateness had served to mark the end of dangers, miseries, and strange high satisfactions, and at the same time to reduce them to their proper scale. Soon they would be the dream, those nights and days of terror and of resolution; the life of this pretty and familiar town would close on him and he would almost forget that such strange things had been and that he had been in the heart of them.

But whether or not he thought about them or remembered them, their mark was on him to support and inspire him, to give him the freedom of a brave new world.

Brave and new it was in spite of everything. This town was beautiful and all the members of his family had seen him now to wrap him, each in a different way, in strength and love. Julia

was beautiful, fuller, more vigorous, more knowing—that work
in the canteen at the station among all the troop trains that came
by. It was a brave new world and she was part of it. She would
be coming now; she had stopped a moment to see the new cook
about supper, then she would come out through the dining room
and up the stair. He could see her now. He could see her coming; her legs, long, delicate, and shining, the honey-colored stockings showing to the knees under the new kind of short-skirted
dress that she was wearing, a dress of thin white chiffon that let
the moving of her flanks appear and followed her small delicate
houlders and small breasts. And she was brave and good besides.
What had been the matter with him? He heard her step on
the stair. He turned his head, he would watch her come in
through the door.

She paused. "Are you up there?" she said.

"Come up."

She came through the door looking as he had seen her in his
mind. "I suppose you want to change," she said. "I'll go right
down."

"Stay here," he said.

"I must go down," she said. "I heard the children calling."
She went to the dressing-table. "Here are all your things. I
suppose you want to change. Will you put on your uniform
again?"

"Oh, no," he said, "I've had it on long enough."

"I suppose so, but you look so imposing. You really do. Aren't
you allowed to wear it any more?"

"Yes, for two weeks," he said, "but there's no sense in it."

"Well, then," she said, "I'll see about your clothes."

"I'll find them," he said.

"They're in the closet," she said, "I had them brought down
from the cedar closet as soon as I got your telegram. That was
the first thing I did."

"That's a dashing dress," he said. "Hot dog!"

"It's the style," she said. "It's just whatever you're used to."

"I don't want to get used to it. Is your hair bobbed?"

"No, it's just tucked up under. I thought you wouldn't like it."

"I wouldn't mind," he said. "I think you've changed."

"Oh, no," she said, "you're just not used to the style."

"Yes I am; we've been seeing girls all the way home."

"You're just not used to it on me."

"You've changed," he said, "and I have too."

"Yes," she said, "I suppose to have fought for a cause like that and gained the victory must give the men that do it something that no one else has."

"It's not that. It's not anything like that!"

"I have often been afraid," she said, "that when you came back I might not be up to you. Such a wonderful experience!"

"Such a wonderful experience?"

"I know," she said, "there are awful things in war; I suppose that's why the cause makes all the difference. I knew that I was missing that. Of course, I did the best I could down in the canteen, but it's not the same."

"I bet you were grand," he said. "How did it go?"

"It was a fine experience," she said. "Some of the men would sometimes—I mean until they knew who you were. But most of them were nice, and nearly all the officers."

She stood now with her hands on the foot of the bed looking down at him seriously. The sunlight fell on her ash-blonde hair, curled strangely back of her ears, and on her pale delicate face. In her flimsy short dress of white, she was tall and soft and slender. She was white and fine and beautiful. He took her hands.

"Julia, we must love each other." He pressed his face against them, they were soft and slim. "We must be happy," he said, "we must have lots of fun."

Her two hands closed over his, her voice was low. "Tommy, dear," she said, "no one could love you more than I do." Her lips were on his hair. "I think God is very good to give you back to me."

A flow of longing, desperate and determined and yet despairing swept him. Like a blind thing he thrust toward her under her lowered head. Almost to himself, in a choking voice, he was muttering her name. For a second she gave, then turned gently rigid. Her hand still held his, but her body seemed to vanish. His face, absurdly, met the cold brass bars.

He felt that the eyes he raised to her were hard and hot. They met her bright forced smile. "Tommy, dear," she said, "I must really go, I promised the children."

He still held to her hands, "Oh, damn the children!"

Her pale lips parted with the shock. "Tommy!" her voice was hard and choked.

"Never mind," he said, "don't say it. I just meant that I love you."

"You didn't say——"

"Stay here," he said, "don't go."

Her hands were almost wrestling against him now. "Tommy," she said, "I must go. The children— Do you know what time it is? It's the middle of the day. The whole town will be coming here to see you."

"Let them come," he said, "they don't own us. Don't we own ourselves?"

She stopped the struggle. In a firm grieved voice she whispered, "Please." Her cold hands slid away from him.

As she went out the door her footfalls sounded slowly on the hardwood floor; and yet to him it seemed as though, still tall and cool and slim and delicate, she were running with great speed.

CHAPTER LIII

DOWNTOWN there was plenty for him to do. "We don't want to hurry you," his father had said the evening of the day that he had gotten home, sitting square and a little incongruous in the cretonne chair under the Maxfield Parrish in the living room. "Certainly we don't want to hurry you and if you and Julia would like to go off for a little honeymoon together——"

"Oh, no," he said, "I guess not, Father. Of course, I haven't talked to her."

"With these new coal properties that we've acquired, there's plenty to do," his father said. "You'll find that out when you get down there. When I look back," he said, "I sometimes don't know how I managed to get through the last two years. But then," he said, "I don't know how you have either." His father's hair was thin, his face was lined and pouchy under the eyes, but his smile was still child-like and warm. When he smiled a different man appeared, a man who was young and kind and rooted deep in happiness. But then, as always, the smile was almost instantly withdrawn. "Your grandfather cannot be active at all any more. To-day, when you saw him, he made a great effort."

"I know," he said, "and even so."

"Yes," he said, "you can see how it is." Sitting dark and firm in the frivolous flowered chair his father looked straight ahead. He cleared his throat.

"My idea is to put you in charge of sales, all sales, practically the whole business as it originally was; then I will take care of the mining properties. That's the part that needs to be watched.

"I am confident," his father said, "that in acquiring them we made the right move. Your grandfather, you remember, was opposed, but naturally, at his age— And we have been able to show a substantial profit. We set up separate books for them which you will probably like to see.

"But the mining business," his father said, "is one that requires

very careful supervision no matter how good your managers are.
I should like to be able to spend more time on it, get down to
the properties." He stood up a trifle stiffly. "I must go, it's eleven
o'clock." His heavy watch-case opened with a tiny click. "Ten
minutes past. I expect Julia will have something to say about
this," he turned pink and shy, "your first night at home."

"That's all right, Father. I'll walk down the bank with you a
little way."

Down on the bank, under a street light between the silent
river and the silent town, his father finally stopped. "This will
do," he said. "Good night. We really must consider Julia."

"Good night, Father." His father didn't move.

"There is one thing," his father said, "that I wish you would
set your mother's mind at rest about."

"What's that?" he said uneasily.

"Why you were not promoted," he said. "Of course, I understand."

"Nobody got promoted over there."

"That's what I tell your mother."

"Everybody was too busy, and they didn't want to break up the
organizations."

"That's what I tell your mother."

"I have seen lieutenants commanding battalions," he said.
"Matter of fact, at the end I commanded the company myself."

"It preys on her mind," his father said. "Of course, it's all
right now, but during the war some of the things she said about
the government might, if reported, have proved most embarrassing. Fortunately, you were decorated; but even so your
mother is far from satisfied.

"For a while," his father said, "everything seemed to be all
right." He gave his warm confiding smile. "And then Gus
Ringler's boy—you know Heinrich, the fat one—came home a
captain."

"Sure I know Heinrich; he's all right."

"Oh, yes, he was in some automobile corps. Well, you might
speak to her."

"You know," he said, "when we marched by this morning
mother didn't seem to see me. She seemed to be having some
kind of rough-house with Uncle Mun."

"She was trying to get down on the sidewalk, I believe; but

your Uncle Mun was convinced that she was going to march with you up the street."

"By God," he said—his father looked startled—"I mean I bet she was. He ought to have let her go."

Next morning in the office there was another small ovation. Mr. Riser, dry and crisp and gleaming, met him and his father at the door. Mr. Wherrill, the hairless little office manager, was close behind him; and then in order of precedence, they came up and shook his hand, beginning with the pale old bookkeepers, in gray alpaca jackets, and ending with silk-legged young ladies that he had never seen before. Then Mr. Riser, in the centre of the circle was uttering well-phrased platitudes at him and placing an imitation jade desk-clock in his hand.

Fortunately the spirit of Commencement Day at Wyomensing had descended on him and he had offered brief, but fluent nonsense in return. The desk clock now sat flanked by three black rubberoid French telephones, by his grandfather's enormous pig-bristled pen-wiper and paper-weights of carved and polished coal, and by a copper ash receiver of a new kind that at a touch opened like a small monster of the deep to receive the ashes into its nether regions.

His father had made sure that this private office would be worthy of his son's new dignity. The walls were freshly painted a light cream; the calendars and faded photographs of tipples had been replaced by a first impression of an etching of the Rand Coal Company's Drift Mouth Number One, done by the Art Department of their advertising agency. And on the floor, there was a remarkable imitation of an oriental rug in inlaid linoleum.

At the close of business he used to stop each day and see his grandfather. His grandfather now sat in his private office in a new-fangled chair that he was very proud of and complained of bitterly. It had various screws and ratchets which Samuel or Levi Mistletoe were always being called on to adjust, although the new position never proved quite satisfactory. He kept a light gray flannel rug across his knees, perhaps to conceal his carpet slippers. The rest of him was as immaculate as ever, white collar open at the throat, heavy blue silk tie, well-cut coat and waistcoat. His hair and beard, thick, neatly trimmed, almost iron gray, were still the same except for a touch of whiteness around the

chin; but his skin had paled and showed a delicate, faintly unearthly, pearly sheen.

At first he used to tell his grandfather what had gone on that
day, re-orders, inquiries, new business; and his grandfather would
respond so courteously, so appropriately that it was some time
before he realized that, for the senior partner, Rand and Company held no further interest. Only once was the gray static
pearly figure roused.

"The mines," he said. "A great mistake."

"But they've shown a profit up to the last quarter."

"In the war everything did." His neat beard stirred. "In the
war your Uncle Mun showed a profit." He looked out of the
window at the river. "Electric power," he said, "oil fuel, and then
labor; especially labor, they've had it all their own way."

"I don't like labor," his grandfather said, "I never have. It's a
mistake to be in a business that's involved with labor."

"But, Grandfather, the men that I was with in France were
labor, I suppose, and most of them were great fellows, remarkable."

"At all events," his grandfather said, "they felt that way
about you."

"Where did you hear that?" he said.

"Samuel."

"Samuel? What's he know about it?"

"He has a niece that's engaged to one of your men, Feibleman."

"Feibleman?" he said. "Well I'll be damned! If Feibleman
thinks I'm all right, I guess the rest do."

"If men are in a tight place and properly led, they will do very
well." His grandfather looked at him approvingly. "Any man
will. Look at General Chinese Gordon. I understand he made
very passable soldiers out of the Chinese; but when the war was
over, undoubtedly they became Chinamen again."

He laughed. "Maybe they kept something out of it though,
too. Anyhow, I'm not going to be the Chinaman I was."

"Yes," his grandfather said, "you've changed." He eyed him
seriously. "You swear more."

"I know; I've got to watch myself."

"Don't. There is altogether too much watching in this family.
The great thing," he said, "is to marry girls of proper ancestry;
then you don't have to watch the children. Take your mother.

Comes from excellent people back in New York State. Excellent people."

"I thought the Worralls came from right around here."

"Your grandmother. Yes, Judge Worrall was a distinguished man; and Claire Worrall was a remarkable woman. You never knew her, I suppose."

"I just remember her."

"She was a MacKenzie from Baltimore.

"The way to get people that amount to something," his grandfather said, "is to breed them. I used to be quite a man for trotting horses in my younger days; I used to follow the Grand Circuit," his grandfather bristled his beard, "until I got tired of looking at the people in the stands."

"But how about Napoleon and Lincoln, for instance?"

"Nothing before," his grandfather said, "and nothing after. Geniuses. It happens on the track as well, but no one would breed a stable on those lines.

"You take us," his grandfather said. "Nothing wonderful; but for two hundred years, reasonably reliable, capable, self-respecting people."

His grandfather showed fatigue. He took a breath and rallied to conclude. "I have known excellent people in every walk of life but when you get outside proved blood lines, you don't know where you're at." He shook his head. "No, you will always have trouble with labor in the end."

He thought of that talk with his grandfather one day in late November when the last leaves scurried down to sift in the cold dust and the river seemed to stiffen and turn sullen under a steely sky. Long lines of people, a fringe almost unbroken, stood in the harsh dry wind along the river bank, along the street that led out to the cemetery to watch the hearse and old John Rand's big silver-handled coffin pass. All kinds of people. He watched their undistinguished faces through the window of the carriage; anonymous America, the silent majority. They stood wrapped in curiosity and uneasy respect to watch the last uninteresting conventionalities of a man they never knew.

How much, he wondered as he looked out the window, had these silent watchers been drawn by some faint notion of his grandfather's integrity? How much by the mystery which his grandfather's shy fastidiousness had thrown about himself and

his career? How much by simple American enthusiasm for ability and power and for the wealth which they created? In any
case, the fact was that there had been no turn-out for a funeral in
Midian to equal this since Senator Beaver died. In this sense then,
his grandfather was finally brought to an equality with the one
departed Midianite whom he least resembled, particularly in his
attitude toward these assembled citizens who now lined the curb
to do him honor and, by their numbers, to raise his funeral in
the traditions of the town to parity with that of the Senator, "a
man," his grandfather said, "whom I regard as the most egregious
mountebank and scoundrel of our time."

They were coming now down near the railroad tracks. Even
the railroad men came out of the saloon to watch them pass.
Soon they would cross the bridge over the canal and climb the
hill, and then soon it would all be over. There was nothing to
regret; one could say that. He had had a long and strong and
satisfying life; had done what he set out to do; had lived till
two great-grandchildren could call him by his name; and died
without pain, and instantly; a fine and firm old gentleman to the
last. Beyond the railroad tracks the waters of the canal were
black and still.

And yet he wished his grandfather could have lived, could have
lived as long as he himself. There was a bond between them.
Left over from a generation of men he had scarcely known, his
grandfather seemed, to the last, freer, fresher, stronger than all
the rest of Midian; a generation of strong simple feelings and
simple strong convictions and devoid of sentimentality, officious-
ness, and nonsense.

Did his grandfather know this, know how he felt about him?
Perhaps; for certainly he talked to him more freely than to any
one except perhaps to his Aunt Clara. "Yes, sir, Mr. Tommy,"
Levi said to him, "Always glad when you come by. Whenever
you been here, old gentleman acts like he feel mighty good." He
had hardly missed a day since he got back from France. Every
day they had talked for perhaps an hour. But he wished his
grandfather had lived; there was still much to say.

The hired hack rose up to the bridge over the canal. Ahead
of them was the settlement of dreary houses, and on the hill the
glint of marble through branches of brown tattered trees. Beside
him he heard a low choked murmur.

"Aunt Clara!" he said. Her fine face was set, but there was a childish tremor to her lower lip. "I know, I know," he said. He took her black gloved hand. Could he think of nothing but himself on this last ride? Here was a lonely woman who had lost her father.

"Oh, these black gloves!" she said; and then began to cry, slow, uncontrollable weeping; no handkerchief and no concealment, head erect.

"There is no use to stop crying," he said, "no use, because there is nothing that any one can say. It was all for the best, the ideal death. He was too old to live much longer. What good is it to say that? Even I am going to be so lonely that I don't know what I'll do. I've just been wishing that he could have lived as long as I do. I wish that we could have grown up together. Well then," he said, "I can guess how it must be for you."

"It's not that," she whispered.

"What?" he said. "Uncle Fitz. I know. I know."

Her handkerchief came out. She blew her nose hard, then rolled her handkerchief in a ball and rubbed her eyes with it like a little boy.

"All right," she said, "no more." She started tugging at her gloves. "I am going to take these off," she said, "I can keep my hands inside my pockets."

He made a gesture toward her with his heavy overcoat. "You can keep one hand inside my pocket."

She rolled her glove off and dropped it on the seat, and slid her hand into his pocket next to his. Touching hands lightly in the warm woolly pocket they climbed the hill to the cemetery.

CHAPTER LIV

WHAT had become of that bright brave new life that he had looked for as the fruit of the world's long suffering, of the nations' battle for redemption? With his grandfather's death the door had finally closed forever, so it seemed, upon an older and a hardier race. Others had gone during the war or shortly after it; Old Captain Mottley, alleged by the godly to have repented on his deathbed, but reported through the underground channels of Midian's backstairs as defiant and salacious to the last; old Mrs. Ringler whose ruddy beaming stupid silence left a far greater gap than they expected; and Gus Ringler, a gray sad mountain on his ormolu inlaid bed, puzzled and inconsolable about his wife and about the brewery, and sending out for people, some-times late at night, to whom he would explain how beer was coming back next year.

His grandfather was the last except for Samuel and Levi Mistletoe, and those two had retired to other quarters of the town on annuities provided by his grandfather's will. From time to time, strangely disguised in handsome business suits, they came to call and to talk of the old days and all those ever-mounting vanished glories. In the spring Levi spaded in Julia's garden. And once a week the year round he took the trolley-car out to the cemetery where he kept the family plot in order and Mr. Fitz-Greene's grave. The disputes between him and the cemetery superintendent were unending. As if the vanished glories had been their only sustenance, Levi and Samuel faded and shrank perceptibly. For them, too, now the time would not be long.

Meanwhile the old house of pressed-brick, high mounting brownstone steps and colored mansard slates stood empty, its big bay windows blinded by sheets of tight-drawn yellowing paper. The grass stood high around the iron stag; and inside, the Numidian maid, the silver George and Martha Washington, the knight in armor on the newel post slumbered amidst swathed pictures and rolled rugs and dusty floors that would echo sadly

496

to a tread. Nobody wanted such houses any more, nor any house
down in that part of town where now the noise and fumes of
motor cars cut off the river and the view and all tranquillity.
People were building now far up in the country underneath the
mountains; and near the Heisdick farm—they still called it that
though Mr. and Mrs. Heisdick died of the flu the second year of
the war and their bad son in Honduras inexplicably had been
killed with the Gordon Highlanders on the Somme—people had
built a country club and a lot of pert girls and snappily flannelled
young men that no one ever heard of were dancing nearly every
night. Sometimes when he was up late at the farm with his Aunt
Clara coming home they would hear squeals and aimless
whoops and see dim figures, two and two, among the bunkers
on the golf course.

This was the war generation he was told. Porky Montross explained it all. One night his first winter at home he had been
sitting in the living room trying to decide whether to read a book
called "The Problem of Coal" or, the poems of Rupert Brooke;
out front a car had stopped, then on the flagstones there was a
sound of a man's steps, measured and even, but differing from
each other—a light step, then a heavy dead one. He was at the
door before Porky could ring the bell. The small mouth and the
round, pink face were smiling at him. "Porky," he said, a wave
swept over him; he grasped the front of the new tweed overcoat.

In the living room he jingled the ice in his glass. "When did
you get home, Porky?"

"This afternoon. Boat docked yesterday, then I had to go down
to the Army Building to get my discharge."

"The last time we saw each other it was different. What was
the name of that place?"

"Cheppy. Isn't it on your citation?"

"Oh, that. No, that was another place called Charpentry."

"That was a queer life; I believe I'm going to miss it."

"You lawyers always have your paper work."

"Paper work is the basis of a happy life, but for perfection you
need other things." Porky looked at his glass. "Is this what
they're drinking here now?"

"Well, yes."

Poray's face fell into grave lines. Gingerly he projected his
snub nose over the edge of the glass and quickly withdrew it.

"Something will have to be done about this; the country cannot go on this way."

Ever since, Porky had come up to spend the evening once a week; usually not for supper; he had no confidence in Julia's transient cooks; and with the children, he had small resources after they had lost interest in his cork foot.

"It's really not cork," he said, "it's a special composition; they make it in England." He tapped the foot with his other shoe to make a mournful, unearthly sound. "Cost a fortune," he said. "You've no idea what a difference. I never use my French foot now, except for ushers' dinners and routine legal work. The man lies on his stomach to watch you walk; in the end he says to the man who takes the moving pictures, 'Wimple, I believe this gentleman's foot is quite as good as His Grace's foot.' He says that to all the customers; I heard him in the dressing room, so I said, 'Which foot?' Confusion. Explanations."

Julia reading the "Forum" under the tall lamp in the corner looked up.

"Was that before you were at the Peace Conference or after?"

"Before. I couldn't have got through the Peace Conference on my French foot. Too tiring to dance on."

Julia smiled with an effort. "But it must have been a wonderful experience. I'm reading about it here."

"It was. It was like being little Nemo in Slumberland."

"Pork," he set down his glass. "How did you get the job?"

"On account of my French."

He picked up his glass again. "How did you get the job?"

"There was a fellow from Princeton."

"What did you do?"

"I was in a room at the Crillon. Everybody there was from Princeton except one Harvard man for appearances and a fellow from Kansas State Teachers to do the work."

"I suppose that was on account of Wilson; all his old pupils coming home to roost."

"What did you really do?" Julia said. "Did you see anything of President Wilson? How was he over there? Magnificent, I suppose."

"All except the shoes. He never could get important-looking shoes. He had the top hat and the morning coat but the shoes were the shoes of my old professor of Constitutional Law."

Julia flushed. "Really I think it's not right to talk like that. After all he did, and the tragedy. Don't you think he was a great man?"

"Yes," he said. "I do, except for his shoes."

Julia returned to the magazine.

"Well, Pork," he said, "it doesn't look so good, this peace of yours."

"It's no good. The Polish Corridor, and a lot of cocky little new nations; Austria, a little crippled monster. But what sort of peace ought to have been made?"

"Free trade, limitation of armaments, no passports, democratic governments."

"All good. But who's to enforce the scheme?"

"The League of Nations."

"Where will the League get its power? It must come from somewhere. No nation though will surrender the necessary power."

"All right. But the League of Nations is better than nothing."

"A lot better. But not in the way intended. It provides a good place where the boys can get together without causing a diplomatic incident. It gets them acquainted and so helps to promote a modus vivendi; like the Midian Kiwanis. But it's useless to expect more."

"I don't know. But it's hard to feel that nothing has been gained by the war."

"If I could only feel that nothing had been lost. You ought to have seen that Peace Conference gang. And behind them stand the different peoples, all ruined, incurably bitter. In the first relief of the Armistice there was a flash of response to Wilson's idealism but in the fundamental situation there never was a chance for a good peace. The dogs returned to their vomit."

"What's the answer?"

"I don't know. In the end the only thing I could think of was to ask Jeanne in to lunch."

"Oh, yes. How was she?"

Julia did not look up from the magazine, but she was listening.

"Fine, she's staying on; on the hospital's permanent staff."

"I guess she's pretty good." His voice was hearty. The ocean would still lie between them: safely.

"Yes," Porky said, "and something of a person besides. The war has brought her out."

"It brought out lots of people."

"Only Americans. Because we were hardly in it. It ruined the real participants."

Julia looked up. "Do you mean that you and Tom weren't in it?"

"A mere interlude—just enough to wake us up. But when you get year after year of it like those fellows; the strain and all your friends being slowly killed." Porky took a sip from his glass. "You come out a dead man. This is better whiskey, Tom."

"I'm glad you like it."

"I don't like it. It's not good. Merely beter than that first. New bootlegger?"

"Two of my men. I run into them at the Legion meetings. They're doing pretty well."

"Who are they?"

"Wendig, he was my bomber, and Feibleman."

"Tell them to come and see me."

"Hear that, Julia?" he said. "Our adjutant is pleased. Or no," he said, "it's no use, Pork; they already have a lawyer: Myrow, in the Sixth Ward."

"Myrow is the man. Protection guaranteed. But is this their territory up here?"

"No, it's Dalvaney's, but I fixed it up. He gets his cut."

"What are you talking about?" Julia said.

Porky pursed his lips. "About our national genius for organization. Already we live under a government outside the law— probably more honest and undoubtedly more efficient. But merciless."

"Do you mean those bootleggers run the town?"

"They will as soon as the big money rolls in."

"I told Tom he ought not to have anything to do with them. We should respect our laws."

"If we respect prohibition we can't get rid of it. It will be successful." He drank.

"But," she said, "what about the younger generation?"

"They call themselves the war generation, I believe."

Tommy took a drink. "Because they weren't in the war. They are desperate and doomed because of the great tragedy they missed. Whereas, the men who were in the war have settled down to what they were before, if anything more so."

"Hold on," Porky said. "Do we see any hope of a better world, of even a possible world?"

"It's fading."

"Yes. But we can stand it because we're grown up. And when we were young we had our chance for dreams. They haven't."

"We had our chance, but nothing came of it."

"That generally happens. But the chance is indispensable. Youth is a tragic period; a boy or a girl needs the chance for dreams to weather it. Do I grow sentimental in my cups?"

"My youth wasn't tragic," Julia said.

"You are fortunate," Porky said, "or were."

"Well," Julia said, "I don't see any excuse for the way they carry on; the way they drink and the way they dance."

"The hip flask," Porky said, "was imposed on them by law, and the dancing started before the war. You and Tom just didn't get around." Porky swayed in his chair making ardent gestures with his arms. "The Bunny Hug and the Grizzly Bear." He sat back gravely. "Already we create a Golden Age before the war. The South did it, England's doing it now. Only the French don't. Not having ever deluded themselves with any golden future, they don't find it necessary to console themselves with any golden past."

"Good boy, Pork," he said, "you see this whiskey's not so bad."

"Be quiet, Tom," Julia said. She turned to Porky, "Go on."

"If I only could," he said; "I'm my own worst enemy. I put things so well at times that people lose patience with me for not doing it always. Not," he said, "that I don't sympathize with their disappointment;" he waved to Julia. "In that you can count on me, absolutely."

"No really," she said, "I wish you'd talk about the French some more."

"Julia, let Pork alone," he said. "Anyhow, he gets it all from a French captain we knew over there."

"I saw a lot of Jaclard in Paris," Porky said, "until I found he was repeating my views on France as his own. It got him quite a name as a coming man."

"What a damned liar you are, Pork."

"No, but I saw a lot of the French. There's no war generation there; a little more freedom and, of course, the sense of
desolation; but in manners and conduct the same amused and
realistic resignation. French youth lacks charm, I grant you, but
not fibre. But really I must go."

"You should have married one, Pork; you would have offset
each other's defects."

Julia smiled at Porky confidently. "You ought to marry. I'm
sure that you'd make the most devoted husband in the world,"
she said.

Porky took her hand and bowed over it "I admit that toward
women I have more devotion than most men, my dear Julia;" he
straightened his short rounded figure and beamed at her, "otherwise, there wouldn't be enough to go around." His figure, neat
and stout and pleased, went through the door.

While other businesses seemed to hum, the coal business,
including Rand and Company, was far from what it should be.
He did everything he could; he bestirred himself, made contacts.
He brought big customers up home for dinner and Julia, if
slightly artificial, was always tactful, interested and kind. He
packed his bag and went to suffer the synthetic and uneasy elegance of houses in Youngstown, Akron, Pittsburgh and Detroit.
His efforts were not fruitful; he was unable to simulate the
passionate false sentiment which had seized upon the country under the slightly comic name of service. Their coal was
good, deliveries prompt, and they were honest. He did not see
why these merits should now be considered unavailing unless
reinforced by emotional fraternization with hard-eyed purchasing agents and by mawkish attentions to elegant dull women of
the industrial cities farther west.

Attempting to add the personal touch by proxy, he let their
advertising agents launch a super-sales campaign. But it encoun-
tered super-sales campaigns of other companies, so that in the
end they were all about where they started with the exception, of
course, of the advertising agents. The super-sales campaign was
discontinued. The advertising agents moved on to super super-
sales. These individuals were the flower and the inspiration of
the new age. Overnight they had risen from the state of newspaper cast-offs and minor clerks, and soared into the empyrean

where, with apostolic authority they created wealth and happiness
and perpetual motion to satisfy all hopes, and with papal infallibility, explained the cosmos from child psychology to Jesus Christ.
To doubt them was the modern heresy. He knew only that the
coal was good and that the sales were shrinking.

The mines that had so flourished in the war passed swiftly
through a negative phase of carrying themselves and slid off into
mounting deficits. His father went to West Virginia nearly every
month. He would leave home on the night train looking old
and grim as though his character and business wisdom would this
time find the secret of the trouble, would track it down tri-
umphantly. But the mines held no secrets not already known
to the office books. There were too many mines, too many
miners; there was too much coal, and every mine, the country
over fighting like a foundering ship to keep its pumps going,
continued mining coal and selling at a loss; two dollars, a dollar
eighty at the pit head. His father came back from these visits
looking merely old. When, in the end, he began to explain the
reasons for having bought the mines, how wise it had been, how
wise it would prove later on, he, himself, to whom his father
had never explained anything before, decided that next time he
would go down to West Virginia and bear his father company.

From the first there was an element of the fantastic about this
visit. It was incredible that he had never seen these mines which
worked for him and for which he worked. Such was the complex unreality of modern business. He had sold half a million
tons of coal from these mines and he had not even a picture in
his mind of what they looked like. At early dawn he raised the
window curtain of his berth and rode then, looking out and
rocking gently on one elbow.

If he were expecting the dramatic, there was nothing; a dark
broken land of desolate ridges too sharp and high for hills, too
small and dull for mountains, and covered with a dreary and
ill-favored second growth. The engine's whistle echoed in the
narrow valleys, and lonely silent little stations passed. Sometimes
there was a store, a row of seedy houses, and sometimes there
were sidings filled with hopper cars.

On the station platform a big pale rangy man met them. He
wore a dark suit, a stiff black felt hat, and a tight black bow
tie. "Always heard a lot about you." His hand was strong with

dark hairs on the back of it. "Glad you're coming down to look us over. You want to bring your bags up to the house? My wife's got breakfast for us."

From the back seat of the Ford he saw the Carbondale Hotel's overhanging balcony; the shotguns, rubber boots, and fishing rods of the hardware store; canned goods and cheeses; a smiling coca-cola girl. They turned back off the main street past barber shops, garages and a long dirty white frame building with a small sign "Rand and Company." That gave him quite a start. So this was what it looked like. "We'll run up by the mine," MacDonald said, "and then come back here after breakfast." The town came to an end, there was a jet black stream beside the road and squalid farmhouses, seemingly deserted. They bumped across a spur of railroad track and climbed.

Steeply rising from the road, two long rows of shacks precariously perched on barren earth. Between the gray shacks a washed-out rutted street was patched with brush and garbage, and on the porches, indeterminate figures were motionless. They climbed around the shoulder of a naked hill; he saw a low dejected range of blunt mountains, a tall black tipple and behind it, as they kept on climbing, a black hole framed in timbers. From the artistic etching that hung in his office he was able to make a far-fetched guess that this was Drift Mouth Number One.

That night when the train came tooting down the valley it was a welcome sound. He stood beside his father on the station platform, his handbag in his hand. He stared at Mr. MacDonald's black bow tie, white shirt and silver belt buckle and listened to Mr. MacDonald's voice. It had been a pleasure to see them. They could see for themselves that everything possible was being done; costs had been cut, men laid off. There was probably not another property in the field that was being more cheaply operated. All that they needed was a reasonable price for coal.

Looking out the window of the smoking compartment he watched rare lights from hillside shanties pass by slowly in the darkness and listened to the locomotive's whistle echo in unseen mournful valleys. This had proved a mysterious, highly complex, and most doleful world. Technically he himself knew nothing. The mines might be well run or not. Under his heavy righteousness, MacDonald seemed on the whole like a good man. All that he himself knew was that if coal went up to where it showed a profit, five hundred other mines would bring production up to their capacity and knock the price right down again.

Next morning when he walked through his white front door with his bag in his hand, there was a sense of refuge and of safety. He closed the door behind him. Further, that sorrowful country could not follow him. A fire burned busily in the living room beneath the Maxfield Parrish boy; to the right the winter sunlight fell on the copper percolator, the electric toaster, the morning paper folded by his plate; the big, but thin, white coffee cups with their rims of blue looked singularly beautiful.

Overhead there was tiny thunder; Jane's voice squeaked like a terrier's. "Daddy, daddy, daddy!" Her flying dress was yellow. Behind her Tad, in his blue suit, took two steps at a time with easy dignity. "Hey, Dad!" he said. Jane's hard, small, ruthless body hurled itself at him; she struck him in the stomach and hung there clinging like a limpet. With her head thrown back and her lips half-parted she fixed her black eyes on him in an attitude intense and histrionic. Tad waited, eyeing her with slightly nauseated reserve.

"Daddy," she said, "we had pink ice-cream!"

"Good for you! Now let go and help me with my bag."

"I'll do it," Tad said. "Did you go down a mine?"

"Yes."

"How was it?"

"It was dark."

"How did you go down?"

"In a little car."

"How big?"

"About six feet long."

"Is that as big as this doorway?"

"Just about."

"Not as big as this hall, though, of course?"

"No, about as long as this door is wide. Now let's go up and have a shave and see your mother."

The very stairs seemed safe and welcoming, yellow pine with white risers, white spindles, and a cherry rail. Behind him he heard subdued and bitter sounds.

"Here, here," he said, "stop punching Tad!"

Reluctantly Jane stayed her fists. "You said I could carry it." Her dark eyes blazed. "Didn't you, Daddy?"

"I said you could help. Here, take this brief case; now you've both got something."

In the bedroom Julia, slim and well-built, in her brown knitted dress, was finishing the coil of pale yellow hair behind her neck. "Tom, dear," she said, "are you all right?" She put a light quick hand on his shoulder and held out a cheek. "I told the children I'd have to speak to you when you got home. Last night Tad knocked Jane down and choked her."

Jane made a small round hole of her mouth. "Ooh, yes," she said.

Tad ran a finger along the edge of his blue serge coat. "I pushed her," he said, "and she fell down."

"All right, what about the choking?"

"So then she laid there——"

"'Lay' there," Julia said.

"So then she lay there and hollered so that mother would hear and come upstairs—she kept looking—so then I just put my hand around her neck enough to make her stop. She could breathe all the time. Come here," he said to Jane. Obediently Jane stepped forward. "Like this," he demonstrated.

"Ooh!" Jane said. "Ouch!"

"You see," Tad said, "she'll holler about anything, and she always tells."

"All right," he said. "Now for you, Jane, no more hollering and no more telling tales." At this débâcle Jane looked deeply crest-fallen and Julia, far from pleased. He turned to Tad. "Come in the bathroom while I shave."

Perched on the turned-down seat of the water closet with one bare knee locked under his chin, Tad's gray eyes followed the razor. A tuft of brown hair fell over his white forehead, his red necktie was almost hidden by his hunched-up shoulders.

"Now, son," he dipped the razor in the bowl, "what's all this about?"

Reluctantly Tad frowned. "She follows me around," he said, "everywhere I go. There's no place in this house."

He brought the razor up and made a preliminary pass. "I know," he said, "it's tiresome."

"Golly, yes."

"What's she do it for?"

"To be mean. I don't know."

"Did you ever see a puppy with older dogs?"

"Up at Aunt Clara's farm, those collie pups."

"Well, when an older dog does something, what do the puppies do?"

"They all do the same thing."

"What for; to be mean?"

"No. I don't know."

"They're trying to learn. So what do the older dogs do?"

'They just kind of stand for it, but they don't like it."

"Of course they don't. But you wouldn't think much of them if they knocked the puppies down and choked them."

"But, Dad, I didn't knock her down."

"If they pushed the puppies so they fell down, and choked them." He made a lathery grimace and scraped away. "No," he said, "think what a baby is and then think what a grown person has to know; to walk and talk and button up clothes, to think, and decide about things. There really isn't time to do it. The only chance is to keep busy. Turn on the water in that bath," he said. "It's tough," he shouted above the rushing spigots, "but what are you going to do? We can't be dogs that bite at puppies."

Tad felt the water and wiped his fingers on the seat of his blue serge shorts. He nodded seriously. "O.K., Dad." His voice rang through the noisy bathroom. "Tell me about the mine."

He still lingered over breakfast in the dining room with the papers spread before him. Tad had put on a brown woollen overcoat and cap and trudged off with his bag of books to school slamming the front door resoundingly behind him. As he read the paper, Julia's voice was in his ears. Her mother had a cold and was in the house. There were a lot of colds going around town; Mrs. Trimble had one and so did Miss Trimble. The leading editorial was fulsome about the merger of the Citizens Trust and the Third National. He skimmed it. Great strength . . . greater service . . . a place among the leading institutions of the state. His eye travelled to the next page. Why didn't they come out and say that you couldn't make a good bank by merging two bad ones? Even Dr. Hartman, Julia's voice said, was confined with a cold; and his nephew, Dr. Speyer, who was taking his practice, had told Maude Westwood that it was the worst winter in Midian for colds that he had ever seen.

"Is that so?" he said. His eye ran on. The ladies of the Eastern Star . . . a silver shower . . . Mr. Fordyce B. Montross has returned from New York City . . . Mr. and Mrs. Guiseppi Malatesta announced the engagement of their daughter Miss Patsy Lou Malatesta . . . Mr. and Mrs. Henry S. Thompson are sailing next Saturday on the *Aquitania* for Paris, France, where they will visit with their daughter, Miss Jeanne Thompson, who occupies an important position in the American Hospital in that city. . . . The building stood up white before his eyes; the trees and the night around were dark—only a dim white front and a dim light somewhere deep inside a lofty corridor; and on the steps, her figure wrapped tight in the dark fur coat above the smooth black satin gown. "Good night . . . good-bye." That was the end of that bright day, of that warm radiant evening, of the long drive through darkness and through shadowy silent trees.

"What are you reading, Tom?" The voice which seemed to rush at him from far away was Julia's.

He raised a quick hand to his face.

"I am down to the social column now." He smiled and fixed his eyes on her.

"I asked you whether we ought to keep Tad home from the children's party."

"Why, no," he said. "What for?"

"On account of all the colds that I've been telling you about."

"Oh, yes," he said, "maybe it would be better. Yes," he said judicially, "I guess that would be best. I expect he'll be disappointed though."

"Perhaps," she said, "but that isn't the point."

"I'll take him out in the car with me. Maybe we can have supper up at the farm with Aunt Clara. Wouldn't you like to come?"

"And leave Jane?"

"Bring her along."

"She'd never get to bed then."

"All right," he said, "either way. Whatever you think best. I'll have to get down to the office."

"Don't you want to finish what you're reading?"

"I finished it."

"What was so interesting; was it a secret?"

"Secret? Good God, no!"

"Tom, please. I don't mind for myself any more, but you'll say it some time in front of the children."

"All right," he said, "I guess I'd better get along." He stood up.

"You were going to tell me what it was."

"Oh, that!" he said. "It just happened to catch my eye—you know how a person's name you know does—I see that Thompy and Mrs. Thompson are sailing on Saturday for Paris."

Her look was veiled, but, if anything, contented. "Yes," she said. "Very sudden; nobody knew till yesterday."

He paused holding to himself. Well, let him say it. "Is anything wrong, do you suppose?"

"Oh, no," she spoke with quiet assurance, "I understand that Mr. Thompson found he could get away."

"Yes, I guess they keep him pretty well tied down. Well, I must get down to the office."

"Tom," she said, "there's something I wanted to speak to you about. I don't think it's quite fair; you read the paper and then you go straight off to the office."

"I am sorry," he said, "I didn't know there was anything."

"Tom," she said, "why can't you forget the war and settle down?"

"Settle down?" he said.

"All the other men have settled down except a few like the Buffer who got to drinking or something. I don't mean your work, Tom, I know you're doing splendidly; I mean your position here in town."

"I thought it was pretty good; better than I deserve."

"Before the war," she said, "you were the most looked-up to younger man in Midian. I hated to have you go in the army, you know that."

"Yes," he said, "you were wonderful."

"No," she said, "I thought it was right. And then when you came back safely, I thought it would be an inspiration to you all your life."

"Well," he said, "in a cock-eyed way, maybe it will."

"For a while," she said, "I thought you were just tired out—No one could blame you for that, Tom—but I thought that afterward you would take up all the things you were interested in again."

"You mean the Boys' Club and the church?"

"It's not only that," she said, "it's the way you go around with

all those men after the Legion meetings. I think it's fine to be
loyal to the men who were with you in the army. And if they
needed anything——"

"I guess I'm the one that needs something; I have a good time
with the gang."

"But every one in town is talking about it."

"That's all right with me."

"But your father and mother don't understand it."

"Have they said anything?"

"Not exactly."

"Well, they haven't said anything to me."

"They won't, they're so proud of you. Father and mother are
disturbed too."

"Well, now I think they have a right to object if I don't treat
you properly, but this is something else."

"But don't you see, you can't divide things that way? It all
comes back on me. And then, being so intimate with Porky
Montross; you never were before the war."

"I never knew him."

"You grew up together here in town. He's brilliant, I suppose,
but he never stood for the things you did. He doesn't believe in
anything. And then when he comes up you feel you have to
give him something to drink because he expects it and take
something yourself, and before the evening is over——" She flushed
unhappily. "Sometimes I don't feel that you're the same person;
I feel as if you are a stranger."

"That is good grounds for criticism all right," he said, "and
probably true. I guess I'm not the same."

Her pale face, lightly tinted, began to work. "Oh, yes you are,"
she said. "It's all my fault; you're not happy." Slowly painfully, she began to cry.

He put a quick arm around her shoulder. "Now, now," he
said. Her pale blonde head came on his shoulder.

After a while her voice, small and choked, came up to him.
"Something is wrong," she said, "it was all so perfect." She was
clinging to him, a puzzled and harried child and beautiful.

"Julia, dear," he said in a low voice, "we must be happy, we
must love each other."

Her head shook gently. "Oh, but we do. I do."

A chill thrust through him. He could only stand there patting
her mechanically. So then there was no hope.

CHAPTER LV

It was a pleasant walk that started from his office that late spring afternoon along the square where the few old locust trees that grew through small holes in the sidewalk were newly green, and the open trolley cars on the siding were filling up with a picnic bound for Prospect Park. He was greeted freely. "Hello, Tommy!" "Thomas!" "Tom!" Shop-girls and stenographers, in their little knee-high skirts, smiled and said, "Mr. Rand." Those smiles of girls, shy or bold; frank or preening and self-conscious; dutiful or mischievous—how many kinds of girls it took to make a world. At the corner, the popcorn man in his rumpled linen duster looked at him over the top of his small, square spectacles. "Chief," he said, "how you doing?"

"Hello, Jeff, let's have a bag," he said. "How do you figure for the pennant this year?"

"Can't see nothing but the New York Yankees. Look who they've got to lead their batting order, with Ruth batting number three and Gehrig in the clean-up position."

"They need some young blood on their pitching staff."

"You watch this Gomez. He's a Cubian, or something, but look what he done already."

"Well, what do you give me the Yankees don't make it?"

"Well, of course, anything can happen, Chief; maybe this Gomez breaks his leg. Make it ten to one."

"That's robbery. There are only eight teams. Make it five to one."

"Well, for you, Chief, a regular customer, make it eight to one."

"Make it six."

"Well, I tell you, I'll make it seven; only don't say nothing."

"All right. How much do you want to bet?" Jeff raised his small spectacles above his eyes as though to study a problem; he massaged his lean, receding chin.

"Ten cents," he said.

"All right, seventy cents to ten the Yankees don't take the pennant."

Without looking at him, Jeff extended his hand. "Shake!" he said. He took a stubby pencil from behind his ear and wrote laboriously on the paper bag. He filled the bag with popcorn. "Hang on to the bag," he said. "It's all wrote down there."

"All right, Jeff."

"That way," Jeff said, "there can't be no argument."

The bag of popcorn felt light and warm in the pocket of his coat. It was a new spring suit of light gray flannel that looked nice, and felt nice too. He walked out to the river bank and up the street. The river was blue and swift under the blue still sky. Tangled, warped shadows fell on the house-fronts and on the dark brick sidewalk; and out under the locust trees the river shone and the islands and the distant shore were green and still and tender.

Ahead, a tall, white figure seated on her marble doorstep, Aunt Clara turned to watch him coming.

"Golly!" she said, "a new spring suit."

"How do you like it?"

"It's good. Turn around. I like that green tie too. There's another mat inside," she said, "if you want to sit down. Crêpe de chine ties are always the best."

"I suppose I ought to have a new hat; this old brown felt——"

"Oh, no," she said; "new hats always look badly on men unless they have vacant pretty faces."

"That settles it. Now what about that suit of clothes you're wearing?"

"It's a hand-woven linen. I got it in Kentucky when I drove out there to see the horses, and then I got the harness-maker to make the belt out of a piece of kid."

"It's absolutely all right."

"Do you really think so?" She smiled. "What a great bond—interest in clothes."

"I'm not really interested. Porky's the man for that."

"One of the nicest things about him. You would be, if you knew how interested others were."

"I don't believe Julia is; but then I'm not very interested in her clothes, I'm afraid."

"You ought to be. She's always beautifully dressed."

"Oh, yes," he hesitated, "but it seems impersonal. It doesn't seem to be aimed at any one."

"Perhaps if you showed interest, it would be aimed at you."

"Perhaps. I must get along. I promised Tad I'd pass a baseball with him."

"Go ahead then. He's a great fellow. You know he's going to be a horseman like your father. I had him on a colt the other day."

"Don't I know. A bay two-year-old named Rumpus and he bucked and he kicked but the bold Tad was his master."

"Roughly speaking. Rumpus is a little pussy cat. But Tad rode him nicely. Oh," she said, "but you must tell Julia. She'll never trust me with Tad again."

"I'll tell her."

"I wondered why she wouldn't let Tad come up with me yesterday. Of course, actually, I was awfully careful."

"I'll tell her. I thought she could guess he was making up a story; the little blow-hard."

"But why shouldn't he? I don't believe any child can amount to anything that doesn't tell stories."

He laughed. "Tell that to Julia. Well, so long, my Aunt."

"So long."

He walked on up the river. Darn that Tad with his big talk.

But the river flowed; the islands stood out green and still, the air, the low beams of the western sun were soft and thrilling. People spoke to him, waved to him from passing cars. He wondered why they all were genial; at any rate it was better than the old distant approval and respect. Business was picking up a little even at this off season. He had a new book of poems in the house waiting to be read, "Second April."

When he got near his home he saw Tad in the park across the street. In his blue shirt and tan shorts, patiently he threw the baseball up and caught it again in his glove. Then he squared off at an imaginary plate and struck a blow, he was running the bases; in a spurt of earth he slid, feet foremost for a tree. Dusting himself off carelessly, he went on throwing the ball again.

He, himself walked slowly, quietly. Here was another person, all complete, obscure, inscrutable, living in a dream world of his own, yet waiting patiently for his Olympian to come. An uneasy thought, that this coming brief moment of his own life, so complex and diffused, should stand for so much to that other. It was like being a dog, to be a child. In some ways worse; the child was filled with heats and passions that must out and yet could often only alienate authority.

Now Tad saw him. There was a flash of radiance, incredulous, exalted, and he was running in a high lope across the street. "Hey, Dad," he stopped, "gee, you're late! What the heck!"

"I came right up. Just stopped for one minute at Aunt Clara's. Didn't even sit down."

"But if you'd had the car." Tad's snub-nosed face turned sombre at the thought of all the glory that car might have saved. "Come on."

In this new spring suit? he thought; but it was impossible to defer again this other person's hope. He could take off his coat.

Tad walked ahead, looking back, as though to draw him faster. "Come on. Can you throw a knuckle-ball?"

"No."

"I can."

"How's your control? We've got to watch out this ball don't go in the river."

In the end there was also Jane to placate. She came out on the river bank, the nurse with her making an elaborate display of caution against automobiles. She too must play ball; fortunately the dark was settling down. "Game called on account of darkness," he said to Tad; for a few moments he bounced the ball off Jane's pink muslin stomach while Tad, munching popcorn, confused her with technical advice. She stood with her hands outstretched and her black eyes on the ball; each time it went through her hands and bounced against her stomach. "That'll do," he said. She marched sedately up to him and wrapped herself around his leg. The three of them crossed the street together hand in hand.

After supper he went upstairs to say good night to the children. Jane lay asleep in her crib in the small front bedroom, one arm outflung, her mouth pursed solemnly as though she still considered the problem of the elusive ball; her black bobbed hair, curled tight around her neck, lay against the narrow ruffle of her nightgown. Under the bedclothes, her figure was small and formless except for the contours of the paunch which still remained as a survival of her babyhood.

He walked along the dim hall past his own bedroom and on to the rear of the house. As he gently opened Tad's door, he thought he saw a light click off. With the door ajar, he listened and as he did he felt that Tad was awake and listening too. Curious, he thought, father and son, silent in the dark, trying to smell each other out like animals.

"Is that you, Dad?"

"That's right." The light came on, Tad sitting up in bed in his pink cotton pajamas was looking at him. On the wall were banners of Yale and the Midian High School and a pennant of the Luray Caverns, and over the bed and the littered table that held the gooseneck lamp was a picture of Robinson Crusoe by N. C. Wyeth; a man on a raft, alone against the sea and sky.

"I was reading," Tad said.

"I kind of thought so. What was it?"

Tad fumbled under the bedclothes. "It's a book of yours, I guess. 'The American Boy's Handy Book.' It's swell."

He sat down on the bed. "Yes, that's my book. My father and mother gave it to me for Christmas."

"I know; it says that in the front. Did you ever make any of these things?"

"Not very much. A kite; and a raft once up on the pond at Aunt Clara's."

"Do you think I could make a boat?"

"Do you mean a regular, full-sized boat?"

"Yes; it says it's easy."

"I know, but you've got to watch these books; they make everything sound easy."

"What about a flatboat, then?"

"That would be easier, but you know there's some pretty strong currents in the river. We don't want anybody to get drowned there."

"But what can I do?"

"What can you do?"

"Yes, mother won't let me ride any more."

"I know, but look here, you got yourself in that jam. You talked so big about the colt that you've gotten your mother scared."

Tad dropped his eyes and stared at the book. A slow flush mounted. "I know," he said, "I guess that was dumb all right."

"Sure it was dumb. And then, another thing; it leaves your mother and me not knowing where we stand; when you say things now we won't know whether we can count on them. You wouldn't like to feel that way about us when we told you things. You see?"

Tad's face remained inscrutable and sombre, but his gray eyes slowly filled. "But you and mother have such interesting things to tell." He pressed his lips. "Gee!" he said, "I just sit there."

He reached along the covers and closed his hand on Tad's blunt knee. It was trembling. "I see," he said. "I guess that's right. That's tough," he said. "But look here, we're just as much interested in you as you are in us; maybe more so. All you've got to do is tell things the way they are. That's good enough for us." Tad nodded. "Now don't you fuss any more about it. I'll fix it all up about the riding. And about the boat, I'll have to see what can be done. I'll tell you what I can do; I know a man on one of the river flats; I could fix it up with him to take you out with him." He shook Tad's knee. "You ought to go to sleep now, son, it's half-past eight. Is everything all right?"

Tad turned on his side, affecting to arrange his pillow. He made a quick pass at his eyes. "O.K., Dad," he said, in a strong husky voice, "much obliged."

So that was that, he said to himself as he went down the dark stairs; and speaking of truth, how true was it that they did pay vast attention to Tad's laborious accounts? He was a fine preceptor for the young. The next best thing was to pay more attention from now on.

In the living room, Julia, in a white crêpe gown, was reading under the vellum-shaded lamp. "Was everything all right?" she said. "You've been a long time."

"Yes, everything's all right." He sat down in the other easy chair.

"It's not good for the children, you know; Tad, especially, he's so high-strung. In some ways he is very difficult."

"Oh, he's all right."

"You only see him once a day and then you give him such a good time."

"I didn't give him a good time to-night. I made him cry." He told her.

At the end, she laid down her book. "I know, it really is pathetic, poor child, but still I think it might have been handled a little differently. It isn't as if he didn't know the difference. I should think you'd be afraid it would be bad for him to get off scot free; if he's to grow up as we want him he must learn to speak the truth."

"The best way, then, is for him to want to speak the truth. I think if we show a little more interest in what he has to say——"

"But, Tom, he'll talk all day. I do show interest as long as I can manage it, and this isn't the first time he's been caught making up tales."

"Well," he said, "we'll just have to nurse it along. A lot of these things come right if you don't make too much of them." His new book of poems, slim and fresh and clean, lay on the table, "Second April." The slim blue letters showed against the gray.

"Oh!" she said, "there's a letter came in the evening mail for you. I put it with the paper."

Across the room, on the small round table beside the fireplace, the paper lay with the letter, a dim square, on top of it. He picked them up together and immediately he knew. The envelope was thin as tissue paper beneath his fingers and, as he went back to his chair, he saw the French stamp and Jeanne's strong, slanting hand. A wave shot through him; he had a hard time not to shout. "Why," he said, slowly and evenly, "it's from Jeanne."

"Yes," she said, "I know. I recognized her hand." She did not raise her eyes from her book.

Confound these flimsy French envelopes; there was no room to get a finger underneath the flap. He fumbled on the table for the paper cutter. Incredible, but he had never gotten a letter from Jeanne before; only that telegram once in France, he could still see the cut-out strip of words pasted on the flimsy grayish form—the letter came open in his hand.

"Tommy, my dear,
"I'm writing to tell you the wonderful news of my engagement."

There was a bright, hard shock and yet a light one, from which he quickly rallied; and then the letter seemed to crawl away into mist and to darkness and he, himself, in deathly sickness to be sinking down through lethal waters; black, heavy and rushing, they blinded him and rustled in his ears; they closed his mouth, his nostrils, throttled him with their weight and blackness and with the sweetish, sickening fumes of gas.

When he rose again, a dead man, the letter still was in his hand and he was able to read it calmly with the detachment of exhaustion and to keep alert for Julia, who with her eyes on her book was, he knew, gathered into an intense and silent focus on him, straining to listen, to hear his breathing, the beating of his heart. He read to the end: "Affectionately, Jeanne." Affectionately. He opened his lips as though to try them.

"Well, what do you think?" he said—there was something horrible in the naturalness of his voice—"Jeanne's engaged. Do you want to see the letter?" With a gesture, he threw the letter across the table. She picked it up and studied it.

"They say he's very nice—an Englishman; much older of course. I suppose they'll live in England."

"You knew about it then?"

She smiled brightly. "Oh, yes."

"You never told me."

"Perhaps I should have." Her voice was casual. "But it was awfully confidential and really not certain. I am awfully sorry if it made any difference."

"When—" He checked himself; he must not use that tone. "When did you know?"

"Meta Trimble told me at the time Jeanne's father and mother went abroad."

"You knew then?"

"It wasn't absolutely sure; I suppose they were going over to see the man."

"Oh!" he said, "it wasn't decided then? I remember——"

"Yes," she said, "you read the notice in the paper."

"And you never told me."

"I've tried to explain; I'm awfully sorry if you're annoyed."

"Oh, no," he said, "that's all right."

"And, really," she said, "I don't see that it would make much difference."

CHAPTER LVI

Down in the office he kept on doing business as if nothing had happened. He went through the motions without an error, alert, intelligent and cool, and all the time he hardly knew what he was doing. He had heard of football players bumped on the head who went on playing without knowing it. In fact, the Buffer, he remembered, had scored a touchdown against Princeton once and wouldn't believe it until they showed him the papers. Even then he was disposed to argue. "Ah, these sports writers," he said, "what a laugh they are. Why not? How does a man get to be one? By failing at everything else. I remember going down under the pile, I tell you, and the next thing I was in the dressing room and everybody was hugging me. The boys just framed it on me to make me feel good. Who was it now? Was it Martinell? He was going good in there."

He, himself, was not unconscious, or if he were, there was a conscious self who watched this unconscious body of his go through the motions and who knew that it would not score any touchdowns.

But what reason had he to feel so? There was no sense to it; nothing was changed. He was here in Midian just as he had been before, and just as he had known he would always be. What had he expected? What had he hoped? Had he hoped that some day Julia— The letter that he was signing swam before his eyes: "Gentlemen: In response to your inquiry—" No, he could say fairly to himself that he had never had such thoughts as that. He had been unhappy, perhaps, isolated and thwarted, but he had not been treacherous. Yet all the time he had been sustained perhaps unconsciously by the thought of Jeanne; by the thought that somewhere in the world there was a woman, far removed and lost to him forever, who knew him through and through, forgave him and loved him as the man he was. And now it seemed that casually with a brief gesture, a few bold pen

519

strokes on a flimsy sheet of blue, she could abandon him and take
another. And so she had been ready to do, undoubtedly, at any
time. At what time then had he meant anything to her? It was
all a farce and he was the buffoon.

But why should he complain in bitterness? Had he not made
his choice long, long ago? How long ago it seemed! Even if
once she had been so, was she to remain forever faithful to the
loyal, earnest husband of another, to the father of another's children? It was too much to ask; and when had he the right to
ask for anything of her?

And yet it was a degradation; a degradation for them both.
By God, she was a common woman just as he had first supposed.
That was the thought, he told himself, which had struck him
down. He now had nothing else to live for. Thinking her
magnificent, he could go on sustained by the thought that she
was magnificent and that she had chosen him. Now there was
nothing, and what thoughts would come to him now he did not
know. He would not think.

Outside the window, in the square, the trolleys banged, a
klaxon sounded and people's feet went slowly along the sidewalks
in the heat. He looked at the letter he had signed: "Gentlemen:
In response to your inquiry for four thousand tons of Pocahontas
mine-run, we would say——"

He looked out the window at the flat roofs, at the painted tin
false fronts of the buildings across the square, at the lumpy
brownstone columns of the courthouse and the big electric sign of
the "Midian Messenger." Above the roofs the sky was brilliantly
oppressive. He should be pleased without a doubt. In these days
mine-run coal was hard to sell.

He heard his secretary's voice, "A gentleman to see you; he says
he's acquainted." He dropped his eyes to the card which lay on
his desk, "Major Thurber Singletarry, The International Products Company." "Oh," he said, "show him——"

"Hi, there, brother," Singletarry said, "how you coming?" He
wore a tan gabardine, a tan shirt and a fawn satin tie.

"Well, Singletarry, I'll be darned."

Singletarry's dark face had hardly changed; his hair still fitted
him like a close fur cap, only deep lines besides his fishlike mouth
made it more petulant. "Brother, you're looking fine," he said, "I
declare. Sit down," he said, "take it easy. We don't need to push
ourselves." He drew up a chair.

"Well, Singletarry, how are you?" He pointed to the card. "Major, I see you're still in the war."

"Oh, that. Don't pay no attention to that. Just a little help to my business. Rand," he said, "I declare you're looking the finest in the world."

"I'm fine. How's everything with you?"

"Well, sir, I can't complain. I'm travelling for a mighty nice proposition, and I'm married."

"You're married?"

"Yes, sir; to the cutest, neatest, little trick that ever came out of Tennessee. I want you to meet that little thing."

"Well, I'd be glad to some time."

"She's right here at the hotel. Travels with me."

"I'll get my wife to go around and see her. It must be kind of tiresome being alone all day."

"Oh, she don't mind. She's a great reader."

"I never would have picked you to marry a great reader."

"She is though. I believe she's the heaviest reader I ever saw, excusing poor old Bill McGuire. Yes," he said, "all I have to do is stop at the newsstand and get all the picture magazines and funnies and that little thing is fixed up for the day."

As he looked at Singletarry in his tight gabardine and legion button, his self-striped sateen shirt and soiled buckskin shoes, against all reason he felt his cold heart warm to this preposterously meretricious figure. "Singletarry," he said, "how long are you here for? We'll have to get hold of you and Mrs. Singletarry."

"My Lord," Singletarry said, "just call her Sally Mae. But what I really came by fo' was about those seven thousand francs. At that time," he said, "there was an uncle of mine in mighty poor health; in fact, I was expecting to get news about him any day. But right then he took a big turn for the better and when the old gentleman did pass, not a one of my own family was named in the will. It turned out he'd had a fuss once with my old man about the Second Coming. Well, he knows whether he's right now, I reckon; and whenever they come to divide up the estate, there was nothing anyway. A first and second mortgage, and the niggers had run off with everything on the place. He was noted for the worst niggers in the entire Charterain section. A mean old God-damn scoundrel, if I do say it myself. Well, sir, then I was getting myself established and married and that's the way things go. But what I aim to do now is to just put something aside every month. A man can do that when he has the right kind of a wife. Let me tell you, Sally Mae is a saving woman. Why, sometimes when we want to go out on a party, it will turn out that she's got more money than I have. Well, sir," he said, "I've got that off my mind and I feel a lot better about it because that was what I really came for. But now that I am here I feel like I ought to show you a little proposition." He reached in his pocket. "Yes, sir, I feel like you would really appreciate this." He brought out a green, imitation-morocco jewel case and snapped the top open with a practised motion. Against the purple satin lay a small steel nut and bolt.

"Take it," he said. "Pick it up. Look at it. I want you to be satisfied. Unscrew it. It can't be done, can it? You can see that for yourself. Now then, just hand that thing to me. You see now how it comes off; just as easy. The Molenko Lock Nut; a Hungarian invention. It's naturally bound to revolutionize every industry in the world where nuts and bolts·are used; and you're a man of practical affairs, you can figure for yourself what that will mean. Why, brother, we're lining up the Baldwin Locomotive Works and the Fore River Shipyards and all such things; we're not fooling with any little stuff. But before we throw ourselves open to the public the Company has authorized me——"

The instant Singletarry left he called up Mr. Good Doggie Trimble at the bank. "Mr. Trimble, there is a man on his way round to see you named Singletarry. I knew him in the army; he saved my life there once, but I don't know anything about him in a business way; not a thing. He's quite a talker though and I was afraid he might bring my name in. The little stock I took was merely for old time's sake."

The voice of Mr. Trimble, a faint harsh quack, came back at him. "I get you. I guess I can handle him all right."

At seven o'clock he entered his living room between Singletarry and Sally Mae, well rouged and buxom in her pea-green taffeta dress with puffed sleeves. "Julia," he said, "this is Mrs. Singletarry and Major Singletarry." Julia stood up smiling in her steel-gray satin gown. Sally Mae left his side and was rushing. "Honey, I sure am pleased to meet you and be entertained in your beautiful home. I feel like I'd known you all my life.

The way my husband goes on about Mr. Rand. There's nothing like being buddies in the war, don't you think so? And the way your Northern men were so sweet to him."

Singletarry bowed from the hips. "Never mind, ma'am, how this child runs on. Sally Mae, don't talk the lady down. But it is a fact that I felt like all the battalion were my brothers. If they'd been Southerners, born and bred, they couldn't have treated me a bit better, and this gentleman here, he was just the finest of them all."

"At any rate, Major Singletarry," Julia said gravely, "he and I will never forget that you saved his life."

Singletarry still held her hand. His brown eyes almost swam. "Why, ma'am, what else could I do? He was my buddy."

With a light, slow flush Julia smiled. "Well, I'm sure we wish there were something that we could do for you. It seems strange to think that you saved Tommy's life and we never see you and never do anything about it."

"Well, lady," he said, "you're seeing me right now, and as for doing something, let me tell you—" Still clasping Julia's hand, he put his arm through Tommy's. "When I came in to see him this morning with a little proposition, the first thing he did was to telephone to Mr. Trimble, the president of the bank." Tommy felt his grin turn rigid.

"Oh, that," he muttered. "Well, that——"

Singletarry gave Julia's hand a shake. "I don't know what he said, all I know is that I came out of there with an order for three thousand shares." He hugged Tommy's arm to his gabardine bosom. "Don't tell me that ain't a buddy."

"Now, darling," Sally Mae said, "don't talk business when you're out in company. Just look around you and see if this isn't the most beautiful Northern home you ever saw."

"Don't pester me," Singletarry said. "I'm satisfied to look at the most beautiful Northern lady I ever saw."

Still flushing lightly, Julia laughed. "So it really is true, then? I've always heard about you Southern men."

"You see, Singletarry," Tommy said, "even being a Southerner has drawbacks. No girl will believe you. How about a little drink?"

"Well, sir," Singletarry said, "it has its good points too. They always offer you a drink as soon as you come in the door."

"But, Tommy, dear," Julia said, "aren't you going to wait for Porky?"

"Wait for Porky?" he said. "The question is will we catch up with him."

It was as he had prophesied, when Porky, in his well-cut blue flannel suit, his linen waistcoat and dark-red foulard tie, stepped with immense confidence•through the door. His round, smooth face and pointed nose were pink and glistening. "Singletarry," he said, "how did you get your first promotion?"

"Why, Captain, this is a pleasure, I declare. Allow me to present my wife, Sally Mae."

"How do you do, I'm sure," Porky said, "or words to that effect." He looked at the two half-empty glasses. "I see you've taken to practically solitary drinking."

"We were just having one to go on," Tommy said.

"Tommy, dear," Julia said, "we really should go in to dinner and I'm sure that Porky has had a drink before he started."

Porky, who was smoothing down Singletarry's gabardine like a head fitter, stood back to admire it. "What was that?" he murmured.

"I said I was sure you had had a drink."

He waved a flipper absently at Julia. "A master of conservative statement," he said. "You know I've never seen my companion-in-arms in mufti before. I think it ought to be let out in the belt," Porky said, "to reduce the prominence of the——"

"Hey, there!" Singletarry jumped. "What you doing, Captain? I swear you make me nervous."

"Now, Porky," Julia said. "Tommy, dear, shall we go in?"

"Go in?" he said, "without giving Porky a drink?" He turned to the side table with Porky close behind him.

"Left to himself, Julia," Porky remarked, "Tommy's judgment is infallible."

Singletarry was close behind him. "I believe I'd appreciate a little of that infallibility myself. After the Captain, of course," he said.

"Spoken like a personal aide of General Robert E. Lee," Porky said. "But what about Sally Mae? Sally Mae!"

"Hey there, Captain!" Sally Mae waved at him across the room."

"Lieutenant," Singletarry said, "whenever you go to pour out Sally Mae's, just make it straight."

Sally Mae wedged herself warmly in between himself and Porky at the side table and took their arms. "I sure do think you boys are awfully cute, both of you. Is that my drink? Thanks, honey."

From near the white double door that led to the hallway and to the dining room, Julia was watching them.

Tommy dropped ice cubes in his glass and poured a good stiff slug. "If Sally Mae is drinking it straight, I don't see why I shouldn't." He looked across the room at Julia standing beside the doorway, impatient and coolly disapproving, spoiling the spirit of the gathering. He took a swallow of the whiskey, oily, hard and raw, and choked a cough. "What's on your mind?" he said to her with conscious insolence. "Come on and join the party."

In the end they carried the bottle of Scotch with them to the dining room. Porky, after solicitously assisting Sally Mae and Julia to their chairs, picked up the bottle. "Anybody?" he said. "Well then." He sat down carefully and helped himself.

"Hold on, brother!" Singletarry said. "We can't let this gentleman drink alone. Honey, hold out your glass."

Sally Mae turned moist and starry eyes on her companions. "Well, what about the Captain here and Mr. Rand?" She leaned toward Tommy. "I think you war buddies are just wonderful."

"Sally Mae," he said, "you're absolutely all right."

"He is a master," Porky on the other side of Sally Mae, gestured at him, "of self-evident truth."

As Sally Mae filled his glass he noticed that the Scotch was running low. This was intolerable; he would go up to his bedroom for another bottle. Then he remembered that he had taken his last two bottles up to the farm. Great indignation seized him; here was Porky, the best friend a man ever had, and Singletarry, a ludicrous, but somehow potent souvenir of great days in the war; and the Scotch was giving out. He pushed back his chair. "I'll be back in a minute."

"Where's that man goin'," Sally Mae asked plaintively. "Is he goin' away?"

"He's just gone to telephone," he heard Porky say, "for a girl for himself. I feel sorry for him," Porky said, "he always has to telephone for his girls. While my girls," he pulled down his linen waistcoat, "just come floating into my life."

From the hallway he could hear Sally Mae's whoop. "I declare, you Northern men!"

Under the stairs he picked up the telephone. It felt extremely light and somewhat fuzzy. "Hello! Is that you, Wendig? Hi there!" he said, "how's everything? Oh, it's Fiebleman? Hi there! How's everything? That's good. Well, now, listen, Fiebleman, here's the situation.

"I know, but damn it, Fiebleman, we've got to have a little action. Action, Fiebleman, is the word.

"What's that?" he said, "an hour. Now you talk like your old self. I said, now you talk like your old self. Never mind, let it ride. I said Okay."

It seemed no time at all till Wendig and Fiebleman were walking into the hall with little heavy bundles sewed in gunny sacking. He jumped up from the table. "Hello, boys!"

Fiebleman took off his slouch hat and shook his head; he raised sad, brown eyes. "Ha, Lieutenant, we took a awful chance on this." From behind him, he heard Porky's voice. "Why not? Aren't we taking an awful chance on it too?"

"Ha, that's Mr. Montross," Fiebleman said. "Now, Mr. Montross, you know you ain't never got nothing from us that wasn't right. You are a very fine gentleman and I ask you please to say whether we treat you right. Lieutenant, where should we put it?"

"Back here in this closet. Who's got a knife?"

In the closet under the stairs they involved themselves with a knife, with gunny sacking, straw and tissue paper. "That's a life saver," he said, as the heavy, shining bottles came out. "I gave away the last of that last case to a friend." Fiebleman rotated a bottle under Tommy's nose. "You see, Lieutenant," he said, "something special. We have a porter, a very fine colored man, that brings it from Canada in an upper berth. Otherwise, you would have to pay maybe one hundred and fifty dollars and then maybe they would fool you; but now if you have just a glass here handy I want you to take a drink of this very marvellous old stuff. It will do you good and then you will be satisfied. Ain't that right, Wendig?"

"All right," he said, "we'll all three have a drink. I want you to stick around; we've got somebody from the old Company to-night; Major Singletarry."

"Well, well," Fiebleman said, "that's a very nice re-union between you and the Major, I bet, and Mr. Montross too. So the Major is here in Midian? That's very fine."

Wendig rubbed his big blue jaw with his knuckles and stared into space. "Jesus!" he said, "him!"

It seemed no time at all till he was carrying the third bottle into the living room. Sally Mae marched behind him, a blue glass pitcher wobbling in her hand. When they grinned at him, he remembered that Sally Mae's hat was on his head and grinned back. "Third relief, boys," he said, "coming right up. Porky?" Porky, with an arm on Wendig's chair, had Wendig pinned back against the wall. With his eyes still on Wendig, mechanically he extended his empty glass. "The orgy is an art," he was saying, "and we have lost it. No nation can be great without it. The Greeks understood that and gave it pattern, form. We try to ignore it, suppress it, and what's the result, Wendig?

"Jesus, Captain, how should I know?"

"The result is that when the urge comes we are unprepared. We are compelled to extemporize. With us, what should be an ample, satisfying ritual emerges merely as an aimless drunk."

Wendig nodded owlishly. "Pretty tough, I'll say," he held out his empty glass.

Tommy cocked Sally Mae's hat over one eye. "In my opinion, Porky, Wendig has the best of the argument. Say when, Wendig."

"Oh, my Lord!" Sally Mae said. She gave a choked whoop. "Don't that sound funny though, 'Say when, Wendig.' Big boy, don't wobble your glass. How can I pour?"

"That's all right, lady," Wendig said. "I was wobbling to try to catch it."

They moved toward the group on the sofa. "What ails that big man, Tommy?" Sally Mae said. "He was rude."

"He's all right; he thought you were making fun of his name."

"Oh, well, darlin'," Sally Mae said. "What the hell!"

Julia sat with Singletarry on the sofa and Fiebleman was in a chair beside her. He sprang up. "So here it comes, another little drink, but the lady should not be doing this." He stretched out his small hand. "Here, please."

"You let me alone," Sally Mae said. "I can pour my own self."

Tommy held out the bottle. "Julia, none for you, I suppose?"

Julia looked at him coldly. "Thank you," she said, "I think a small drink would be very nice."

"Well, I'll be——"

Fiebleman darted across the room; his voice trailed behind him. "Ha!" he said, "I'll get a glass." Singletarry reached out a thin, dark hand and patted Julia's shoulder. "Lady, now I know you're perfect." He fixed his brown eyes on her. "The only thing that was on my mind was that this beautiful lady would allow a man to drink alone."

"So here we are then." Fiebleman held out the glass. "Mrs. Rand, this will positively do you good and to-morrow morning, too, you feel fine." He handed her the glass. "You needn't have nothing to worry about; an absolutely special brand."

Singletarry held out his glass. "Just a touch, brother." He turned his face, now slightly white around the pettish mouth, to Julia. "The finest evening of my life."

Tommy whacked the meagre gabardine shoulder turned toward him. "You're all right, Singletarry. Do your stuff. It will do her good."

"Sure it does them good, Tawm," Sally Mae observed, "but what good does it do me?" She took his arm. "Well, what the hell, darlin'; can you stand on your head? I can. Sure enough, do you want to see me? Let's go out in the hall."

"You've got to hold my skirts up," she said, as they went through the door, "in case that somebody else might come by."

It must have been somewhat later that they started drilling with sticks and umbrellas in the hall. Sally Mae, in his old trench coat and derby hat, was showing how a drum-major twirled his baton and making tremendous brass effects through solemn, tight-pressed lips; and Fiebleman, with a malacca cane, did the Manual-of-Arms in front of the hat-rack mirror. Through the doorway he could see Julia and Singletarry on the sofa, and Wendig, alone, still sitting motionless against the wall. Then, Porky challenged him to a duel. They took off their coats and Sally Mae put lipstick on the ends of their canes and kept the score until two canes were broken.

After that they marched out through the kitchen where Sally Mae added a dishpan to her equipment, and then around the house with military commands and martial music.

Back in the hall they started dancing; in fact they invented a dance of their own. Sally Mae put her arms around him and Porky, and he and Porky put their arms around Fiebleman. In a tight ball they revolved slowly, singing "The Old Grey Mare," and jumping high at every fourth step.

From time to time he thought he heard the ringing of a bell and then there was a pounding on the front door and an unmistakable silhouette against the glass. "Don't give your right names," Porky said.

"Hello, Mr. Rand," the policeman said. He took a look at Tommy and then put a broad hand over his mouth and slowly brought it down. "I hate to disturb you," he said, "but some of the neighbors here—" he frowned; "me," he said, "I wouldn't have done nothing but they telephoned up from headquarters."

Tommy took a deep breath and removed Sally Mae's hat from his head. "Why, certainly, Harry." He was dignified but hearty. "That's perfectly all right. We were just having a little re-union. All these men here were in the war together. You know how it is. As a matter of fact, we were just about to break up."

"Sure, Mr. Rand, I know how it is. I was in it myself."

"Why, absolutely you was in it," Fiebleman said under Tommy's elbow. "You was a corporal in the 709th Ammunition Train."

"I bet he was a mighty fine soldier too," Sally Mae observed. "He sure does look it."

Gravely, Tommy handed Sally Mae her hat. She clapped it on her head. "Thank you, honey." He turned to the policeman in time to catch his grin. "Harry," he said, "we were just breaking up."

"Well, that's good, Mr. Rand, because when they telephone up from the station like that——"

"Yes, yes, I know. A man's got to do his duty, but if you've got just a minute—Porky," he said, "where are those glasses?"

"I can't stay but a minute, Mr. Rand."

"That's right, Harry; a man's got to do his duty. Just step inside the door."

Harry closed the door behind him and took off his blue cap.

He patted his ruddy, glistening brow with a red bandana hand-kerchief. "Kind of warm out to-night, Mr. Rand."

"Lord, Lord!" Sally Mae said. "Look at that man; he could carry me off to jail right now."

In a stately manner Porky, still in his shirt sleeves, was bearing a bottle with glasses on a tray. "Sally Mae," he said, "you'd be a wonderful girl if you could just let yourself go."

Tommy picked up the bottle and a glass. "Here you are, Harry. I guess it's all right or we wouldn't be here."

Harry looked at Fiebleman. "Yeah," he said, "I guess it's all right."

"Well," Tommy said, "we'll just have a nightcap and call it a day. As a matter of fact we were just about to break up."

"That's fine, Mr. Rand. I hope there ain't any hard feelings."

"Certainly not. In fact, I appreciate the way you handled this thing, Harry. We just happened to get together and being in the war together——"

Through the door he saw Wendig rise with smooth swiftness and disappear toward the sofa. He heard his voice; "Here you punk, take your hands off that lady"; and Singletarry's, "Why damn me, you Polack." As he started for the living room, the policeman took one step beside him. "I'll wait here," he said, and dropped behind.

They were all three on their feet, and Wendig, standing in front of Singletarry, seemed to nurse his big fists lovingly.

"All right, Wendig," he said, "I can handle this. Singletarry," he said, "the party's over. There's a cop in the hall to close it up."

Fiebleman came running. "You hear, Wendig?"

"What's that to me?"

"It's Harry Morton; now you see? We better have sense."

Wendig and Fiebleman went out the door. He heard Fieble-man's, "Well, Harry, everything's absolutely all right."

"Come on, Singletarry," he said.

"Good night, ma'am." Singletarry bowed coldly but with great precision. "It looks like your Polish friend cannot hold his liquor."

"Singletarry," he said, "come on."

"Now, darlin'," from the doorway Sally Mae nodded owlishly, "you listen to Tawm. Honey," she called at Julia's rigid figure, "good night. We sure God had a lovely time."

CHAPTER LVII

THE sun was already high and hot when he came down the next morning balancing his head delicately against the least unnecessary jar. In the living room the maid, with a towel around her head, was pushing furniture and rolling rugs. Across the hall a hot light fell on the percolator and on the centre-piece of wilted asters. His place was still set at the table. He sat down gingerly before his orange juice and gingerly explored the roof of his mouth with his tongue; there was no change for the better. He raised the glass; the orange juice was warm. He shuddered. Was it possible that Porky felt this way every morning of his life? He would stop on his way downtown and ask him; if he could get that far. The swallow of orange juice had met no favorable reception. He tried the electric percolator, pausing for a moment to place his clammy hands around its warmth. A brown stream trickled into the white blue-banded cup. He pulled the cup toward him. No sugar; sugar turned to alcohol. No cream either; there was something oily about cream.

As the first hot, bitter swallow braced him, the pantry door swung open. Julia wore an old blue linen dress and apron. "Here is your egg," she said.

"Thanks." He hoped his smile was not too sickly.

"You haven't drunk your orange juice."

"I'll get around to it. I just came down."

She set the egg down on the table. He was sorry to see that it was fried. "I heard you when you came down," she said.

He took another drink of coffee.

"Don't you want cream in your coffee?"

"No." His voice was a husky moo. He cleared his throat. "No," he said. "This is perfectly all right, thanks." He took another sip and dared to breathe more deeply. "Sit down," he said.

"Sit down!" she said. "I've got to help Susan in the living room. I've sent for the dry cleaners to take the big rug, and

Jadwin's coming to see what he can do about the cigarette burns in the floor.

"Gosh! Were there cigarette burns?"

"It was mostly your friend, Mrs. Singletarry. Generally she stepped on them but sometimes she forgot."

"I'll be darned! I didn't notice that."

"I don't suppose you did."

"I guess it's an old Southern custom."

"Major Singletarry didn't do it."

"He didn't need to. He was on the sofa with you."

"I don't see what that's got to do with it."

"Never mind," he said; "there was an ash-tray handy, that's all." He took another drink of coffee. This was no way to start; he set the cup down. "Julia," he said, "that was a fool performance last night."

"I don't know what you mean."

"I mean my performance, the party, the whole thing. I don't know how I got into it. My intentions were good but I just seemed to drift from one thing to another and before I knew it the whole thing was cock-eyed." He poured himself more coffee. This coffee was doing him good and the way he was talking now would do him good. "It was a mess," he said, "and I feel terribly about it. You see, I felt I ought to ask Singletarry after that business over in France and I didn't know anything about his wife till I brought them up here; then in the middle of dinner I remembered I was short on Scotch and so I telephoned to Fiebleman. Well, then, when they got here I felt that having both been in the Company I ought to ask them at least to have a drink; and then after that things sort of got out of hand. It was a fool performance," he said, "and I'm glad it's over." He looked up at her and grinned. "But at that, I guess some of it was pretty funny. Did you see Fiebleman drilling himself in front of the mirror in the hall?"

"So that's what you think?" she said.

"What?"

"That it was funny."

"I didn't say that. I said it was terrible, only there were funny things about it."

"I wasn't going to speak of it now," she said, "but since you think it's all so funny I want you to listen to this."

"Why, Julia, I don't think it's funny! I said I'm awfully sorry."

"When I married you every one said I was the luckiest girl in Midian. You were the most respected young man in town; every one looked up to you and if you had kept on you would have a wonderful position in Midian to-day."

"What's the matter with my position in Midian?"

"Last night," she said, "you were disgusting. You were—" she hesitated, "you were drunk and you were making love to a nasty, cheap little girl that you had brought up here into my home, and you were running around with two bootleggers who ought to be in jail, and making such a noise that the neighbors had to send for the police. And you ask what's the matter with your position in Midian!"

"I know," he said, "it was a fool performance. I admit it; but it was only once and I'll tell you this right now, it won't happen again; so don't have that on your mind."

"It was only once, but it's just the end of what's been going on since the war. I could see it coming and I've spoken to you about it but you wouldn't listen. I've tried to get you back into the church work and the Boy's Club, and the things that are worth while; all the things," she said, "where you used to be such an influence for good; and now," she said, "if you wanted to be a leader in them they wouldn't have you. It's been so gradual that you haven't noticed, but that's how far you've gone."

"Oh, come on," he said, "you're taking this too hard. One fool evening doesn't make a man's life."

"It's not just last evening, although I can tell you that when I sat there last night and saw those people in my house, and when I came down this morning and saw the whole place looking like a pigsty, I felt as if my home had been taken away from me. Don't you think a woman has a right to have a nice home and to have only nice people in it?"

"Look here," he said, "we'll get hold of Jadwin and have everything fixed up. We'll have the whole floor done over, if necessary, and if there are rings on the tables——"

"I've sent for Jadwin. That's not what I'm talking about; it's

you. Don't you suppose that I feel it? that people notice the kind
of man you have let yourself become?"

"Sure, people notice, and some of them don't like it and some
of them do."

"Who like it? The bootleggers and the town bums, and the
Singletarrys and Porky Montross."

"Well," he said, "there's good in all those people except the
one you picked."

"No, no," he said, "I didn't mean that; I just said it to be
disagreeable."

"You're always taking cracks at Porky but when a bird like
Singletarry comes along—" His voice trailed off. "Oh," he said,
"let it go. I'm sorry. I know it was nothing."

She continued to stare at him, her pale face rigid and
unappeased.

"Julia," he said, "we mustn't go on like this."

"We?"

"I, then. We must try to help each other; we must try to make
each other happy." He took her hand. "Don't let's argue; let's
just do that. Arguments are no good," he said, "they're worse
than no good."

Her hand was stiff and unresponsive. "I didn't know there was
an argument."

"Quarrel, then."

"I don't see why there need be any quarrel," she said. "I have
my beliefs and I try to live up to them. You have them too;
you were brought up in them, and if you had followed them
everything would have been all right. Don't you admit that's
so?"

"That's like admitting that if I had been a different man
everything would have been all right."

"If you had followed them you would have been a different
man."

"I don't want to be a different man," he said; "I want to be a
happier one."

"No one can be happy," she said, "that doesn't live in accordance with what we know is right."

"Well," he said slowly, "there is something wrong with the
system somewhere. The church has been going for a long while
in this town and all it seems to do is to turn live human beings

into wooden Indians. The only time it came to life was in the war and then it was to ballyhoo recruiting."

"That's just an excuse. You believed in the war then."

"About the war, I don't know the answer. It may have been necessary for man, but I don't believe it was necessary for God."

"You still believe in God then?"

"Oh, yes."

"Why don't you believe in His Word then and His church?"

"Now," he said, "we're getting into another argument."

"Well, then," she said, "what do you believe?"

"I don't know," he said; "I guess I believe that people should love each other and have fun."

"Is that all?"

"It's the main idea."

"Well," she said, "what else?"

"That's about all," he said. "I think we ought not to do other people harm if there's any way of helping it."

"Don't you think it does me harm to act the way you did last night?"

"Yes," he said, "I guess it does. That's why I said I was sorry."

"Don't you think it does the children harm to have you act that way? All this morning," she said, "I've been putting off their questions about what was the noise last night, and why the house looked like this this morning."

"I guess it does," he said, "but I can't be sure."

"You can't be sure! What are you trying to do? make fun of me after all I've been through?"

"I was thinking," he said, "that if my father had gotten tight and had had the cops in the house just once we might have gotten on better together."

"So you really have changed then even about your own children. I suppose I might have expected it; I've noticed for a long time that you have no interest in how they are brought up, or what principles they learn."

"I don't want them to learn anything that isn't so. They start under handicaps enough already."

"I see," she said. "Well, what is so?"

"That, I don't know."

"You see," she said, "it amounts to the same thing. You have no principles to teach them."

"At least," he said, "they'll start with a clean slate."

"You don't believe in the Word of God, then?"

"I believe it would turn out to be true if we could find it."

"You never go to church," she said; "you never read any books on the spiritual life, and yet you seem to think that you know more about it than the men who have given their lives to it. All you do is talk to Porky and read those books of poems. I read the last one," she said, 'Second April.' "

"Yes," he said, "where is it?"

"I put it away on account of the children."

"The children?"

"I'm no poet," she said, "but I can read plain English, and so can they. The book offers promiscuity as a cure."

"Not as a cure—as a disease. And even so I don't think I believe her."

"I should hope not," she said disdainfully. "It would be better to have no beliefs than to believe that woman. I suppose the truth is you have no beliefs."

"Julia," he said, "we're going round in circles."

"I'm not," she said. "I know what I believe and I know what I feel." She paused. "I've been patient with you, but I can see now it was a mistake. I ought to have listened to my father and mother and some of my friends, but I thought it was my duty to keep quiet. No one can say that I haven't done my duty as a wife and mother. I've given you everything that a woman should and it seems that you have just taken it for granted and gone your own way. The reason I speak of it now is that I see it isn't good for a man to be allowed to act that way. I'm afraid now that I am partly to blame for your having become the way you are."

"Oh, shucks!" he said. "I'll take the responsibility." He looked at her intently. "Julia," he said, "have you ever been in love?"

"Now," she said, "you are insulting." She colored. "If my father were here you would not dare to speak to me that way."

"You're talking by the rules," he said. "Now that we've started all this, let's talk about ourselves as we really are. How do you really feel about me?"

For the first time her face lit up, but the gleam was of a zeal impersonal and fatuous. "I know that you are really fine at heart," she said, "and I think that all this is just a passing phase, and every night I pray——"

He sat there silent, eyes on his plate, and listened to her. It was incredible that they had lived together all these years, had courted, married, kept house, had children. What was the joke that was passing around—"it must have been a couple of other fellows"; for now, as he saw themselves, he was a mortal wandering desolate in the darkness of an uncomprehended world, and she was a being bearing merely some resemblance to the earth he knew; a being strange and sexless, descended out of interstellar space, or if a woman, then a woman from some dim, frigid valley of the moon.

CHAPTER LVIII

HE sat alone in the living room. It must be late. Through the open window he seldom saw the lights of passing cars. Now and again one passed, moving slowly, silently along the starlit river; and one raced by at high speed trailing shouts and laughter.

Here in this room last night there had been shouts and laughter, too; high antics and a great unmeaning din, beating in vain against his isolation and despair. The starlight fell in dim mist on the river. Another car passed slowly, silently; two figures close together, motionless. What was there for him now? Jeanne was gone; she had betrayed him in one swift, unbelievable gesture; thrust him through. It was still night in England; at this very hour in a strange man's house she lay— He got up from the easy chair and walked out to the closet, in the darkened hall. He felt among the straw and gunny-sacking. "A touch of dog-hair," Porky used to say. He came out with a smooth and heavy bottle in his hand. From the second floor Julia's hushed voice, coldly patient, dropped down to him. "What are you doing? Why don't you come to bed?" There was a silence; he stood motionless holding the bottle, listening. "I should think you'd be tired after last night."

"I'm all right," he said, "go to sleep."

Back in the living room he poured a little whiskey in the glass and took a sip of it. It was really horrible; better than most, perhaps, this stuff of Feibleman's, but essentially horrible; raw and greasy with a taint of sweetish, musty grain; and, once drunk, moving men to infantile or brutal savagery. The thing to drink was wine; as he had drunk champagne with Porky in the army; as he had drunk the thin still gold in the hotel dining room in Paris. Thin still gold in the fragile glasses and high above them gilded beams and crystal chandeliers; and leaning her strong arms on the table, turning her strong laughing face to him in her close black satin gown— Ah, she was like the rest. He had

538

been right about her from the first. Let him go back to his first thoughts of her and be content. They were all alike, the women of that sort, unstable and unfeeling, children of their own inscrutable whims. A man perhaps could make a life with one of them, but it would only be a matter of luck, of nothing happening to come along to change her toward him. He wondered what luck that Englishman would have; for she would change; she had always set her cap at every man.

They were all alike, that kind. The only kind that did not change were women without passion; the hard, cool, bloodless women of the moon. She lay above him now, this calm perpetual stranger in his house, and while she might complain of him and of her lot, he knew and she knew that all advantages were hers; the advantage of immunity to suffering, to gusts and heats of passion, to the slow drain of loneliness and longing, to the bewilderment, the desolation of unrealized dreams in a world that could not find its gaiety and splendor. To be free from heats of the flesh and of the spirit, to have a mind too small and cool and firm to grasp them and so to be immune to all the puzzlement, the strain, the self-doubt that comes from understanding—that was what made a woman strong, armored at every point, no crevice in the smooth completeness of her obtuse self-righteousness; and within that armor, within that moderate placid heart no flicker of desire that could not be satisfied; perfect contentment based on small arrangements; a church, a cook, a well-thought-of friend or two to tea; and growing from the soil of that contentment the tough-fibred flowerless plant of self-esteem.

In all this hard, well-rounded little world of hers, he was the only flaw; he was the only thing that could not be arranged. And always, for years now, he was growing worse, a greater trial to her. He reached his hand out, took a drink; the liquor tasted better. Yes, slowly he had come to understand and resist this woman and all those like her. In America misguided chivalry had done too much for them; had reduced them from their natural state of human beings and bred them up as somewhat simple-minded demi-goddesses, devoid of knowledge of mankind and inclined in seeking their incomprehensible objectives to overestimate their nuisance value.

All this was most amusing. He felt that at this moment he could hold his own with Porky. But it got him nowhere. America was full of men his age that permitted themselves guarded and timorous reflections on their wives as a secret relaxation from lives of alert docility.

Actually he was no longer a young man. He stood on the middle ground between his youth and what would some day be called the latter part of his life. He had spent his youth in a vain endeavor of honest principles and high hopes; he had tried to make a marriage that would match all that was best in him and now he had come to recognize the degradation of this lofty enterprise. Curious that she had never seemed to feel it too, not in the sense that he did. A thick hide covered that ethereal soul of hers. How could one, knowing the warmth and beauty of living bodies, of all the glory and tenderness the world might show, go plodding unconcerned through life; go plodding unconcerned yoked to a life and a companionship unvarying, savourless, and without hope of gusto. That, again, was her strength; to all these thoughts she was impervious from birth, and so she would remain. But why should he be doomed to minister, superfluously, no doubt, to her obtuseness? It was a sacrifice out of proportion to any benefit to her. Her pride would be injured and her so greatly valued standing in the town; though there again she might become a heroine and martyr; but in any case those were not objects that a man should be asked to give his life for. And he would give his life if he stayed on. He was still young in spirit and certainly not old in body, but if he stayed on he could see from now on the declension; the American husband till death did them part.

The liquor slowly flowed in him and with its flowing, as with the chemical that slowly spreads in a retort and then abruptly changes all the contents, suddenly his life seemed simple. All these complexities and bonds that baffled him were mere assumptions erected through the centuries by dint of man's industrious and senseless talent for involving himself in the superfluous. In point of fact, there was nothing to hold him; the window was open to the night; the door was open. Beyond the shadowy bank, the river flowed down to the sea through towns and sleeping farms and cities, and on the ocean ships were stealing through the night to ports where no one would ever ask or care about a stranger's name. Once a man sensed reality, he saw that nothing was easier than for him to step out of this life of his, this chrysalis whose vast complexity of tiny fibres hemmed him in. Simply to step out, leaving the chrysalis intact for the benefit of those who still enjoyed its smothering protection. It would be fair all round. The home here would remain and an ample allowance would come to Julia every month. Her church, her fads, her children, all that she prized in life would still be hers. In the office he was little more than an exalted clerk and the mines, so jealously guarded by his father, would not even know that he had gone. He wondered how much that men called their duty was really a delusion of conceit maintained subconsciously to buttress their self-esteem; a delusion made possible only by the kindly provision of nature, which kept them from learning, when they died, how microscopic was the hole they made. But since he had no such illusions, why not take advantage of the fact? His investments would take care of Julia; he would turn his interest in the business over to his father to do with as he liked. He, himself, could always earn a living; it would be interesting to see what it would be, where he would do it. He took a breath. Merely the prospect was charged with excitement and the sharp air of freedom.

His heart slowed down, turned leaden. He wished he felt better about the children, or rather he wished that he felt worse. He would miss Tad's "hi, Dad!" and his manly gesture of salutation copied from his own; he would miss the whirl and shock of Jane against his legs. But this unhappiness was muffled and remote like a sad memory of something long ago. Some nerve had died in him, leaving him strong, even stronger in himself, but cut off from mankind. He could take care of himself and make his life, but he no longer cared to carry other lives in custody. It was just as well. He had nothing to offer them and would have less as time went on, as he sank into his solitary trance, and as they came to see that he was living, dead to their mother and numb to them. And he was not good for them; Julia was right to that extent. He nullified her teaching and confused them. They loved him now as children love all those who play with them, but some day they would be brought to face their own confusion, would trace it back to him and hate him for it. Long before that they would hate him for a home from which all life had gone; a home

inimical to all that sportiveness and gaiety which children, for the
solace of their secret grief, sought with such eagerness and passion. Not that Julia by herself would offer sportiveness and
gaiety, but life in the home would be peaceful and harmonious,
easy for them to make adjustment to. They might find more
stimulating pleasures elsewhere, but their home would be a
refuge comprehensible and to be counted on. And Julia took the
most excellent care of them. He was always the one who was
letting them catch cold.

Far down the river he heard the long-drawn whistle of a locomotive. That was the midnight Eastbound; wailing, it died
away. Through the still summer night he could make out the
train's swift even rumble on the bridge across the river. The
whistle sounded again; died away. He had missed that train.

At the desk at the far end of the room he took out a sheet of
smooth gray notepaper and looked at the letter heading, "1717
River Street."

"Dear Julia:" He picked up the other pen but it, too, was in-
tolerably sharp-pointed like all of hers. He went on scratching.
"Some of the things you said to me are certainly true and I
suppose I could have said things that were true, or would have
seemed so to me, but argument would not have changed them.
If anything about us could have been changed it would have
been changed by our life together, and so I see no chance and
therefore no use of trying to keep on. If this seems sudden,
remember that you too have seen this separation of our lives
developing for quite a few years. I feel that we ought to recognize it. To keep on as we have can only be bad for both of us
and also for the children, in the end, when they find it out. I
have no plans; just now I simply want to get away. You will
hear from me soon. Meanwhile, I want to tell you that everything that I own in the world is yours and that I will make the
proper arrangements without delay. For every reason you are
entitled to all that I have; I recognize that, and so for myself the
only thing I want is a chance to see the children from time to
time. As for the rest I know you will be happier in the end and
that this house will be at peace."

He crept up the dark stairs with the letter in his hand, pausing
to listen when they creaked. But she was a heavy sleeper for one
so frail, a heavy eater too—almost greedy.

The door was half-ajar. He slipped inside and paused again. Without emotion, he stood for the last time in the dark familiar room. Slowly he moved among the shadows, intent only that she should not wake up. That was his only feeling, the immense, the critical necessity of leaving the note where she could find it, and getting clean away. If she roused up, turned on the light, he would be caught, condemned forever to a life of servitude.

Her breathing now was close. He stretched a hand out and felt the glass top of her bedstand. There was her wrist watch and her handkerchief. He laid the note down softly; with infinite caution he backed away.

Outside the house his footsteps fell noiselessly across the grass. The softness of the night was overhead; the highway shone black and polished under a distant street light. He stepped across it on tiptoe, raised a foot for the whiteness of the curbing on the farther side, and was walking on grass again beneath the dark and brooding locust trees through whose soft branches he could make out scattered stars. The river flowed in placid silence under its faint mist, and on the dark and distant shore a single farm-house light still burned.

He walked downstream; the dim, soft locust branches passed by overhead. The street lamps threw their hard sharp light at intervals to send long shadows of the trees across his feet, and show beyond their own fierce moth-ringed brightness, the close-built sleeping house-fronts of the town. These house-fronts, now dim, now sharply lit, passed by him like a wall. He had passed beyond the wall; he was outside it and was moving, silent and free, beneath the trees beside the river; he was moving with the current, silent, free, almost as if he floated down the stream. It was easy, incredibly simple. All that he had needed for his freedom was his hat; this old hat he wore; the one Aunt Clara sometimes spoke well of, a shapeless thing but rakish and with an air. It had acquired a certain standing in the town. All that a man needed to be free was to take his hat from the hall as he had done. With a hat, a man could voyage the world unquestioned. He had no idea it would be so simple.

If there were reproaches afterward, they would be far behind him here in Midian. They would never reach him, or if they did, they would have no more weight with him than the town's obtuse esteem. These people did not understand either the good or bad in him. They lived only to thwart each other by convention, a joyless and aimless conspiracy of dogs in the manger. And bitches. He laughed aloud. When he knew where he was to be, he would get Porky to come and visit him.

How his Aunt Clara had kept herself from this contagion was a mystery. It could be done then, he supposed, but he was not the man for it; he had tried and failed. But then he had that load to carry; she was free.

The house-fronts passed by. He was walking fast. A distant clock struck two. He would be downtown in half an hour, in plenty of time to catch the four-fifteen. He would stop in at the Greek's for a cup of coffee; he would sit at the counter drinking coffee and maybe eating a toasted Swiss sandwich, and discuss with the Greek the ball team and the Balkan wars, and how the health inspectors shook the cafés down. Then he would catch his train and the Greek would never know till afterward that he was talking to a free man.

It was a sickly, foredoomed life, this life of towns and villages. They all in some fashion had passed beneath the yoke; his father and mother, his grandparents and doubtless generations that he never knew, all had been warped and thwarted by the narrow iron shell of life in this and other little places. Some took refuge in the church where they contrived for themselves an ample, more consequential life with God. A man like his grandfather simply withdrew, puzzled but uncompromising, into a solitude of his own devising. A girl like Julia found every limitation of this world exactly suited to her. Only his Aunt Clara had been able to savour it with warmth and gusto and at the same time to maintain immunity, just as her house—he was coming to it now—remained unostentatious but charming, neat and cordial, in a portion of the town which now was partly running into shabbiness and partly breaking out in impersonally vulgar new apartment houses.

He saw the gleam of the white front door, the brilliant marble doorstep. The house was dark but immediately he knew what he would do. Once he had come there late at night before, long, long before, and had thrown pebbles against her upstairs window. Sitting on her bed he had told her with sophomoric ardor

of his love for Julia, and in the end, to his stupefaction, she had
had a fit of crying. He stopped. Prophetic tears.

On the black gleaming roadway there would be no pebbles
now. He fumbled among the shadows underneath the trees and
found a small stick which he broke in pieces. The crackle
sounded clear and sharp in the still night.

The first stick missed her window; the second tapped lightly
on the screen and fell down lightly to the sidewalk. Immediately
her light flashed on and then, just as it had that time so long
ago, her tall slim silhouette stood framed in the soft yellow
square.

"Is that you, Tommy?"

"Yes."

"Any trouble?"

"No."

"That's good," she said. "I'll be down."

Along the narrow hall and up the narrow stairs he followed her
white figure in the belted cotton dressing-gown.

"We'd better sit in my room," she said. "The breeze comes off
the river. Have you got cigarettes? All right then."

In the cretonne-covered armchair he looked around him. The
dim light from the vellum-shaded lamp threw faint gleams on
her dressing-table of mahogany and its silver fittings, and on the
brass rods of her bed. On the walls he saw the white and dim
blue of the Della Robbia, the dark mass of St. Mark's Square in
Venice and a faded photograph which he knew to be his Uncle
Fitz and the Aurelian Club at Princeton.

She sat down on a cherry rocking-chair and locked her arms
around her cocked-up knee. Her hair, now faintly gray, was
still soft and wavy and fell down abundantly around her waist.

"Well?" she said.

He took a package of cigarettes from his coat pocket. "I'm on
my way," he said.

Her big deep eyes were on his hands as he got out a cigarette
and tapped it on his knee.

"It's gotten that bad, has it?"

"Yes," he said. "I'm through. Are you surprised?"

She watched him light his cigarette. "I know how you feel."

"Right now," he said, "I feel fine. I've just walked out in nothing but the clothes I wear. She can have everything. I want to be fair to her. Of course," he said, "she's never cared for me; I don't know if she has it in her. All I know," he said, "is that I was turning into a dead man."

"Where are you going?" she said.

"I have no idea."

"Just going?"

"That's it."

"What about money?" she said.

"I've got forty dollars and on the first stop I can cash a check."

"I have some money in the house. You can have that if you want it."

"No thanks," he said, "I want to go just as I am. Just to walk out, by God!"

"I'll write, of course," he said, "to father and turn over my interest in the business, and I'll write to mother right away."

"Oh, yes," she said, "we must never let them know that you came by here."

"I know," he said; "I just wanted some one to know what it was all about."

"Yes," she said, "what happened? Or don't you want to talk about it?"

"I don't mind. It sounds grotesque though. Yesterday, that fellow Singletarry, remember? blew into town, and so we had a party."

"Yes." She threw her head back with a quick grin. "I heard all about it by ten o'clock this morning."

"Well, I heard all about it by ten o'clock this morning too," he said, "from Julia."

"You couldn't expect her to like it."

"I was a goat," he said, "but she kept on and on and suddenly this evening, when I was by myself, it came over me that my life was a farce. I'm dying on my feet," he said. "It's been coming on a long time. Last night was just the Sarajevo."

"What happened before that?"

"Nothing; only the usual vacuum between us. It sounds absurd, I suppose," he said.

Aunt Clara looked at him. "It sounds not so," she said.

"You don't believe me?"

"I believe it as far as it goes."

He was silent.

"I saw you three days ago," she said, "something had happened then."

A knife thrust through him. He turned away from it, leaned forward and threw his cigarette in the empty fireplace. "Oh, that," he said. "It has nothing to do with this business."

"It was bound to happen some day," she said gently. "Any woman could have told you that a girl like Jeanne was bound to marry."

"A girl like Jeanne!" he said. "I guess so."

"Well," she said, "you can say anything to me."

"Well, then," he said, "I thought that she was different. I asked too much maybe. But that does not make it any easier."

"What should she have done?"

"I know," he said, "there's no sense to it, but I think she really cared for me."

"Yes," Aunt Clara said, "I always thought she did."

"Well then," he said, "if she feels that way and goes off with another man, what does it make her?"

"So you loved her, too," she said. "Ah, I'm sorry."

He stared at the smoke which wavered from the tip of his slightly trembling cigarette. "I guess I did," he said, "but now I know I'm lucky."

"To think that," she said, "will never make you happy."

"When I came in here," he said, "I was happy enough."

"It was no good though. You'd been drinking."

"Just a couple." He grinned at her. "Just three or four. You don't think I'm tight?"

"Not a bit," she said, "but it's no good to drink when you're unhappy. People should drink when they're happy; that's what drinks are for."

"Well," he said, "I'm sober as a judge."

"You are, but you're trying to dodge."

"What's that?"

"If I were a man," she said, "this is what I would say to myself, that the girl that I might have married and I had missed each other, partly through our own faults and foolishness, and largely through the unreality of my whole upbringing." Slowly she shook her head. "You must be merciless to yourself if you want peace. Some people can fool themselves. Not you. So go on.

Say that Jeanne forgave you when you married some one else. Now she has married. There are all kinds of love and some of the greatest women love different men in different ways. No one, perhaps, will ever mean to her precisely what you did. That's an injury which chance and your family tradition did her through you. If she has been able to recover from this injury you should be glad if only on the lowest ground that it will ease your conscience."

"That's a good theory," he said, "and some of it is true. But not the important part. Not for me."

"We all change and grow," she said, "if we are any good, and try to fulfill ourselves. Why do you want to call a girl who can find the strength and warmth to make a new life for herself a low woman? Why not be proud of her?"

"You have all the reasons. Only you don't know how people feel."

"Explain it."

"It's no use. I'm on my way."

"Explain it. You have always been able to say anything to me."

"It's not that. You have to live through things like that."

"I've lived through things."

"I know. Uncle Fitz. Terrible. But that was an accident. Something outside. It's not the same."

"It was not an accident," she said. "He killed himself."

"Killed himself? Why——"

"Listen," she said.

.   .   .   .

Outside the river ran in the soft night. The muslin curtains swayed to a breeze that brought the sound of frogs from the dim dark islands.

"So that was how it happened," she said.

"Why," he said, "I never—Ah," he said, "that was horrible."

"Not at the end," she said. "But before. So I know about misery," she said.

"Yes," he said, "you do. But what can we do about misery?"

"Bear it."

"Of course. What else could I do? She's married."

"Decide whether leaving home will ease your loneliness."

"That's another question."

"No, the same. Unless you see that, you can't decide."

"I know enough to save myself."

"You had beliefs," she said. "Some true, some false. So did I. The hard thing when you find out some are false is not to scrap them all."

"Whatever you do," she said, "you will never be happy till you forgive this town and your parents and me."

"You?"

"I should have done something. But I didn't want to lose you. So I cried and kept quiet. You remember?"

"Yes. I thought of it to-night."

"I might have saved you; probably not. But whether I had or not you would never have forgiven me. So I didn't try."

"But you could always say anything to me."

"Because I never did. I was the only person who didn't try to save you. And always I wanted to most of all. Then when the chance came I didn't dare. I'd lost your Uncle Fitz and you were the person now that I depended on."

"For what? I've never done anything for you."

"For happiness. Then, too," she said, "you must forgive yourself for the wrong you did to Julia."

"To Julia?" he said. "Well, by God!"

"You imposed on her," she said. "She was a girl who wanted a stuffed shirt and she was entitled to have one. You made her think you were one. Gradually you undeceived her."

"And myself."

"Yes. But that doesn't make it different for her. She might have had a happy life."

"She might have had one anyhow. If there was just a little sap in her."

"Does she still expect much in the way of family attention?"

"Still? She never has. That's what I'm talking about."

"Good."

"By God," he said, "you're easily pleased."

"I was thinking of the children."

"That's one thing you needn't worry about. There won't be any more."

"Of Tad and Jane."

"Ah," he said. "Them. That's the one bad thing. But I'm no good to them."

"Julia," she said, "will never let Tad ride now and Jane ought to be starting. I found a pony for her when I was in Lexington, and got a price on him."

"That's too bad," he said, "good ponies are hard to find."

"Yes," she said, "I've been on the lookout for a year."

"I don't suppose she'd ever be as good as Tad. Too nervous."

"She might be good, but he's exceptional; much better than you were at his age."

"Do you think so?"

"Oh yes! I think he'll be even better than your father."

"How much does that pony cost?" he said.

"Two hundred dollars."

"Is he really all right?"

"Yes. I rode him every day I was in Lexington. He's ten years old, well bred and sound. He's really a little horse; about 13-1. Plenty of rein, a light mouth and——"

"Never mind the sales talk," he said. "You're good at it, I know." Outside the window, a faint gray streak edged the dark hills beyond the river. "I've got to go," he said. "I was going to get some coffee at the Greek's."

"I'll make you coffee."

"I haven't time," he said. "Get the pony. I want to give it to them. Send me the bill. I want to pay for him. How much will the freight be? What about a saddle? I want to get that too. Will he carry Tad? Would Tad like him? Send me the bill."

His eyes were on his trembling hands. From far away he heard her voice. "I thought I'd get a felt pad with little stirrups on it. Yes, he's big enough for Tad. And he jumps like a little hunter. You can pay me when——" Now she was coming with a rush; she was kneeling down in front of him, and at the touch of her light arms around his shoulders he was shaking horribly. A rending seized him, twisted his stiff face and bursting its bonds brought him down to a dark and breathless cavern of despair. He clenched his teeth; try as he would he could not still those strangled noises in his throat.

In the end he felt her warm, soft hair against his face and her two hands gently gripping him. He turned his head aside and came up panting. Her hands slid away and took his own, still tightly clenched, smoothed them and lifted them against her face.

He looked at her head, bent down in front of him. She was really turning gray. A faint gray light was in the room; and out the window, beyond the dusky islands where his Uncle Fitz-Greene had drowned himself, beyond the dark hills of the farther shore, a delicate, mild lavender suffused the sky.

"Here, here," he said, "I must go. The sun is coming up."

"Must you?" she murmured.

"I left a letter for her beside the bed. I must get back."

She sat back on her heels and looked at him seriously. "Oh," she said, "you must run!" She smiled at him softly, sadly; "But wait," she stretched her hands out toward him. "Hold still," she said, "your tie."

The sky and the flat, smooth-flowing stream was turning pink as he went up the river. The birds were stirring with light chirpings, and down below the highway bridge he heard the soft, thin puffing of a flatboat. The house-fronts showed pale and empty in the morning light. Under the branches of the maple trees that still held the dregs of dusk, he saw the big bay windows of his father's house, shrouded and sleeping like all the other houses.

Over the front door of his grandfather's a sickly blue light glowed; it was a private hospital. He was glad that house was not dead, that it still lived and had a function; and if, as was suspected, the genial and dissolute old semi-quack who ran it was not above extending aid at times to damsels in distress, so much the better. Children should be wanted. They knew that much in Russia anyway. If they were wanted, they gave life its indisputable meaning. He would start to ride again. He wondered how high that pony could jump. There were a number of roads in the hills behind the farm; they could be cleared out and a few small fences put across them; very small at first. In that way they could take a different ride and jump a few fences every day.

Gray curtains were drawn in the bow window of the red brick house they still called "Old Judge Worrall's." His Uncle Mun now lived there all alone, quarrelling with his German housekeeper and giving small select dinners at long intervals; small dinners with choice wine and beautifully cooked, after which he would be ill for days.

He passed by the late Senator Beaver's brownstone front and by Gus Ringler's Byzantine façade, where Heinrich Ringler now lived in kindly solemn state with a Dusenberg car and a spangled wife from Jersey City.

The sky was red now and he was walking fast. From an alley-
way he heard the echo of heavy footsteps, then saw a policeman's
cap and a trudging figure.

"Hello, Harry," he said. The policeman turned his ruddy face
and waited for him. "Hello, Mr. Rand, you're out early."

"Yes," he said, "this is the best time of the day."

Swinging his nightstick the policeman walked beside him.
"Yes," he said, "it's all right. I'm due for the day shift by rights,
but I told 'em I was satisfied. Of course," he said, "in winter it's
different, but even then," he said, "I don't mind. I get to take the
kids to the pictures and things like that. If they're kept in
though, I don't take 'em; not even Saturday. They know that.
One of them won't work and the other one is kind of dumb. He's
a good kid though. Don't you think that sometimes dumb kids
turn out all right too?"

"Sure, I do. Lots of kids keep on going after the bright ones
have stopped and pretty soon they're beyond them."

"I guess that's a fact," Harry said. "I know they always used
to say when I was a kid I was awful dumb. Say," he said, "I'm
sorry about last night, night before, I mean, but I guess you
know how it was."

"Why, Harry," he said, "you were fine. It was a break for me
that they didn't send some one else."

"Any one else would have treated you just the same."

"It might not have been so good though if I'd gotten some one
I didn't know."

"That wouldn't make no difference; they all know you. No,
sir," he said, "nobody ever better try to pull anything on you.
The town wouldn't stand it. Of course," he said, "there's always a few mean old bastards like the one who telephoned; he
didn't give his name but I'm having the call traced, see? And
believe me, in the end, we'll get him on a parking ordinance or
something."

"No, hold on, Harry, let it ride. There was no harm done.
Forget about it."

The policeman spun his nightstick and caught it deftly. "Well,
just as you say, Chief," he said reluctantly. "I turn off here."
He grinned and made a half salute. "Any time we can do
anything for you——"

CHAPTER LIX

I<small>F</small>, at the time of his return that early morning, up the river bank, he thought that his virtue, which was the name he sometimes liked to give his instincts, was to be rewarded, there turned out to be nothing in it. Julia remained incredibly unaltered, though after the first flush of his new allegiance to his home, he admitted that she of all people could least be expected to respond to a drama of his spirit of which she was ignorant. But it did annoy him to have her take his improved behavior and greater interest in the children as the results, only partial but admirable so far as they went, of the talkings-to she gave him. In fact, she was encouraged to make quite a practice of them; and he, on his side, found to his slowly dawning and profound surprise that they made his life a little easier. He had only to listen and agree, to nod his head—here her obtuseness was an asset—and she, refreshed and stimulated by her achievement, would make concessions.

There were a few set rules—no unexpected guests to meals, and she must know where he was going so that she could find him, which he soon found out she never tried to do. And in most arrangements of their lives, not being interested in matters of the spirit, she was open to negotiation. In fact, she was a woman not difficult to get along with, once a man had given up all idea of being fond of her.

Through the hills behind the farm he and the children rode. Ahead, down the leafy wood road, the small bay pony switched his narrow tail and put his black feet down quickly, delicately, among the dried leaves, the enormous hoof marks and dead sticks. His sharp ears pointed forward, twirled back when any of them spoke. Above the pigtails, Jane's head was dark and small and domed. She chattered freely but unanswered, and, in fact, incomprehensible, as she never turned her head. From time to time she hitched a strap of her overalls over her thin shoulder

and addressed herself to the pony whom she had insisted upon
naming "Clara."

Behind her Tad sat, proud and easy, on a chunky sleepy gray
that had almost won a cheap race at Pimlico before he broke
down. Tad stared ahead at the babbling Jane, then looked back
at his father woodenly and shook his head. The gray took the
occasion to snatch a bunch of green leaves. He grinned at Tad
and kept the old chestnut brood mare from nipping the gray's
inviting rump. Behind him on the saddle a flour sack held the
provisions for their lunch.

The pony and the horses grazed in the clearing while Tad and
Jane cooked chops over the fire they had made, and ate the re-
sulting combination of cinders and raw meat with satisfaction.
But even with them his life was not an idyl. With greater
familiarity, Jane had become a pert and tireless talker, an inexhaustible fount of questions, designed not to gain information
but to attract attention to herself. And Tad, as he grew older,
proved a master of good advice, of critical suggestions and of
explanations of the obvious. The two of them fought endlessly
over the most far-fetched and inconsequential trifles; in this
field their talent for involving themselves in an inane redundant
labyrinth amounted to a sort of demented genius. For a long
time he was patient and very logical, and all to no avail. But
when one day a wave of fury swept him and he told them he
was sick of them and one more peep out of either and he would
knock their heads together, they listened with respectful understanding and showed afterward an increase in their affection.

Toward his children, toward Julia, toward his father and
mother, even toward Porky, and so on down to Harry, the cop,
and Jeff, the popcorn vendor, in the square, he felt like a stranger
returned from some more brilliant, desperate world; and yet
returned only to join himself as he had been, and always would
be, to the end. If any of them guessed the violent and fantastic
journey he had been on, it was most unexpectedly his father. Not
that his father knew the possibilities that once had entered his
dutiful son's well-ordered life, but he began, partly, perhaps,
because he sensed the impending failure of his own powers, to
treat this son of his as though he were a man. He began to talk
about the problems of the mines and then to take him with him
on his trips to West Virginia. And on these trips, sitting in the
meagre superintendent's office at the drift-mouth, or around the

cylindrical nickel-plated stove in Mrs. MacDonald's parlor, he would say, "Well, MacDonald, my son and I feel——"

Now and again his father dropped out of these monthly trips; and then insensibly he drifted back to the sales end. "Here, I'll take care of these inquiries," he said; "you'd better answer this letter of MacDonald's. He wants to know if he can try cast concrete instead of timbers on that new entry."

"All right, Father, but what's the answer?"

"If I knew the answer, do you suppose I'd give the job to you?"

From then on, the village street of flat-roofed stores, the narrow valley teeming with life, yet lonely, the double row of company houses on the gullied hill, the grotesque tipple, the dark unchanging labyrinth underground, became increasingly the centre of his world. On the business side he merely, and all too confidently, stepped into a fragment of a boundless chaos. His own position was uncomfortably ridiculous, at least in his own eyes. All the others there at Carbonvale seemed to accept this as an inevitable, even a natural phenomenon. He had been part owner of these mines for years; he had sold their coal by countless thousand tons, and he knew nothing whatever about them; about Mr. MacDonald or the bosses, or the men that worked them, or about the art and craft of mining. All that he knew was that the general state of the coal business was fantastic and impossible, and that from the Jacksonville agreement, down to the latest wildcat mine that had just been opened on a shoestring by two insurance men from Parkersburg, the industry was a welter of waste and exploitation.

If anything, the introduction of an amateurish absentee owner into an already hopeless situation did, he supposed, more harm than good. MacDonald had his system and the world of Carbonvale had apparently become adjusted to it. They knew that as manager for those mysterious owners who existed somewhere in interstellar space, Mr. MacDonald's method was never to spend a cent if it could be avoided. This they accepted as a logical effort on his part to hold his job, and continued to struggle along with resignation; while Mr. MacDonald, maintaining underground a division between Americans, foreigners and negroes, derived from his arrangements added confidence that they would not combine against him.

However, when the young heir-apparent owner of the mines

began with increasing frequency to impinge in person upon their consciousness, it raised all sorts of questions in their minds. It was Mr. MacDonald's simple, fervent hope that he would go away again; and undoubtedly that would have been the easiest solution; but to go away again was the one thing which he could not consider. The dreary village street, the shabby company houses, the ruined hillsides drew him strongly. He made excuses to stay over, pretending to be studying past records in the offices, but really because from the Superintendent's office window he could see the big wheel of the tipple turning, the pump-house engines throw their wisps of steam, the cars trip up against the sky and, at the close of day, the blackened night shift, with cap-lamps and dinner buckets, come trudging out through the drift-mouth door. Here was a life again where men were doing work, and though he never could be part of it, he caught for a minute an echo of the days when he, himself, had worked and fought and suffered filth, and hunger and fear with other men.

Back home in Midian, he watched the children grow and watched his father fade. The women altered less; Aunt Clara toward him, not at all, though he felt that in affairs of business she might be growing slightly adamantine. Perhaps she realized that only a certain time remained to make up for the trimmings which, as a solitary woman, she had suffered in her early struggles with the business world. His mother was convinced that with the exception of his father's illness, the world was growing better; and that her son was the proof of it. He had saved the world in the Great War and come home a hero; he was happily married to an estimable, if at the same time, quite unworthy girl; he had two darling children and was making a most extraordinary success with the mines; not that her husband had not done wonderfully with them too. And yet he sometimes wondered whether all this were not part of a rôle in which she, long ago, had cast herself as the most feasible answer to a life whose dark recesses and complexities were too much for her. She had moulded her husband and her son on a model which she had never questioned while she was at work. Certainly now was no time to question it.

As Jane grew up her congenital garrulity blossomed into a sort of conscious and exasperating charm. Her nose was pointed like her grand-mother's and her eyes were brown and quick; and while she had an artificiality of manner it was, he concluded, a natural artificiality, a child-like and instinctive attempt to express a sense that the world was colorful and gay. He could not claim that this discovery was his own. It came improbably enough, through Porky who, having exhausted the possibilities of his composition foot as a topic, had politely but firmly resigned from intercourse with the children. But now that Jane was twelve, Porky began to time his visits so that he should encounter her and she quite shamelessly would make excuse to wait outside the house to meet him.

Sitting in the living room, he would hear the alternate footfalls of Porky's shoes and then Jane's triumphant greeting; and often while he waited on he would hear their footfalls mingle on the walk, passing to and fro, and the murmur of their voices engaged in the discussion of affairs.

One night when Julia, involved in a church supper, had left the house, Jane sat between him and Porky in the living room while they waited for dinner to be announced. In her blue serge dress with broad white cuffs and collar and her dark hair tousselled around her brown face, she looked like the young son of a cavalier; but when she moved to turn and listen it was with the grace and lightness, though still awkward, embryonic, of a girl.

"Look here," he said, "what about bed?"

She shook her head at him. "Eight:fifteen." She turned to Porky. "He knows that."

"Well, what about home work?"

"I've done it."

"Frankly, I don't see when you could have."

"Well, though," she said, "I always get good marks." She looked at him compellingly. "Don't I always get good marks?"

"Yes," he said, "unfortunately, you do."

Porky stirred. "Julia is out," he said, "Jane should preside at dinner."

"Oh, my," she said, "I'd love that." Her face was tragic. "But I've had supper already."

Porky nodded his head at her. "A very wise precaution for a hostess."

In the dining room she sat in her mother's chair in front of the white mantel and the gilt-framed round mirror between the silver bracket-lights above it. Sitting on her right, Porky moved a cut-glass candlestick to get a view of her. "That's a pretty dress," he said.

"This?" she said, "oh, this is just my school dress. I have one much prettier."

"How do you know?"

"It's a party dress."

"I am still not convinced. What's it like?"

"It's flowered crépe de chine," she said; "yellow roses with a pink bow."

Porky mastered himself. "Well," he said, "I imagine that is pretty, too, but this is really right. Do not," he said, "allow the dressmakers to delude you. For you, simplicity of color and severity of line."

"I don't think I like that."

"I was afraid so, but that has nothing to do with the question."

"But I like to wear dresses I like."

"Do you choose your clothes?"

"Not yet."

"Even so," he said, "you are no worse off than any other woman. May I have another roll?"

"Yes, indeed." She rang a silver bell beside her plate. The maid's long, sad and discontented face was thrust from the pantry door. "Mr. Montross would like a roll, please." The face was withdrawn.

"Three men in Paris choose women's clothes," Porky said. "I suppose it is for the best. It prevents all kinds of deplorable atrocities, but at the cost of all originality. Thank you," he looked up at the maid. "Did the cook make these rolls?" She nodded sadly. "Please give her my compliments. Tommy," he said, "here is a girl that should dress in her own style, don't you think?" The maid looked startled.

"Some day maybe she will."

"Simplicity of line," he said. "It is our forte here in this country and yet how scared of it we are. Look at the ax-handle; look at the clipper-ship; American inventions and each a perfect form. And then we turn around and do state capitols and gingerbread and Byzantine and Queen Anne, bastard Gothic in the colleges and bastard Spanish in the subdivisions." He buttered his roll, his face pursed with the labor of impending pronouncements. "We are supposed to be a practical people," he said, "and yet we can't get it through our heads that mere ugliness for its own sake is not enough."

"What about some of those French villas that we saw, Porky?"

"I know," he said, "and I have visited some of the towns they have rebuilt in the devastated regions." He shook his head. "They are the real atrocities of the war. It is incorrect," he said, "to say that nations have the defects of their qualities. They seem to have other defects quite inconsistent with them. Otherwise why should the most intelligent and military of all nations have gone into the war wearing bright red pants? And yet," he said, "they can teach us the most. Jane," he said, "do you study French?"

"Yes," she said. "We're reading 'Lettres de Mon Moulin.'"

"That must be a good school. Generally they read 'Le Cid' and 'Hernani.'"

"Oh, we read those last year."

"Do you like 'Lettres de Mon Moulin'?"

"Yes," she said. "All except about the little goat. That's too sad."

"You don't like sad things then."

"Not about animals. About people, I don't mind."

Porky wiped his small round mouth. "Do you regard your father as a person or as an animal?"

She gave a short sharp laugh and then looked down the table across the ivy centre-piece at her father with a half-smile, mischievous and warm. For once she had nothing to say.

"She regards me, Porky, as a mythological figure combining the best features of each."

"A centaur perhaps," Porky said. "Would it be a centaur, Jane?"

She shook her head. "No," she said. "Not a centaur. A centaur can't fall off his horse."

Porky flew back in his chair and clapped his napkin to his mouth to muffle the hisses. He came up breathing hard. "My old friend," he said, "my old White Knight I might have guessed it. How long has this been going on?" He turned to Jane. "How often does he do it? Is it fun to watch? May I come, too?"

But Jane was no longer smiling. A dark flush mounted, her eyes were on her empty plate. "It was only once," she murmured, "and the mare fell, too." She looked up at her father with swift appeal. "Didn't she?"

He smiled. "Well, not exactly. She stumbled badly but she didn't fall."

She looked away unhappily.

"Well, that's another matter," Porky said gently. "When a horse starts to go down the best thing is to get clear. I've no patience," he was firm, "with these people who stay on too long."

She looked at him acutely. He met her glance with firmness. "It's just asking for trouble," he said.

She smiled a little and nodded seriously.

Afterward in the living room she sat in the fiddleback chair behind the silver coffee tray. "Sugar, Mr. Montross?"

"One lump, please."

"Cream?"

"No, thank you."

Her hard and somewhat scrubby little hands moved delicately among the silverware and the small gold-rimmed cups.

"Father," she said, "you take two lumps."

"That's right," he said. He watched her firm small hand and the dark jet of coffee from the curving spout. "And now," he said, reaching forward for his cup, "you've served the coffee and it's quarter of nine. Your mother may be here at any minute."

"Gosh," she said, "I guess so." She got up with a scramble and stood in front of Porky on the sofa. "Good night, Mr. Montross," she said. "It has been a very pleasant evening."

Porky put his cup down and stood up. He held out his immaculate stout hand. "For me too," he said. "Good night."

She gave his hand a quick handshake like a boy and let it go. "Daddy," she said, "will you come up?"

"When you're in bed," he said, "you holler."

In her straight narrow dark-blue dress with the white cuffs and collar she walked out of the room.

Though Julia inwardly changed little, in appearance she aged fast. Perhaps her ash-blonde hair and pallor lent itself to grayness; perhaps age finds it easier to establish itself in those who were never young. And then one day when he was down in

West Virginia at the mines; it was a late Fall day of scanty yellow leaves and wet bare branches in a driving rain, Tad's second year in high school; a telegram had come. And when next morning he had stumbled into the cold darkness of the train shed, his mother met him with both small hands stretched out before her purple satin coat. "My dear son," she said, "you must be brave." She gripped his hands. "At three o'clock this morning," she said. "We did everything that we could."

He could not think of anything to say. He stood stunned, not knowing what to make of all the feelings that beset him— sorrow, and awe, pity and a sense of freedom; a faint and fragrant unexpected sort of love; and suddenly a vile regret that it had come far, far too late. He burst out with a strangled frightened voice. "What was it? Why, when I left home——"

"It was pneumonia; just a little cold three days ago." The porter had his bag now and he and his mother were walking slowly, hand in hand. "And yesterday morning her lungs seemed suddenly to fill. The doctor says he's never seen anything like it." She gave his hand a little shake of emphasis. Together they climbed the stairs to the waiting room.

"Did she—" he said. "Was she in pain?"

"Oh, no"; she said. "Dr. Julius thinks not. He was wonderful. He did everything. We all did everything. He had oxygen tanks, and he has a doctor from Johns Hopkins coming in on the morning train from Baltimore. Son, dear, I can't keep up—these stairs."

"Oh, I forgot," he muttered. "We'll stand here on this step." He faced her. "Was she—was she unhappy?" He cleared his throat. "Was she frightened?"

"Oh, no, dear," his mother said. She still was panting. "Nothing like that. You mustn't think that. Except for the breathing, she seemed to just pass into a sleep. Dr. Flowers was there, of course, and spoke to her. Mr. Wyman, his assistant, was there too, but he did not go up."

Going through the waiting room, he was conscious that his mother was trotting and clinging to his arm. "I'm sorry, Mother," he said, "I forgot."

"Go on," she said, "I'll keep up. It was just those stairs." In front of the taxicab, he started to reach in his pocket. "No, sir,

Mr. Rand." The redcap's brown hand came out and gently pushed him toward the car. "You go right along."

The river, cold and dark in the early autumn morning, passed by the taxi window. His mother still tightly gripped his hand. She was strong for one so small and old.

"The children are all right," she said. "They're waiting for you."

"Yes," he said.

"Clara's there."

"That's good," he said, "I'm glad of that."

"She has the spare room. I should come up myself, but your father needs me."

"Yes," he said, "how is he?"

"He feels the shock, of course."

"How are you? You've had no sleep."

"Those poor children," she said. "We must all try to make them happy."

"Yes," he said. He looked out the window at the steely river and the dark hills. What was happiness, how obtained, how transferred to another? There was nothing he would not do if he could give those two a source of happiness that they could keep. But the intention was in itself of no avail. There was nothing his mother, here beside him, would not have done at any moment from his birth to give happiness to him, yet she had always been, and dimly guessed it in her grieved and craving heart, no more than a loved and loving alien. Julia, too, would have died to make him happy, at least to make him happy in a way that she approved of. And her way, now at this gray moment beside the steely river, crowned by the dignity of death, brought into focus by irretrievable finality, suddenly took on form and meaning. No meaning that carried conviction to him, truly, but an integrity and pattern of its own. She had given, had been ready to give him all she had, only to encounter his changed and, for her, impossible demands. On her side, too, she had in favor of her way of life, however thin and flat it tasted to him, not only her own feelings and her lack of them but also tradition, not to be despised, and the authority of good sense and of logic.

So equipped, as she must have thought at first, for all of life's contingencies, she had found herself confronted by problems she had no reason to expect and, facing them and the changed man who was their author, she had, with unimaginative courage, done the best she could. She had even, he saw it now with pity and astonishment, tried once to enter the distant repellant life of his for which he had left her. He saw it now. Through the rowdy night of Singletarry and the little gang, she had sat while they roused the neighborhood and had never warned them of the children. She had even taken a drink or two herself; as if she thought that in the noxious potion lay a mystery that would make her free of her husband's love once more; only to find herself no less deserted, and so next day to harry him in her defeat. She was not wise, not generous, not clever, but she had been brave and pitiful and he had been too pleased with his own new insight into the more obvious shabby corners of humanity to reflect that prigs as well as wastrels need forgiveness.

Now he would always think of her, trying, while he got drunk, to enter into the incredible evening. And in a sense succeeding. What feelings had stirred her at Singletarry's addresses, however egregious, what thoughts nebulous and tragically belated, that there was a world of men and women which she had missed? And what thoughts had been hers in the critical years since then; and at the end just now, alone with death and Dr. Flowers?

He gripped his mother's hand. No, he had wronged her. Wronged her in more ways than one. Poor child, poor child! He smiled with sadness, almost with bitterness. She had had a right to ask that he remain the same or else make love to her like Singletarry.

In the hallway Tad was standing in his gray long trousers and dark-blue soccer-team sweater. His brown hair was shaggy and there were dark lines under his gray eyes. His snub nose stood out boyish and incongruous in the face of a desolate, self-controlled young man.

"I was just telling your father, dear," his mother put in quickly, "how wonderful you'd been."

"I'll take your bag, Dad," Tad said. With the bag in his hand, he hesitated, flushing unhappily; it could not go up to the familiar room.

"That's all right, son. Leave it in the hall. We'll have some breakfast. Where's Jane?" In a silent rush, her long thin legs were flying downstairs. Her dark-blue serge dress fell against him; her dark braided hair was on his shoulders.

"There, there," he said, "you must be a good girl." He stroked the long dark braid. "I should have been here," he said, "if I'd only known." She flung her head back, her pert, mischievous face was white and tragic. She searched his own face through her tears. "Now we have only you," she said, and dropped her head again down on his shoulders. His mother, watching, fumbled and dabbled with her handkerchief.

And all the while he knew that these were Jane's dramatics, and yet like Tad's stolidity, they too were a defense against unbearable disaster.

At last, Jane freed herself and stood scrubbing at her eyes with her deplorable handkerchief; a mere, dejected little girl again.

"I'll go upstairs," his mother said, "and talk to Clara. The maid has breakfast ready."

The lights were on in the dark dining room. Jane took her mother's place behind the coffee percolator, and after sitting for a while, deferring to the silence and her grief, began to eat tremendously. "Can I have coffee, too?" she said.

"If you want," he said, "but you ought to get some sleep."

"I'll have mostly hot milk," she said, "with a little coffee in it." She was determined to have at least some coffee on this occasion.

"Tad can have coffee, too, can't he?"

"I often have coffee," Tad said.

"Not very often," Jane said. "Hardly ever."

He looked at the two of them, then Jane flushed, and lowered her eyes. "I'm sorry," she said, "I'll stop."

"If you do," Tad muttered with an effort, "I will."

While Jane was cleaning up her bread and jam, Tad left his plate untouched.

"Don't wait, Tad," he said to him, "if you want to go."

"I'll wait," Tad said.

"Now, Sis," he said, as Jane wiped her mouth and pushed back from the table. "You ought to get some sleep. I'll tell you what you do; take off your things and rub yourself down with some of that alcohol." He checked himself; the alcohol was in his own bathroom beyond the bedroom.

"Wait," he said, heavily, "I'll get it."

"It's in our bathroom now," she said. "Aunt Clara moved the things."

When she was gone, Tad waited silently for him to finish; then he raised his serious eyes.

"Dad," he said, "I've got to ask you something."

"All right, son."

"Well," he said, "you see we play the Newtown High a week from Saturday. It's for the Second District Championship." He looked away. "I guess I ought to let them know, so they can work another guy into my place."

"Well, how do you feel about your playing? Do you think you'd be able to swing it?"

"Oh, I guess I'd be able to turn in a good game, all right."

"Well, then," he said, "I think the harder you play, the more your mother would be pleased." He took a final sip of coffee from the white, blue-banded cup. "Don't you think so?"

There was no answer. When he looked up, Tad's snub nose was crinkled back, his eyes were squeezed together tightly. Silently, blindly, he was stumbling from the room. His shoulder struck the door frame, and he was gone. He heard his stumbling footfalls in the back hall.

The yard behind the house, now graying in the late wet fall, was empty. He walked down to the weathered tool-house at the end and gently pulled against the creaking door. The dark-blue soccer-sweater was bowed down among the pots and rusty spades and stove wood.

CHAPTER LX

From then on, he did not go to the mines so often. He stayed at home with the children, and often his Aunt Clara stayed with them. In the office he was taking charge of everything. His father lived on milk now and could not get to the office every day. When he did it was to say, "You stay here where you're needed; there's no one here that knows the game—just clerks, that's all they are. Down there, MacDonald is a first-class operating man, one of the best. I picked him out myself. He was just a youngster and I sized him up."

And it was true that without him the mines were doing better. In 1926, they earned sixteen percent, and if it had not been too late, Tad could have gone off to boarding school. Jane did go off to Farmington next year, and the year after Tad was a freshman at Cornell. He supposed that Tad ought to have gone to New Haven, but there was this boy from high school that was going to Cornell, and then there were the mines. The boy was bound to be a mining engineer. He read all the books in the house and subscribed on his own account to "Modern Mining," marked copies of which he sometimes presented to his father for his instruction. "Dad," he would say, "you ought to get this." And worst of all, he showed a talent for bringing a conversation on any subject around to mining. It was too soon to tell whether he would turn out to be a mining genius, or merely a bore. In either case, it would not help matters to thwart him. The summer after his senior year at high school, he and his friend, Red Perrin, a son of the manager of the Armour Storage Plant, drove down to West Virginia in a Ford which they had bought for eighteen dollars. When he came back there was only talk of mining; they had kept the office letters to Mr. MacDonald in their pockets and gotten jobs with the track gang. And then a miner's buddy had fallen sick, and Tad had been taken on.

"How could you do that work? A fool performance. You don't know—" He stopped; he was getting old and talking like his father. "How did you make out?" he said.

566

"Swell," Tad said. "You ought to see me load a shot. Of course, Grandpa had to decide about the drilling. His real name was Mr. Harrelson. We had a kind of tricky roof in there, but Grandpa knew his stuff and when we fired the shot you ought to see that face come off."

"My God!" he said. "What did MacDonald think of this performance?"

"Oh, him," Tad said. "I never saw him. Told them my name was Tad Smith."

So Tad went off to study mining at Cornell and wrote back home to say that he was doing fine; that, in fact, he knew most of the stuff that they were teaching already, and also, having worked in a mine, a good deal of practical stuff that the Profs were not aware of. He was out for the freshman soccer team and thought he'd join Psi Upsilon. They would take Red Perrin in too; and he had been up to the house and on a tablet in the hall had seen the name of William G. McGuire among the others who had died in the war; and would somebody send him his fur-lined gloves.

In the dark hospital room his narrow mattress, as he stirred to ease himself, gave off a faint rustle. The starched skirt of the night-nurse rustled, too. Her face, a pale blur above her blue cloak, came toward him. "Are you awake?" she said. "Well, you had a good sleep." Her pale face and pale rustling skirt passed him by. There was the tinkle of a tiny chain and then the hooded night-lamp on the table sprang into light; within the sharp, brilliant circle her hands moved to the thermometer in the half-filled glass. The glass rod came out, dripping, was shaken smartly, deftly and disappeared toward him into the dusk. He opened his mouth; the smooth wet glass, faintly indented, slid beneath his tongue: Miss Wesson's fingers in one motion fell to his wrist and hung there, lightly tenacious. Rustling, she bent her head to see her wrist-watch, now shining in the small ring of light.

Under those cool, impassive fingers, he felt his pulse jump as though again it would babble a secret message to the outside world. The poor blind worm that was his body and that knew so much and knew so little, still struggled to convey its meaning. Let it desist, let it be at peace, its message had long since arrived,

had been deciphered. Rest, worm. It is all right. They know.
I know.

The fingers left his wrist. The worm, resigned, now ceased to
tap its hurried code.

"How am I doing?" he mumbled around the glass rod in his
mouth.

"You mustn't talk," she said. "You're doing fine. All that
can be expected."

"Good," he said. "And what do you expect?"

"If you talk," she said, "I'll have to leave it in longer."

"Come on," he said. "Isn't this a minute thermometer?"

"No, it is not," she said. "It's a three-minute thermometer.
Minute thermometers are not reliable. Don't talk." He lay there
mouthing the glass rod, trying to count the tiny indentations
with the tip of his tongue. The block of night against the window was quartered by the sharp reflection of the night-lamp,
and of Miss Wesson's arm and hand. "Anyway," she said, "it's
bad for you."

The thermometer cocked up with his grin. "What's good for
me?" he said.

"Now, Mr. Rand," she said, "I mean it. Is it under your
tongue?" He stared out patiently then into the night. She had
her work to do.

Her fingers plucked the rod from his mouth, tilted it to the
light, turned it microscopically. With a faint click it slid into
its glass: there was the scratch of Miss Wesson's fountain pen
on paper.

"We can't take care of you," she said, "unless we keep your
chart correctly, can we?"

"That's right. This hospital has certainly made a fine job
of my chart."

The light clicked off. Her voice came from the rustle as it
crossed the room. "Try and see if you can sleep again."

He closed his eyes. From the distant river a steamship raised
its dull, gruff voice. It sounded close. His eyes came open. Out
there was nothing but the night and far up-stream the string of
lights across the enormous bridge.

Across this river, far out to the West, where night had fallen
hours after this dark here, Tad was somewhere now spending
his last summer vacation in Colorado, looking over the copper,

gold and silver mines in furtherance of his modest ambition to know more about mining, if he did not already, than any other living man. And to the East, where dawn had come, Jane, with three other girls from Farmington, and a teacher whom they liked was perhaps in some country inn in France. He and Tad had come to see them off; that was two months ago, here in New York. There had been flowers and books and baskets of fruit, and candied ginger and marrons glacés, all obviously unnecessary as the ship had a large and flourishing shopping district of its own. And there had been a little sophomore from Harvard, well poised and earnest, who had privately assured him that his daughter was a very remarkable girl. At last the deep hoarse whistle, the sweet rich bugle sounded. The sophomore shook hands warmly and went away. He and Jane and Tad sat in a row on the berth in the small gray stateroom. In her brown knitted dress, Jane stood up; with her brown hair tousled around her dark eyes, she looked a little like a girl pretending to be a woman, or almost like a woman who had not lost and perhaps would never lose the spirit of a child. Abruptly she sat down on his knee. He felt, almost with dismay, the mysterious warmth and lightness of a girl. "Oh, Daddy," she said suddenly, "it's all so big and lonesome."

"It's just that way at first. Wait till you get started."

"Oh, no," she said, "I wish I were staying home with you. I wish Tad were going in my place."

Tad withdrew his eyes from the green moss of the piling outside the porthole and glanced briefly at the other littered berths. "What?" he said, "sleep in here with those two Janes! Not me! They've got the place messed up already."

"Oh, dear." Her light strong arm came round his neck. Her warm soft hair was in his mouth and eyes. "I feel so ungrateful to be acting this way." He heard Tad's voice. "A mess. Somebody's going to get a nasty jolt when he marries them."

"I'm going to bring you a silk dressing-gown from Paris," she said. "Tad, would you like one?"

"If you want to be really useful," Tad said, "go round to the Bureau of Mines there and get all the reports for last year. Of course, if you could get a chance to visit some good property——"

He roused himself. "Son, I won't have her going down one of those French mines."

"All right, then," Tad said, "I guess that's right. The miners wouldn't like it. They think it's unlucky, and anyhow, she wouldn't get anything. But actually," he said firmly, "their safety factor is three times as great as ours. No, sir," he observed impressively, "we don't know it all."

She raised her head and looked at Tad. Her little sunburned nose was sharp and impudent. "Surely, Tad, darling, you don't include yourself."

"All ashore!" a steward's voice echoed down the corridor.

As the great high wall of shining plates drifted slowly from the pier, he ran his eye down the crowded rail till it met with a shock, the small brown figure in the knitted dress. She was waving blindly with both hands and crying without restraint or shame. He fixed his face in a grin and waved until the figure could no longer be distinguished in the long and close-packed row which drifted slowly, turned, slowly, then gained momentum down the tide.

Tad's voice was in his ear. "She's a great kid; but we've got to admit that she really loves a good cry."

"Oh, for God's sake, Tad," he said.

"Ah, no," Tad said. "She really is the best I ever saw. What about that Harvard bird?"

"He seemed like a nice boy."

"Sure," Tad said. "Democratic, too. He absolutely forgives the rest of the world for not being Harvard men."

Back in Midian he was lonely in the house and, living alone there, he began to feel that he had reached, if not old age, at least a certain age; an age after which he would make no new friends, think perhaps no new thoughts and achieve no success of any sort that required youthful spirits. He and his age had served their purpose, if any purpose ever had been theirs, a point which modern commentators seemed to doubt. And now the world, or what was left of it, was in the hands, God help it, of Tad and Jane. Well, he had had the fun of watching them grow up and they had had the fun of being watched by some one who, with whatever reservations, intrinsically believed in them.

On the warm spring evenings he would sit shirt-sleeved on the front doorstep in bourgeois fashion, reading the paper, and gaining disproportionate satisfaction from the exchanges of stere-

otyped banalities with neighbors who passed by. One evening, his
heart rejoiced at the sound of alternate footfalls in the dusk.
"Hey, Porky," he said, "I thought you were at Narrangansett."
Porky's blinding Palm Beach suit swam into view. He placed
his panama on the top step and then sat down with hesitating
care. He was getting bald as well as stouter.

"Just a few days' business," he remarked, "and then I'm going
back again."

"Is that so? Who's the girl?"

Porky's small blue eyes met his. "This time," he said, "it
really is a girl."

"Well, I'll be darned!"

"A widow. Charming, well-to-do and generous."

"Good Lord, Pork, is this serious?"

"Only in the highest sense of the word. She is a remarkable
woman. She saw at a glance that I was worthless, which took a
great load off my mind to start with. Since then she has proved
an unfailingly good companion; and her burgundy is probably
the best in America. Her brandy is, unfortunately, mediocre, but
perfectly potable." He drew a silver cigarette case from his
pocket. "In short, I foresee a warm and mutually agreeable relationship, uncomplicated by the harassments of immorality."

"Well, as to that, Pork, we can only hope for the best. For
some women, I suppose you still have charm, and in any case a
man can never tell."

Porky had a cigarette between his small pursed lips now, and
the end of his silver case had proved to be a lighter.

"Pork," he said, "that's quite a trick you've got there."

Porky snapped the lighter shut. "The latest thing," he said,
"cumbersome and impractical. She insists upon my using it."
He put the cigarette case in his pocket. "Don't feel," he said,
"that my remarks about her burgundy make it useless to offer
me whatever you have in the house."

They sat till the passing cars grew scarce and the crescent moon
was standing overhead. Porky set his glass down on the silver
tray between them.

"Another Tom Collins, Porky?"

Porky shook his head. "Thomas," he said, "have you ever been
in love?"

"Well, yes," he said slowly. "I guess I was once."

"I thought so," Porky said. "For you it was a tragedy." He stood up in the moonlight and carefully pulled down the front of his white Palm Beach coat. He glanced at the blue-silk handkerchief in his pocket to see that the proper amount was showing. "Even so," he said, "I envy you. I must get along."

It was late in the afternoon, about a week later, that he sat alone in the hot and dusty offices and looked out at the fading light on the dusty square. The yellow trolleys bumped and groaned and in the middle of the square late returning office people stood, patient and heavy, in the hard hot light.

He was writing to Tad in Denver to tell him how the mines were doing, and that a bundle of official documents in French had come for him marked "Tad, with love from Jane." Outside in the dark old wooden hall there was a whistle and a scuffling step and then a knock on the outer office door.

"Come in!" he shouted. His voice sounded unreal and far away in the empty offices.

The telegraph boy removed his sharply tilted cap and gave a thin and pasty grin. "Hello, Mr. Rand." He pulled his shirt off his damp, meagre chest and shook it till the pencils in his pocket rattled. He took a yellow envelope from inside his cap and threw it, damp and hot, down on the desk. A pencil and a receipt book flashed: "Sign here."

"So long, Mr. Rand." The footfalls clumped through the empty offices. The glass door banged. The whistle, remarkably high and piercing, went on down the hall. But instead of dying away it seemed, as he sat there staring at the message, to prolong itself indefinitely in his ears. The words of the telegram by now were sharply bitten in his mind and yet they seemed to have no meaning. His mind was stunned and in its palsy clung with insensate persistence to the last high notes of that unmeaning melody.

And yet, of course, it really in some secret chamber of its own was moving fast and lucidly. He had the telephone and called the numbers. The cook would pack his bag and he would send a taxi for it. Was this the ticket office? . . . "That's right. A single occupancy section." . . . "Is that you, Father? We've got a wire from MacDonald. Are you feeling pretty well? Well, here it is: 'Explosion Number five entry, nine-forty-five A.M. All men out but twenty-one (Stop) Unable reach or signal them account rockfall (Stop) Mine rescue car due seven-twenty P.M. Doing everything will advise.'"

He heard his father's voice sounding small, fierce and resonant. "Of course you ought to go. But I want you to remember that you'll be a lot more use outside than under-ground. Do you understand me? Don't get down there and get carried away. Do everything possible, you understand me, anything they need, but remember: you're no miner." The small fierce voice muttered an aside and then turned loud again. "Your mother is here in the room and she approves of every word I say."

"All right, Father." Half-smiling, he hung up the receiver and glanced again at the damp yellow message. It was only then that his whole mind for the first time grasped what had happened. In his brain a sort of quick bright humming started. A swift reiteration, nauseating, and at the same time subtly and horribly stimulating. He felt doomed yet stirred and eager, sickly yet strong, while in his ears, over and over, hummed words which now in their turn had lost their meaning: "Twenty-one men."

The mournful locomotive whistle in the narrow valley woke him in a thin green dawn. The Pullman rocked and groaned around the curves and stopped interminably at little mine-town stations. At the next, half-dressed, he swung down hurriedly.

"Have you heard anything from Carbonvale?"

"Hear it's pretty bad," they said with slow relish. "The whole day shift, they say; a hundred and twenty men. Maybe they'll get some out," they said. "The rescue car come by here last night running special."

When he got off the train, the town in the hot early morning light looked artificial, static, like a set in a play. There was no sound or movement as he strode along the coal dust of the platform searching for a sign. A green sedan was parked in front of the Carbonvale Hotel. There was a barrel of trash by the door of the hardware store and a newspaper on a bench in front of the grocery window, but nobody came out on the street to watch the train or stopped to look at Myrna Loy under the canopy of the Palace Picture Show. Through the open station window he could see the agent in his eyeshade sitting motionless at his key, staring at the train that already had jerked at its couplings and started creeping on its way. The last car passed him, gaining speed and sucking coal dust off the track, a brakeman standing motionless against the wicket of the vestibule. He had come all this way, it seemed, and had arrived, keyed up for all emergencies, only to find a vacuum.

Down hill from around the corner of the grocery store beyond the hotel, a car was coming, fast. It burst out on the main street on two wheels, turning and throwing coal dust out behind it, an ancient sedan, high and black and prim. It stopped beside him with a rattle of its ample glass and Mr. Rodmeyer, the company bookkeeper, bald-headed and still wearing his alpaca coat, peered at him through his spectacles and flung back the door.

"Mr. MacDonald sent me; he's up at the mine, of course. Plenty of room for your bag, sir."

He sat down on the clean striped-linen cover of the seat.

"How's it going?"

"No change as yet, sir, I understand. Would you wish to go by the hotel?"

"No, no," he said. "Let's go on to the mine."

Impassively Mr. Rodmeyer spun the small hard tires and sat rigid while the sedan shot ahead and rocked alarmingly around the corner. The shoemaker's, the barber's, and the dirty white siding of the company offices flashed by.

"Have you been up there, Mr. Rodmeyer?"

"Well, no sir, not exactly. I started up. But then, of course, we've been quite active down here." Almost imperceptibly he inclined his dry brown head back toward the offices just left.

"How did it happen?"

"Well, sir, I believe the cause is not really known."

"Well, what's the situation? What do they say?"

"Well, sir, of course we don't hear much. I understand there was a rockfall."

"Yes, yes," he said. "MacDonald wired me that."

"Yes, indeed," Mr. Rodmeyer said. "In fact, I sent the wire for him. Mr. MacDonald, of course, has been pretty active up at the mine since yesterday."

"What's happened since then? What are the chances?"

"I understand," Mr. Rodmeyer said, "that they are working on the rockfall.

They were out in open country now and doing forty-eight. He and Mr. Rodmeyer swayed dangerously, high aloft in the heavy rattling glass aquarium. The dirty coal-black stream, the dingy farmhouses were flowing by. "That," Mr. Rodmeyer said, "is what they would do." Impassively he took a hair-pin turn. "It is most unfortunate," he said.

They turned right-handed with the railroad spur and climbed around the shoulder of a dingy hill. To their left the double row of miners' shacks perched among the rubbish and the gullies of the steep naked street. There, too, the signs of life were few. A brick flue breathed faint smoke. A baby crawled on a flimsy porch and one slow trudging figure with pail and cap-lamp lurched down the footpath over the shoulder of the hill. He opened the rattling door of the sedan.

"What's the news?" he shouted. "How's it going?" The black squat figure stopped and stared at him till he was ought of sight.

Around the humped fold of the next bald hill the rank sparse grass was grayish, and then he saw the mountain and the tipple, tall and dark, against the sky. On the siding below the tipple, the long mine-rescue car stood empty except for a negro cook in khaki who watched them from an open door. They flung across the railroad tracks and shot up toward the shaft-mouth. The ring of people behind the ropes turned in silence and looked at them.

"You can get in by the tram-track," Mr. Rodmeyer said. "They have a guard there." He snatched at the emergency and came to a smoking halt.

"Yes; much obliged for meeting me."

"A pleasure, sir." Mr. Rodmeyer's voice behind him took on animation. "It's my own car."

With his felt hat in his hand he hurried past the line of staring faces.

Inside the circle of rope where deputies with badges paced, there was nothing. It was as if they guarded nothing; as if the crowd, who stared at nothing, waited for nothing, too. The drift-mouth door was shut and in the low brick power-house beside it the dynamos were humming as usual, and farther back along the hill the pump-house engine muttered as it always did. All was the same except for the silent crowd and the silence of the tall black tipple.

Mr. MacDonald came out of the little office in the power-house. His shiny blue serge suit was buttoned tightly; his black bow-tie was square and tight, but his collar was dirty and his big white face showed stubble. He pushed the office door back as he nodded.

"Come in," he said. "This is Mr. Sorenson, in charge of the rescue car."

The straw-haired man in khaki reached out a heavy hand and fixed him with bright blue eyes.

"Mr. Sorenson," he said, "how do we stand?"

"It's quite a rockfall, but I have seen lots worse. We are using all the men we can. We've only a five foot eight top there and seven foot six from wall to wall. We may break through at any time. Can't tell, of course."

"What about the men?"

"First class," he said, "good workers: oh—well, we haven't heard from them. But, then, we haven't stopped to listen. It just wastes time."

"Is there anything you need?"

"No."

"How about you, MacDonald?"

"Nothing."

"Where's the Super?"

"He went down with an extra shift to load the rock on cars."

"Any gas?"

"No."

"No fire, I suppose?"

"No fire."

"Does the telephone work?"

"As far as the mine-boss' station."

"See if you can get him."

MacDonald cranked the handle, listened, cranked again.

"He's probably down at the entry. That's where the rockfall is; right at the entry. Like this." With his free hand he drew on the back of a stray envelope. "Say this is the main entry—" the moving pencil stopped. "Hello, is that you, Mac? This is MacDonald. . . . All right. . . . That's good. . . . That's good. . . . O.K." He turned slowly, heavily, but his eyes were brighter. "He says he thinks they're breaking through."

In the corner Sorenson was silently climbing into his miner's overalls. He put his cap on with its battery cap-lamp and slung his gas mask on his chest; he reached under the high old-fashioned desk and brought out a little canton-flannel-covered cage. Raising the cloth sides, he stared at the canary bird who fluffed his feathers once and stared straight back at him. Satisfied, he folded the cover neatly on the desk and, holding the cage in front of him by the ring, he walked out the office and toward the drift-mouth door. There he raised his hand to his cap. The battery lamp shone wanly in the daylight. With another look at his canary bird he pushed on the door and disappeared.

He and MacDonald sat on the two hard chairs in the little office now beginning to warm up under the rising sun.

"This is the toughest part," he said. "We ought to hear pretty soon. Have you had breakfast?"

"What about you, Mr. Rand?"

"I'm all right."

"They've got a hot-dog stand. You can get hamburger and coffee too."

"A hot-dog stand?"

"News travels fast," Mr. MacDonald said. "There was quite a crowd here yesterday; there'll be plenty more to-day. This fellow moved in here last night."

"Is he on our property?"

"Oh, yes, he's right outside the ropes."

"Why, the son of—— Throw him off."

"If that's the way you feel, Mr. Rand."

"Who is he? Turning this disaster into a circus!"

"He's a Greek from Parkersburg. He's been giving coffee to the miners. Of course he's making plenty. But I mean he means all right."

There was a knock on the door; a white and scrubby little face craned forward.

"Coffee, Misser MacDon?" The Greek came forward, carrying a steaming paper cup and a paper plate with a napkin over it. Putting them on the desk he fixed Tommy with sharp, serious eyes. "Big boss?"

"Here," he said, "what the hell do you mean by turning this disaster into a circus?"

The little man shook his head. "Me? No. Pipples come. So must eat." He shook his head. "Bad trouble. My, my. You like coffee? Hamburger? Mustard?"

"Oh, God," he said. "I guess so."

In the hot office, greasy with the smell of hamburger, he went over the blue prints. MacDonald's big white finger with tufts of black hair above the knuckles traced the details which, in their thin white lines on the blue ground, seemed highly regular and simple. Here at the edge they had reached the end of the workable seam. That was in March; then they had started robbing back, cleaning the rooms out one by one, taking pillars, everything. The top had come down after them, of course, but slowly; it looked good. There had been no gas, here was the safety boss's record. A little dust perhaps—maybe a little more than common, the men were getting out the coal so fast. The blast had come about an hour after the men had reached their working places. It might have been caused by anything, bad tamping, a hung shot, an overcharge of powder to make up for careless drilling—all miners were incurable the way they took chances. Anyhow, immediately the entry roof came down and that was all they knew.

"Could any of the men still be alive?"

"Oh, yes, in the other rooms."

"How had conditions been there?"

"Normal."

"Were the dead workings bratticed off?"

"To some extent."

"Why not all?"

"There was a lot of it and brattice cloth was an item."

"What about props?"

"Normal. All the men wanted."

"All they wanted? But won't they skimp on props if they have the chance?"

"The mine inspector passed it."

"When was he here last?"

"Six months ago."

"Before you started robbing back?"

"Well, yes."

"In other words, more could have been done?"

Mr. MacDonald's finger left the blue print and pointed at him.

"Mr. Rand, there is no limit to the money that can be spent on a mine. Conditions here are better than lots of properties. I could show you properties——"

He stood up under a thrust of rage and agony. The safety

factor slighted. "By God!" He looked down at MacDonald. The big hand lay on the blue print. MacDonald stared at it. The big man was growing old. He sat stooped in his flimsy serge like a faithful dumb animal. What thoughts went through his dark grizzled head? A good manager with a good record. Thirty years with the Rands and always saving money for them. He sat down. "I wonder when we'll hear," he said.

MacDonald stirred. Here was something he could speak about. His thick gold watch on a silver chain came out.

"Sorenson's been down an hour."

They sat together after that in silence.

Outside the power-house the tramway wire began to hum.

"That's the motor," MacDonald said. "I guess it's Mac with his load of rock."

They rose together.

The drift-mouth door swung open; there was the flash of a headlight in the depths; a groaning hum and the low-hung motor crept out like a lizard into the light of day. The three low, box-like cars were filled with blackened silent men. The train came to a halt. From the crowd, now large, close-packed behind the ropes, a tight breathless murmur took up where the motor left off. "Have you found them? . . . found them?" There was a woman's sharp broken cry. The black men shook their heads. Slowly they swung their legs over and stood up heavily on the ground. The reflectors of their cap-lamps showed bright above their grimy clothes and faces. They looked at Mr. Mac-Donald, and Mr. MacDonald, silent and steady, looked at them. One of them opened gray lips in his black mask.

"Gas," he said.

"Much?" MacDonald's voice was quiet.

"Plenty."

The men, a row of monsters, all studied MacDonald to see how he would take the news. Their faces were stolid, ludicrous and filthy, but their eyes were bright and glittering and hard.

"When did you get it?"

"Just now when we broke through."

"You're through then?"

"Yeah."

"And there's nothing but gas?"

"Yeah."

Mr. MacDonald's voice remained unchanged. "All right," he said. "Go get some rest."

The pile of figures started trudging toward the rope. A deputy in sleeve-garters and a new pearl-gray Fedora waved his club aimlessly. "Now then, folks, stand back there. Let 'em out, folks; don't push. Now then, folks, you're hurting this lady."

CHAPTER LXI

It was night now. The second endless night. All of the day before and the long night before there had been no change. The shifts went in and came out, silent. The crowd grew thin and swelled again, and now since early afternoon there was a woman who wailed. Voices of other women murmured to her, then her slow cry would take up its beat, pitiful yet inhuman, meaningless and maddening. Under the naked globe in the little office he watched the yellow pencil in Sorenson's square hand tapping on the blue print. Outside a soft glow came out of the canvas of a First Aid tent and, farther on, the gasolene flare of the Greek's hot-dog stand showed scattered silhouettes that moved and ate and talked, or hung against the ropes.

The pencil point ticked lightly on the blue print. The high stool creaked as Sorenson shifted his small hard bulk. "Mr. Rand, this is all we know."

"But what about the men? The men is all I care about."

"That's right," Sorenson said. "Sometimes owners don't talk that way. You'd really be surprised," he added patiently. He picked the pencil up and put it in the breast pocket of his khaki shirt. He looked up with his honest, literal blue eyes: "but in this kind of work, let me tell you; never talk about the men, never think about them; you must act like you are doing a contract job with a penalty clause and a bonus for every minute saved." He took the pencil from his pocket and waggled it in a gesture of negation. "If you think about the men, you will do foolish things." The pencil point came toward the blue print. "Now here," he said, "we are using judgment and making all the time we can." The pencil rose from the blue print and waggled affirmation. "In a mine disaster, always act as if every man in there was still alive," the pencil point fell down, "until you know different"; Sorenson looked up firmly, "and I mean know."

"Well then, what's your judgment of the situation?"

581

"When we broke through yesterday—" He watched Sorensons reddish, impassive face with the stiff straw hair and little white hairs on the jaw—so that was only yesterday—"No, sir, not so favorable. There was gas enough in there to wipe out everything. So then we went through with our helmets and found the second rockfall. Now, we don't know. It may be just a gas pocket between the two rock-falls."

"Wouldn't you expect to hear them signalling?"

"Well, maybe you would, but every mine is different; and miners act different, too, sometimes. Maybe they hear us. If they can hear the way our men are working, they know we're doing the best we can, so why signal? Maybe that's the way they figure"; Sorenson looked at the blue print where blackheaded pins showed the supposed location of every miner and his buddy in their working places; "or maybe they signalled and did not get an answer, so they quit. We're making plenty of noise down there. Or maybe a crack has opened in the roof so the rock won't carry sound."

"In that case, they can't hear us either."

"Maybe not, but we're making a lot more noise than they could. Then maybe, of course," Sorenson said, "they have got some gas on their side. In that case, they may be laying on the floor and afraid to raise up." The pencil point ran between the pins along the edge of Entry Number Five. "You've got a stream in here; they may be laying with their faces close to it."

"How long could they last that way?"

"That's hard to tell. Sometimes these streams carry quite a little air along with them, and then it depends on the man too, if he don't get excited."

"If there's as much gas on their side as we have now on ours, there's no chance?"

"No chance; even if they had masks."

"What if there is no gas? Then we're all right so far."

"I guess you could put it that way," Sorenson said slowly. "If they have no gas they have bratticed themselves off so our gas won't leak into them. Then it's a question of how long the air in there will last them. That may be why they haven't signalled."

"Saving themselves?"

"Too weak. A hammer weighs ten pounds."

He was silent. So then perhaps they were just sitting there—silent, staring at the dark. He roused himself. "Have you figured how much cubic footage they have got?"

Sorenson shook his head.

"Why not?"

"You figure, and then when the time is out you can't help slacking off, and then you may be wrong. We don't know how far the rockfall runs back, so we don't know what the cubic really is. Half the men may be gone, then the others have twice as much air. The explosion may have opened up air pockets in the rock."

"What about sinking an air shaft to them?"

"I have gone over the cores of the old test drills and checked up on the topographical. From the nearest surface point you have twenty-seven hundred feet, fifty-four per cent rock. It would take ten days."

"Is there a possible chance that it might do some good?"

"You can never say that there's no chance, but ten days from now—" Sorenson rubbed the back of his straw-colored head and shook it. "It's one chance in ten thousand."

"All right," he said, "I'll 'phone down to the office and have them wire for a drill rig."

"If you have no one in mind, Casey at Red Oak is all right. Have an understanding with him, in case he sets up and don't have to drill. We might break through to-morrow."

"You think we might?"

"I only mean we might; we don't know how much rock we have got ahead of us, and the men can only work for thirty minutes in that gas. It slows you up to change shifts so often."

"Do you need more men?"

"We don't need any more men, but we'll need some fresh men soon. The masks are all right, but after a while the gas gets into them and slows them up." Sorenson slid off the creaking stool and started putting on his miner's overalls. "That's why I don't stay down there longer. You begin to make dumb decisions." He looked up, friendly but remote. "I guess it looks funny, though, to an outsider."

Later that night, Mr. Rodmeyer came in his high, prim sedan and drove him back to town. He passed through the hotel office, lit by a single bulb, where the night clerk snored in his chair behind the desk; his frowzy head hung down against his breast.

Up in the small hot room, he stared at the rosebud wall paper, the varnished trim, the sagging iron bed, as though they were strange and fascinating phenomena. He roused himself, and in the bathroom shaved his dirty-looking jaws and took a bath in water that was tepid and filled with dark-brown sediment. At last he lay in the hot darkness on the creaking springs and wondered what more there was that he could do. At times an insect struck lightly against the dark, encrusted window screen; and once, incredibly, a car passed filled with youngsters singing. He wondered what had been left undone; what knowledge, foresight, better method, might have saved those twenty-one now lost, and perhaps forever lost, to the world of living men. He made himself stop this, and lay there weak and empty, wishing that Tad were here to give him good advice and backing; but if Tad were here he would be down the mine. No one could stop him. So he wished then that Tad were simply here in this room, and nowhere else. Then he thought of Jane, and it seemed was seeing her again in the cabin of the ship. He was really there sitting on her berth, the hard edge of the board under the backs of his knees; and she, in her brown knitted dress, was standing by the folding basin in the narrow space between the berths; her little brown nose was tilted down at him; her eyes were brown and warm. Faint sunlight fell through the porthole on her hair. She was tender, young and loving; she was touching in her sweet, yet confident immaturity; and he was happy. And yet a shadow lay on him. This was a ship and he felt portents in his heart. They were together in the cabin, but in this ship anything might happen. Suddenly there were clanging sounds of great disaster. He woke up shouting. The noise still beat against his ears. The dawn was creeping through the dirty screen, and as he stumbled toward it he heard the violent tumult of a tractor and saw, long and dim in the dark street, the drill rig going past the corner.

By noon there was no change, except that around the mine the crowd was bigger and some of the men in it were slightly and reverently drunk. The rock was coming out in driblets, and they had sent for more men from the High Gap mine up the valley. The High Gap manager, himself, had come down with them; a big bald man in thick gold spectacles. "Anything we can do, Mr. Rand?" He took a cigar from his wide mouth and inspected the pulpy end.

"Much obliged," he said. "I guess that's all, unless you have any ideas."

"I don't think that I'd have any. Mr. MacDonald knows his mine." He put his black felt hat on carefully, shook hands, and went away.

Up at the pump-house they were watching gauges and oil cups, keeping up all the steam that they could carry, oiling fan bearings and listening to the hum; but down below the gas seeped in. They could not get clean air. The Greek from Parkersburg brought hamburgers into the stifling office. He wiped the sweat off his face with his greasy apron. Underneath, the bulge of money showed in his trouser pocket. "That's all right, boss. You no pay. You feel bad. Me too. You get the men out, I say Okay, fine." He made a gesture with his apron and nodded solemnly. "Get men out. Hell with-a business."

"That's all right, Mike," he said. He looked at the fat, dripping hamburger. Suddenly, almost revoltingly, in the midst of sorrow, misery and disaster, nothing had ever seemed so good. "Bring me two more of these," he said, "and plenty of mustard."

At three o'clock the telephone rang. He seized it. "Yes?"

"Is that you, Mr. Mac?"

"No, this is Rand."

"This is the mine boss. We're sending out a man."

"By God, you've found one?"

"No, this is one of the workers—Angelo. Too much gas."

"Oh," he said dully. "All right." He sat back sick and heavy and waited, staring at the drift-mouth door. At half-past three it opened: a hush fell on the crowd. Two dark bent figures carried a stretcher and on the stretcher a man with a pale-blue face and dead eyes, under hanging lids, jutted his mouth in a funnel and drooled. A murmur, almost like applause, ran through the crowd. The flap in the First Aid tent fell behind the stretcher. Inside they could hear the light hiss of the inhalator. The crowd stood silent, listening. In the humming silence there was a scuffling sound. She was through the ropes and running fast, a big girl with fair flying hair; two deputies were running. At the drift-mouth they caught her. The three wrestled silently, her rocking head bowed down between them, reared up fiercely, her voice was tiny, desperate. "He's in there. I'm going to get him. I'm going——"

"Here now," they muttered. "Easy." They wrestled again. At last her head dropped down and with her fair hair hung around her face she stumbled back between them.

"MacDonald," his voice sounded tight and tiny. He cleared his throat. "How's Angelo? Will he be all right?"

"Oh, yes; they think he'll be all right." MacDonald walked on into the office. "But the gas is getting them. We ought to lay off our men for a while. They've had enough."

Outside the office, the foreman's voice called: "Next shift." Silently and slowly, but with no hesitation, the line of fifteen miners trudged past the window. They held their arms akimbo, putting on their gas masks as they went toward the drift-mouth door.

"They're all right," MacDonald said, "but they've been going now since day before yesterday."

"What about those High Gap men?"

"There are only twenty of them and they are going to quit. I can feel it coming. They didn't know how bad it was. It's no use to blame them; it isn't their mine and they have families. No," Mr. MacDonald said, "we ought to have one hundred fresh men all the time to keep the four shifts going. I've sent over to the Pocahontas field, but they won't get down here until tomorrow." He moved a thumb toward the window. "There are a lot of miners out there in that crowd. I think I'll call for volunteers. Sometimes you get the best men that way."

"You've got one bad one right now—me."

MacDonald turned on him with slow, patient anger. "Mr. Rand, you can't go down there."

"I can't stay up here any longer."

"Mr. Rand," he tried to make his voice conciliating, "you're much more use up here."

"For what?" he said. "What can I do?"

"Well," he said, "I was just thinking that you could go round and see some of the wives of the men who are in there."

"Yes," he said, "and what could I say?"

"Well now," MacDonald said, "you would know what to say, I guess."

"Do you know the only thing that I could say—that I was sorry we had been a little short on brattice cloth." Mr. Mac-Donald's face turned to a set white mask. "When I say we, I mean the owners, too. What kind of work goes on down there exactly?" He waited. "I said, what kind of work?"

A little color came back to MacDonald's face. "The men in front are working on the rock. There's only room for four. Then we have men behind them passing the stuff back and loading it on cars. Then they push the cars to a dead entry this side of number four."

"It doesn't take a miner to load rock."

"It takes a man that's used to heavy work."

"What have they done with Angelo's outfit?"

"It's in the First Aid tent."

"I'm going to get it."

Mr. MacDonald's arm took his above the elbow. "Mr. Rand, it's your mine and I can't stop you, but you'll be no use."

"For a while I will and then I'll quit. That's fair."

Mr. MacDonald still held his arm. "I don't like it. I've been in the mining business forty years and I never heard of an owner going down during a disaster." Mr. MacDonald continued to stare at him. "Where are your matches?"

"Here."

"Throw them away."

Squatting with the others against the power-house wall in Angelo's stiff, greasy cap and overalls, he watched the volunteers file through the ropes—sharp-faced West Virginians and pink-faced boys, two ox-like Polacks walking close together, and four Italians in a group, squat but jaunty; a negro edged in, slow and shy, in a stand-up collar and saffron neck-tie. Mac-Donald wrote their names down in his book, and then they went to the far side of the First Aid tent and got their brand-new overalls and masks and lamps.

There was a stir in the crowd and mingled voices. "Here comes Grandpa." A small bent man, in a neat black suit and a clean white shirt without a collar, came through the ropes. The row along the power-house stirred and grinned. "Hey, Grandpa!" He gave a slow pull at his sparse goatee and peered at them with pale, sharp eyes. "Fellows," his voice was thin and musical, "how you all?"

"Why, Grandpa," Mr. MacDonald said, "you don't want to go down there. This is young men's work."

"That's right, Grandpa," they said, "you better stay out." The old man turned to them. "You may call me grandpa, fellows," he said in a gentle voice, "but I could be a daddy right to-day if I'd a mind." The old man waited placidly while their wild laughing cheer lingered and died away. "If he had a mind," a voice said, "oh, my Lord!"

Squatting against the wall, he grinned and pulled at the peak of Angelo's cap. He wondered, what if the men down there should hear their laughter. They were men, too; perhaps they would not mind. Grandpa nodded at them with dignity. "Well, fellows, so I could. I have always lived a moral life," he observed. He turned back to Mr. MacDonald. "Put down my name, my right name."

Mr. MacDonald shook his head. "It wouldn't be right," he said, "you're over seventy."

"And I know more about this mine than all you young whippersnappers put together. You mean well," Grandpa conceded tranquilly, "but I was mining here with mules and hand-cars when you were a puling babe in arms. I was getting out my seven cars a day ten years before you knew enough to button up your breeches. When you——"

"All right," MacDonald grinned and reddened. "All right, here goes your name." Grandpa started for the First Aid tent. "I will go down and look at that rock," he remarked, "and tell you all what to do."

When Grandpa came back toward them slowly, his cap set squarely on his head, his small, slope-shouldered figure in new overalls, a size too large, he made room for the old man against the shaded wall. Grandpa sat down creakingly beside him. The men leaned forward and grinned at him. He raised a hand politely. "Fellows," he said. He turned. "A hot day, friend."

"That's right."

"It will be nice and cool down there." With a thin finger, he fluffed up his goatee.

"That's right. Is your name William Harrelson?"

"Yes, sir; that is my name."

"Did you have a boy named Tad Smith working for you four years ago?"

"A tall, dark-haired boy? Yes, sir; I remember him all right. He was a remarkable boy."

"Is that so?"

"Yes, sir; the biggest liar I ever knew. Yes, sir. My buddy took sick and this chap came along and told me all the mines he had worked in and what he could do. And when I got him down there, he didn't know as much as your grandmother's kitten. I reckon he had run away from a farm."

"No; he was my son."

"Well, then, he told me that much truth."

"He told you I was his father, did he?"

"He said his father was a miner."

"Oh."

"He was an untruthful boy," the old man said, "but he was willing and he had good manners. Maybe he will turn out all right."

"Next relief," Mr. MacDonald called.

"Are you on this relief?" the old man said.

"Yes."

"What is your first name?"

"Tom."

The old man reached a thin hand up to him. "So long, Thomas," he said. "Be a good fellow."

The drift-mouth door swung shut behind them and, in the darkness, the file of swaying cap-lamps trudged on ahead. The gas mask smelt warm and rubbery and the air inside the rubber mask was hot and close, but he could feel on his wrists and on the back of his neck that here in the blackness underground it was cool. The lights ahead were rising up a gentle slope. The footfalls of the men threw long hushed echoes along the blackened walls. He felt that he was climbing gently, and then he saw the lights in front of him level out; and from a dark hole on his right he felt a warm blast against his wrist and ear. That was the air-shaft. From now on the gas would probably be heavy, but that would make no difference. The rubber air his mouth was sucking through the tube would be the same, and he was getting used to it and to walking slowly, steadily under the batteries across his shoulders

and under the smooth, enormous roof of slate, an inch above
his head.

The lights in front of him were slanting downward now; the
ground was falling away. He walked out feeling strong and
eager. He felt a switch and a curving track beneath his feet and
passed the blank mouth of entry number one. The blue print
came before his mind. He wished the men would step out faster.
They had come five-eighths of a mile and were half-way there.
He began to watch the wall on his right for entry number two.
When he passed its silent, staring mouth he said to himself:
"Seven-eighths of a mile," and settled down to count his footsteps and estimate the length. If he were stepping two feet and
there was five-eighths of a mile to go, say half a mile, that
would be one-fourth of five thousand, two hundred and eighty,
and at a hundred steps a minute they would be there in ten
minutes now. He raised his wrist watch to his cap-lamp. It was
eleven minutes after four.

Ahead, above the tramping, he heard a faint reverberation, the
rumble of a mine-car's wooden sides and the dull thump of rock.
Again he looked at the blue print spread out in the office now far
behind him. That noise was from the dead entry that they were
dumping into. The lights ahead moved to one side, and distant,
tiny, yet sharply seen as though through an inverted telescope,
two small cap-lamps were pushing on a mine-car. As he came up
to them, all other sounds were drowned in the dull tight rumble
of a loaded car. The cap-lamps turned their masks aside, big,
blankly staring eye-pieces set in black rubber faces that ran down
into shaking snouts; like two grotesque and diabolical marion-
ettes, they disappeared, still pushing, into the dead entry's long,
resounding tunnel. The rockfall was not far ahead.

He felt that they ought to run and, in fact, they had begun
to step out faster and hurried toward more approaching rumbles
and passed more masks and cap-lamps, leaning and trudging and
pushing on the loaded cars.

Suddenly an entry opened and deep inside it there was a glow,
a constellation, of many lights and many shimmering reflections
against the dripping walls. It was sooner than he had expected.
He took a deep breath of the rubbery air inside the mask. The
world was far behind. He was a good mile under ground, at

the face of the rockfall. The trudgers ahead of him moved up and mingled with the other lights. Like ants, they seemed to touch each other and know what they should do. Up there, the sounds of sliding rock and of light, thin clinking went on unbroken. The old shift started drifting back. Behind him he heard the hollow wooden sound of empty mine-cars coming up.

The four men in front of him had halted and seemed to be conferring, each in turn. In turn their masks and cap-lamps nodded together, their blunt dark figures seemed almost to embrace. The man in front swung round at him, crouching, and holding a rock against his knees. By instinct he crouched, too, and took its weight into his lap, then waddled three steps to the mine-car, arched his back and threw the black, enormous slippery weight over the wooden side.

After that the rocks came steadily and most of them were smaller. He felt that he was doing well so far, but he was glad that he had got a pair of canvas gloves from MacDonald. He couldn't handle rock with naked paws the way the miners did. Sometimes the empties had not come, he had to pile the rock along the track and lift it up again. He tried to figure a way to get the empties there on time. But with the rocks always coming and his face shut up inside the mask, he could not think it out. Perhaps there was no answer. The empties had to be switched back along the main haulage line and held there while the loaded cars were run into the dead entry. Sometimes when he had rock piled up, the car men would help him load, and sometimes they lay down on their backs, relaxed, to make their breathing easier. He didn't blame them. At first he thought they had given out, but as soon as the car was loaded they got up and started pushing, with bent backs and a short hard scuffle to get the car in motion. He got to know the men who would help him by their figures and the way they moved.

Once a man came along the line of rock-passers, walking very slowly and turning his gas mask from side to side. As the man went by, he recognized between the back of his cap and his mask-strap the straw-colored hair of Sorenson. He called out soundlessly to himself, "Hello, Sorenson! Here I am."

Once a rock was too big for him to handle; he hung there, rigid, unable to raise it to the car side. Two hands stole around his, the rock seemed to rise from him and fall into the car; he caught a flash of a palm. It was the negro. He nodded to him and the negro bobbed his mask in answer and made a shy, brief, drooping gesture with his hand; then he went back, shambling, to his place in line.

The rock kept coming, the full cars rumbled dully, the hollow empties rattled back. Some of the smaller rocks seemed heavy now. Not all. He could not tell which rock it would be. The big excitement was all over now. This was work. It was aimless, endless work. And maybe hopeless. The rockfall might run back a quarter of a mile. It would take two weeks to move it. And the men inside would have been buried underneath. He wondered when the next relief was due. He kept looking back down the entry and when he saw the string of swaying masks and cap-lamps he didn't slack off work, but he was glad.

The first figure in the line of apparitions was Grandpa—no one could miss him. He reached out as the old man passed and touched him with a friendly gesture. The old man inclined his head in its gas mask, a nod that was distant, stately, ludicrous. But then he remembered that Grampa could not recognize him. The rest filed in; he threw a small rock on the car and eased his cracking knees. Now for the long tramp back.

It was some time that night and he was passing rock again. This was the fourth time he'd been in. He wished he'd made a mark at his old place to see how much they had gained. Perhaps it was just as well. That thought and the rock, the gas, his mask, the roof, weighed him down. Even inside the canvas gloves his hands were getting raw, his loins were wearing out, his mouth was foul, his feet were wet and filthy. MacDonald knew: he should have listened to him. He'd only worked four shifts and now he'd have to quit. He'd not take up space down here if he couldn't do the work. But he was glad he'd tried.

He felt that his ears had been plunged in a vacuum and wondered whether the gas was getting him. But, no, there was no sound. A hand, the negro's hand, reached out and touched him. Then it pointed. Up at the fall the men were standing motionless. He stood up stiffly, straightened his back and, like the others, hung there in a trance. And then the faint slow sound came, incredible, mysterious, a sound of terror and of pity, stirring him wildly, horribly moving, high through the locked vastness of the stone above, thin and vague and far away, a faint slow knocking. It stopped. He felt the hackles rise on his back like a dog who sees the dead. He saw Sorenson make a snatch and swing a hammer against the roof three times. They waited, again suspended in their trance. Thin and vague and far away, came three slow knocks.

CHAPTER LXII

A BIG swift dawn was coming through the window of the hospital. Far down below him roofs and towers caught the light. A shaft of light fell high up on the green wall of his room. The river and the far rock parapet were faintly luminous. He stirred and tried for breath. His heart was shaking. He felt the oppression of the mask, the gas. As the tension eased, he looked out at the city and the growing day. His heart still pattered, but only with an echo of that moment in the mine. His mind had slipped off into blurred contentment. They had broken through that night. The company doctor was down there then in his neat gray business suit and gas mask, and they had a car of masks and stretchers ready, but nearly all the men inside could walk. They had used their clothing to brattice the rock pile against gas and come out, crawling over the heaped rock in the gas masks, that had been passed in to them, and their dirty drawers. Two had been killed by the explosion in their working places, and no one ever found the cause of it. All the rest were saved, if you counted one Hungarian who appeared to have had his mind affected.

He, himself, had not lasted out to see the rescue. After they heard the knocking they had jumped into their work with fury, and when the new relief came down, some of them would not quit. They shook their masks at Sorenson and kept on passing rock. He was one of them and, as he looked back on it now, he still felt that it was not all foolishness. By doubling up with the other shift, they were able to take turns in resting frequently, to walk back up the entry and to stretch out on their backs in the wet gutter beside the tracks and lie there, relaxed, and breathing easily, while the cars rolled past, three inches from their shoulders.

He had had a couple of rests like that and was doing fine. His hands were sore and the canvas gloves were sticking to them, but his muscles seemed to have gotten their second wind.

He was proud of himself when he saw a man slip down against the wall, and he helped to put him on a half-loaded car and send him on his way.

But then a rock turned vague and furry in his hands, and all the cap-lamps wavered off and came back sparkling; then many drifts and tunnels stretched away on every hand, and in them all the lights were moving, the mine-cars rumbled. He picked out one and hurried to it. The lights were vanishing and when he got there he found nothing but a face of solid rock. Rock crumbled down behind him and left him walled in there alone with Jane, who stood in the cabin between the berths and smiled at him, a light, faint green from the moss on the piles outside the porthole, playing on the low white ceiling above her brown head.

When he woke he saw the nickelled cupola of Mrs. Mac-Donald's parlor stove and the edges of a flowered sateen quilt drawn up beneath his chin.

But though he had not lasted out until the rescue, he saw it just as clearly. He saw the dirty figures in their drawers and gas masks being helped on hands and knees under the great stone roof across the tumbled rock. He saw them lying jumbled in the empty mine-cars and being covered with brown army blankets. He felt in his tender eyes the hard, sharp light of day and heard the crowd begin to cheer. They were lifting up the children. Fierce, silent women were breaking through the ropes. He saw all this. It would be easy for a man to be a liar. It was far sharper in his mind than anything that had happened since. Now it was all behind him, and there were damage suits and a smart Italian lawyer and hearings before the Board of Mine Inspectors. The Board's opinion was that the Company had shown no negligence whatever and should exercise greater care in the future. And he, himself, received a handsome tribute to his valuable services and his devotion. He laughed out loud. In the easy chair, Miss Wesson threw back her long blue cloak. She stood up, trying not to yawn. "Well," she said, "we're doing splendidly. Have we had a good sleep? The nights are short," she said. "It is only a quarter of five. Perhaps if I pull down this shade—" She stood looking out the window. "It's a beautiful day again."

"Yes," he said, "I'm having great luck with the weather."

"It's lucky for me, too," she said. "I've a gentleman friend that wants to take me driving out to Rockaway." The green shade came down slowly, shrouding the room. "He drives one of those Imperial sedans." He turned on his right side, stretched out his arm and closed his eyes. It was not the breathing that bothered him; it was shallow, but as long as he did not push it, there was no pain. But he never knew if the blood would start again, would well up in his breast, his throat, to drown him. It was his heart, too, the doctor said. Yet that was strange. His heart seemed all right in its way, only it seemed small and faint and far away like the tapping in the mine. It seemed as though he were being kept alive by a tiny stream that was being pumped from far away. He opened his eyes. Miss Wesson was looking at him attentively. Instantly she smiled. "Perhaps we can get a little more sleep." He closed his eyes again.

When he woke up the shaded room was hot. The little fan was going almost noiselessly. In the easy chair there was another figure now in a rough brown coat and old gray flannel trousers. He saw the tanned face and the dark, rough hair on the fine, high, narrow head. The young man's gray eyes swung to him. "Hello, Chief," he said.

He tried to raise up in the bed, but his furious, joyful heart seemed to rise at him and knock him down. He stretched a hand out. "Tad," he said, "how did you get here? . . . Your hand feels tough," he said. "You've been working."

"They wanted a little mineralogy out there. Simple stuff."

"How did you get here?"

"I guess you're not supposed to sit down on the bed."

"That's all right."

"Flew in from Cheyenne. Left there yesterday at five-ten mountain time."

"What did you do that for?"

Tad swung an old, well-polished shoe. "Oh, I was through out there, and as far as cost goes, when you figure Pullman fare and meals, you are not much better off. You ought to have seen the sun coming up over the Alleghenies. Chief," he said seriously, "it's the only way to travel. Look here," he said, "why didn't you let me know?"

"I've only been in here six days."

"I mean before that."

"Before that, I was feeling fine. A cough, but I thought that was from the gas. And then I came over here on business, and suddenly on the street— So here I am."

"Couldn't be in a better place. This looks like big-time stuff. But you ought to have let me know."

"I kept thinking every day—" he said.

"Oh, well, it's nothing to fight about." He sat there silent on the bed, his brown calloused hands hung over his sharp knees, his knowing, boyish face suddenly fallen into soft grave lines. Only his foot was swinging nervously. "How do you feel?" he said.

"I feel fine."

"That's good," he said dully. "That's fine." He stretched a lean arm out of his sleeve and studied his wrist watch intently. "They told me only five minutes after you woke up. I'll be back in a little while."

"How soon?"

"I'll find out. They've got all their rules." Slowly and heavily he started to rise. "When I come in again I want to hear about the mine." He turned his blunt nose, his dark-gray eyes toward the bed and forced his sharp young mouth to smile. "I wish I'd seen you down there."

"You couldn't have seen me; only a gas mask and an old suit of overalls."

"What kind of masks did they use?"

"M. S. A.'s from the mine rescue car."

He nodded. "That's right. That's the best. Well," he said, "you got them out. They can never take that away from you, or me either. I was hot stuff in Colorado when they heard the news."

"They would have gotten them out just the same."

"Maybe so. But I guess it put some heart in them when they heard the old man was down there passing rock."

"Why shouldn't I? The real joke is that I own the mine and that was all I was good for."

"Maybe so, but it's a joke that most other owners wouldn't see. I'd like to stay," he said, "but I told them that after five minutes I'd come out under my own power." But still he stood there.

"Son," he said, "what's on your mind?"

"There's a girl," he said. "Her name is Constance Holden. I

want to bring her up here. She wants to see you. She was at
the airport when I got in. She lives in Morristown."

"And weighs, I suppose, about one hundred and twenty-five
pounds."

He turned for an instant with a swift, crooked grin, and looked
away again. "She looks a little like Jane will when she grows
up, if she learns to hold her shoulders straight. She is like Jane,
too, only more strongly built and not dramatic."

"You wouldn't like that."

"No. She comes from good people all along the line. Some
fellows never think of that. Her father is a consulting chemist."

"Do you love her?"

He turned a white face. "If you don't like her, I don't know
what I'll do." He turned away. "I want you to see her. She
wants to see you." Quickly he walked to the wide door and
swung it back and went out from the room. The long, dark
head was up; under the brown rough coat, the limber shoulders
were firm. But, lying on his side in the high bed, he knew that
his son was crying bitterly.

His mind fixed on the girl. So life was going on; his life, his
blood was going on. What was she like though? Like Jane;
not tall; quick, strong and a little sturdier. A little, perhaps, like
Jeanne, but quieter, more gentle, endowed with a fastidiousness,
with a slow, sweet wisdom, like Aunt Clara.

He smiled to himself. In his premature dotage he was making
her the girl of his dreams, combining every strength and grace
and loveliness, and he was half in love with her already. Poor
child, when she came what chance would she have to hold her
own against such a rival? He must not expect too much; he
must, in fact, prepare himself, steel himself for anything. Tad,
unlike the young men of his own youth, was free of the world
of women; before girls he was hard, astute, critical; and yet
this business of love could lead the best of boys to unpredictably
grotesque results. He only hoped she had fine eyes; he would
be willing to compromise on that; but if she had a silly eye—
not likely perhaps; her father he had heard of. He stood high in
his line. He must be a good man. But there was, of course, her
mother who might be any sort of person. But if she were, the
boy would have noticed it. His genial ruthlessness was not con-

fined, by any means, to women of his own age. But his first picture of her persisted and seemed, as he reasoned with himself, to float and hover in the background of his mind. He found it pleasant to contemplate and looked up crossly when the day nurse came in with milk in a covered glass and a glass tube on a tray.

"Well," she said, "you had a visitor."

He felt more kindly. "That was my son," he said.

"I know," she said. "We knew it right away. You don't have to move. I'll hold the glass down.'

He put his lips to the glass tube; the cold milk flowed into his mouth.

"You couldn't miss it," she said. "We knew it right away."

He opened his mouth. The milk flowed back down the tube, leaving a pale film behind it. "He doesn't look like me."

"Well, not exactly, but he reminds you of you."

"How's that?"

"Well, you know what I mean. That's what one of the nurses was saying. How old is he?"

"Twenty-one."

"Drink your milk."

"He just graduated from Cornell. He's going to be a mining engineer. He's been working out in Colorado this summer."

"Is that so? Now drink your milk."

He drank.

"Well, he certainly made a stir among the probationers all right."

He let go the tube. "That's ridiculous. He's not good-looking, really; not with that nose."

"No," she said, "I suppose not."

"Of course he's well set up."

"Yes," she said, "he is. Well, I don't know what it is. He even had the Nurse Superintendent coming along to show him the way. I bet she's sixty-five years old."

"Well, he's not a bad sort of boy."

"I'll say he isn't," she said. "Now drink your milk."

Afterward, he lay in the warm, shaded room, comforted by the milk and by the thought of Tad's triumphant progress through the small probationers, and also by the thought of the girl, Constance Holden, who now made a definite and most charming image in his mind. The cycle of her life and of Tad's was almost just beginning. From now on the circle of her existence and of Tad's would be nearly concentric; at least by a miracle of love and character and temperament, that might be possible. At worst, there could hardly be the disillusions of his generation. They lacked the ample basis of his own youth's unreality to build their disillusions on. Their way of life together, its freedom, humorous mutual contempt and easy license was destructive in other more immediate ways. Yet those who survived it were tempered and sure, as he had never been, as he was not now. He wondered what new mistakes they would invent and bequeath to succeeding generations as the characteristic of their age.

Thinking of his son and of the future, he had forgotten the past few days, the long backward journey of his mind, the object of his search. And now that object seemed far less important, at least as far as the future was concerned. If there was some sort of other life ahead of him, he did not know that he would choose it. He smiled to himself. God knows what new and even more insoluble complexities it might offer; and if, by any freak of nature, there remained a consciousness of what was going on below—instinctively he used the phrase below; he still remained a provincial, as he had been raised, of this terrestrial sphere—that would be tantalizing, possibly tormenting, impotently to watch the children in their unpredictable dilemmas. He was confident, however, that this could never be the case.

But as far as the past went, he could say to himself that his search had been somewhat rewarded. His life and the lives of those around him had none of them been more than partially, some microscopically, successful; and one at least had been a tragedy. Happiness, too, had been at best fitful and deceptive. But something deeper than happiness could not be so dismissed. There was in all those he had known and in himself some fragment of divinity, small enough, one might well say, and sometimes atrophied or walled off by the chances of this world; but otherwise, like radium, possessing, however minute, a potency beyond belief for good, and also, if misunderstood, for evil. And in the light which this mysterious essence gave off, as from this lofty room he looked down on the world and on his past, no matter what mean, ludicrous or terrible effects defaced the scene, his last impression of mankind was one of splendor.

The fan hummed softly. He wondered when his son would bring that girl.

He was wakened from his light sleep by a circumstantial rustle. His nurse and the head nurse stood beside his bed. The head nurse took her pince-nez off and rubbed the red marks on her thin white nose. "You've had a good sleep, Mr. Rand," she said. "Now you must take your medicine. And now that you're awake," she said while he still blinked at her, "I have a visitor for you." The head nurse smiled with vague benevolence and put her pince-nez on.

"Aunt Clara," he said.

She was wearing a soft dark dress with cuffs and collar of fine lace: there was a touch of deep red in the narrow leather belt. Under her small black hat, her hair was white, but she was tall and straight and as she came into the room she picked a straight chair up and set it by the bed. She sat down silently and took his hand. Her hand was strong and cool. The skin on the back was translucent and blue veins stood out in high relief. She wore nothing but her wedding ring.

She sat silent in her stylish small black hat. The color in her cheeks was natural, and she had made no effort to conceal the tiny wrinkles around her dark, firm eyes. She looked like a great lady, he thought, and also still looked like a gay, brave girl.

"How do you feel?"

"I feel fine. Tad's here."

"I know. I saw him. I was waiting till it was time for you to wake up."

"He told me about a girl."

"I saw her."

"Well?"

"Ah," she said, "you'll like her."

"What is she like?" he said. "I understand she lives in Morristown. But I can't find out how much she weighs."

She squeezed his hand and smiled. "Wait till you see. It will be all right. She's fine. I can always tell. A gong rings."

"Yes," he said, "you can."

"Yes," she said, "don't you worry."

"I don't," he said, "not about him; about Jane."

"She's having a grand time. I got a letter yesterday."

He turned and looked out under the window shade. He could see the sunlight and the sky and the edge of a thundercloud. She had him by the hand. There was no need to play a farce; he could lay his burden down. "I'm afraid I'm not going to make it," he said.

Her hand was steady. Her voice was low and steady. "I know, my dear, that's what they say."

"I guessed it long ago."

"You would, of course. They told me not to tell. What nonsense with a man like you."

"Yes," he said, "they're pretty silly in here."

"I suppose they don't like to say. They may be wrong."

"If I could get well—" he said. "But that's out. I know that, and I don't want to be an invalid. There's nothing on my mind but Jane."

"Would you like it if she came to live with me?"

"Yes."

"That's settled, then."

"I must go," she said, "I mustn't spend too much time in here."

He grinned at her. "What are we saving it for, I wonder."

"Your father and mother will want to come."

"Yes," he said, "poor people. Before you came in," he said, "I was thinking over my whole life. In the last two days, I've thought over all of my life and most of yours."

"And what do you think about it all?"

"I think it was fine."

"So do I," she said, "though sometimes I didn't."

"I, either."

"That's where you came in. You were my child," she said, "or let me feel you were. And now your children will soon be having children of their own. And so I can feel that life goes on. Like other women."

"What do you think it's like out there?" he said.

Her hands closed quickly over his. "Ah, my dear, are you frightened?"

"No," he said, "not a bit."

"There may be nothing, I suppose," she said, "though to me that seems impossible."

"Yes," he said.

"But if there's anything," she said, "I know it's fine." She put her cheek down on his hands and quickly sat up smiling. "Look what we have made here from so little."

The door swung open slowly. The nurse was beckoning.

Date Due

MAY 23		
JI 1 '42		
JI 1 '42		
JI 29 '42		
O 12		
N 8		
De 5 '42		
N 9 '43		
DEC 12 '44		
MAR 1 '45		
MAY 5 '51		
FEB 23 1966		